KT-527-914

select
editions

Reader's
Digest

Reader's Digest

The names, characters and incidents portrayed in the novels in this volume are the work of the authors' imaginations. Any resemblance to actual persons, living or dead, events or localities is entirely coincidental.

www.readersdigest.co.uk

Published in the United Kingdom by Vivat Direct Limited (t/a Reader's Digest), 157 Edgware Road, London W2 2HR

For information as to ownership of copyright in the material of this book, and acknowledgments, see last page.

Printed in Germany
ISBN 978 0 276 44668 9

select
editions

THE READER'S DIGEST ASSOCIATION, INC.

contents

author in focus

The Edgar Allan Poe Awards—popularly called the Edgars—are presented every year by the Mystery Writers of America. C.J Box was a recipient of this prestigious award for best novel of 2008 with *Blue Heaven*, which is currently being made into a film, and he is fast becoming one of the hottest American mystery writers on both sides of the Atlantic. But whether he's at an awards ceremony in New York, or at the Beartrap Café, Wyoming, where the best-selling author dreams up the latest adventure for game warden Joe Pickett, C.J. Box is never so happy as when he's at home in Cheyenne with his wife and family.

in the spotlight

Having her debut novel published was a dream that Natasha Solomons believed she would never realise, for when she was a child she struggled with dyslexia. 'The written word was for me as awkward as trying to wind a watch while wearing boxing gloves,' she recalls. The person who best understood her battle with language was her refugee grandfather, Paul, who encouraged her to translate the ideas in her head into sentences. 'People often ask me who inspired Jack Rosenblum, the hero of my novel. They presume it was my grandfather and they are right in a way—Jack is a refugee from Berlin who longs for England to be his home. But Jack is also me. I understand his relentless pursuit of a dream. Seeing my novel in print does feel like a particularly large miracle.'

SEAL OF THE PRESIDENT OF THE UNITED STATES

SAM BOURNE

Maggie Costello, an adviser to newly elected US President, Stephen Baker, is happy to be working for a leader she trusts—a man who she and millions of fellow Americans believe will make the world a better place.

So it comes as a terrible shock when a man called Vic Forbes surfaces, making damaging revelations about Baker's past. More devastating still is the news, a few days later, that Forbes has been murdered.

Suddenly, Maggie's top priority is to find where the truth lies . . . and just who is pulling the strings.

PROLOGUE

New Orleans, March 21, 23:35

He didn't choose her, she chose him. At least that's how it seemed. Though maybe that was part of her skill, the performer's art.

He hadn't stared at her, hadn't fixed her with that steady gaze he knew freaked the girls out. He didn't want to make anyone uneasy. So he pretended to be like those out-of-town guys, cool and unbothered. On a business trip, only visiting a strip club so they could say they had tasted the true New Orleans experience—letting their hair down, sampling a little sin. The city didn't mind those guys. Hell, New Orleans had made a living out of them.

So he did his best to act uninterested, even glancing down at his BlackBerry, only occasionally stealing a look at the stage. Not that that was the right word. The 'performing area' was little more than a jetty pushed out among the low-lit tables, a few square feet with barely enough room for a girl to peel off her bikini top, jiggle the silicone on her chest, bend over and show her G-stringed ass before blowing a few kisses to the men who had slotted a twenty under her garter belt.

The thrill of these places should have faded long ago, but somehow he kept coming back. This spot had been a fixture, once a week, for years. It wasn't really about the sex. It was the dark he liked, the anonymity. He didn't want any strangers recognising him. He didn't want to chat. He needed to think.

Be calm, he told himself. Things are on track. He had dropped the bait and they had picked it up. So what if there was no word yet? He should give it time. He stared into his glass, raised it to his lips and knocked the bourbon back in one sharp swallow. It burned.

He glanced back to the stage. A new girl, one he'd not seen before. Her hair was longer, her skin somehow not quite as plucked and smooth as the others. Her breasts looked real. She was looking directly at him. Had she recognised him, perhaps from the TV?

He fiddled with the BlackBerry again, the device slick from the moisture in his palm. He fought the urge to look up, only to surrender a few seconds later. She was still holding him in that steady gaze. Not the fake leer perfected by the girls who know how to kid a bald, drunk guy that he's hot. This was something more genuine; friendly, almost.

Her spot was over and she was gone, ending with the obligatory shake of the rear. Even that seemed aimed in his direction.

To his relief, the machine vibrated in his hand, forcing him to be busy with something else. A new message. He scanned the first line. Another media request. Not what he was waiting for. He scrolled through the rest of the day's email.

'You know what they say: all work and no play—'

'Makes Jack a dull boy.'

He interrupted her even before he had seen her face. She had pulled up a chair at the small table he had made his own. Even though he had never heard her speak, he knew from the first syllable that it was her.

'You don't look like a dull boy.'

'And you don't look like a stripper.'

'Oh, really? You don't think I've got the goods for—'

'I wasn't saying that. I was saying—'

She placed her hand on his, to silence him. The warmth he had seen in her eyes on stage was still there. Her hair hung loose, falling onto her shoulders. She could have been no more than twenty-five—almost half his age—yet she exuded a strange . . . what was it? Maturity? Or something like that.

Then, in an accent that was not Southern, perhaps Midwest, maybe California: 'So what kind of work do you do?'

The question brought a warm wave of relief. It meant she didn't recognise him. 'I'm kind of a consultant. I advise—'

'You know what,' she said, her hand still on his, her eyes searching for the door. 'It's too stuffy in here. Let's walk.'

He said nothing as she led him out onto Claiborne Avenue, the traffic still heavy even at this late hour. He wondered if she could feel, just through his hand, that his pulse was racing.

Finally, they turned down a side street. It was unlit. She walked a few yards, turning left into an alley. It ran along the back of a bar. He could hear a party inside.

She stopped and turned to whisper into his ear. 'I like it outside.'

The blood was surging towards his groin. The sensation of her voice, her breath in his ear, flooded him with desire.

He pressed her hard against the wall, reaching for her skirt. She pushed her mouth against his, kissing him enthusiastically. Her hands moved upwards, heading for his face. She was touching him, her fingers gentle. They moved down to his neck and suddenly pressed on it hard.

'You like it rough,' he murmured.

'Oh yes,' she said, her right hand now firmly on his windpipe.

He heard himself rasping. He tried to prise her fingers off his throat, but there was no budging them. She was remarkably strong.

'Look, I can't breathe—' he gasped.

'I know,' she said, her left hand joining her right in fully circling his throat, as she choked the life out of him. He fell quietly.

She straightened her skirt, reached down to remove the BlackBerry from the man's jacket pocket, and headed off into the night.

1

The previous day: Washington DC, Monday, March 20, 07:21

Maggie Costello twisted her wrist to get another look at her watch. No getting away from it: 7.21 a.m. She was going to be late. But that was OK. It was only a one-to-one meeting with the White House Chief-of-bloody-Staff.

She pedalled furiously, feeling the strain in her calves and the pressure on her lungs. No one had said cycling was going to be this hard. So much for the fresh start. New job, new regime, she had told herself. Healthy eating; more exercise; quit the fags; no more late nights. If there was a plus to finding herself suddenly single, it was that she could now start each morning bright and early. And not just normal-human-being early. No, she would start her day Washington early, so that a meeting at 7.30 a.m. would feel like an ordinary moment in the heart of the working day.

That had been the plan, at any rate. Maybe it was because she had been born and raised in Dublin, only coming to America as an adult, that she didn't fit. Whatever the explanation, Maggie was fast coming to the conclusion that she was innately out of sync with all these bright, shiny Washingtonians, with their impeccable self-discipline. No matter how hard she tried to embrace the DC lifestyle, getting up at the crack of dawn still felt like cruel punishment.

So here she was, whistling down Connecticut Avenue, willing Dupont Circle to come into view but knowing that, even when it did, she would still be at least three to five minutes away from the White House. And that was before she had chained up the bike, cleared security, dashed into the ladies' room, torn off her T-shirt and swabbed her armpits, wrestled her body into her regulation Washington uniform—a feminine version of a man's suit and shirt—and somehow altered her appearance from under-slept scarecrow to member of the National Security Council and trusted Foreign Policy Adviser to the President of the United States.

It was 7.37 a.m. by the time she stood, still red-faced, before Patricia, secretary to Magnus Longley, who had summoned Maggie to this meeting.

'He's waiting for you,' Patricia said, peering above her glasses just long enough to convey a sharp look of disapproval—for her lateness, of course, but for other reasons, too. That cold, lizard's glance had found Maggie's appearance sadly wanting. Maggie looked down and realised that her trousers, ironed so carefully last night, were now unacceptably creased and marked at the ankles by a line of cycle grease. And then there was her autumn-red hair which she kept long and tousled in a town where women tended to keep it short and businesslike. Maggie passed her hand through her hair in a futile bid to impose some order, and stepped inside.

Magnus Longley was a veteran Mr Fix-it who had served either in the House, the Senate or the White House since the Carter era. He was the requisite greybeard appointed to balance out—and allay any anxieties over—the President's youth and lack of Washington experience.

His thin, aged head was down when she came in, poring over a pile of papers, a pen in his hand. He scrawled a comment before looking up, revealing a face whose features remained always neat and impassive. He still had all his hair, now white.

'Mr Longley,' Maggie said. 'I'm sorry I'm late, I was—'

'So you think the Secretary of Defense is an asshole, is that right, Miss Costello?'

Maggie felt her throat run dry.

'Shall I repeat my question?'

'I heard the question. But I don't understand it. I never—'

'No time for games, Miss Costello. Not in this office. And no time for such infantile behaviour as *this*—' the word punctuated with a loud flick of the fingers against a single sheet of paper.

'What is that?'

'It is an email you wrote to one of your colleagues at the State Department.'

Slowly a memory began to form. Two nights ago, she had written to Rob, over on the South Asia desk at State. He was one of the few familiar faces around, like her a veteran of aid organisations and UN peace missions in horrible, forgotten corners of the world.

Longley cleared his throat, theatrically. '"Intel on AfPak suggests close collaboration with Islamabad", et cetera, "none of which seems to be getting through to the assholes at the Pentagon—especially the chief asshole, Dr Anthony Asshole himself".' He placed the paper back on the desk and looked at her, his gaze icy.

Maggie's heart fell into the pit of her stomach.

'As you can imagine, the Defense Secretary is not too happy to be described in these terms by an official of the White House.'

'But how on earth did he—'

'Because—' Magnus Longley leaned forward—'because, Miss Costello, your friend at State forwarded your proposal regarding intelligence cooperation with Pakistan to colleagues at the Pentagon. But he forgot to use the most important button on these goddamned machines.' He gestured in the direction of his desktop computer. 'The delete key.'

'No.' The horrified response came out as a whisper.

'Oh yes.' He handed her the print-out.

She took one look, noting the list of senior Pentagon officials who had been cc'd at the top of the email. How on earth could Rob have made such an elementary mistake? How could she?

'He wants you gone immediately. This morning.'

'It was just one word in one email. It's just office banter.' She could hear the desperation in her voice.

'Do you even read the newspapers, Miss Costello? Or perhaps you are more of a *blog* reader?' He said the word as if he had just caught a whiff of a soiled dishcloth.

Maggie decided this was part of Longley's shtick, playing the old fart: he couldn't be as out of touch as he liked to pretend, not when he had stayed on top in Washington for so long.

'Because you may have picked up that our Defense Secretary is—how can we put this?—not one of the President's loyalists.'

'Of course I know that. Adams ran against him for the nomination.'

'You *are* up to date. Yes. The President has assembled what is admiringly referred to as "a team of rivals". But as Lincoln understood, it may be a team, but they're still rivals. So Dr Adams wants to flex his muscles, show that his reach extends beyond the Pentagon. He's not going to let this go.'

'Which means he wants me out.'

The Chief of Staff stood up. 'That's where we are. The final decision is not Dr Adams's, of course. It rests in this building.'

What the hell did that mean? *This building*. Did Longley mean he would decide—or that whether Maggie kept her job or not would be settled by the President himself?

'Does the President know about this?'

'You seem to have forgotten that Stephen Baker is the President of the United States of America. He is not a *human resources* manager.' Longley's mouth seemed to recoil, as if uttering such an absurd, new-fangled term might stain his lips. 'Miss Costello, there are hundreds of people who work for the President. You are not of a rank at which your employment would be of concern to him.'

So that meant the final decision rested with Longley. She was finished.

'I have someone waiting for me, Miss Costello. No doubt we will speak again soon.' She was dismissed.

MAGGIE WAITED TILL she was in her own rabbit hutch of an office before she would even breathe out properly.

Was this going to be the story of her bloody life, having a magical opportunity in her hands, only to screw it up royally? Not that Adams wasn't an asshole: he was, First Class. But it was absurdly naive to put it in an email. How old was she? Nearly forty, for God's sake. When would she learn? For a woman who'd made her name as a diplomat—a peace negotiator, with all the sensitivity and discretion that required—she really was an idiot.

When she had got back from Jerusalem nearly three years ago—hailed as the woman who had made a breakthrough in the Middle East peace process—she had been swamped with job offers; every think tank and university had wanted her. And, much to her amazement, things had worked out with Uri. They had come together during the strangest and most intense week in Jerusalem. She had learned long ago to be suspicious of relationships hatched on the road, especially those lent glamour by the presence of danger and the proximity of death. Love among the bombs felt delicious, but it rarely lasted. Yet when Uri had invited her to share his apartment in New York she hadn't said no. True, she had kept her apartment in Washington, planning to divide her time between the two places. But when it came to it, both she and Uri simply found that they wanted to spend most nights in the same city—and in the same bed. There had seemed to be no reason for it ever to stop.

But somehow, just weeks ago, she had found herself sitting on the steps of the Lincoln Memorial, looking out at a gleaming Washington DC—scrubbed up and ready for the inauguration of a new president—with Uri at her side, his voice cracking, saying that they had run out of road. That he still loved her, but that this was no longer working. 'The bottom line, Maggie, is that you care about Stephen Baker more than you care about us.'

And, even though the tears were falling down her cheeks, she hadn't been able to argue. He was right: she had dedicated the last year to helping Stephen Baker become—against all the odds—the most powerful man in the world. She had thought that once things got back to normal, she would concentrate on her relationship with Uri. But suddenly it was too late: he'd made his decision and there had been nothing she could say.

So now here she was, yet again, another relationship officially screwed up, and on the verge of losing the very job that had sabotaged it. She put her head in her hands and muttered to herself, again and again: *Idiot. Idiot. Idiot.*

This bout of self-loathing was interrupted by a vibration somewhere near her thigh. She dug out her cellphone. Where the number should have appeared it just said: RESTRICTED.

A voice spoke without saying hello. 'Is this Maggie Costello?'

'Yes.'

'Please come to the Residence right away. The President wants to speak to you.'

WALKING AS FAST as she could without triggering a security alert, she headed off through the press-briefing room and then outside along the colonnade towards the White House Residence, home for little more than two months to Stephen Baker, wife Kimberley, their thirteen-year-old daughter Katie and eight-year-old son Josh.

The Secret Service agents ushered her through without a question, clearly expecting her, and suddenly she was in what looked like any other American household at ten past eight in the morning. There were cereal boxes on the table, school bags on the floor, and childish chatter in the air. Except for the armed officers posted outside the door, it looked like a regular family home.

Stephen Baker was standing in the middle of the kitchen, jacket off, with an apple in his hand. Standing opposite him, three yards away, was his son Josh—clutching a baseball bat.

'OK,' the President whispered. 'You ready?'

The little boy nodded.

'Here it comes. Three, two, one.' He tossed the apple, slowly and at just the right height for it to make contact with the little boy's bat. Struck firmly, the fruit went flying past the President's hand and splattered into the wall behind him.

A voice came from the next room, raised to full volume. 'Josh! What did I say about ball games inside?'

The President made a mock-worried expression for the benefit of his son and then, conspiratorially, put his finger to his lips. He called out, 'All under control, my love,' as he retrieved the apple from the floor and wiped the pulp from the wall.

He was a striking man. Six foot three, with a full head of brown hair, he was always the first person in the room you noticed. He was lean, his features fine and sharp. But it was his eyes that grabbed you. They were a deep, penetrating green, and even when the rest of him was animated they seemed to operate at a slower pace, gazing levelly.

And now they were looking towards her. 'Hey Josh, look who's here. Your favourite Irish aunt.'

'Hi Joshie. How's your new school?'

'Hi Maggie. S'OK. I play baseball, which is cool.'

'That *is* cool.' Maggie was beaming. Josh Baker was a contender for America's cutest boy and, having first met him nearly two years ago, she felt as if she had almost seen him grow up.

That first encounter had come on a summer Saturday in Iowa, at the State Fair in Des Moines. Stephen Baker had been there with his family, as the candidate tried to endear himself to the people of Iowa. Baker was then the rank outsider in the Democratic field, the little-known governor of Washington State.

Still, Rob—Maggie's old pal from her Africa days, who had ended up in the State Department and who had just dealt the deathblow to her nascent career—had been insistent. 'Just meet him,' he had said. 'You'll know right away.'

Maggie had resisted. Maggie Costello? Working for a politician? She had ideals, for God's sake, and ideals had no place in the snakepit of modern politics. First as an aid worker, latterly as a behind-the-scenes diplomat, she'd seen what politicians had done to godforsaken bits of Africa, the Balkans and the Middle East. As far as she was concerned there was only one mission that mattered: trying to make the world a better place, especially for those on the sharp end of war, disease and poverty. The way she saw it, politicians tended to get in the way of that process. And anyway, what did she know about US presidential politics?

'It doesn't matter,' Rob had insisted. 'Just meet him and you'll see what I mean. He's different: he's special.'

So she had gone to Iowa and watched Baker in action. It didn't take long to see he was a natural. His manner was easy, his interest in people shone through as genuine, not the synthetic sincerity of the blow-dried politicians usually deemed presidential material. And whatever quality it was that had won over Rob, it seemed to be working on the folk of Des Moines. Baker had the crowd in his thrall: they watched him eagerly, reflecting back the warmth they felt from him. And unlike other candidates, who seemed to have been parachuted in to such events from another planet, he genuinely seemed to be making real human contact with people.

Finally she stepped up to say hello.

'So you're the woman who brought peace to the Holy Land,' he had said. 'It's a pleasure to meet you.'

'Nearly,' she had replied. 'Nearly brought peace.'

'Well, nearly's a lot further than anyone ever got before.'

They snatched moments of conversation as he shook more hands, posed for camera-phone snaps or exchanged banter with a local reporter. Eventually he asked her to hop in the car that would take them to his next event. Kimberley and the kids would be in the back; she could ride with him up front. When she looked puzzled as to how there would be room, he smiled. 'I have the most crucial job on the "Baker for President" campaign: I'm the driver.'

They talked for the entire two-hour journey, until the three Bakers in the back were fast asleep. He wanted to know how she had started, asking her more about the work she had done as a volunteer in Africa, straight after graduation, than about the high-level shuttle diplomacy that had made her name in Jerusalem.

'You don't want to know this,' she had said eventually, with an embarrassed wave of the hand.

'No, I really do. Here's why. You know who I'm going to be in this campaign? I'm going to be the hick. "The logger's son from Aberdeen, Washington". I've got to convince Georgetown, the *New York Times* and the Council on Foreign Relations—all that crowd—that I'm not too provincial to be President.'

Soon he was telling her how, once he'd got a scholarship to Harvard, he'd spent vacations back in Aberdeen working shifts in the lumber yard to pay the bills.

'Eventually I got away. And I went to Africa. Just like you. I was in Congo. Jeez, I saw some terrible things. Just terrible. And it's still going on, if not there, then somewhere else. Rwanda, Sierra Leone, Darfur. The burning villages, the rapes, the children orphaned. Or worse.' He glanced at her. 'I believe I can win this thing, Maggie. And if I do, I want to dedicate some of the enormous resources of this country to stopping all this killing.

'I'm not talking about sending our army to invade places. We tried that already. It didn't work out so well. We need to think of other ways to do it. That's why I need you.' He let that sentence hang in the air while she stared at him in disbelief.

'Something tells me that you never forgot what you saw when you were twenty-one, Maggie. It's what makes you work so hard, even now, all these years later. Am I right?'

Maggie looked out of the car window, picturing the conferences and endless meetings of which her life now consisted. Each day she felt she got further away from that angry twenty-one-year-old woman she had once been. But he was right. What fuelled her still was the fury she had felt then about all the violence and injustice—all the sorrow—in the world, and the determination to do something about it. She turned back to him and nodded.

'And that's how I am, too. I never forgot what I saw out there. And I'm going to have a chance to do something about it. Something big. Will you be with me, Maggie Costello?'

NOW, NEARLY TWO YEARS later, the President was reaching for a red plastic lunch box with one hand and opening the fridge with the other. 'So what's it to be, junior? Apple or pear?'

'Apple.'

The President put the fruit into the box, clipped the top shut, then placed it in his boy's hand. He bent to kiss his son.

'OK, young man, scram.'

Just then, Kimberley Baker came in, blonde and pretty as a peach, clutching a bag bulging with gym gear.

The political cognoscenti had decided that she was an enormous asset to her husband. Female voters, in particular, liked what it said about Stephen Baker that his wife was a real, rather than artificially flawless, woman. That she was from Georgia, thereby connecting him with the vote-rich South, was an added bonus.

She had been worried about life in the White House from the start, anxious about an eight-year-old boy and a thirteen-year-old girl entering the most vulnerable time in their young lives in front of the gaze of the entire world. During the campaign, Stephen Baker always got a laugh when he joked that the only two people who truly wanted him to lose the election were his opponent and his wife. But Kimberley was making an effort, chiefly for the children's sake.

Now Kimberley was fussing over Josh and her shy, gauche, pretty teenage daughter, bundling them out of the door and into the hands of a casually dressed, twenty-something woman who looked like an au pair. In fact, she was Zoe Galfano, one of a Secret Service detail whose sole duty was the protection of the Baker children.

'Maggie, something to drink? Coffee, hot tea, juice?'

'No thanks, Mr President. I'm fine.'

He checked his watch. 'I want to talk about Africa. I saw your paper. The killing's starting up again in Sudan; there's hundreds of thousands at risk in Darfur. I want you to work up an option.'

Maggie's mind started revving hard. Magnus Longley was all but certain to take her job away, and yet here was the President offering the opportunity she had always dreamed of.

She was about to reply when a head popped round the door frame. Stu Goldstein, Chief Counselor to the President: the man who had masterminded the election campaign, the man who occupied the most coveted real estate in the White House, the room next to the Oval Office. The veteran of New York City political combat who stored a million and one facts about the politics of the United States in a phenomenal brain atop a wheezing, morbidly obese body.

'Mr President. We need to go across to the Roosevelt Room. You're signing the VAW act in two minutes.' A small turn of the head. 'Hi, Maggie.'

Baker took his jacket off the back of a kitchen chair and swung his arms into it. 'Walk with me.'

'What kind of options are you after, Mr President?'

'I want something that will get the job done. There's an area the size of France that's become a killing field. No one can police that on the ground.' As they walked, a pair of Secret Service agents hovered close by, three paces behind.

'So you're talking about the air?'

He looked Maggie in the eye, fixing her in that cool, deep green. Now she understood.

'Are you suggesting we equip the African Union with US helicopters, Mr President? Enough of them to monitor the entire Darfur region from the sky?'

'It's like you always said, Maggie. The bad guys get away with it because they think no one's looking. And no one *is* looking.'

She spoke slowly, thinking it through. 'If the AU had state-of-the-art Apaches, with full surveillance technology, then we could see who's doing what and when. There'd be no place to hide.'

'And if people know they're being watched, they behave.'

Maggie could feel her heart racing. This was what anyone who had seen the massacres in Darfur had been praying for for years: the 'eye in the sky' that might stop the killing.

He smiled. 'Give me some options, Maggie.'

By now they had arrived in the West Wing, standing in the corridor just outside the Roosevelt Room. An aide applied dabs of face powder for the

TV cameras. Someone asked if he was ready and he nodded.

The double doors were opened and a voice bellowed out, 'Ladies and gentlemen, the President of the United States!'

Sneaking in discreetly, in the tail of the entourage, Maggie watched as a packed Roosevelt Room rose to its feet, applauding him, a room full of some of the most senior politicians in the country, smiling wide, satisfied smiles. Sprinkled among them were a few faces she did not recognise. Women, not dressed in the tailored suits favoured by their Washington sisters. It took Maggie a moment to work out who they were. Of course. The victims.

Crisply, as the applause was still subsiding, Stephen Baker began directing those in the first row to gather behind him. Knowing the drill, they formed a semicircle, standing as he sat at the desk. Maggie identified the key players: majority and minority leaders from the Senate, whips and committee chairs from the House, along with the two lead sponsors of the bill from both chambers.

'My fellow Americans,' the President began, 'today we gather to see the new Violence Against Women Act signed into law. I'm proud to sign it. I'm proud to be here with the men and women who voted for it. Above all, I'm proud to be at the side of those women whose courage in speaking out made this law happen.'

There was more applause. Maggie glanced at the people she had joined, lined up against the wall nearest the door, the traditional zone occupied by the aides to the President. The Press Secretary, Doug Sanchez, young and good-looking enough to have caught the interest of the celeb magazines, had his head down, barely paying attention, scrolling instead through a message on his iPhone. Aware he was being watched, he looked up and smiled at Maggie.

President Stephen Baker reached for a pen on the desk before him, then signed his name. 'There,' he said. 'It's done.'

The guests were on their feet again, cameras clacking noisily. The President had come round in front of his desk to shake hands with those who had come to witness the moment.

Aides were now beginning to nudge the President towards the lectern, to take questions from the press. This was an innovation that Baker had insisted upon. Traditionally, presidents made themselves available to the press only rarely, doing occasional, set-piece press conferences; now a public event would end with a few minutes of light interrogation. The Washington punditocracy gave this fresh, transparent approach a life expectancy of about a fortnight.

'Terry, what you got?'

'Mr President, some people are saying this might be the first and last legislative achievement of the Baker presidency. This was the one thing you and Congress could agree on. After this, isn't it going to be gridlock all the way?'

He flashed the wide signature smile. 'No, Terry, and I'll tell you why.' Maggie watched as the President went into a now-familiar riff, explaining that, though his majorities in the House and Senate were narrow, there were plenty of people of goodwill who wanted to make progress for the sake of the American people.

He took another question, this time on diplomatic efforts in the Middle East. Maggie felt a surge of anxiety, a leftover from the election campaign when it had been her job to make sure he didn't stumble on the subject of foreign policy. No need for her to worry about that now.

Then Sanchez leaned in to say, 'This will be the last question.'

Baker called on the cable news channel MSNBC.

'Mr President, did you deceive the American people during the election campaign, by failing to reveal a key aspect of your medical history—the fact that you once received treatment for a psychiatric disorder?' There were perhaps two seconds of frozen silence as the question cut through the air like a missile before impact.

Every head in the room swung round to look at Stephen Baker. His posture remained the same. But, Maggie saw, he was gripping the lectern so tightly his knuckles had turned white. They matched the pallor spreading over his face as the blood drained from it.

He began to speak. 'Like every other candidate for this office, I released a medical statement during the campaign that included all the details my doctor—' Baker paused, looking down at the lectern as if searching for a script that wasn't there. He looked up again. 'All the details he deemed to be relevant. And I think now is the time to attend to the business of the American people.' With that, he turned on his feet and headed for the door, a long snake of aides at his heels, leaving behind a loud chorus of 'Mr President!' bellowed by every reporter.

The staff scattered in every direction. En route to her office, next to the

Press Secretary's, Maggie hesitated, looking in at those charged with handling the media: the scene was crazed, every person on a telephone, each simultaneously hammering away at a computer. She could see Tara MacDonald, Director of Communications, and Sanchez talking intensely. She turned to leave, taking one last glance at the TV screen. The *Breaking News* tag along the bottom conveyed a devastating sentence: *Source tells MSNBC: President Baker received psychiatric treatment for depression.*

The word *psychiatric* reeked of political death. Americans could tolerate all manner of weaknesses in each other but not in a president. They needed their president to be above all that, to be stronger than they were.

Voters would be rattled by this news, whoever was in the White House, Maggie knew that. But Stephen Baker had been lionised, ever since his campaign took off in the depths of the Iowa winter. Word had spread that a different kind of politician had arrived: one who really did seem to talk straight. YouTube clips of him telling audiences what they didn't want to hear became cult viewing. Soon the press was writing up Baker as something more than a regular politician. He was a truth-teller, destined to lead the American people out of a dark moment in their history. Yet now he had been accused of failing to level with the nation. And instead of knocking back the charge, he had paled at the very words.

Maggie was stepping into her office when she saw Goldstein heading towards the press area. No matter that he was way above her in the Washington food chain, Maggie regarded Stu as one of the few unambiguously friendly faces round here. They had whiled away many hours on the plane during the campaign. She figured that if anyone knew the truth of the MSNBC story, it would be Goldstein—the man who'd been with Stephen Baker from the start. She walked down the corridor so that she could meet him halfway, then cut to the chase. 'We're in the toilet, aren't we?'

'Yup. Somewhere round the U-bend and heading underground.' He carried on walking. Given his bulk, he was advancing at quite a speed.

'How bad's it going to be?'

'Well, as people used to say back when Dick Nixon was using this place to turn the Constitution into confetti, it's never the crime, it's always the cover-up. Most folks won't mind if the President's a real loony, so long as they knew it before they pulled the lever.'

'They'll be angry he didn't reveal it in the campaign.'

'You betcha,' he said bitterly.

She couldn't tell whether Goldstein was irritated that something he'd long known had leaked, or whether he was disappointed that the President had kept a secret from him.

It came back to her then, the brief flap over medical records during the campaign. Mark Chester, Baker's much older opponent, had refused to disclose his, issuing a terse 'doctor's summary' instead. Most expected Baker to seize the moment and release his records in full, waving his clean bill of health in Chester's face. But he had done no such thing, choosing to issue a doctor's summary of his own. Everyone gave Baker credit for that: he had shown compassion, sparing the embarrassment of the older man.

Maggie had never considered that Baker might have taken the chance to avoid full disclosure to cover up his own embarrassments. But it was what everyone would be thinking now. MSNBC would either have to be flat-out wrong or Stephen Baker would have to come up with a good explanation for why he hadn't told the truth.

She headed back to her office and sat at the computer.

The blogs were obsessed. She went to Andrew Sullivan.

> This could be a defining moment for the republic. Mental illness is one of the last great taboos, and yet one in three Americans is affected by it. Stephen Baker should be brave, tell the truth and call for an end to prejudice.

She next went rightwards, to The Corner.

> Normally it takes at least a few years for a Democratic politician to start falling apart. Credit to Baker for speeding up the process.

Maggie sat back in her chair. She knew it would have been risky, verging on suicidal, for a candidate to start blubbering about his time on the psychiatrist's couch in the middle of a presidential election. She knew why he hadn't come clean with the voters. But he should have come clean with *her*. She had jacked in her job and gone to work for him in the days when his staff could fit into a minivan. They had run up tens of thousands of air miles together. She had eaten in his home, played with his son and daughter and chatted with his wife. She had put her faith in him. And so had the country.

She glanced up at the TV. The *Breaking News* ident was flashing. Maggie reached for the volume control. 'Word just into us here at CNN: the President is to make an emergency statement.'

AT SANCHEZ'S INVITATION, she watched it in the press room.

'My fellow Americans,' he began, his voice steady, his face calm and businesslike. 'I am not here to deny what you heard today. I am here to tell you what happened.

'Long ago, in my early twenties, I hit a difficult patch. I have not spoken about it before because the source of my unhappiness involved another person. As you know, my mother died a few months back—in the very last week of the campaign, as it happens—so perhaps now it can be told. I tremble at the thought that I might be dishonouring her memory, but you need to hear the truth.

'When I was a teenager, I suspected my mother was an alcoholic. It took me some time to reach that conclusion but, by the time I was in college, I knew for certain. This knowledge began to eat away at me. Was I fated to follow in her path? Would I too become an addict of alcohol? I was laid low by these thoughts. And, yes, I sought professional help. The help of a psychiatrist.

'Eventually I came out of this "slough of despond". But it was not the doctors who lifted me from that dark place. My mother, on hearing that I had sought help, was shaken out of her own disease. She joined AA and got sober. When she died, she had gone twenty-four years without a drink. It was a great achievement. I'm as proud of her for that as she was of me for getting to the brink of the presidency. But it was private. And I chose to honour that.

'Perhaps that was a mistake. But now I hope you understand why I needed help and why I did not rush to tell you, the American people, all about it. I cannot know how you will react to this news. But I am taking the risk that you will respond as so many American families do when confronted with news that disappoints. With the generosity of spirit that makes us a great nation. Thank you.'

Maggie stood, barely daring to breathe. In the silence, she heard the sound of a single pair of hands clapping. Then another and then several more, until there was loud, sustained applause. She heard Tara MacDonald give a single whoop.

Sanchez passed her his iPhone, already open at the Sullivan blog. She only had to read the first sentence:

> Stephen Baker has just reminded the American people why they chose him to be their president last fall.

'OK, people,' Tara yelled, silencing the last few claps of applause. 'We're not out of the woods yet. Fox and the others are going to be yakking all night about "the questions that still need to be answered". We need to be ready. I want names of surrogates ready to be in front of a camera heaping praise on President Stephen Baker for being honest and for being a devoted son. Now get to it.'

Tara MacDonald was right to be cautious, but Maggie had lived in America long enough to know that the public would like what they had seen. They would not turf out a new, young president for the crime of loving his mother and worrying about the inheritance she might have passed to her son.

She was right, too. The cable networks were kind, hosting discussions about whether alcoholism was hereditary and on the usefulness of therapy. The consensus in the White House was that Baker had dodged a bullet. Indeed, the relief lasted until the next day. Except in the Baker household. Where it was about to vanish in the cruellest way possible.

Washington DC, Monday, March 20, 19:16

Jen, those new sneakers are COOL!

Katie Baker read the messages on her new friend Jennifer's Facebook wall and was all set to add her own. But her fingers hesitated over the keyboard. Her mom had told her she had to be triple careful. 'Remember, sweetie: no names, no pictures that show you, your brother or your friends. Nothing that identifies you.'

Why did she have to be the one who was different? Oh, yes. Because her father was President of the United States, that's why. Which was cool, no doubt. She had already met several of her favourite stars and she had been in *People* magazine.

She clicked out of Jen's and back to her own Facebook page. There was a message from her friend Alexis.

Hi K, hope you're feeling OK this evening. Sorry today was so hard. You seemed to be coping really well though. You're one tough chick!

Katie read it again, checking the name. It was definitely from Alexis, but it made no sense. Alexis hadn't been at school today. How would Alexis know how she'd been coping?

She typed out a reply.

I don't understand! Aren't you in bed with that yucky bug thing?!!

Katie was about to click open another window when she heard a light knock on the door. Her Secret Service agent, Zoe, poked her head round the door. 'Your mom says it's time you came down for dinner.'

''Kay. Be right there.'

The door shut and Katie was about to close down Facebook when she heard the message alert announcing Alexis's reply. She glanced back towards the door. It would only take a minute.

THE FIRST LADY looked over at her husband, now chopping garlic for a tomato sauce. He was sitting on a stool tucked up against the breakfast bar, both tie and shoes off. Whenever she regretted her husband's choice of career, Kimberley Baker fell back on this consolation. As he had put it in a dozen interviews, 'At least I get to live above the shop.' So she tried to savour this little scene of domesticity—the four of them having an evening meal together.

Actually, it was still just the three of them. Katie had not yet come down despite Zoe's summons. Kimberley was poised to shout for her daughter to come to the table, when the door swung open.

The girl was staring straight ahead, every last drop of blood drained from her face.

'Katie, what is it? What's happened?'

Instinctively, Stephen Baker looked to the door. Had an intruder broken into the White House Residence? Zoe, having quietly entered the room behind her charge, read the President's expression. She shook her head. *We've seen nothing.*

He knelt down, so he could look his daughter in the eye.

'Was it something on the computer?'

She nodded.

'One of your friends, saying something mean?'

'I thought it was. At first.'

The President and his wife looked at each other.

'What did they say?'

'I don't want to tell you.'

The President stood up and gestured towards Zoe. Swiftly, she left the room, returning seconds later holding an open laptop computer, its shell a blaze of psychedelic swirls. Teen chic.

Kimberley took the machine from Zoe and looked at the screen. It was her daughter's Facebook page. Katie had begged to be allowed to keep it and her parents had eventually relented, with strict conditions. No real names. No contact details. An IP address arranged through the White House comms department revealed only the United States as her place of residence, with no city specified. Only her closest friends knew that Sunshine12 was in fact the daughter of the American President.

Stephen Baker scanned the screen, searching among the multiple open windows, banner ads and thumbnail photos for what had so distressed his daughter.

And then he found it. A message from one of Katie's schoolfriends.

No, I'm not really sick. And I'm not really Alexis either, to be honest. But I am sorry about your dad. Must have been a shock to find out Grandma was a pisshead and he had to go to the head doctor because he was a mental case. My apologies for spilling the beans. Oops, silly me. But I wonder if you would be a doll and take a message to him from me. Tell him I have more stories to tell. The next one comes tomorrow morning. And if that doesn't smash his pretty little head into a thousand pieces, I promise you this—the one after that will. Make no mistake: I mean to destroy him.

2

Washington DC, Tuesday, March 21, 05:59

Maggie got the call before 6 a.m.: Goldstein, sounding caffeinated. 'Put on MSNBC. Now.'

She fumbled for the remote, down at the side of the bed, and stabbed at the buttons until finally the screen fired up.

'It's an ad for car insurance, Stu.'

'Wait. We got a heads-up.'

There was the portentous sound of a station ident, a whizzy graphic and then the morning anchor. The image over her shoulder showed the President, the words across the bottom of the screen: *Breaking News*.

'Papers seen by MSNBC suggest Stephen Baker received campaign contributions that came, indirectly, from the government of Iran. Details are still sketchy but such a donation would constitute a serious violation of federal law, which prohibits candidates from receiving contributions from any foreign source, still less a government hostile to the United States. Live now to . . .'

Iran? They could not be serious. Something truly bizarre was going on here. Bizarre and sinister. 'What the hell is going on, Stu?'

'Two stories, two days running, on the same network. That doesn't happen by accident, sweetheart. That means they have a leaker. A *source*. Someone who's out to destroy this presidency.'

'Stuart,' Maggie said, now out of the bed and walking towards the shower. 'I'm glad you called, but why me? Shouldn't you be speaking to Tara?'

'Did that thirty minutes ago. *Iran*. You're our Middle East gal, remember. Need you to think about the angles. If this does not turn out to be bullshit, then who might have done this at that end? Government or rogue? And—Shit.' Goldstein's cellphone rang. He must have put the call on speaker because she could hear a voice at the other end. She couldn't make out all the words but she could hear the urgency.

'. . . a doorstep at the Capitol, demanding a special prosecutor.'

Stuart's response was instant and ferocious. 'That prick. Was he on his own or with colleagues?'

The voice: 'One other. Vincenzi. You know, bipartisan bullshit: one Republican, one Democrat.'

Maggie tried to say goodbye, but it was clear Stuart was not listening. He was absorbed in this new conversation, apparently unaware that he was still holding the receiver. She hung up.

They had now, she understood, entered a new realm of seriousness. If a Democrat was calling for an independent counsel to investigate a Democratic president, there was no way he could fight it. Baker would have to agree. In the space of a few weeks he had gone from St Stephen—the coverline on a British magazine story about the new president—to Richard Nixon, under investigation.

They had all been so euphoric that evening in November when Baker had won. Maggie had been caught up in it, accepting the ribbing from Stu and Doug Sanchez, as they mocked her earlier pessimism. 'Oh ye of little faith, Costello, who said it would never happen,' Sanchez had said as he embraced her.

She had tranquillised her doubts, allowed herself to believe that this time it would be different. Her own experience told her that politics was bound to end in failure. But she had got it wrong. Again. Politics would always rise up and strangle hope. She had been stupid to think it would be any different this time.

By now, she was out of the shower and standing in a towel, staring at her wardrobe, wondering what you were meant to wear for a full-blown political crisis. A special prosecutor. Jesus.

The cellphone rang again. Maggie grabbed it.

'Excuse me?' A woman's voice. 'Is this Maggie Costello?'

'Yes.'

'Can you hold for Magnus Longley?'

Maggie felt her guts clench.

'Miss Costello? I'm sorry to disturb you so early but I thought it best to let you know of my decision immediately. I'm afraid Dr Adams insists that you be removed from your post. And I see no alternative but to bow to his wishes.'

Maggie felt as if someone had plunged a needle into her neck, mainlining fury directly into her bloodstream.

'But just yesterday the President asked me to—'

'You should come in early this morning and clear your desk. And you will need to surrender your pass by twelve noon.'

'Don't I get at least to—'

'I fear my six forty-five meeting is due to start. Goodbye, Miss Costello.'

She stood there a full five seconds, the rage rising. How could they do this to her? After all she had sacrificed?

She turned round, raised her arm and was about to hurl the phone at the bedroom wall, when it began to ring. She looked at the display: RESTRICTED.

She hit the green button. A woman's voice again, different this time. 'Please hold for the President.'

A second later, it was him. A voice known to millions, though in a tone heard only rarely and by those closest to him: 'Maggie, I need to see you. Right away.'

BAKER HAD INSISTED they meet in the Residence: him, her and Stuart. Maggie called Goldstein immediately and explained that she'd just been fired. 'I've got to surrender my pass by twelve noon, for Christ's sake!'

'OK,' he said. 'That means we've got a few hours.'

'Is that meant to be funny?'

'No. And Maggie? Come to my office first. I need to give you a heads-up before we go in.'

She was there twenty minutes later. Stuart was tearing his way through a memo, his eyes red and agitated.

She spoke from the doorway. 'Is that the file on the Iranian?'

He didn't look up but kept his eyes fixed on the document on his desk. 'Known in this country as Jim Hodges, resident in the state of Texas.'

'He's a US citizen! So then we're off the hook.'

'But he's also Hossein Najafi, citizen of Iran. Who just happens to be a veteran of the Army of the Guardians of the Islamic Revolution, better known as the Revolutionary Guard.'

'But how was anyone to know that Jim Hodges was really—'

'Because we're meant to check these things!' Now Goldstein was looking up, his voice raised. 'We're the White House. The President of the United States is meant to know who he meets, for Christ's—'

'He *met* him?'

'Yes! Some fundraiser. During the transition.'

'So there'll be a photograph.'

Stuart's reply came in a quieter voice. 'Yes.'

'And people will ask why we didn't know we were letting an Iranian spy get close to the President-Elect.'

'Yes. And why on earth the Iranians would want to give money to Stephen Baker.'

'It's a nightmare,' Maggie agreed.

'But that's not why he wants to see you. Us. Not completely.' Stuart told Maggie about the message sent to Katie Baker via Facebook.

'Jesus.'

'Oh yes.' Stuart checked his watch. 'He wants us over there right now.'

Inside the Residence, the difference in mood from the previous morning was palpable. Kimberley Baker had taken the children to school early. The President was in the kitchen, pacing. Maggie had seen Stephen Baker receive all kinds of bad news during the campaign, and on all but a handful of occasions he had remained calm. He would keep his voice down when others would raise theirs; he would stay seated when the rest would be jumping to their feet. But now he was pacing.

'Thank you both for coming.' He nodded towards two chairs but remained standing. 'Maggie, I take it you have the full picture?'

'Yes, Mr President.'

'The crank who wrote that message to my daughter. He warned there would be another big story "tomorrow morning". And there was. Which means he's no crank.'

Goldstein now spoke. 'Or at the least he's a crank who knows how to hack computers.'

'We need to know who this man is. Fast,' Baker said.

'Can't the Secret Service help?' Maggie asked.

'The agent assigned to Katie is running a trace.'

'Good,' said Maggie. 'So we'll see what she finds out.'

'I need someone I trust involved, Maggie.'

'You can trust the Secret Service.'

'They will investigate the threat to my *life*.'

Stuart leaned forward. 'But this is not just a physical threat. This is political. Someone is out to destroy this presidency. We need our own person on it. Someone who cares. Someone who has the resources to do, you know, unusual work.'

'What do you mean, *unusual*?'

'Come on, Maggie. We know what you did in Jerusalem. Put it this way, you weren't just drafting position papers, were you?'

'But I don't even work for you any more!' It had come out louder and angrier than she had planned.

'I'm sorry about that,' the President said quietly.

'Longley runs his own show, you know that, Maggie,' Stuart said. 'But it doesn't mean you can't help. If anything, it's better. You have distance.'

The President drew himself up to full height and let his eyes bore into her. 'I need you, Maggie. There is so much we hoped to achieve. Together. To do that, I need to stay in this office. And that means finding this man.'

She held his gaze for a long second or two in which she thought of the conversation they had had twenty-four hours earlier. She thought of Darfur, of the helicopters that this president was ready to send and the lives they would save.

'All right,' she said.

As they walked back to the West Wing, Maggie turned to Stuart. 'We'd better start drawing up a list.'

'A list of what?'

'Of everybody who wants to drive Stephen Baker from office.'

Washington DC, Tuesday, March 21, 09:16

In the office of the junior senator from the state of South Carolina, they liked to pride themselves on the knowledge that a visitor had only to cross the threshold to feel as if he had stepped inside the Old South. The receptionist was blonde, under thirty, and always ready with a welcoming smile. Outside that door, you entered the swamp that was Washington DC. But here, once you were a guest of Senator Rick Franklin, you were south of the historic Mason–Dixon Line.

In the waiting area, the visitor's eye would be caught first, perhaps, by the bronze plaque depicting the Ten Commandments. Not for Senator Franklin the niceties of separating Church and State in a public building. Then he would spot the TV monitor tuned, not to CNN or MSNBC, as would be the case in most Democrats' offices, nor even Fox News, as in most Republicans', but to the Christian Broadcasting Network. Midterm elections might be nineteen months away, but there was fundraising to be done—and it paid to give the folks the right impression.

That was the outer area. Once a visitor had entered the private office of the Senator, he would get a rather earthier glimpse of the realities of political life. In here, it was Fox or MSNBC, usually the latter. 'Know thine enemy,' Franklin would say.

In the last twenty-four hours, however, it had hardly felt like an enemy. The network, usually pilloried in Franklin mailings as news for liberals, had been making the weather on the Baker presidency; and for those on Franklin's side of the aisle it had felt like sunshine. First, St Stephen revealed as some kind of wacko, in need of treatment. And this morning the Iranian Connection. Iron law of scandal: gotta have a good name. 'The Iranian Connection' did the job perfectly. Sure the details were obscure, but that only made it better. Folks would conclude that Mr Perfect President was no longer as pure as the driven snow.

Which is why he had got on the phone to his Democratic colleague within minutes of the story breaking. He knew Vincenzi would be a reliable ally. And calling for an independent counsel was the no-risk move. If the investigation found nothing, Franklin could claim to have performed a public service, getting to the bottom of baseless rumours. If it found something, then bingo!

Vincenzi's presence at his side would give Franklin the lofty, bipartisan patina the media could never resist. 'This is above party politics,' they had both said in their statements.

So Senator Franklin felt able to hum 'Happy Days Are Here Again' as he straightened the blotter on his desk. Things were going according to plan.

There was a gentle rap on the door. Cindy, his Head of Legislative Affairs, coming in with a smile. It always gave him pleasure watching her move, her rear end tightly contained in a skirt that was never any lower than the knee.

'I can see you come bearing glad tidings, sweetheart.'

'I do, sir, I do.'

They played these games, the Southern gentleman and the demure young lady, with dialogue sub-*Gone With the Wind*—but only when the political weather was clement.

'Pray tell.'

'I do declare, Senator,' she said with a girlish flutter that sent electricity to his groin, 'that the source of MSNBC's recent tales of woe has been—what's the word—*outed.*'

'Already? What the hell's happened?'

'Seems some liberal hacker broke into the MSNBC system and found the emails between their Washington bureau and the leaker. Then went ahead and named him on his own website.'

'And what have they found out about him?'

'All they have so far is that he's late forties, white and from New Orleans.'

Washington DC, Tuesday, March 21, 14:26

'Aren't people going to talk?'

'What? About you and me?'

'Yes. Me, in here.'

'Something tells me, Maggie, that people worked out long ago there's not a chance of that happening: you're not my type.' And with that, a smile spread across the large, flushed, wobbling face of Stuart Goldstein, the first smile Maggie had seen in what felt like weeks but was actually less than thirty-six hours.

At his request, she had returned to his office. He had had to put her on the visitors' list at the tourists' entrance; she had had to show her passport to gain admission to the White House.

Fifteen minutes earlier, Goldstein had received a call from a contact inside MSNBC warning him that the network was about to air a live interview with the source of its two recent stories on Stephen Baker. The source had been named as Vic Forbes of New Orleans, Louisiana.

'Here's what I don't understand,' Goldstein said, while they were waiting for the TV to deliver what it had promised. 'The shrink thing. How did this Vic Forbes find out?'

'Maybe he spoke to the shrink?'

'Difficult. He died fifteen years ago.'

'There would have been records. Papers. Bills.'

'Nuh-uh. None. Put it this way, yours truly did not come down with the first shower of rain. I made sure in Baker's first race that the enemy couldn't dig up any surprises.'

'Because you had dug them up first.'

'Exactly.'

'What about Iran?'

'Well, that couldn't come up during the campaign 'cause it hadn't happened yet. That took some serious digging. Somehow Forbes knew what we didn't know ourselves.'

'Were we set up? Someone sent Hodges in to embarrass us?'

'Maybe. Maybe the Iranians did it. Make Baker look like a fool. Right now, though, the thing that bothers me about Hodges is how Forbes knew about him. And about the shrink.' He stared at the TV. 'I want to know who this bastard *is*.'

In the end, they were disappointed. Vic Forbes did not look like a monster or a pantomime villain. In truth, his face, as he stared dead-on at the camera, conducting a satellite interview from New Orleans, was forgettable. His nose seemed to be pinched, too thin at the bridge. He was bald, save for some slight grey at the temples.

Describing himself as a 'researcher', Forbes insisted he was aligned with 'no party and no faction'.

'I am a truth-teller, if you will,' he said. 'I had this information, and I felt guilty that I wasn't sharing it with the American people. They have a right to know who their president really is.'

'But *how* did you get it?' the interviewer asked. 'Surely the American people have a right to know that too?'

'Well, Natalie,' he began, 'would you reveal your sources, if your network had broken a story like this? Of course you wouldn't. That's a basic principle of journalism.'

'Yes, but you're not a journalist, are you, you scumbag!' Stuart hurled an empty Styrofoam cup at the TV.

Stuart's phone rang. He stabbed at it, putting it on speaker. 'Hey, Zoe, whaddya got?'

Maggie heard the agent's voice.

'It's still very early in our enquiries, Mr Goldstein.'

'I know. And I also know that electronic data of this kind is complex and searches can take weeks. But I need to know—what have you got?'

'OK. We think the person who sent that message to Katie Baker's Facebook page was white, male, extremely adept with computer technology and from New Orleans, Louisiana, sir.'

He hung up, shooting a glance at Maggie, then back to the TV.

'So, Stu, he's the same guy, right?'

'Confirmed,' Goldstein said, watching Forbes perform. 'How come this guy's so good? Where did he come from?'

Without taking his eye off the screen, he reached for the remote and hit 'pause'. (A set-top box, allowing the pausing and rewinding of live TV, was now an essential tool of the trade: it meant never having to miss an enemy gaffe again.). He rewound and watched the last minute again.

'What are you looking for?' Maggie asked.

'I don't know,' he murmured. 'But I'll know it when I see it.'

There he went again, more guff about his 'duty' to lay out the facts before the American people. People should know he was serious and the President should know he was serious.

But on this second viewing Goldstein saw what he had glimpsed so fleetingly. Maggie could see it too. A movement of the eye, no longer looking as if trying to meet the gaze of the unseen interviewer: he was, instead, looking into the audience. More than that, he seemed to be addressing someone specific.

Goldstein hit 'pause' once more, freezing Vic Forbes at the moment he lifted his eyes, the signal that he was speaking to an audience of one:

'The President should know I'm serious. Deadly serious.'

For the third time in two days, Maggie was in the White House Residence. This was an emergency meeting, called by the President. He wasn't pacing this time; his exterior, at least, was calm and cool. Maggie looked round the room. Four of them had been called here—Goldstein, her, Tara MacDonald and Doug Sanchez.

'Thank you for coming,' Baker said, steadily. 'This is not a White House meeting. This is a discussion among my campaign team. Old friends. I need your advice. This presidency is under assault.' He paused. 'Stuart, remind us what we know.'

'Thank you, Mr President.' Stuart Goldstein moved to the edge of the sofa he was on so that he could have a line of eye contact with everyone in the room.

'Vic Forbes, from New Orleans, Louisiana, supplied MSNBC with two stories, both calculated to cause maximum damage. At the same time, he has made personal contact with the White House. Last night someone posing as a friend of Katie Baker's sent her a message via Facebook.'

Both MacDonald and Sanchez sat to attention.

Stuart went on. 'This message effectively claimed responsibility for both the first MSNBC story and, in advance, the second. He also made a very direct and personal threat against the President.' He began to read. '"... Make no mistake: I mean to destroy him."'

Tara MacDonald gasped, suddenly looking like the mother of four that she was, an angry and protective matriarch, as she shook her head and muttered, 'That poor child.'

Stuart continued. 'Secret Service Agent Galfano traced the communication to an IP address in New Orleans. She also examined the data records of the so-called liberal blogger who so ingeniously hacked into MSNBC's emails, thereby revealing their source.'

Tara MacDonald shook her head. 'Don't tell me. New Orleans.'

'Yep. Forbes. He's the same guy.'

Sanchez whistled. 'The guy outed himself.'

'Seems so,' Goldstein said.

Sanchez crinkled his forehead, in a way that recalled the precociously bright teenager he had obviously been all of seven or eight years ago. 'Why would he do that?'

Now Maggie spoke. 'So that we'd listen to him.' All heads turned to her. 'He knew what we'd do. He knew we'd trace his message to Katie.

He *wanted* us to match him up to the MSNBC source.'

Stuart came in behind her. 'First rule of blackmail. It's not enough to have the goods. Your target has to *know* you've got the goods.'

Baker decided he had heard enough. 'Thank you, Stuart. Everyone, that is the background to the decision we need to make this evening. Who wants to go first?'

Tara MacDonald didn't wait for the customary polite silence. 'I wanna be clear what exactly it is we're talking about here. Are we discussing *negotiating* with a blackmailer?'

Sanchez fiddled with his watch. 'Doesn't it depend a little on what we think the guy might have?'

Maggie felt the air suck out of the room. You had to admire the guy, the fearlessness of youth and all that. But there was only one person who could answer that question and you didn't want to be the one to ask him.

There was, to everyone's relief, a knock on the door. A butler. 'Sir, I have an urgent note from the Press Office. For Mrs MacDonald.'

Baker beckoned the man forward and he presented the piece of paper to her. She pulled on the glasses that hung round her neck on a chain and read rapidly. Then she cleared her throat. 'Forbes has just released a statement. It reads as follows. "I want to make clear that the further information I hold on Stephen Baker is about his past. An aspect of his past that I think will shock many Americans. An aspect of his past he may not even have shared with his own family."'

Maggie felt a new mood enter the room: embarrassment. What mortifying secret might the President have kept from his own wife? No one could bring themselves to look at him.

Maggie stole a glance at Stuart. She could see that his embarrassment was compounded by something that shook him much more: political panic. How much more of this could this new presidency take?

Her voice dry, Tara spoke again. 'There's one last paragraph. "I do not plan on providing the full details today. I just wanted everyone following this story, especially those following it real close, to know that I have them."'

The gall of it was stunning. Vic Forbes was using a combination of live television and the Internet to present a blackmail demand to the President of the United States.

Stuart did not let the silence linger. 'Ideas for what we should do, people.'

Tara MacDonald spoke first. 'I say we go to the police and then we go on

TV. We expose Forbes for what he is, a cheap scumbag.'

'I worry about that,' said Sanchez. 'Initial response can be positive, but once you go public with something like this, people can say what the hell they like about you. Makes it legitimate.'

Tara MacDonald stepped in again. 'If we say nothing, Forbes is gonna keep coming at us, letting off these bombs. If we try to fess up, then the bomb's gonna be going off anyway. OK, it's gonna be us pressing the detonator and that helps. But we still don't know what damage it's gonna do. Which leaves—'

'All right, all right,' Stuart interrupted. 'We get the idea. A series of dead ends. But right now, somehow, we need to be inside Vic Forbes's head. Whatever he has—'

But he didn't get to finish his sentence. Stephen Baker, the cool, steady, unflappable Stephen Baker, the man who had barely put a foot wrong in a two-year presidential campaign, the man who had never broken a sweat even when his poll numbers were in the tank and his bank accounts dry—Stephen Baker finally snapped.

He slammed his fist onto the table and raised his voice. 'Vic Forbes! VIC FORBES! I don't want to hear that man's name again. Do you understand me?' Then, his voice much quieter, he murmured, almost to himself: 'I want him gone.'

Washington DC, Wednesday, March 22, 06:35

'Maggie. It's Stuart. Did I wake you?'

'No. Not at all.' It was a reflexive lie. No one in Washington ever admitted to being asleep, not even at 6.35 a.m.

'Sorry about that. Anyway, put the TV on.'

'Is this like some kind of daily service? Because I don't remember signing up.'

'Now.' There was a kind of manic energy in Goldstein's voice.

'Hold on.' Maggie fumbled for the remote. She aimed it at the small box in the corner and waited for it to glow into life. It was tuned to MSNBC.

Still squinting, she gasped at what she saw. 'Bloody hell.'

'My sentiments exactly.'

She couldn't say anything else. She simply couldn't speak. All she could do was stare at the words streaming across the bottom of the screen: *Breaking News: Vic Forbes found dead in New Orleans.*

3

Maggie kept staring at the screen, which showed a residential street in New Orleans, with the house clearest in vision behind yellow and black tape that read: POLICE LINE DO NOT CROSS.

She could hear Stuart breathing heavily into the phone, waiting for her to speak. She turned up the volume on the TV.

' . . . few details at this hour, Tom. What sources are telling this network unofficially is that the circumstances in which Mr Forbes was found were bizarre.'

'Bizarre?' echoed Maggie.

Stuart was still on the phone. 'Let me in and I'll tell you.'

'You're here?'

'Cab just pulled up.'

'Can you give me five minutes?'

'Two.'

As Maggie rushed to pull on a pair of jeans and to find a sweater, she kept one ear on the tale tumbling out of the TV.

What on earth had happened to Vic Forbes that they couldn't give the details? Last night she and the others had sat there facing a series of brick walls. Whichever path they took, Vic Forbes had stood there blocking their escape. And now he was gone, helpfully magicked away and in the nick of time.

She heard the knock on the door and the unmistakable sound of Stuart Goldstein's breathless panting outside.

'Stuart,' she said, ushering him in.

She headed straight for the kitchen to put on a pot of coffee.

He joined her, impatient to get on with things, pulling out a chair tucked into the small kitchen table and lowering himself into it. Maggie did the same. Their faces now just a few inches apart, the words raced out of him.

'Forbes was found hanged in his bedroom in New Orleans.'

'Right . . . '

Stuart lowered his voice. 'He was wearing women's underwear. Stockings, garters, the whole deal.'

'Jesus. Is this some kind of a joke?'

'Do I look like I'm joking? The police say it's not as uncommon as you'd think. Starving the oxygen to the brain gives you a rush. "Autoerotic asphyxiation" they call it. One theory is that Forbes was getting off on the success of his little project. Making contact with the President, interviews on cable TV. Seems like he was aroused.'

'Is that what the police are saying?'

'No. All they know is that he'd been in the news during the last forty-eight hours, as the source for a couple of stories damaging to the President. Do you have any breakfast cereal?'

Maggie stood up and passed him a box of Cheerios. He immediately plunged a hand deep inside and fed himself a large mouthful.

Neither of them had said what she knew he and everyone else in the White House must be feeling. 'Solves a problem, though, doesn't it, Stu?'

'I was worried you'd say that. If you're saying that, so will plenty of other folks. In fact, they've already started.'

'What do you mean?'

'Blogs. Wingnuts mainly. But that's how it always starts. On the margins, then spreads inwards.'

'They're claiming Baker had something to do with this?'

Goldstein reached into the pocket of his triple-extra-large jacket and pulled out his iPhone. A few stabs at the screen, and he was reading:

> '"Napoleon said he wanted generals who were neither courageous nor brilliant, but lucky. Seems as if Stephen Baker is one of life's lucky generals. Just when he was staring into the abyss, the guy who was going to push him over the edge wakes up dead. You've got to admit it, this Prez has someone up there who likes him. Though they say you make your own luck . . ."'

'So?'

'Come on, Maggie. "You make your own luck"? We know where this is heading.'

Maggie said nothing. She understood perfectly. She poured herself a coffee, then returned to the table.

'We had seven senators calling for an independent counsel *before* this broke,' he said bitterly. 'It won't just be Rick Franklin talking about a special prosecutor now.' He fed himself another fistful of Cheerios. 'Thanks to Forbes, people who used to trust the President now don't. They think he might be crazy and in the pay of the ayatollahs. So now they'll be ready to believe he is capable—'

'—of murder.'

Stuart looked at her hard. 'You heard what he said last night.'

Maggie hesitated. Of course she had heard what Stephen Baker had said last night. 'But no one on the team would leak anything.'

'It's still a disaster!' Stuart's usually cheerful, gnome-like countenance was gone, transformed by sorrow or anger, Maggie couldn't quite tell which. 'Maggie, do you know how long a presidential term is? In days?' He didn't wait for an answer. 'It's fourteen hundred and sixty days. We've had sixty-one. Can you imagine if he has to stagger on for fourteen hundred days without the trust of his most senior advisers? If they think what you were thinking?'

Maggie stared into her coffee, reluctant to meet Stuart's gaze. She could not deny what he had just said.

'We have to know the truth, Maggie. We need to get the facts, the full story. Otherwise the Baker presidency is going down.'

Maggie held his gaze and then, brisk and businesslike, she began working through the questions to be answered.

'First, we need to know if it was a suicide. Then we need to know if Forbes was alone. If he was part of a team, the threat is still there.'

'Right. Who are they? Is this Republican dirty tricks? Foreign? Someone we haven't thought of?'

'And what is this nuclear secret he was about to drop?'

Goldstein pointed his finger directly at Maggie, a sign that she had asked precisely the right question. 'What indeed?'

Her mind was whirring now, rattling through multiple questions, each of which spawned dozens more. The diplomatic negotiations that had dominated her professional life worked the same way: you had to consider each path the parties might take, and then work out which tributaries and detours might lead off each path. But before any of that there was one large fork in the road.

'OK,' she said, finally. 'You'd better go. I need to leave now.'

'Where are you going?'

'Where do you think? I'm not going to get any answers here, Stu. I'm going to New Orleans.'

EMAIL CHATTER, intercepted by the National Security Agency, Maryland. Thought to be a statement issued by a key leader of violent jihadism, whereabouts unknown:

> I bear witness that there is no God but Allah and that Muhammad is his messenger. The head of the infidels worldwide has a new face, but the rotten heart is still the same.
>
> We are now in a new struggle, to prevent brothers and sisters being tricked by the smiling face and honeyed words of the deceiver Baker. May God find a way to remove this man, so that Muslims may see the true face of America once more.

New Orleans, Wednesday, March 22, 18:15 CST

The billboards on Interstate 10 told her she was in a different country, a universe away from the buttoned-up pieties of the capital. One sign promoted a gun show, the next a burlesque club.

'This your first time in N'Awlins?'

Maggie nodded, not wanting to get into conversation with the cab driver just yet: she needed to think.

She had asked for the French Quarter. It made for useful cover. She could be a tourist from Dublin too naive to know anywhere else to stay. Or she could be a journalist.

It was a message on the machine from Nick du Caines, the dissolute New York-based correspondent of a much-loved, if ailing, British Sunday newspaper, that had given her the idea. If Nick was to be believed, there was no one and nowhere a journalist could not gain access to.

If Nick was to be believed, that is. Part of his charm was the grey zone he inhabited when it came to the truth. Or *la véracité*, as he would doubtless refer to it, resorting to his comedy French accent whenever he wanted to skirt round a topic that might be awkward. ('Mags, it's late, you're gorgeous, I am full of *ardeur*, so what about a little *liaison dangereuse* or otherwise?')

She had tried calling him as soon as she left home for New Orleans. She called his cellphone at least three times. From what she could divine, Nick du Caines didn't work during the week at all, instead building himself up to a fever which crested on Friday night as he hammered away at his keyboard until dawn on Saturday—just making the lunchtime deadline in London. So where the correspondent would be on a midweek morning was anybody's guess. Though you'd get good odds for the bed of a lonely expat European—the wife of the Belgian ambassador, perhaps.

But now, as her cab was navigating its way down streets with improbable names like Abundance, Cupid and Desire, she finally got through.

'Mags! My long-lost comrade! What the hell is happening at the White House? Just heard about your unwanted *au revoir* from there. Sounds like you got out just in time. Bastards, though, for firing you. Is there anything your Uncle Nick can do?'

'Well actually, Nick, there's something I need.'

'I can't tell you how long I've been waiting to hear those words, Mags my love. Shall I come over at eight? Or right now?'

'Not that, Nick. I need some advice.'

'OK.'

'About being a journalist. I can't tell you much about it yet, but I promise when I can you'll get it first.'

'A story? Oh, bless your little Irish heart. What is it you need to know?'

For the next ten minutes, Nick du Caines proceeded to teach a crash course in journalism's black arts. They agreed that she would be Liz Costello of the *Irish Times*: if anyone were to check up on her via Google they would at least find something. The fact that the Costello byline would be attached to witty, albeit out-of-date reports on Dublin nightlife would be a problem, but a surmountable one.

'Say you're writing it for the travel section: a post-Katrina piece, "Return to New Orleans",' Nick advised. 'And remember you never write, you *file.* It's never an article, it's a *piece.* And don't save anything onto the machine. My laptop was once crushed under a motorbike by some hairy biker: lost a three-thousand-word feature. Save everything online, Mags. In the ether.'

Nick warned her that the city would be swarming with journalists after the Forbes death. She was to head for the hotel where all the reporters would be staying. There's always one, he explained. He would call his mate from the *Telegraph* and find out the name. Within two minutes, there was a buzz on her BlackBerry: The Monteleone.

The second she got out of the cab, she was hit by a scent that reminded her of Africa: the subtropical tang of damp and decay, with a hint of sweetness. She looked around, instantly hit by the lushness that seemed to tumble off every Paris-style balcony, vivid purple bougainvillea or trailing plants of dense green.

It was still early, but Nick had told her to head for the bar: thanks to the time difference, the European hacks would all be off deadline by now. The Carousel Bar was the kind of place that would normally make Maggie recoil: it had, God help us, a theme—the circus, complete with a spinning merry-go-round in the centre of the room. But there were also portraits of past guests, among them Tennessee Williams and William Faulkner, which made her feel rather more forgiving.

She spied a group of half a dozen—five men, one woman—at a corner table. Past experience told her this was the foreign press corps, and she was right. There, sipping at a vile-looking concoction, was a man who matched Nick's description of his *Telegraph* pal—sandy-haired, gawky, probably ten years her junior.

'Tim?' she asked, prompting the man to his feet, simultaneously putting down his drink and offering a handshake.

'Hurricane?' he said, raising his glass with a smile. 'The post-Katrina cocktail of choice, apparently.' Remembering Lesson One in Nick du Caines's journalism for beginners course, Maggie insisted she would get this round—taking orders for more Hurricanes from the rest of the table. As she did, she noticed a man at a corner table, alone. Dark-haired, thin-faced and older than the others, he had a laptop open. Was he a journalist too?

By the time she came back to the table, Tim had already filled everyone in: she was Liz from the *Irish Times*, a pal of Nick's.

'Where we got up to, Miss Costello,' explained Francesco, a bald man in his forties from *Corriere della Sera*, 'was the police statement today that they are "looking for no one else" in connection with Forbes's death.'

'Means they are treating it as suicide,' added Tim keenly.

'And what do we think of that?' said Maggie, taking a sip of her cocktail. Sickly sweet, it made her gag: how anyone would want to drink this over a glass of Jameson's was beyond her.

'I don't see how they could do anything else,' said Francesco. 'There was no sign of a break-in at the apartment,' he said. 'There were no fingerprints except his own.'

'The coroner might call it death by misadventure.' It was the woman, who was, apparently, the New York correspondent for *Der Spiegel*. 'It's not suicide if Forbes didn't want to take his own life.'

'It seems,' said Tim, 'as if our Mr Forbes was so thrilled at his success that he wanted to celebrate, as it were.'

'And we think Forbes was into the whole autoasphyxiation thing?'

'Oh, yes. We have a piece from our medical correspondent which says Forbes fits the profile—risk-taker, thrill-seeker, loner. And don't forget the New Orleans factor.'

'What's that?'

'N'Awlins!' Tim attempted a Southern drawl, without success. 'The Big Easy, the Big Sleazy. He lived just off Bourbon Street, for God's sake. This is sin city, and he was right in the middle of it.'

'Is that what the *Telegraph* is saying tomorrow?'

'That's what *I'm* saying. The editor loathes Baker. He asked the foreign desk to get me to write "The ten clues that say Forbes was murdered". Been reading too many blogs.'

'That would be a cracking story, though,' Maggie said, before noticing that the woman from *Der Spiegel* was staring at her.

'Don't I know you from somewhere?' the woman said.

'I don't think so. Not unless you spend time clubbing by the Liffey.' Maggie could hear her accent change, dialling up the Irish.

'No, you definitely look familiar.'

Maggie didn't like where this was going. 'Actually, I get this a lot. I have one of those faces. People say I look like a lot of people.'

'Must be that then.'

Maggie smiled in what she hoped was a sisterly fashion. She glanced down at the pile of BlackBerrys and phones on the table: it would only take a couple of searches of the name Costello and this woman would soon have her rumbled.

A phone call came for Francesco and, thankfully, the moment was broken. Seizing his chance, Tim turned to her and suggested the two of them go out for a bite of dinner. 'We could compare notes on the story, if you like.'

Maggie remembered another of Nick's rules: better to hunt in packs, at least if you're a novice. She needed to tag along with someone, so it might as well be someone eager.

She got to her feet, accepting the table's collective gratitude for getting the round in, and followed Tim out.

They headed down Iberville Street, hearing the jazz riffs that curled like cigarette smoke from each doorway. Eventually they reached the Acme Oyster House: she had a plate of chargrilled oysters, while he gobbled up a pound of spicy boiled crawfish.

After dinner they walked along Bourbon Street, trading speculation on the Forbes case. Was he a Southerner? A native of New Orleans?

'Can we go to his house?' Maggie said suddenly.

'It's sealed off. Crime scene and all that. No media access.'

'I don't mean to go in. Just to look from the outside.'

Tim, who had visited earlier that day, was only too happy to play tour guide, leading Maggie a few blocks east to the tree-lined and residential Spain Street. The homes were decent enough, timber-clad in pastel colours, but they were small, and without the ornate, wrought-iron balustrades that made the French Quarter alluring. It suggested that Forbes had been anything but wealthy.

'There it is,' said Tim, gesturing ahead. Ribbons of yellow and black police tape still barred the front porch and the three-step walk-up; a couple of TV satellite trucks were parked outside.

Maggie gazed at it, trying to imagine the life of the man who had lived there. Just then, she spotted some activity. A policeman was approaching and behind him what appeared to be a colleague in plain clothes. She turned to Tim—'Isn't that . . .?'—but he was off chatting to one of the technicians by the TV truck.

Maggie took another look. It was the thin-faced man from the Monteleone bar, being ushered into Vic Forbes's house, a place that was off limits to the press. Yet he had been among the journalists. What was going on? The simplest explanation was that the man was a plain-clothes cop who had been at the Monteleone bar undercover. But why? Surely he hadn't been eavesdropping on the hacks: of what possible value could that be?

Tim was back at her side and Maggie said nothing. She scribbled a few lines in her notebook, then agreed that they stroll back to the Monteleone together.

Back at the hotel, Maggie reluctantly agreed to return to the Carousel Bar, where the table of international journalists had re-formed. This time, she insisted on whiskey.

Within twenty minutes, the thin-faced man was back, once again taking a table on his own, once again pulling out his laptop as if to begin journalistic work.

Maggie excused herself from the group and, with no clear plan, strode right over to the man. 'Excuse me,' she began.

'What is it?' he said. American, the accent rougher than she was expecting. Not Southern; closer to New Jersey.

'Who are you?'

'I'll tell you if you tell me.' He cracked a smile, showing bad teeth.

'My name is Liz Costello. *Irish Times*.'

'Lewis Rigby. I write for the *National Enquirer*. Freelance.'

That was not what she was expecting. 'As in the supermarket tabloid?'

'Yeah, the supermarket tabloid that broke the biggest political story of the last year, thank you very much.'

'Mark Chester's love child? That was you?'

'Not me personally. But yeah. You wanna sit down?'

Maggie pulled up a chair, forming a new strategy in light of this information. 'So,' she said, her voice friendly now. 'You here on the Forbes story?'

He smiled, as if licking his lips at the prospect. 'You bet.'

'Right,' Maggie said slowly. 'It's just I had a tip that earlier today a reporter for the *Enquirer* bribed a serving officer of the New Orleans Police Department in order to gain access to a crime scene. You know that's a felony in all fifty states.'

He turned ashen. 'Jesus Christ.'

'Don't worry. I'm not going to blab. We've all got a job to do.'

He let out a long gulp of air.

Maggie continued. 'Just so long as you share whatever you've got with me.'

'You gotta be kidding. There's no way the *Nat*—'

'—*National Enquirer* is going to want to face charges of corrupting a police officer. Too serious. Which is why you're going to get on the phone to your friend and ask him to arrange another visit to the house. With me as your pal.'

THE TV TRUCKS were still there but, Rigby counselled, one was local and, at this hour, off the air, while the other was Japanese: nothing to worry about. Still, Rigby insisted on waiting across the street, standing in the shadows where he would not be seen. Eventually the policeman Maggie had seen earlier came into view. Rigby stepped out to meet him. He nodded his head towards Maggie and uttered the word 'colleague'. The cop shrugged, as if to say 'Like I give a shit'.

In silence he led them under the tape and up the steps, acting as if this were perfectly normal police procedure. Once inside, he handed them each a pair of latex gloves. He put on a pair too, then turned on the lights. 'You know the rules: you don't move anything, you don't take anything. You got five minutes, max.'

Maggie's eyes swept over the room, trying to capture as much information as she could. Minimal furniture. Paintings on the wall: Holiday Inn prints rather than art. It looked unlived in, like a corporate rental.

Rigby had already moved across the ground floor and was on the spiral staircase to the bedroom, apparently grateful for the chance to take a second look round, even if it had cost him an extra few hundred dollars. Maggie followed. She clanked her way round the wrought-iron staircase, emerging onto a small landing giving onto three rooms: bathroom, bedroom and a small study.

Maggie darted into the bathroom and opened the medicine cabinet: empty, save for one tube of toothpaste and a can of shaving foam. Across the landing, she could see Rigby standing in the centre of the bedroom, taking photographs.

She looked into the study. Side on was a glass desk, dominated by a vast computer screen. It was flanked by two others, each angled into the other. She looked under the desk to see a curtain of cables, connected to nothing. So those were just monitors on the desk; the police must have taken the machines.

She heard a creak, the sound of Rigby leaving the bedroom.

She passed him on the landing. 'I'll just take a quick peek.'

'You want to focus on the beam by the window,' he said. 'That's where it happened.' Then he headed for the study.

She stepped in, bracing herself. But there was no need. This room was as soulless and empty as the one downstairs. A bed, a side table, an old-fashioned armoire. No photographs anywhere. If there had ever been anything in this place that might have shed light on Vic Forbes, the police had clearly removed it.

A raised voice from halfway up the staircase. The cop: 'We need to clear this premises in the next ninety seconds.'

It was then that she heard it.

The first sound came so soon after the policeman had spoken that she assumed that it must somehow be connected to him: perhaps an alarm he had triggered. But when the second buzz came, she could tell that it was much closer. It was inside this room.

No longer moving gingerly, she yanked open the armoire. A row of suits: mostly grey. She rifled through them, each one revealing precisely nothing.

She squatted, checking the floor of the closet, her hand furiously feeling in the dark for anything that might explain that noise. Straightening up, she checked the top shelf. Nothing.

Then it came once more, a low buzz.

'Come on.' Rigby was at the door. 'We're leaving.'

The cupboard door was still open, standing as a barrier between them, preventing him from seeing her hands. She began groping at the pockets of the suits, one after another until, at last, inside a jacket she found what she was looking for.

Turning to face the man from the *Enquirer*, she shone what she hoped was her warmest, most engaging smile—even as one hand took the small device and slid it into her own pocket.

Washington DC, Wednesday, March 22, 22:15

'So now it's your decision. You've spoken to colleagues. They say you'll have the full weight of the Republican party in Congress behind you.'

'They *say* that. You know how much verbal agreements are worth in this town.'

'I do, sir. They're not worth the paper they're written on.'

That one word had done it, as she surely knew it would. *Sir.* He felt his loins stirring. She was playing this little routine expertly tonight, the demure-yet-pert Southern belle with a hint of sauce. She only had to call him 'sir' in that eyelash-fluttering way and he was transported back to the nineteenth century: he was master of the house and she was bending over to submit to his will . . .

He looked at his watch: ten fifteen. He would have to act fast. 'If this is to work, Cindy, then the Forbes stuff is critical. Our folks have to be dead certain that Stephen Baker had Forbes killed.'

'We don't have many allies down there. Governor Tett is ours, obviously, but he's surrounded by Democrats. But the good news is that the *National Enquirer* is sniffing around.'

'That *is* good news.' He looked out of the window. 'This is the big one, Cindy. If we get it right, Baker will be finished.'

'And you, sir, will only just be started.' She fluttered her eyelashes again. 'Strike me hard if I'm wrong.'

That was it, the surge of lust was now too great to resist. Senator Rick Franklin glanced down at the portrait on his desk, the one that showed him and his four children smiling warmly at the lens, while his wife of eighteen years gazed adoringly up at him. He turned the picture face down and looked at his watch. If they were quick, there was time.

'Now, Cindy, I am about to follow the rules of this house and administer the punishment that you deserve.'

They were practised enough, the Senator and his aide, that they could run through the whole ritual in a matter of minutes.

Once it was done, he felt ready to make the move that he knew would define his career and might well alter the course of American history. He dialled the number Cindy had put in front of him, heard the operator answer and realised, with a rush of adrenalin, the import of what he was about to do.

'This is Senator Rick Franklin. I need to speak to the President.'

New Orleans, Wednesday, March 22, 23:45 CST

The device she had found had been burning a hole in Maggie's pocket for the best part of an hour. Lewis Rigby had insisted they have a drink. Throughout their conversation, though her eyes didn't waver, Maggie did not listen to a word the grubby little hack was saying. Instead all her brainpower was channelled into her fingertips, as she turned the object over and over.

It was round and flat, a disc. It was too thin to be a cellphone. There were no buttons, nor one of those clamshell flaps that might conceal them. A moment of panic seized her. What if she had reached into the wrong pocket? What if she had had the chance to grab Vic Forbes's cellphone, only to come away with a flipping bar coaster or whatever this was?

They finally got back to the Monteleone, where she made her excuses. Once upstairs, having closed the door, she plunged into her pocket and pulled the thing out. Hell, if it wasn't actually a poxy coaster after all. From the 'Midnight Lounge, S Claiborne Avenue'.

She threw it on the bed, convinced that she had screwed up royally. What the hell was she doing here? She was an analyst of international relations, a diplomat, and here she was, playing at being Sherlock Holmes. And she was crap at it. She could curse—

There it was again. The buzz. The coaster was buzzing.

She picked it up and stared at it. At last she smiled. She hadn't seen one of these things in years: a pager handed to customers while they waited for a table. Get a drink at the bar; when the pager buzzes, you can be seated.

She wondered how the police could have missed it: but perhaps it would only have started going off again late in the evening, as the Midnight Lounge opened for business.

And if it was still buzzing now, its batteries still alive, did that not suggest Forbes had picked it up recently, maybe even *very* recently?

She glanced at the bed, with its enticing offer of rest after an exhausting day, and then back to the coaster.

Mind made up, she went downstairs, stepped outside and hailed a cab. 'Midnight Lounge on South Claiborne Avenue, please. As quick as you can.' In her haste, she didn't notice the man watching from the other side of the street flag down a second cab, so that he could follow her into the New Orleans night.

Washington DC, Wednesday, March 22, 22:55

As Stuart Goldstein made his way to the Residence, he had no idea what to expect from the late-night conversation they were about to have. Would Baker be as anxious as he had been last night, or would he have found some relief in the fact that Forbes had indeed now 'gone'?

As it turned out, the President spoke about the First Lady's spirits rather than his own. He said Kimberley was grateful that the lowlife who had dared prey on Katie would never bother them again.

'And you? What do you think about it?'

'I think, Stuart, that a problem which was already consuming far too much White House time need distract us no more.'

'It's a relief, right?'

'Yeah, it's a relief.' He allowed himself a smile. 'Those stories were giving me a headache. And there didn't seem to be any easy solution.'

'Except the one that landed in our lap.'

'Not sure I would put it like that, Stuart.'

'No. Of course not.'

There was a pause. In the silence, Goldstein reminded himself that whatever history they shared, Baker was now in another realm, one that prevented him talking like a buddy, even if he wanted to. But he couldn't leave without asking the question.

'Mr President, is there anything at all that I should know about Vic Forbes and his death?'

'Stuart, you've known me a long time. In my entire political career, every path that I've taken, you've known about. You know all there is to know.' The President picked up the papers at his side, a gesture that signalled the meeting was over.

Goldstein had just reached the door when the phone rang.

Baker gave Goldstein a raised eyebrow. Who could be calling who would be put through this late? Some foreign leader? He picked up the phone, silently indicating that Stuart should stay.

'Yes. Good evening, Senator.'

Goldstein made a face. *Who?*

Baker mouthed back a single word: Franklin.

Franklin? What the hell was that prick doing phoning here, and at this time? Goldstein watched his boss listening intently. Then he saw a change in him he had never witnessed before. The conversation ended with Baker saying, 'Senator, I appreciate the courtesy of the call. Good night.' Stuart was transfixed by the sight of the President of the United States turning the colour of death.

New Orleans, Thursday, March 23, 00:06 CST

The cab threaded its way first through the streets close to the hotel, then it left the French Quarter behind and the streets slowly became wider and more desolate. Soon they were passing boarded-up shops and whole blocks that seemed abandoned.

Maggie leaned forward to speak to the cab driver, an African-American whose hair was tipped with grey. 'Where are we going?'

'Just where you told me to go. Not many tourists come round here. This is the Ninth Ward.'

'I see.' Everyone in America knew of the Lower Ninth Ward of New Orleans, the part of the city where Katrina had packed her hardest punch. Maggie had seen the footage on the news a hundred times, but still it was a shock to see that so much of the area looked as if the hurricane had only just struck.

Eventually there were a few lights at the side of the road: a gas station, a liquor store, and then a single-storey building of grey corrugated steel decorated by a vertical sign: THE MIDNIGHT LOUNGE. The illuminated graphic of a curvy, thick-lipped stripper might have conveyed glamour once. Now it just looked forlorn and tatty.

Maggie paid the driver, nodded to a bouncer the size of a fridge on the door, as if she came to places like this all the time, and walked in.

Save for a few feeble table candles, the place was cast in a deep gloom. A stage area, dully lit in low purple, faced a clutch of small tables, all of which lay under a blanket of darkness. A strip joint, designed to spare the blushes of the audience and—judging by the performer bending into an improbable angle at that moment—to spare nothing of those on stage.

'You here alone?'

She looked up to see a waitress wearing a strip of material that few would recognise as a skirt and the skimpiest of bras, inside which were two unmoving globes of not-quite-flesh.

Maggie had her response ready. 'I need to talk to your manager. A personal matter.' Nervous, but doing her best to be friendly.

The human blow-up doll inclined her head towards a table near the bar and slunk off.

It was impossible to see who was at the manager's table until she was just a few feet away. A woman, short blondish hair, Maggie's age, dressed—to Maggie's relief—in actual clothes. Black cigarette pants, a spangly top.

'Can I help you?'

'Can we speak in private?'

'This *is* private.' The voice was firm but not quite harsh.

Maggie leaned in closer, then lowered her voice. 'I need to speak about something personal. Very personal.'

'It's going to have to be right here.'

'OK. Can I sit down?'

The woman gestured her into the seat opposite.

'I know you have your rules about privacy and all,' Maggie began, her voice wavering just as she intended it to. 'But I need to know if my husband was here last night.'

'I'm sorry, we have a strict pol—'

'I knew you would say that, but this is different.' Maggie hoped her eyes were full of desperation and, to her surprise, she saw something that was, if not quite warm, then at least not cold, in the eyes scrutinising her. 'You see,' Maggie whispered, playing her trump card, 'I'm pregnant.'

The face of the woman opposite softened.

'And I need to know what kind of man I am married to. He said he had stopped all this: coming to strip clubs, seeing hookers. He promised me months ago. I told him I needed that if we were to be a family.'

'But you think he's been coming round here?'

Maggie nodded mutely, trying to look as distressed as possible.

'I tell you, honey, if a woman didn't hate men before working at this joint . . . Like I say, I'd really like to help. But we don't exactly take names at the door.'

'You have CCTV though. I saw it on my way in. Why not let me just see the tapes for last night? That's all I need. Please . . .'

'There must be, like, a million rules against that.'

'Then at least I'll know if I'm being taken for a sucker or not.' She laid her hand on her stomach. 'Just let me look.'

The blonde woman shook her head, with a small, world-weary smile. 'There's not a man in this town who would let you go anywhere near those tapes. I must be an idiot.'

Maggie let out a sigh of relief and extended her hand across the table in thanks. The manager clasped it, holding it for a long second or two. Finally she stood up and Maggie did the same.

Maggie followed the manager down a flight of stairs and through a door marked 'Authorised Staff Only'. Inside was a corridor with three glass-panelled doors, all opening onto offices.

They stopped at the third. One side was dominated by four TV screens. Barely watching them, preferring to concentrate on the *Puzzler* magazine in front of him, was a man Maggie identified as the companion bouncer to the fridge she had seen upstairs.

'Frank, this lady is a friend of mine,' the manager said. 'She wants to see the tapes from last night. Give her whatever she needs.' With that, she turned and gave Maggie one last look. 'I have a twelve-year-old daughter at home. She hasn't seen her father in ten years. You're smarter than I was. Best of luck.'

Frank pulled out a swivel chair from under the desk, and nodded for Maggie to sit in it. As he punched the buttons that would bring up last night's recordings, Maggie's BlackBerry chimed. A message from Stuart:

Call me urgently. Situation grave.

'Anything here, ma'am?'

She forced herself to come back to the moment. She had to concentrate. She looked at the screen for what felt like ages. A procession of heavy men, thin men, black men, white men, men who looked furtive, men who looked like wife-beaters—no wonder the manager had grown to hate the entire sex. And Maggie had only been staring at an hour's worth of customers, and that was at twice normal speed.

Halfway through the second hour something caught Maggie's eye.

It was not a man but a woman. Tall, with dark hair, she instantly stood out from the rest: classier than the handful of other women the CCTV had picked up that night.

Not that Maggie could see her face; she kept her head down. But she walked elegantly. And with something else too. Purpose.

And now she could see why. Walking a pace behind her was a man in a flat golfer's cap and a dark grey suit. As he came out he looked left and right, exposing his face to the CCTV camera. His eyes were almost bugging out with desire.

There was no doubt about it. She asked to freeze the frame, so that she could take a good, long look at the man who had stared so knowingly from the television set yesterday. For there, caught on tape, was none other than Vic Forbes.

Trying to sound as nonchalant as she could, she asked the guard next to her, 'Do you recognise this man?'

'He looks kinda familiar, yes.'

'You know who that is?'

'Well, I couldn't tell you his name, if that's what you mean, ma'am. We're not meant to know anyone's name. We never ask.'

'But you've seen him before? Is he a regular?'

The guard nodded.

'And what about her?' Maggie nodded towards the frozen image on the screen.

The guard rewound and played the sequence back at half-speed. 'Hard to tell,' he said. 'Oh, OK. I can see who that is now. She's a dancer. Started a couple of days ago, I think. But she didn't turn up for work today.'

'And do you remember her name?'

'The girls have names,' he said, allowing himself a small, patronising smile, as if explaining to a naive child the ways of the world. 'But they're bullshit names. Mystery, Summer, all that shit.'

'So what was this one called?'

Before he had a chance to answer, the door swung open. It was the manager. She smiled at Maggie. 'You got what you wanted?'

'I wouldn't say it was what I wanted.'

The woman shifted her features into a pose of earnest concern. 'No, of course.'

Frank, eager to seem helpful, gestured for his boss to look at the screen. 'The lady wants to know who this is. I said she was new.'

The manager leaned in for a closer look at the monitor. After a second or two, she spoke. 'Frank's right. She's new. Started this week. She dances under the name of Georgia.'

'You don't know her real name?'

'I never ask.'

'And she only started this week?'

'Right. She came in day before yesterday, I think. Offered to start right away. It wasn't a hard decision, if you know what I mean.'

'What do you mean?'

'I just meant that she was—' She hesitated, unsure how to put it. '*Unusual.* In this place, I mean. Most of the girls in here *look* like strippers. Their nails are fake, their boobs are fake, their hair's fake. The college boys like those girls plenty, but the more upscale guests are looking for something real. Kind of the whole natural beauty thing. They'll come back for that again and again. She was gorgeous, no doubt about it.' She looked at Maggie, who was furrowing her brow in a show of wounded wifely love. 'I'm sorry.'

Maggie collected herself. 'And where is she now?'

'I don't know. She didn't show up for work this evening,' the manager said. 'I called her. Her phone just rang.'

Maggie looked down at her hands, digesting what she had heard.

The woman spoke again. 'Listen, sweetheart, I'm sorry you had to find out like this. But better to find out now than later. Take it from me, that ain't no fun. Not for you, not for your child.'

Maggie collected her things, digging into her bag for a tissue which she used to wipe away fake tears, thanked Frank and let the manager show her out.

Once outside, she exhaled deeply, refreshed to be away from the stale, soiled air of the Midnight Lounge. She fought the urge to phone Stuart. Not yet; this was still not nailed down. She looked across the street, seeing a man in an idling car. He glanced directly at her, then away. Not a cab, then.

While the bouncer on the door called her a taxi, she began to pace. Surely what she had just seen could mean only one thing. The time stamped on the CCTV recording had been 23:35. She tried to remember what Telegraph Tim had said earlier. There had been so many details, but he had told her, she was sure of it. Twelve-thirty. The estimated time of death. Vic Forbes had been in a TV studio, then sat somewhere—maybe at an Internet café—and issued his 'statement' threatening to reveal a shocking aspect of Stephen Baker's past. And then later he had come to the Midnight Lounge where he had picked up a girl. And not just some stripper, but a beautiful woman who just happened to have started work at this place—where Forbes was a known regular—one day earlier and who had now disappeared. They had left together and, an hour or so later, he was dangling from a rope.

There was only one way that could have happened, wasn't there?

What if it was a real pick-up? Theoretically possible. But Maggie remembered that the only fingerprints they'd found at the house had belonged to Forbes. If she had just been a hooker, she'd have left her prints everywhere.

No, there was only one plausible explanation. It was a classic honeytrap—though with a lethal sting.

The police were wrong. Forbes had not killed himself.

Victor Forbes had been murdered.

FROM THE PAGE, Thursday, March 23, 00:03:

> Impeachment! Republicans to table articles of impeachment through House Judiciary Committee accusing President Baker of 'high crimes and misdemeanours'. Massive and developing story.

Twenty minutes later, from politico.com's Playbook column:

> I'm hearing that Senator Rick Franklin placed a call to the White House in the last hour, notifying the President of his intention to proceed with impeachment.
>
> This has only come about because of the death of Vic Forbes. Sure, that name won't appear on the charge sheet when it comes before the House Judiciary Committee in the morning. Franklin and his pals in the House will make the Iranian Connection the heart of the legal case against the President. But make no mistake, the rumours, the suspicion at the undeniably convenient timing of Forbes's passing, all that has created bad atmospherics for Baker.

And, if Franklin is serious, he must reckon he can peel off enough conservative Democrats to make this thing pass. Let's face it, there's no shortage of Democrats who never liked the President—and all his idealistic talk of America showing an outstretched hand rather than a clenched fist to the world. The Democratic majority is so slender, Republicans need only a couple of Democrats to waver and the Judiciary Committee could agree to submit articles of impeachment for a vote of the entire House as soon as next week.

4

New Orleans, Thursday, March 23, 01:22 CST

Maggie was in the cab on the way back to the hotel, her mind racing through the implications. Only one question mattered, though the answer made her blood run cold. Who would want Forbes dead? In response, a single sentence kept repeating itself.

I want him gone.

It was the most obvious explanation. Who benefited more from the death of Victor Forbes than Stephen Baker?

For the fifth time in two minutes, she hit redial on Stuart's number. Still busy. *Situation grave*, he had said. What the hell was happening over there? Her BlackBerry, now set on silent, vibrated. She seized on it. 'Stuart? Is that you?' But the vibration had announced not a call but a message.

Stuart:

> Can't get hold of you. Things insane here. Franklin and the Republicans launching impeachment proceedings in the morning. You have to get us something fast. HE'S depending on you.

She felt her throat dry. Impeachment. How dare they? At long last, a truly decent, good man emerges from the swamp of politics, and what is their reaction? To tear him down, using the dirtiest tricks imaginable.

Her job was clear. She had to find something that would prove that the President had committed no crime. She needed to establish beyond all doubt that Forbes had taken his own life. And what had she done? The very opposite. She had found evidence suggesting Forbes had been murdered.

Calm down. That fact alone did not necessarily implicate the President. Baker had allies, including those who would have seen Forbes as a threat to their own interests. What if one of them had decided to do Baker a favour and take Forbes out? Or might someone have dispatched Forbes not to help Baker but to *damage* him, by making him look like a Mafia boss whose enemies mysteriously ended up dead?

Two minutes after she got back to her hotel room, the phone vibrated again. Stuart. 'Stu, what the hell's going on? It can't happen, can it? He hasn't got the votes. I mean, we're the majority party.'

'By a whisker. And that whisker is made up of conservatives who will vote with the Republicans if they feel that's where the wind is blowing. Maggie, you gotta find something to help our boy here.'

Maggie swallowed. 'Well, I've found something. But I'm not sure it helps.' There was a strange crackle on the line. 'What's that noise?'

'Gherkins,' Stuart said, crunching audibly. 'I keep a jar in the office for emergencies. So hit me, Maggie. I can take it.'

'Forbes was at a strip club the night he died. He left with a woman about an hour before the time of death.'

'Jesus.'

'It's not cast-iron proof but it adds up. There were no fingerprints at his house except his. The woman was a dancer at the club, but she'd only started the day before Forbes died. Exactly the time Forbes started spilling the beans. And she hasn't been seen since.'

'OK.' She could hear him chewing and thinking. Finally: 'The thing is, and this is about the only good news we have round here, New Orleans Police Department are winding up the investigation. The coroner says there's no evidence to alter his verdict of suicide. Seems like some people down there are trying to be helpful.'

'Who's being helpful?'

'It's a Democratic town, Maggie.'

'Stuart, at Forbes's house the police have removed all the computer stuff. We know Forbes did everything by computer. What Forbes knew—it's going to be on those machines. If we could—'

'Can't be done. That's gonna look like the White House poking its nose into a criminal investigation. Besides, Zoe—you know, the Secret Service agent? She reckons Forbes didn't store it on a machine, just on the Internet.'

'Oh, I get it.' Maggie remembered Nick's hairy-biker story.

She could hear Stuart still munching. It must have been his sixth straight gherkin. 'You need to find another way into this, Maggie. If Forbes was murdered, you have to find out who did it.'

'There's the woman who picked Forbes up.'

'What, the stripper? If she was some kind of hired gun then it's not the gun we're interested in, is it? It's who did the hiring. That's what we need to find out. And what bag of shit Forbes was about to tip over our heads. *Urgently.*'

'I know.' She wished he would stop telling her how much pressure she was under: she knew. Her mind had been churning with this and this alone for nearly nineteen unbroken hours.

'Maggie?' His voice was softer now. 'We've kind of given our lives up for this guy, haven't we? I have a wife and all, but I spend more time with CNN than I do with Nancy. And let's face it, you're married to the job.'

Maggie felt a sting of something like shame. Hadn't Uri said exactly the same thing? If the Baker presidency collapsed, it would all have been for nothing.

Stuart spoke again. 'We can't let this thing go down. He's hardly had a chance to do any of the things we dreamed of.'

Injecting confidence into her voice, she said, 'We're not going to let it go down. We're going to survive this. Just like we survived everything else. Remember, when Chester—'

'This is different, Maggie. We both know it. In the morning, I'm going to start counting the votes. See if Franklin has enough of our guys—even potentially—to win this thing.'

'And if he does?'

'I was thinking of telling the President he should resign.'

'Jesus Christ, Stuart.'

'Think about what it would mean to fight on. Wading through all this shit. Better to leave with some dignity. But then I think about you and me. If he goes, what's left of us? Actually, you've got plenty. You're smart and you're beautiful.'

Maggie didn't know what to say. She felt her eyes pricking with tears. Stuart had never spoken like this before.

'But there wouldn't be much left of me, would there? For twenty years, I've been Stuart Goldstein, the guy behind Stephen Baker. Without Baker, there's no Goldstein. Who else is gonna hire a big fat Jewish guy who eats gherkins out of the jar?'

She could hardly bear to listen. 'Stuart, don't. We're—'

'So what I'm trying to work out is, if I'm being selfish for wanting to fight this. If I'm doing it for my sake, not his. Maybe the best thing for him is if we let him walk away.'

'Enough, Stu. Enough late-night maudlin talk. I can get that in Ireland.' She wanted him to laugh but he didn't.

'You're right. I know. I know. I'm just so tired, that's all. We've worked so hard . . .' His voice tailed off, exhausted.

Maggie felt her heart swell. 'Go home and get some rest, Stu. I'll call you in the morning. Things will look better then, trust me.'

'Good night, Maggie.'

Washington DC, Thursday, March 23, 07:55

'I love the smell of fresh bagels in the morning.'

Senator Rick Franklin and his Head of Legislative Affairs, Cindy Hughes, had just stepped out of the elevator onto the fifth floor of the building on L Street which, to the naked eye, looked like a regulation 1970s-built office block. Functional and dull. To those in the know, however, it was—every Thursday morning, at least—the epicentre of American conservatism.

This was the Thursday Session, when a conference room would host the activists, lobbyists, congressional staffers, movers and shakers who together represented Washington's key 'movement' conservatives. At the back of the room, jugs of coffee and trays of bagels alongside bowls of cream cheese. If you were fifteen minutes early, you'd load up a plate and take a seat. Any later than that and you'd be standing at the back or spilling into the corridor.

When Franklin appeared, something happened that he had never seen before: a spontaneous round of applause which turned into a standing ovation. Already his push to remove Baker had made Rick Franklin a star, anointing him as de facto leader of the opposition.

He waved aside the offers of a seat: he was far too humble for such gestures of deference. Instead, he stood close to the door. His body language was politician's semaphore for 'I'm here to listen'.

Matt Nylind, the activist who had turned this meeting into the dominant force it had become, called for order. Franklin took a good look at him. Classic behind-the-scenes operative; looked like an overgrown college student. One tail of his shirt was edging over the waistband of his trousers; his glasses were smeared. Just the fact that he wore glasses: no politician would wear glasses. But these dweebs who crunched the numbers, drafted the Republicans' policies and never stopped working to advance the cause—these guys could look awful. No one ever saw them. Men like Franklin—with their gleaming white teeth, full heads of hair and pretty wives—would be front of house while the elves stayed hidden.

Nylind was making his introductory remarks: '. . . some big news overnight, but before we get to that I want to run through other items on our agenda. First, governors' races in Virginia and New Jersey. Baker stole both of those last fall but we're trending just two points behind. And that was before last night.' There was some bullish laughter and a smattering of applause in Franklin's direction, which he duly acknowledged by inclining his head minutely. Humbly.

Nylind resumed. 'OK, the banking bill. Polling is horrible for us on this right now. Suggestions for how we can turn it round?'

Immediately a voice piped up. 'We gotta death-tax it,' the voice was saying. 'When the Democrats called it an "estate tax" it was popular. Once we called it a "death tax", we killed it. We need to do the same with this bill.'

'Who is that?' Franklin whispered to Cindy.

'Michael Strauss. He's the head of the American Bankers' Association. Lobbyist for the entire financial services sector.'

Nylind was asking for new names for the banking bill. A woman close to the front suggested the 'anti-wealth bill'. Nylind nodded, but without enthusiasm. 'Let's remind ourselves of its core elements. This bill will cap bonuses till these banks have paid back the federal government every last cent they owe. Which could take decades. It will be the biggest cap on wealth and individual freedom since Leonid Brezhnev.'

'Why don't we call it the Brezhnev bill?' asked the woman.

Nylind muttered, 'Yeah, that will play really well with eighteen to twenty-fours.' Then, his volume duly adjusted: 'Let's get to the matter of the moment. Republicans on the Hill have set a remarkable lead, showing an aggressive response to the Iranian Connection with a move to impeach the President.

'Clearly that's gonna depend on pulling in moderate Democrats. Which means shifting public opinion to our side of the issue. I suggest the climate will depend less on the technicalities of donations from Iran and more on the general mood created by the Forbes episode. Where do people think we've got to on that?'

A man standing directly opposite spoke up, identifying himself as a producer of one of the nation's best-known talk-radio shows. 'There's still plenty of flesh on that turkey,' he began, with an accent Franklin placed in Alabama. 'And what was this bomb Forbes was gonna drop? Folks are mighty interested in that, I can tell you.'

Towards the back, a woman stood up. Franklin recognised her. She was a former prosecutor turned TV talking head.

'Are we too prim here to talk about the other dimension of the Forbes case?'

'The other dimension?' Nylind was smiling, enjoying himself.

'Yes, Matthew. The very *convenient* demise of Mr Forbes.'

Nylind surveyed the room. 'Do we want to go there?'

'There is a risk to it.' The talk-radio guy again. 'It can make us look wacko.'

'There's another problem.' All heads turned towards the chief aide to Congressman Rice of Louisiana. 'There'll be a coroner's report today, declaring Forbes's death a suicide. I got off the phone from the New Orleans Police Department just before I came here. They're going to announce this morning that their investigation is formally concluding.'

Loud tuts and several shaking heads.

Nylind jumped in. 'Let's not forget that there are a lot of Democrats in Louisiana. Since Katrina, most of the state officials, in fact.'

The lawyer spoke up again. 'I don't think that should shut us up. Just because a few party hacks are closing this thing down to help their buddy Stephen Baker. If anything, it makes it worse.'

A few hands rose, but Nylind moved to wrap things up. He wanted to talk about the chairmanship of the Federal Reserve.

Franklin looked at Cindy and signalled that they should leave.

In the cab back, he stared out of the window.

'You know what I'm thinking, Cindy?'

'What's that, Senator?'

'I'm thinking that it's interesting that the Democrats down there in N'Awlins are shutting down the investigation. Like my mammy used to say, if you see a woman get out a broom, chances are there's a pile of shit somewhere that needs cleaning up.'

'Well put, Senator.'

'It also means that this is the moment of maximum vulnerability for the White House,' Franklin said. 'I think it's time to put some serious pressure on Baker—and those who work for him.'

New Orleans, Thursday, March 23, 09:12 CST

'Good morning, Liz. You are cordially invited to a funeral.'

'A funeral? Whose?'

As Maggie contemplated the breakfast buffet, Telegraph Tim excitedly explained the morning's developments.

Forbes appeared to have left no family of any kind. In most cities, that would be a bleak and lonely state of affairs. But not New Orleans. This city still had the Paupers' Burial Society, a relic of the ante-bellum days of plantation owners doing good works.

'They left a pot of money. The fund is still there, still paying out, for anyone who dies alone within the city limits of New Orleans. If police can find no next of kin, the Paupers' Burial Society step in.'

Maggie smiled. 'Must be a pretty liberal bunch, given the way Forbes wound up.'

'Apparently they don't care. Anyway, it wasn't their decision.'

'No?' Maggie said, choosing between grapefruit juice and orange.

'No,' said Tim, hovering behind her. He explained that while most cities would have wanted the Forbes episode to fade away as quickly as possible, the mayor and tourist board of New Orleans had, after Katrina, a what-the-hell attitude: they had nothing to lose. They reckoned there was a marketing opportunity to be had. With so many journalists in town, why not lay on a show? Prove to the world that the city was still a place with party in its soul.

AN HOUR LATER, Tim was bouncing from one foot to the other in his delight. This was what any editor in London wanted from a story out of New Orleans. 'Liz,' he said to Maggie, 'truly we have been blessed on this one. Sex, death, men in tights—and now this!' Standing on the kerb, he swept his hand at the procession getting under way on the street.

Leading the way was a trio—clarinet, banjo and tuba—playing a slow, mournful spiritual. Behind them was a larger group, bearing trombones, trumpets and saxophones. These musicians were not yet playing, but moving in a stately fashion, a sort of graceful shuffling in time to the music. Finally, behind them, came the hearse.

When they got close to the media huddle, a woman with a clipboard—a PR for the tourist board, Maggie guessed—had a quiet word and the march drew to a halt.

Now more men, all black, gathered round the hearse. After a minute of pulling and shoving, they emerged holding the silver casket. The refrain kept playing, but the volume was rising. And, as if lifted by the music, those round the coffin made a sudden, swift move, raising it high above their heads. But the pallbearers didn't hold it still; they made it sway. Then they brought it down again, to waist level, where they began shifting it from side to side. The PR girl explained that this was another tradition of the jazz funeral: let the deceased dance one last time.

The procession headed down Bourbon Street, towards the cemetery. The TV guys hoisted their cameras onto their shoulders, while the reporters scrambled to catch up. Maggie did the same.

By the time they reached the burial ground, Maggie had drifted from the journalists. She put her notebook away and watched as the long snake of people now turned into a thick crowd at the gates of the cemetery. A priest said a few words of welcome, dwelling on New Orleans and its customs. He then added a quick mention of Vic Forbes before suggesting that they all head to the graveside.

Maggie hung back, close enough to hear but far enough away not to be visible. She looked around, only belatedly realising that someone was standing next to her. A man with white hair, sixty or so, in a grey suit. He had no notebook. And he wasn't dressed like a tourist. Could this man be the one true mourner for Vic Forbes?

She gave him a solemn look. Trying her luck, she whispered, 'Hello. Did you know him well?'

His gaze remained firmly ahead, watching the priest, but he spoke immediately, not answering the question, but asking one of his own. 'What line of work you in?'

An instinct told her not to claim to be a journalist, not now. 'I'm in the foreign service.'

Now he looked at her. 'Did you know him from the Company?'

Intuition took care of her answer. 'That's right.'

'You here as the official representative?'

This was one trick Maggie had learned in a thousand negotiations. However hard you were scrambling to assimilate new information, you had to give no sign of it. So she looked impassive as she processed what she had just heard. *The Company . . . the official representative.* 'I'm here to pay the Company's respects, yes.'

The man exhaled, as if he had just peeled off a protective layer. 'Figured you must be. Bob didn't have many friends.'

Maggie nodded stiffly. Her mind, though, raced with a single word. *Bob*.

'But he was good at his job. Even in some tight spots. Honduras, El Salvador, Nicaragua.'

Maggie turned her face towards him, a three-quarter turn meant to convey warmth. The penny had now dropped fully. 'That was important work. The nation owes you a debt. Both of you.'

'Funny that he ended up in New Orleans. Had no idea.'

'You weren't friends, then?'

'Hadn't clapped eyes on him in nearly twenty years. Then I see him all over the tube this week. I was thinking I should get back in touch—for old times' sake. Next thing I know, he's dead.'

They both paused, watching the priest throw a handful of earth on the coffin. Maggie had to fight the urge to bombard this man with questions: she had to do whatever an official representative of 'the Company' would do. And that, she decided, meant playing it ice cool.

The funeral party was turning away from the grave now, and Maggie sensed her chance was about to slip away. She would have to push her luck. 'I confess we did not quite know what to make of this . . . latest outburst.'

'Oh, he could be an asshole. That was the thing with Bob Jackson. Marched to his own drum.'

Bob Jackson. Was Vic Forbes his true identity, or a fake? Filing that away to be wrestled with later, she pushed again. 'What about his death? The police here say it was suicide.'

'I know. But after the guy had been threatening the President like that, you gotta wonder, haven't you?'

Maggie kept her face impassive. The band was now playing a raucous version of 'When the Saints go Marchin' In'. She turned as if to head back, praying that he would not take that as his cue to say goodbye. But he walked alongside her.

'Look, I would not rule it out. Jackson was not always the most popular guy around. Loner. Kind of obsessive. He might have made some enemies, even before this Baker thing. But anyone who knew Bob would know that he would do what we were all trained to do.'

The trumpets and trombones were making it hard to hear. 'I don't follow.'

'The blanket. No point taking out a guy like Jackson. Or any of us. Not if you're worried about what we know. He'd have prepared his blanket.'

'Of course,' Maggie said, even as she thought, What the hell is a blanket? They were now back by the cemetery gates.

She was about to press him further when she felt a hand on her shoulder and turned to see Telegraph Tim behind her. She made a face that she hoped said *not right now*. He looked a little offended, but to her relief he moved away. But when she turned back, the man had vanished, lost in the crowd.

She had to call Stuart right away. This information could be just the breakthrough they needed. Hurriedly, she thumbed the buttons on her phone, trying his direct line at the office. Straight to voicemail. Next she tried the mobile. *I'm sorry but this phone is no longer in service.*

Goddamn it! Now she dialled the White House switchboard. 'Stuart Goldstein, please,' she said.

The operator's voice was hesitant. 'May I ask who is calling?'

'My name is Maggie Costello, I used to be on the—'

'Ms Costello, I've been told to direct your call to Mr Sanchez. Please hold.'

There was an interminable delay, filled by piped classical music. Finally Maggie heard the voice of Doug Sanchez, though with none of the pep she was used to.

'Hi Maggie. I have some very bad news, I'm afraid. Stuart is dead.'

DIPLOMATIC CABLE: From the Embassy of the Islamic Republic of Pakistan, Washington DC. To the Head of the Army of the Guardians of the Islamic Revolution, Tehran:

TOP SECRET. ENCRYPTION SETTING: MAXIMUM.

Situation for SB deteriorating. Following our previous conversation, I can report that SB is now without the advice of his chief aide. We may not have the problem of the 'outstretched hand' for much longer. Ends.

5

New Orleans, Thursday, March 23, 11:23 CST

His voice wavering, Doug Sanchez explained that two joggers had found Stuart's body at six o'clock that morning in Rock Creek Park. Initial examination suggested he had died after swallowing thirty tablets of Dextropropoxyphene—a painkiller whose packaging warned against use by those with a history of 'depression with suicidal tendency'—and then slashing his left wrist. The police were about to issue a statement saying they were not looking for anyone else in connection with his death.

Maggie was too stunned to speak. She had worried about Stuart's life expectancy almost from the first day she had known him. She often imagined him keeling over with a coronary. But suicide? The very idea of Stu Goldstein, who gobbled up life the way he gobbled up food, killing himself would have seemed absurd.

Until last night. That last conversation they had had unnerved her. She had never heard Stuart sound so utterly defeated before.

Why hadn't she recognised that he was a man on the edge? What sort of a friend was she?

Sanchez was still speaking. 'Listen, Maggie, the President has told me what you and Stuart were working on. He's asked me to continue Stuart's work. From now on, you and I are to liaise, except where there are things for you to discuss directly with him. In fact he told me to transfer you over to him once we'd spoken. OK? We'll talk later.'

'OK.' There was a click and the sound of hold music. Telegraph Tim and the other reporters were looking over at her now, appearing curious. Maggie waved for them to go on without her. She found a quiet spot. The cemetery was almost empty, save for one or two stragglers, including a white man in a dark suit standing by the gates, also talking into his cellphone.

'Please hold for the President,' came the voice on her BlackBerry.

Another click and then: 'Maggie, I'm glad we've reached you.'

'Yes, Mr President.'

'This is a terrible blow for us all. I know how close you were to Stuart.'

'You were too, sir.'

'Yes. I was.' He paused, as if fighting to keep the lid on his emotions. 'He was not himself yesterday, I know that. But Stuart was not a quitter.' His tone changed. 'I just can't believe . . .' The sentence trailed away. 'Suicide: not Stu—'

'You're not saying that . . . someone might have done this?' It came out as barely more than a whisper.

'I'll tell you what I think, Maggie. I think this presidency is under assault. And we have to fight that with all we've got. It's not about me any more. This is about the Constitution of the United States. If they can remove an elected president, then they can do anything.'

Maggie tried to focus, to put Stuart out of her mind. 'Sir, it's unconfirmed but I strongly suspect that Vic Forbes was in fact Bob Jackson, a former agent of the CIA.'

A sharp intake of breath at the other end of the phone. 'Jesus Christ. Where did this come from?'

'I've just been at the funeral. I met a former colleague of his who repeatedly referred to "the Company". He said they worked together in Honduras, El Salvador and Nicaragua.'

There was a silence, two or three beats. 'You know what Stuart would say, don't you? "At least with Kennedy, they waited a few years. Gave the guy a chance."'

'You don't think—'

'Well, what does it look like, Maggie? An ex-CIA agent? That's who they use, for God's sake. I can hear Stuart saying it. "The Watergate break-in? Who were the plumbers? Who were the dirty-tricks squad? They were ex-CIA." Jesus.'

'So you think Forbes was working for—'

The President spoke more softly now. 'We're missing Stuart already, aren't we, Maggie? He would say that the plumbers—they were ex-CIA but they weren't working for the CIA.'

'Which leaves the key question: who was Forbes working for?'

'That's what you need to find out, Maggie. Tell me again, when was Forbes in the Agency?'

'He was Bob Jackson then. Started decades ago. He would have been in his twenties. He was forty-seven when he died.'

'I'll put Sanchez on it. See if he can get that confirmed. And stay safe, Maggie. I'm relying on you: we all are.'

'Thank you, Mr President. I'll do everything I can.'

Her hands were trembling. She felt a desperate need to be back home, in a hot bath, with none of this happening.

She headed for the roadside, and as she climbed into a passing cab, she reached for her BlackBerry. Without thinking, led only by need, she entered the area of her phone's alphabetised contacts where she only rarely dared tread: the letter U. For Uri.

He picked up. Without missing a beat, he said: 'Hi. How's my favourite ex-White House official?'

She swallowed, determined to get a grip. 'Stuart's dead.'

'Oh God. I'm so sorry. What happened?'

'I don't know. They say it's suicide. But I just can't believe it.'

'I know how close you were, Maggie. You always said he had such a big heart.'

At that, she let out a full sob. These last few days had, she realised, left her like a coiled spring; she had been wound so tight.

'Do you want me to come down to see you?'

That was what she wanted more than anything in the world—but it was impossible. 'I just needed to hear your voice.'

'OK, so I'll talk,' he said. Just hearing his accent, still alien even after all the time he had spent in the States, triggered something in her—despite everything that had passed between them.

'I was thinking of you today,' he said. 'I was looking at some footage of Baker at the Iowa State Fair . . .' He was shifting the subject to safer ground, giving her something else to focus on. He was like that, Uri: sensitive.

She tried to pull herself together, engage in the conversation.

'You doing the Baker film?'

'Didn't I tell you? PBS want ninety minutes. The full life story.'

She did her best to sound enthusiastic. 'Wow. That's really good, Uri. Big job. You'd better hurry, though.'

'It's not looking good, is it? I don't get it. The guy was Mr Invincible and now he's fighting for his life.'

'I wish I could talk about it. But I'm on assignment. You know, usual rules apply.'

'Mother's the word.'

'*Mum's* the word.'

'Oh, yeah? And how's your colloquial Hebrew getting on?'

She smiled, imagining the dark curls of hair on his head. She felt the tears rising again. 'I'd better go, Uri.'

'OK.'

'Thanks, Uri.' She pressed the red button, ending the call. A moment later, the phone rang. Sanchez.

'We need to meet, Maggie. Urgently. Come back to Washington. Not here. I'll text you the time and place. There's something I need to give you. As quick as you can.'

She hung up, her heart pounding, thinking, Now what?

And thousands of miles away a man she had never met was listening to every word.

Undisclosed location, Thursday, March 23, 18:00 GMT

'Are we on a secure line?'

'Yes, sir. Maximum encryption.'

'Good.' He leaned forward, resting his elbows on the table, bracing himself for the start. The technology was state of the art, but he still preferred to look a man in the eye. Or several men, in this case.

He envied his predecessors. They had operated at a time when all this would have been done face to face. Not in a windowless room, deep underground, staring only at a bank of monitors.

Still, there was no alternative. The discussion was urgent and this was the way it would be done.

'Gentlemen, we've all been following recent events. I know there is some concern about—how shall I put it?—the law of unintended consequences.'

A voice chipped in, on the line from Germany. 'I worry that the cure might be worse than the disease.'

'I agree.' Another voice, this time from New York. 'My colleague in Germany is right. Removing Victor Forbes has created at least as many problems as it has solved.'

He felt the need to establish command. 'Gentlemen, my strong view is that we removed a problem that posed an absolute and immediate threat. If it had been allowed to stand, our entire project would have been jeopardised. Now, admittedly, that move has left us with other challenges. But they are manageable.'

'What about Goldstein?' Germany again.

'As the chair of this group, I acted on live intelligence. The risk that he could have rendered our project void was too great.'

'All right,' said the voice from New York. 'I'm happy to accept the decisions that have been taken. But it's time to secure our asset, as it were. Otherwise, we risk defeating the whole object.'

'Understood,' he said. 'That will be the next phase of our work. One last thing, gentlemen. It seems as if there is someone looking more closely at the Forbes case than we might have hoped. A woman. I wanted everyone to be clear that we will ensure she causes us no trouble.'

'Make sure we do.' A first intervention from London.

'You have my word,' the chairman said. 'She will be removed from the picture if necessary.'

Washington DC, Thursday, March 23, 19:41

Doug Sanchez's instructions had been clear. The information he had to give her could not be conveyed over the phone or by email or by fax. They had to meet face to face. She was to take the next plane to DC and then head to Union Station and stand facing the Amtrak departures board. In happier times she might have laughed at the intrigue of it all. But it was clear Stephen Baker felt he could no longer trust anyone.

There was a sudden flurry of movement, as waiting passengers suddenly took off in a hurry. She looked up at the board to see that it had at last revealed the track number for the Acela Express to New York. In the throng of people, she felt herself jostled. She looked to her left and there was Doug Sanchez, handsome in raincoat and scarf, looking straight up at the board.

He kept his gaze upwards, prompting her to do her own bit of play-acting. She pulled out her BlackBerry, smiling and saying hello as if it had just vibrated with a new call.

'Maggie, listen. This is radioactive. It is a federal crime to leak the identity of a CIA agent, even a dead one.'

'So I was right. Forbes is ex-CIA.'

His gaze was still fixed on the board. 'Took a whole bunch of crap to confirm it, but yes. The number three there sent me a summary of Forbes's personnel file. He did more than was required. I asked for a simple yes or no. Was Forbes an agent or wasn't he.'

'What's it say?'

'That you were right. Jackson is the same age as Forbes. He retired three years ago. Served everywhere, Saudi, Pakistan. Central America in the eighties. There's a full résumé. I didn't read it properly. We need deniability. I've been wondering if this is some kind of set-up. Send it to us, see what we do with it. We have to ensure there is no record of me passing this information to you.'

'So how do we do this?'

'I'm going to drop the stack of newspapers under my arm. You'll bend down to help me out, you'll give me everything back except the brown envelope. Ready?'

'OK.'

He dropped the papers. A whole pile went from under his arm: the *Washington Post*, two blue document wallets, a pile of A4 computer printouts. Instantly, Maggie bent down so that she was opposite Doug as he apologised profusely.

'I'm such an idiot,' he said. 'Thank you so much.'

'I'll call you right back,' Maggie promised her imaginary friend on the phone. 'There you go,' she said to Doug. She handed him back a wad of paper, keeping hold of the brown envelope.

Under his breath, he said, 'Don't let us down. We need you. He needs you.' Then he turned and walked away.

SHE RODE THE METRO home, itching to look in her bag. But she didn't dare risk it. Back in her apartment she opened up a kitchen cabinet, took down a bottle of Jameson's. Drop or two of water, a sip standing up, then she moved over to the couch and let herself fall into it. Blood pumping, she pulled the envelope out of her bag.

Inside was a two-page document, stapled together, the crest of the Central Intelligence Agency in the right-hand corner. In the top left, a small mugshot that she recognised as a young Vic Forbes. He had hair then, brown and straight; a moustache too. Large glasses of the kind everyone wore in the early 1980s. In the centre in bold type, it stated the subject's name: Robert A. Jackson.

It began with a summary of his education: high school in Washington, then college at Penn State. Spanish major. Three years in the Marines, then recruited to the Agency. Deployed to Central and Latin America. Then a long stint back at Langley, stretching through the late 1980s and into the next decade.

On the next sheet were the personal details which revealed only how little there was to reveal.

Marital status: single. Children: none.

Significant associations: negligible activity of which the Agency is aware.

Maggie took another glug of whiskey. Christ, she still had her coat on. She should have a shower, maybe eat. She got up and turned to head for the bathroom. As she did, she saw the winking light on her answering machine. Reaching over, she pressed 'Play'.

'Could have sent you a text, or an email or a bloody Tweet,' the message began, the accent unmistakable. 'But something told me you'd want to hear a human voice on your return from the Lost City of Atlantis. Mags, it's Nick here, sweetheart, keen to know how my brightest pupil performed in her Journalism for Beginners practical. With flying colours, if Tim from the *Telegraph* is to be believed. As luck would have it, I'm in DC for a few days. Call me if you fancy getting together.'

Her response surprised her. So often she would give Nick the brush-off. But tonight she wanted to see him. It wasn't simply that she needed company, though she did. She needed help. This thing was too big for her, there were too many angles. Her head was swimming. Too many hours alone.

Not that she could be open with Nick du Caines. Nick might have the best of intentions, but if he was drunk, or trying to get some Dutch intern at the World Bank into bed, who knew what he might say?

THEY MET AT the Eighteenth Street Lounge, a place where the corners were dark enough, and the couches sufficiently battered, to play to Nick's Hemingway fantasies: the seedy, world-weary ex-war correspondent. He leapt up when he saw her come through the unmarked door, embracing her and letting his hands run up and down her back. Trying it on before she'd even got her coat off.

They talked about New Orleans, Nick urging her to describe her skilful integration into the press pack, taking it all as a compliment to his teaching skills. 'Now, Mags, are you able to tell me what any of this is about, so that the beloved and historic newspaper that I work for might at least have something resembling a story?'

'It's nothing you can use yet, but I can tell you something.'

Light spread across Nick's face, his eyes widening in an expression of childlike joy. 'Hallelujah,' he bellowed. 'The words I've yearned to hear from your lips more keenly than any others—save, of course, for "Nick, will you undo my—"'

She gave him a look.

'Sorry. I'm all ears.'

'At this stage I have no actual proof. But I really do think Forbes may have been killed. Something tells me it was done professionally.'

He sat up straight: if he'd been a dog, his ears would have pricked up.

'What I want you to look into is whether there is any evidence of involvement by the,' she dropped her voice to a whisper, 'CIA.'

'Blimey.' He took a swig of his drink. When he looked at her again, his expression was serious. 'You wouldn't be asking this unless you already had some evidence. I can't proceed unless I know what it is.'

Maggie smiled, remembering that Nick du Caines hadn't won a hatful of awards for investigative reporting by accident. 'I can't show you anything. All you can know is that I have reason to suggest you look in that direction. Anything you find, you need to share with me first. Publish it before it's ready and there'll be no more from me.'

'That's not such a massive threat, Mags. The CIA bumping off a US citizen who happened to have criticised the President is quite a big story all by itself.'

'Not if it's only the tip of the iceberg.'

'What are you saying?'

'I'm saying, be patient. Wait till you see the whole picture.'

'I like what I'm seeing right now,' he said, licking his lips.

She let Nick walk her home—swiftly, through years of experience, swivelling her head to offer her cheek when he moved in for the good-night kiss. As always, his slobber was worse than his bite. He reached for her hand, kissed it and walked off into the night.

Once in her apartment, she pulled out Jackson's file. Something had been niggling at her all night.

She turned back to the first page and read it again, slowly. What the hell was it? She looked at the first few facts, which she had skimmed over. The date of birth, the school, the college.

The school. James Madison High School, Washington. The name was familiar, but she had no idea where from.

She found her BlackBerry and Googled it. It produced a list of dozens of

James Madison High Schools, some in DC, some just outside. Hold on, what if . . .

She went to the pile of books stacked on the floor by the bookcase: the new ones, for which there had been no room on the already jammed shelves. She rifled through them.

At last. *Running Man: Stephen Baker, His Insatiable Quest for Power and What it Means for America.* By Max Simon PhD.

It was a hatchet job, which had been torn apart by a legion of liberal bloggers. She had never got round to reading it; after the Baker landslide it suddenly didn't seem quite so relevant. But she'd given it a glance and remembered that it did at least pretend to be a proper biography with a cursory chapter on Baker's childhood. Now she was flicking the pages furiously.

In those days Cliff Baker lived a nomadic life, pitching up wherever work could be found . . .

Some padding, which she skipped. Here it was.

. . . logging meant Washington State and for the teenage Stephen that prompted yet another move, starting at a new high school. He enrolled, for what would be his last two years of education before attending Harvard, at the James Madison High School in Aberdeen, Washington.

That was it. Jackson hadn't been educated in Washington DC but in Washington *State.*

Finally she had found a connection between the President and the man she had seen buried in New Orleans earlier that day.

Stephen Baker and Vic Forbes had been at school together.

Washington State, Friday, March 24, 11:11 PST

Maggie left on the dawn flight to Seattle the next morning. Thirty-five minutes after landing she was in a rental car driving along I-5. Soon she would arrive in Aberdeen. Washington State was as far away from Washington DC as you could be, on the other side of the country. The drive had been long, but that gave her a chance to think. She couldn't stop thinking about Stuart. The initial shock and sadness had given way to new feelings: anger—and fear.

She had accepted without question that Stuart Goldstein had cracked under pressure, heading to the park in the early hours to slash his wrists. But now she wondered at the convenience of it. Baker was in desperate trouble and Stu his most trusted and capable lieutenant. If the President was right—that they were facing an attempted coup d'état—then it was not out of the question that the enemy might see fit to kill Goldstein.

The notion that Stu could have been murdered filled Maggie with fury. Who could have done such a thing? If these men's motive was the thwarting of Baker's efforts to defend himself, then surely there was every reason to remove her. She wondered if her conversations and texts with Stuart had been secure. They had been using the White House's encrypted communications system. But if Stu had been murdered, it had been done professionally; and people like that would have their ways of listening, watching, following . . .

She checked her rearview mirror. There was a truck behind her. But behind that? She couldn't tell.

The landscape outside, while unchanging, was easy on the eye. Mile after mile of tall pine trees, scraping the sky like sharp pencils. She had passed mirror-clear lakes, and forests dusted with Christmas-card snow. She checked the mirror once more. Still the same truck. She strained to see the driver, but the angle was too steep.

She had flown to Seattle without calling Sanchez. She knew she was meant to 'liaise' with him, but she wasn't going to start deferring to a twenty-seven-year-old guy whose place of work prior to the White House was Starbucks, Dupont Circle branch. Besides, if she were honest, she didn't want him trying to talk her out of it. What did she have? Little more than a hunch.

As she clocked up her hundredth mile from Seattle's airport, the pine forests gave way to a lake and a sign saying WELCOME TO ABERDEEN. A thin strip of new signage had been added just below: *One-time Home of President Stephen Baker*.

She had punched the zip code for the high school into the satnav and now it led her straight into the car park. She checked her watch. Thanks to the three-hour time difference and her early flight, it was still only early afternoon. She looked over her shoulder: no sign of that truck—or of any other vehicle she recognised.

There was a framed photograph of Stephen Baker in the hallway and, next to it, an eighth-grade art project, 'Dear Mr President', in which students of James Madison had expressed, through a drawing or a poem, their hopes for their most famous alumnus. These children were being inspired by their new president. A lump rose in her throat, reminding her why she was here.

'Can I help?'

Maggie spun round to see a smiling woman with long straight hair. 'Oh yes, I'm looking for the Principal's office.'

'I'm the Principal's secretary. He's busy with students right now. What's your question?' The smile remained fixed.

'It's about a former pupil at the school.'

'Are you a journalist? All media enquiries go through—'

'No, I'm not a journalist,' Maggie said, with what she hoped was a warm grin. 'And it's not about him. My name is Ashley Muir. I'm with Alpha, the insurance company. I'm here because one of our policyholders has, sadly, passed away. He left insufficient instructions as to beneficiaries and I—'

'Do you have ID?'

'I have my business card.' Maggie opened her bag and pulled out the card she had been handed by Ashley Muir, of Alpha, at a Sunday brunch in Chevy Chase. He had called too, a couple of times, suggesting they go out on a date. She had said no but she was grateful to him now for giving her the only business card in her desk drawer that combined insurance and a female first name.

The secretary studied it for a moment. 'So what is it you want?'

'I'm starting at the beginning, you see,' Maggie said. 'Which is why it would be an enormous help if I could see the school record of the policyholder in question.'

'Well,' the secretary said. 'You'd need to fill out a form and we'd have to process the request, then I'd have to get Terry—our janitorial manager—to go down to the basement and retrieve it. So if you were able to come back, say next Thursday, then I—'

Instead of a frustrated grimace, Maggie managed to give her an apologetic smile. 'The problem, I'm afraid, is that I'm based in Washington DC. I can't be here for a full week.'

'We could mail it to you. If you just leave your address—'

'Sadly, there is a degree of urgency. The courts will need notification of intestacy, before we can proceed to probate.' She saw the baffled expression on the secretary's face and pressed ahead, dredging her memory for jargon that would sound suitably intimidating. 'It's a legal process and the courts could issue a subpoena against any person or individual who obstructs that process. Which could mean this school. Or you.' She felt cruel doing this to the poor woman, but there was too much at stake to play nice.

The smile had gone now. 'So what would you need exactly?'

'All I would need is for you to take me to wherever those files are kept, so that I can take a quick look at the one belonging to our client and then I will be on my way.'

'That's all?'

'That's all. I'm in the business of friends and family. That's what I'm looking for—friends and family.'

The smell of bullshit was filling her own nostrils, but somehow Maggie sensed it was working.

THE LIGHT WAS FLUORESCENT, the smell stale. Upon rows and rows of metal shelves were hundreds of cardboard boxes. Each one was labelled in the thick but fading ink of a marker pen.

The secretary had been called away to deal with a boy with a nosebleed. Maggie was left alone, accompanied only by the gurgling of hot-water pipes. She didn't have much time. With her head angled, she read the sides of these old brown boxes. 1979–80, 1978–79 . . . Turning the corner, she found at last the right year. She pulled the box down, set it on the ground and knelt beside it.

Inside was a series of dark green files. She did a quick flick through the Bs: the Baker file was gone, no doubt removed during last year's campaign, when journalists kept asking for it. A few Cs, a large number of Ds; on and on until, at last, there it was.

Jackson, Robert Andrew. There was a home address, which Maggie swiftly scribbled in a notebook. There was a mother, Catherine Jackson, but by the word 'father' only a blank.

Copies of his school report, including praise for his leadership of the debate team. High scores for history and for Spanish. Not what she needed. She turned the pages fast, hoping something would pop out, something that—

What was that?

A sound, close by. Metallic, but not the banging of a pipe. It came from farther away and yet it was definitely down here, in the bowels of this building. It sounded somehow *deliberate.*

She scoured the file, speed-reading. There was another reference to the debate team, written by a Mr Schilling. The date was three years after the first one: Jackson would have been seventeen.

Robert's contribution to the debate team has not been quite as enthusiastic as it was previously. I suspect the loss of the captaincy of the team made him a little sore. If he is to pursue a political career, he needs to learn that every career includes its defeats!

A political career. Maggie kept going. A letter to Mrs Jackson from the Principal, suggesting a meeting at the school to resolve the 'disciplinary matter we discussed'. A rejection letter from Harvard.

Keeping the file on the floor, she was just replacing the box on the shelf when she heard the same metallic sound again, this time nearer. Inside the room.

Suddenly aware that she was alone in a closed underground room, she felt a desperate need to get out.

The sound came again, closer. She turned round. There, framed in the light between two rows of shelves, just a few feet away from her, was the outline of a man. Fixed, still—and staring at her.

Washington DC, Friday, March 24, 12:00

'Are we on a secure line?'

'Always, Governor. We have our own encryption equipment in this office.'

'That's smart, Senator. You sure you're not from Louisiana?' A loud thunder of laughter down the phone: the sound of a big Southern man who could fill a room with his own charisma. Conventional wisdom said they didn't make them like that any more, but Governor Orville Tett begged to differ.

'I want to thank you for getting in touch, Governor.'

'You're the main man on this Baker stuff. You're leading the troops into battle.'

'Yes, I started this fight and I mean to finish it.'

'Well, that's the kind of fighting spirit we need in our party. That's why I want to help.'

'Glad to hear that, sir.'

'Here's the thing. You know that cesspit down in N'Awlins is run by Democrats. So they've canned the investigation into Forbes's death. But there are still a few good, God-fearing men in New Orleans. And one of them's been my eyes and ears down there. Found out something mighty interesting too.'

Franklin could hear a rustle of papers.

'Let me just get my reading glasses here a moment. OK, here we go. He noticed a woman down there, snooping around. Claimed to be press, but was doing her own thing. My man kept a close eye on her. Turns out this woman's not press at all,' Tett went on. 'She is, in fact, Maggie Costello, until this week a foreign-policy adviser to one Stephen Baker. President of these United States.'

'Oh, that's good. Very good,' Franklin replied, resolving to keep this information to himself until the moment was ripe.

'Question you gotta ask yourself is: was she the dustbuster? Did Baker send her in after Forbes was taken out to cover their tracks?'

'Of course, Governor, it may turn out that Forbes did take his own life after all.'

'Yes, Senator Franklin, it might. But it might be too late for Baker to matter by then. And whoever gets that head on the trophy wall, he's going to look pretty good in three years' time, ain't he?'

'Well, I'm not thinking about that, Governor.'

'You should, Senator. You should. And when you do, you remember your good friends down here in the great state of Louisiana, won't you?'

'I will certainly not forget this kindness, Governor Tett. One last question: where is Miss Costello now?'

'We have that covered, Senator. Remember, I have sympathetic counterparts across the entirety of this great country of ours. Governors with eyes and ears everywhere. Put it this way, Senator. Wherever Miss Costello goes, there'll be someone watching.'

Aberdeen, Washington, Friday, March 24, 15:24 PST

'I see you've already made yourself at home here.'

Maggie's breath came in heavy, pounding gulps. 'You gave me quite a start.'

'Did I? I am sorry.' The voice was old, but steady. In the basement gloom, Maggie could still not make out a face.

'My name is Ashley Muir, from Alpha Insurance,' she brazened.

'Yes. So Mrs Stephenson said. I have to tell you, I don't like people coming down here. Not without me.'

Desperation made her cut the politeness. 'Who are you?'

'My name is Ray Schilling. I am the principal of this school.'

A wave of relief broke over her. 'Oh, good. I am glad to hear that.' She smiled a wide smile. 'Can we perhaps talk in your office?'

'SO YOU CAN UNDERSTAND my wariness, Ms Muir.'

'Completely,' Maggie said, a mug of coffee in her hand.

'We didn't have many journalists last summer—Stephen Baker was a student here for such a short while. But those that did come: devious people, Ms Muir. So when I heard this story about insurance claims and whatnot, well, I thought, "Here we go again".'

'Of course you did. As it happens, I was not looking for Mr Baker's file.'

'Someone has died, I understand.'

'That's right. Robert Jackson.'

The Principal sat back in his seat. 'Robert Jackson,' he repeated.

'Yes. He would have been here thirty-odd years ago.'

'Exactly thirty. I should know. I taught both of them. Baker and Jackson.'

'Of course!' Maggie smiled. 'You're the Mr Schilling on the report. You ran the debate team.'

He smiled too. 'Such a long time ago. I was very new here then.'

'And now you're the Principal.'

'Fifteen years in this job. Time for me to quit soon. But what a thrill, to see one of our students do so well. One day this will be Stephen Baker High.'

'So you remember him when he was here?'

'I remember all the students I teach.' He paused, then leaned forward. 'Stephen was always something special. No one forgot him. You couldn't.'

'He certainly is very charismatic,' Maggie said. 'And Robert Jackson. Was he memorable in any way?'

'Well, I remember him, but that probably has more to do with Stephen Baker than it does with him. Anyway, I'm sure this is irrelevant for your purposes. An insurance claim, was it?'

'I'm trying to build up as full a picture of the policyholder as I can. There's a large sum of money involved, no apparent beneficiaries. I need to find out if there's something we're not seeing. In my experience, the unlikeliest information can prove useful.'

'As I remember it, Jackson was not a bad debater. He could be sharp and precise. But he was so *overshadowed*.'

'Overshadowed?'

'He used to be the captain of the debate team. He got far in several competitions. And then Stephen Baker arrived. I remember they got on well. Both interested in politics, in history. Stephen used to call him by his middle name: Andrew. Like the president.'

'Stephen Baker and Robert Jackson were friends?'

'I would say so, yes. Same class, same interests. They began debating together, a tag team if you will. They were very effective.'

'So what went wrong?'

'Well, Stephen had true star quality, even then. A tremendous magnetism. It struck me that with Baker as captain, our debate team might finally have a chance of success.'

'So you replaced Jackson with Baker.'

'Yes.'

'Did it work?'

Schilling smiled. 'Big time, as the students would say now. James Madison won the statewide cup. You have to know what that meant to a small town like Aberdeen. Things were already pretty depressed back then. And then, there was this . . . *star.*'

'So you talent-spotted a future president of the United States.'

'That's what I tell the reporters who come here. But Robert took it very badly. It broke his friendship with Stephen Baker instantly. And he retreated into himself. He became bitter. His resentment of Baker became unhealthy. People don't realise how fragile kids are at that age. These are the formative years. A young man can be shaped by what happens to him at that age.'

'And what happened to Robert Jackson?'

'I would say he developed an obsession. I ran into Robert a year or two afterwards, and he had a file with him. He showed it to me. Inside were clippings about Stephen. Items from the local paper, neatly cut out and filed in date order. It made me shudder.'

'Did they still know each other then?'

'Well, Stephen's father still worked here, in the timber trade. So Aberdeen is where Stephen came back to during the vacations.'

Maggie tried to collect her thoughts. 'And you feared Robert Jackson would do something . . . something he might regret?'

'You've just reminded me of something I said to my wife at the time. An obsession like this only ends in destruction. Jackson will either destroy Stephen Baker—or he will destroy himself.'

Clinton, Maryland, Friday, March 24, 13:23
It was windy and noisy and the ideal place not to do an interview. But Nick du Caines's source had insisted on it.

They were in a piece of scrubland, standing in front of a tall wire fence. To reach it he had had to pull off the freeway and into a rest-stop, park up, then walk through a thicket of overgrown weeds until he found a small clearing. The loud hum of traffic was constant.

They'd met here, not because Daniel Judd was wary of meeting in a public place, but simply because this was his place of work and any time away from it he regarded as a waste.

Nick knew better than to interrupt Judd when he was working. On the other side of the wire fence, about two hundred yards away, a crew in overalls were fussing round two stationary aircraft. Another man was driving a small electric buggy. To anyone driving past it would have looked like a regular working day at the small private airport known as Washington Executive Airfield.

Judd raised a pair of binoculars to his eyes, then mumbled a number into a tiny digital recorder: 'N581GD.' Without breaking his gaze he reached for the long-lens camera that hung on a second strap round his neck and took pictures of one of the two planes.

Judd was an 'airplane spotter', one of these people who stood near runways watching planes take off and land, anoraks who could get genuinely excited by pencilling a serial number into a notebook. But it turned out they were right to get excited. For it was geeks like them around the world who had discovered the phenomenon of 'extraordinary rendition': the secret flights by which suspected terrorists were spirited away in the dead of night from the streets of Milan or Stockholm to nations whose intelligence agencies were ready to do whatever it took to 'persuade' these suspects to talk.

It was Judd and his pals who had noted down the number of a plane that had landed first in Shannon, Ireland, then reappeared in Sweden before reaching its final destination in Amman. The spotters had then visited the Federal Aviation Administration's website and clicked on the registry of aircraft licensed to US owners. There they could find not only a full archive of flight plans for every registered aeroplane, but also the owners of each aircraft.

The plane that had touched down in Shannon en route to Amman had been the property of a small aviation company based in Massachusetts. A few clicks later and Judd had the names of the company's executives. But these businessmen proved to be curiously shy. Instead of giving an address, each one had supplied only a post-office box number. That piqued Judd's interest, not least because these PO boxes were all in northern Virginia. Which happened to house, in Langley, the headquarters of the Central Intelligence Agency.

After that, Judd had enough to be certain. Over a drink, seated in the dark at a corner table, he had provided the dates and registration numbers that enabled Nick du Caines to reveal to the world the plane he and his newspaper called the 'Guantánamo Bay Express'. He had won three awards for that one.

'You got that look on your face, Nick.'

'What look?'

'The look that says you want to cause trouble.' Judd raised the binoculars to his eyes. 'You didn't come out here into the middle of nowhere on a freezing day to look at my pretty face, now did you?'

'I did not.'

'So, what is it you want to ask?'

'Would you be able to see if a CIA team flew into New Orleans?'

'This about that guy who was spilling the shit on the President?'

'Christ, you don't miss much, do you? OK. Yes, it's about that. I have reason to suspect that Vic Forbes did not kill himself. I think he may have been helped, if you see what I mean.'

For the first time Judd turned away from his view through the chicken wire and looked Nick du Caines in the face. 'So why do you think they used an airplane?'

'The truth is, I have no reason to believe that at all. But you're the only person I know who's ever found out a *thing* about what the CIA gets up to, so I'm starting with you.'

'Fishing expedition.'

'Total. I'm thinking that if by some chance they *did* use a plane, then that's something we can find out. *You* can find out.'

'OK, I'll look. But it's a long shot. Chances are, they drove there. Or flew separately, on commercial.'

'I know. But you'll look? I owe you one, Dan.' With that, Nick du Caines returned to the battered Nissan that served as his car.

But, like all those who see themselves as observers, neither Judd nor du Caines imagined that, at that very moment, they were themselves being observed through a long lens.

The watchers being watched.

Aberdeen, Washington, Friday, March 24, 18:23 PST

Maggie concluded the meeting with a few bureaucratic questions that she thought Ashley Muir, life-insurance agent, might ask.

'What about his parents? Are they alive or deceased?'

'Both dead,' Principal Schilling answered. 'Robert's father died even before he came to the school. Robert's mother died long ago. More than twenty years, I think.'

'Besides the debating, was there anything else that might have made Jackson stand out as a student?'

'He was bright. Not a star, but accomplished. I guess Robert was what today's students would call a "geek". He was fascinated by computers. No one had computers in their homes back then, of course, but Robert was very knowledgeable.'

Maggie wrote it all down in her notebook.

'You've been very generous with your time.'

'I hope it's helped, Ms Muir.'

By the time Maggie had pushed through the swing doors and stepped outside, twilight was setting in. The thought of driving back to Seattle now—her original plan—suddenly lost its appeal. She was exhausted. Safer to find a motel in Aberdeen and make tracks in the morning.

She was walking towards her hire car when she froze.

There, standing in the gloom beside her car, was the outline of a person—man or woman Maggie couldn't tell. The figure was standing, quite still, facing towards her. Was this how it had happened to Stuart—a man in the shadows, waiting for the moment to strike?

Then a voice, carrying over the empty asphalt of the parking lot: 'Am I glad to see you!'

A woman. As Maggie stepped nearer, she could see that she was older, early sixties at a guess. She felt her shoulders drop in relief. Either a veteran teacher or a grandmother of one of the pupils, Maggie guessed. Grey-haired, bespectacled and in a terminally unfashionable coat. A less frightening person it was hard to imagine.

'Gosh, I am so relieved, I can't tell you. My battery's dead—again!—and I desperately need someone to give me some help.'

'Of course I'll help. Mind you, I'm not sure I have any jump leads. This is a rental.'

'Oh, don't worry about that, dear. My son gave me everything. I have it all in the trunk. All I need is another car that works.'

Maggie watched, impressed, as the woman went round the back of her silver Saturn, opened the boot and emerged carrying two cables. She then lifted the hood, talking throughout.

'If I've made that mistake once, I've made it a thousand times. I park the car, I collect my handbag and then—'

'Don't tell me,' said Maggie, watching as the woman placed the crocodile clips on her car battery. 'You left the lights on.'

'Oh no, dear,' the lady said. 'I learned that lesson a long time ago. No, I left my key in the ignition.'

'And that gives you a flat battery?'

'It does, yes. It runs the radio or something, I don't know. My son is the mechanic in the family. He knows about these things. Now, let's get your car moved alongside mine and then get that hood open.'

Maggie drove the car in a near circle, so that it ended up facing the Saturn, nose to nose. Then she turned the engine off and began looking for the latch for the hood. Feeling in the dark under the steering-wheel column eventually revealed a small lever. She pulled it, heard the click and then watched as the woman hoisted the hood up to full height.

'OK, don't turn the engine back on just yet! Wait for me to give you the word.'

Maggie waited.

'OK! Let's give this a go!'

Maggie turned the key and heard the car spark into action. She watched the lady move to her own car and slip into the driver's seat. A second or two later came the sound of her engine revving back to life. A moment later both were out of their cars.

'We did it,' Maggie said, a wide smile on her face.

'I'm so grateful to you,' said the woman. 'Now I can pick up my grandson from football practice. Is there any way I can thank you?'

'I'm glad I could help. Go pick up your grandson. And remember to keep the engine running!'

Having watched the Saturn turn smoothly out of the lot, she headed to the highway that had brought her here, looking for signs for the centre of town. Traffic was thin, just a few lights brightening the dark. She wondered if this was going to be one of those American places that had no real centre—just a sprawl. Maybe she should just keep driving, waiting for the first motel that popped up.

There were some up ahead and on the left. In readiness for the exit, she eased down on the brake, but her speed didn't alter. She pressed down harder and this time the car jerked when it should have slowed down. Bloody rentals. When the exit came into view, she moved into the right lane, gently squeezing the brake.

The car did not slow down.

Maggie pressed down again. Still nothing. The car kept rushing forward at full speed, utterly beyond her control. She slammed her foot on the brake. Nothing!

The road curved round suddenly. She gripped the steering wheel as tightly as she could, swerving round a road meant to be taken at half this speed.

Finally the road straightened but still she was going too fast. She could see that up ahead was a red light at a crossroads. Already there were two other cars waiting at the light—and she was heading at full motorway speed towards them.

She had only one option, but the fear of it almost paralysed her. It was only the sight of two heads low down on the back seat—children—that finally prompted action.

Gritting her teeth, she swerved off the road and into the indistinct blackness beyond. A thicket of trees and a tangle of branches came at her, the car bumping and thudding at thunderous speed.

Instinct took over as she reached for the clasp holding her safety belt and, with one hand still on the wheel, unpopped it. Then, seeing what loomed ahead, she opened the car door and hurled herself out, even as she could see the ground passing rapidly beneath her.

Perhaps a half-second before she hit the ground, she saw two things, one clearer than the other. Less clear was the thick tree that her car had just rammed into, crumpling the entire front end. Clearer, and in her mind's eye, was the face of the woman with kindly eyes who had persuaded her to open the hood of her car.

After that she saw nothing.

6

Virginia, Friday, March 24, 18:25

Daniel Judd logged into his email account, typing an alias formed out of his own middle name, his wife's maiden name and a bogus middle initial—Z—that he hoped would throw any snoopers off the scent. Of course, if the CIA really wanted to hack into his email they could, but there was no reason to make it easy.

He sent a message to his contact in New Orleans. He worded it carefully. Even if he took precautions, there were no guarantees that his fellow enthusiasts were as careful. In the era of federal wiretapping, he worked on the assumption that there was always someone looking over his shoulder.

Euphemism was the key. No word that would be flagged automatically by the authorities' word-hunt programs.

> Hope you're well, big guy. Question for you. If our friends at the Company were planning to take a little working vacation in the Big Easy, what would be their best initial destination? Am assuming Louis Armstrong International too crowded etc. What would you advise?

He got a reply within four minutes.

> No one but tourists uses Louis. They'd go for a place they Knew.

Neat. Just that capital K was enough. He called up the Federal Aviation Administration database, waiting for the right page to load before typing the word KNEW. Instantly the four letters were recognised as the call sign for Lakefront Airport, located 'four nautical miles northeast of the central business district of New Orleans'.

He went to the airport's website and read the spec: general aviation, with special provision for charter and private flights. That would be ideal for a black op, Judd decided.

He glanced down at the dates Nick had given him, then keyed in the details he needed to call up the flight plans for aircraft that had used Lakefront in that period. As he expected, a long, long list of N-numbers appeared. One by one, he checked to see if any of those numbers also appeared on the list of planes he and his fellow spotters had determined constituted the fleet leased by the CIA.

Not one.

He would have to go the long way round. He decided to call his buddy Martin, whose greatest asset was that he was not burdened by domestic obligations. Martin had no kids, no wife and, so far as he could tell, no friends save for Judd himself.

As always, Martin answered on the first ring. Judd walked him through the problem and they agreed to split the list. Judd would check the midnight Sunday to noon Wednesday flights and Martin would do the same for the second half of the week. 'First one to find it gets free beer for a night.'

That had been close to 6 p.m. Now, shortly after eleven, he felt the first nibble on the end of the line.

Every other N-number traced back to a regular commercial air operator: licensed, well-known, all-colour website, the full deal. But here was one, N4808P, owned by Premier Air Executive Services, an operator based in Maryland, whose site gave only the sparest of details—and named no executives.

Judd headed to the registry of company records. The entry for Premier Air listed three officers. A further search on these three men yielded their social-security numbers—all issued when they were over the age of fifty. The rendition saga had taught Judd that when a social-security number is given to someone in their fifties, that someone is creating a new and fake identity.

But the company records contained one more curious fact about Premier Air Executive Services, one that, he guessed, would particularly interest Nick du Caines. He reached for his phone.

Aberdeen, Washington, Saturday, March 25, 10:05 PST

When Maggie opened her eyes, she saw only a white wall. There were no lines she could make out, in fact nothing that could make her certain it was a wall rather than just empty space.

She moved her head and felt a surge of pain at the base of her skull. She must have let out a noise because within a few moments a nurse had scurried into the room, filling up the white space.

'Well, good morning.'

Maggie answered, 'Good morning.' It sounded slurred.

'Do you know where you are?'

Maggie tried to shake her head, sending more shooting pain up from her neck. She heard a yelp come out of her mouth.

'OK. We should start at the beginning. What is your name?'

With vast effort, Maggie croaked, 'Maggie Costello.'

The nurse—fair-haired and large-armed—checked her notes. 'Good. Who is the president of the United States?'

Before the answer, a sudden onrush of memories and the emotions they aroused. She saw the den in the White House Residence, Stuart Goldstein, Stephen Baker . . .

'Don't worry, he's still very new. His name is Stephen Baker. How many states are there in the United States?'

'Where am I?'

'I'll come to that. I just need to ask you these questions the instant you wake up. That's our protocol. How many—'

'Fifty. Stephen Baker won last November with three hundred and thirty-nine electoral college votes, defeating Mark Chester. Now will you tell me where I am, please?'

The nurse, whose eyes had widened, now let her face relax. 'You're at the Grays Harbor Community Hospital in Aberdeen, Ms Costello. Do you know why you're here?'

Maggie tried letting her head fall back into the pillow, but even that small movement made her wince. 'I was in a car accident.'

'That's right. Last night.' She looked at her watch. 'Nearly sixteen hours ago. And you are very lucky to be alive. The police officer who found you says the front of your car looked like it'd been through a trash compactor. Are there people you'd like us to contact? A partner, perhaps? A family member?'

'Not just yet, thank you.'

Maggie asked for some time to think and, then, for her phone. The nurse left the room only to return a second or two later.

'Are you sure you had your phone with you, Ms Costello?'

'Yes', she said, still slurred. 'It's always on me. It would have been in my bag.'

'We have an overnight bag. Also two earrings, one lip balm—' she was scanning an inventory of some kind—'no phone.'

A suspicion began to grow, like a spreading stain.

'Do you have a notebook on that list? A laptop? Wallet?'

The nurse scanned it up and down.

'No.' The woman shook her head apologetically.

Maggie felt a shudder pass across her skin.

'I need to make a telephone call. An urgent one.'

'There'll be plenty of time for that.'

The nurse stepped forward and reached for Maggie's right hand. The main vein was punctured by a cannula, a small tube attached in turn to a long, clear line. The nurse checked it, then produced a cuff to measure Maggie's blood pressure.

'I'm in bad shape, aren't I?' Maggie said.

'You fell from a fast-moving car, so that would be a yes. You have a couple of broken ribs, but your legs and arms are intact. And we'll keep checking that head of yours. Try to get some rest.'

The woman in the car park had fiddled with the engine, hidden by the hood. She, or her accomplice, must have followed Maggie onto the highway, watched her careen towards what they assumed was her death and then rushed to the car, stolen the vital items and fled—all before the police had got within a hundred yards of her.

She tried to think through exactly what information was in the hands of those who had tried to kill her, starting with her phone. The recent calls list was a disaster: it would immediately implicate the White House. It would also reveal calls to Nick du Caines. Maybe Uri. The laptop didn't contain much. But her notebook would have everything that Schilling, the school principal, had told her. If she was in a race against these people, she had just lost.

She turned onto her side and, ignoring the pain spreading across her chest, reached for the side table where there sat a chunky beige phone. She grabbed for it, her hand flailing vainly. She pushed herself towards the edge of the bed, extended her arm once more and this time made contact. The receiver was hers and she used the cord to reel in the rest of the phone. She pressed nine and immediately a computerised voice cut in:

'We're sorry, but you have no credit for calls on this line. To get credit, please contact your operator . . .'

Shit. Her wallet had been stolen, with everything inside it. And of course she couldn't remember her credit-card number.

With great effort, she pressed zero on the phone's keypad.

'I need to make a collect call, please.'

'Excuse me?'

She was still slurring. She tried again, giving the number.

The White House operator must have been expecting her call. 'Miss Costello, is that you? I have instructions to put you straight through to the President.'

There was a delay. Finally a decisive click on the line.

'Maggie? Where are you?'

'It's a long story.'

'You sound terrible. Has something happened?'

'I think you were right, Mr President. About Stuart. Someone sabotaged my brakes last night. I think they were trying to kill me.'

'Good God. Where are you now?'

'Grays Harbor Hospital, Aberdeen. Your home state.'

'We've got to get you out of there. I'll call the governor—'

'No, sir. With respect, I don't think that's a good idea. That will confirm that what I'm doing is for you. Besides, sir, there's a lead here I need to follow.'

'In Aberdeen? What has Aberdeen got to do with any of this?'

'Robert Jackson, sir. You were at school with him.'

Maggie listened hard to the moment of silence that followed.

Finally he spoke. 'Robert *Andrew* Jackson? That was him?'

'You didn't recognise him when you saw him on TV?'

'They barely looked like the same person. You sure?'

'I'm sure, sir.' *Shure, shir.*

'I used to call him Andrew at school. I just didn't make the connection. What on earth's this all about, Maggie?'

'I wish I knew, Mr President. But I intend to find out.'

'What do you need, Maggie?'

'They stole my wallet and my phone.'

'OK, Sanchez will send you everything.'

'Thank you, sir. But make sure he leaves no trail. Tell him to be careful.'

'It's you who has to be careful. I can't afford to lose another person I trust. There are too few of you left.'

'Thank you, Mr President.'

She must have dozed off after the phone call. When she woke up, a handwritten telephone message had been left by her bedside from a Mr Doug of

Dupont Circle. She smiled at Sanchez's attempt at discretion.

The door creaked open. Maggie looked up, struggling to focus. She could see that a woman had entered, middle-aged, but in the dark it was hard to make out her features.

'What an unexpected surprise to see you again. There you are, dear,' she said.

Maggie created a fist, a futile gesture for a woman with two broken ribs and a tube in her arm, but it was a reflex, the result of the bolt of fear and rage that had just coursed through her.

Now the woman was coming nearer, approaching the bed. She had a syringe in her hand. Maggie recoiled.

'No need to be scared, Maggie dear. No need to be scared at all. I have something that will make all the pain go away.'

Maggie reached for the cup of coffee, still hot, that had been left at her bedside. The woman was looming over her. If only Maggie could grab hold of it, she could throw the steaming liquid in her face. She stretched . . .

And at that moment she saw the woman's face clearly. Grey-haired, yes, but not, after all, the apparently kindly lady who had sabotaged her car at the school.

'There really is nothing to be frightened of, dear.'

'I'm sorry,' Maggie panted. 'I thought you were someone else.'

'It's easy to get confused, dear. I was in the ambulance bay when they brought you in. You'd had quite a scrape. Now the doctor says you should take these painkillers. I can either do it intravenously'—she held up the needle—'or with tablets. What would you prefer?'

Maggie nodded towards the tablets. She took the tiny paper cup from the nurse and put the pills on her tongue, then knocked back a swig of water.

'Well done, dear.'

The instant the nurse's back was turned, Maggie popped the two tablets out of the side of her cheek where she had lodged them, and tucked them under her pillow. She waited for the door to creak shut.

Right, that was it. Whoever it was who had tried to kill her would doubtless try again. She would not stay here a moment longer. Lying here she could be poisoned or smothered: it would be so easy.

Grimacing from the pain, she removed the needle in her hand, grabbing a tissue from the box by her bed to staunch the blood.

Next she pulled back the duvet. She saw that she was wearing a standard hospital robe. With a massive exertion, she swung first one leg and then the other off the edge of the bed and slid her bottom forward till her feet touched the ground. Gingerly, she transferred her weight onto them and to her relief, realised that she could walk.

She made it across the room to the chair where her overnight bag sat. She unzipped it, finding trousers and a shirt inside. It took nearly ten minutes to dress herself.

She retrieved the note from Sanchez, still by the bed, then moved towards the door. There, a mirror projected back an image that stopped her short. Her right cheek shone with a red bruise and there were dark, deep lines round and underneath her eyes.

Cracking open the door, she began to make her escape. With all the strength she could muster, she walked past the nurses' station, determined not to look back.

She was just a few feet from the double doors leading away from here . . .

'Miss? Excuse me?'

Over her shoulder, as nonchalantly as she could manage, she called out: 'She seems much better! Thanks.' She pushed the doors open and left.

The signs offered little help. Geriatrics upstairs, obstetrics downstairs. And then, separately, student halls of residence. She hobbled in that direction, wincing at the pain as she headed down two flights of stairs. Before long she was in a series of corridors. Finally she found an exit sign. Her hunch had been vindicated. The medical students had their own separate entrance—one that, Maggie hoped, would not be monitored by whoever was watching her.

The walk to the main road was long and agonising. She dreaded how easily, out in the open, she would be spotted by her pursuers. At last she flagged down a cab and slumped into the back seat.

'Where can I take you?' the driver asked.

'Heron Street.' She tried to smile, then saw the driver look her over in the rearview mirror.

'You OK?'

'I'm getting there.' She pulled out the message from Doug and looked at it properly for the first time.

There is a safe way to do this. Go to Heron Street. And remember, we always believed in Western unity.

The road was wide, more a highway than a street, and as the driver passed Sidney's Casino and several open-air car dealerships, she felt her brow furrow. Why would Sanchez send her here?

And then she saw it, the tall flagpole-style sign for Safeway. She smiled and asked the driver to wait, forming a guess for the last piece of Sanchez's puzzle.

She only had to look round the supermarket for thirty seconds to see it. A counter below the instantly recognisable yellow and black sign: Western Union.

She gave her name to the young, much-pierced girl behind the glass window who promptly asked for ID. Maggie began to explain, that was the whole point, everything she had had been stolen—

'Hold on, there's a note on my system here? Says I'm meant to check your face against this?' The same upspeak Maggie would have heard back home, on O'Connell Street.

The girl produced an envelope which bore the crest of the State of Washington. She tore it open and out fell a credit-card-sized rectangle of clear plastic: a driver's licence, with Maggie's face on it. Good old Sanchez.

'So that's your ID, which means I can give you this.' The girl disappeared, returning with a wad of clean, crisp banknotes. She counted off five thousand dollars and sent Maggie on her way.

She paid off the cab and slowly made her way to a hair salon. She wondered about a cropped, peroxide number but decided it was likely to attract too much attention. So she went halfway, asking the stylist to turn her russet-brown, shoulder-length cut into a mid-length bob with blonde highlights. She didn't love it, but she looked different and that was all that counted.

She had a few more things to get. At the top of her list was a bulk order of extra-strength painkillers, a BlackBerry, a new laptop, some basic cosmetics and a place to stay.

She decided on the Olympic Motel, which looked suitably down at heel and anonymous. She unlocked the door to her room. It would do perfectly. The bed invited her to sleep for the rest of the day. But she knew she had to get to work right away.

She held the BlackBerry, shiny and new, and dialled the one number, other than the White House, she remembered by heart.

'Uri, it's me. Maggie.'

'Maggie! I tried calling you. Over and over. What happened to you?'

'I was in an accident, but—'

'What! Are you—' He sounded genuinely alarmed.

'I'm fine, really.' She strove to keep her voice steady. 'I'm OK. I just need your help.'

'Do you need me to come there, because—'

'No. I need to ask you about . . . intelligence.'

He had always refused to provide more than the sketchiest details, but she knew that Uri Guttman had performed his military service in Israel in the intelligence corps. So now, swiftly, she gave him a very thin outline of what had happened to her.

'Jesus. You and danger, Maggie. It's like some chemical attraction or something.'

'I thought you wanted to help me.'

'OK. Another time. What do you want to know?'

'At the funeral in New Orleans, the retired man from, er, the Company said a whole lot of stuff I didn't understand. He said there would have been no point killing the man we're talking about because "He'd have prepared his blanket."'

'Exactly those words?'

'Yes.'

'OK, we have something different in Hebrew but it sounds like a similar idea. We call it *karit raka*. It means a soft pillow. Like it guarantees you a soft landing if you get in trouble. Normally you only use the *karit* in an emergency. Inside your pillow will be information that might help your organisation find you and get you out of trouble. But you could also use a *karit* another way. Let's say I know something sensitive. And I think there would be people willing to kill me to keep whatever I know secret. Then I might make up a *karit* that would sit somewhere, a bundle of information that would be released automatically the moment I died.'

'And the potential killers would know you had done it, so that would deter them from killing you. Because once you're dead, whatever they were trying to keep hidden would come out anyway.'

'Precisely.'

Maggie was trying to think through all the questions now rushing into her mind. 'But it obviously didn't work. The guy I'm talking about died. It didn't stop his killers killing him.'

'Either he hadn't prepared his blanket, and the bad guys knew that. Or he had, but they felt sure they could get to it before it was made public. Or it's still out there. And they're desperate to find it.'

'Let me ask you something, Uri. If it were you. If you had a blanket, a *karit*, where would—'

'I was never at the *karit* level. But my father was. And you know what he used to say? About all intel things. Again and again, the same quote. From some Brit. "If you want to keep a secret, announce it on the floor of the House of Commons."'

'I don't follow.'

'Hide it in plain sight. The one place no one thinks to look. If Churchill wanted to give the code for the D-Day landings, he'd do it in a speech to Parliament. What German would look there?'

'Hide in plain sight. That's good. Thanks, Uri. For everything.'

He was telling her she didn't have to thank him, but she wasn't listening to his voice. She was listening instead to other sounds coming through the phone. She had heard a door closing, the bustle of another person in the room and then a change in the register of Uri's voice. That confirmed it: a new girlfriend, in the apartment Maggie had once regarded as home.

'Maggie, listen, if—'

'Gotta go! We'll talk soon.' She decided to expel from her mind the sound she had just heard, the sound of domesticity and intimacy between Uri and a woman who was not her.

Hide in plain sight. Concentrate on that.

She could see how that would work for Winston Churchill. He was famous, everything he did was in plain sight. But what did that mean for Vic Forbes/Robert Jackson, for a man who had spent most of his life hiding in the shadows?

A wave of aching tiredness fell over her. She slowly lay down on the bed, feeling the pain in her ribs afresh. It felt good, though, to rest her head on the pillow and close her eyes.

The whole point of a blanket, if she had understood Uri correctly, was that the information it contained could be retrieved by others after one's death. If it were too deeply hidden, it would serve as no kind of deterrent. That meant there had to be some kind of timing mechanism, like a safety deposit box programmed to pop open a certain number of hours or days after his death.

Such a device would work only if it somehow knew its owner had died. How could that happen?

It could be held with a lawyer, who would know to release it in the event of his client's death. But that didn't seem likely. Everything Forbes had done, he had done alone.

What had been the motif of his assault on President Baker? Technology. He had hacked into Katie Baker's Facebook account. He had even contrived to hack into MSNBC's system. What had the school principal said about young Jackson? *Robert was what today's students would call a 'geek' . . . fascinated by computers.*

Of course Forbes would have hidden his blanket online. And there the timing mechanism would be simple. You'd create some site that you made sure to visit every day or every week. If you didn't log in, the site would know. A technical wiz like Forbes would have no problem programming a site to email his blanket out to those who would know what it meant and what to do with it.

Maggie felt a surge of energy run through her. She was sure she was right. But one question remained. Where the hell was it?

She opened the new computer and typed in the most obvious place she could think of: *vicforbes.com*

Nothing. Nothing for .net or .org either. Same with victorforbes and robertjackson, robertandrewjackson, andrewjackson and bobjackson.

How the hell was she meant to crack this?

And then it came. The one person who would know the answer.

She looked at the clock. The eight-hour time difference meant it was already past midnight in Dublin. She hesitated.

In the old days, she'd have happily called her sister Liz at three in the morning: she would either have just come in or been about to go out. But the arrival of her son Calum three years ago had put Liz's clubbing days behind her. The drug she craved now was sleep. Calling her at this hour was what you'd call a high-risk operation. She dialled the number from memory.

'Liz? It's Maggie.'

'Uggh? Maggie? It's the middle of the night.'

'I know. I'm really sorry—'

'Where are you? Has something happened?'

'I'm in Washington. But not that Washington. It's a long story.'

'Are you drunk? You sound like you've got your head in a bucket.'

'No, not drunk. I was in an accident.'

Instantly, Liz's tone changed: she was a whirlwind of sisterly concern, offering help, wanting to know what the doctors had said. It was simultaneously touching and stressful.

'I don't need anything, Liz, I promise. Nothing like that. Actually, I need your brainpower.'

Liz croaked out a laugh. 'You mean you're not calling for a recipe for courgette mash. It's nice that someone remembers the real me.'

'Too many coffee mornings?'

'And playdates.'

'Poor you.' Then Maggie explained what she was looking for.

'What kind of man was he, Maggie? What did he do?'

'He was retired. But he had been in American intelligence.'

'When?'

'Eighties and nineties.'

There was a pause. Then she heard her sister clear her throat, as if fully waking herself up, ready for action. 'Now. Have we ever had the darkweb conversation?'

'I don't think so.'

'OK. When you look something up online, you think you're searching the whole Internet, right?'

'Right.'

'That's what everyone thinks. But they're wrong. In fact, you're searching just three hundredths of one per cent of the entire web.'

'So where's the rest?'

'That's what I'm talking about: the darkweb. Or the deep web. The places that are hidden. What most people see and use is the tip, but there's this massive iceberg underneath.'

'And what's in it?'

'A whole lot of it is junk, websites that have stopped working, addresses that have fallen into disuse. Sometimes it's legitimate, maybe a database that's blocked to search, because it contains commercially sensitive information. And sometimes it's vile. Like dirty address spaces that get taken over by crime syndicates. You gotta imagine it like this vast underwater landscape, full of old shipwrecks and derelict buildings that have fallen into the sea.'

Maggie, lying on the bed, made a silent grimace as she shifted position, sending a new ache through her ribs.

'And the other stuff you find—kind of lying on the seabed—are addresses that were set up right at the beginning, when the Internet was just starting, and then abandoned. And you remember who started the Internet, right?'

'The US military.'

'Yep.'

Maggie pulled the covers tight and hugged herself against a sudden chill. 'And is there any way to probe all this stuff?'

Maggie listened, taking notes as Liz gave her a step-by-step guide. She would follow the instructions and they would speak again in the morning. Dublin time.

Maggie hauled herself upright and with the sheet of paper at her side and the computer on her lap, followed Liz's first instruction and Googled 'Freenet'.

Two clicks later she was at a site that looked grey and basic. The welcome paragraph declared that Freenet was free software allowing people to browse anonymously, to publish 'freesites' that would be accessible only via Freenet and to 'chat on forums, without fear of censorship'. Maggie followed the prompts, downloading and installing the Freenet software.

She came to an index, much more basic than anything you'd find on the regular web. It listed freesites, those that would remain utterly hidden to anyone above the surface.

Before long she had found *The Anarchists' Cookbook*, the book spoken about in whispers even when Maggie was a student, and, more of a shock, *The Terrorist's Handbook*. Maggie rapidly concluded that the darkweb she had just entered was bound to be home to radicals, but also to those charged with hunting them down—the natural habitat of both cat and mouse. Everything she knew about Vic Forbes told her he would have felt right at home.

She did a search for Vic Forbes and was taken to a URL page that didn't look like any she had seen before. It took a while to load up, and then it was there. Maggie recoiled, astonished by what she saw. Not that it was such an arresting image. Just the fact of what it represented. For here was confirmation that Vic Forbes had prepared for his own death by hiding his most precious secret in the deepest recesses of the Internet.

She looked at the website address, so simple and so obvious. All she had had to do was type in victorforbes.gov and there it was.

Doubtless, he had been one of those pioneers who had been in on the Internet from the start, able to create a personal domain when next to nobody knew what such a thing was. The front page consisted of a single, full-face photograph of him. Not the Vic Forbes who had been on television in the hours before his death, nor the young, moustached Robert Jackson on his CIA dossier. This was Forbes seven or eight years ago: that was Maggie's guess.

She clicked on it, expecting it to link her through to other pages, but nothing happened. There were no other links round the side or at the bottom. Indeed, there was no text at all.

There was something missing. Yet, that this was the hiding place, the locker into which Forbes had stashed his blanket, she was more certain than ever.

There was only one way to break in. She looked at the clock: 7 p.m. on a Saturday night in Aberdeen, Washington, three o'clock on Sunday morning in Dublin. She had promised her sister faithfully that she would leave her in peace.

She looked at the web page. That man had set out to destroy the presidency of Stephen Baker. There, on that screen, was the land mine he had buried deep—and it was still ticking.

She loved her sister, she really did. But some things were more important than Liz's unbroken sleep. She dialled the number.

The phone rang twice. Then a croak remarkable for its coherence—and hostility: 'This had better be good. It's gone three in the morning!'

'I'm sorry, Liz. But I am desperate. Can I remind you that somebody did try to kill me last night? I think there's something they're trying to find out. My only chance is if I can work it out first.'

'Maggie, you seem to think that if you just know whatever it is you're not meant to know, then you'll be OK. Whereas the exact opposite is the truth. I don't know anything and no one's after me, are they? Mrs O'Neill on Limerick Street, she doesn't know a thing and she's sound asleep right now. You see how it works? If you stay a million miles away from all this crap, then nothing happens. Simple.'

'It's not quite as simple as that—'

'No, I can well believe that. I can see it's way more complicated than that. This is about you needing adrenalin in your life, isn't it—to convince you your life is worth while?'

'What are you talking about?'

'I'm talking about you, Maggie. I'm talking about this insane way you live. Always travelling to the back end of arsehole, always dodging bullets. Why do you do it?'

'Liz, I'm exhausted. I'm on my own in a shitty motel in the middle of nowhere. I hurt everywhere. I just need some help and I've turned to my sister. Is that too much to ask?'

'I remember all the bullshit answers, Maggie. "Making life better for children in war zones", all that Miss World shite. But I don't believe a word of it. Maybe once, when you started. But now it's something else. You're trying to make up for what you don't have. For the husband you don't have, for the—' and now Maggie heard the first silent note of hesitation in what had, until then, been an unstoppable flow.

'And what else, Liz? What else am I compensating for?'

But they both knew. 'That's why I reckon you phone me in the middle of the bloody night, Maggie. You want to wreck what I have because you're jealous.'

'That is NOT TRUE!' The sound of her shout echoed round the motel room. 'Of course I'd love to have what you have—a great husband, a lovely boy. But for reasons I can't sodding well be bothered to go into, I don't have that option right now. I do what I do because I'm good at it. OK?'

There was silence down the phone, both of them as shocked as each other by what they had just heard. Maggie cracked first.

'Liz! I'm serious. I wouldn't be calling unless I needed your help. Now will you help me or not?'

There was another long pause. Then Maggie heard the pop of a bedside light being switched on. 'What do you need?'

Maggie explained the dead end she had hit. Liz responded with a grunted 'hmm'. In anyone else, you could put that down to sibling fury that had not yet subsided. But Maggie knew—having grown up in a house where the fiercest rows could pass as quickly as a summer storm—that it meant only that Liz had been confronted by a technical conundrum.

A series of noises down the phone confirmed that Liz had fired up her computer. 'All right, I'm in. I've gone to the dark side. Give me the URL again.'

A few keystrokes later and Liz was muttering again. 'Creepy-looking guy. But there's nothing here, Mags. Just that picture. It's your classic single-page site. Just a flag in the soil. You know, Forbes reserving that domain for himself.'

'Are you sure? This really is my best shot.'

'That's the thing about the darkweb. It's mainly full of crap. This is probably just some site your man set up in the eighties and forgot about.'

'But this picture is more recent than that. He was in the CIA, Liz. Couldn't he have—'

'Oh, that is so cool. That is genius. I've read about this.'

'What is? Liz? What are you talking about?'

Maggie could hear a furious hammering of keystrokes.

'Liz Costello, you may never have cracked breastfeeding but you have cracked this.' Liz's excitement was infectious. For the first time in days, Maggie felt herself smile properly.

'Steganography, Maggie. The coolest encryption ever thought of. Instead of a code that everyone knows is a code—so they immediately start trying to break it—you conceal your information in such a way that no one even suspects there's a message there.'

'Liz, you've completely lost me.'

'That program didn't work. Don't worry, there's tons more.'

'What are you talking about?'

'Steganography. Means concealed writing. It's when a message seems to be something else entirely. You think it's a shopping list, but the real message is written between the lines—in invisible ink.'

'So there are words hidden in this picture? How the hell could he have done that?'

'Basically every pixel in a digital picture is made up of colour values, formed by strings of ones and zeros. If you change one of those ones to a zero it will be invisible to the naked eye. The picture will still look the same. But all those little ones or zeros you've changed can contain some extra information, besides the colours. You just need a program to piece it all together.'

'So you reckon that's what Forbes did to this picture?'

'Yep. In the massive data of this picture, there'll be a parcel of hidden data. Apparently al-Qaeda use it. You send a holiday snap; guys at the other end run it through a program and, bingo, you've got your instructions telling you to blow up the Statue of Liberty.'

'So is that what you're doing, running it through a program?'

'I am. I'll remote access you.'

'You'll what?'

'I'll take over your computer and run it from here. Then you can see what I'm seeing.'

'You can do that?'

'Easily.' Methodically, Liz ordered Maggie round her computer telling her to open up System Preferences one moment, then to choose an option from the pull-down Tools menu the next—one baffling step after another.

'There,' said Liz at last, invisibly moving the cursor round Maggie's screen. 'I'm on. Here goes.' Liz made a tum-tee-tum sound, the noise a tekkie makes when they're waiting for a computer to perform a function. Eventually she said, 'Oh. It's encrypted.' A box, familiar even to Maggie, had appeared in the middle of the screen. It demanded a password.

'Let me do this, Liz.'

Maggie allowed herself a second smile. Without hesitation, she typed in the letters that, she felt certain, would unlock the code.

S-T-E-P-H-E-N-B-A-K-E-R

7

Washington DC, Sunday, March 26, 08:41

'That you, Senator?'

'It is.'

'Honour to be speaking with you, sir. Sorry to be calling you at home on the weekend. Caught you before heading off to church?'

'You have.' Rick Franklin marvelled at the absurdity of Washington etiquette. Elected office always ensured formal deference, even from those who so clearly wielded greater power. Nylind's Thursday Session made him a genuine force in this town. In the business of political influence they were at least equals. Yet here was Nylind, touching the forelock.

'I have quite a few items, Senator, if that's OK with you.'

'Fire away.'

'Banking bill. Democrats are foaming at the mouth on that one. Reckon they've got the numbers.'

'In the House?'

'So they say.'

'Right,' said Franklin. 'So this means—'

'— that we need to switch to the Senate.'

'You mean, wreck the bill there so that it voids whatever comes out of the House.'

'Wouldn't put it quite like that, sir. Prefer to say that a strong pro-growth Prosperity for America bill needs to come out of the body that looks to America's long-term interests.'

It was part of Nylind's genius, this. He never crafted so much as a tactic, let alone a policy, without framing the language in which it would be sold.

'I hear you,' Franklin said. 'But, as I know you know, I am not the ranking Republican on the Senate banking committee.'

'How can I put this, Senator? Whatever the formal hierarchy might be, the movement regards you as the lead man on this.'

If Nylind was aiming to flatter, he had succeeded.

'I'd need some back-up,' Franklin said. 'My staff have never led on a bill this size before.'

'You got it. Economists, lawyers, number-crunchers. Heck, we've even got a bill drafted!'

'Oh, yeah? Where'd that come from?'

'Well, as you know, sir, there are a lot of people in this town who have a direct interest in ensuring that Congress gets this issue right. They see the wisdom in sharing resources.'

Translation, thought Franklin: *banking industry lobbyists have drafted the bill*.

'OK. Well, let's fix a meeting. Cindy from my office and whoever you recommend from yours.'

'Good to know, Senator. Next item: some of us feel we might be losing momentum on the impeachment project.'

'How do you mean?'

'We still don't have our Democrats on House Judiciary.'

'That has to be a matter for the House leadership,' Franklin shot back. 'That surely is their responsibility.'

'Agreed, sir. But for that to happen, they need more on Forbes.'

'But we don't have any evidence on that. Until we do, allegations implicating the President in Forbes's death cannot be part of the case for impeachment. Right now the articles of impeachment relate only to the Iranian Connection. That's all we got.'

'Technically, that's true, Senator. But Forbes is the mood music, the *soundtrack* for the impeachment.'

'The trouble is,' said Franklin, adopting the superior tone of the man in the know, 'it seems someone may be at work cleaning up all that mess. A dustbuster.'

'That's what I hear too, Senator.'

'That's what you *hear*?'

'There's not much that goes on that I don't know about.'

How was this possible? Franklin had told no one, bar Cindy, about that Costello woman. He was holding on to that particular nugget, confidentially provided by Governor Orville Tett, so that it could be deployed at the moment of maximum effectiveness.

'What exactly is it that you're hearing?'

'There seems to be some kind of lone intelligence-gathering operation. By a woman formerly at the White House.'

Shit. So he really did know.

'Our worry is that this hurts us with the impeachment push. We need that stuff, sir, and she's getting in our way.'

Irritated now, resentful that this *activist* was as well informed as he was, Franklin demanded, 'So what is it you're asking me to do, Matt?' *Matt.* Put him in his place.

'I suppose I'm suggesting we need to step it up a gear. We need to get ahead of this thing. Take radical action if necessary.'

If only he knew, Franklin thought to himself. But all he said was, 'OK. Was there something else?'

After they'd discussed a few more items, Franklin hung up and rubbed at his temples. Everything about the phone call suggested progress. He was to be entrusted with a key task on the banking bill; he was seen as the lead player in the Forbes business. It all spelled career gold.

And yet, something nagged at him. It was not just Nylind's apparent omniscience, it was his manner—as if he were the general and Franklin a subordinate, expected to take instruction. Above his paygrade, as they said in these parts.

Franklin needed to get to work right away.

Aberdeen, Washington, Sunday, March 26, 08:55 PST
'Looks like we're a pretty good team, Mags,' Liz had said, as they wrapped up what had been an hour's phone call.

The password had worked immediately. Once she had keyed that in, the image at victorforbes.gov had suddenly appeared to turn into a square of dark, dull grey. Almost black. Liz had checked a site on steganography and read that the apparent fade to black was a familiar trick. She had only to turn up the brightness on Maggie's screen and a new image revealed itself.

Though it was not really an image at all. Just six large numbers at the centre of the screen, separated by two slashes.

A date; American format. The month, the day, the year.

Working back, Liz discovered that the website was programmed to a timer: if the site remained unvisited for more than three days, then it would slowly emerge from Freenet onto the regular web.

As it happened, four days had passed since Forbes's corpse had been found, and the website's underlying code had changed in such a way that soon the site would turn up on a search conducted by anyone who typed the name Victor Forbes into Google.

Maggie sat there, staring at the screen. March 15, just over a quarter of a century ago, when both Robert Jackson and Stephen Baker would have been graduating college. She was certain that whatever Forbes had been trying to tell her from the grave must relate to the shared past of these two young men.

More research to be done, and quickly. But starting where? Local papers from the time . . . She typed the words 'Aberdeen Public Library' into the search engine and the website told her that the library was open on Sunday mornings. What was more, the library did indeed keep the archive of the *Daily World*, the magnificently named newspaper of Aberdeen.

By 10 a.m. she was standing outside the entrance of the public library on East Market Street, waiting for opening time. Once the door was unlocked, she headed straight for the newspaper archive. 'No longer bound copies, I'm afraid,' explained the librarian. 'They are on microfiche.'

Maggie explained that she only needed to see the paper for specific days in a specific year: the editions of March 15, March 16 and March 17. The librarian showed her to a first-floor room, then reappeared five minutes later with boxes containing spools of film. He loaded the first one into the machine and then left her to it.

Maggie started scanning the front page for anything relevant. A story on a budget crisis at the state capital; a report on a resignation from the Aberdeen school board. Inside, car accidents, a high-school basketball player set for a scholarship to Duke, and a recipe column.

She was not deterred. Logic had warned her that whatever had happened on that day might well not be reported until the next day or the day after. She spooled forwards to March 16.

She read slowly, searching for the words Forbes, Jackson or Baker. She peered at every photograph, leaping when she saw a page-four headline 'Destined for Greatness' above a group shot of smiling young people. They were around the right age: Washington State students set to embark on the then-novelty of a junior year abroad. There was not a Baker or Jackson in sight.

She looked at the next page: six. Nothing there either. Mainly ads on seven, letters on eight, more ads on nine and then an advice column, financial tips and, eventually, sport. The paper for March 17 proved just as empty.

She spooled back, reviewing what she had seen. Then she did the same for the March 16 edition. Page one, news: nothing there. Two, an ad. Three, international news items. Four, that picture of smiling young Washingtonians heading to Europe. She stared at the faces. Was one of them Forbes, under yet another name? Was Baker there? But no matter how hard she stared, she could not conjure them up.

Next was page six, a preview of a vintage car rally. Then the ads on page seven.

She went back. What had happened to page five? Had she nudged the controls on the machine too fast?

She lined up page four and inched the control wheel along. Up came page six. There was no mistaking it. There was no page five.

She tracked the librarian down.

'You see,' Maggie demonstrated. 'Four. Then six. No five.'

'Well, that is odd,' he said. 'I've never seen that before. I'll need to report that right away. This is library property.'

'Are there any other copies of that day's newspaper around, do you think? What about at the office of the *Daily World*?'

'The *World* digitised some of its archive. So if you know what you're looking for, you can search their database.'

'The whole point is I don't know what I'm looking for.'

He gave her a look.

'What I mean is, I'll know it when I find it. It relates to this town or this area on that day.'

She saw the librarian looking at the bruise on her forehead. 'Maybe you need to take a break and come back tomorrow . . .'

Maggie took a deep breath. Of course, she looked like a wreck; worse, even: mad. She had an idea. 'Forgive me for being so demanding. And thank you for your help. It's possible I've made a mistake with the year. Do you think I could trouble you for microfilm copies of the same dates—but for the following year?'

This time she checked the page numbers first. All three sets were complete. She started with the newspaper for March 15, exactly a year after the date Victor Forbes had gone to such trouble to secure for posterity. The front page once again offered nothing of obvious relevance. More mundane, local tedium on the subsequent pages.

Maybe the event Forbes had in mind was some national or international happening, far away from Aberdeen and the little Jackson–Baker soap opera. Perhaps she needed to be searching not the Aberdeen *Daily World*, but the *New York Times* or *Washington Post*.

She would check one last time, working from the last page back to the front. Sports, agony column, letters, financial, ads, puff piece about a local hotel reopening . . .

Maggie had not read the story properly first time round, just taking in the headline and scanning the text for names. But this time she caught the caption:

Staff at the Meredith Hotel prepare for today's grand reopening, one year to the day since the blaze that nearly destroyed the establishment.

MAGGIE TRIED FIRST to do it the official way, to see if there was a paper trail left by institutions and follow that, but she hit a series of dead ends. She called the Aberdeen Fire Department and asked if they kept records of their work. A duty officer said they did keep such records, though they couldn't just show sensitive information to a member of the public: it would require the written consent of the Chief. The police department gave the same answer.

So she went to the Meredith Hotel.

'I know this sounds like a very odd question,' she asked the concierge, an Asian-American man close to sixty. 'But I wonder if you could tell me who is the longest-serving employee at this hotel?'

'Longest serving? That would be me, Miss.'

Good. Just as she had hoped. 'I'm researching the history of this area and I wonder if you could help me with something. I understand there was a fire here many years ago.'

'Before my time, Miss.'

'I thought you said you—'

'I've worked here fifteen years. But that was—'

'More than twenty-five years ago.'

'Right.'

'And there's no one else here who has memories of that night? What about the owners?'

'Changed hands eight years ago. This hotel is part of a chain owned out of Pennsylvania now.'

Maggie's face must have displayed her disappointment because he seemed eager to please. 'What do you need to know?'

'Anything you can tell me.'

He leaned on his desk. 'I heard it was a very big fire. Destroyed the interior of the hotel. They say it was cigarettes, set the curtains on fire. On the third floor.'

'But nobody died.'

'Where did you hear that?'

Maggie pulled from her pocket the photocopied *Daily World* cutting about the reopening she had taken from the library. With a quick glance, she checked it. Nowhere did it mention any fatalities. She looked back at the concierge. 'Do I have that wrong?'

'I think you do, Miss. The anniversary was a couple of weeks back, right?'

'Yes. It was.' She smiled. 'I'm impressed you know that.'

'Well, it's difficult to forget. The family of the person who died come here every year. They lay a wreath outside the hotel. Very polite, always ask permission.'

'What's the name of the family?'

'Oh, I don't know, Miss. They never say.'

'And do you still have the wreath?'

'I threw it out just yesterday.'

Damn. She thanked him for his time, handed him a five-dollar bill and left. Five minutes later she was in the loading bay behind the hotel, with its giant trash cans. Bracing herself for the stink, she flipped open the lid of the first dumpster. Just glass bottles. There was a blue one full of paper and then, next to it, a large black one.

She heaved the black dumpster open and was assailed by the stench. It was full of black bin bags, but several had burst, with food scraps and rotting peelings leaking out. She gingerly pushed a bag to one side and leaned further into the bin, tearing at each bag.

She had all but given up when she glimpsed the dark green edge of it. She hooked it out. The wreath was in a sorry state, the flowers dead, the greenery wilted. But there was a small, white card still attached to it, though it was damp and buckled. Chucking the wreath back into the garbage, she examined the card. It bore a single word, handwritten in ink that had run but was still legible.

Pamela.

SHE HAD BEEN HOPING for more, a last name at least. She wondered if she was travelling ever further down the wrong path, piling error upon error, taking one false turn after another. What if Forbes's date referred to something else entirely, nothing to do with Aberdeen?

She caught a reflection of herself as she left the hotel—the new hair, the bruise—and wondered what the hell she was doing. But then Maggie reminded herself that the sweet lady who had sabotaged her car had been ready to kill without discrimination. And the President was relying on her. She owed it to Stephen Baker, to Stuart and to herself to find out who was behind this.

She pulled out her BlackBerry. If there was any man who, on principle, would ensure his number was in the local phone book, it would be him. She called directory assistance and asked for the home number of Principal Ray Schilling.

After an apology for disturbing him at the weekend, she went straight in. 'Mr Schilling, something you said stayed with me. "I remember all the students I teach." Could I test you?'

'Go ahead.'

'Pamela.'

'You'll need to give me more than that, Ms Muir.'

'I'm afraid I don't have a last name. Best I can give you is that she was a contemporary of Robert Jackson and Stephen Baker.'

'Let me try to picture the class. That's how I do it, I visualise the class as I taught them.' He began muttering names, as if taking a register. 'No. As I thought, no Pamela in that class.'

'What about the year below them?'

'Let me think.' More muttering and then he said, 'Do you mean Pamela Everett?'

'I'm not sure. Who was she?'

'Well, she did stand out. She was extremely pretty. The students called her Miss America.' He paused. 'Terribly sad. She died just a couple of years after graduation.'

'And how did she die?' Maggie's pulse began to race.

'An illness. I forget the details. Very quick apparently.'

'An illness? Are you absolutely sure about that?'

'Yes, of course. It all happened very suddenly. The parents asked me to read a lesson at her funeral.'

Maggie was thinking fast. 'Do you think I might speak with them?'

'They left Aberdeen very soon after Pamela died.'

'Do you have any idea where they went?'

'I'm afraid I don't.'

She was about to ring off, but there was something about the way Ray Schilling was breathing into the phone that suggested he was hesitating. Maggie kept silent, not wanting to scare him off. Eventually, and warily, he spoke.

'Ms Muir, I have not been completely frank with you. I *do* know where the Everetts are. We have kept the address on file all these years on the strict understanding that we share it with no one.'

'I see.'

'But when you came to me on Friday, you told me that a large sum of money is involved here. I am working on the assumption that you would not be asking me questions about Pamela Everett if the late Robert Jackson had not remembered her in his will.'

Maggie said nothing, hoping he would take her silence as confirmation.

'I could not in conscience stand in the way of some financial comfort coming the way of the Everetts. Lord knows they have had their share of misfortune.'

'You are a good man, Mr Schilling.'

'Now I hope you have your snowshoes with you. If you think Aberdeen is the middle of nowhere, wait till you hear where the Everetts live.'

Undisclosed location, Sunday, March 26, 16:00 GMT
'My thanks to all of you for making time for this conference call: I know that the weekends are precious.'

A murmur of agreement, conveyed through the desktop speaker.

'I wanted to brief you on the latest developments in the case we discussed last time. I am glad to tell you that we have sent in some very experienced . . .' he hesitated, unsure of the appropriately delicate term for such work, '*personnel*, and I am assured that there will be results very soon.'

'How soon?' Germany again. Of course.

'Well, put it this way. If you read your newspapers over the next twenty-four hours, I don't think you'll be disappointed.'

'That's good to hear.' Manhattan.

'Can we say we are back on track?' A new voice, Middle Eastern.

'We are not out of the woods yet. As we all know, politics is an unpredictable business.'

'Except that's what we're all here for, isn't it?' said Germany. 'To make politics as predictable as possible. Am I right?'

8

Coeur d'Alene, Idaho, Sunday, March 26, 20:55 PST
In normal circumstances Coeur d'Alene would have been a perfectly lovely place to visit. Not that Maggie could remember what normal circumstances were. But a weekend here, in this snow-covered ski resort of a town, with its alpine chalets and cosy, crackling fires, would have been a treat. With the right person.

It had taken two tiny planes to get to here, first the short hop from Aberdeen to Seattle, then a connection for the longer flight to Coeur d'Alene.

Maggie thought about the upcoming encounter with the Everetts. Should she stick with the story Mr Schilling had imagined for her? That she was an insurance agent needing to check out a claim that might lead to a windfall? Too cruel. So she came up with something else. Not brilliant, but it would have to do.

The cab turned off the main thoroughfare through the town onto a lane that wound its way far up a mountainside. She checked her watch. Nearly 9 p.m. It was crazy to do this in the evening—who wanted to open the door of their remote home to a stranger emerging out of the darkness?—but urgency drove her on.

The street lighting had long gone and the last car they had seen had passed nearly ten minutes ago. Maggie looked over her shoulder: some distant headlights still twinkled.

They drove on, climbing ever steeper, until the satnav told them their destination was approaching on the right.

Maggie asked the driver to pull up twenty yards away and to stay: she would pay him once they were back in Coeur d'Alene.

She stepped out into the bracing air. Standing there listening, she became aware of a sound she had probably not heard in years: complete silence. The darkness was total, too. The only light to break this darkness came from the stars and the lamp above the entrance of what she hoped was the Everett residence.

The house was timber-fronted, with a two-step walk-up and a porch with two neatly arranged outdoor chairs. The porch light was encouraging, but it was hard to tell if there was any light within: heavy curtains were drawn across the windows.

Maggie closed her eyes for a moment, then knocked on the door.

That the woman who opened it was the mother of Pamela Everett, Maggie could tell instantly. Principal Schilling had told her Pamela was pretty. This woman had the fine features of a long-ago beauty queen.

'Hello.' Maggie smiled, hating herself for what she was about to do. 'My name is Ashley Muir. I'm so sorry to disturb you so late. But I've come a long way to fulfil the wish of a dying man. My late husband. This is something I promised him I would do. Are you Mrs Anne Everett?'

The woman looked aghast, but she did not slam the door. Maggie pressed on. 'My husband died a month ago. In one of our last conversations he told me about his first love. Your daughter, Pamela.'

Now the woman's face turned white, and it was as if she had aged by twenty years. 'How did you find me?'

'My husband did that. Worked that computer for months, I don't know how he did it. Mrs Everett, could we speak inside? I promise this won't take long.'

Staring at her as if at an apparition, Anne Everett widened the door to let her in. Maggie stepped inside hesitantly, wanting her body to convey what she felt: that she was treading carefully here, not wanting to bring more pain to this house of loss.

There were reminders everywhere: a large photograph of Pamela Everett in the costume of high-school graduation, several photos of a girl at the seaside, on a rocking horse, blowing out birthday candles. Mrs Everett ushered Maggie into a sitting room organised round a TV set. Maggie sat on a couch. Anne Everett perched on the edge of her chair.

'My late husband was in the class below your daughter. He told me she'd never even have noticed him. But he had a crush on her. His first.' Maggie smiled, the rueful smile of a widow. 'He said he had hardly thought about her for years, until he got his diagnosis. And then he remembered the "beautiful Pamela", and how she had died from a sudden illness. And it hurt him to think that maybe people would think your daughter had been forgotten. Because she hadn't. He had remembered her. And it was so important to him that you knew that. Because—and this is what he said—if people remember us, then it means a little part of us lives on.'

Maggie had told herself it was a white lie, but that did not reduce the shame she felt. When she saw the tear falling slowly down the cheek of Anne Everett it made her loathe herself all the more. Nothing could justify this. She began to stand up, mumbling an apology.

'Please don't go!' The woman spoke with such urgency that her voice pushed Maggie back onto the couch.

Anne Everett wiped the tear from her eye and, to Maggie's great surprise, revealed the beginnings of a smile. 'Young lady, I have waited twenty-six years for this day. I have waited for someone to come and say what you just said. That my daughter *lived.* That her life meant something. I was never allowed to believe it.'

'I don't follow.'

'Of course you don't. How could you? No one ever knew. Except me. And Randall.' She was animated now, leaping up from the chair. 'Are you a whiskey drinker, Mrs Muir? I am,' she said, without waiting for Maggie's answer. From under the side table, she produced a bottle, now down to its last third, and a used glass. She poured herself a healthy measure and downed half of it.

'My daughter's only "illness" was to have a beautiful face. That was her illness. Pamela never had a day's sickness in her life. We *said* that she had got sick. That was the deal.'

'The deal?'

'That's what he made us say. After the fire.'

Maggie felt herself shudder. 'What fire?' But she knew the answer already.

'There was a fire at the Meredith Hotel in Aberdeen. Huge blaze. They said that everyone survived.' She paused, a shadow falling over her face again. 'But it wasn't true.'

'Pamela was in that hotel?'

Mrs Everett nodded. 'We don't know who with. Some boy, on spring break. Using her for sex. She was cursed with a body that men hungered for. We didn't know she had been in the hotel. We thought she was having a sleepover with her girlfriends.'

She smiled a bitter smile at her own naiveté.

'Early the next morning, we were just waiting for her to come home, like she always did on a Sunday after a Saturday night. And then there he was, at the door.'

'Who was there?'

'The man. From the hotel, I thought—at first, anyway. He explained there had been an accident, a fire. Pamela had been killed.' The last word came out in a croak. 'I'm sorry.'

'You take your time.'

Anne Everett poured the rest of the bottle into the glass and swallowed it whole. 'You see,' she said, 'I've carried this for so long. Randall never would let me tell. But it's eaten me alive, this secret. He took it to his grave, but it killed him too.

'The man said Pamela was dead. And there would never be anything we could do to bring her back. All that would be left was her reputation. She could either be remembered as a "good-time girl" who had died in someone's bed, or as prom queen Pamela Everett of James Madison High. It was up to us.

'All we had to do was tell people, starting that day, that Pam had come down with something. Then, a week or so later, we should say it was serious. That she was being transferred to Tacoma. No visitors allowed. Then, a week after that, there would be an announcement of her death. And in return he would pay us a lot of money, more than Randall would make in five years. To show he was serious, he had one of those attaché cases with him. And inside it was cash. A lot of cash. I don't think I'd ever seen that much money in my life. And he promised there would be more.

'Well, Randall threw him out, of course. Said it was blood money. How dare he? But the man left the case there, with a card. The hours went by and we were sobbing about our daughter, our little baby. But we were also looking at that money. Might have been fifty thousand dollars in that bag.'

Now she hunched over, making small, noiseless sobs. Maggie crossed the space between them and placed a hand on her shoulder. Mrs Everett grabbed it and held it tight. Raising her head, she let out a howl of anguish. 'I said we should take the money! God curse me for it, I accepted it.'

'I understand,' Maggie said, shaken.

'I believed what he said, you see. He said we could use the money to set up a memorial for Pamela. Perhaps a scholarship. Some way of keeping her memory alive. So we said yes. We called the number on the card. Randall made the call.

'Of course we never did set up that memorial. We were too ashamed. Imagine lying about your own child's death. We deserved to be cast out. So that's what we did. We cast ourselves out. As far away as possible. But you can't run away from your own shame. It stays with you.'

Maggie spoke softly. 'The money? Did the man ever pay more?'

'Oh yes. It kept coming into the bank account, month after month. I can't bring myself to spend a penny of it, of course. Nor could Randall. It's filthy.'

'And who did it come from?'

'Like I said, we never knew. We were too grief-stricken to ask. Too stupid, too, probably.'

Maggie had a question burning on her tongue. 'And what about this . . . boy she was with that night? Did you ever—'

Anne Everett shook her head furiously. 'Never did, never wanted to. We would have killed him if we'd have found out who he was.'

'Do you have your suspicions?'

'Well, it's funny you should ask that. This last year or two, I'd been wondering when somebody would knock on that door and ask about Pamela. I thought a journalist might come here.'

'Why a journalist?'

'Because the boy my Pamela loved when she was at high school, the boy she adored until the day she died, was Stephen Baker.'

The words sent a charge of electricity through her. Instantly Maggie assumed the obvious: that Vic Forbes knew what had happened to Pamela Everett and believed that Baker had been involved in her death. That was why that date represented Forbes's blanket. But none of that could explain a stranger appearing at the Everetts' door ready to hand over serious money to protect the reputation of a lad barely out of his teens, twenty-one at most. Why would anyone go to such lengths to protect him?

Anne Everett was watching Maggie's face, studying her reaction. 'If you're thinking it was him, you're wrong,' she said firmly. 'Pamela was in bed with someone at the Meredith Hotel that night, but it wasn't Stephen.'

Maggie frowned. 'How can you be so sure?'

Anne Everett got to her feet. 'Come with me.'

She led Maggie up a narrow staircase, and opened a door that instantly released a cloud of spare-room must. Maggie shivered as she looked around. Posters of Prince and Jimmy Connors on the wall, a teddy bear on the bed.

'But didn't you move here after . . .?' Maggie said.

'Yes, we did. Randall didn't want me to do this. He said the whole point of coming here was to move on. But you can't always move on. Not everyone can do it.'

Pamela's mother crouched on the floor by the bed, lifted the valance and tugged at the drawer that was revealed beneath. Inside was a large, black-bound scrapbook. She pulled it out, then perched on the end of the bed and opened it. She patted the space next to her, encouraging Maggie to sit down. 'Look,' she said.

Glued into the scrapbook was a yellowing two-page spread from the *Madisonian*, the newspaper of James Madison High. At the centre was a prom picture of Pamela Everett in a ball gown.

She turned the page, to what Maggie recognised as a cutting from the *Daily World*. 'Blaze at Downtown Hotel' read the headline. The story described a late-night fire at the Meredith Hotel, how a drill had brought all the guests out into the streets in their nightclothes as the 'inferno gutted several storeys of the hotel'.

'This is what I wanted to show you,' Mrs Everett said quietly. She turned a couple more pages of the scrapbook.

Another page from the *Daily World*.

'There he is,' Anne Everett said.

Sure enough, there stood a young Stephen Baker shaking the hand of some older, distinguished man. Below was a caption:

> *Washington's senior US Senator, Paul Corbyn, greets the state's first winner of a Rhodes scholarship since Corbyn himself nearly forty years earlier. The lucky young man is Stephen Baker, graduate of James Madison High School and, this summer, Harvard University. The photograph was taken in Senator Corbyn's Washington DC office on March 15.*

Maggie looked at the date at the top of the page: March 18. 'This photo proves it wasn't him,' Maggie said softly.

'That's right,' Mrs Everett agreed. 'He was on the other side of the country that day. I often think how different things would have been if Stephen Baker had taken Pamela out that night—instead of that *bastard*.' She spat out the word with the venom of a woman who never swears. 'Then Pamela would be alive today, I am sure.'

New York, Sunday, March 26, 23:01

Late nights suited him. Best time to work: no email, no phone calls, no distractions. There was a glass by the side of the computer, amber with whiskey. But he had barely touched it: he was absorbed in his work.

He hadn't heard from Maggie for a while, but that only served to motivate him further: she was clearly in a bit of trouble here, and so he was duty-bound to do whatever he could to help. Besides, with Maggie it was never just duty.

He moved the cursor across the screen and clicked open the information that had, at last, caused the penny to drop. He reached for his phone and punched in Maggie's number and it rang and rang and then went to voice-mail. Yet again. He shoved the phone back into his trouser pocket.

He sat up. Was that a noise? A muffled metallic clang? Must have been outside. He needed to think how best to organise this material, for maximum impact. What would work best? He imagined relaying it to Maggie, watching a smile of recognition spread across her face, as she understood the pattern he now understood. That smile could make a man fall in love with Maggie Costello.

There it was again. Not the same noise, more of a creak this time and, if anything, louder. 'Hello? Anyone there?'

Nothing.

He checked the clock at the top of the screen. Past eleven.

He reached for the glass of whiskey, glancing at the darkness of the window as he did so.

The sight of a man's face peering in made him jump. Idiotically, he wondered how someone could be outside—here in a fifth-floor apartment. It took him a second to understand that the face staring at him was a reflection of a man standing just behind him.

By then it was too late. The man's hands were on his shoulders, pinning him to his chair, and then on his neck.

He writhed and clawed at his attacker, but the strength in this man's hands was insuperable; he was, he could tell instantly, a professional. Suddenly, and with horrible certainty, he knew he was going to die.

But if they were ready to kill him, they would be ready to kill Maggie—and that thought gave him determination. Letting his hands fall, as if in submission to his fate, he dug into his pocket and then gave a sharp lurch to his right to shake the man off.

As his attacker stumbled backwards, he gulped down oxygen. All his concentration was on his left hand. Adept at using the phone when he wasn't looking at it, he jabbed at the buttons. The strangling hands were back on his neck now, attempting to get a grip as he writhed, while his own left hand remained deep in his pocket, searching for the green key that would start the call. He needed to wait for the machine to pick up and the message to play.

Now. He would do it now. With his right arm he tried to lash out—backwards—at his assailant and, once again, the man had to take one hand off his victim's neck to fend off the diversion.

'*Ennnnnn!*' he rasped, in what sounded like an exhalation of desperate pain.

His attacker had forced him now onto his knees, so that he bore the full weight of his brutal killer on his shoulders. Somehow he had to find the strength to cry out once more. '*Ayyyy!*' he shouted.

The attacker now took his hands off his prey's neck and punched him hard in the jaw. Even so, he did not flinch, instead seizing on the chance to cry out, *'Seeeeeeeee!'*

Somehow he found the energy to force his executioner to interrupt the job of asphyxiation often enough that eventually he had cried out five times. Then his strength left him. He could flail no more at the man who was squeezing the life out of him. At last he surrendered, and ended up on the floor, curled up and lifeless.

There was a noise outside in the hall. The attacker, unnerved by the sound of neighbours returning to the next-door apartment, moved swiftly—using the device he had been given to wipe the computer's hard drive.

The knock at the door interrupted his effort to frisk the man he had just killed. 'Hello? Is everything all right in there?' The knocking continued and was getting louder.

Hastily, the killer scanned the apartment for the fire escape, eventually finding it in the kitchen where a door led out to the iron staircase that zig-zagged down the exterior of the building. Taking the stairs two at a time until he had reached ground level, he fled.

Five floors up, the dead man's fingers curled round his cellphone as if gripping the hand of a loved one.

Coeur d'Alene, Idaho, Sunday March 26, 22:55 PST

To her great relief the cab driver was still outside. He had waited nearly two hours, with only a radio and the car heater for company. But he had waited. Maggie asked how long it would take to drive to Boise. He wanted to see the cash before he agreed to go any further. Maggie took pleasure in pulling out five hundred-dollar bills and agreeing on that as the rate for the evening's work.

The darkness of the Idaho sky and the emptiness of the roads reminded her of those countless night flights she had endured during the campaign. It was where she had done some of her best thinking.

For a brief, blissful second she had believed she had finally unravelled the knot bequeathed by Vic Forbes. The young, handsome Baker had taken the adoring prom queen to bed in a downtown hotel, and there, somehow, she had died. Vic Forbes knew of it and was ready to use it. But this theory had been shattered by that photograph of Baker with Senator Corbyn taken on the same day as the fire. Could Forbes have made such an elementary blunder?

That was not all that nagged at Maggie. Why was that single page missing from the library archive? Who had removed it? And if it wasn't Baker who had left Pamela Everett to die, who was it?

Maggie desperately needed to talk this through with someone. For at least the third time, she dialled Nick du Caines's home number, the only one of his she remembered. Voicemail, yet again. Where the hell was he?

She checked her watch. Midnight in Idaho, 8 a.m. in London. Worth a shot. She used the browser of her BlackBerry to find the London number of Nick's Sunday newspaper, dialled and asked for the foreign desk. A secretary answered. 'Unusual call,' Maggie began in her politest voice, explaining that she was a regular Washington contact of Nick du Caines and that she had unfortunately mislaid his mobile number. She had a story that she was sure he would be interested in. Was there any chance they might help?

'I think you'd better speak to the foreign editor,' the woman said, an edge in her voice that Maggie didn't like.

There was a delay until a man came on the line.

'I understand you're a friend of Nick's?'

'That's right.'

'I'm afraid I have some bad news. We've only just heard. Nick is dead.'

9

Boise, Idaho, Monday, March 27, 04:13 PST

The shock of Nick's death was beyond tears: Maggie was numbed to the bone. Emerging from the taxi as it pulled into Boise Airport, she was hardly able to breathe.

The foreign editor had told her there had been a break-in at Nick's apartment, and that there had been signs of a struggle. His body 'bore all the hallmarks of death by strangulation'. Police were interviewing neighbours. But so far there were no witnesses.

Of course there would be no witnesses, Maggie thought. The people who had killed Nick were like the people who had killed Stuart. They were pros: they would leave no trace.

With hours to wait before the first morning flight out, she knew she should try to sleep. She tried curling up on a hard plastic chair, but no matter how exhausted she was real sleep would not come.

She started walking around, scrutinising everyone she passed. Are you a part of this? Are you? After some minutes she noticed a man, apparently immersed in the *Idaho Statesman*, standing by the Departures sign, and wondered how long he had been there.

Think, she told herself. She had asked Nick to look into an aspect of the Forbes story: was there any evidence to link the CIA with his death? She hadn't considered that a life-threatening question to ask, not when Nick had won himself a shelf-full of trophies investigating CIA conduct in the war on terror. Clearly whatever he had found had struck a nerve that was too raw to be tolerated.

Shortly after four thirty in the morning, she felt the vibration of a text arriving on her BlackBerry. It was from her sister:

Call me urgently. Something strange is happening. Liz.

She was halfway through dialling the Dublin number when another message arrived, this time from Sanchez.

The police want to see you. Now. Take the next plane to New York.

New York, JFK Airport, Monday, March 27, 14:41

They met her off the plane, a detective in plain clothes with two uniformed officers. They led her away from the other passengers, towards a blank room containing a desk and three chairs.

The detective introduced himself as Charles Bridge. In his early forties, African-American and unsmiling, he got straight to business. 'Thank you for coming to New York right away. We appreciate that.'

Maggie nodded, her heart throbbing. What was this about?

'It took us a while to get hold of you, you know,' the detective said. 'Tried your cell, that just rang out. No response on email. Seemed like you'd just disappeared.'

'My phone was stolen. Along with my wallet and computer.'

'That right? Do you know why we wanted to see you, Miss Costello?'

'I know that my friend Nick du Caines is dead.'

'That's right. Why else? If you had to guess.'

'I don't know.'

'Because, Miss Costello, the last call Mr du Caines made was to you. To your home number.'

'To me? When?'

'His phone says he placed the call at three minutes past eleven last night. Your answering machine confirms that. And, based on what the neighbours have told us about the noises coming from Mr du Caines's apartment, we think that's the time of death.'

'Did you just say my answering machine confirms that? How do you know that?'

'We tried to contact you by all available means. We contacted your former employers at the White House, and they had no idea how to reach you. We had no choice but to obtain a warrant and make an entry into your apartment and impound the machine.'

'You broke into my apartment?'

'Our colleagues in Washington made an entry on our behalf, yes.'

Maggie's mind was racing as she thought of what was there, what might have been seen. Had she left anything out that might point to the Forbes business? 'And did you find anything—on my machine, I mean?'

'We'll come to that, Miss Costello. Right now, I'm puzzled why a man who is being beaten and strangled would call your number in his death throes.'

'What are you suggesting, Detective?'

'I'm not suggesting anything. I'm just wondering. I mean, he didn't dial your cellphone, did he? He called your home number. Almost like that was the only way he could lead us to you.'

'Lead you to me? I don't understand.' Maggie could feel her face growing flushed. 'I don't like what you're insinuating, Detective. Nick du Caines was a very dear friend of mine. And I was on the other side of the country when he died.'

'I'm not insinuating anything, Miss Costello. I'm just asking some questions.'

'I want to hear this message. He left it for me.'

'This is evidence in the case now, Miss Costello, I can't—'

'That answering machine is my legal property. And right now I am a witness, no more. If you want to arrest me, go ahead. Until you do, I have the right to hear what's on that tape.'

The detective pulled out his phone and retreated to the corner of the room to make a call, apparently to a superior. He returned to his chair, looking glum. 'Apparently, the advice is that we should play the message to you. See if you can shed any light on it.'

He produced a laptop computer, pressed a few keys and then clicked on an audio file. From the machine's small speakers, Maggie heard Nick, bellowing in pain. *Ennnnnn!*

It was terrible to listen to, the horror of it real and direct. Even distorted by transmission to the audio file, she could hear the thud of blows to Nick's body followed by exhalations of pain: *Ayyyy!*

It was as if she were there, watching as the breath of life was squeezed out of him. It lasted another full, murderous minute, until there was a last gasp from Nick—*Phwaw!*—and finally it was over.

Maggie's head was dipped low as she stared at the floor. The detective spoke again. 'It's harrowing to hear, I know. But why would he do it? Like I said before, he doesn't do anything except leave a recording of his own death. There's no message to you.'

A small spark suddenly broke through Maggie's grief. 'Can you play it again, please?'

'Why? Did you hear something?'

'I'm not sure. Maybe.'

He clicked on the file a second time, watching Maggie closely as she listened. Ninety seconds later, he raised his eyebrows. 'So?'

'I'm sorry, Detective. I was wrong.' She had to look away from him as she lied.

'Any idea why he would call you at such a time?'

'Look, Mr Bridge. This is awkward. I had a drink with Nick last Thursday. He was an old friend but he always wanted it to be something more. He said some things to me last week.' She looked up briefly at the detective, so that their eyes met. 'Romantic things. I wonder if Nick was just trying to say goodbye.'

The detective held her gaze and Maggie willed herself to meet it without flinching. Then, apparently satisfied, he nodded to the uniformed men that the interview was over and showed Maggie to the door.

Released back onto the airport concourse, Maggie tried to walk away as nonchalantly as possible, in case the cops were watching her. She forced herself to be patient, to take the elevator to another floor before whipping out her computer and acting on the information Nick du Caines had passed to her as his last, dying act.

She would stay here, surrounded by people. Surely that would make her safe.

She said the sequence over to herself once more, repeating it as she had heard it. There was no doubting it. It was N-I-C-K-4.

Nick died trying to make contact with her. There was a message within that message: of that she was now sure. She marvelled at the strength and ingenuity of such a feat and, not for the first time that day, felt glad to have known Nick du Caines.

She had remembered how Nick, in his little masterclass on journalism, had confessed that he wrote everything online, storing it up there 'in the ether'. She flipped open her computer, watching as it latched on to the airport's Wifi signal. A few keystrokes and she was at the Googledocs website. She logged in, typing Nick's name without spaces: nickducaines. Then the password he had cried out: Nick4.

Incorrect name and password.

She tried again, this time spelling Nick's name in capital letters.

Incorrect password, insufficient characters.

Damn. Nick's effort, valiant though it had been, had been in vain. He had not lasted long enough to convey the last few letters.

She stared at the screen. Nick4. What might 4 refer to? *Think.*

Then a teenage memory returned. They had all done it, carving it on park benches and on school desks. She had done it herself once: Maggie4Liam. Was it possible that Nick du Caines had been that soft-hearted? She typed Nick4Maggie.

She was about to press enter when something stopped her. She could hear Nick's voice. *Now listen, Mags, when are you finally going to start moving those luscious lips of yours into the shape of a story for my newspaper?*

Mags. Carefully, she retyped so that the password read simply Nick4Mags. Without fuss, as if it had been waiting for her, the page transformed itself, offering a list of documents. She was in. Poor, sweet Nick. She had never taken his interest in her seriously.

At a glance, she could see all his most recent stories. And there at the top, a document entitled *New Orleans*. She clicked it open, expecting a long, detailed memo. Instead there was a single line. Daniel Judd, aviation expert—followed by a phone number.

Maggie pulled out her phone and dialled. After two rings, a voice answered: male, cautious.

'I'm a friend of Nick du Caines,' she began. 'He left a message on my machine just before he died. I think he—'

'Died? Nick? What happened?'

'I'm sorry, I thought you might have known.'

Maggie explained the circumstances that had led to her call. There was a long silence and then he said, 'How can I trust you? How do I know you didn't kill Nick and now you're after me?'

Maggie was flummoxed. 'All I can tell you is that Nick went to great lengths to let me know how to reach you. He used his dying breaths to leave a message on my answering machine. It was—'

'All right, get off this line. Call me on a payphone in thirty minutes. Number is—' There was a shuffling of paper, then he rattled off a number at her. 'Go buy pay-as-you-go phones, as many as you can afford. Call me from one of those. After that, throw it away. Never use any of them twice. And don't give the number to anyone.' He repeated the number of the payphone and hung up.

Maggie did what she was told, rushing to a cellphone store in Terminal 3. She bought five phones with her now-dwindling cash supply and punched in the payphone number.

He picked up on the second ring.

'Listen, Mr—'

'No names on the phone!'

'Of course, sorry. Listen, it was me who put, er, our mutual friend onto the, um, issue that I think he was discussing with you. I think he wanted me to know whatever it was you told him.'

'This is some serious shit you're wading into here, Missy, I can tell you. I'm gonna do this real quick and I'm only gonna say it once. Are we clear?'

'We're clear.'

'Right then. Once only. At midnight thirty local time on March 22, a jet departed from Lakefront Airport, New Orleans, Louisiana, carrying seven passengers. The number of the aircraft was November-four-eight-zero-eight-Papa. That aircraft is registered to one Premier Air Executive

Services, an air operator based in Maryland. Its prior history indicates use by the Company.'

As Maggie suspected, the CIA.

Judd wasn't done. 'That was its *prior* use. Two years ago it shifted ownership. It is now entirely at the service of a single client. Premier runs private jets exclusively for AitkenBruce.'

Maggie couldn't repress her surprise. 'AitkenBruce? The bank?'

But Judd was in no mood for discussion. He had one more fact to convey. 'Today Premier submitted another flight plan. They have a Gulfstream 550 jet departing Teterboro, New Jersey, for Washington Reagan at nineteen hundred hours. Looking back through the flight history, there's only one person who makes that journey on that aircraft. And that's the chairman of the bank.'

After the call ended, Maggie's thoughts whirled. A bank? What on earth could any of this have to do with a bank? It made no sense.

The phone she had bought in Aberdeen vibrated, making her jump. She pressed the green button to answer the call.

'Maggie? Is that you?'

Uri.

Panic flooded through her. She spoke fast, thinking of Stuart and Nick. 'Don't call this number again. Give me a number where I can call you.'

Her abruptness shocked him; a sudden wariness in his voice, he replied, 'I'm in an edit suite.' He gave her the number; Maggie scribbled it down, then ordered him to hang up.

She binned the phone she'd used to call Judd, picked another and called Uri back.

'Maggie, what's going on?'

'Uri, anyone who talks to me is in danger. Grave danger. Remember my friend Nick? He was killed last night.'

There was a beat of silence. 'Jesus. I'm sorry, Maggie.'

'I so want to talk, Uri, just talk for as long as we like.'

'Where are you?'

She hesitated. She knew it made no sense to say it out loud. But it was a virgin phone; it should be safe. 'I'm at JFK.'

'I'm coming. Right now.'

She tried to argue, but he bulldozed through her resistance and she told him exactly where she was sitting.

She turned back to the computer, still open at Nick's Googledocs account. Focus, she told herself. Focus. She went to the search field and typed 'AitkenBruce'. She had heard of the bank, of course. It was famous for its squillionaire executives, rewarding themselves with telephone number salaries and even fatter bonuses.

Google led her to a long piece in the *Sunday Times* magazine headlined: 'The True Masters of the Universe: Inside the World's Richest Bank'. It revealed an institution whose assets topped a trillion dollars and whose top brass routinely went on to take up posts in the heights of the world's economies—US Treasury Secretary, German finance minister, head of the European Central Bank.

Maggie scrolled down, looking for anything which might connect AitkenBruce to Forbes, let alone explain why a Company jet might have been dispatched to New Orleans to assist in his murder. Had Forbes been blackmailing the bank as well as the President?

She lingered over the section which detailed how AitkenBruce made its vast fortune. AitkenBruce didn't waste its time with the little guys: its customers were governments, multinational mega-corporations and only the very richest individuals.

But knowledge was its secret weapon. If an investor was thinking about getting into, say, timber, AitkenBruce could help because it counted the world's biggest timber companies among its clients. In addition, major investors in the same field were probably also paying the bank for its advice, so the bank knew what they were up to, too. AitkenBruce had every angle covered, which could only help when the bank came to decide how to invest its own money.

She scrolled past a photograph of Waugh, the boss—fiftyish, bald—and came to a paragraph written nearly a year before Stephen Baker had been elected. 'No one doubts the extraordinary influence of an institution like AitkenBruce. Its links to the White House are solid. And the bank will be watching the coming presidential contest closely. Once again, the money-men are covering all their bases. AitkenBruce gave donations to both Democrats and Republicans.'

Maggie moved her cursor to the Search field and typed 'Stephen Baker + Roger Waugh'.

The first entry was billed as a 'News' result. It took her to a page on politico.com listing the President's appointments for the next day. There at

9 a.m. was 'President Baker meets representatives of America's financial community', listing the personnel involved.

So that was why Waugh was travelling to Washington tonight. He was going to meet the President.

And yet Waugh was somehow tangled up with the death of Forbes. A sudden alarm drove through her like a surge of electricity. It would be madness to let Waugh come within a hundred yards of the Oval Office before the President understood what the hell was going on. And that meant Maggie had to find out.

She opened up a new tab and checked out Teterboro Airport. It was a tiny airport very popular with 'private and corporate aircraft', just twelve miles from midtown Manhattan. Slightly farther from JFK, but she could make it if she got going right away.

Just then there was a tap on her shoulder.

She froze. And then she heard his voice.

'I nearly didn't recognise you. What's with the haircut?'

She hadn't planned it; she'd had no idea how this moment would feel. But the sight of him now, in his trademark dark jeans and white shirt, his full head of lustrous, almost-black hair, made her stand up and close her arms round him.

They stood like that, holding each other, for a minute or longer. It had been so long since she had felt his touch. She wanted to breathe in the smell of him, the scent that instantly transported her back to the thousand different moments of love they had shared.

It was Maggie who eventually broke the embrace, stepping back to look at him. She smiled, childishly pleased that he hadn't let go of her hand. 'So what couldn't wait that you had to rush over here?'

Uri sat on the stool next to hers. 'You know the Baker film I'm making? I've come across something—I don't know—odd. Do you know how Stephen Baker became Governor?'

'I know he won big.'

'Very big. Massive, in fact. Ran against a total nobody. You know why? Because the Republican opponent he was meant to face imploded three months before election day. During the campaign his divorce papers suddenly surfaced; showed he had a thing about filming his wife having sex with other men.'

'I really don't see—'

'But that's not all. Baker was never even expected to *be* the Democratic candidate. Everyone thought he'd lose the primary. He was up against a really popular mayor of Seattle. Except someone produced a tape of the mayor talking on the phone, saying there were too many "chinks and spics" in the city. Baker just glided to the nomination.'

'Where's this going, Uri?'

'I don't know. It just seems that—until all this impeachment stuff—somebody up there really liked Stephen Baker.'

She was ready to hear anything that might help explain the bizarre chain of events that had unfolded this last week. Not that she could yet work out how this fitted in. 'Uri, I have to leave here any minute now. If I need to reach you, where will you be?'

'In the edit suite. I can't get any work done at home at the moment. My sister's visiting from Tel Aviv.'

A different cog in Maggie's mind started turning. 'Your sister?' So that had been the woman Maggie had heard in the background on that call to the New York apartment. Not a new lover after all. She felt a knot deep inside her—one she had only been dimly aware of until this moment—begin to loosen and unravel.

'Are you sure I can't come with you, wherever you're going? I might even be useful.'

'I know, Uri. And I'm really grateful. But I've drawn too many people into this mess already.'

'OK. But take care of yourself, Maggie.' They were standing now, close together. 'I mean it.' He leaned forward and kissed the top of her head. Then he turned and walked away.

She looked at her watch: she would have to leave right now if she was to get to Teterboro in time. But she had the guilty, nagging sensation of something she was meant to do. She was about to switch off the computer when it came to her: call Liz. Her sister had sent that text hours ago.

She picked out one of the disposable phones and dialled Liz's number.

'Christ, thank God Almighty.'

'Liz, what is it?'

'Jesus, Maggie, you had me worried.' Now the phone was filled by the noise of a child sobbing. 'Oh, it's OK, Calum pet.' There was rustling and more sniffing. 'There you go, love. Oh look, *Peppa Pig*'s on.'

'Liz, I can call another time.'

'No! You've got to see this. Get your computer out, get online.'

'Hang on. I haven't any time, I've—'

'This won't take a second. Go to the Freenet page where . . . You know what, forget it. I've still got remote access, I'll do it.'

Maggie watched as the cursor moved, apparently by magic, round her screen. It directed itself to the Freenet and from there to the eerie, unsmiling portrait that constituted victorforbes.gov. Maggie could see that Liz was typing in the password—rendered as asterisks—that transformed that image into the page that glistened with just a single date. March 15, a quarter of a century ago.

Now, though, the image appeared to be slowly fading away as square by square it was replaced by another. A photograph was materialising. As the pixels filled out, Maggie saw what she was looking at. It was an old black-and-white newspaper shot of the Meredith Hotel, the night it all but burned to the ground. And there in the foreground were the guests, milling around on the street in pyjamas or bathrobes.

On an electronic post-it which Liz had somehow thrown up on the screen, the cursor began typing. Do you see who I see?

Maggie looked closely at the picture whose resolution was improving with each second. A cluster of three people were in sharpest focus, their faces wearing panicked expressions. And now, with a shudder, she recognised him.

There, watching the Meredith Hotel burn down, was the man whose face the American people and now the world, had come to know. Younger, unlined, but undeniably the same person.

She was looking at Stephen Baker.

FROM MUCKRAKER, posted at 16:45, Monday, March 27:

> You've gotta love this. With exquisite timing, one of the President's key tormentors has just suffered what you might call an ethics malfunction. Sen. Rusty Wilson was all set to play the role of Grand Inquisitor alongside Rick Franklin had the impeachment proceedings against President Baker moved from the House to the Senate. Republicans will be revising those plans now.
>
> For Sen. Wilson has just been on the sharp end of a rather unfortunate leak: to wit, the transcripts of every email exchange and phone conversation

between himself and a thirty-seven-year-old pharmaceutical industry lobbyist from his state who, as luck would have it, is a chesty blonde among whose qualifications for such a policy-intensive job include past service as a waitress at Hooters. The transcripts reveal the senator as a breathy and demanding lover.

Maybe this is why they call Republicans the Grand Old Party.

Teterboro Airport, New Jersey, Monday, March 27, 18:42

For the best part of forty minutes Maggie had sat on the edge of the rear passenger seat, willing the cab driver to go faster. He had given her a series of disapproving looks, as if her angst were so much cigarette smoke fugging up his cab. Taking out her compact, she could see why. She looked appalling, pale and drawn and raw round the eyes; hardly a suitable guise for the next stage in her plan. She repaired as much of the damage as she was able to, brushing the unfamiliar hairstyle into some kind of order, applying dabs of concealer, mascara, a touch of lipstick.

For the rest of the journey she had stared at the photograph which she had kept up on her now-offline computer screen.

Could it have been doctored? Forbes wouldn't have gone to such lengths to protect a bogus photograph. This was the insurance policy designed to protect his life. The photo must be real. Yet, she had seen the picture showing young Baker on the other side of the continent, on the very same day as the hotel fire. It made no sense.

Eventually the cab passed a sign for the General Aviation building and Maggie jumped out, thrusting a wad of bills into the driver's hand. She looked at her watch: the plane was due to take off in fourteen minutes.

She did her best to straighten herself out and to walk tall. She needed to look like the kind of woman who knew her way round a private airfield for the highest-paying corporate customer.

She strode up to the reception desk. 'This is very urgent. I'm here for the AitkenBruce flight to Washington that leaves in a few minutes? I have some important documents to deliver to them.'

The woman tapped away at her computer. 'It's runway nineteen. I'll let them know you're here.'

Maggie turned and headed for the door, the receptionist calling after her: 'Excuse me! Someone's coming to meet you here. You're not to go out there. Miss!'

She passed a sign for Runway 1 and, a full five minutes later, Runway 6. It was no good. There was just too much ground to cover. She looked at her watch. Six minutes to takeoff. She broke into a jog, cursing all the damage that cigarettes had done to her poor lungs. Her sides heaved; her battered ribs complained.

Finally, she saw a marker indicating that she was at Runway 19. Three minutes to takeoff.

Before her, separated by a grass strip perhaps seventy yards wide, was a Gulfstream jet, the mighty engines already revving up. Parked just alongside the open cabin door and the descended staircase was a black Lincoln Town Car. She was in no doubt that the plane belonged to AitkenBruce and that inside that car sat its chairman and chief executive, Roger Waugh.

Should she just stride up to the car, waving a sheaf of fictitious papers? Then what? She was uncertain what to do. A question popped into her mind: What would Stuart say? She was just forming an answer when she felt the sudden and tight grip of a hand on each of her upper arms. A half-second later, there was a hand over her mouth and then—darkness.

10

'Now tell me this isn't the way to travel.' The accent was New York, the manner self-satisfied. 'Forgive me. Where are my manners? Guys, you can take all that stuff off now.'

As the black hood was lifted off her face, one of the two bodyguards who had dragged her on board the plane sharply pulled back the strip of duct tape that had sealed her mouth, so that her first audible sound was a howl.

'Welcome aboard, Miss Costello. We'll be taking off any moment. I don't need to tell you to fasten your seat belt.'

At that, Maggie tried to move, only to realise that she was tied to the armrests at the side of her chair. Her legs would not move either: they were tied to each other.

She could feel the plane straightening on the runway. Now it began picking up speed. 'This is kidnapping. What the hell do you think you're doing?'

'I like to think of it as a meeting. You clearly didn't come to that armpit in New Jersey to admire the scenery: you wanted to see me.'

Maggie stared at this man directly opposite her, his face corresponding with the picture she had looked up of Roger Waugh. He was bald, with small, mischievous eyes, vole-like, wearing, to her surprise, a rumpled suit and a tie of drab blue. You would never have guessed that this was the boss of the largest banking group in the world.

'How do you know what I wanted? How the hell do you know who I am?'

His eyes seemed to bore right into her. 'Oh, come on, Maggie. You don't get to be me if you don't know what's going on. We've been following you. New Orleans, Aberdeen, Coeur d'Alene, JFK this afternoon. You knew we were there, right?'

Maggie thought of the man across the street from the Midnight Lounge; the headlights in the distance on the way to see Anne Everett. Her instincts had been right all along.

'So why didn't you just kill me, like you killed Stuart and Nick? It's not like you didn't try.'

'An act of overzealousness. Call it irrational exuberance.' He quirked a smile, as if they were co-conspirators sharing a joke. 'I'm afraid I was feeling a little pressure from colleagues. And though I detest failure, there was an upside in this case. I came to see you're of greater use to us alive.'

His smile widened, as if he expected her to be intrigued.

But Maggie refused to play along. Turning her head, she looked out of the porthole. Who were these 'colleagues'? And in what way could he possibly think she was of use to them? Unable to process it all, she asked simply, 'Where are we going?'

'We'll come to that. Now why don't you ask me what you came all this way to ask?'

At that moment, an absurdly pretty woman appeared with two flutes of champagne. She nodded sweetly at Waugh as she placed his glass on the table before him, then did the same for Maggie, apparently oblivious to the fact that this particular passenger was in shackles, and then discreetly withdrew.

He sipped his champagne. 'Mmm. That's good. You really ought to—oh, sorry, you can't. Silly me. Would you like me to help you?'

Maggie glared at him.

'Please yourself. I always find a meeting goes so much better with champagne. So, to business. I gather you've spoken to Mrs Everett. So now you know almost everything.'

Maggie stared back at him. 'I know that someone—probably you—paid her a lot of money to keep quiet about what happened to her daughter. But I don't think she has any idea why.'

'Which is as it should be,' Waugh said.

'Now why is that?'

Waugh put his champagne glass to one side. 'Let me ask you a question, Miss Costello. You're a clever woman. You have a grasp of politics. So tell me this. Have you never thought about how the great political leaders made it to the top? How the luck always seemed to go their way?'

Maggie thought suddenly of her conversation with Uri.

Waugh was warming to his theme. 'Take Kennedy. He won in 1960 by a whisker. Nearly seventy million votes cast, and JFK edges it by a hundred thousand votes—which just happen to turn up late in the day in Chicago. Could so easily have gone the other way.

'Or in Britain, that nice, smiling guy with the teeth, remember him? He was prime minister for ten years—all because his party leader had a heart that gave out at the crucial moment.

'Or Florida in 2000? Bush loses the popular vote but ends up getting two terms in the White House. All thanks to a ruling of the Supreme Court that came down to the decision of a single judge.'

'What's your point?' Maggie's head was throbbing. She told herself it was the shock, the shoving and gagging at the hands of Waugh's meatheads. But she feared it was something else: the anticipation of a truth she did not want to see.

'There are no accidents, Maggie. There is no luck. There was a pattern to all those events.'

Waugh looked out of the window, his earlier smile gone, and suddenly the affable vole was replaced by a reptilian predator. Maggie shivered. This was a dangerous topic, and for her, probably lethal. She had seen what happened to anyone who knew too much.

'Why are you telling me all this?'

He turned back to face her. 'Oh, we always tell them in the end. We always find a way to let them know. Those we choose.'

'Choose?'

'Maggie, you're being very slow. Yes, *choose*. We spotted Stephen at high school. We have our people everywhere, you know, in high schools, in colleges, keeping an eye out for the smart ones, the charismatic ones, the future stars. They saw it straight away: captain of the debate team, so handsome, so clever. And that backstory. The son of a logger! He sounded like Abraham Lincoln.'

'You were aware of Stephen Baker when he was at *school*?'

'Oh, it wasn't me then, Maggie. It was my predecessors at AitkenBruce, just like their predecessors before them. It's not just AitkenBruce either. We work together, all the big banks. We have the same interests.

'And it's not just America any more, like it was in the early days. It's a global economy now, money floating across borders like clouds in the sky. So we work with our colleagues in London and Frankfurt and Paris. And in Asia too: can't move without Tokyo or Beijing. And the Middle East of course, even if the regimes are a little, shall we say, unsavoury. This is a global enterprise. It has to be.'

'And what exactly is this enterprise?'

'Talent-spotting. We're the best talent-spotters in the business. Always have been. The original Aitken made his name that way, more than a century ago. That's what we do—what we've always done. And we did it with Baker. We spotted him at high school and we watched him. By the time he was at Harvard, we had made our decision.'

'What decision?'

'That he was to be it. Our chosen one. Let me correct that. He was *one* of our chosen ones. There are always several. Dozens of them, in fact, in each generation. To allow for all eventualities. But of that cohort, Baker was our preferred one. He was the one we wanted in the White House. And, despite a couple of hitches along the way, all went to plan.'

Waugh smiled, then took another sip of champagne.

Maggie felt her throat turning to dust. So Baker was a hired gun, bought and paid for by the world's biggest banks. So much for all that grand talk of ethics and ideals, of changing the world.

Disappointment gave way to anger. 'So it was you who got those opponents out of the way, in the governor's race?'

Waugh put his glass down. 'Well, yes and no, Maggie. Yes in the sense that it was us who released the relevant information. And no, in that it was not me or my colleagues who forced the Republican nominee to film his wife having sex with other men. He did that all by himself. Same goes for the Mayor of Seattle.' He smirked. 'We very rarely force anybody to do anything. That's the joy of politics. It's a human business. There's human error.'

'And Chester's love child: was that you too?'

'Well, it was his rather than mine, but yes.'

'That revelation changed the presidential election. Chester never stood a chance after that.'

'That's true.'

'But why would you work so hard to get Stephen Baker elected? He doesn't even *agree* with you. He wants to take on the banks.'

'That, Maggie, only makes him more credible. For the day he vetoes the banking bill that threatens to cripple my business.'

A small light dawned in the darkness. Was it possible that Stephen Baker did not *know* he had been chosen? Maybe it was *him* who had been played all along. Maggie shook her head, confused. 'He'd never do it. Why would Baker veto a bill he believes in?'

'Ms Costello, when are you going to get *smart*? Come on. How could I know with absolute certainty that he would veto that bill? Because one day, we'd tell him what we have on him.

'We'd show him the photos of the Meredith Hotel, burnt to a crisp. Remind him we knew he was there. Maybe we wouldn't even have to do that. We'd probably just have to say a single word.' His voice dipped and he let out a breathy whisper: 'Pamela.'

'But there's a photo of him in Washington in the *Daily World*, taken on the same day.'

'Senator Corbyn was always a good friend to our industry. If we asked him to shake hands with a bright young man from his home state, why would he refuse? And as for the date, well, the editors of the *Daily World* accepted the information they were given. They didn't have the advantage we had: a copy of the photograph duly date-stamped, proving that that meeting actually took place on March 17. Two days *after* the fire.' Waugh paused for effect, infuriatingly self-satisfied. 'So we'd show him what we have and we'd give him a choice: veto the bill—or we reveal that you left a young girl to die.'

Maggie felt as if she had been punched, hard, in the stomach. She had clung to that photo of the young Stephen Baker shaking hands with the veteran senator just as tightly as Anne Everett had. But now she could not escape what Waugh had told her.

'So Vic Forbes was working for you,' she said finally. 'That blackmail message was really from you.'

He smacked his palms on the table so hard that the crystal glasses wobbled. 'Christ, no! What Forbes did was cheap and nasty.'

'So he didn't work for you?'

'Forbes? As it happens, he *did* work for us. A long time ago. He gave us the tip-off about the hotel fire, stalking Baker there probably. And he told us about the shrink, which enabled us to destroy all the files and billing records so that they never came to light.'

'How did you do that?' Maggie asked, astonished.

'A break-in at the doctor's office. No big deal. So Forbes gave us some early help. But after that, no. He joined the CIA, went to Honduras. He was off our radar. And then, last week, he pops up all over the TV making those wild accusations.'

'Not on your orders?'

'Are you crazy? He was ruining everything! The guy had gone rogue, doing his own thing. I don't know why. Maybe it was just plain jealousy. He did hate the guy's guts. Anyway, we knew he had to be stopped. He was threatening to throw away our greatest asset. We'd have been powerless to control Baker.'

Maggie was thinking hard, despite the ache in her ribs growing ever more intense. She desperately needed to move. She shifted the inch or two her shackles allowed. 'You say he'd worked for you in the early days. So how come he knew about the Iranian donation?'

'Well, that was confirmation he was off the reservation. Because even *we* didn't know about that. Our information suggests that was an initiative out of Tehran, the mullahs wanting to embarrass Baker. But the guy was an obsessive. Not impossible that he traced every donation Baker received. He was crazy enough.'

'So you got him out of the way. Sent some bait into that strip club, led him away and that was that.'

Waugh said nothing.

'It wasn't such a smart plan, though, was it?' Maggie persisted. 'You bumped off Forbes and the next minute, the whole blogosphere's lighting up with claims that Baker's Tony Soprano.'

'Call it the law of unintended consequences.'

'He's facing impeachment!'

'I think you'll find things are back on track now.'

'You mean, the . . .' She shook her head, too numbed to complete the sentence. So even this latest boost to Baker, the story of the Republican senator and the pneumatic lobbyist, had come from Waugh and his pals. They were behind everything. At that, Maggie's fatigue and pain were replaced by anger. 'So why Stuart? And why Nick? Why did you have to kill them?'

'With Stuart, we were left with no choice. Not after that phone call you had with him where he threatened to urge Baker to resign. We could not have that. Not until the banking bill was dead and buried.'

'So you killed him?'

'The coroner's report says he took his own life. As for Nick,' he continued. 'I'm afraid that was your fault. You involved him. He found out about this'—he gestured at the smooth, noiseless interior of the jet—'and New Orleans. We couldn't risk him publishing that in a newspaper. No way.'

'So why not kill me?'

Waugh gave her the hint of a smile. It was chilling. 'I repeat, Maggie dear, that you're more useful to us alive than dead. Because you're going to work for us. Negotiate the deal. Isn't that your forte? Maggie Costello the great negotiator?

'Besides, we know you're close to Baker; you're one of the few people he trusts. In ten minutes this plane will land in Washington DC—and you're going to see the President.'

Washington DC, Monday, March 27, 20:16

The car hummed along sleekly, gliding down George Washington Memorial Parkway with its view of the Potomac, now glittering in the moonlight. They had taken away her phones, so she couldn't call ahead. She would have to turn up at the visitors' entrance to the White House and explain herself.

Waugh had not let her go without a warning. Standing on the tarmac in a corner of Reagan National Airport, waiting to step into one of the two glistening limos that had pulled up, he said, 'Maggie, I'm trusting you to live up to your reputation: to achieve better terms than I could; to convey what I have said so that Baker understands he has no choice in this matter.

And if there are any heroics, he and you will pay. Severely. And so will those you love.'

With that, he stepped into the Lincoln and drove away, leaving her with just one of the bodyguards for company.

THEY WERE AT the White House now. The bodyguard nodded at her, nudging her to get out and complete the task she had been set.

She got out and approached the security station. A guard beckoned her to open the glass door and enter. She began her explanation, that she was Maggie Costello, former official of the White House, and that Doug Sanchez was expecting her.

The guard scanned his list of scheduled appointments and shook his head. She told him to call Sanchez's office. While she waited for him, she tried to digest all she had heard in that vile flight. The scale and comprehensiveness of their operation was breathtaking. They had thought of everything, not just paying hush money to Pamela Everett's grief-stricken parents, but getting a United States senator to pose with young Baker so that he would have a perfect alibi, printed and published in the local newspaper. They had taken the time to remove the relevant page of the *Daily World* from the archive in Aberdeen, such was their determination to leave no trace.

'Maggie! Is that you?' It was Sanchez, looking as if he had lost ten pounds in weight and had had only ten hours of sleep in the several days since she had last seen him. He opened his arms for a hug. Maggie let him hold her, hating herself for what she was about to do.

'So what's this, you go off the grid in the Pacific Northwest and change your whole look?' Sanchez said, as he walked her towards the Press Secretary's office. 'What the hell happened, Maggie?'

'It's such a long story, Doug. And the only person I can tell it to right now is the President. I'm sorry.'

He gave her a long, compassionate look which left her feeling more guilty than ever. Then he suggested Maggie take a seat in his office and embarked on the short stroll down the corridor to the President's secretary.

Maggie looked at the TV, tuned to MSNBC.

'. . . the word of the hour is "exit strategy". House whips say the numbers are just not there on Judiciary for the Republicans to move forward with this thing. Democrats are closing ranks behind the President and those two crucial waverers are no longer wavering. So the pressure is now on the Republicans to find a way out of this without losing too much face.'

Maggie sighed, knowing that everyone in this building would be jubilant at that news, believing it to be a rare stroke of good fortune. Believing that Baker's lucky streak had at last been restored. But all she could think of was Waugh's smirking face. Sanchez appeared in the doorway. 'He's ready for you now.'

Washington DC, Tuesday, March 28, 10:58

Somehow, despite herself, Maggie had had a decent night's sleep. Baker had only given her one assignment and that she had promptly delegated to Uri. He had agreed to do it on the strict understanding that she went straight home to bed.

Her meeting with Baker had been awkward, no doubt about it. He had blanched when she uttered Pamela Everett's name. He had shaken his head, murmuring that this was what he had always feared.

Maggie could see from his eyes alone that condemnation from her was unnecessary: he was judging himself harshly enough.

He had then picked up the telephone on his desk and asked that all his meetings be cancelled until further notice, all calls held unless it was a matter of national emergency.

He had listened in growing disbelief as she told him what Waugh had told her: that he, Stephen Baker, had been their chosen one. Growing ever more pale, he said quietly, more to himself than to her, 'My whole career has been a sham.'

Then she spelled out Waugh's ultimatum: veto the banking bill or he would tell all. Regarding it as her duty, she forced herself to assess and walk through each option that faced him. She wanted to put aside the shock of the moment and speak practically. She wanted, in other words, to do what Stuart had trained her to do.

He listened to it all and probed at the right places, responding as she sought to approach the problem from all angles. At the end of the meeting, he simply nodded and said he had a decision to make.

They parted with a handshake, the President thanking Maggie for her 'remarkable' service. His last words to her were, 'I know I've let you down. But I will find a way to make this right.'

And now Sanchez was on the phone, telling Maggie to switch on the TV.

The President was about to make an address to the nation.

A pit began to grow in Maggie's stomach. She didn't know which option he was going to choose. Would he announce a delay in the banking legislation, a move that would at least buy some time to take Waugh on? Would he opt for the other, riskier scenario she had put forward: that he veto the bill as Waugh had requested, only then to embark on a covert effort to find the congressional votes needed to override his veto and pass the bill into law anyway?

If he did that, she would have to admire his courage, but it would spell disaster for her—and for Uri. And maybe even for Liz and Calum, too. *You will pay and so will those you love*.

Yet she knew it was wrong to think of her own safety, when something so much larger was at stake. If Baker caved in, what would that mean for the country? Waugh would have neutered Baker, he would have destroyed him.

What was he going to do? She had no idea. Suddenly, there he was, at his desk, the Stars and Stripes behind him.

'My fellow Americans. You have all been through quite a week. I apologise for my part in those events. I promised to bring a spirit of calm to Washington, and these last seven or eight days have been anything but calm.' He flashed that dazzling smile of his.

'Last night I finally discovered the true explanation for a chain of events that began with the shocking revelations made by the late Mr Vic Forbes about my past and my political funding arrangements. These events went on to include unfounded rumours linking me to his death, calls for my impeachment and the apparent suicide of my closest adviser, the much-cherished Stuart Goldstein.' He looked down at the table, seemed to gird himself, and carried on.

'The details of all this will come out in due course, and there will be consequences for those involved. But let me speak about something for which I alone am responsible.

'As you know, I spent my late teenage years in a small town called Aberdeen, Washington. I went off to college but I always came back for the vacations. I'd get a job, usually in the lumber yards, to pay my way. And during one of those vacations I met a girl by the name of Pamela Everett. She was very sweet, she was very beautiful and though we were too young to get engaged, I loved her very much and she knew it.

'Well, one night we were in a hotel together, asleep in each other's arms.

In the early hours, I suddenly woke up to see smoke seeping under the door of our room. I could feel the heat and I could smell the flames. I shook Pamela—but I did not stay long enough to see if she was fully awake. In the panic of that moment, I rushed out and saved myself. And though I told the fire-fighters she was there, I did not go back to save her. In the end, it was too late and Pamela Everett died that night.

'Not a day goes by when I do not think of what happened. I should have been honest about this terrible truth a long time ago—but I never said a word about it. Not even to those closest to me.

'I'm telling you this now not because I'm seeking your forgiveness. What I did was so wrong, I don't think I deserve that. I'm telling you because I have discovered that a handful of men have known about that grave mistake of mine for many years. And now they are using it to blackmail me.'

Maggie gasped with disbelief. They hadn't discussed *this*.

'They want me to abandon a key part of my programme—a programme you, the American people, voted for in your tens of millions last fall—in return for their silence. They believed that faced with that choice, I would save my own hide rather than do what's right for this country I love.

'Well, these men—who spend their lives calculating profit and loss, nickels and dimes—calculated wrong. I know I did a dreadful thing and I intend to pay for my actions. That is why I shall resign the presidency effective at noon tomorrow. Vice-President Williams will be sworn in as President at that hour in this office.

'May God bless his presidency. May God bless you. And may God bless the United States of America.'

Maggie sat, her palms flat against both sides of her face, shaking her head. She couldn't move. She was frozen, not so much by shock as disappointment. In truth, it was more than that: it was heartbreak.

That explained the assignment Baker had given her. He had asked her to draft a short summary of Bradford Williams's career, as personal as she could make it: 'triumphs and tragedies', he had said. Uri had worked on it for her all night.

She had feared this was the reason Baker had asked for such a paper. But that made it no less awful to hear. He had resigned. He had sacrificed everything he had worked for his entire life.

And then, a guiltier thought. Baker had defied AitkenBruce—and that meant she would pay. She and those she loved.

Twenty minutes later the phone rang. A female voice, level and calm: 'Please hold for the President.'

There was a click, and then: 'Maggie, I'm sorry.'

'So am I, Mr President. And there are lots of people who feel the way I do, all over the world. Was there no other way?'

'I thought about it, Maggie, I really did. But I couldn't see it. Remember, no one is indispensable, Maggie. Not even me.'

'But what about everything we believed in?'

'Williams believes in all that, too. Truly he does. He's a good man, Maggie. The work will go on.' There was a pause. 'He and I are already collaborating on a file detailing the evidence that links AitkenBruce and the other banks to the deaths of Forbes, Stuart and Nick du Caines. Lawyers at the FBI are already on the case.'

'I'm glad to hear that.' Then she asked, 'What will you do now?'

'I don't know, Maggie. I need to think a while. But I do have one immediate plan. I'm going to fly to Idaho tomorrow and see Anne Everett. Apologise to her in person.' He cleared his throat. 'I've also been thinking about you, Maggie. How to protect you. We need to give you what Forbes gave himself.'

'A blanket, sir.'

'That's right. A blanket. I think I may have found a way for you to have some peace of mind.'

'How?'

'One of the advantages of being President is that I have access to the database of the National Security Agency. Ever since 9/11 they've had satellites watching all our airports in real time. "Eyes in the sky" they call them. Record everything.'

'I don't see how—'

'It means, Maggie, we have footage from Teterboro Airport which shows you being assaulted and then bundled into an aircraft registered with AitkenBruce on which Roger Waugh was the listed passenger. That footage will now be lodged with the Secret Service. If anything happens to you, Waugh will be the prime suspect.'

'Thank you, Mr President.' She didn't feel that she could voice her worry that that might not be enough. Even if Waugh was incapacitated surely there were others who would come after her. And Uri. And Liz—and Calum. She shuddered.

'It's me who needs to thank you, Maggie. I know you risked your life for me these last few days. I will never forget that, Maggie. Just like I will never forget your passion, your devotion to those who have no other voice but yours. You are truly a remarkable woman, Maggie Costello. I hope one day to find a way to repay you.'

'I don't know what to say, Mr President.'

'I also need to thank you for that paper you sent over this morning. On Vice-President Williams. Very helpful. It confirmed what I had suspected, which made me feel all the more comfortable handing over to him.'

'And what had you suspected, Mr President?'

'Well, you saw what kind of career he's had, Maggie. Tried and failed to get into Congress three times. Was forty-two years old before he got elected to anything. No one smoothed Bradford Williams's path, did they? He got there all by himself. It means nobody will have a hold over him. Except the voters, of course.'

Maggie smiled. 'I think you're right, sir.'

'And do you know why that is, Maggie? I have a theory. Our friends the bankers didn't spot Bradford Williams's talent. And I suspect that was for one very simple reason. They never believed a black man could become President.'

WIRE STORY from the Associated Press, posted on March 28, 11:45 EDT:

> Police in at least four cities across the globe have launched raids against the headquarters of some of the world's biggest banks, in internationally coordinated action triggered by outgoing President Stephen Baker's resignation announcement.
>
> The key target of the arrests is AitkenBruce Bank. Its premises in London, New York, Frankfurt and Dubai were raided within minutes of each other, as international law-enforcement officers impounded computerised records.
>
> Federal agents have arrested Roger Waugh, Chairman and Chief Executive of AitkenBruce, at his $35m Long Island home. In front of waiting photographers, Mr Waugh was led out in handcuffs and leg-irons—a signal that prosecutors plan to level 'the gravest charges' against the banking giant and its boss . . .

One week later

'Ladies and gentlemen, the President of the United States!'

Maggie watched senators and congressmen on both sides applauding wildly, as Bradford Williams waded through the thicket of people jamming the entrance to the chamber.

It took four minutes for all four hundred and thirty-five representatives and one hundred senators, along with the nine justices of the Supreme Court as well as the Joint Chiefs of Staff, to still their applause. When they did, Williams began.

'My fellow Americans—all I have I would have given gladly not to be standing here today. The departure of Stephen Baker was a deep blow to our nation, one that seemed to shake the foundations of our entire system. It was a shock not only because this nation had given him a mandate to govern just a few short months ago. It was a shock because we discovered that there had been a conspiracy to deny the American people their right to be a free and sovereign people, a conspiracy to hold to ransom the man this nation had chosen as its president. Tonight I am here to tell you and those behind that conspiracy, wherever they may be: this will not stand.'

A thunderclap of applause. Maggie sat forward.

'Tomorrow I shall put a bill before you that will regulate these banks. I plan to curb their reckless dicing and slicing of our money. No longer will our nation's economy be used as a casino.'

By now he was drowned out by waves of applause. But he rode right over them. 'I plan to cap their pay, so that it reflects the real world the rest of us live in—so that those who work hard can get on, but those who lie, steal and cheat are no longer rewarded for their efforts.'

Maggie watched all but a handful of die-hards applauding. The politicians knew how such a populist message would be playing with their constituents back home: they'd be fried alive if they dared to disagree with what Williams had just said.

He talked for a while about education and the environment. And then he turned to international affairs.

'I cannot promise to be the same as my predecessor. We are different men. But Stephen Baker was full of great plans and some of those now fall to me. One in particular I want to mention tonight.

'A slaughter has been under way for too long in Sudan, a terrible war against women and children and men who want only to live in peace.

Tonight I am ordering the Department of Defense to dispatch three hundred of our best-equipped helicopters to the African Union. They will be eyes watching over that troubled land. If the killing continues, those killers should tremble—because they will be watched.'

Maggie shook her head in delighted incredulity. She had assumed that the Darfur plan she had discussed with Baker had been buried the instant he resigned. Yet he had clearly handed their plan to his successor. And then she remembered Baker's parting words to her: *I hope one day to find a way to repay you.*

Washington DC, three months later

Maggie knocked back the dregs of whiskey in her glass and surveyed the crowd in the Dubliner bar. Uri had texted to say he was running late, so there was no point in watching the door. But still she kept glancing up, hoping to see him come into the bar. He would be in a good mood: the distributors had just told him his documentary—*The Life, Times and Curiously Short Presidency of Stephen Baker*—had been picked for the Toronto Film Festival.

But still she could not help feeling a little on edge. Why had Uri suggested meeting here, rather than at the apartment? You only selected a neutral venue if you thought negotiations were going to be tense and complicated; she had learned that long ago. So what choppy waters did Uri want to negotiate?

It was true that the last few weeks had not been great. After those lunatic final days of March, they had decided to get away, to go on holiday together. They plumped for the Aegean island of Santorini.

At the insistence of Zoe Galfano, the Secret Service agent tasked with what was officially called 'aftercare', the US consul in the region had been notified and a 'discreet' security presence arranged. When Maggie had objected, protesting that Roger Waugh and his pals were now behind bars, Zoe had said plainly that former President Baker had been adamant: Maggie Costello had earned the protection of the US government.

She would like to be able to blame the guards for what followed, but it was hardly their fault. They had indeed been discreet: close enough to deter anyone planning mischief, distant enough that no regular person would even spot that they were there.

It had started off well enough, Maggie relishing the chance to catch up on sleep, food and . . . Uri. They would wake up late, and eat an unhurried breakfast together. They would make slow, tentative love in the afternoon—slightly unsure of each other after their time apart—then walk and talk until sunset. After a few days of the quiet and peace, though, she had found herself itching to pick up the BlackBerry. At first Uri merely rolled his eyes.

'What are you doing?'

'Nothing.'

'A special kind of nothing that requires a handheld device.'

'The *New York Times* is running a series on Williams's first hundred days.'

'And you want to read it. Even though you're on vacation. I don't know why you can't lie on a beach and relax like a normal person.'

'I don't like being in the sun, that's why. I'm Irish. I burn.'

'But you're in the shade.'

'That's so I won't burn.'

Those clouds would pass eventually, but as the week wore on they came more often.

'What about a swim?' Uri might suggest.

'I don't want to swim. I don't want to jog and I don't want to get sunburn. I want to *do* something.'

She smiled about it now, recalling that Liz had always said her definition of hell would be a two-week holiday with her sister. She had been impossible, no doubt. Irritable, scratchy and bored.

Since then, Uri had been working flat out finishing the film. She had spent some time with him in New York, and he had come down to DC for a few last-minute interviews. And now it was completed, he had needed to be in Washington for a dinner with PBS executives to discuss transmission dates. He had suggested they meet for a drink afterwards.

She was about to go to the ladies to sort out her hair, when she saw him walk in. Those eyes—at once those of a strong, brave man and a haunted boy—melted her the way they always had. He sat down next to her at the corner table. But when she tried to kiss him on the lips, he offered her his cheek. That alone gave her a small shiver of anxiety.

'So, well done on Toronto!'

'Thanks.'

'Who knows, this film might go down in history as the one successful achievement of the Baker presidency.'

'Don't forget "Action for Sudan". The helicopters. Your legacy, Maggie.'

'That's true.' She felt a stab of guilt at what she hadn't yet told him, then ordered drinks. Another whiskey for her, a beer for him.

He took a swig straight from the bottle, then said, 'Maggie, we should talk.'

'That sounds ominous.'

'Hear me out. Remember that night on the beach in Santorini, when we'd finally settled in and we went for a walk by the sea? There was a full moon.'

'Of course I remember.' She felt her throat turn dry.

'I had a whole speech prepared that night. I was going to tell you that I couldn't bear being apart and that we're meant to be together. I was going to say that life is so short and so precious, and at some point we just have to choose. I'd made my choice. I was going to say, "I want you, Maggie. You're the one I choose."'

'And what happened?' She sensed what was coming.

'You know what happened. You were itching to get away from the moment we got there.'

'I don't think that's fair.'

'You're always so restless, Maggie. You start a job at the White House, and then, before you know it, you're jetting round the country, dodging killers in New Orleans and the Northwest and—'

'That was an insane, crazy week, Uri.'

'It's always insane and crazy with you, Maggie. Something always happens. When we met in Jerusalem you were fleeing for your life. And then here you were doing the same thing.'

'Come on, that's just a coincidence. When—'

'Is it though, Maggie? Really? Because I'm not sure I believe in coincidences any more. I think on some level you *need* it.'

'Oh, for God's sake—'

'It keeps happening. You try to come back, settle into a normal life, have a job that would have you sitting at a desk and keeping regular hours and then something always goes wrong.'

'I was fired, Uri!'

'For calling the Defense Secretary an asshole! Who writes that on an email, unless they want to sabotage everything they've got? And it worked too. The next minute you're off nearly getting killed.'

'Someone was out to destroy the President!'

'I'm not saying it's not a good cause. I'm just asking why it always has to be you. You once told me that even though there were people dying all around you, and you went to sleep to the sound of sniper fire, you were never happier than when you were in Africa.'

'That was bloody years ago. I was young.'

'I saw it myself, Maggie. In Jerusalem. You were that close to death every day and you know what? You were loving it. You even said it. "I've never felt more alive."'

It was true. She said, 'So what are you saying?'

'I'm saying I want you, Maggie. But I also want a life. To live in one place. To have children.'

'But I want that too!'

'But you'll always want something else more. To save the world—or at least not stay in one place long enough to get bored.'

She couldn't say anything to change his mind, just as she could never say anything to persuade Liz. Because she knew there was an element of truth in what they were saying. Even at the worst moments, whether driven off the road in Aberdeen or coming face to face with Roger Waugh, she had felt the adrenalin thumping round her system. What Uri said was true: she had felt alive.

She looked at him, his eyes dark and intense, his face unmoving. He had tried hard to be with her and she had wanted so much to be with him, but they had driven into the same roadblock every time. She remembered the call she had received—but not mentioned to Uri—from President Williams's Chief of Staff, offering her the job of coordinator of the Action for Sudan plan. She could accept it on one condition: that she be on the ground, in Africa. She had been pushing the thought of that offer away, as if it were a guilty treat she was not meant to open. She could see that now.

She turned to him, forcing the tears back. 'You know what, Uri? I *do* need to know that what I'm doing matters. And let's say you're right and I do get off on the thrill of danger. Is it such a crime, Uri? Really? Is it such a crime to have seen such terrible things that I want to use every ounce of energy I've got to make things better?' She looked into his eyes. 'You know,' she said. 'I wanted to be with you, I really did. But I can't be someone else, Uri. It's taken me a long time to see it, but this is who I am. I'm sorry.'

She leaned across the table to kiss him long and hard on the lips. And then she stood up, quickly gathered her things and strode towards the door before the tears could fall.

EPILOGUE

That same night . . .

Senator Rick Franklin put aside the memo he had just received, detailing the results of a poll which asked likely Republican voters how they rated a series of leading party figures. To his team's delight, he had come in second, just behind the party's rock-star former vice-presidential candidate who always topped these surveys.

He knew how this had happened. Even if most of the country had been distraught at Stephen Baker's removal from office, among the hard-core American right it was a day of celebration, and Rick Franklin was rapidly hailed as its hero. He was the man whose persistence had driven Baker from office. The pundits were all as one, anointing Senator Franklin as the front-runner for the Republican nomination to take on the unelected President Bradford Williams in the election that was now little more than three years away.

His supporters were ecstatic; so was his wife. Only he felt a knot of anxiety at all this presidential talk. He had seen Baker having to confess to those misjudgments from his past. They had broken him. And wasn't he, Rick Franklin—family man, poster boy of the Christian right—just as vulnerable? His affair with Cindy had gone on for nearly two years; there was nothing they hadn't tried, some of it illegal in several states. He would be destroyed.

It was a good thing she was away for the week, at that conference in Colorado. She would enjoy herself and, when she was back, he would tell her it had to end. His mind was made up.

Twenty minutes later, there was a call from Charleston.

'Senator, it's Brian.' One of his aides, sounding anxious.

'What is it, Brian?'

'It's Cindy, sir. We've just had a call from—'

'What's happened?'

'She's dead, sir. In a skiing accident.'

Franklin felt his heart thumping. Was he about to have a heart attack? He put down the receiver slowly and carefully and took several deep breaths.

He told himself this pain in his chest was grief and, in part, it was. He'd been very fond of Cindy: she was a lovely girl, with a body shaped by the Lord's own hand . . .

But there was more to that tension in his chest than sorrow. A thought was brewing. Was this Providence stepping in to remove the last serious obstacle between him and the White House? Could this have been the work of the same beneficent God who had lent a helping hand at so many other awkward times in his career?

Rick Franklin spent the evening making dutiful calls, to Cindy's parents and to his staffers. But in between, he stole another look at that memo and those poll numbers.

They really were very encouraging.

In among all the calls was one he hadn't expected. It came from that veteran creature of Washington, Magnus Longley, the man who'd served as Baker's Chief of Staff and been around longer than the Lincoln Memorial.

'To what do I owe this pleasure, Mr Longley?'

'Senator, I just heard about the loss of your very talented Head of Legislative Affairs.'

'You are on the ball, Mr Longley: that hasn't even been announced yet, just immediate family and friends.'

'I believe I was among the first to know.' A pause. He cleared his throat. 'Anyway, my condolences. I was hoping that we might have a conversation.'

'Of course. Yes. I—'

'Let me begin by saying—and this may surprise you—that my colleagues and I hold you in the highest possible regard, Senator Franklin. We always have . . .'

sam **bourne**

RD: What was the starting point, or the inspiration, for *The Chosen One*?

SB: The starting point came during the 2008 US election, specifically at the moment when Barack Obama's campaign seemed to be derailed by the incendiary comments of his former pastor, The Reverend Jeremiah Wright. Every day, Wright made a new outburst that damaged Obama more gravely. I began to imagine what Obama's team must be feeling: what can we do to make this man shut up? If it had gone on much longer, some would surely have grown desperate and started thinking the unthinkable. So that was my starting point: what if someone hugely threatened a candidate or president—and then mysteriously ended up dead. Wouldn't everyone—including the politician's own inner circle—suspect that their boss might have had that person murdered?

RD: Stephen Baker, in the novel, is very reminiscent of Barak Obama. During your years working as a journalist for the *Washington Post*, did you ever—or often—visit the White House, and have you met Obama?

SB: I worked for the *Washington Post* for just a few months, on a fellowship programme when I was twenty-five, but I was later *The Guardian's* correspondent in Washington for nearly four years. During that time I visited the White House frequently for my work, though I can't pretend to know every nook and cranny: that took research. As for Obama, I followed his campaign closely during 2008, and saw him up close throughout that year. But I have not had a one-to-one conversation with him—yet.

RD: In *The Chosen One*, the part played by the banking fraternity, reminds the reader of the global financial collapse, and the subsequent demand for new regulations to prevent it happening again. Do you feel strongly that the banks should be much more tightly controlled?

SB: I do—and I'm lucky enough to have a day job, as a *Guardian* journalist under my own name, where I've been able to make that argument in print. I think that too many people have forgotten that Britain's current deficit woes were mainly caused by the banking collapse—itself caused by sheer greed—rather than by government overspending. As one Labour politician puts it, 'This crisis was caused on Wall Street not Downing Street.'

RD: Apart from the ability to write, do any of the qualities required to be a successful journalist also help in the field of thriller writing?

SB: I think there is a great overlap. First, thrillers are very often grounded in reality, and that takes research, which is what journalists do. Second, a good journalist is fundamentally nosy, curious about other people—and a novelist similarly needs to be fascinated by people: what makes them tick, what drives them to extremes? I won't say that, thirdly, both jobs require the ability to make things up. That would be a terrible slur on me, and my colleagues!

RD: Which of your thrillers to date are you most fond, or proud of?

SB: I have a soft spot for *The Righteous Men* because it was my first novel—and also because it did find such a wide audience. I'm especially proud of *The Final Reckoning* because it tells the story of a fascinating and true episode from the Second World War—one that amazes most people who hear of it.

RD: Has your Jewish heritage had a big impact on your life and/or character and, if so, in what ways?

SB: It has had an enormous, shaping influence on my life—so influential, in fact, that I wrote a book about it. *Jacob's Gift* also explores what the inheritance of Jewishness means in the modern world. For me, it has meant having not only a set of ideals which has informed my political outlook, but a kind of anchor—a sense of where one belongs in the world. In these dizzying, globalised times, that offers great stability and comfort.

RD: Are there any cities, or places in the world, where you would like to live?

SB: I've lived in Washington, but never New York. I'd like to try that. As an eighteen year-old I lived in Israel for a year: I'd like to do that again, with my wife and children this time.

RD: What are your favourite ways to relax?

SB: Playing cricket in the garden with my two boys, now aged nine and six, or just spending time with my family, especially in the outdoors and in the sunshine.

RD: And, finally, can you give any hints about the subject of your next thriller?

SB: The next book will once again turn on a little-known historical episode from the Second World War, at the heart of which is a secret that I think many, especially in Britain, will find shocking.

Mr Rosenblum's List

Natasha Solomons

When Jewish refugee Jack Rosenblum arrives with his wife and daughter at Harwich in 1937, he is handed a 'Helpful Information' leaflet, explaining how to become English. Desperate to blend in, Jack follows its advice to the letter, but his wife, Sadie, doesn't want to forget their past or the family they've lost.

It's not until Jack leads a reluctant Sadie to Dorset, to a world of woolly pigs, bluebells and jitterbug cider, that they both finally find a place they can call home.

CHAPTER ONE

'It will be cloudy and dull this evening and tonight, periods of rain, the rain being moderate or heavy in many districts. Fog will be extensive on high ground with fog patches along the south coast. Tomorrow, more general and heavy rain will spread from the southwest with temperatures of approximately fifty-seven degrees. That concludes the weather summary; a further news bulletin may be heard at a quarter to . . .'

Jack Rosenblum switched off the wireless and nestled back into his leather armchair. A beatific smile spread across his face and he closed his eyes. 'So there is to be more rain,' he remarked to the empty room, stretching out his short legs and giving a yawn. He was unconcerned by the dismal prognosis; it was the act of listening to the bulletin that he savoured. Each evening during the weather forecast he could imagine he was an Englishman. When the forecast was stopped through the war he grieved on behalf of the British, aware what loss this absence would inflict, and when it started again he listened in religiously. The national preoccupation with the weather had been rightfully restored and, in his soul, Jack rejoiced.

He stared out of the window, watching the rain trickle down the pane. Beyond, the garden ran up to a dilapidated fence, and on the other side was the heath. The fence had been falling down since 1940 but there was no new wood with which to mend it. He could have found some on the black market, but the simple truth was that he, like everyone else in London, had ceased to notice the shabbiness of his surroundings.

Jack was not like the other refugees who, in the most part, were quite happy to build their own tiny towns within the great city. He agreed with his neighbours that the role of the Jew was not to be noticed. If no one noticed you, then you became like a park bench: useful, but you did not stand out. Assimilation was the secret. *Assimilation*. Jack had said the word so often to himself. He was tired of being different; he did not want to be doomed like the Wandering Jew to walk endlessly from place to place, belonging nowhere. Besides, he liked the English and their peculiarities. Their city was crumbling all around them; the people dressed in utility clothing, there were only wizened vegetables, dry brown bread and miserable slivers of bacon from Argentina in the shops; yet the men shaved and dressed for dinner and their wives served them the grey food on their best patterned china. Even as the Empire collapsed and the pound tumbled, the British stood tall in their trilbies or bowler hats and discussed the weather.

Jack had aspired to be an Englishman from the very first moment he and his wife Sadie had disembarked at Harwich in August 1937. Dazed from the journey and clutching a suitcase in each hand, they had picked their way along the gangplank, trying not to slip in their first English drizzle. Sadie's brand-new shoes made her unsteady, but she was determined to arrive in her host nation smartly dressed and not like a *schnorrer*. Her dark blonde hair was plaited into neat coils around her ears and she wore a neat woollen two-piece. Elizabeth, barely a year old and unaware of the significance of the moment, slept on her mother's shoulder. All the refugees, with their piles of luggage, clutches of small, sobbing children and pale-faced Yiddish-speaking grandparents, were herded into haphazard queues.

Seeing others with parents, cousins and brothers-in-law, Jack had experienced a gut-punch of guilt. Acid rose in his throat and he gave a small burp. It tasted of onions. He cursed in German under his breath. Sadie had made chopped liver and onion sandwiches for the train ride into France. He hated raw onions; they always repeated on him. That whole journey, he had watched with an odd detachment as Germany vanished in a blur—God knew if they'd ever see it again. '*Heimat*'—the idea of home and belonging—was gone. Yet as the train rushed through Holland and France, all Jack could think about was the taste of onions. Sure enough, he arrived in England in his best suit, shoes polished to a gleam, hair neatly trimmed, and his breath reeking.

The refugees had waited beside the dock in the falling rain, none daring to complain (they'd learned the hard way to fear the whims of bureaucrats). A man walked along the lines, pausing to talk and pass out pamphlets. Jack watched his progress with fascination. He had the straight back of an

Englishman and the self-assurance of a headmaster. Jack himself was slight with soft blue irises (hidden behind a pair of wire-rimmed spectacles) and sandy hair receding rapidly into baldness.

Reaching Jack, the man had handed him a dusky-blue pamphlet entitled *While You Are in England: Helpful Information and Friendly Guidance for Every Refugee.* He gave another, identical, to Sadie.

'Welcome to England. I'm from the German Jewish Aid Committee. Please study this with great care.'

Jack was so taken aback that this man with his twirling moustache was both an Englishman and a Jew that he stuttered, quite unable to talk. The man gave a tired sigh and switched effortlessly into German.

'*Willkommen in England. Ich bin—*'

Jack shook himself out of his stupor. 'Sank you. I will learn it hard.'

The man beamed his approval. 'Yes, jolly good.' He pointed to the pages in Jack's hands. 'Rule number 2. Always. Speak. English. Even halting English is better than German.'

Jack nodded dumbly, carefully storing this piece of advice.

'And this? He will truly tell me everything that I must be knowing?'

The man smiled tightly, impatient to be moving down the lines. 'Yes. It tells you everything you need to know about the English.'

Jack clasped the flimsy pamphlet in trembling hands. He glanced along the rows of refugees sitting on travel trunks, glancing at newspapers in half a dozen languages. Did they not realise that they had just been handed a recipe for happiness? This leaflet would tell them—Jews, Yids and *Flüchtlinge*—how to be genuine Englishmen. The booklet fell open upon the list and Jack read avidly, his lips mouthing the words, 'Rule 1: Spend your time immediately in learning the English language . . .'

JACK SPENT HIS FIRST few months in London living according to the rules set out in *Helpful Information*. He took English lessons; he never spoke German on the upper decks of buses and joined no political organisations. He never criticised government legislation and would not allow Sadie to do so either, even when they had to register with the local police as 'enemy aliens'. He obeyed the list with more fervour than the most ardent bar mitzvah boy did the laws of kashrut, and it was while adhering to it that he had an unexpected piece of good luck.

Sadie had sent him out to buy a rug or a length of carpet to make their flat above Solly's Stockings on Commercial Road a bit more homely. Jack strolled along Brick Lane, idly sucking the salt crystals off a pretzel. He was aware that he ought to be eating an iced bun but, as he recited item number 9, 'An Englishman always "buys British" wherever he can', he consoled himself that in this *shetetl* buns were hard to come by. Boys peddled newspapers, trolley-bus conductors yelled for passengers going to '*Finchley-Straße*' and stallholders hustled for business. The air was thick with Yiddish, and Jack could almost imagine himself back in Schöneberg. With a shake of his head to drive away this stray homesick thought, he scoured the stands for carpets. He spied clocks and watches, barrels of herring, *heimische* cucumbers, a broken hat stand and then, at last, a length of mint-green carpet. He pointed to the roll.

'Him. The green carpet. Is he British?'

The stallholder frowned in puzzlement, his usual sales patter forgotten.

Impatient, Jack flipped over the roll to inspect the underside and to his delight saw a Wilton stamp and the Royal Warrant of His Majesty the King.

'Super! I take it all, please-thank-you.'

'Right you are. I got more if you want it, guv? A bloomin' trailer load.'

Jack thought for a minute. On the one hand, he had only ten pounds to his name. On the other, he could see the potential in selling on the rest of the carpet, if he could get a good price. He glanced back at the Royal Warrant—surely this was a sign?

'Yes. I take everything. I pay two pounds and I must be lending trailer.'

Sadie was appalled when Jack returned home with twenty rolls of carpet in shades from mint to mustard and magenta, but that trailer load of carpet marked the beginning of Rosenblum's Carpets. At first, Jack acted as a middleman, selling on remaindered stock to other refugees looking to add homely touches to squalid apartments, but soon he realised that there was enough demand for him to open a small factory right there in the East End.

Sadie observed her husband easing into their new life with a mixture of wonder and concern. For her part, she felt off-balance in this new place. Jack insisted that they spoke only English (something from that cursed pamphlet for sure), but speaking with her husband in her disjointed newcomer's tongue transformed him into a stranger. He looked the same, but the easy intimacies were lost.

He'd already changed his name. He was Jakob when she fell in love with him, and Jakob when she married him, but when a clerk wrote down 'Jak' on his British visa, he accepted it.

Sadie perched on the settee sipping a cup of coffee. There was a murmur as Elizabeth woke from her nap, and then a little cry, 'Mama. Mama!'

Sadie put down her cup, spilling a few drops on the new mauve rug in her hurry to fetch her daughter, and gave a little tut of discontent that Jack had taught her baby to call her 'Mama' instead of 'Mutti'. Tonight, when he returned from the factory and could mind Elizabeth, she would go to Freida Herzfeld for some *Kaffee und Kuchen*, kitchen gossip and illicit German chatter. Then she might go to the synagogue—the only place in this city where she felt at home. When she closed her eyes and listened to the deep song of the cantor, she imagined herself back in Berlin with her mother beside her in the women's gallery, fussing as to whether Emil was behaving himself in the room below. Sadie could almost make out the off-key intonations of Papa as the cantor mumbled his way through the service.

ROSENBLUM'S CARPETS outgrew its cramped workshop and expanded into premises off Hessel Street Market, until it was the largest carpet factory in London's East End, supplying some of the best middling hotels in the city. Half the men in the Rosenblums' street were gone, and goodness knew where—Canada? The Isle of Man? Even Australia, if the rumours were true.

The police came for you at dawn. It was a haphazard system, and sometimes if you were out they never came back. Sadie fretted that Jack would be taken and, to humour her, he agreed to an unconscionably early walk to the factory. But when he arrived at the factory that September morning, he realised he'd forgotten his breakfast. Sadie always packed him a paper bag with matzos and a sliver of rubbery cheese from his weekly ration. His stomach growled. '*Mistfink*,' cursed Jack, resorting to German in his exasperation. He pictured the brown bag on the kitchen table and decided to go back for it.

The police were waiting for him on the doorstep. Jack didn't even try to turn around. They'd found him and it wouldn't be British to run like some coward-criminal.

THE STENCH from urinals always brought it back—one whiff of ammonia and mothballs and he was back in 1940 in a makeshift cell in a London police station with five other refugees all facing internment. Jack had sat with his head in his hands and wondered how it was that he, the most promising Englishman of all his acquaintance, could still be labelled a 'class B enemy alien' (possible security risk) and arrested. With his knowledge of marmalade and Royal Family history going back to Ethelred the Unready, it scarcely seemed possible that he could be anything other than a 'class C' (loyalty to the British cause not in question).

Jack couldn't understand how this had happened. He'd obeyed the rules to the letter and they'd still taken him—clearly the points in *Helpful Information* weren't enough to make a chap blend in. He fished out the pamphlet and began to make his very first addendum:

REGARD THE FOLLOWING AS DUTIES TO WHICH YOU ARE IN HONOUR BOUND:

1. SPEND YOUR TIME IMMEDIATELY IN LEARNING THE ENGLISH LANGUAGE AND ITS CORRECT PRONUNCIATION. *Have done so but it is not so easy. Even English lessons do not assist. German accent* IMPOSSIBLE *to lose.*
2. REFRAIN FROM SPEAKING GERMAN IN THE STREETS AND IN PUBLIC CONVEYANCES AND IN PUBLIC PLACES SUCH AS RESTAURANTS. TALK HALTING ENGLISH RATHER THAN FLUENT GERMAN—*and do not talk in a loud voice. (Unless talking to foreigners when it is the done thing to shout.)* DO NOT READ GERMAN NEWSPAPERS IN PUBLIC. *Do not read them* AT ALL *or you will be considered a 'class A threat' and a spy.*
3. DO NOT CRITICISE ANY GOVERNMENT REGULATION, NOR THE WAY THINGS ARE DONE OVER HERE. *Very hard to manage at times like this.*
4. DO NOT JOIN ANY POLITICAL ORGANISATIONS.
5. DO NOT MAKE YOURSELF CONSPICUOUS BY SPEAKING LOUDLY, OR BY YOUR MANNER OR DRESS. *Don't gesture with your hands when talking. Keep them stuck to your sides or the English will think you strange and overemotional.* THE ENGLISHMAN GREATLY DISLIKES OSTENTATION OR UNCONVENTIONALITY OF DRESS. *Remember, 'bland is best'.* THE ENGLISHMAN ATTACHES VERY GREAT IMPORTANCE TO MODESTY, UNDERSTATEMENT IN SPEECH RATHER THAN OVERSTATEMENT. HE VALUES GOOD MANNERS. (YOU WILL FIND THAT HE SAYS 'THANK YOU' FOR THE SMALLEST SERVICE—EVEN FOR A PENNY BUS TICKET FOR WHICH HE HAS PAID.) *Always apologise, even when something is plainly not your fault.*
6. TRY TO OBSERVE AND FOLLOW THE MANNERS AND CUSTOMS OF THIS COUNTRY, IN SOCIAL AND BUSINESS RELATIONS. *Yes—but what* **ARE** *the manners and customs? This point requires some significant expansion.*
7. DO NOT EXPECT TO BE RECEIVED IMMEDIATELY INTO ENGLISH HOMES, BECAUSE THE ENGLISHMAN TAKES SOME TIME BEFORE HE OPENS HIS HOME WIDE TO STRANGERS.

8. Do not spread the poison of 'It's bound to come in your country.' The British greatly object to the planting of this craven thought.

A policeman banging on the bars of the cell interrupted Jack's scribbling. He looked up with a start to see his wife and daughter standing outside, and flushed with humiliation. He didn't want them to see him caged and stinking. The first week he'd been here, they had met in the visitor's room, but now thanks to Mr Churchill's exhortation to 'collar the lot', every room in the police station was full with refugees waiting for transfer to internment camps.

Sadie reached through the bars and stroked his unshaven cheek.

'*Meine Liebe . . .*'

'In English, darling,' murmured Jack, with an anxious glance at the guard.

'The little one misses her papa.'

Elizabeth peeked out from behind her mother. Jack planted a kiss on the back of Sadie's hand and did his best to seem cheerful.

'It's not so bad. I'll sausage through. Did you speak to Edgar?'

'*Ja*. I visit him at his office, just like you say. And Freida, she tell me he visits police every day and he goes to see magistrate and he shout. Then he drink whisky.'

Jack tried to smile, knowing his friend was doing all he could. If anyone could help him, it was Edgar Herzfeld.

When she left, Sadie slipped a small package wrapped in a handkerchief through the bars. Jack sniffed at it. Apple strudel. Sadie and Mutti, her mother, always baked strudels on Fridays in Berlin. Today must be Friday. He took a bite and his teeth tingled on the sultanas. Sadie's younger brother Emil hated sultanas. He always picked them out and lined them up in neat rows along his plate—it drove Sadie crazy. 'Think of all the currants you've wasted!' she used to say. 'If you lined up all the currants you've not eaten, they'd stretch all the way to the *Zoologischer Garten*.' Jack closed his eyes, and felt a crushing sadness against his ribs. He swallowed, trying not to cry, but a tear escaped and trickled down onto his strudel. He worried about Emil and Mutti and the others left behind, but right then, he had space only for his own unhappiness. He was cold, the cell smelled of piss and he was homesick.

At dawn one morning the prison was emptied and he was herded into a second-class compartment of an extra-long passenger train at Waterloo Station. Jack knew he should be concerned about where they were taking him. Instead, after three weeks sealed into a damp, high-windowed cell, he felt a tingle of excitement in his belly.

The train rattled through the city, an endless warren of brick streets and grey skies. Plumes of smoke still smouldered from last night's *Heinkel* raid and he saw people crawling over the wreckage of crumpled houses. The lurching rhythm of the train lulled him to sleep.

Then someone was shaking him awake, offering him a piece of stale bread that he did not want. Jack turned back to the window and realised he had woken in another England. This one was green. Before they left Berlin, he had imagined that this was what Britain was like. He smiled—so England was meadows and sheep, thatched roofs and silver rivers after all.

The train pulled into a station and Jack was shoved onto the platform by the throng. The air smelled of salt and he could hear the sea. The afternoon sun was so bright to his prison-accustomed eyes that it made him blink, and it took him a moment to realise that someone was calling his name.

'Jack! Jack Rosenblum!'

Jack peered into the crowd and saw a figure frantically waving a wad of papers.

'Edgar?'

A slight man with wild grey hair hurried towards him, pushing aside the unwilling bodies and enfolded Jack in a crushing embrace.

'I've done it! You're safe, Jack. I can take you home to Sadie.'

Jack swallowed and stared at Edgar, as his legs began to tremble.

'I went to a judge and I tell him, "This man, this Rosenblum of Rosenblum Carpets, is a true ally against the Nazis. On the day war is declared this man turns his profitable factory over to the British war effort. Do not question Jack Rosenblum's loyalty!"'

Jack nodded dumbly, unable to speak.

'The judge agreed. You are now "class C" alien and can go home.'

Jack's tongue stuck to the roof of his mouth. 'This place? Where am I?'

Edgar gave a shrug. 'Dorsetshire.'

'Pretty,' said Jack, as a tiny bird with dappled feathers landed on the fence next to him. It flapped its wings and took off in a gust of song.

FROM THE MOMENT he arrived home, Jack devoted his spare time to expanding meticulously the bullet points in the *Helpful Information* pamphlet, until there was no room left and he had to insert supplementary pages at the back. There was nothing he liked more than to make another little note, an observation upon English customs such as, 'the British housewife makes a purchase of haddock on Friday mornings'. Jack prided himself that, should another booklet be commissioned, the German Jewish Aid Committee could turn to no greater expert than himself.

The factory continued to grow, the looms churning out parachutes and kitbags and canvas tents, so that the Rosenblums were able to move into a terraced house in Hampstead, with a brass door knocker and a cobbled patio backing onto the heath.

The end of the war meant that, no longer limited to utility garments, Jack could now acquire the proper attire of the Englishman and he decided that this meant nothing less than a bespoke suit from Savile Row. In his neat hand he recorded this as item 106 on his list. Jack went to Henry Poole for the first time in October 1946. It cost him a small fortune just to acquire the requisite number of clothing coupons, let alone the cost of the clothes, but it had been worth every halfpenny: that suit was the livery of the English gentleman.

The suit was delivered twelve weeks later, wrapped in crepe paper inside a pearlescent box with the Henry Poole crest emblazoned in gold. His pattern was to be kept in the company vaults alongside those of Churchill, Gladstone and Prince Albert. When he put on the suit, he felt taller than his five feet three inches, his bald head appeared to shine less and his nose felt less pronounced. It was how the emperor would have wished his new suit to be.

As car production increased once more, Jack was able to complete item number 107: An Englishman drives a Jaguar. The summer of 1951, Jack took delivery of a Jaguar XK120. He had been on the waiting list for two years, and when the moment arrived he was overwhelmed. The night before he had stayed awake and imagined himself driving along Piccadilly in his Henry Poole suit, at the wheel of his racing-green Jag, beside his wife with her purple rinse and perfect nails.

However, item 108 (An Englishman's wife has a purple rinse, nice nails and plays tennis and bridge) was problematic. Sadie was devilish at bridge but did not play tennis and refused even to consider the rinse, complaining that it was an unnatural hue to have upon one's head. Knowing his wife's temperament, he decided not to press the point. He would have to be English enough for the both of them.

Apart from the deficiencies in his wife, Jack had fulfilled nearly all the items on his list. He had the suit, the car and the house in a leafy part of the city. He procured his hat from Lock of St James's and tried his best to adjust the brim to precisely the correct degree. He ate lunch three times a week in the best of the squalid restaurants in town, took his wife to Covent Garden and to Wigmore Hall and made donations to the right charities as well as the wrong ones—giving equally to the fund to restore St Paul's Cathedral's roof as well as to the fledgling Israeli state.

There remained one more item on Jack's list. He knew it to be the quintessential characteristic of the true English gentleman and without it he was nothing. Item 150: An Englishman must be a member of a golf club.

For Jack, membership of a golf course was proving troublesome. He flicked a catch concealed in the carved Griffin of his Victorian desk and a drawer popped out a few inches. This was where he kept his correspondence with the golf clubs of England. The communication consisted of a copy of each application and a polite, but firm, response from the club secretary declining his admittance. Jack was persistent to the point of stubbornness; he had arrived in London with nothing but his suitcases and twenty pounds in his pocket. Within ten years he had one of the biggest carpet factories in London, so a single rejection from a snide official of a golf club was not going to dissuade a man like Jack Morris Rosenblum.

To his dismay, the single rejection rapidly turned into five, then ten, until every course in a twenty-mile radius had turned him down. It was time he took advice. He spoke to Saul Tankel, the jeweller, who was considered to be a source not only of diamonds but information.

'It's no good, no good at all. They'll never let you in. Not with that *schnoz*.'

Saul pushed back his thick, jeweller's spectacles onto his forehead, and waved his hands with enthusiasm. He looked like an alarmed grasshopper.

'There is us and them. And they will never, ever let you in. Anyway, what will you do? They play on Saturdays.'

The problem of playing on Saturdays had already occurred to Jack, and did not unduly concern him. He hadn't yet the courage to tell his wife, but he considered golf as an excellent alternative to a tedious morning spent at synagogue. Saul seemed to sense his thoughts.

'You know what would happen if you did get in?' he asked, jabbing a surprisingly large finger two inches from Jack's controversial nose. 'You will play on a Saturday, when everyone else is in *schul* praying to Him,' Saul gestured to the heavens, or rather a light bulb hanging inches above their heads, but Jack took the point. 'And you will play the best game of your life. And finally you will get the hoop-in-one.'

'A hole,' Jack corrected.

'What?'

'A hole-in-one. Golf has holes not hoops.'

'Ah. So, then you will get the hole-in-one. And you will be able to tell no one. Because you played on Saturday, against His wishes on the day of rest!'

Jack was not convinced, but the information was useful. The next letter he signed under the pseudonym Professor Percy Jones. The professor received a much more favourable response.

February 1, 1952

Dear Professor Jones,

Thank you for you kind enquiry concerning membership of the Lawns Golf Club. We are indeed open to new members. I sincerely look forward to making your acquaintance.

Regards,
Edward Fitz-Elkington, Esq.

Jack turned the letter over and over until it grew quite worn along the folds. He decided to write back to the club secretary under his own name, mentioning that his good friend Professor Percy Jones had been told membership was not full, but the reply was inevitable.

Dear Mr Rosenbloom,

I am sorry to inform you that there has been a misunderstanding. Membership is now full. I would be pleased to place you on the waiting list, but I must warn you that the current wait is approximately twenty-seven years.

Yours sincerely,
Edward Fitz-Elkington, Esq.

It was hopeless. He could not produce the evidence of the professor's letter without admitting that he had impersonated him, to which he imagined the secretary would not take kindly.

Jack wrote one final letter to the Sanderson Cliffs Club, offering free carpets for all the buildings. Considering the scarcity of good carpets, in fact the scarcity of everything, Jack knew it to be a generous proposal—and he even had a precious letter of recommendation. He was more hopeful than he had felt for months because Mr Austen, a woollen merchant, had actually offered to nominate him for membership. Jack was elated; this was fate. The Sanderson Cliffs was the perfect club; their course was legendary, the best in North London. Even during the war they had retained twenty greenkeepers to nurture the grass and, according to legend, they used tweezers, nail scissors and water imported from the Nile, so smooth were the greens.

So optimistic was Jack that he finally bought a set of clubs. He had never actually played a single round of golf; he had never even been on a golf course, nor had he held a club, let alone taken a swing. He put on his Henry Poole suit and went to Harrods. He rode the elevator to the sports floor in a state of hushed reverence, and the shop assistant led him to the selection of golf clubs. The room was oak panelled with dim overhead lights, and in the gloom the steel of the clubs seemed to glow. The assistant passed him a club.

'Try this six iron. Beautifully balanced, sir. Specially designed to make striking the ball that bit easier.'

Jack held it in his hands and he felt his throat catch. He hadn't wanted anything this much since he was a small boy and had saved up for a bright red steam engine that really worked. The assistant passed him another.

'This nine iron has fine grooves. Used by Bobby Jones himself.'

That was it. Jack had to have them.

'Excellent choice, sir,' cooed the assistant as he wrapped them and Jack counted out the crisp pound notes. 'Will sir require a new bag to put them in?'

Jack selected one in a rich tan with a crimson stripe stitched along the side. He thought they were the most beautiful objects he had ever seen.

The clubs rested in the corner of his office, still in their wrappings. Jack would sit behind his desk and gaze at them. Then, when he could bear it no longer, he would cross the room and reverentially pull out the nine iron or the sand wedge and grip it in his hands. After a few minutes—he never risked a swing, as he didn't want a single graze on that metal—he would meticulously rewrap the club and tenderly place it back in the bag.

ON FRIDAY, Mr Austen paid a call. While Mr Austen was fond of the odd round of golf, he couldn't fathom Jack's fixation. That was because Mr Austen was born an Englishman. There were Austens in Hampshire going back twenty generations—there was even a rumour that they were distantly related to that greatest of English novelists. Edward Austen knew never to leave home without his hat, but to remove it immediately on entering a church. He could tell by the cut of a man's suit or the angle of his hat, as easily as by the tone of his voice or the wax of his moustache, where he ranked in the social order compared to himself. Such men as Mr Edward Austen never worried about membership of golf courses. They presumed their superiority above every other nation, as confidently as they knew that the 7.03 to Waterloo stopped at Clapham Junction.

Jack waited for Mr Austen in his small office, off the main factory floor. One wall was entirely covered with samples from the new season's range of innovative tufted carpet, in a rainbow of colours. Rosenblum's Carpets might not have the cachet of a Wilton or an Axminster but Jack was secretly sure that his product was quite superior. Hearing a loud knock on the door, he rose to greet Mr Austen and shook his hand with enthusiasm.

Mr Austen liked the outlandish little man and his perpetual cheerfulness. He always found his accent surprising; those Germanic vowels and softly hissing consonants had not faded one jot over the years that he had known him. He felt sorry for him—it must be awful to sound like the enemy.

'Ah, nice clubs. May I?'

'Of course.'

Jack watched, concealing his concern for his treasure, as Mr Austen pulled out a short iron and stood—legs slightly apart, shoulders tilted—and raised the club. He brought it down in a controlled arc, a proper golfer's swing.

'They're a good heft. Where did you get them?'

'Harrods.'

Mr Austen laughed unthinkingly. 'Really? You didn't? My good fellow, no one actually *buys* clubs at Harrods.'

Jack flushed, embarrassed. He stared at his clubs in their white tissue paper. Their shine no longer looked radiant, but taunted him.

Mr Austen slid the iron back into the bag and reached into his pocket. There was no point putting it off any longer. He pulled out a sheet of stiff notepaper embossed with the Sanderson Cliffs emblem.

'I've heard back. Not good news, old man. It's a no-go. Terribly sorry.'

Jack sat down, dumbstruck. It couldn't be true. Mr Austen had recommended him, and he was one of *them*.

'You needed more nominations; my paltry one wasn't quite enough.'

'But you said others had been admitted. That membership was still open.'

Mr Austen fiddled awkwardly with the label on the golf bag. He wished old Rosenblum would hide his disappointment better—it made this damned uncomfortable—always so emotional, these continental Jews.

'Think that was part of the problem. Apparently the quota's full.'

'Quota?'

'Yes.'

Quota. Jack turned the word over slowly. He hadn't heard that for a while, and with it he knew the game was lost. They would never, ever admit him to any golf course inside or outside London.

'You told them about the carpets?'

'Yes,' said Mr Austen. He was longing to leave. He'd done his bit, really he had. The suggestion of free carpets had gone down particularly badly. 'Think they can buy their way in anywhere, don't they?' The club president had complained. He did not mention this to Jack.

'I'm very sorry.'

The door swung open and Fielding, the factory manager, entered, staggering under a tower of files. 'Sorry to disturb you, sir. Shall I come back later?'

'No. It's quite all right, I'm just leaving,' said Mr Austen, relieved to have an excuse. He closed the door quietly behind him.

Fielding dumped the pile of paperwork on the desk. 'I need you to make a decision on these new machines, Mr Rosenblum.'

'I'll look at them later,' said Jack, shooing away the young man.

There was no room left in his mind for business; it was full with this latest disappointment. He was disconsolate and needed to wallow for a few minutes, which involved pouring a large whisky and reading the paper. He settled into his armchair and flicked through *The Times* to the sports pages but something in the property section caught his eye: a large cottage with tangled roses growing up the walls and a thatched roof. Next to the picture of the house was another one of a view taken from the top of a hill looking down over a patchwork of fields that lay under a cloudless sky. The photograph was black and white but Jack could tell that it was the bluest sky he had ever seen. There were flowers at the front of the frame peeping out among the hedgerows and dots of sheep in the distance. He peered closely at the small print. 'House offered for sale along with sixty acres of land. Splendid aspect. Apply Dorset office.' Sixty acres. And in Dorset. He could hear the birds singing as he looked at that photograph.

There was a distant chime as the bells of Bow Church struck the half-hour.

Hurriedly Jack got up, put on his hat and left the office. The golf course was the last item on his list, and pursuing the list had not led him wrong yet.

The carpet factory was situated in the East End in a large redbricked Victorian warehouse with posters for '*Rabenstein Ltd. Kosher sausage manufacturer for first-class continental garlic sausage*' and '*Hats, Frocks and Fancies by Esther de Paris*' pasted all over the walls. Jack sniffed: change was coming—he could smell it as a hint of turmeric and cumin mingled with the yeasty scent of baking challah. There were holes where buildings used to be, a single missing house in a terrace like a knocked-out tooth, and vast craters filled with rubble. Such was the scale of the repairs that the cleanup had barely started, and nature had crept back into the East End; there were wild flowers springing up among the waste, memories of the meadows that once covered the ground.

He was considering this, alongside his other more serious concerns, when he walked right into an idea. He had turned left down Montague Street and seen the sign. It read in Yiddish: 'MILCH, FRISH FUN DI KU.' Years ago, those living in the East End couldn't get milk from the countryside and so had their own herd in the middle of the city. The last cow had departed long since but the sign remained, hanging haphazardly on the disused gates, to serve the purpose of providing divine, or bovine, inspiration for Jack.

'That's it! Milk fresh from the cow!'

The sound of birdsong echoed in his ears again and for a moment he almost muttered a prayer under his breath. If you couldn't get milk from someone else's cow, you had to get your own. No golf course would admit him and so he must build his own.

CHAPTER TWO

'And tell me, *mein Broitgeber*, since you know everything—why couldn't we go to Israel?' Sadie muttered at her husband as the green Jaguar wound its way along the narrow country lanes. She was younger than Jack, still in her forties, but had long since resigned herself to a premature old age. She had neat grey-blonde hair and on the rare occasions when she laughed, the rolls of fat around her middle wobbled ever so slightly. Now they shook with agitation. 'You want to be like everyone else. So let us go to Israel, where everyone is like us!'

Jack said nothing. He liked being called '*Broitgeber*', or 'my Lord and master', but wished her tone was more sincere. 'Israel is a place for the young and I am old. It's too much to build a whole new country. A golf course is enough for me.'

He had bought the cottage unseen, and without telling Sadie, which in hindsight may have been a miscalculation. He had known she would have railed against it, and he knew with quiet self-assurance that this was the right thing to do. He had also taken the rather dubious decision of not telling her that their house in London was up for sale. So when, while reading the *Jewish Chronicle*, Sadie discovered that her house was 'under offer', she was more than a little surprised.

'And why could you not build this thing in London? Why this godforsaken place?'

'London's full. And fresh air is good for nerves.'

'What do I care for fresh air?' Sadie's words came out in a sigh as she sank miserably into her seat. 'You sell my house from under me, you take me to *alle schwartze yorne* and then you have the nerve to mention my nerves! *Du Blödmann*.'

'You will be better away from it all,' replied Jack.

The Rosenblums' lives were divided into two—a neat line severed each half. There was the old life in Germany that was *before*. Then, there was the new life in England, which was *after*. Sadie thought of her existence purely in these terms of *before* and *after*, but this left no room for *right now*.

The car reached a straight stretch of road and Jack hit the accelerator, forcing Sadie to clutch the scarf covering her hair. She frowned and burrowed even further into her seat. Most of the luggage was in the removal van but she had insisted on her box being placed carefully in the boot of the car. That box was all that was left of *before*. It contained half a dozen photographs: there was one of Sadie, aged eleven, and her brother Emil, aged three, as well as pictures of each of Sadie's parents. There was also a tattered Hebrew prayer book that once belonged to her grandpa, Mutti's recipe book and a neatly folded white linen towel. Her family had been in Germany for 500 years and that box was the sum total of her history. Only she remembered how Emil used to cheat at chess, and that they had hoarded their treasures under a floorboard in the maid's room: a shiny *Pfennig*, a piece of green glass, a lump of elephant dung stolen from the zoo. Sadie wondered if they were still there. Did Emil look at them again before they took him?

Unless she looked at the photograph, Sadie could no longer quite recall her brother's face. She couldn't remember whether his eyes were blue or grey. The only thing worse than remembering, she decided, was starting to forget.

Sadie liked the Jewish calendar because it was all about memory. She had a list of her own: remember to keep the Sabbath; remember to keep the dietary laws as they remind you that you are a Jew; at Yom Kippur atone for your sins; and, most importantly, do not forget the dead. During life there is the birthday and afterwards Yahrzeit, the day of death. She knew as she celebrated her birthday each year that there was this other anniversary waiting, like an invisible book end.

Jack was humming under his breath beside her, and she pulled her scarf closer over her ears in an attempt to block out the sound. The narrow lanes frothed with cow parsley that brushed the side of the convertible. Sadie glowered and said, 'We're lost and I hate the countryside. *Du Dumpfbeutel*. No one will come and see us, not even Elizabeth.'

Jack winced at the mention of Elizabeth. She was soon to start her studies at Cambridge University and the thought that she would not visit them in their self-imposed exile was terrible. 'She will come,' he insisted, 'we will sip champagne and eat strawberries on the lawn and then I'll drive her to Cambridge.'

Elizabeth had gone to Scotland with a girlfriend for the summer but had promised to come and see them before term started. It was now three weeks, ten days and seven hours since she had gone and Jack experienced a pain in his gut whenever he thought about her absence.

He tried a conciliatory tone, 'Sadie, doll, try to be happy.'

She frowned—after all these years, he still did not understand. 'I don't want to be happy.'

They reached a ramshackle set of crossroads and a blank signpost.

'You see, silly old man, this place doesn't even have a name.'

'Of course it does. The signs were simply painted out during the war and no one's replaced them. Everyone in this village knows where they are. Probably aren't enough strangers passing to warrant replacing them.'

They passed the village hall where a small group of men were hammering wooden tent pegs into the sun-baked ground. They all stared narrowly as the Jaguar passed. Jack was perturbed—it was part of his grand scheme of assimilation that they would simply seep unnoticed into village life, like rain into damp earth, and he did not like their scrutiny.

He steered the car round to the left, turned by a steep hill and then noticed a broken gate leading along a roughly hewn dirt track. 'This is it!' he cried, recognising this to be a great moment in their lives—in years to come when he stood at the front of the driveway and ushered in the chauffeured cars to his golf club for the Wessex Cup or the qualifying match for the British Open, he would remember the moment when he saw the place for the first time.

He steered the car up a potholed driveway lined with beech trees. 'Need to get this fixed,' he said resolutely. His course would need a proper road.

He pulled the car up beside the front door of the house. It looked rather different from the picture that was sitting snugly in Jack's breast pocket. The thatch was still there, but even with scant knowledge of thatching, he felt that it shouldn't have bald patches. The limewashed exterior was grimy in the sunlight; the roses grew feral and obscured the boarded-up windows. The walls were made of wattle and the house gave the impression that it wished for nothing more than to slump back into the earth. Jack furrowed his brow, climbed out of the car and ripped away the rotten wood nailed to the window frames. There was a tinkle of broken glass as a pane fell out. 'Need to fix that,' he muttered, less resolutely than before.

Sadie hadn't moved; she sat fixed in her seat and stared at the house curiously, breathing in deeply—there was a familiar scent, something she knew well but had not smelled for a long time. Jack plucked a rose from the wild tangle round the door and presented it to her. She ignored him.

Unperturbed, he opened the car door for her and offered his arm, which she rejected, brushing past him to stalk across the drive to the front door.

'The house looks sad now but with a lick of paint it will be perfect,' he called, producing a bunch of old-fashioned, cast-iron keys. 'Ready?'

He slipped one into the big keyhole on the studded door and as he turned it there was a satisfying click. He heaved open the door and entered the dark hallway, Sadie close behind him. She gave a little scream. '*Scheiße!* Something touched me!'

Jack wedged the door so that a shaft of light illuminated wisps of a torn cobweb. 'See, it's nothing, doll. Nothing but us.'

Glancing up, Sadie saw the low ceiling was crisscrossed with hulking beams, stained black with soot and age. On the walls the lime plaster was beginning to flake and where the sun fell it shone upon spots of mould and creeping damp. She ducked under a low archway leading into a rudimentary kitchen—it certainly wasn't Sadie's idea of a kitchen. There was a filthy stove, a heap of wood to fuel it, a worn oak table with a few broken, upended chairs and, as she looked about her, she saw there was no sink. In fact, not only was there no sink, there was no tap.

Jack had followed her and was heaving against the stable-style door that lead to the back garden.

'Just a minute. Nearly got him. Oh . . .'

His voice trailed away as he saw the land stretched out before him. Wordless, he seized Sadie's hand and, oblivious to her protests, led her outside. The fields lay under a shimmering heat haze and the bees hummed in every bush. The lawn sloped gently into fields full of waving grass tinged with buttercups, and high above their heads a kestrel hovered.

Here was his golf course. Jack walked ahead, narrowing his eyes and, whether it was the effect of the sunlight or sheer excitement, he could hear a wireless commentary—'*Well, this is the first British Open to be held at the new course at Pursebury Ash. It is a fine day for it. Here comes Bobby Jones with the owner of the course, that well-known English gentleman, Mr Jack Rosenblum. Ah yes, it's going to be a great competition.*'

Realising that Jack was lost in a daydream, Sadie turned to go inside. A voice from inside the hedge made her start.

'Mornin'.'

An old man was squatting in the shadows behind her, camouflaged by leaves and cow parsley. His face was the colour of wood stain, and he looked as if he was growing out of the hazel boughs. Sadie took a step back.

'*Ja*, hello, may I help you, Mr . . .'

'Curtis. Jist Curtis. You can help if yer likes. I is huntin' for pignuts, Mrs Rose-in-Bloom.'

Sadie stared at him. 'You know my name?'

'Aye.'

He offered no more explanation, and Sadie continued to gaze at him.

'Them last ones flew away,' he added conspiratorially.

'I am sorry? I beg your pardon?'

'Them last ones what lived in your house. They flew away.'

Sadie did not understand. 'They took an aeroplane?'

'Nope. Beds a-made of pijin feathers. 'S bad luck to sleep arn pijin feathers. They's wings grow back in the night and then they flies away. With you in bed or not. They is very dangerous things, pi-jins.'

'Pigeons?'

The man tapped his nose.

'What about goose feathers? I have an eiderdown of goose, will they fly away, too?'

The man screwed up his face in concentration. 'Nope. Don't think so. Jist pi-jins.'

He stood, clambered out of the hedge, gave Sadie a little tip of his hat and wandered away down the hill.

Aching with tiredness, all Sadie wanted was to lie down and sleep. Attempting to ignore the fustiness of the house, she climbed the wooden stairs and tried the nearest room. A cast-iron bed covered with a moth-eaten quilt rested in the middle of the room. She knelt to open the low window but the catch was stiff and splinters of rotting wood broke away as she forced it ajar and wondered aloud, 'How did I get here?' A wind blew into the bedroom carrying tiny seed cases and the same odd scent; it was something familiar from her childhood. She sighed, drew the curtain and lay on the bed, scrutinising the thick oak beams in the sloped ceiling above her head. On the floor lay a pile of faded books and she reached out to take a volume from the top. The cover was damp-stained and it smelled vaguely of mould, but she opened it anyway and idly read the Contents page. It was a collection of folklore: 'The Dorset Oozeer', 'Apple Bobbin' at Midnight', 'The Drowners', and she skimmed through the titles, searching for any reference to pigeons. There was none. The rest of the books were novels by Thomas Hardy and must once have been a smartly bound nineteenth-century set, but now they were scarred by brown watermarks. She got up, shoved all the books in the corner of the room so that their dank stench could not reach the bed, lay back down and closed her eyes.

SHE WOKE with a jolt to find that it was dark and, for a moment, she was back in Bethnal Green underground station in the midst of an air raid. She reached out automatically for Elizabeth—the child always slept curled against her hip, oblivious to the booms overhead—but Sadie's fingers brushed the wiry hair on Jack's leg, and she remembered where she was. She sat up, on the edge of the bed, and listened to the rasp of Jack's breathing. There was another sound, too: a soft thudding and flapping. She tried to shake Jack awake but he would not stir. The scrabbling grew louder and screeching cries came from the wall. She dug her nails into her palms—she was a middle-aged woman and would not be tyrannised by night-time noises.

She slid out of bed and followed the sound to a door built into the wattle wall in one corner of the bedroom. As she fumbled with its bolt, the door burst open and looming grey shadows poured out and flapped across the ceiling. She could not tell if they were outsized bats or birds. There was only the *thud*, *thud* as they flew into the walls or collided with the window glass. She ran to the window, flung it as wide as she could and then escaped from the bedroom, slamming the door behind her.

She raced downstairs in the darkness until she reached the hall, where the flagstones felt icy cold on her bare feet. She didn't like to think of Jack asleep in the room with all those creatures—supposing they flew away with him? Then she would be left alone. She laughed aloud at her silliness, but her voice echoed in the empty house as she padded into the sitting room. Their furniture had been safely delivered but was still covered in white sheets. She could make out the shape of their sofa, an old high-backed Knole. Jack had bought it after reading that the Knole sofa boasted a proud aristocratic lineage. Ladies had to be careful whom they sat next to on a Knole sofa as, with a pull on the cord, the sides and back came tumbling down to form a makeshift bed. Right now, it proved very useful and Sadie gladly removed the sheet, tugged on the cords and lay down. She wrapped herself up in the dustsheet, shut her eyes and waited for sleep.

JACK WOKE the next morning feeling disorientated. He was lying in a neat, low bed in an unfamiliar room. Light grey-blue feathers lay scattered across the floor and a dead bird rested next to the window. He yawned, got out of bed and went downstairs to the small back parlour that he had decided would be his study. It was dingy, the walls were smoke-stained and the thick layers of dust made him cough. A half-burned fire mouldered in the broken grate. A box of his papers rested on the floor. He removed the lid, rifled through them and found what he was looking for.

A Guide to the Old Course at St Andrews, Scotland
By Mr Tom Morris
1884
Printed for T. R. Johnson in St Paul's Churchyard.

It was a yellowed and dogeared pamphlet, which he had discovered in a secondhand bookstore off Piccadilly. He had read it at least fifty times and was almost word perfect. He stroked the battered pages with affection. It was like the commandments given to Moses on the Mount—the blueprint for his destiny. With the wisdom of Tom Morris he would build the greatest golf course since the end of the war: an Old Course in the West Country. He didn't have the sea—that was the only slight hitch and it probably couldn't *officially* be a links course with only a duck pond—but other than the lack of ocean, the differences in topography, soil, wind direction and grass, it would be a perfect copy of St Andrews.

He went out into the garden, and listened to a cuckoo calling from a distant copse. He unfolded the central pages of the pamphlet to display a map of the Old Course, which he held up to the prospect before him. He wondered how long it would take until it was all finished—five months, six? The holes couldn't take too long to dig—it was the greens that would be tricky. They needed regular watering and he would have to find out where the springs on his land lay.

'The springs on my land.'

The words caught in his throat. He stared at the ground before him, awed that this patch of green belonged to him and Sadie. He would be the perfect country gentleman and take good care of these fields. What he needed first was a tweed cap and a walking stick with a bone handle—that was the wardrobe of a country gentleman with sixty acres (rule number 5: Always adhere to English conventions of dress). He returned to the house shouting, 'Sadie, I'm off to buy a hat.'

Sadie was already up; she had fallen into a fitful sleep but had risen at dawn to begin the immense task of cleaning the house. There was, of course, no hot water and the large tin bath in the kitchen also provided a dismal hint that there was no bathroom. Yet the bare, grimy house with its lack of electric light and strange nocturnal sounds reminded Sadie of her childhood. As a girl there had been long holidays in Bavaria with her family, in an ancient house on the edge of a wood. The childhood holiday cabin was full of privations: a well in the garden, candles for light and no maids. Back then it had seemed like an adventure. She was older now, had a twinge in her knee, her back ached at night and she liked ease but somehow this house reminded her of *before*. She thought she could lose herself here.

She did not share these feelings with Jack—he would not understand. She resolved to accompany him, and since she knew he would not want her to come, this gave her a kernel of pleasure. From the landing she called down to him, '*Broitgeber*, you must wash before we leave.'

Jack frowned—he had taken a notion to buy a hat, and once fixed upon something there was no time for distractions. He followed the voice of his wife upstairs. She had disposed of the dead bird and was tidying the bedroom, making the bed.

'Jack, you must get a man in to fix the ceiling. It's an aviary up there. And the birds fly down into the cupboard.'

Jack kicked a feather with his toe, disinterestedly. 'I'm going. You stay here and worry about the birds.'

Sadie studied her husband. He was still wearing the clothes from yesterday; he had grass stuck to his back, a feather on his cheek and stubble across his chin. She gave him a sly look. 'You wish to make the correct impression, hmm? They'll think we're slovenly foreigners unless you wash.'

Jack knew that she was right—it was rule 37 on his list (Englishmen of all classes take great pride in excellent personal hygiene). He couldn't possibly risk the condemnation.

LATER THAT MORNING, as the Rosenblums drove down the lane towards the village hall, a burly man in a stiff wool suit stepped into the road and waved at them, forcing Jack to brake sharply. The man stood in front of the car, looking them up and down with steady interest. He seemed to be waiting for something, and then, clearly losing patience, he snapped, 'Well, Mr Rose-in-Bloom, are yer comin'?'

Jack experienced the same confusion as his wife had the day before. It must be the local custom here to know everyone's name. So, not knowing the man before him, Jack felt rather awkward and searched for the suitable English phrase 'I don't believe I've had the pleasure, Mr . . .'

'Jack Basset. But I is jist called Basset. None of yer misters.'

'Glad to make your acquaintance, erm, Basset.'

Jack offered his hand, which Basset shook. He made no move to get out of the way of the car. Peering round him, Jack noticed a crowd gathering in the shade of the hall, the women dressed in floral frocks and wide-brimmed hats and the men sweating uncomfortably in hot, special-occasion suits.

Basset waited for a moment and then cleared his throat. 'Well? Are yer?'

'Of course.'

Jack had no idea to what Basset referred but did not want to cause further upset so enquired, 'May I ask where the car park is?'

'Car park? He wants to know where the car park is!'

Basset started to cough with laughter, a button popped off his shirt and a fleshy triangle of hairy stomach poked through. Embarrassed, he straightened and pointed to a field across the road.

'That there is the car park. I'll get gate.'

Jack steered his beloved Jaguar through a flock of nonchalant sheep and parked under a tree, eyeing the animals suspiciously. The Rosenblums allowed Basset to lead them onto the village green, where a battered white marquee was erected in the centre of the grass. Peering inside, Jack glimpsed plump girls selling fat hunks of red meat. Mounds of dark hearts, piles of kidneys and blue-tinged ox tongues lay on steel trays. Beside them rested baskets filled with misshapen vegetables and trays of grey fungi.

Basset ushered them inside the tent, where it reeked of cider and warm bodies. 'This is Mr and Mrs Rose-in-Bloom,' he announced, guiding them into the midst of the crowd.

Jack stood quite still and let them all stare, while Sadie took a small step closer to him. A ragged woman viewed them suspiciously, eating the biggest peach he had ever seen; it took him a moment to realise what the fruit was—it had been so many years since he had seen one.

'Rose-in-Bloom's a funny name,' said the woman, 'sounds English but yoos foreign, ent you?'

'We are British now. We love England,' Jack declared.

The woman wasn't to be deterred. 'What was you before, then?'

Jack hated this part, the declaration of his otherness.

'We were born in Berlin. We came to England before the war.'

'Berlin—that's in Germany.'

He nodded. 'Yes, it is.'

The ragged woman was not impressed. 'So, you is a Kraut.' She corrected herself, 'You *was* Kraut. You sounds Kraut.'

'No. I am a British Citizen.'

'Why 'ave you come to Pursebury?'

'To build a golf course.'

This was unexpected.

'A what?'

'A golf course.'

Jack was standing in the centre of a growing crowd, where he was proving to be the most popular attraction at this fair—this did not please him, as he was trying to be inconspicuous. He never understood how, when he always obeyed the list to the letter, dressing in the uniform of the English gentleman, he was instantly identified as a rank outsider.

'I shall build the greatest golf course in the South-West.'

The faces in the crowd stared at him dubiously.

'This ent golfing country. It's skittling country,' said Basset. 'Ever played skittles?' he asked with a note of challenge.

'No, I haven't.' Jack was intrigued—an English game he hadn't heard about. He was filled with instant enthusiasm.

Seeing this, Basset smirked. 'I'll learn you,' he said and led him away with a glint in his eye.

Choosing not to witness Jack's latest escapade, Sadie wandered from the tent into the village hall. It was an unusual building; the pitched roof and walls were all made of corrugated iron while inside it was wood-panelled and decked with multicoloured flags. Framed photographs of the Royal family adorned every wall, the pictures of King George all draped in black crepe. A small army of women stood at the back of the hall guarding the tea table.

Sadie was used to London where good food was scarce; in contrast, the table in the church hall was heaving with sandwiches of rare beef, cakes, bowls of cream and trays of bright strawberries. She became conscious of someone staring at her, and turned to see a thin woman, hair swept into a severe bun, standing very close.

'I'm Mrs Lavender Basset. Secretary of the Parish Council and chairwoman of the Coronation Committee. Will you be wantin' some tea?'

'Thank you. That is very kind. I'm Mrs Sadie—'

Lavender cut her off with a snort, 'Oh. I knows who you are, Mrs Rose-in-Bloom.'

She led Sadie to the front of the hall and filled a plate for her with a fat slice of Victoria sponge. Sadie didn't want to eat. She always felt self-conscious eating in front of strangers, but Lavender was scrutinising her through owlish spectacles. Glancing round the hall, Sadie realised that all the women were waiting, teacups poised on saucers, watching. Feeling a little sick, she took a bite and forced a smile.

In the field beside the hall, Jack was not faring well at skittles. He shook his head in total bemusement. Curtis, a tiny old man, gave him a friendly tap on the shoulder.

'Nope. Like this, Mister-Rose-in-Bloom.'

Curtis clasped the rock-hard ball, took a run up and, falling to his knees, then slid along the wooden alley on his belly.

The ball rolled from his hand and collided with the skittles, knocking them flying in a perfect strike.

'Now, that there is the Dorset flop. Nothing like the piddling Somerset wump. Much more effective. 'S why we beats them nillywallies every time at t' Western Skittlin' championship.'

'Yer turn to try,' growled Basset, who had come over to watch. He thrust the ball once more into Jack's damp palm.

'Trick is to let go of the ball at last minute,' said Curtis.

Others grunted in agreement at this advice. Jack rubbed the ball against his trouser leg and prepared to bowl again. The rules were beyond him; he knew only that the aim was to knock down as many skittles as possible and that somehow, whenever it was his turn, the skittles remained resolutely upright, while, when Curtis, Basset or one of the others bowled, the skittles clattered to the ground. Steeling his nerves, he took a deep breath, stepped back a few paces and began his run-up along the grass. Reaching the wood of the skittle shoot, he threw himself onto his belly, knocking all the wind out of his lungs. He slid two yards along the ramp and stopped. Jack opened his eyes, and realised that everyone apart from Curtis was laughing.

'Yer forgot to let go of the ball,' the old man said. 'An ersey mistake.'

'Loser 'as to drink,' said Basset thrusting at Jack a brimming mug of a sweet, apple-scented alcoholic drink.

As the afternoon wore on, the combination of home-brewed cider with hot June sunshine was making Jack's vision cloud. He sat down and closed his eyes for a moment, and heard a voice mutter, ''Ee's a goner. Skittled. 'Ee'll be seeing Dorset woolly-pigs soon.'

There were sniggers and hissing mirth. Then another voice. 'Dorset woolly-pigs. Them is idiots wot believe that.'

There was a derisive cry from Curtis, 'Don't mock. Yer doesn't josh about the Dorset woolly-pig. A noble beast of strength and savagery. I saw it. More 'an thirty yer ago. But I saw it.'

Jack struggled and with supreme effort opened his eyes. The sight that greeted them made him think that he was indeed skittled. A tree was standing in front of him: a huge knot of branches covered with leaves and woven with drooping flowers swaying on a pair of stout legs. There seemed to be a man inside, but he was almost entirely hidden by the vast framework of twigs. Unsure if he was in the midst of a dream, Jack closed his eyes again.

'Git moving, you drunken bastard,' yelled a voice.

Concerned that he was being addressed, Jack opened one eye to see the tree-man sway and stagger across the field where he paused, and then slipped into a ditch. There were shouts, and a rush of children surged towards him, yanked him out and then, clutching the branches, pulled him onwards. A minute later the strange procession disappeared up the hill, the crowd resumed their business, and Jack drifted back into his stupor.

When he woke up, the field was quieter, the crowd had thinned, and his wife sat on the ground by his feet.

She did not look pleased.

'Scold later,' he murmured.

She studied him for a moment and then heaved him upright, but his legs were as weak as a newborn lamb's, and he slid back down.

'Just get me to the car. I can drive us back up the hill.'

Sadie pursed her lips in profound annoyance, and half dragged, half carried her husband up the lane.

The car's dark paintwork shone in the afternoon sun and Jack shambled to it, fumbling in his pocket for the key, but sitting in the driver's seat, eyes shut and chewing happily, was a large woolly sheep. The words burst out of him before he was aware of it. '*Mein Gott. Scheiße! Kaput!*' He lapsed into German only at moments of extreme stress, as he prided himself on what he considered to be his great emotional self-control.

The sheep looked at him in surprise, scrambled to its feet and leaped out.

'They is not used to such luxury,' said a voice.

Jack looked round to see a youth with a lopsided grin standing next to him.

'Well, no harm done.' Quickly he recovered his temper. 'Jack Rosenblum.' He shook the young man's hand.

'Max Coffin,' said the boy.

Jack thought for a moment through the apple haze in his head.

'What do you do, Max?'

'Work at farm.'

'How would you like to earn some extra cash?'

Max flexed his arms awkwardly. 'Always want extra cash.'

Jack liked this bit and felt his mind sharpen, and the sense of bleary sickness subside. He was good at striking a bargain—pay what you have to and add a little bit extra so that the man really wants to work that bit extra for you.

'What do they pay you at the farm?'

'Three pound a week.'

Jack paused for effect; this was part of the process—the boy needed to feel that this was a real negotiation and he was being taken seriously.

'I am creating the greatest golf course in the entire South of England and I'm going to offer you the opportunity to share in that triumph.'

The lad stared at him blankly.

'Come and work for me,' Jack explained. 'I'll pay you and your friends,' he gestured to the young men folding away tables outside the village hall. 'Three pound ten a week. Go and discuss it with the lads.'

Jack watched Max saunter back to the village hall. The lads huddled in animated discussion.

'Are you sure this is a good idea?' Sadie asked, concerned.

'Of course.'

Max returned, hands in his pockets, clearly relishing his sudden elevation to negotiator and spokesman.

'Five of us wants to help.'

'Wonderful,' said Jack, 'The course will be the jewel of England.'

'But we wants three pounds twelve.'

Jack whistled and Max looked stricken, as though he knew he shouldn't have pushed it.

'It's a deal. I shall see you on Monday.' Jack shook the young man's hand and studied him for a moment as he returned to the others.

'It has started,' Jack said to Sadie. 'They will help us build our golf course.'

'Your golf course.'

'I am sure they can help on the house once the course is underway.'

They climbed into the car and Jack started the engine. Sadie surreptitiously knocked a shiny, round sheep turd off her seat.

CHAPTER THREE

Sadie spent the next day scrubbing the house. It had been deserted for years, save for the birds and mice that she could hear scratching at beams in the attic. She did not know from whom they had bought the place but she liked not knowing. It made the house belong more to her; the only history that mattered now was theirs. 'I don't have space for other people's memories,' she murmured as she crouched, washing away the years of neglect. Later, she decided, she would bake.

Jack sat in the sunshine listening to the birds. He thumbed through a copy of the '1951 Golf Year Book', scouring the advertisements for tools and brands of fertiliser. There were captions proclaiming the virtues of 'DORMAN SIMPLEX JUNIOR PNEUMATIC SPRAYER' and telling others him to 'OBTAIN THE FINEST TURF OF ALL FROM SUTTON'S GRASS SEEDS—THEY **ENSURE** SUCCESS!' He wondered whether he ought to buy some for his greens—he didn't want the grass to grow either too long or too coarse, it had to be just right.

Lost in this reverie, he started when the gate clattered loudly and half a dozen men stomped along the driveway. He recognised them from skittles but now they were unsmiling and had changed into stout leather boots.

Trying not to be alarmed, Jack strolled through the garden to greet them, just as Basset began to hammer furiously on the ancient front door.

'Why did you do it?' Basset shouted, jabbing a finger accusingly at Jack, who stood there whitely on the porch, dropping his golfing annual in shock.

'I beg your pardon?'

'That's right. You should beg my bloody pardon. The lads won't work now. Not less I give 'em another fifteen bob a week which I ent got. So what am I going to do? Watch my harvest rot in them shittin' fields?'

Basset paused for breath. He flushed with anger and struggled to articulate the words through his rage.

Jack shuddered and stared at the man swollen with anger before him. From his muddy boots to his red-veined nose, Jack Basset was an Englishman. And Jack Rosenblum wanted to be part of his village—he was going nowhere.

Jack swore to Basset that he wouldn't lure away the farm boys until after the harvest was in. The farmer grunted a grudging assent, and led his friends away. Retreating into his study, Jack poured himself a medicinal whisky, and breathed a heavy sigh. It was June and, according to the leather-bound copy of the *Encyclopædia Britannica*, the boys would be busy until late September. Jack was sorely disappointed; the coronation of the new Queen was set for the following June and he was resolved on having the finishing touches completed well before then. He would invite a selection of gentlemen—Mr Austen as well as Edgar Herzfeld—to partake in a small tournament dedicated to Her Majesty. He could already see the gleaming silver cup laid out on a long table covered with a white cloth and piled high with bottles of champagne, trays of sandwiches, pickles and poached salmon. If the men only began in October, they would barely have started the course before winter arrived, and he knew from reading Tom Morris that new grass had to be planted in mild weather. At present, the fields were full of meadow flowers and long grass and it would need a great deal of mowing to transform them into greens like those at St Andrews.

Jack made a decision and, needing someone to announce it to, walked into the kitchen where Sadie was carefully flouring her hands.

'I am going to build the course by myself. With these two hands I shall dig my way to victory!'

Sadie shook her head in contempt and brushed her fingers through her hair leaving two white streaks of flour like badger stripes.

'My mother warned me that craziness ran in your family. I should have listened but no, I was young and foolish and easily impressed by your red bicycle and your thick hair.'

She gave a rueful cry and turned her back on her husband. He waited, disappointed by her unsatisfactory response, and then retreated in silence.

OVER THE NEXT MONTH, Jack's study metamorphosed into a labyrinth of plans, maps, drawings and letters. He joined Stourcastle library and ordered every title on golf that he could find. They lay stacked in tottering piles across the floor, partly submerged by detailed drawings of various Scottish, English and American courses. He was captivated by Bobby Jones's account of the transformation at Augusta. There were botanical sketches of the flowers he had used and detailed layouts of the planting and water features.

Jack decided that the course at Augusta was man's perfection of nature. Jones was an omnipotent magician; at his command woods vanished, hills subsided and valleys rose. A canvas of verdant green provided the background, like the painted backdrop of an Old Master, and into this was woven a thread of glittering streams filling large pools, which reflected the wide-open blue of the sky. Then there was the miraculous marriage of water and scented azaleas and dogwoods—reds, pinks and gold—sparkling in the mirror ponds so that Jack could smell the fragrance rising off the photographs. There was a vista from every rise—a glimpse of a trickling stream surrounded by blooming camellias, or the curve of a yellow bunker echoed in the angle of a lake. This was living art: man creating beauty in flowers, water, earth and sky.

Yet Jack was also transfixed by Robert Hunter, author of the celebrated tome *The Links Courses of England and Scotland*, who declared, 'it should be remembered that the greatest and fairest things are done by nature and lesser by art'. Hunter was a Romantic and valued the sublime on the golf course. Bunkers were only true hazards when formed from sand blown in by the turbulent North Sea. The rough should be toughened blue seagrass and the greatest vista was that of the crashing waves against the horizon. Hunter's ability to utilise the natural obstacles provided by the terrain was compelling. Jack's land was full, overflowing in fact, with natural obstacles: there were the water meadows at the base of the valley filled with sprouting bog plants, and the slope of the hill was an incline of approximately twenty per cent, which, Jack understood, already made his course one of the more challenging. The edges of the course were tightly wooded and hedges divided the land into thin strips.

He reached a decision. He must combine the two great models: he would create a links course according to the wisdom of Robert Hunter but using the techniques of Bobby Jones. He would create a St Andrews in the Blackmore Vale—even if he had to demolish Bulbarrow Hill.

There remained one niggling doubt, however, that was like a small stone in his shoe, and so Jack decided he must do what any logical man would—write to Bobby Jones for advice. He went over to his desk, pulled out a piece of crisp white writing paper and reached for his pen.

Dear Mr Jones,

I have recently purchased sixty acres of land in the county of Dorsetshire, which I have undertaken to turn into a golf course. I am a great admirer of your triumph at Augusta, and hope that you will condescend to bestow upon me a little of your advice.

I intend to have my course completed before the following summer. I enclose a map of the land. My only slight inhibiting factor is that currently I must undertake all work myself. I do not wish this to impede any suggestions you may decide to bestow. Please be assured, sir, that I am five foot three and a half inches of sheer tenacity.

With regards,

Your humble servant, Jack M. Rosenblum

Jack sealed the letter. He did some rough calculations in his head. Presuming that the letter went into the first airmail post tomorrow, it would still not reach Mr Jones's publisher until a minimum of four weeks later and a delay of anything up to twelve weeks was certainly very possible. He then assessed that it would sit in a secretary's in-tray for another week and would not be forwarded to Mr Jones for at least another fortnight. All in all, he would consider himself fortunate if he heard back at all before Christmas. He simply could not wait that long. While he would incorporate Mr Jones's advice the instant he received it, construction must begin right away.

He stood up. There was no more time to waste—he'd already lost a whole month in preparation. He must start this very instant. He went straight to the ramshackle barn at the side of the house that had been converted into a toolshed. Unable to procure any labour from the village, the previous week he had requested two caretakers from the London factory to come to the country. In seven days they had plumbed a bathroom and fixed up his toolshed. He surveyed the gleaming racks of tools; he had no idea what most of them were, but they looked wonderful. There were five different types of hoe as well as rakes, trowels, mowers and a fearsome array of heavy rollers and, on a hook, rested a steel spade with a red-painted handle. Retrieving it, he headed for the door.

He hurried out to the field and stood in the biggest of the meadows with his local Ordnance Survey map, surveying his land.

He closed his eyes and tried to visualise Tom Morris's plan of St Andrews. He had stared at it long enough that he could see it in his mind and, as he opened his eyes and gazed at the landscape once more, he saw it with St Andrews superimposed on top. To the north, where the sea should be, was the part of the original that Jack recognised he could not recreate. There was a rise to the south at St Andrews but on his land there was a pond. There was also a strange hollowed-out path cut into the side of the hill, just where he wanted it level for the first green. On the Ordnance Survey map it was labelled 'the coffin path'. He supposed this was the route used to take the dead to the little church and the centuries of use with heavy, lead-lined boxes had sliced a deep gouge into the earth. Interesting, but it'd have to go. Well, then, he decided, that was a good place to begin. On balance, he considered it would be easier to fill in the path than empty the pond. He would pack it with earth and level the ground. Buoyed with enthusiasm, he hurried over and thrust his spade into the soil. Instantly there was a crack as metal hit rock. He bent down to inspect the damage and saw that the spade had struck a piece of flint. He hesitated for a moment, removed it with his hands and tossed it aside. From his pocket he retrieved a crisp pocket handkerchief and meticulously wiped his muddy hands.

'There now, that's what it's all about. Getting one's hands mucky.'

He thrust the spade into the earth once more and again there was a clink as it collided with stone. He bent, plucked out the object, cleaned his fingers on the dirt-smeared pocket handkerchief and stood upright, slightly painfully this time. An hour later, there was a low pile of stones and a hole but the sunken path was no less hollow.

'How on God's earth am I supposed to fill these blasted holes without digging more holes for earth to fill them?' It was a real conundrum.

He was damp with perspiration and his fingers were blistered. He sat down with a tiny sigh on a tufted molehill, and put his head in his hands, inadvertently smearing mud across his cheeks. Old grassed molehills covered nearly an acre, rising out of the ground like giant, mossy pimples.

'That's it!' He jumped up in excitement. 'I will dig up the molehills and use them to fill the holes! That'll kill two birds with one stone.'

It was genius in its simplicity. What he really needed was a giant cheese wire. There were enough molehills to plug the voids. 'It's going to be a triumph—I can sense it.'

MOVING THE MOLEHILLS was a gargantuan task and he made slow progress, inching around the field like a shadow on a giant sundial. The cheese wire plan had worked. He'd found a piece of wire and managed to work it through the base of the mound. The molehills, however, proved to be extremely heavy, forcing him to construct an elaborate pulley system in order to lift them. This took several hours and many buckets of water from the pond to use as counterweights. He had been at work for a month now and there were bare brown circles where the molehills had been removed. Word spread throughout the Blackmore Vale about the Jew's quest to construct a golf course on Bulbarrow. At first he was dismissed, but then, when his molehill contraption was glimpsed, it was decided that here was a sight worth seeing. Jack never took a day off to rest, his task was too important, and so on Sunday afternoons people gathered with picnics on the brow of the hill, and stared happily at the peculiar little man with his giant cheese wire invention. They clapped as the pulleys lifted the tufts right off the ground, but no one offered to help. It seemed to them that here was a man devoted to a unique and solitary calling.

Away from the crowds on top of the hill, Sadie watched her husband quizzically. She hardly recognised the sunburnt figure with muscles showing through the thin skin on his arms. At dusk he crossed the fields and opened the kitchen door with a bang, collapsing onto a high-backed chair.

'So, you come inside only for meals now?'

He shot her a beseeching look. 'Too tired to argue.'

Sadie hid a tight smile. It was more fun if he didn't enjoy it. 'You're an old man, you work all day and for what?'

Jack only nodded.

'We live in the same house, at the edges of each other's lives. Nearly twenty years of marriage and it has come to this,' said Sadie, slapping the table with her palm for emphasis.

Still he said nothing. This irked Sadie; she was plaguing him and he was not fighting back. She fetched a loaf of bread and some cold beef from the larder, slapped it onto a plate and handed it to him. He ate hungrily. He would have to stay and listen while he ate.

'Thank you,' he said and smiled.

This was too much for his wife.

'*Mein Gott!* Always so cheerful! Why can't you be even a little bit miserable? Then, maybe, we'd have something to talk about after all these years.'

'Why do you have to chew over everything like a piece of gristle? The past is in the past. For pity's sake, let it stay there.'

There was a note of anger in his voice that pleased Sadie. At last, she had got to him. 'You are sunshine at a funeral.'

Jack gave a sharp laugh. 'And what is wrong with that?'

'Everyone wants good weather for a wedding, but at a funeral the sky should have the decency to be overcast. It is simple respect.'

Jack finished his bread, sent his wife a wary glance and stalked out of the kitchen. She gave a sigh of exasperation and contemplated following him into his study to torment him further, but, deciding against it, she sat down.

Despite the usual quarrels with her husband, Sadie felt more peaceful than she had for many years and certainly since Elizabeth had left. In the mornings she was woken by the scent of roses seeping in through the open windows. The sounds of the wood pigeons in the roof no longer alarmed her. Butterflies and bees moved among the tangled flowerbeds and snails left their silver trails across the damp earth. Sometimes she did not get dressed; she would come downstairs in her curlers and nightdress and lie on the dew-damp ground and stare at the clouds drifting across the changing sky. There was still that familiar scent in the garden, a flower that smelled of her childhood. Finally, she traced it to a rose—an unremarkable yellowing bloom with dark leaves marked with blight. Its fragrance was of endless summer holidays a long time ago. It made her melancholy and yet it reminded her of a time *before*, when she was happy.

The garden was thickly overgrown. She had cut back a few of the unruly shrubs and trimmed the plum tree's lower branches to open up the view from the kitchen window, but the rest of the garden remained covered with brambles. Sadie neither planted nor weeded; Hitler had declared the Jews weeds and plucked them out wherever he found them. She knew that a plant was only a weed if unwanted by the gardener, so she refused to move a single one, and they sprouted up wherever they wanted.

On rainy days Sadie turned her attention to the inside of the house. The front door had been waxed and the great iron knocker glistened. Every room was limewashed, the flagstone floors cleaned with lemon soap and the curtains rinsed and rehung. The cottage's crooked sign had been reforged and 'Chantry Orchard' hung proudly on the gate. The thatch had been patched and it would be redone next spring. In the kitchen, the ancient kitchen table had been restored so the knots shone and a black enamel range with four hot plates nestled in the inglenook and threw steady heat out into the room.

Until the new bathroom had been fitted, Sadie had been strip-washing over the sink, and the pleasure of a hot, bubble-filled bath had not yet lost its novelty. She climbed the stairs to her new bathroom with the same excitement Jack experienced each morning as he went to dig his golf course.

The bathroom had an elegant, claw-footed, cast-iron bath, framed prints of tea roses on the walls and a polished wood floor, but the best part of the room was the low mullioned window with a view across the Stour Valley. Sadie ran the bath, the water thundering against the metal sides like an express train, and poured perfumed salts into the steam. Slowly, she unfastened her blouse and unclipped her skirt. Naked, she stared at her face in the mirror—it was the face of a woman in middle age.

The face didn't feel like it was hers. It belonged to someone else; it wasn't the face that her family had known. They wouldn't recognise her now. She had never seen her mother as an elderly woman; soon she would be older than her mother had been when she died.

Sadie climbed into the hot water and looked out across the fields. The landscape already looked different from when they had first arrived. She was aware of the weekly changes in the countryside in a way she had never noticed in the city. In London there were only four seasons, and she had handbags for each. Here, summer was a thousand shades; the elderflower bushes found in every hedgerow and copse had smelled sweetly in the middle of June and now, a month later, they were all brown and withered. Yet the honeysuckle and the jasmine were in full bloom and their scent lingered in the air.

As she got out of the bath and dried herself, she studied the large cracks in the wall, running all the way from the heavy oak beam in the ceiling right down to the floor. They had called in a builder when she first noticed them but he found their concern entertaining and explained, 'They is like livin' things, these old houses. The stones move. It don't matter. Supposed to. These old 'uns like to move. Stretch a bit.'

Sadie had never thought of a house as a living thing before—it was a thing, which one filled with other things, like furniture and books. Yet the walls here were painted with limewash so that the stone could breathe and at night the house did feel almost alive.

On her way to the bedroom, there was suddenly an almighty crash and a rumbling clatter from close by. Clad in her bath towel, her feet still bare, she followed the noise to the sitting room.

Jack was kneeling on the hearth from where he had been laying a fire, black rubble and grime pouring out of the chimney and onto the floor. As Sadie watched in dismay, he changed colour; his hair went black and his face turned grey, except for the shining whites of his eyes. A moment later the tide slowed.

Sadie stared in horror. 'I've just had a bath.'

Jack did not turn round. 'Hope you kept the water. Think perhaps I might need a wash.'

Noticing something, he reached in to the back of the chimney. 'There's a shelf here. And there's something on it.'

He pulled out a charred object and laid it on the mat. Sadie peered at it from a safe distance and felt a little sick. It was a skeleton of some sort. Jack gave it a poke. 'What is it?'

While Jack had been reading endless books on golf, Sadie had read the volume on ancient folklore.

'It's a cat. People put mummified cats up the chimneys. Thought it kept out evil,' she said.

Looking closely at the bones, Jack could make out the shreds of bandages.

'And there should be a Bible. The cat keeps away witches. The Bible is for Him.' Sadie gestured to the ceiling.

Jack was intrigued as he picked out another object, which was indeed a book. He murmured a *Brocha* to humour his wife and opened it with reverence. He read a line to Sadie.

'"Asylum: a place of refuge; a place of protection. Atheist: one who disbelieves in the existence of God."' He paused, rubbing his nose and leaving a black smear on his spectacles. 'The Christian Bible is more different from the Torah than I had thought.'

Sadie took it from him, flipping to the front page and read, '"*Johnson's Dictionary of the English Language*. To which are added an Alphabetical Account of the Heathen Deities. Published 1775." Hmm. Funny sort of Bible.'

Jack gave a short laugh. 'I'll bet you the hole in my *beigel* that whoever put it up there thought it was a Bible.'

Sadie smiled. 'The words are the same, just in a different order. I am sure He can rearrange them.'

Jack chuckled and Sadie turned, laughing with him. She looked pretty, he decided, with her wet hair curling around her face and in this light, her eyes were quite green. In these brief interludes Jack could almost remember the woman his wife had once been. He recalled the first days of their courtship when, half in love, they were still shy with one another. In a fit of boldness he'd confessed that he liked Christmas carols and secretly always wanted to go to the service on Christmas Eve in the *Berliner Dom*. Sadie had laughed and challenged, 'Well? Why don't we?' They'd snuck in and sat in the very back pew, their thighs brushing, as the congregation bellowed the refrains of 'O Tannenbaum'. Somewhere between the third and fourth verse, Jack had realised that a gloved hand was sliding into his. He clasped it, his heart beating like butterfly wings. Afterwards, exhilarated by their daring, Jack had kissed Sadie for the first time. They stood beneath the Christmas tree in the *Gendarmenmarkt*, cheeks flushed with excitement and cold, and Jack leaned towards her, wondering if he ought to remove his spectacles.

Jack chewed thoughtfully on his lip. In half an hour he would return to the field and she would sink back into her silent gloom but, for an instant, they were in the same place, and he did not want the feeling to pass, not just yet. 'Let's put up the mezuzah,' he said.

Ordinarily, Jack despised the trappings of religion. They only served to show up one's differences. He was willing, however, to humour his wife in order to maintain this fragile equilibrium. Besides, he reasoned, a mezuzah was only a small brown box by the front door—another Jew would recognise it while an Englishman wouldn't notice it at all.

Sadie looked at him, surprised and pleased. Clutching her towel, she went into the kitchen and fetched a carved wooden box, a few inches long and with a space at the top for a nail. She held it up and shook it so that the parchment inside rattled.

'What are the words on the paper in the mezuzah? Do you even know?' Jack enquired, hoping that he was not jeopardising the peace.

'No. But they're supposed to ward off evil and bring good fortune to the household.'

'With a cat, a dictionary and a mystery prayer, I believe we are very well prepared for all eventualities.'

He placed a handkerchief on his head as a makeshift yarmulke and Sadie handed him a prayer book. It was evening now and the house martins zoomed under the eaves to their twittering young. Jack's voice mingled with the birds as he sang a Hebrew prayer. His song was ancient; it sang of Israel and a desert land of milk and honey. The village of Pursebury Ash had never heard such a song before. Jack hammered the mezuzah to the doorframe in a single movement, his arm rising like Abraham's, ready with the knife.

JACK WORKED as the long ears of corn turned golden and the days became slowly shorter. As July slid into August, he finished moving the molehills. He retired his pulley system to the barn, fetched his mowing contraptions and, for the first time in years, the grass was cut. He left it long around the edges so that the rough remained strewn with frog orchids, goose grass and bright pink ragged robin. He read about the different kinds of grasses for the greens, the advantages of seed versus turf and ordered long hoses to keep everything watered. The pond would not be drained; it was filled by a spring whispered to have magical properties. He could not tell how deep the pool was, as the surface was covered with giant buttercup lilies.

By the beginning of September, the first hole was nearly finished. In the gathering dusk, Jack carried a large watering can from the pond to his green and poured it over the young grass. He had planted the finest seed he could find, ordered specially from Switzerland. He knelt down, tenderly stroking the soft stems, now three inches high and ready for their first cut. Unable to wait, he went to the barn and fetched the mower, a hand-pushed roller with hundreds of tiny blades and, with the utmost care, slid it across the precious surface. At midnight, he had finished mowing and the green was smooth, like a shot of silk in the moonlit darkness.

He was so tired that his muscles trembled. 'Must carry on . . . must carry on,' he chanted, clenching his fists in determination. Elizabeth would be here in a week or two, and he was resolved on having the hole finished.

He felt a flicker of excitement in his belly—finally, he was ready to cut the first hole. He had purchased a special tool for this: a long metal tube with a serrated top that lay in readiness by the pond. He ran his finger along the sharp edge, cutting himself, and a drop of blood fell to the ground. He licked his finger and removed his torch and the map of Bulbarrow from his jacket. Trying to avoid smearing it with blood, he spread the map along the ground, weighted it with rocks and with a pencil marked with an X the spot where the hole was to go. It corresponded to the first hole on Tom Morris's plan of St Andrews; Jack had laboured mightily to get the land to match, and the stream trickling down from the pond haphazardly mirrored the Swilcan Burn running in front of the first hole on the Old Course.

There were drawbacks; the Bulbarrow stream ran at a different angle to the Swilcan Burn and instead of skirting the green, it simply cut it in two. Try as he might, he simply could not get the green level and although he removed the molehills, the incline remained sharp—a ball placed at the top rolled straight down into the pond at the bottom. Similarly, the fairway remained bumpy as, despite all his watering and a hefty dose of summer rain, the molehills did not go. They remained grassy lumps, wedged into the furrows and dips of the land. These minor impediments aside, he was thrilled by his miraculous progress.

Clutching his map in one hand and a brass compass in the other, he walked carefully across the new grass to mark the position of the hole. He gazed learnedly at the compass and searched for the North Star. He wasn't absolutely sure how to use a compass but the cowboys in the pictures always looked at the stars.

'Here. The hole will go here.' He plunged a stout stick into a random spot declaring, 'I shall decide by instinct.'

Instantly the stick hit a rock, so he shifted it a little to the left where it sank into the wet earth with ease. 'Clearly, this is the right spot.'

He slid the hole cutter into the ground and hammered it in with a piece of wood. Heaving and puffing, he hauled it out to leave behind a neat, round hole, a foot deep and perfect.

'Now for the cup.'

He fished an old soup tin out of his pocket, parcelled in newspaper and preserved especially for this purpose. Gingerly, avoiding the jagged edges, he slid it into the hole. Finally, it was ready—this was the part he had been waiting months for. As he picked up a black-painted pole with its neat blue and white chequered flag and slotted it into the hole, he felt a twinge of regret that Sadie was not here to watch his first triumph. He would have liked this moment better if his Sadie and Elizabeth were here.

The flag fluttered in a tiny breeze. Jack stood back and admired his handiwork. Eventually, after all his effort, the first hole was finished. He had felt a similar sense of achievement when his factory produced its first roll of carpet, but this he had done with his own hands. 'One hole made—only seventeen to go.'

He felt slightly dizzy at this thought and craved sleep. In the morning, he would drink ginger beer for breakfast to celebrate and then he would play his very first hole. He wondered how he could persuade Sadie to join him. To have his wife toast his success with a ginger beer, and then walk round the course with him (shaded by a white parasol and marvelling at his every shot) would be very pleasant.

He hoped Sadie would be impressed by the brilliance of his swing. After all this time and hard work, he still had not played any golf—he had been determined to wait until the first hole was ready. He'd tee off tomorrow morning, after breakfast.

He staggered back up the ridge to the house, so tired that he felt as if both legs had turned to lumps of clay. Reaching the house, he climbed the stairs and, removing only his mud-caked shoes, slumped into bed next to his sleeping wife. He tucked himself in beside her and stroked her back. 'I know you are not pleased now, but you will be,' he whispered. 'This is for both of us. Wait until the course is full with people and then you'll feel better. You'll see.'

He kissed the nape of her neck, something he would never dare to do when she was awake. As he went to sleep, he saw himself teeing off and hitting a ball high up into the far reaches of the sky, where it became a shooting star and disappeared into the black night.

JACK WOKE LATE to the sound of bells; it was nearly twelve o'clock. The room was empty and he could hear Sadie in the kitchen. He waited until it was silent, signalling she was in the garden, and then traipsed into the bathroom to wash.

He cleaned himself carefully, washing the dirt from his ears and hair and taking a brush to his fingernails. He had been careless of his appearance the past few weeks but this morning, for his hole of golf, he needed to be pristine. He whipped up a lather and shaved meticulously, then took the scissors and comb from the bathroom cabinet and trimmed the hair protruding from his nostrils. He dabbed cologne behind his ears and on the top of his head, and scrupulously scrubbed his teeth with peppermint powder.

Clean and sweetly scented, he padded along the landing to the bedroom. Hanging in the wardrobe, wrapped in tissue paper, was his new suit. It was a green and yellow golfing tweed with plus fours, a matching cap and canary-coloured socks. He pulled it on and scrutinised his reflection in the long mirror. He looked just right, a proper golfer. Once it was a little more lived in it would be perfect. He laced up his brown leather studs and clattered down to the kitchen, leaving small holes in the wooden tread of every stair. The ginger beer was set out in readiness and Sadie had left some bread and fruit on the table. He cracked open a bottle and took a gulp; it was fiery and made him hiccup.

'Well, is today the day?' demanded Sadie, coming into the kitchen.

Unable to speak, Jack nodded.

'Do you know what to do?'

Jack scrambled to his feet in excitement at her interest. 'I've been reading all about the perfect golf swing. First there is the grip, the *Vardon* grip.'

He grabbed a saucepan from the countertop and clasped it in both hands to demonstrate.

'It's all about power. You need to place your hands in a neutral position so as to deliver the force flush to the back of the ball and send it whooshing down the fairway!'

He swung the saucepan through the air and knocked a chair flying. Sadie frowned, unimpressed, but Jack's enthusiasm could not be stopped.

'Do you remember—we saw a reel of Bobby Jones at the Masters?'

Sadie wrinkled her forehead. 'Yes, I think so. It was at the front of a Veronica Lake picture.'

Jack barely recalled the film—some weepy that Sadie had wanted to see—but the newsreel footage of Bobby Jones was something else. He had gone five times just to watch that swing: the elegant poise, feet shoulder-width apart, elbows in, head still, left arm straight, wrists cocked and then the sheer force, hips pivoting, as the club swept down in a perfect symphony of coordination with muscles, joints and mind all working together.

'Bobby Jones's swing—that's as close as a man can get to magic.' He shook his head, awed by the thought of his hero. 'I mean, I realise that mine won't be like that, not at first. I'll need to practise, but I have a course of my own, well, a hole, to learn upon. Maybe in a year or two, I can enter the British Open as a gentleman amateur, like Bobby Jones.'

Sadie stared at him, and wondered if she should knock sense into him or pity him.

Jack, unable to read the thoughts of his wife, was once again overwhelmed with the unfamiliar sensation of desiring her company. He felt almost shy, a bashful suitor once again.

'Will you walk round with me? Watch my first shot, *mein Schatz?*'

She dismissed him with a tiny shake of her head.

JACK RETREATED TO the barn to collect his clubs. He would have liked Sadie to accompany him but perhaps it was for the best, just in case he wasn't a natural. His clubs were propped in a corner, carefully wrapped in two old blankets to protect them. With the tenderness of a new father, he peeled off the layers and hoisted them gently over his shoulder. Smiling broadly in the morning sunshine, he walked down to the field. Everything was leading up to this moment; the orange lilies in the flowerbeds had burst into bloom that morning especially for him. Tiny white butterflies floated before him like a guard of honour. How many Englishmen could say that they had played their first hole on their very own golf course?

He paused on the rise leading down to the first tee, closing his eyes in the warm sunshine, and felt tingles of happiness. In a few days Elizabeth would come to visit and he would stand on this spot and show her the golf course. He was proud of his daughter, and he wanted her to be proud of something he had achieved. She would look at the hole he had dug and the land he had heaved, and she would realise that her father was a man with vision. Finally, with his golf course, he would be the kind of man a daughter could admire. He would drive her to Cambridge and they would talk about the magnificence of his achievement.

With a grunt, he repositioned his clubs on his shoulder but, as a shaft of sunlight illuminated the tee, he stopped dead. 'No. No. It can't be true.'

He rubbed his eyes, certain that he was not seeing right but, as he looked, he realised with a tightening of his stomach that it was true. His beautiful new grass had been torn up in great chunks; deep gouges ripped up the fragile green and the turf was yanked back. Massive holes were furrowed across the rough and the fairway, some several feet across. The molehills had been wrenched up and scattered, and a vast pile of twenty or more lay mouldering in a heap on the middle of the green. For a whole minute he stood paralysed with horror. Then, dropping his clubs, he ran up to the ruins, tripped and fell. He heard something crack underneath him and for a horrible moment was sure it was a bone in his leg but feeling no pain he eased himself up. On the ground lay his flagpole snapped in two, its chequered flag torn and spattered with mud. A shout of rage snarled from him like the war cry of some wild beast.

'Bastards! Jew haters!'

His brand-new trousers and dapper jacket were smeared in filth and stained with grass. He was heartbroken. How could they do this to him? What had he done to so offend them?

Despair rolled over him in dark waves. It would take months to repair the damage. And what next? He could repair the spoilt hole, nurture the greens, smooth the land, water the grasses, only to have them destroy it all again? But who? In his mind there was no doubt: Jack Basset. He fixed all his fury and hatred upon him. So English, so self-assured, he would surely take pleasure in the misery of a foreign Yid. He would find the . . . the . . . here Jack faltered, trying to think of a word strong enough to convey his wrath. English failed him, '*Jack Basset ist ein Schweinehund!* Pig-dog bastard!'

He wondered what day it was—he had lost all track of time during the past weeks. From the hill above came another peal of bells. Sunday? It must be Sunday and that meant Basset would be in the pub. They all went there after church—Jack had seen them on previous Sundays walking down the lane in their best clothes, talking and laughing.

His cheeks flushing with anger, he made his way across the fields towards The Crown. It was only as he crossed the stream that fury gave way to worry. All he wanted was to be one of them and, failing that, to be ignored. He did not want trouble—that was dangerous. If only he'd got to play a hole and try out his swing, then perhaps he could have forgiven them. All that work and not a single shot—it was too much to stomach.

He gave a sigh, rage subsiding into unhappiness. Above him the humped back of Bulbarrow Ridge lay like a sleeping giant beneath the sky. In the distance was the ringed hill-fort of Hambledon; the Iron Age earth walls made deep cuts into the side of the hill, its outline jagged and roughly hewn like a badly thrown pot. The woodlands were a series of dark green shadows on the hillsides and he stared at them, wondering what forgotten beasts lay hidden in their depths.

When he reached The Crown it was teeming with people. He recognised several of the faces by the bar. Jack felt himself redden as all the heads turned to stare, before returning to their conversations and their pints.

Now he was here, the urge to shout at Jack Basset and threaten worldly violence upon his household did not seem the best way forward. He found Basset in the gloom of the pub. He was a large, tall man and, despite the protruding belly, there was power in those shoulders. For a second Jack found himself wondering whether Basset would have a fine golfer's swing.

Jack had good bar presence; he was neither tall nor aggressive but with a forced smile he was the next to be served. He put money down on the bar. 'I'd like to buy all these gentlemen a drink.'

The elderly barman grunted—he wasn't used to this. 'Please yerself.'

'They won't want a drink?'

There was a shout of objection from Basset. 'What you sayin', Stan Burns? When 'ave we ever turned down free booze?'

There were snorts of laughter and poor Stan began topping up pint glasses along the bar. Basset clapped his arm around Jack and pulled him into a corner where a group of men were huddled. They were the same bunch who had trounced him at skittles. He half wondered whether he ought to buy a skittle set and make an alley in his barn, so that he could practise and then thrash them all.

Basset slapped Jack on the back, making him stagger forward. 'A toast. A toast to our new friend, Meester Jack Rose-in-bloom.'

The men raised their mugs and drank to the bottom. Jack tilted his and took a small sip, all the while watching the others.

'We seen what happened to your land and offers our condolin-ses,' Basset slurred through his pint of bitter.

Jack felt the hair on his neck prickle. 'So you admit it then? You ruined it all? All this spite from such a big man. I thought only women and girls did such things.' Angry again, he spluttered carelessly.

'Now, now, easy. Some might git offence at that,' warned Basset.

'We ent guilty. Twasn't us,' confided a man in a patched suit.

Jack snorted derisively.

'It was the—' started the man.

'Hush, Ed.' Basset placed a thick arm around Jack again. 'I think it is time to tell our new friend our secret,' Basset said in a stage whisper.

The men gathered closer as though they didn't want to be overheard as Curtis gave a loud hiccup and slid off his bar stool. Standing, he barely reached Jack's shoulder. Jabbing a finger at Basset he hissed, 'Don't ee start that. Leave the man alone. What's 'ee done to yoos?'

He was instantly hushed by the others and Basset leaned in so close that Jack could smell the beer on his breath. 'I is about to tell you that which 'as never been shared with no stranger. The . . .' he paused for dramatic effect, 'Legend. Of. The. Dorset. Woolly. Pig.'

Jack took another sip of beer and shuddered. He detested beer, especially bitter—much preferred whisky—but it was important to blend in, so he had better go along with the game. 'What is a Dorset woolly-pig?'

Basset gave an elusive smile. 'The Dorset woolly-pig is a beast found only in the heart of the Blackmore Vale. Only true-hearted Dorset men 'ave ever seen 'im and then only rarely. 'Ee is a majestic beast of unusual savagery. Could eat a small child if he wanted. 'Ee 'as the snout of a pig, tusks of a great wild boar an' the fleece of a ram an' can be killed only with an arrow of pure gold.'

Jack played along. 'And have any of you gentlemen seen one?'

Curtis had dozed off but he awoke with a start when Basset nudged him. The old man stared at Jack, taking in the spoilt suit, mud-streaked hair and tired blue eyes. He cleared his throat and spoke in a rumbling voice. 'I sawed him. Twas three score year ago. I were mindin' sheep on top of Bulbarrow. It was so 'ot that I thought I'd 'ave a little nip o' special cider like, before goin' home for my supper. I must have fallen asleep, cos of the sunshine, mind, and when I awoked—well, there 'ee was. The great beast were starin' at me. 'Is eyes blazed like a burnin' wheat field and 'is woolly coat glowed as if it were a snowy January. Never seen anything like it.'

Jack's eyes narrowed. 'What kind of tail did he have?'

Curtis stroked his stubble—it was years since someone had listened this intently to his story. He was fed up with the others and their teasing, but this new chap had respect. Rose-in-Bloom seemed like a bright fellow.

''Ee had the curled tail of a pig. And great curved tusks. Like those but on his chops.' Curtis pointed to the head of a ram with magnificent curly horns that was mounted above the bar.

'Weren't you afraid?'

Curtis furrowed his brow and took a sip of cider to help him think.

'No,' he said slowly. 'No. I don't remember that I was. 'Ee was like nothing else. I jist looked at 'im and 'ee looked at me. And then 'ee were gone.'

As he said 'gone', he blew on his fingertips and opened his hands to reveal his empty, if slightly grimy, palms. Jack turned to the rest of the men. 'Has anyone else seen him?'

They looked at each other.

'Old Tom Coffin did.'

'And Matthew Clinker.'

'Aye, but they's dead now. Long since—may God rist their souls.'

There was a general muttering among the fellows—a prayer or curse, Jack couldn't fathom.

'I is the only one left,' said Curtis. 'An' trouble is—you 'ave to really believe in 'im an' be pure of heart. That's why these noggerheads ent seen 'im.'

The others didn't seem to take offence at the insult.

'We is truly sorry for the mess in yer field. It's a nasty shame. But only a woolly-pig can make that much trouble. An' a big 'un at that,' said Basset.

'Aye. Was the woolly-pig what done it. No doubt at all.'

Jack glanced round the sombre faces. So, they were going to blame their barbarous savagery on a fairy tale. Well, he would go along with their ludicrous game. He surveyed the ram's head on the wall and, for a moment, he felt that the glassy orange eyes were staring back at him.

CHAPTER FOUR

When he arrived home Sadie was waiting on the doorstep, her expression compassionate. Jack was touched, and reached out and brushed her cheek with his fingertips. 'Thank you.'

Sadie flinched and stomped inside the house, 'Not your stupid course. I would have dug that up myself if I'd only thought of it. It's Elizabeth. She's not coming home.'

Jack went cold. He felt the last remnants of optimism trickle out of him.

'She telephoned to say that Alicia Smythe's father will take them both to Cambridge. She said it would be easier—save you the long journey.'

'It would have been no trouble.'

'I told her that. She was very insistent.'

Jack crumpled—the anticipation of Elizabeth's visit and then driving her to university had carried him through all the hours of hard labour. The trip was to have been an adventure for them both, but Mr Smythe had stolen it from him. Jack thought of Arnold Smythe: banker, six feet tall, handsome, blond moustache and a hearty handshake. He would get to take both girls to tea in Cambridge and walk with them through those ancient quadrangles. With a pang, Jack wondered whether Elizabeth had planned this all along. Was she so embarrassed of her father and his foreign voice and looks?

Yes, he could understand her preferring Mr Smythe as a stand-in father.

Jack was tormented by the idea that Elizabeth was mortified to be seen with him. He had thought that he was different from the others. He was the one chap in their circle who knew to buy marmalade from Fortnum's, and who realised that Lux was the only brand of soap flakes that would pass muster (and was not to be confused with a kind of smoked-salmon *beigel*). Yet, it seemed that his own daughter knew him to be a fraud and a foreigner. He must return to his list, and rehearse the subtleties of Englishness.

This had to be done properly, and so he found a concealed spot in the garden, carried out his list, the wireless, the papers and a bottle of whisky, set down a canvas chair and took up his studies once again.

It was over a month since he had last glanced at a newspaper (item 49: An Englishman studies *The Times* with careful attention) and the City and financial crisis seemed oddly distant. As he turned to headlines about the 'Chronic Housing Shortage', 'National Debt Crisis' and 'Expense of the Health Service', he realised that he was no longer a man who cared about such things.

He yawned, switched on the wireless and took a large slug of whisky. Number 71—An Englishman listens to the BBC—felt natural to him. He'd been desolate when his set was briefly confiscated during the war (they would have taken his bicycle, camera and car, too, if he'd had them). The local bobby had been under orders to remove wirelesses from all 'class B' enemy aliens. He had given Jack a ticket, and promised to return it the minute he was reclassified as a 'class C'. Six months later, the wireless was indeed returned unscathed by the same policeman, along with a bag of almond biscuits baked by his wife. The incident had remained in Jack's mind as a symbol of the vagaries of government legislation (not that he'd ever criticise), and the kindness of the ordinary Englishman.

The clipped tones of the announcer introduced John Betjeman and Jack nestled back into his deck chair, closing his eyes in anticipation. He remembered his programmes during the war—Betjeman, like the great Churchill himself, had reminded the public of what they were fighting to safeguard: a resolutely English way of life. Jack felt himself to be one of the broadcaster's select society of ardent Anglophiles, devoted to the preservation of everything great about this little island. Quietly, he promised himself trips to St Ives, Brownsea Island and the Isle of Man, and swore allegiance to Betjeman's quest to block the march of the prefabricated bungalows across England's green and pleasant land.

Betjeman's fascination with churches he could not share. However ancient, ivy-clad or pretty the weathered tombstones in the churchyard, churches remained a symbol of Jack's un-Englishness. He listened to today's talk on churches obediently but, unlike those on every other subject, he did not weep with sympathy. He fidgeted, trying to pay attention until finally, in an admission of abject failure, he switched off the wireless.

He folded up his chair, trapping his finger in the hinge, and his temper snapped in a torrent of German obscenities, '*Himmeldonnerwetter*', before he recovered enough to curse in English, 'Shit and skulduggery.'

He stormed into the house and lurked sullenly in his study, irked by his own shortcomings and worrying about Elizabeth. He wanted her to be pleased by her English father and here he was abandoning his studies. He must try harder. He pondered the other topics Betjeman had touched upon: seaside towns, the architecture of Bath, Victorian novelists. Now, that was a good one; he could cultivate his admiration of the novelists. Jack realised that being an English gentleman was a state of mind and, while it was too late for him to attend Eton or Cambridge, he must cultivate his mind with the reading of a gentleman nonetheless.

After all, was not Elizabeth reading English Literature at Cambridge? Jack flushed with joy at the prospect of discussing voluminous tomes with his daughter and impressing her with shrewd insights. He drew up a reading list according to the principles of Mr Betjeman, who was very specific about the importance of the Victorian novelists above all others. He listed them: Thackeray, Dickens, Mrs Gaskell, Thomas Hardy. Yes, he would begin with Hardy because he was the author of Wessex. The house conveniently contained, in seventeen dusty volumes, the complete works of Hardy.

He scanned the titles: *Tess of the D'Urbervilles*, *The Mayor of Casterbridge*, *Far From the Madding Crowd*. Then, one caught his eye: *Jude the Obscure*. 'I didn't know Hardy wrote about a Jew! *And* an obscure Jew.'

In an instant Jack went from feeling excluded by his Jewishness to glorious exultation. The Great Victorian Novelist of Dorset had written about an obscure Jew like him. 'This is me!'

He attempted to read *Jude* over breakfast the next morning but gave an unhappy sigh and pushed the book aside, miserably adding 'Victorian novelists' to 'English churches' on the list of things he could not properly appreciate, despite their having been recommended by Betjeman. He considered that at this rate, when Elizabeth finally returned, she would notice no difference in her father at all, and began to butter his toast with such aggression that it disintegrated into a mush of crumbs.

Jack rubbed his aching temples; he loved England but there would always be people who did not want him and who tore up his land pretending it was the work of a giant pig. It was not the first time, or even the second or third that such a thing had happened to Jack. His factory in the East End had been vandalised on countless occasions. It had occurred continually in the run-up to the war, as people did not like a Jew (and a German) making money in their city. The walls had been daubed with paint, bricks tossed through the windows and, every Monday morning, Jack had helped clean up the damage. It got better during the war; vandalism then was an unpatriotic act, especially on a parachute factory. In the vast, anonymous city such petty hatred was impersonal and he accepted that his position as a new arrival made him the perfect scapegoat. Here, among the dappled clouds and cooing wood pigeons, the hatred punctured his idyll and disturbed him.

He sat in the kitchen miserably chewing his toast and slurping a cup of black tea. Sadie bustled around, scrubbing pots and muttering under her breath, until finally she fixed Jack with a hard stare and demanded, 'When are you going to start work again on that wretched course?'

'It's broken. *Kaput*. Finished.'

'So, you must fix it.'

While Jack's obsession irked her, Sadie discovered that this miserable man, who refused to shave and dripped from study to deck chair like a cat caught in a rain shower, was even more bothersome.

'How can I?' Jack gazed steadily at his wife. 'I don't want to rebuild because I cannot bear them to destroy it again.'

There was a dull bump as the post hit the doormat, and he went into the hall to collect it. He recognised the handwriting of Fielding on a white envelope, and opened it with a sinking feeling. The letter from the factory manager contained the usual requests for new machinery. The looms were near-obsolete (everyone wanted tufted and pile carpets nowadays). Fielding was pressing him for a decision, but Jack had no room in his mind for such things and guiltily slipped the letter to the bottom of the pile.

Then he noticed something most unusual. Among the usual bills there was a cream envelope made from expensive watermarked paper. He took it into his study—such a pretty piece had to be opened with the silver letter knife. He fumbled in the drawer and pulled out the shining blade, carefully slicing open the envelope to remove a smart cream 'At Home' card.

Piddle Hall

Dear Mr and Mrs Rosenblum,

My wife and I are hosting a little gathering for drinks on Friday. We would be delighted if you both could join us. We look forward to welcoming you to our delightful piece of country. Be so kind as to come at seven.

Regards,

Sir William Waegbert

Jack's hand shook with excitement. This was a letter from a real English knight, not a mere gentleman but an actual member of the aristocracy.

He marvelled over the invitation; did it mean that he was finally about to be accepted as an Englishman? He wished again that Elizabeth was there—then he could have shown her the card and she would realise he was a proper gentleman. Still trembling, he reread the invitation, admiring Sir William Waegbert's close hand and genteel loops. He must strive to make his own handwriting more gentlemanlike. Clearly, his was far too easy to read—one must work to decipher the words of a real gentleman. Jack tried the name aloud, 'Sir William Waegbert'. Much smarter than 'Arnold Smythe', and a fragment of Jack's jealousy of that man vanished.

There was one slight difficulty with the otherwise delightful invitation—Sadie was also invited. Jack realised it would take all of his persuasive powers to get Sadie to agree to accompany him; the party was on Friday night and she never went out on *Shabbat*. She would not even pick flowers, for the law states that nothing shall be broken into two halves on the Sabbath. Jack ventured into her territory to plead his case and found her kneeling among the flowerbeds cutting the dead heads off cala lilies.

Without a word, he squatted down beside her and handed her the invitation. Putting down her shears, she read it in silence and passed it back to him, leaving a bright yellow smear of pollen across the pristine surface. He winced but uttered no reproach. 'Well, will you come?'

'It is on *Shabbat*,' she said by way of answer.

'Ah, well, no, not quite.' He had been thinking about this on his way into the garden. 'It states an arrival time of seven o'clock and dusk is not until eight thirty. And, therefore,' he gave a little cough, 'by my calculations *Shabbat* will not be in until nine thirty.' He actually had no idea when dusk was, but he spoke with such assurance that Sadie did not question him. She simply picked up her scissors and continued to snip away at the flowers, placing the fallen heads into a bucket.

'Please,' said Jack, 'please.'

Sadie did not seem to hear him.

There was the sound of knocking on wood, like a tiny, powerful fist against a massive door. Above them a brilliant woodpecker, white and red, hammered with his beak against the bark of a tree.

'I like his outfit,' said Jack, pointing to the bird's brilliant plumage. 'He's a dapper little fellow. And an excellent percussionist. I'm sure with the right contacts, he could perform at the Wigmore Hall.'

Sadie's face brightened until she was almost smiling. She rocked back onto her heels and glanced up at her husband.

'Very well, I'll come,' she said and carried on snipping.

JACK WAITED FOR FRIDAY like a small child waiting for sweets to come off ration. When it finally arrived, he dressed himself meticulously in his Henry Poole suit and carefully selected a lilac silk tie.

Sadie was waiting for him by the car. He was relieved to see that she was very respectably dressed in a pale olive frock, with a white cardigan and matching shoes. She clutched a bouquet of garden flowers. 'We mustn't go empty-handed. We're not *schnorrers.*'

Jack smiled, pleased by her good thinking. The evening was warm and Jack had peeled the top off the car. He gripped the steering wheel tightly to hide the slight trembling of his hands. If only he had finished *Jude* then he would have something suitable to talk about.

Jack had memorised the map and was confident of the route but, in case of misadventure, he had allowed an extra half-hour for the fifteen-minute journey. They arrived in fourteen minutes, shortly before half past six. The invitation strictly stated seven o'clock, so he pulled the car to the side of the road and they waited in silence. In front of them were the gates to the house. They were elaborate wrought iron and supported by two towering gateposts, each one topped with a screeching, weather-beaten eagle. A wall, seven feet high, ran from the gates all around the estate, so they could not see what lay beyond. A narrow driveway led away and immediately wound tightly to the right, heightening Jack's sense of expectation.

At six fifty-five Jack started the engine and they drove slowly along the gravel drive. It was lined on both sides with towering bushes of rhododendron and ancient magnolia trees. The land sloped down to a lake and parkland dotted with spreading oaks, and Jack noticed a herd of deer grazing in the distance. In a minute they reached the house, a handsome stone manor, the front façade covered with tumbling wisteria, the evening sun glinting off the windows. They drew up to the main steps, whereupon an elderly man in a grey suit slowly descended. Jack leaned out of the car, trying to shake his hand, 'Delighted to make your acquaintance, Sir William Waegbert.'

The man gave an almost imperceptible bow, 'Thank you for the compliment, sir, but I am not the illustrious Sir William. My name is Symonds. The butler.'

Jack flushed with embarrassment—his first blunder and he'd not even parked the car.

'Would you be good enough to leave the automobile by the stables, sir?' said Symonds, pointing to a low building around the corner.

Jack steered the Jaguar to the smart stables at the back of the house. They had recently been reroofed with black slate tiles and the wooden walls were newly painted duck-egg blue. Two horses wearing nosebags gazed nonchalantly at the newcomers. Jack parked alongside a line of other vehicles in the far corner of the yard. There was an Austin, its bodywork battered by what appeared to be hoofprints, the wheel arches eaten away by rust. Next to it was a Rolls-Royce, but it was a model dating to before the Great War—its exhaust was missing and there were holes in the leather upholstery where tufts of horsehair stuffing poked through.

They walked back through the yard, Sadie stumbling on the cobbles. Having taken to walking barefoot over the grass, it felt strange to her to be wearing shoes at all. Symonds was waiting for them at the front of the house.

'May I show you into the rose garden? Sir William and Lady Waegbert will join you shortly, Mr Rosenblum, Mrs Rosenblum.'

They followed the servant into the formal garden at the front of the manor. Jack still found the English manner of speaking most peculiar. They continually spoke in rhetorical questions—'would you?', 'may I?'—when what they truly meant was park here, wait there. They liked to give you the illusion of choice, when really there was none.

'Will you be quite comfortable here, sir? May I bring you a drink, sir?'

'Yes. Thank you. A whisky.'

'With soda or ice?'

Jack paused, wondering which was the correct answer. Which would give him away as a phoney and a foreigner? 'A dash of soda, please,' he said, trying to sound casual.

Symonds gave a tiny bow and Jack relaxed—he had chosen wisely. He must remember that. No more neat whisky: whisky and soda.

'And for madam?'

Now it was Sadie's turn to look stricken. Nice, middle-class Jewish ladies didn't drink. She had once tried a sip of gin and tonic and had rather liked it but Mrs Ezekiel had seen her, and she had told everyone at *schul* on Saturday that Mrs Sadie Rosenblum liked a gin. Gin, Sadie decided, was a danger to one's reputation. Jack, however, knew better; only yesterday on the wireless Mr Betjeman had described how gin and tonic with a slice of lemon was one of the great joys of an English summer's evening. Betjeman explained that it evoked the old days of Empire, and noted wryly that even English ladies enjoyed a little 'G and T' among friends.

'A gin and tonic, with a slice of lemon if you've got it,' said Jack firmly.

Sadie opened her mouth to speak and then shut it again meekly, smoothing an imaginary crease in her dress. She was still clutching the flowers.

'May I take these, madam?' asked Symonds.

Sadie hesitated. 'They're for Lady Waegbert.'

'The man doesn't think they're for him,' said Jack irritably.

She allowed Symonds to take them from her, watching as he vanished into the house. They were left standing on a lawn, neatly clipped and rolled into smart stripes. Pyramids of yew were planted in straight lines across the grass and loomed above them. She wondered whether it was usual to be left hanging about in the garden, waiting for one's host.

In fact it was not. Lady Waegbert liked to greet her guests personally—however unwelcome. She could not see why her husband had invited such ludicrous people to her house—just because people were odd it was no guarantee of their being entertaining. And now, they had arrived so outrageously early that no one was ready to receive them.

'Surely *everybody* knows that seven o'clock means seven thirty,' she complained bitterly to her husband.

'Darling, they are foreign, *Germans*.'

The Rosenblums, in the shadow of the yew pyramids, were oblivious to their violation of social niceties. Nor did Jack realise that they had been invited solely for entertainment value. The other ten guests had all been asked to stay for dinner, and Jack was intended to provide the pre-dinner cabaret. Sir William was not a cruel man but he enjoyed the bizarre or ridiculous, and he had heard the strange tales about the Jew of Bulbarrow, who was trying to build a golf course in forty days and forty nights with only a shovel. This was too good an opportunity to forgo, so risking the wrath of his wife he had dispatched a rash invitation.

Sir William, growing tired of his lady's complaints, went out into the garden to meet his guests. He rubbed his hands in delight as he saw them standing together. They were better than he had hoped—she was merely old-fashioned-looking, a plump woman in a faded frock—but he was very promising. To Sir William's eye, Jack's treasured Henry Poole suit was garish and the lilac tie lurid. The fact he wore a suit at all for what was merely drinks was also highly entertaining. A gentleman wears a jacket and tie for drinks and a suit only for dinner. Sir William, however, was the model of perfect breeding and, as he shook their hands with profuse apologies at his own lateness, Jack and Sadie suspected nothing.

The remainder of the guests arrived punctually late at seven thirty. They appeared on the lawn with Lady Waegbert just as Jack was attempting to steer the conversation to the first four pages of *Jude the Obscure*.

'*Jude*, eh. No, never read it. Tried *Tess* once. Heard she was quite a gal, a real corker,' confided Sir William with a wink.

Jack made a silent promise to read *Tess* next. The combination of whisky, sunshine and nerves was making him feel a trifle faint. The men drew around Sir William, eager to meet the promised Jew, like a crowd gathering for a circus act. He introduced Jack to several smart-looking gentlemen, including Mr Henry Hoare, a man of about sixty in a patched flannel jacket and heavy horn-rimmed spectacles.

'So, do tell us about this golf course, then. The only reason we've come to this ghastly pile at all is to hear about it,' said Mr Hoare.

Jack looked worried—he recognised this to be an instance of English wit but did not like it and hoped Sir William had not taken offence. The baronet, however, remained unperturbed and smiled encouragingly.

'Well, the course will be the greatest in the whole South-West. It is the most important labour of my life,' Jack declared.

He looked at the expectant faces and took another sip of whisky. It was nearly a week since he had stopped construction but he found his enthusiasm for the project returning in great waves as the alcohol warmed his throat.

'I am following the example of Mr Bobby Jones—in my view the greatest player and designer of courses in the whole of golfing history.'

'Jones is a gentleman, too. A true amateur, none of your *sporting professionals*,' added a man in dull green tweed.

Sir William gestured to Symonds, who scuttled over to take a whispered order, reappearing, as if by magic, moments later with another glass of whisky and soda for Jack. As he sipped, Jack felt warm and pleasant, and became expansive.

'There is no one quite like Mr Jones. He truly is a remarkable man. His is a gift straight from Himself,' said Jack, in a voice quivering with emotion, as he raised his eyes to the cloudless sky. 'Augusta is paradise on earth. There are flowers in red and yellow and gold and blue and silver lakes with multi-coloured fish. The sand in the hazards is so fine it feels like ground silk. Parrots roost in the trees and help to find any lost balls. When the light is just so, the grass looks blue, and you believe you are playing a round in the sky.'

'Jones, you say?' Sir William asked, caught off-guard by Jack's description.

'Yes, Mr Bobby Jones, Sir William Waegbert.'

'Oh, please, please, just plain old Sir William.'

Jack grinned, gratified at the perceived honour of calling a knight by his abbreviated title. He was relaxing with Sir William's kindness and the growing effects of the liquor.

'And you say that your course will be the greatest?' demanded the man in mossy tweed.

'Yes. For the very first time in the illustrious annals of the sport, I am combining the two great models. Not only am I using the inspiration of Mr Jones's brilliance at Augusta, but also the triumph of Tom Morris and the revered wisdom of Mr Robert Hunter. I shall create a links course on the side of Bulbarrow. It will be a perfect copy of St Andrews.'

'Links are by the sea are they not?'

Jack sighed and plunged his hands into his pockets. 'Yes. I may have to dam the Stour. We shall see.'

Sir William beamed. His eccentric guest was proving most amusing and he rewarded him with a benevolent smile.

His confidence growing, Jack risked an observation. He phrased it as a question, in the English way. 'Waegbert is a German name, is it not?'

'Good God, no! It does sound Germanic—I'll give you that. Bit like Wagner or what-not. No. It's Anglo-Saxon. There have been Waegberts at Piddle Hall since 973.'

Jack nodded, overwhelmed by this sense of history. He fully expected that Noah had had two Waegberts on his ark.

Sir William was usually quite happy to talk about the grand ancestry of the Waegberts at some length, but he wanted to hear more about the golf course. 'When will it be finished?'

Jack frowned—he did not want to admit to the catastrophe, as that would show weakness. And that was not British. Rule 64: An Englishman keeps his head in a crisis *no matter what*.

'In time for her Royal Highness Queen Elizabeth's coronation. I shall hold a competition to celebrate the momentous occasion.'

'Excellent. Can anyone play?' enquired Mr Hoare, rubbing his palms.

Jack considered this—he had not resolved the finer details of his plan yet. 'No. I believe I shall restrict play to members only.'

'Jolly good. Well, we shall have to become members then, Sir William, eh?' Mr Hoare gave his friend a nudge.

'If we are accepted, Henry. We do not know the conditions of membership,' said Sir William seriously, with an appeal to Jack.

It was one of the proudest moments of Jack's life. A knight, a real live knight (with stables, horses, a Rolls-Royce and a family going back to 973) was asking him, Jack Rosenblum, if he could have membership of his golf club. His cheeks turned pink. He wished Elizabeth could hear this. Some men at this point may have demurred, wanting to slight a man who was part of a class that had universally rejected his own applications to a hundred golf clubs, but Jack was not such a man. Friendship was too precious a commodity to refuse in this sad world. A tear trickling down his cheek, he clasped first Sir William's hand and then Mr Hoare's.

'Of course. Of course. I would be delighted,' he said, his voice cracking with emotion. 'You will be my very first members. I shall have your names put up on the board in the clubhouse in gold letters.'

The two men were taken aback by the emotional outburst of the slight man. Sir William did not know whether to laugh or take offence at the notion of the Waegbert name being sullied on a board in a common clubhouse.

Across the lawn Lady Waegbert tried to get a better look at Jack's shoes, which, as she rightly suspected, were made of suede. This was really too much for Lady Waegbert, who viewed suede as a symptom of moral degeneracy. That her husband had encouraged these people into her house was quite unbearable. Sadie's skirt length, cut at the knee instead of midcalf in the New Look, merely revealed her to be a woman without style; at least she had let her hair go grey, instead of indulging in one of those dreadful blue rinses that the middle classes all seemed so wild about. It was nearly eight thirty and time for dinner. These people should have gone by now. The middle classes or Jews—they were all the same to her—never knew when to leave. It was most unpleasant. If they did not go soon, she would be forced to ask them to stay, and that would be frightful.

'Do stay and dine. My wife would be simply delighted,' said Sir William.

Jack glanced over to Lady Waegbert—it pained him to refuse such an elegant woman but he had promised Sadie that they would return home before the start of the Sabbath. So it was with genuine regret that he politely declined Sir William's invitation.

They made their farewells and left the party on the lawn.

As they walked back to their car, Jack felt easier than he had all summer; he was tired of being the Jew and the Yid—it was lonely and dangerous. He had tried again and again to impress the need for assimilation upon Sadie. 'We need to become part of them. If *they* come back'—by which, Sadie knew, Jack meant the Nazis—'whom do you think they will give up first? Us! Us! You and me! Only if we become like them can we hide among them. We must not be poppies in the wheat field.'

'I need the lavatory,' announced Sadie.

'Can't you wait?'

'No.'

He frowned. 'You ask. I'll wait here.'

Sadie scowled, and he knew that the tentative truce of the evening was over. He watched as slowly she went up the front steps of the house and disappeared into the murk of the house.

Ten minutes later she had not reappeared and, growing restless, he ventured into the manor. It was still, except for the wafts of laughter coming from the terrace where Sir William and his guests were now being served supper. Jack stood in a large, oak-panelled hallway hung with a dozen or more portraits; austere men and women glared at him from their frames, their hands resting on the heads of supercilious-looking dogs.

A minute later he began to fidget; where on earth was his wife? A door was ajar and he pushed it open to reveal a large, panelled room with a vaulted ceiling stained black with smoke and age. Dangling from one wall was a tapestry of a hunting scene; silken men rode on horseback, accompanied by a pack of woven hounds all chasing an animal into a forest.

On the opposite wall was a massive stone fireplace, the mantelpiece hewn from a single slab of rock and supported by two elaborately carved sidepieces teeming with magical creatures. There was a unicorn, a ho-ho bird and a pair of griffins whose clawed feet made the bottom of the pillars. Beneath the mantelpiece was engraved a forest of twisting branches, some in leaf, others in bud. Peeking from between two branches Jack noticed another beast. It had the head of a pig and carved tusks that were entwined with the magnificent horns sprouting from its skull. On its back grew a woolly fleece which, even chiselled in stone, appeared to him soft and white.

'It's a Dorset woolly-pig' said a voice behind him.

Jack turned to see the elderly servant standing in the doorway.

'He is a myth of this county,' explained Symonds. 'The older people in these parts still believe in him.'

'Do you?'

Symonds only smiled. 'There he is again.' He pointed to the tapestry and Jack realised that the poor creature pursued by the hunters was none other than the woolly-pig. In the medieval work the brute was as large as the horses the men rode and its eyes were woven with crimson fury.

'Why would you harm such a magnificent beast?'

The servant gave a sad smile. 'They were said to be plentiful during ancient times and could grant the pure-hearted their true wish. But then the knights hunted them for sport and the woolly-pigs grew angry and refused to grant any more wishes, pure of heart or not. They hid in the depths of the oldest forests and gored any who tried to find them. As the trees were hacked down and the woodlands became smaller and smaller, they died of sorrow. A few are said still to wander the forests bleating of their sadness.'

Jack thought of his wife, filled with nothing but sorrow, wandering the earth, remembering the dead and happier times.

LATER THAT NIGHT, Jack surveyed the wreckage of the opening hole and wished it really were the woolly-pig who was to blame. Postwar Europe was a drab place, and a mysterious creature surviving from antiquity to create a little havoc in the modern world was an appealing thought. A wild pig destroys hedges and golf courses out of rage that they are in his way—Jack couldn't imagine that a pig gave a fig whether the land belonged to a Yid, a Kraut or the Queen of England. For the first time in months, he thought of Berlin. He saw the city with a towering barbed-wire fence splitting it in two and imagined a woolly-pig crashing through the night, tearing up the wire as if it were a bramble hedge. Yes, the world would be much improved with a dash of magic.

He sighed and loosened the knot in his tie. With a vast yawn that made his jaw crack, Jack slumped upon the heap of molehills. His eyes were slowly adjusting to the darkness, and he watched the tiny undulations on the surface of the pond; it was never still and never the same. There was something remarkable about the way the water trickled out of the ground that seemed as mystical as any seam of gold or imagined mine filled with precious gems. He bent down and washed his hands in the cold, fresh water.

On the banks of the stream, he noticed several prints in the mud. He studied them carefully. Several looked like rabbit and he recognised a bigger set that he guessed was deer. Then he saw something else. Embedded in the earth were two neat trotterprints. They were ten times the size of an average pig and could belong only to a giant boar.

The adrenalin surged in Jack's veins and then, half a second later, it vanished. Of course there are prints, he reasoned. They wanted to blame the mess on a woolly-pig so they would place the evidence; they must consider him a simpleton to think he would believe such childish stories. There were no bootprints that he could make out in the darkness but he supposed Basset and the rest must have waded up the stream to disguise their tracks. 'I wish I could catch the sneaky bastards,' he muttered, and that gave him an idea. Traps. They were pretending that it was the woolly-pig, and he was pretending to believe them. So, he must go a stage further and lay traps all over his land, purportedly to catch the beast. He would place them everywhere as he rebuilt the course and then, if they tried to destroy it again, the traps would imprison the real culprits!

Under the whispering leaves, he flopped onto his back and lit one of his rare cigarettes. Catching the perpetrator would be satisfying, but the most important thing was to protect the course. Time was ticking away and to have any hope of a game on Coronation Day, he needed to make progress and he simply did not have the time to dig man traps. What was required was a deterrent. Basset and the others needed to *believe* he had traps. Then, he could quietly restore his poor butchered fairway in peace.

AT NINE O'CLOCK on Saturday night, Jack decided to go to the pub. He had not seen Sadie all day, only heard her singing to herself, and he slipped out so as not to disturb her.

The doors of The Crown had been thrown open and people had spilled into the garden. Jack Basset perched on a wooden bar stool like a great heron on a pebble. He drank his pint with ardent concentration and, on seeing the other Jack, greeted him like an old friend.

'Evenin', Mister Rose-in-Bloom. Found any woolly-pigs yet?'

Jack shook his head. 'Not yet. But I will.'

The men looked up in surprise. Jack was pleased. '*Good*,' he thought, '*let them all believe I am a crazy Jew-Bastard*.' He cleared his throat and met Basset's cornflower-blue eyes. 'I am going to capture the woolly-pig.'

There were suppressed muffles of laughter and a small gaggle of men gathered around Jack.

'How?'

'Traps, Mr Basset.'

'Wot sort, mind?'

'I have a few designs . . . what would you recommend?'

Basset liked to be consulted. He took a drink. 'He's too big for a badger trap. 'Ee'd break it with his tusks. What d'you use for bait?'

'A pit and leaves. Tis only way. Mush-rooms are best for bait. Nothin' but mush-rooms,' Curtis piped up, elbowing his way to the front of the group. He seemed about to speak again, then changed his mind.

Jack reached into a pocket and pulled out his hand-drawn map of Bulbarrow, marked with a series of red crosses that looked a little like grave markers. 'These denote the position of the traps,' he explained, waving the map in front of them quickly and then hiding it from view—he didn't want them to go searching for a trap that wasn't really there. 'I believe I shall stick with my own designs. They are more dastardly.'

He slid a hand into his jacket and produced another sheet, decorated with a diagram of the supposed contraption to catch the beast. A large cage was concealed in the earth and just beneath the ground was a set of vicious serrated jaws, ready to snap if the wire was touched. 'It's a hair trigger. A mere snuffle from the creature and *wham!*' He clapped his hands shut and surveyed the curious faces, wondering if he had pushed it too far. 'I don't mean it any harm. I only want to catch one. Put Pursebury on the map.'

'Tis already on the map, Mister Rose-in-Bloom,' said Basset.

Jack knew they were laughing at him—all of them except Curtis, who was staring at him with an odd expression. The old man was the smallest grown person he had ever seen; he was the size of a child but wizened and thin. He'd entered into that part of old age where it becomes impossible to fathom the person's precise number of years. Even Curtis wasn't sure. The baptismal records for the last century had been removed to the county office and he had no other way of checking; he guessed that he was somewhere between eighty-five and one hundred and thirteen. His face was creased with more lines than usual because he was worried.

'Yer really want to see the beast?' He spoke quietly, almost in a whisper.

'Yes,' answered Jack. The word came out before he was aware that he had spoken and, at that very moment, it was true—he did want to see a woolly-pig. It would mean that the men in the village had not ruined his hopes and had not lied, and that the world was not such a grey place.

Curtis shook his head, 'Won't find 'im with traps. Yer believe in 'im. That's summat but that's not t' whole apple cake. Come.' He beckoned with a stubby finger and pointed to the door of the pub.

In a minute they were on the road outside. The old man raced along on his short legs so that soon Jack was panting to keep up.

'Where are we going?'

'Your house. Pick up t' car.'

'Why do we need the car?'

'We is goin' to Hambledon. It's three miles and I ent walkin'.'

They reached the Jaguar, which stood gleaming, reflections of clouds moving across the bonnet. Curtis ran a hand lovingly along the shining paintwork. 'Ent she a beauty.'

Jack tiptoed inside to get the keys, wondering if the expedition was actually a ruse so that Curtis could go for a drive in the car. Not that he minded—he would have quite happily taken him, although probably not at half-past eleven at night for a trip up an ancient hill-fort.

He started the engine and peeled back the hood. Curtis climbed onto the rear and perched upon the curved boot, his feet resting on the front seat.

'Are you sure that you're quite comfortable?' asked Jack.

'Yup. I likes to feel the wind in my ears.'

They drove along the roads without seeing another soul. At the foot of Hambledon Jack slowed when Curtis gestured for him to park.

'Stop 'ere.' Curtis nimbly hopped out. 'We is goin' up there.'

He pointed to a narrow, tree-lined track that fell away into the darkness, and led the way at his usual rapid pace. Jack kept tripping over tree roots as he struggled to keep up. Trees grew on either side of the pathway, their canopies spreading and meeting in the middle like the fingertips of two hands touching. The green-tinged tunnel was sunk ten feet below the trees.

'Why is the track in a ditch?'

The old farmer gave a snort. 'Ent no ditch. This path is two thousand years old. These is the wearin's and tearin's of all those feet an' carts.'

They emerged from the tree tunnel and reached a gate, which Curtis vaulted. He then began to climb the sharp incline as Jack scrambled after him. Jack must have been at least thirty, maybe as many as fifty years younger than Curtis but there was no question as to who was the more agile. The hill was sheer, the slope even steeper than that of Bulbarrow, and into the side were cut deep, circular grooves many yards deep. Jack gasped for breath and he had a stitch. He felt like he had been climbing for an hour, though it couldn't have been much more than twenty minutes.

'Righty, stop 'ere. We is at top.'

Jack flopped down and closed his eyes. 'You climb so fast. You're not even out of breath,' he gasped, his own coming in rasps. He heard the sound of a bottle being unscrewed and then a flask was thrust into his hand.

'Drink,' commanded Curtis.

Jack took a deep glug; it was like drinking apples set on fire. It made him cough and want more at the same time. Curtis snatched away the bottle.

'That's enuff. Yoos ent used to it yet,' he explained, not unkindly.

'What is it?' Jack's eyes were watering.

'Jist a special cider brew. Apples and thingy,' he answered cryptically.

Jack lay on his back and felt the stuff warming him all the way down to his toes. He closed his eyes and was suddenly very sleepy.

'Are you ready, Mister Rose-in-Bloom?'

'Ready for what? Are we waiting for a woolly-pig?'

'Nope. Not tonight. Tisn't t' right time. And yoos isn't ready.'

Usually Jack would have objected to this: he was perfectly ready and this was exactly the right time. But, whether it was the heat, his drowsiness or the effect of the special brew cider, he was happy just to lie there and listen.

'Open yer eyes.'

Summoning all his energy, Jack opened them. The moon was high and bright and the stars were so clear that he felt he could reach out and touch them. Jack knew that he was gazing across time to stare at light that had travelled billions of years to reach Dorset. He stared at one hovering star that emitted a pale green glow. It danced in the air, floating above his head before disappearing. Then he saw that there were scores of them—not in the sky but near to the ground—tiny, pale green lights that flickered and floated as they swayed upon long grass stems. He reached out to touch one and it twinkled just out of reach before drifting away.

'W-what are they?' he stammered.

'Worms. Glow-worms. Jitterbugs. What we are seein' is a jitterbug orgy.'

'A what?'

'An orgy. Them is the female ones that glow to attract a mate. Tis jitterbug mating season.'

Curtis handed him the flask and he took another swig. The green lights began to blur and sway like a miniature firework display.

'In years gone by, hignorant people thought these is fairies,' Curtis scoffed.

Jack could see why. There were no wings on the glow-worms, but he could hear a soft batting, like the whirring of a clock. Curtis pointed with a stubby finger. 'Only males 'as wings an' they doesn't usually glow. They is right lazy bastards.'

Jack stared at another pale light nestled in the prickly palm of a thistle. As he watched, the light dimmed. He blinked and it was dark.

'Ah,' said Curtis, 'once she's mated, she puts out 'er light. She lays her eggs, she fades and then she dies.'

Through his alcohol haze, Jack wondered whether the male jitterbug was performing a dance of grief for his dying mate.

Jack and Curtis lay in a large ditch, which formed part of a series of Iron Age trenches designed to defend the fort against marauders. Each dugout had grass walls nearly fifteen feet high and Jack marvelled at their construction.

'How did they dig these ditches?'

Curtis took a swig of cider. 'Antler horns and wooden pickaxes.'

The place felt ancient; they were lying in a fort nearly 2,000 years old. Jack could hear the whispers of the earth and knew that here was deep time. The woolly-pig was part of that world, a remnant from another, older age.

Curtis heaved himself onto his elbows; his battered hat perched at an odd angle and a clump of burrs was stuck to his shirt.

''Ave you 'eard the legend of Arthur and the Round Table?'

'Yes. Don't they think it was at Cadbury Castle now and not Glastonbury? I read it in *The Times*.'

Curtis spat on the ground in disgust. 'Those Somerset folks. They nickered our 'istory. Tisn't Glastonbury nor Cadbury Castle neither. Tis Stourcastle. Dorset. That's where the Saxon King were—old Wessex.'

Jack rubbed his eyes and tried to focus. 'King Arthur was in Stourcastle?'

Curtis nodded. 'Aye. But 'ee wasn't called Arthur, mind. 'Ee were Albert.'

Jack closed his eyes and dreamed of King Albert. He was a mighty woolly-pig with tusks of gold, and when he opened his mouth a stream of green lights poured out and filled the sky with stars.

CHAPTER FIVE

Jack woke the next morning in his own bed, with no memory of getting home. He felt as if he had been asleep for a hundred years and was now roused from an enchanted slumber. Putting on his leather slippers he wandered downstairs and went outside to check the car. It was parked neatly in the driveway, paintwork unscathed. Then he noticed the driver's seat: it was pulled all the way forward as though a child had been driving.

Despite the drinking and the late night, he was filled with more exuberance than he had experienced for over a week. As he changed out of his pyjamas and into his work clothes, he decided that now it seemed appropriate he hadn't yet played a hole. It was right and proper that the first hole should be played on the morning of the coronation. That was to be the greatest British Event since the end of the war and would mark the beginning of a new era: the Illustrious Elizabethan Age.

He collected his molehill contraption from the barn and wheeled it along the rugged track down to the field. For the first time in nearly a fortnight he was not disheartened by the monumental task before him. Humming 'Land of Hope and Glory', he loaded up the first bucket of water and tugged on the pulley. He hoped the threat of traps would be enough to ward off saboteurs but, just in case, he had bought several from a gamekeeper. They lay bundled in a sack by the pond, since he could not quite bring himself to set them. The bucket of water wavered and the first molehill was hoisted up; he swung the contraption and dumped the heap of earth into a ditch. One down. He turned to the next molehill, but Curtis was sitting on it.

''Ow has the woolly-pig hunt bin farin'?' he asked Jack.

Jack winced; he did not like lying to the old man but could not confess that when confronted with daylight and a clear head, he did not believe in the woolly-pig. Saying nothing, he pointed towards the sack by the pond. Curtis picked it up and tipped out the traps so that they lay in the long grass, a heap of glistening metal jaws. He gave a shudder.

'I was told they were humane,' Jack said, sounding unconvinced.

'Aye, very humane,' said Curtis. He lifted his trouser leg and showed an angry red scar all the way round his ankle, where the skin was mashed up like flesh-coloured marble.

'*Zum Kuckuck!* That was from a trap?'

'It is. Found a pheasant—weren't poachin', it jist flew into a sack I 'appened to be 'oldin' like and then *crack*.' He smacked his hands together to show the movement of the trap shutting on his leg. 'I were lucky them trap didn't take my leg off.'

Jack was appalled. 'I don't want to kill them. It. The woolly-pig. I don't even want to hurt it. I want to trap it.'

'Well then, don't use them things. Evil buggers,' said Curtis bitterly.

Jack paused. Much as he did not wish to maim another man, he also did not want his course destroyed. He thought for a moment. 'I want to see a woolly-pig, but I don't really need to catch one.'

To his surprise the old man jumped up and began to shake his hand.

'Tis good news. No noggerhead can never catch one of them nanyhow. Yer might be from forin lands but yer gets the beast and 'is thinkin'.'

Jack held onto Curtis's arm, 'I won't use any traps. But perhaps you could tell Jack Basset that I am using these things to catch the woolly-pig. Then he will leave me alone.'

'Yer wants me to tell folk that yoos is an evil and nasty bastard not to be buggered with?'

This was not quite how Jack would have put it. 'Yes.'

Curtis tapped his nose confidentially. He helped himself to one of the shovels and, with a neat thwack, sliced off part of a molehill, lifted it and dumped it into a ditch.

Jack watched, amazed at the tiny old man's strength.

'Righty ho?'

Jack agreed and turned back to his machine. The ground was hard and they could dig only a few inches at a time, scratching away layers of dried dirt. Curtis dug twice as fast, but it was still very slow. The wind was strong and whipped the mud flecks into their faces, so that soon Jack began to tire. He felt a hand on his shoulder.

'Here, 'ave a nip,' said Curtis, drawing the flask from beneath his jacket.

Too tired to argue, Jack took a small sip. Instantly, he felt fiery strength burn along his veins. He seized the bucket and poured the contents over a patch of cleared green. Then he filled up another and another, until, in half an hour, he had tipped fifty loads of water over the brown grass.

EVERY MORNING for the next month Jack found the older man waiting for him. Working side by side, they heaved the last of the molehills off the spoilt green and into the ditches, smoothed the hillocks as best they could and carefully watered the withering grass. Curtis had the strength of a much younger man and together their progress was swift. Jack enjoyed the companionship, although he tried to avoid the topic of the woolly-pig, worried that the only reason the old man had bestowed his friendship was in the mistaken belief that Jack shared his faith in the creature.

Jack was usually too exhausted to find his way up to bed and for the third time in a week, fell asleep in his chair in the study. He was vaguely aware that he'd not seen his wife for several days. He heard her in the garden and noticed that the larder remained stocked for him to pillage for meals, but he was too busy with his golf course to worry himself with her. He felt a little uncomfortable about the neglect of Sadie but—as with all things that were unpleasant to him—he tried to think about something else.

SADIE THREW THE BEDCOVERS off, too hot to sleep, and realised she was alone yet again. She reached for the bedside clock: midnight. With a yawn she climbed out of bed, put on her dressing gown and tiptoed downstairs, unwilling to disturb the darkness. She retrieved her box from the kitchen dresser and sat down at the table. The moon was so strong that she didn't need any other light in order to see the picture of her brother. Emil smiled up at her from the curled, brown print. His was a face that would never grow old.

Next she picked out a white linen towel, stiff with starch and with an embroidered rose in the right-hand corner. It was neatly ironed into folds and wrapped in tissue paper. Mutti had given it to her when she left for England, insistent that a lady always needed a clean towel. Sadie never could bring herself to use it and it had remained pristine in the neat folds of her mother's ironing, still smelling of lavender soap and starch.

Sadie sighed and wondered whether she ought go back to bed, but knew she wouldn't be able to sleep. Murmurs were coming from Jack in the study—he was so tired from digging, from trying to become one of *them*. She went to the open window and gazed out across the night-time garden; it was growing bare now. Come the winter, she would tuck up the plants in armfuls of straw and wait for spring. The flora would return, undamaged by death and a sojourn underneath the earth. She inhaled deeply, and breathed in the cinnamon perfume of her favourite rose.

Sadie returned to the table and removed the last item from the box: Mutti's cookery book. Opening the worn pages, she noticed cooking spatters from long ago and imagined Mutti bustling in her Berlin kitchen, pans bubbling. Her mother had been a great cook and had ordered her life entirely round meals: breakfast, lunch, tea and supper. Things were either before breakfast, after lunch or between tea and supper. A time like three o'clock meant nothing—it was instead that space shortly before apple strudel and freshly made peppermint tea. Then there were the recipes themselves that fitted into neat categories: the conventional ones like 'dishes so that you can tell it is summer', 'meals for times that are cold and wintry', but there were others like 'biscuits for when one is sad', or 'buns for heartbreak'.

Sadie stroked the battered volume. The spine was coming away and the cloth cover hung loose. She glanced through the index, neatly inscribed in her mother's curling hand and smudged with mixtures from a hundred mealtimes, until she found the one she wanted: 'Baumtorte'—part of a category called 'cakes to help you remember'. Unlike Jack, Sadie preferred German to English because she liked the literal meanings of the words. 'Baumtorte' was a good word, meaning tree (*Baum*) cake (*Torte*), since it is made of layers like the rings of a tree. Sadie, like her mother and grandmother before her, had baked a Baumtorte whenever she needed to remember. She'd baked a cake after Jack kissed her for the first time that December night, another when he proposed (in a noisy train carriage on the way back from Frankfurt, so that she couldn't hear him and he had had to repeat himself), another when they were stripped of German citizenship and one more after Elizabeth was born. She made the last one with Mutti on the day they received their exit visas. They'd asked for six (Jack, Sadie, Elizabeth, Mutti, Papa and Emil) but there were only three. They hadn't cried—they'd baked a Baumtorte.

Sadie read out the recipe, 'Whip together a batter made of eggs, the right amount of sugar, sufficient flour and the perfect quantity of vanilla.'

The quantities were never more precise than that—she had to know the correct amount in her heart before she began. 'Oil a tin and heat up the grill, spread a thin layer over the bottom of the pan and grill until it is done.'

More and more layers would be ladled on and then grilled until the side of the cake looked like the rings of a tree. Sadie glanced at the clock on the kitchen wall—nearly one o'clock. There was time to bake another Baumtorte. She would bake a layer for everyone she needed to remember.

She went into her larder and counted out three dozen eggs. She had started to keep chickens as their shit was good for her beloved plants.

'A vanilla pod.'

She had just one and it had travelled with her all the way from London. She had bought it in the days before the war, had kept it all those years and, upon giving it a sniff, happily discovered that it had not lost its scent. A mountain of butter given to her by Curtis rested under a tea cloth; she did not ask whose cows it had come from. There was a sack of flour from the mill and a large enamel flask filled with milk, which would be useful if she needed to loosen the batter—all she wanted now was a basin big enough to mix the ingredients. None of the kitchen pots was sufficiently large and then she remembered the tin bath that was in the house when they first arrived; she would give that a good wash.

Still clad in her pink floral dressing gown, she began to whip up the batter. She did not weigh any of the ingredients, trusting her instincts. She mixed them in the echoing bath; at first she used a wooden spoon but finding it too small, she carefully washed her feet with soap, dried them on a clean towel, hitched up her dressing gown and climbed into the bath to stir the batter with her feet. She found the widest cake tins in the cupboard and put layer after layer of the oozing mixture under the grill, and when each tin was completely full, carefully removed the cake inside and smothered it in a layer of sharp lemon icing. Each cake was placed on top of another and then another until, when dawn came, there was a cake towering many feet high with a thousand layers of rings; every layer holding a memory.

Sadie fell asleep on the kitchen floor, still holding her spatula. When Jack rose half an hour later, he did not see her lying hidden in the shadow of the kitchen range. Helping himself to a glass of milk, he disappeared into the field to carry on digging.

While Sadie slept, the smell from her baking drifted out into the lane where several women from the village were walking. Jack was not the only person in the village counting down the days until the coronation; the women who had formed a Coronation Committee were busy pinning posters to trees along the lane when the scent of baking overwhelmed them. It had a strange smell, not merely cake mix or sugar, but the fragrance of unbearable sadness.

'We should ask Mrs Rose-in-Bloom to join us,' murmured Lavender.

The women followed the smell along the driveway leading to Chantry Orchard, like several middle-aged Gretels searching for the gingerbread house in the wood. The kitchen door was open, and they saw Sadie stretched out on the floor, still fast asleep. On the table above her stood the Baumtorte. It was as tall as Curtis, and the women stared, uncertain.

'Should we wake her?' asked Myrtle Hinton, a portly woman with greying hair, tied back with a scrap of yellow ribbon.

'Well, we can't be leaving her sleeping 'ere. Poor soul will catch cold,' tutted Lavender.

Mrs Hinton gently shook Sadie awake, 'Mrs Rose-in-Bloom?'

Sadie opened her eyes, alarmed to find her kitchen full of women.

'We are the Coronation Committee. Would you join us for a meetin' in the village hall?' asked Lavender primly.

Bleary eyed, Sadie nodded. 'I must dress.'

'No, dear. It's only us. Put on a housecoat.'

Sadie shrugged and buttoned up her dressing gown. She glanced at the Baumtorte—it was a thing of magnificence; she had used the juice of three precious lemons for the icing. A cake like this should be shared.

'Help me carry the Baumtorte,' she said.

AS THOUGH PART of a stately parade, the women filed to the village hall. Several others were already waiting for them, busily setting out chairs and handing round sheets of paper, but they all paused to watch the procession of the Baumtorte. It was placed on a table at the front of the hall while they discussed the day's business. Lavender chaired the meeting.

'Now, I've been requestin' suggestions about how to mark the coronation. I have had only a few, and only one that I am able to read in polite company. It is from Mr Jack Rose-in-Bloom. He wishes to propose a game of golf be played at 'is new course in honour of Her Majesty.'

Sadie looked up in astonishment; Jack had not confided his plans to her. Lavender appealed to her but Sadie shook her head, embarrassed.

'I know nothing at all. My husband tells me nothing.'

Lavender smiled—Mr Basset never told her anything, either. It seemed men were all the same—English or foreign. 'Well, if there are no objections, perhaps Mrs Rose-in-Bloom would be good enough to tell Mr Rose-in-Bloom that the Coronation Committee approves the idea.'

It was time for tea and Sadie went to her Baumtorte. The table it rested on was bowing under its weight. She cut slices for each of them with a huge knife—the thinnest that she could manage. The women ate, and it was the most remarkable cake that they had ever tasted. It was sweet and perfectly moist with a hint of lemon but, as her mouth filled with deliciousness, each woman was overwhelmed with sadness. Each tasted Sadie's memories, her loss and unhappiness, and while they ate, Sadie was, for once, not alone in her sorrow.

JACK WAS TOO PREOCCUPIED with his golf course to notice the unusual behaviour of his wife. Parading towering cakes through the village while wearing slippers was not blending in, but Jack was driven by his obsession and was therefore spared the bother of being embarrassed.

Jack and Curtis had restored the opening hole on the golf course; it was more battered than before and the grass still needed time to recover, but the damage had been repaired. Jack checked the post each day for a letter from Bobby Jones, eager to hear from his hero. There was none, just an ever-growing pile of anxious letters from Fielding at the factory.

> Dear Mr Rosenblum,
>
> I have nothing good to report. I'm very concerned about the looms. The machines are getting old and finicky. Soon one is going to break down beyond repair. The emergency funds are almost empty—please wire more cash. When are you coming back?
>
> Yours truly,
> George Fielding

Jack did not reply. He was reluctant to wire money to the factory—he needed every farthing for the course. Surely the looms would be fine for another season or two? They could sausage through. He felt a pang of guilt at his neglect of the business, but he had room for nothing in his mind except the golf course, and the possibility of a letter from Bobby Jones.

He knew it was too soon to expect a reply from America but still he hoped. That afternoon he confided his disappointment to Curtis.

'He might be a busy man, but I am in serious want of advice.'

Curtis paused for a long moment, leaning on his spade.

'Tis my 'pinon that tis time to write him another letter. Tis always the danger that Mister Jones were not in receipt of yer first epistle. Besides 'ee might like gitting letters.'

Jack stopped digging and gazed at his friend—this was something he had not considered. He always told his employees that persistence and determination were the most important rules in business and yet here he was, hesitating, when he ought to be tenacious.

'You're quite right, my friend. Very right, indeed. I'll write to Mr Jones tonight and then, I think, I'll write each week to tell him of our progress.'

Curtis smiled, revealing a set of surprisingly strong white teeth. 'Tis an excellent idea. Only good will come of it.'

That evening the friends tripped into Jack's study to write to Bobby Jones. There was no sign of Sadie, but she had left out an apple strudel, which Curtis munched as he helped Jack compose the letter.

Dear Mr Jones,

I am not sure if you received my last letter, so I thought I had better write you another one. I am building a golf course in Dorsetshire with the assistance of my good friend Mr—

Here Jack paused, realising he knew Curtis's first name only. 'Mr Curtis? Is that correct?'

'Aye, well, Curtis Butterworth,' the old man replied, through a mouthful of apple and pastry.

—Curtis Butterworth. We have completed the first hole, using Tom Morris's map of St Andrews as a model. We do not have the sea to make this a true links course but we do have the advantage of an excellent pond. I had hoped to have the benefit of your advice before proceeding much further, but my course must be finished in time for Her Majesty Queen Elizabeth's coronation on June the 2nd next year, so I am trusting that you have not taken offence that I was forced to commence without the benefit of your inspirational wisdom. Here is a drawing of our first hole. It is a little hilly, but I hope that will merely add to the challenge. We are proceeding at a pace—

'Tell 'im 'bout the trouble with the woolly-pig,' interrupted Curtis.

'Are you sure? I want to seem professional.'

'Tis an unusual difficulty, but twould be a lie not ta even mention it,' said Curtis, directing a hard stare at his friend.

Jack sighed. He could not risk the old man discovering that he did not believe in the woolly-pig—let Bobby Jones think him crazy, it could not be helped.

—and despite tremendous difficulties with a vicious woolly-pig that wreaked havoc and destruction, we are now doing well. Please write back very soon with your recommendations, even though you are a very busy man.

With regards,

Your humble servant, Jack M. Rosenblum

Jack folded up the letter and put it into its envelope, already addressed and waiting. He poured a whisky and settled back into his chair.

The two men sat for a moment sharing a contented silence. 'If only we had more men to help. We are three times as fast with the two of us,' remarked Jack.

'Aye. Tis a right shame.'

THE NEXT DAY, Jack went down to the field at daybreak. The air was cool and the first of the blackberries were covered in thick dew. He glanced about for Curtis but, unable to see him, decided to start alone. As he reached for his spade, he heard a voice.

'Mister Rose-in-Bloom, come, come!'

Curtis stood on top of a rise pointing towards the road. Jack scrambled up beside him and squinted into the distance. Coming up the lane through the early-morning mist was a giant combine harvester. It was bright red, with glinting teeth like a colossal mechanical dragon.

''Eard 'ee was comin',' said Curtis sagely, ''Ee's from America.'

Jack frowned. 'It won't fit through the gate. Too narrow.'

'Nope. But that don' matter—they'll rip out all them 'edges. All of 'em, so they can plough the whole side of Bulbarrow.'

Jack shuddered; it sounded barbaric. Then he noticed Curtis staring at him.

'You isn't thinking. Use yer noggin,' said Curtis, tapping his head with a grubby forefinger. ''Alf the tennants in Pursebury will be put out to grass.'

Jack sighed. It was a sad world when men could be put out of work by a machine. Yet, such was civilisation and progress.

'Where will they be?'

'Pub.'

It was early in the morning, yet The Crown was already full. There was a hum of agitation as men in work clothes gathered at the bar. No one looked up when Jack came in, but then he no longer looked different from them, dressed as he was in mud-spattered trousers and a stained sunhat.

Curtis clambered up on a bench by the bar, and called for quiet. Then he announced: 'Mister Rose-in-Bloom wishes ter offer any of yer put out by the arrival of the beast from h'America gainful employment.'

The men turned to look at Jack with tired faces.

'He'll 'ave to join the queue.'

Jack noticed two suited men seated by the bar. A pair of cheap trilby hats rested on the counter, and the men were not drinking. One of the men, a fellow with sandy blond hair and a wisp of a moustache, turned and gave him a thin smile.

'Good morning. I represent Wilson's Housing Corporation. If you are in need of a job, I'll take you on at five pound a week for general building.'

Jack frowned. 'What are you building?'

'Bungalows. We have permission for forty in the water meadows at the edge of the village. Want them up sharpish. Hence the generous wages.'

Jack's frown deepened into a scowl. He did not like this young man, nor did he like bungalows being built on ancient water meadows. He knew people needed somewhere to live, but he could not understand why they did not rebuild the ones that had tumbled down at the bottom of the lane.

'Five pounds?'

'Yes. But *you*'d have to prove you can work a full day. No offence, but you're not in the first flush of youth. And since you're not English, we'll put you on probation for a few weeks. Just to make sure you don't slack.'

His companion sneered. 'Lazy foreign bastards. All the same. Just remember. We. Won. The. Bleeding. War.'

Jack reddened with rage; he had not been this angry since they mutilated his golf course. Curtis moved to stand beside him, lips drawn back into a silent snarl.

'Well,' said Jack, trying to control the furious tremor in his voice, 'if this man will pay you five pounds, I'll pay you five pounds and ten shillings.'

The farmers in the bar looked at Jack in surprise. Hunched in the corner, Jack Basset stiffened. The blond man in the suit was taken aback by the unexpected competition. Wordlessly, his companion wrote a note and slid it across the bar. The fair-haired man glanced at it.

'We'll pay five pounds, twelve and sixpence.'

Jack swallowed. He did not know how on earth he was going to pay them this much, but he had to win.

'Five pounds and fifteen shillings,' he whispered.

The first man stood up. His companion was desperate to up their offer but he put a hand on his arm to restrain him; they had no authorisation to go higher. He snatched his hat from the bar, and addressed the room.

'Fine. But remember you'll have to work for a Kraut. When he goes broke and you come crawling back to us, we'll pay you only four pound a week and not a farthing more.'

They left, crashing the heavy wooden door behind them. Jack sat down in shock, scarcely aware that Basset was buying him a drink. He trembled as he considered the consequences of what he had just done—he would need to take out a loan to cover the cost of the wages. And use the carpet factory as collateral—he couldn't possibly wire money to Fielding now. He grasped the glass in front of him and drained the contents. 'I'm a *Dumpfbeutel*. Emotion is always bad in these situations.'

'What?' Basset motioned for Stan to pour Jack another drink.

Jack drank and as the liquid warmed his gullet, he gained confidence. He took Basset's hand and shook it warmly.

'It is a good day. You're very right,' forgetting that Basset had not actually spoken. 'With all you splendid fellows, I'll actually finish the golf course. For sure I will. For sure.'

TWENTY MEN had been put out of work by the great machine. Jack learned from Curtis that Basset and the others were only tenant farmers, permitted to work the land in return for hefty rents.

'All the little farms is bein' gobbled up by the big 'uns. Them giant machines can plough whole o' the buggerin' hill in a single day.'

Jack agreed sadly. 'It's a new era, Curtis. Britain and her hedgerows must make way for progress. I don't like it. I don't like it all.'

Jack wrote a careful list of the men he was hiring and added them to the payroll of the London factory. It was cripplingly expensive and Fielding was irate, penning Jack a furious letter, which he scanned guiltily and shoved in the back of his desk. The bank agreed to a loan, but he had made none of the investments he ought to have over the past few months and the quarterly profit was down. He was concerned, more for those who relied on him for their wages than for himself, but he signed the loan papers nonetheless, sent them back to the bank and tried not to think of them again.

The rate of progress on the course rapidly increased. These countrymen had worked on the land all their lives, and understood the quirks of soil and scrub. Basset informed Jack that the marsh at the bottom of the course could not be drained—the soil was clay and there was nowhere for the water to run. For the first time Jack had an expert on-site; Jack Basset's brother, Mike, had actually played a round of golf while on holiday in Margate. Jack and Curtis listened to him attentively. He advised them that a stream cutting the green in two was highly unusual. He also persuaded Jack that nine holes would be ample—'Players who wants eighteen 'oles can jist go round again, like.' Jack agreed to this solution with relief.

Yet, something had shifted within Jack and he no longer dreamed of demolishing Bulbarrow Hill in order to mirror the Old Course. The slow beauty of the country had crept up on him, and he wanted his course to be defined by the rise and fall of the landscape. Jack listened to the men, and learned to listen to the landscape, until it seemed to whisper the direction they should go, and the positions of the holes. He did not want to dig too deep and disturb the ridges of the hill; it was best to go around them, and let the edges of the mounds and ditches define the rough.

While the men laboured in the afternoon, Jack drew Robert Hunter's *The Links* from his pocket and sat down. Two hours later he called them together.

'Before Robert Hunter, very little had been written on the art of golf course construction,' he told them. 'It is a very elusive subject. I would like to share with you, my friends, the rules I have devised from his methods:

'Number one: Select well-drained, slightly rolling land.

'Two. Avoid clay soil.

'Three. Do not go into hilly country at any cost.

'Four. Shun also that country broken by streams and ponds. They are most objectionable.'

At the end of this little speech Jack coughed. 'I am aware that the land here on Bulbarrow does not quite conform to Mr Hunter's recommendations, but sometimes the most beautiful things are created in the most unusual places. Think of a pearl found in the belly of a fish.'

'Aye. An' I once found a nest o' blue robin eggs in middle of a dung heap,' added Curtis. 'Lovely they wis.'

Jack grinned. 'You thieved the words from my mouth, my friend.'

The men listened to Jack, intrigued by his passion and energy. Here was a man who disobeyed the rules he himself devised; his golf course was in the worst possible site and had every known drawback. Yet, he believed in it and had absolute faith in their ability to produce a modern-day miracle.

AT THE END of three weeks two holes were complete and Jack and Curtis sat on a bank at the top of the hill, surveying the landscape. Jack was worried; every Friday he paid the men but he did not pay Curtis. They had been working on the course for so long that he did not know how to broach the topic.

'My friend, I do not wish to insult you. But I would like to compensate you for your hard labours.'

Curtis wrinkled his face in displeasure. 'Friends durst pay.'

'Friends also do not take advantage of one another. That is not friendship.'

The old man continued to scowl but Jack knew he was right.

'Let me give you a gift then. Choose something of mine, anything at all.'

Curtis shrugged; he was not hungry or cold and therefore was quite content. Putting an end to the discussion, he got to his feet and started to walk down the hill. Jack followed. They passed the two neat flags of the completed holes and reached the marshes at the bottom of the valley when suddenly, with a flash of light, a ball of fire hovered above the bog.

'A will-o'-the-wisp!' Curtis gasped in excitement.

The ball of light drifted in the air, weaving between the reeds. The water looked as though it had caught fire, and the flaming reflection trembled on the surface. Jack watched in awe as the wisp singed the tall reeds and he thought of Moses and the burning bush. Then, it flickered, and was gone.

The two men retreated to Jack's study, where he set about his weekly letter to Bobby Jones. It was an unusual predicament for Jack, to write letters without knowing if they would ever be read or answered, but it was also strangely liberating, and he found he confided all his fears to the legendary golfer.

Dear Mr Jones,

It has been a long week. I confess that I am worried we will never finish in time. Winter will come and turn the fairways to mud and we will be able to dig no more in the fierce frosts. I am also running out of money. This is a secret. Even my wife does not know how little we have left. I must finish by spring.

This evening I saw a will-o'-the-wisp. I knew it to be nothing but a ball of phosphorescent light but I wanted it to be magical, or mystical. Wouldn't you like to live in such a world, Mr Jones? A world of magic instead of concrete and bungalows?

Regards,

Your humble servant, Jack M. Rosenblum

Curtis sat quietly while his friend wrote. He waited until Jack sealed up the letter, and had placed it carefully inside his jacket pocket.

'I can have anything?' Curtis was referring to their earlier conversation.

'Yes, of course.'

'I'd like 'im,' said Curtis, pointing to Jack's gold watch lying discarded on the bookcase. Jack had taken it off the first week he arrived in the West Country and had not used it since. He pulled out the old timepiece and pressed it into his friend's hands.

'Please. I would be honoured. It is yours.'

Reverently, Curtis slipped it into his pocket. ''S excellent. Won't be late no more. Time-keepin's very important.'

SADIE WAS BUSY COOKING her way through the recipes in her mother's book, and the house became filled with scents of her childhood. Sometimes, she took her baking down to the village hall for the women to eat. Each time she ventured into the wood-panelled room, Lavender Basset tried to persuade her to stay: 'Come an' have a nice cup o' tea wi' us, Mrs Rose-in-Bloom. Her Majesty's Coronation Committee could do with an outstanding baker like yerself.'

Sadie would set down her tray of almond macaroons or cherry and coconut pyramids and shake her head, avoiding the eyes of the smiling women.

'Very kind, Mrs Basset. Much obligated, I'm sure. But I can't stay.'

The Coronation Committee met only on a Wednesday, so the rest of the time Sadie left cakes, biscuits and loaves of honey-coloured bread out on the table in the kitchen and forgot about them.

Jack and Curtis, passing through the kitchen on their way to the study, presumed that the offerings laid out were for them and always ate hungrily. Jack did not realise that this new burst of cooking was another act of remembrance and took the vanilla crescents, the sand cakes and *Pfefferkuchen* as tokens of a well-concealed affection. He suspected that in some wordless way she understood he was in a spot of bother—being nearly out of money—and that these sweetmeats were a silent symbol of companionship.

'WHAT DAY IS IT?' Sadie asked Jack one day.

Jack peered at the date. Why was she asking him? The woman had eyes of her own. 'Twenty-second of September.'

'*Nein, du Mistkerl*. In the Hebrew calendar.'

He was late—Curtis and the men would be waiting for him and he did not like them to start without him, but Sadie was not to be dissuaded. She pulled out a tattered Hebrew almanac and flicked through the pages.

'I've forgotten. How could I forget?' Sadie raised her eyes to the heavens and muttered an apologetic prayer.

Jack continued to look at her blankly.

'It's Rosh Hashanah, Jewish New Year, the Day of Judgment, the Day of Remembrance . . .' she snapped.

'Yes? And what does it have to do with me?'

Two pink spots appeared on Sadie's cheeks and her eyes flashed with anger. 'Go. Go to your fields and your new friends, then. I'll say Kaddish for the dead. I am sure they'll understand.'

Jack stood up sharply. On the table was the fruit of Sadie's sleepless night: a plaited loaf of challah, studded with currants, sprinkled with cinnamon and warm from the oven, with a jar of honey resting beside it. He studied the bread, and considered his wife. One. She scolded him. Two. She was stubborn and indifferent to happiness. Three. She baked for him during the night, making all the treats and sweets he recalled from their brief months in Berlin—they were happy then, ignorant of what was to come. Jack picked up the challah, tore off a piece, dipped it in the honey and popped it into his mouth. He chewed pensively, took another bite and then another. In ten minutes the entire loaf was gone.

'I'll sit with you,' he informed Sadie with a puff of resignation.

Sadie's lips flickered into an almost-smile. She liked the ritual of Rosh Hashanah and liked to think of all the other Jews, busy with their own recollections; it was a rite of shared sorrow, *The Day of Remembrance*. Most days, she thought about *before* alone, in silence, but this was a whole day dedicated to remembering. She thought back to the final Rosh Hashanah in Berlin, the last with her family. Back then, she had not known that soon she would be saying Kaddish for them. She had been late to synagogue, arriving in a flushed hurry of joy, and apologised to the disapproving women as she squeezed her way through to Mutti, who scolded her for her tardiness, that day of all days. Sadie had claimed it was because she couldn't find her coat but it was a lie. She was late because her new husband had persuaded her back to bed to make love. She had not known it then, but that day, Elizabeth had begun to grow in her belly. Perhaps that was why she had become so unhappy, because she conceived on the Day of Remembrance?

The dead that she was too busy to remember grew alongside the child in her womb and, long after she gave birth to her daughter, wormed their way into her consciousness, insisting that she say Kaddish for them every day.

Once she had confided this thought to Jack and he had become angry: 'Life, that is the most precious thing! Life. It takes the place of death. Wedding has precedent over funeral. I choose joy over pointless sorrow.'

The shofar-blowing was Sadie's favourite part of New Year: the eerie note of the hollow ram's horn calling through the centuries. It sang of the symmetry of time and was one constant in an ever-changing world.

Back in their kitchen, Sadie looked up. 'Let us go and cast away our sins into the river.'

Jack perked up; he had abandoned any thoughts of working with the others on the third hole today. While he was dubious about the prospect of ditching his sins into a body of water, at least it meant going outside and quietly checking on the course.

Together, they walked down towards the pond at the bottom of the large field. It was a damp, misty morning, and the air smelled moist and earthy. Jack peered up towards the third hole where he could see several men digging and Basset leading two great cart-horses, hitched to a pair of stone rollers, down the steep slope.

He was reassured that they were managing spectacularly without him. A few more weeks at this pace and Jack would have another hole done. There was a chance, if the winter was not a cold one, that he would have all nine holes completed by spring. He uttered a little prayer to heaven: 'Listen, please don't be offended that I don't really believe in you. But, just in case, I would be most obliged if you could make this winter a mild one. I'd very much like to finish my course. Otherwise, there is a very good chance that I'm finished—*fertig*. And, if you really are there, I am sure you don't want that. There is enough unhappiness.'

He was not sure whether this was the right tone for a prayer—it had been quite a while since he'd last addressed God. He thought as a concession that perhaps he ought to cast off a few sins. If the slate was clean, God might be more inclined to favour his request.

Jack helped Sadie climb over the stream to reach the pond.

'Are you sure there are fish?' she asked. 'A fish's need for water symbolises the Jew's need for God and, as a fish's eyes never close, so His watchful eyes never cease.'

'Quite certain.'

'Then empty your pockets over the water.'

'Really?'

'Yes. And feel contrite.'

Obediently, Jack emptied his pockets. There was a piece of string, a receipt for straw and a bag of humbugs. He tried his best to be contrite, but it was hard because he always tried not to dwell on regrets, although he did regret the humbugs that were slowly sinking to the bottom of the pond—they were still on ration. He watched Sadie, her eyes closed and her lips moving in prayer, as she turned her pockets inside out and flapped them over the water.

'Hey, there's nothing in them. They're already empty,' he objected.

She opened her eyes and stared at him. 'Of course. I don't want actually to throw anything away. You cast away your sins *metaphorically*.'

'Oh.'

'Say Kaddish with me, Jack.'

He sighed, but he supposed, as the English would say—in for a penny in for a pound. Round his neck he wore his battered sunhat on a string—it would have to do this time for a yarmulke. He placed it on his head and started to sing, his voice mingling with the cries of the birds and the falling rain. Yet, there was a strange sort of harmony to the sound.

'*Yis'ga'dal v'yis'kadash sh'may ra'bbo, b'olmo dee'vro chir'usay v'yamlich malchu'say.*'

'*The dead are held in our memories; we carry them with us through life; one generation to the next, so that our people live on in the minds of our daughters and our sons.*'

Jack sang the names of those they had lost while Sadie pictured their faces and, for a few brief moments, saw them on the water before her.

Then there was another sound: the rich long note of a horn.

It rose up through the mist and echoed against the hillside.

Sadie clutched Jack's arm. 'A miracle! Thank God! It's a miracle!'

Tears ran down her cheeks. God had sensed her loneliness and here, in the wilderness, He had found them and sent her the sound of the shofar. They were alone no more.

For a moment the mist cleared. Jack moved to the edge of the pond and stared towards the horizon. There was the sound of barking and pounding hooves, and then a pack of hounds raced into the meadow below, closely pursued by red-coated riders on thundering horses. The horn cried out again and the hunt disappeared back into the haze. In the distance the note rang out for a final cry, and then silence.

Sadie was sobbing now. Jack passed her a rather grubby handkerchief and noisily she blew her nose.

'It's a miracle, Jack, isn't it?'

He reached for her hand, 'Yes, darling, a miracle.'

CHAPTER SIX

Autumn slid into winter. The leaves fell to the ground, blew into piles, turned crisp in the frost and rotted away. Jack dug out extra blankets from one of the boxes and they huddled under them at night, hostilities suspended as they clutched one another for warmth.

The ground froze one night and did not thaw the next day or the day after that. There was nothing to do on the golf course, except wait. Jack paced his fairways, admiring the five chequered flags, each one frozen midflutter. He now realised his course was rather testing (though he was sure it would be much admired by expert players). From each tee the respective hole was invisible, hidden behind the slope of the valley or masked by scrub. The greens were uneven and steep. The rough was a mixture of wild grass, dog-wood and gorse and a ball entering it would be lost for ever. Despite these drawbacks, the view across the countryside was vast and open, and Jack enjoyed feeling his smallness against the great expanse of earth and sky.

November eased into December, bringing the thickest frost of the year, and Elizabeth. Jack was filled with joy at the prospect of seeing his daughter.

Elizabeth knew she was her parents' connection to the alien, English world and was not above exploiting their ignorance. Most girls went home for the weekends and when at college they were strictly supervised, but she was expert at circumventing rules and avoiding home visits. Even so, she was deeply curious about her parents' strange journey into rural England. They had never really done anything interesting before: her father made lists and sold carpets, while her mother gossiped and wept when she thought no one was listening.

Sadie cleaned the house and made up the little bedroom under the eaves for her daughter, filling it with all her old childish things. There was the school desk, scratched with ten years of homework, and volumes of Dickens and Shakespeare. In a packing crate she discovered a stash of bedtime stories that she used to read to Elizabeth. Jack didn't want his daughter speaking German—it was the first and second rule on his list. But Sadie had wanted Elizabeth to hear a little of her language and so read *auf Deutsch* the pranks of Till Eulenspiegel and the macabre adventures of Struwwelpeter. She wasn't sure the little girl understood every word, but Sadie wanted her to know that *Deutsch* was also a language of stories and magic. The child promised her mother that she wouldn't tell Papa about the German storybooks. Sadie cherished their secret. As a girl Elizabeth shared everything with Jack—they were forever laughing at some joke or disappearing off to cafés without inviting her—but those forbidden bedtime books belonged solely to Sadie and Elizabeth. During those minutes, she could be *Mutti* at last.

LEAVING HIS WIFE FUSSING, Jack left early to collect his daughter from the station. There was a deep frost, the leaves coated with white and the grass hidden beneath an arctic layer. The Jaguar was parked inside the barn, covered in a horse blanket, but even so it took him a good ten minutes to fire it up.

Elizabeth was waiting on the platform, stamping her feet to keep warm, her hands buried in a pair of red woollen mittens. For a moment Jack didn't recognise the young woman in the smart caramel-coloured coat; every last trace of the schoolgirl had vanished. He was the same: small, balding, bespectacled and smiling. Elizabeth ran to him and planted a kiss on both cheeks. He received her affections awkwardly and bashed her nose with his, not expecting the second kiss.

'Let me look at you, Daddy.'

She stood, hands on hips and gazed at her father, who shifted from foot to foot under her scrutiny.

'You're thinner. And browner. Your hat's on funny.'

She reached out and fiddled with Jack's trilby for a moment, took a step back and shrugged. 'It never sits right,' she sighed.

Jack felt himself flush like a schoolboy and walked briskly behind the porter with the luggage to hide his mortification. All his hats were purchased from Lock of St James's, the best hatter in London, and yet they never sat right. He wished she wouldn't always draw attention to it; he was trying as hard as he could and he hated it when he shamed her.

They caught up with the porter, who loaded the bags into the trunk as Jack slipped him sixpence. Elizabeth rolled her eyes in mock exasperation.

'Oh, Daddy, when will you learn not to tip so much?' she said when the porter was out of earshot.

Jack winced; she'd told him that before—people sneer at you, if you tip too much.

'But it's nice to be generous. It's Christmas.'

'Only Americans tip that much. The English are mean.'

'Thank you for coming, love, it means so much to your mother.'

She smiled at him, the quick, bright smile that made dimples form in either cheek and she looked happy. Jack relaxed. '*It's all right*,' he thought. '*It's all right. I'm a klutz but love has brought her back to me*.'

Elizabeth wiped away the condensation from the window and watched the English landscape unfold—the trailing rivers iced over and the frost hanging in the rushes on the river banks. She barely heard her father chattering as she stared in amazement at this new world. Smoke puffed from every chimney and the cottage doors were festooned with wreaths of holly.

Sadie was waiting anxiously at home; she'd been checking the window for signs of them at least an hour too soon. Then, in a crackling of gravel, they were there. Elizabeth flung open the heavy front door and embraced her mother, burying her face in the familiar soft cheek and neck. Sadie always smelled softly of Chanel No. 5, and there it was, but mixed in with it was the heady scent of damp earth and wood smoke.

'*Mein lieber Schatz! Mein Kind*,' exclaimed Sadie, her face buried in her daughter's hair. She covered her face with exuberant kisses, and ushered her into the kitchen. Sadie felt a tug of joy at the prospect of feeding her little one, and sat at the table to watch her eat, hiding her smile behind her hand as Elizabeth demolished half a dozen vanilla crescents. And yet, she felt that Elizabeth was different—a young woman now, beginning her own life and exuding confidence. In contrast, Sadie felt middle-aged and tired. She remembered when she was young like Elizabeth, with thick hair and smooth skin. Elizabeth looked English: she had dark, Jewish hair but bright green eyes and the creamy pink complexion of the classic English rose, and now she spoke with the self-assurance of a student of one of The Universities. No one would guess that she was conceived in a tiny apartment in a Jewish suburb of Berlin. She listened to Elizabeth chatter about new friends, the tutors she liked and the ones she didn't, new words peppering her conversation. Sadie didn't understand but did not like to expose her ignorance to this smart new daughter who drank tea with milk.

JACK MARCHED INTO the kitchen, a scarf wrapped around his face, his eyebrows covered in frost. Elizabeth smiled—he looked like a peasant from a storybook *shetetl* in his layers and woollen cap.

'Come see my course.'

Swaddled in her coat and woollen scarves, Elizabeth followed Jack outside. The winter's moon hung low in the sky. The frost was so thick that it shone white, bathing the countryside in a ghostly light. It was a good night for stories, so Jack told his daughter all about the legend of the woolly-pig. She listened in silence as their feet crunched through ice on the iron ground. It coated the spindly trunks and dangled from the branches like silver streamers. In this strange other world of glittering white, Jack could almost believe in the tale of the woolly-pig.

'Perhaps there really is such a creature. It might be a wild boar. After all, they still have them in France,' conceded Elizabeth.

Jack was delighted; he loved it when she believed his stories.

'Come, you must see the first hole. I dug it all myself.'

SADIE SAT ALONE in the kitchen. They had been gone for an hour and she was starting to worry. There was a chicken roasting slowly in the oven as a special treat and soon it would go dry. She felt like crying. It was always the same—they would go off and forget all about her. Every Sunday in London, Jack had taken Elizabeth to the Lyons Corner House in the high street. Not once had they thought to ask her.

Nearly an hour later, Jack and Elizabeth flung open the kitchen door and erupted into the room in a flurry of noise, treading wet bootprints across Sadie's clean floor.

'Well, sit down. It's all ready.'

Sadie lit the candles on the kitchen table and the room basked in the flickering glow. As Jack and Elizabeth sat, Sadie reflected on how she had wanted everything to be perfect tonight but instead, she was simmering with resentment. Elizabeth reached for the mashed potatoes and took a huge spoonful as Sadie watched. She remembered when she used to be able to eat like Elizabeth. She flung the vegetable dish on the table. For a moment rage bubbled inside her. It wasn't fair—Elizabeth had everything: youth, the possibility of happiness, and Jack. Sadie watched as Jack gazed at his daughter, his eyes wet with love. Once, long ago, he'd looked at her like that. She slammed down the gravy jug.

'The chicken's dry. Everything's spoilt.'

LATER THAT NIGHT Jack waited until his women had gone to bed, enjoying the few moments of stillness and watching the embers dying in the grate. He would like a fireplace like Sir William's, decorated with mythical beasts and woolly-pigs. A little magic was a good thing.

He hadn't seen Curtis in several days. It was as though when the cold came he disappeared into hibernation, like the badgers and ferrets. Jack yawned—it was getting late. He stretched luxuriously and ambled into the kitchen to fetch a glass of milk before bed. He sloshed it into a mug and as he wondered whether or not to warm it, he noticed Elizabeth's exam results lying on the table. Picking them up, smiling in anticipation—he presumed she had done well or she would not have left them out for him to peruse. Then he noticed the name on the envelope. This was not *his* Elizabeth—this was another girl. Elizabeth Margaret Rose.

Jack placed the letter back on the table. This was what he wanted: an English daughter with an English name. Now she had the first names of a queen and a princess, and the last name of the most English of all flowers.

She was not even the first to change her name, he reasoned. At nine days old she was named Ilse after her great-grandmother by the rabbi at the synagogue in Berlin. In spite of his wife's railings, Jack had insisted that Ilse had her name altered to the English version, Elizabeth, when they reached the shore at Harwich. Sadie had been furious. Names were important; the history of the Jews is carried forth through names: *Jack son of Saul, and Sadie daughter of Ruth*. Jack had broken the chain. He objected; he had merely translated her name into English. He did not want his daughter, so tiny and brimming with promise, to be crippled by a German-sounding name.

Sitting in his warm kitchen years later, Jack reasoned, he had no right to be unhappy that Elizabeth had changed her own name once again. He was sad nonetheless: she no longer had *his* name. Most fathers had to wait until their daughters were married to receive this blow, but for Jack it had come early and he felt it bitterly.

He tiptoed upstairs to Elizabeth's bedroom and pushed open the door.

She was not sleeping, but curled up in her mother's rocking chair, chewing her plaits and reading a magazine. Christmas carols played softly on the wireless. She did not hear him and, as he watched the small figure, he felt his heart within him ache.

'Well done. A good result, Elizabeth Rose.'

He said her new name, trying it out in his mouth like a new taste. It sounded very fine. She looked at him sharply, trying to read his thoughts.

'It's easier for other people to say, Daddy,' she said, her green eyes appealing to him to agree, not to contradict her.

'Sure, sure,' he said nodding. He understood: she was tired of always being the Jew. She did not look like a Jew—only the name betrayed her and without it, she was free. He had done this, he started her on this course to Englishness, and it was what he had wanted. It had driven him to write his list and made him come here, to the countryside veiled in ice to build his golf course, but for the first time in all his years in Britain, he felt a sense of loss.

He crossed the room and took her warm hand, brushing it against his lips. 'You're quite right, my darling. Mr Rose does sound better. Mr Rose sounds rather English. In fact,' he added with a rueful smile, 'I think I should add it to my list. Item 151: An Englishman must have an English name.'

His heart filling with tears, Jack vanished to his study. It was time to write to Bobby Jones again.

Dear Mr Jones,

The weather here has been terrible. I don't suppose you in sunny Augusta know the bitter chill of a midwinter freeze. My bones creak, and I feel like Captain Scott, only with more tinned soup. My daughter has come home. I don't know if you have children, Mr Jones, but they grow away from you so fast. We name the things we love. God created the world and then he named it—'Let there be light, and there was light' and so forth. God named us, in love, according to my wife who believes such things. A man names his child, and at that moment she a person. It is sad when a father is no longer allowed to give his child her name. What else have we to give?

Your friend and humble servant, Jack Rose

And with that, after hundreds of generations of Rosenblums, the name was severed. Jack Rose took half the name, made it English and anonymous, and another little piece of history disappeared.

JACK TRIED HIS BEST not to think about the matter of the name but found that it troubled him. It haunted him even more than his money troubles or the cold weather halting progress on the golf course, and he was relieved when distraction arrived a few days later in the form of Freida and Edgar Herzfeld. They were visiting cousins in Bournemouth and had decided to make a short detour and stay the night with their good friends the Rosenblums.

Edgar was partial to a game of golf. His fascination was not synonymous with a wish to be considered an Englishman; he merely liked the click of the ball and eagerly joined a Jewish golf club. He appreciated what he took to be Jack's passion for golf, but could not understand why the man needed to build a course of his own. Edgar liked the Jewish club, where they served excellent schnitzel, everyone was familiar and nothing needed to be explained.

Jack was very fond of Edgar and was eager to extend membership to him as soon as the course officially opened. In the meantime it was very pleasant to show his old friend his triumph. He walked him up to the fifth hole, where from the tee the entire Blackmore Vale could be glimpsed. It was damp and dark, the sky seeming to hover only a few feet above the muddy fields. Edgar was impressed.

'I like it. I like it very much. How many members do you have?'

Jack pondered this. 'Well, there is Sir William Waegbert and Mr Henry Hoare and yourself. So three.'

Edgar thought the position was charming, or would be in spring, but he was concerned at the steepness. He wanted to help Jack; he suspected that he was not an experienced golfer and would benefit from a little advice.

'I'd dearly like to play a few holes. I think it'd be useful. Test them out.'

Jack considered this. Trying the course sounded like a good plan. If there were any changes, they could be made when work resumed. He did not want Edgar to know that, as yet, he had not played a round himself.

'Yes. I should like a second opinion. But, I will walk round with you. I'd rather listen to your thoughts than be worrying about my own game.'

Edgar was surprised. 'Well, if you really prefer. I'll fetch my clubs.'

Jack wanted to be the first to play, but he considered that since Edgar was only trying out a few holes and not the completed course, it did not really count at all. The sky turned black and then white as snow fell to the earth in a silent avalanche of flakes.

'Oh! This is too bad,' exclaimed Edgar sadly, returning with his clubs, 'I'll just have to come back in the spring.'

Jack was perturbed. Now that Edgar had suggested the course ought to be played, he was not willing to wait. A touch of snow would not deter the man who had single-handedly built a golf course.

'It's not bad,' said Jack, looking optimistically at the sky.

'Are you sure? I don't want to damage your greens,' said Edgar looking doubtfully at the looming clouds.

'It'll be fine but we should go right now.'

He hoisted Edgar's bag of clubs over his shoulder and led him towards the first hole. Flakes were fluttering to the ground in kaleidoscopic patterns. Jack blinked to brush flecks of snow from his eyelashes. Edgar was losing his enthusiasm. He was cold and a little hungry, and this no longer seemed like a good idea. They could barely see more than a few feet as the valley disappeared behind a solid bank of fog.

'Which club do you want?' enquired Jack through muffled layers.

'What does it matter? How the hell do I hit the ball?'

Jack paused to consider. With the utmost care, he placed the bag on the ground and began to build up a little pile of snow. He stopped when it was a few inches high and popped the ball on the snow-tee.

'Here.'

Edgar selected his driver and got ready to take a swing. Jack admired his stance; he wasn't Bobby Jones but he looked respectable enough as he lifted the club high above his shoulder, turning his hips, and then swung down to the ball. There was a click, and they watched the ball fly off into the mist.

'Good shot,' said Jack in awe.

'How can you tell? We have no idea where it went.'

'Well, we'd better look then.'

Jack hoisted the bag back onto his shoulder and took off along the ridge. Edgar followed him, using the driver as a walking stick to stop himself from slipping. The ground was now completely covered in snow and only the flags flickering through the haze indicated that this was a golf course at all.

Bent against the wind, Jack battered through the falling flakes, pursuing the direction he thought the ball to have taken. The temperature was dropping fast, and his fingers were getting stiff and numb.

'Come on, Jack, let's go inside. It's too cold. We'll never find it. Looking for a white ball on white snow. It's madness.'

Jack saw something on the surface of the pond, a round object with a small cap of gathering snow.

'Look! It's your ball. See how far you hit it!'

Sitting proudly on the top of the frozen water was Edgar's ball; he had sent it a good 300 yards.

'I've never hit a ball so far in my life. *Wunderbar*. What a course!'

Edgar laughed, pumped Jack's arm and slapped him on the back. The two men marched back to the house leaving two neat sets of footprints. As they approached the back door, they could see a figure waving to them.

'Who's that?' said Edgar,

Jack was not sure. There was a tall man wearing a deerstalker, certainly not Curtis. 'Sir William Waegbert?'

The aristocrat stamped and waved his arms partly in greeting and partly to keep warm. The tips of his moustache had a light dusting of white.

'Yes. Yes. Happy— um, whatever it is that you do and all that. Your wife said you'd gone of to play a round of golf.'

Jack shook his head sadly. 'Not a whole round. Course isn't finished.'

He opened the door to the kitchen and ushered his companions inside. The snow melted off their boots and formed little puddles on the flagstones. Unconcerned, Jack trotted to the larder to fetch his bottle of whisky. They sat around the table as he sloshed some of the liquid into three glasses.

'Soda, Sir William?'

'Good God, no. Far too bloody cold.'

Jack grunted his agreement and took a deep swig.

'So, how is the course? I've come to investigate.'

'Wonderful,' announced Edgar, his cheeks flushed from freezing air and the excitement caused by his great shot in the blizzard. He was a gentle man, calm and cautious; his game of golf in the driving snow was the greatest act of daring he had undertaken in the past ten years and he felt like Shackleton in the Antarctic in his audacity.

'Best course. It will be fantastic. Super-incredible.'

Jack smiled, filled with happiness. Here he was, sitting with his old friend, glorying in his achievement, and his new friend, a knight of the realm. Sir William raised his glass to the others, and took a gulp. Edgar followed and toasted Jack.

'To you, old friend.'

Edgar was aware of the shortcomings of Jack's course: the tees were blind, the greens steep and the hazards poorly placed. He was not usually prone to exaggeration or wanton praise, but he was unused to the powerful effects of whisky and as he drank he became loquacious in his enthusiasm.

'You mark my words,' he said, jabbing a finger in the vague direction of Sir William, 'it is going to be the triumph of the South-West. Everything this man does turns to gold. You want a good carpet at an excellent price. Only Rosenblum's will do.'

Here Jack fidgeted uncomfortably on his hard wooden chair.

'Rose's. It's just Rose's.'

Edgar raised an eyebrow. 'Oh?'

'Yes. I've changed the name. Not yet, but I will. It's Elizabeth's idea. Jack Rose. Less of a mouthful. Don't know why I didn't think of it before.'

Edgar continued to contemplate his friend in astonishment but Sir William gave a slow nod.

'Probably for the best. No point having a Kraut name if you can help it.'

Edgar swallowed, momentarily lost for words. With another sip of whisky he recovered and returned with enthusiasm to his original topic.

'This place will be his next big success, mark my words! You did a smart thing getting membership now, my friend.'

Jack watched as Sir William stretched his legs comfortably under the table. It was very pleasant in the warm kitchen. Sadie had been baking at her usual pace and he sliced Stollen into fat chunks and placed it on the table, taking it as a great compliment when Sir William helped himself to a large piece. Glowing contentedly with single malt in his belly and from Edgar's effusions, he was feeling particularly optimistic about his course.

'I will have nine holes by spring. I want this to be a course for champions. The British Open will be played in the Vale of Blackmore!'

Thinking this was a toast, Edgar raised his glass and drained it. 'The British Open! To the Blackmore Vale!'

Sir William leaned forward confidentially. 'And Bobby Jones. I believe you mentioned he was the chap whose designs you were following?'

Jack fidgeted awkwardly in his chair. He had been checking the post every day for a reply from his hero but still none was forthcoming.

'Yes. He is the greatest of them all. A true champion in our dreary age, but he is a busy man, a very busy man,' he added sadly.

Sir William stayed until the whisky bottle was empty, then climbed back into his decaying Rolls-Royce and drove away into the snow.

BY CHRISTMAS EVE the house was buried in two feet of snow. The bright white dazzled Jack every time he went outside but it was oddly peaceful; time seemed to have slowed with the snow. Everything took longer; walking down the lane for a pint of milk was an expedition. The boundaries beyond Bulbarrow signalled another far off and unreachable realm. Pursebury Ash was a miniature, ice-filled island.

Sadie looked out of the kitchen window. A robin was balancing along a sugar-coated branch with a bright berry in its beak, trying not to drop its precious cargo. The wind blew, and flakes fluttered from the bough of a birch tree in spirals to the ground. She could hear Elizabeth and Jack in the sitting room arguing over backgammon.

Alone in the quiet kitchen, she opened the sturdy farmhouse dresser, took out her box, removed the lid and laid out her family on the battered table. Her brother's face smiled up at her and she felt a twist in her stomach. Next, she took the picture of her father and placed it on the table. It was tattered at the edges, beginning to yellow and curl. It was taken when he was a young man and Sadie still a baby. He had a neat black beard in the photograph but he had shaved it off when she was small and she didn't remember it. Yet this was the only picture she had of him and, as her memory began to fade, the face in the photograph seemed to loom where once her father's had been.

She placed the picture of Mutti beside her father. It was taken shortly before Sadie left for England and showed a fretting, middle-aged woman doing her best to look cheery for the camera. She wasn't worrying about things to come—this was no premonition—she was concerned whether she had picked up enough chicken schmaltz for supper. The mismatched photographs presented an odd couple: her father glowering in his twenties and her mother twenty years later, so that husband and wife looked more like mother and son. Sadie reached into the box for another picture: a studio print of Jack, Elizabeth and herself taken several years ago for the holidays. She arranged all the photographs in a circle, her family together.

'Sadie Rose. Sadie Rose,' she said, to the pictures, introducing herself. This new name was strange; it had an unpleasant taste like strong mustard and burned her tongue. It was one more thing to take her away from them, to separate her from *before*. Her family had known her as Sadie Landau and later, when she married Jack, as Sadie Rosenblum. This Sadie Rose was someone new, and they would never be able to find her.

THAT AFTERNOON, the Roses walked together by the banks of the River Stour. It had frozen over and boys in greatcoats and girls in mufflers skated over the still surface. Jack shuddered: he did not like deep water, solid or not. Elizabeth, ignorant of this aversion, took his hand and dragged him resisting out onto the river. He wobbled, his feet sliding away from him.

'*Scheiße!* Let me go. I don't like this at all.'

Elizabeth laughed and pulled him along. 'Look, we're like Moses, see!'

Sadie smiled and shook her head, 'No, no, he parted the sea *then* walked.'

Jack succeeded in crawling back to the bank where, breathless, he rested against an alder tree. 'Even Moses would not walk on water. It's not natural.'

The air was punctured by the happy shouts of children on toboggans and makeshift sledges made of coal sacks, which left dirty smears on the white ground. The poplars were so laden with snow that they leaned forward heavily like stooped old men. The willows on the banks dangled down into the river, their branches frozen in a silent waterfall.

Jack and Sadie perched on a tree stump on the shore, watching Elizabeth skate, her red hat a crimson streak against the blur of white.

When the sun dipped behind the bank of bare trees, the Roses picked their way back along the meandering river.

'*Snow is a white, white word,*' sang Elizabeth into the darkness.

She took hold of her mother's hand and tried to make her run and skip. Sadie stumbled to keep up, unaccustomed to moving so fast and young. Elizabeth skidded to a halt. 'Look,' she whispered, still clasping her mother's mitten.

A clamour of rooks rested in the shadow of a dead tree. There were hundreds of them, black against the snow.

'They is nasty creatures,' said a voice.

Curtis appeared in their midst. Expertly, he skimmed a large stone, which bounced across the ice and hit the tree carcass with a hollow crack. The rooks beat their wings and rose into the sky, circling with angry caws.

''arbingers of death,' he added cheerfully.

Elizabeth laughed.

'And them mare's tails sproutin' in the frost. Terrible omen, for sure,' he said, pointing to where a green brushlike plant poked through the snow.

Elizabeth snorted. 'Do you know any tales that aren't nasty?'

Curtis was crestfallen. He thought for a moment.

'Well, I does know that comfrey flowers is an excellent cure. Can't remember what for 'xactly. But tis excellent. Also, you mustn't wash on New Year's Day, or yer'll wash yer family away. That's a good 'un.'

He reached into his pocket and passed his flask to Jack.

'It's a night as dark as a badger's backside,' said Curtis. 'Yer shouldn't linger here. The Drowners will get 'ee.'

Elizabeth laughed into her mitten. 'The Drowners?'

Curtis swiped the flask from Jack and fixed Elizabeth with a hard stare. 'They puts out precious things upon river bank. Yer know, things that yer have treasured and lost. Then, when yer creep down to the edge of the water to grab it, they snatches yer and pulls yers under.'

Jack shuddered.

'You shouldn't say such things in front of my girl,' Sadie scolded Curtis.

'She don't believe me anyhow. Modern wi-min.'

They reached the gate at the foot of the hill leading to the golf course. Curtis leaned against it and, steadily ignoring Elizabeth, waggled a finger at Jack and Sadie.

'Lost people in this village to the Drowners. I 'ad a cousin who 'ad a lovely gold watch, present from his granpa. Went out drinkin' one night and lost it. Was very upset, got a big hidin' from his pa when 'ee got home. Then, a year later, 'ee's walking home an' sees 'is gold watch on river bank. It'd bin snowing like, and it were twinklin', and he bends down to git it, and then . . .'

His voiced trailed off and he gave a little wave into the darkness.

'And then what?'

'Well, 'ee was niver seen again, was he,' said Curtis crossly.

'If you never saw him again, how do you know about the watch and the Drowners?' said Elizabeth.

'Hush,' said Jack.

Curtis scowled, offended by the impertinence of the girl; he did not want to be dismissed as an old fool. Sadie took Elizabeth's arm and gently pulled her towards the house. Jack and Curtis watched as the two women trudged across the garden and then a few moments later, the lights flickered on in the kitchen. The two men paused companionably in the night air.

Jack stared at the crisscrossing tracks littering the white field; there were marks from the sledges of the village children and deer prints, but next to them, lying deeply embedded in the snow, was a large round trotterprint. Was it possible? He pointed to it. 'A woolly-pig print,' he said, with an air of conviction to mollify his friend. '*Yom Tov* woolly-pig.'

His voice rang out into the night. For a moment he waited, and then he was sure he heard a deep-throated grunt echoing a reply across the snow.

NEW YEAR CAME and the ice stayed, snow drifting against the ancient walls of the cottage. The flags on the golf course were dotted across a white ocean and, as he dug narrow walkways across the endless snow, Jack found the tiny, frozen bodies of birds.

It was fortunate that Sadie, schooled by rationing, was in the habit of hoarding food or they would have gone hungry. Luckily, her pantry was piled high with tins, buckets of flour and crocks of eggs, which Jack traded for pitchers of milk.

The hot-water pipes froze and Sadie boiled kettles on the kitchen stove. Jack refused to wash—'I need my dirt to keep me warm'—but on New Year's Day, Sadie decided that it was time to bathe. She had never seen in a New Year dirty. With a scowl, she placed her hands on her hips and cleared her throat.

'*Broitgeber*, I believe it is a rule on your list. An Englishman is always clean, is he not?'

Lying in bed later that night, he decided the water had gently broiled his innards, since he was less cold than usual. He went to sleep with ease and dreamed he was at Augusta, lying contentedly in the sunshine, listening to the trickling of temperate streams and the pock of golf balls.

When he awoke, it took him a moment to realise he was still in the midst of the dismal British winter and not in the great Georgian pleasure garden. He was disappointed only for a moment and slid smiling out of bed and into his slippers. He adjusted his fleece-lined dressing gown and bounded onto the landing. There was a powerful draught whistling along the staircase and he concluded that a window must have blown open in the night. Rubbing his hands for warmth he scurried down the wooden stairs to close it, before Sadie or Elizabeth caught cold. Oddly, he could hear the wind howling in the kitchen and hurried to the door to open it.

Mayhem greeted him: the ceiling had come down in the night. Plaster and debris were strewn everywhere and melted snow pooled on the flagstone floor. There was a large hole above his head and he could see the thatch sagging ominously.

'*Mistfink*. Shit-heaps and buggering hell.'

THE FAMILY SURVEYED the wreckage as snow fell gently into the kitchen, turning the dust and rubble into a thick, rancid mess. Jack was almost out of his mind. He needed every penny for his golf course and did not have money for roof mending. Perhaps he could offer the thatcher membership of the course in lieu of payment.

Sadie and Elizabeth shovelled armfuls of ceiling plaster, scraps of wood and liquefied black dust into large, wet piles, which Jack scooped into sacks. After an hour, the flagstones had turned to mud and they began to skid along the floor. Sadie slipped by the kitchen dresser, grabbing hold of the base to steady herself. She noticed the low doors were ajar, and frowned. She knelt down in the dirt and shoved the wood with her fist. The cupboard door bounced open and water poured out. Snow from the roof had melted and run into the dresser, flooding every cabinet. The crockery was covered in slimy filth but she didn't care about that, or the vases or the linen tablecloths. She cared only about her wooden box. She eased it out and left the kitchen without a word.

She crept into the hall, feeling bile rise in her stomach.

'Please let them be all right. *Bitte. Bitte*,' she murmured.

Her hands trembling, she lifted the carved lid. The photographs floated in water, the faces blurred and featureless, all drowned in the deluge. Sadie picked out the picture of her mother, rubbed it gently against her sleeve and held it up in the daylight. The face was gone—she had wiped it off. There was only a piece of soggy, grey paper on the floral swirl of her housecoat. She reached for the other pictures and tenderly laid them on the ground. Every one was ruined.

She picked up the sopping linen towel, Mutti's last gift, and held it to her face and breathed in, but the scent of her mother's starch and soap was gone. Sadie had preserved that small towel immaculately in its tissue paper for nearly twenty years and now there was nothing left.

She sat down on the stone floor and was sick; she retched and vomited again and again until the muscles in her stomach ached. Then she lay down, the stone cool against her cheek. Without the photographs, she would forget their faces. They had no graves, no names engraved in stone; they needed her to remember them. She closed her eyes. Perhaps if she slept and then woke she would still be in bed and this wouldn't have happened. She opened her eyes. She was still there. The box was still spoilt.

Suddenly, eyes feverishly bright, she sat up. Through the closed door she could hear the happy chatter of her husband and daughter. She had an idea; she knew where to look for her photographs.

She fastened her robe tightly around her waist and, clasping her box, slipped out of the back door. The snow was knee-deep, and she had to stoop against the battering wind. It lifted the flaps of her flannel dressing gown, making her pink nightdress flutter like a great moth. Her slippers were instantly sodden but she did not notice. It was midmorning but the sky was pumice grey, filled with murky half-light hinting ominously of blizzards to come.

Sadie crossed the garden and opened the gate out into the blank expanse of the field. The still rooks on the dead tree at the edge of the river eyed her as she passed.

Breathless, she paused and craned upwards to look at the sky, and remembered winters like this at the old house in Bavaria. They were snowed-in one December and stayed in the house in the forest, marooned from the outside world. Sometimes, in her dreams, they were all still there in the cabin in the wood. Mutti hunched over the stove, Papa sleeping in his chair and Emil building models out of balsa wood in front of the fire. She was late, and they were waiting for her.

She manoeuvred past a fallen branch blocking the path along the river bank and sat down to rest on a stump, not bothering to brush the seat clear of snow. She was exhausted without being tired and wanted to slip down into the downy whiteness and close her eyes. Her fingers were turning blue at the tips, and she could feel them tingling uncomfortably, but she liked the pain—she was supposed to suffer. The others had stayed and died, therefore she deserved to be unhappy. Jack did not understand this, however much she tried to show him, and so she placed burrs in his socks to give him blisters to mar the unbroken cheerfulness of his day. When she bothered to cook his supper she made all the food he disliked eating: kidney pie, rabbit, and marzipan tarts. It was good for him, she reasoned; he needed to be a little sad. Making Jack a tiny bit unhappy, and nurturing her own hurt, were acts of love in Sadie's eyes.

She stared indifferently at the river and waited. The trees creaked under the heaving mass of snow, and the ice on the river groaned and sighed. That moment she saw it: on the bank of the river fluttered a photograph. Not daring to blink in case it disappeared, she stole through the snow to the edge. Her back stiff from cold, she bent down and peered at the paper.

There, lying on the ice, was the picture of Mutti, her face unmarked by water or dirt.

Sadie reached out for the photograph. She grasped it with both hands and studied the familiar face, the grey hair and friendly eyes. Lovingly, she cradled it to her chest, and smiled. She must place it safely in her wooden box, but just as she moved away from the bank, she saw a flicker as another piece of glossy paper caught a stray beam of sunlight.

It was just out on the ice of the frozen river, partly submerged in snow. She slipped the first picture into her pocket and sat down on the edge of the bank. There was a drop of several feet, and she tried to ease herself down but she slid faster than she intended, tearing her housecoat on a tree root as she fell.

Sadie picked herself up, and stood bruised and uncertain, trying to balance on the black ice. Forcing herself not to hurry, she glided on her slippers across the solid river to the second picture, and crouched down to peel it off the surface. This picture was of her father and she smiled between chattering teeth as she placed it carefully in her pocket, confident now that there were more to find.

Dark ivy clung to a gaunt elder overhanging the river. As she grabbed a strand to steady herself, she spied another photograph. She let go and skidded uncertainly further out, but this one was more difficult to reach and her slippers slid in every direction. She was dizzy from the bitter cold and the hard exercise, and saw the rooks surveying her with black eyes. Voices in her head urged caution, but, unable to resist, she edged onto the centre of the river and, kneeling down, reached for a corner of the picture. Her fingers were so cold that she could not command them properly, and the paper fluttered away. It was snowing now, her path onto the river obscured. The paper was lifted by another gust of wind and floated along the river towards the opposite bank. She cursed loudly, '*Verdammt Scheiße!*'

The photograph lodged in a drift by a shivering willow. She took another few steps and came to a halt by the tree. Her cheeks were red raw from the wind, her lips tinged blue and her hair a tangled mass. Holding her breath, she reached up for the photograph wedged in the bank of snow. As her fingers brushed it, she felt herself being pulled downwards by invisible hands. They grasped at her, yanking her hair and clawing at her feet. The ice cracked open and Sadie fell slowly into darkness.

JACK AND ELIZABETH had cleared away most of the rubble. The hole was patched haphazardly but at least it was no longer snowing inside the kitchen. Elizabeth gave the stove a cursory wipe, put the ancient kettle on to boil, and when it began to sing, she made two steaming cups of tea. Jack took his and sat hunched at the table.

'Are there any biscuits?' said Elizabeth.

'In the larder.'

'I've looked. I can't find them.'

'Ask your mother.'

'I can't find her either.'

This was more surprising. Where had his wife gone? This was not a morning to be anywhere except by a warm fire sipping hot tea. He opened the back door and saw a set of partially obscured tracks leading through the garden to the gate.

'I think she's gone outside.'

Jack saw that Sadie's stout walking shoes remained neatly by the door. Her woollen coat and oilskins hung limply on the wooden peg. Jack had a nasty feeling in his belly. Sadie liked to make him cross, to worry at him like a blister, but she never tried to frighten him. She could catch a nasty chill going out in this arctic weather without proper layers. Jack pulled his overcoat over his pyjamas, put on some coarse woollen socks, his felt hat and three knitted scarves.

'I'd better check she's all right. Best put the kettle on again.'

He hoped he sounded casual; he didn't want Elizabeth to worry. She said nothing, but he felt her watching from the doorway as he ventured out into the blizzard. He could just make out Sadie's route across the land to the river and, as the feathery layers hid her tracks, he followed the stream to the edge of his land. What madness or stupidity made her venture out in this?

Grimly, Jack realised that people had frozen to death on warmer days and with a fierce pang of guilt he remembered all the times that he'd wished she would leave him alone. He thought ruefully of the cakes she left out for him on the table, those little markers of concealed tenderness. He must find her to thank her for the baking. He loathed her cooking; she always forgot the things he did not like and was forever making him rabbit stews, but he knew that she revealed her love for him through her pastries. Years afterwards, he'd learned that those strudels she'd brought him in prison had used up her entire week's ration of butter. The whole time he was away, Sadie and

Elizabeth had managed on a meagre half-portion of butter, so that he could have his strudels. So that Sadie could show she loved him.

His face stung with cold. He drew his coat tight around his shoulders and pulled his hat down low over his eyes. Where the devil had she gone? He reached the gate at the bottom of the field, clambered to the top rung and peered into the distance. Nothing moved.

Unable to see any sign of her, he climbed back down and began to trudge the path along the river bank. The jutting branches and fluttering bird shadows cast weird shapes upon the snow.

'I would like to sit in my house with my two women—my daughter and my wife.' His voice sounded thin in the big afternoon and he felt a little sick as he realised how much he wanted the company of his wife. He did not need to try and be English with her. She did not care. She had known him as the little Jew in Berlin and had loved him enough to marry him. He was suddenly light-headed and felt himself sinking into the snow. He cursed himself and his stupidity, yelling so loudly that his throat hurt, 'I am a fool!' *Fool, fool, fool!*

His words echoed across the frozen river as he surged onwards through the gathering drifts. He passed a rook perched on a bare bough of a tree. The bird cocked its head on one side and stared back curiously.

'Tell me if you have seen her,' he called in desperation.

It looked at him for a moment and then flew away. With an eager cry, he chased after it, buoyed by the wild hope that it would lead him to Sadie.

'Wait, my friend. Wait!'

The bird took no notice and vanished into the white void. Jack swallowed hard, and felt a painful lump in his throat. He must not give up. He must find her. He gritted his teeth, adjusted his hat again and stomped on.

The snow was coming thickly now and he could see only a few inches in front of him. He knew, rather than saw, that the river was still beside him and, moving as quickly as he could, trudged on through the falling snow. His mind began to fill with sinister thoughts: what if he never found her? What if he found her and she was dead? Jack raised his eyes to the dark sky and through chattering teeth tried to bargain with the God he did not believe in.

'If you help me find her and she lives, I promise I will be a better husband. I will let her be a little sad. I promise I will be good to her. *I promise.*'

The trees groaned in the wind and a heavy fall of snow landed on his head. Losing his balance, he staggered and there was a sharp crack.

Looking down, he saw Sadie's wooden box splintered beneath his foot. Fingers stiff, he gathered the shards and shouted into the storm.

'Sadie, it's me! Sadie.'

No one answered.

'I've come. Sadie, Sadie, I've come.'

Still no one answered.

He saw a snatch of pink fabric from her housecoat dangling from a twig on the bank—she must be nearby. His heart pounding, he slid down onto the river and struggled across the ice. Another flash of pink. Jack slithered urgently towards it.

She was lying on the ice, half buried by snow. With the fury of a wild bear, he cleared it from her body, and brushed her pale cheek with his hand.

'Sadie. Sadie. *Mein Schatz. Ich liebe dich*.'

Jack wrapped his arms around her and stroked her damp hair. She was so cold. There was only a faint tickle of breath on his cheek.

'*Mein Gott, mein Gott*,' he muttered. '*Was soll ich nur machen?*'

It would take too long to fetch help; he needed to get her into the warm as quickly as possible. He took off his coat and laid it down on the ice. Then, he knelt down beside her, unpeeled her sodden clothes, undid his dressing gown and wrapped her in it. Jack heaved her onto his fur-lined coat, untied his scarves and wrapped one around her head, another on her feet and slipped the third through the collar on the coat. Holding on to this scarf like a handle, dressed only in his red-striped pyjamas and heavy boots, he began to pull the makeshift sledge along the frozen river.

They reached the bottom of the field that led to the golf course and the pond. The snow had compacted to form a ramp. Panting, Jack used it to drag Sadie up the river bank to the path, his pyjamas damp with sweat and steam rising from his back into the freezing air. His muscles burned, the air seared his lungs and throat and set his teeth on edge. He struggled to keep his footing as he carried Sadie through the field back home. At last they reached the garden and he dragged her the final few steps to the back door. Thumping on it with his fist, he called for Elizabeth.

'Help me . . . carry her.'

Elizabeth came running from the kitchen and threw open the door. She froze at the sight of her mother. Sadie's face was only a shade darker than the snow covering her. She was cocooned in white, like a giant chrysalis.

'Elizabeth!'

Shaking herself out of her stupor, she helped her father carry her mother over the threshold. They laid her in the hallway, and Jack leaned against the wall, struggling for breath.

'In the sitting room . . . put her . . . is warmest in there.'

His voice filled the narrow hall and he could hear the sob stick in his throat as he spoke. Together they carried Sadie into the living room. With trembling fingers Elizabeth unbuttoned her from Jack's coat while he stoked the fire into a fearsome blaze.

'I'll stay with Mummy. You go into the village and send for a doctor.'

Jack shook his head, dazed with grief. 'I can't leave her. I won't.'

Elizabeth gave a small nod and was gone.

Jack stripped off his dripping pyjamas and climbed onto the sofa next to his wife, wrapped himself around her, rubbing her arms and legs to warm them. He was naked and cold but she felt colder still.

'Don't die, Sadie,' he whispered. 'Don't leave me. Please, please.' He clung to her, his teeth chattering, terrified that if he let go, she would die.

THEY LAY TOGETHER in front of the fire as the shadows grew long. Jack did not release his grip but slowly fell asleep. He dreamed they were back in London. They were so poor, Elizabeth slept in a drawer in their bedroom. It was their anniversary but he had no money to buy his wife a present. In his dream, Jack climbed again the rickety, cast-iron stairs to their fourth-floor flat and put the key in the lock. As he turned it, he heard Caruso crooning love songs on the gramophone next door. He paused to listen, then pushed open the door to their apartment.

Sadie was standing stark naked on the table and when she saw him come in she began to dance. She swayed in time to the refrain lilting through the thin plaster wall. She was small and slender, her dark hair snaked down her back and she wore nothing but a pair of red high heels. 'Happy anniversary, darling,' she whispered. '*Mein lieber Schatz*. Do you like your present?'

Jack stood, his back against the door, gazing at this girl-woman, silent with love.

HE WOKE, embarrassed to discover that he had an erection. He was both aroused and sick with guilt; how could he have wanted this woman to disappear? She was still the girl in the red shoes. The fire had burned low, the embers orange.

'Jack?'

'My darling, you're awake.'

He pulled her tightly to him and began to cry.

'I am so tired,' murmured Sadie, her voice rasping and thin.

'Then sleep. But first you must promise me. Never to do it again.'

'Do what?'

'Leave us,' he whispered, 'promise me that you will never try to leave us ever again.'

'Oh,' murmured Sadie, 'so that is what I did.' She was warm at last, and it was so pleasant in Jack's bony arms. 'I promise.'

Jack kissed her mouth. His rough cheeks grazed her skin, and he touched the creases around her eyes with his fingertips.

THE DOCTOR DIAGNOSED PNEUMONIA and advised complete bed rest for a month. Jack told Elizabeth that it was an accident; her mother had neglected to put on her boots and slipped and fell on the ice. He nursed Sadie with forgotten tenderness; he brushed her grey hair and brought basins of hot water to warm her feet.

Yet, something had happened to Sadie on the ice. She remembered falling into darkness, floating under the frozen film and looking up at the heavens. She fell further, down through the middle of the earth and then another sky, until she had emerged in a dark wood. A gnarled oak tree stood before her, and she breathed in the scent of Bavarian pine. Lights twinkled inside a cabin and somewhere she could hear Papa singing. She walked through the cabin door and Emil had grinned up at her from the rug, before returning to pasting stamps in his album. Mutti patted the cushion beside her, saying, 'Come, you must dry yourself by the fire and have something to eat.' Sadie had kicked off her wet slippers and padded across the floor.

Lazing now, by the Dorset hearth, Sadie understood that she'd left a piece of herself in that other place. She knew none of this was possible, yet she felt different: same eyes, same nose, same round belly, but something minute had shifted inside her and, to her surprise, she realised that she was glad Jack had found her. She liked sitting on the sofa, reclining on plump cushions and toasting tea cakes on the hot fire. She liked Jack combing the knots out of her hair, and listening to the click, click of Elizabeth's knitting needles in the afternoon.

The incident had triggered another revelation. When Sadie closed her eyes, she was overwhelmed by a passionate longing for turkey meatballs. Her mouth watered, and she could almost smell them frying on the stove. She remembered that Mutti had made them when she was small and they had been her favourite thing as a child, then in the course of time she had forgotten them. One afternoon, when Jack left Sadie alone with Elizabeth, she confided her yearning to her daughter, who took the task seriously.

Elizabeth listened as her mother explained how the taste hit her tongue, until she too could hear her grandmother in the kitchen bashing spices with a rolling pin. She followed the instructions in the battered recipe book with its magical amalgamation of German and Yiddish, but the quantities were vague and imprecise. The book required her to cook with instinct, to imagine the flavour she wished to create and then use the book as a companion and guide. Her mother refused to eat the early attempts—if the recipe was wrong, Sadie would forget the taste once more.

Elizabeth was a small baby when they had fled Berlin and had no memory of her grandmother, but she began to know her through the book. The meatball method was in a chapter entitled 'food to soothe troubles' and slowly she learned to listen to her voice. She procured some turkey, ground it carefully, and then she heard a whisper, 'Mustard seed, mustard seed.' She pounded it with the old farmhouse pestle, added it to the sizzling meat and then presented it proudly to her mother, confident that this was perfection.

As Sadie ate, her face was radiant. 'This is a good thing,' she decided, comforted by the scents wafting from her kitchen. History could be carried forward in tastes and smells. Elizabeth was learning to cook from her grandmother; her children would know the tastes of the *shetetl* and the world *before*.

JANUARY WAS DRAWING to a close and it was Elizabeth's last evening before returning to Cambridge. As the snow retreated, shrinking first to the edges of the garden and fields, hiding under hedgerows, then disappearing altogether, Sadie rose from her bed. She took a long bath, washed her hair, dried it by the fire, put on a green stuff skirt, a cable-knit sweater and went into her kitchen. Jack was not pleased.

'Go back to bed. You've been ill. Lie by the fire.'

'No. The doctor said I could get up when the snow was gone.'

She pointed out of the window. The evidence was irrefutable: drizzle dampened the ground, and the meltwater had turned the trickling stream into a torrent. There was something Sadie needed to cook before Elizabeth left for the station; the meatballs were an excellent start, but she wanted to teach her how to make a Baumtorte.

It was gathering dusk, the lights were lit and the stove was burning when the two women lugged the tin bath inside to scrub it clean. They counted out the eggs, weighed the butter, flour and sugar and mixed them together. Tired from her illness, Sadie sank onto a kitchen stool, unfastened her stockings and washed her feet, then she climbed into the bath and began to tread the batter slowly between her toes, the mixture oozing creamily.

'Let me do that,' said Elizabeth.

Sadie shook her head. 'I must do this one. The next one is yours.'

Taking her time, she blended the ingredients, feeling them grow smooth and slippery beneath her skin. Elizabeth watched as she spooned the buttery mixture into great tins and toasted each layer under the grill. The cake grew tall, sprouting like a sapling, while dusk mellowed into nightfall.

The church bells struck midnight and Jack came into the kitchen carrying his bottle of Scotch. The sweet scent of baking pervaded the house, and disturbed him—the fragrance of Baumtorte was always tinged with sorrow.

Sadie surveyed her cake-in-progress, chewing her lip. Once assembled, it would be as high as the one she had baked last summer, but this time it needed one extra layer. Tiers of cakes were spread out across the kitchen table. She spooned the final coating of batter into one of the tins and put it under the grill. She was no longer tired; she was hot and her arms felt sore from lifting and beating the eggs, but she felt a surge of energy as she lifted out the last tier and set it down on the table to cool.

Together they piled the tiers on top of one another, using the icing to bind them, until finally the Baumtorte was ready.

'You should have the first piece,' said Elizabeth.

Sadie shook her head. 'I made it for you.'

Standing on a chair, Sadie cut her a slice, as thin as her little finger but several feet deep. As Elizabeth bit into it she felt a wave of sadness. She considered how lonely her mother must be, to bake cakes in order to remember. It was both strange and sad, and a fat tear trickled down her cheek.

Seeing her daughter cry, Sadie believed Elizabeth finally understood, and was comforted.

CHAPTER SEVEN

Jack and Sadie went to bed in winter and woke to discover spring in the garden. They inspected the garden arm in arm, pointing out the sprouting stems to one another, each patch of plants a treasure hoard. Pinpricks of snowdrops grew in icy clusters beneath the apple trees and, as they began to fade to brown, primroses crept into view and shone like tiny suns.

After the primroses came clouds of daffodils, golden with bright orange trumpets. Sadie picked armfuls and brought them inside until every room was filled with vases of happy daffodils. In Berlin they had been banned from the parks, so in their first English spring they had circled round and round Regent's Park, marvelling at all the flowers. Back then, she and Jack were still dazed and she was silent, unable to speak English. Not knowing it was forbidden, Sadie had picked one white daffodil, and it smelled of freedom.

As he went to his course each morning, Jack found himself walking with his mouth open, taking great gulps of clean, moist air. One day, he gathered the men on the field by the fifth hole; this was the one with the most splendid aspect, the land falling away beneath them and the tall grass glimmering in the morning light. They were not the only ones working—in the distance, on the edge of the village, the bungalows were going up. Wilson's Housing Corporation had been true to their word and prefabricated buildings sprouted up across the cleared meadows. Jack sighed. When the course was finished he would plant more trees, white ash and elm, to shield his land from their ugliness. He stood on a mound, drew himself up to his full height and cleared his throat, since he wanted very much to be inspiring.

'Friends, we must press on, full puff ahead. I need nine holes finished before June. This will be the greatest golf course in the whole of England. We must work like hedge sparrows building their nests or the honeybee gathering nectar. We will triumph! And a bottle of Scotch to the man who moves the most molehills.'

He was determined that the course be finished on schedule; it was a matter of necessity as he was nearly out of cash. He must be brave, like the champion Bobby Jones himself, hold fast and not lose his nerve. From first light he worked so furiously that the others marvelled at his energy.

He did not rest but laboured by the light of the bright spring moon, breaking up clods of soil with his spade. There was power in his small frame and he laboured relentlessly—raking, cutting, smoothing. Dropping his tools in exhaustion, he halted shortly before dawn and traipsed back to the house where Sadie had left a tall glass of milk and apple strudel on the table. He drank the milk down in a single gulp then licked the buttery pastry off his fingers and, half in a dream, picked out all the currants, lining them end on end around his plate. Leaning back in his chair, he gazed at the neat row and thought of Emil. Hearing the kitchen door creak, Jack looked round to see Sadie standing behind him, her eyes bright. She leaned over and rested her chin on the top of his bald head.

'You remember, too,' she said. 'I never knew.'

BEFORE HE CLIMBED the stairs to bed, ready to sleep for a few hours next to the warm body of his wife, he retreated into his study to write to Bobby Jones. The sun was stealing over Bulbarrow Ridge as he pulled out his sheet of paper, and began.

Dear Mr Jones,

I really hoped to hear from you before Christmas so either your American postal service is slower in coming than the Jew's messiah, or the aeroplane delivering my letters is tipping them out in the middle of the Atlantic.

Jack decided not to acknowledge the third, most likely possibility, that Bobby Jones discarded his correspondence with no intention of ever responding at all.

I've been tardy in writing (though not so much as you, Mr Jones, if you will forgive this gentle reproof) as the Michaelmas season was eventful. My wife was ill but I am pleased to say that she is now much better. I am working very hard on the golf course. To tell you the truth, if it is not finished soon I am in the shit, as they say.

I am holding a golfing tournament in honour of Her Majesty on the morning of the coronation and, on behalf of the Pursebury Ash Coronation Committee, I warmly and most cordially invite you to attend as our guest of honour.

Your friend, humble servant, etc., Jack Rose

He sealed the envelope and placed it reverently on the stand in the hall, ready to go to the post office. Worn out, his hands raw with blisters from shovelling, he went upstairs to bed.

MARCH GAVE WAY to April and with it came the bluebells. Mr Betjeman described the bluebell as the quintessential English flower and the bluebell wood as a snippet of magic left behind as an oversight from the ancient world. Jack decided this was something that he ought to investigate, and so agreed to spend an afternoon with his wife in search of them. They drove to the top of Bulbarrow with the roof of the car down for the first time that year.

They had never seen anything like it: there were thousands upon thousands of bright blue flowers, as though the sky had fallen to earth beneath the trees. Sadie had thought she was too old for new things but the striking beauty of the place stirred her. It was like being a little girl again and seeing the sea for the first time. They picked their way through the trees but it was impossible not to crush the bluebells—the wood breathed with them—and Sadie wondered if her cheeks would turn blue with the scent. She picked one and tucked it behind her ear.

'You mustn't, my darling,' Jack chided her. 'They're dying out.'

They laid a blanket beneath the trees, unpacked a box of vanilla biscuits and poured sweet Madeira wine into china teacups. Jack was nicely warm and lay back on the rug. He did not like to think of the fate of the bluebell, disappearing in the onslaught of progress. It was the fault of those wretched bungalows. This was a disappearing world and he was glad to be old—he would not live to see it all ruined. Shafts of sunlight fell to earth and illuminated clumps of the flowers. In the sunshine they were bright blue while in the depths of the shade they turned to deep indigo or shades of wine. He watched Sadie while she dozed, noticing the fine lines around her eyes and a mottled mark on her cheek, which he traced with his finger. He treasured these markings of age—they were like rings on a tree. He gave a wide yawn and, in the pleasant warmth of the wood, overcome by the scent of flowers and sweet wine, he succumbed to drowsiness and slept.

As they dozed, curled side by side on the picnic rug, the afternoon crept on. The sun disappeared behind a bank of cloud, the air grew cold and the sky turned black. There was a terrific crash of thunder and, a moment later, a powerful flash of lightning illuminated the heavens. Jack sat up with a start and adjusted his spectacles, as another roll boomed out in the sky.

'Wake up. It's going to rain,' he said, shaking Sadie and scrambling to his feet.

Immediately the air vibrated as another bright crack of lightning danced through the sky. Sadie began to stuff the picnic things back in the basket, while Jack haphazardly folded the rug. Then the rain came: huge pellets of water hurled from the sky, battering the leaves and stinging their skin.

'Dance with me, Jack?'

'Are you a *messhuggenah Hund?*' called Jack, already racing back to the car and slipping on rotting foliage.

'Are you a hen?' shouted Sadie after him.

Jack stopped and turned around. 'You mean am I chicken-shit?'

'Hen-shit, chicken-shit, *alter kacker*, it's all the same to me. Dance with me, old man,' she added with a smile.

Jack dropped the rug and, grabbing her round the middle, whirled her about, crushing bluebells, which released their scent, thick as smoke.

'You are a terrible dancer,' complained Sadie as he crashed her into an oak tree.

He leaned forward and kissed her on the nose. 'And still you married me. Foolish old woman.'

THE RAIN LASTED for three solid days. Jack stared miserably out of the bedroom window—it having the best view of his course—and wondered how much harder he would have to work to make up the lost time. Even Sadie baking 'wet weather treats' could not console him. He turned the bed into a model of Bulbarrow and, making the contours with eiderdowns and pillows, used knitting needles to mark the position of the holes.

Sadie came upstairs carrying a mug of tea to find him trying to visualise the eighth hole. Sadie stared out at the mist-covered golf course. A sigh came from Jack, who uncharacteristically ignored the biscuits she had placed on the saucer. She needed to cheer him up.

'Show me the course.'

'It's too wet. We'll drown.'

'Use the model.'

Jack looked at her in surprise; she had shown no interest in his plans before. Pleased, he took her hand and led her to a patch of emerald baize.

'This is the first fairway. See. Down there is the pond.'

He pointed to an old hand mirror of Sadie's that twinkled away, nestled in the eiderdown. She gave him a smile of encouragement and he gestured to a knitted turquoise scarf that meandered along on the edge of the quilt.

'This is the stream. It will be marvellous.'

'What's that?' She pointed to a round purple stain by the knitting-needle flag on the third fairway.

Jack frowned, 'That, I think, is a patch of strawberry jam.'

Sadie's face lit up. 'A strawberry patch. That would be nice. If you get peckish in the middle of a game, you could pick strawberries.'

Jack was uncertain whether this would be feasible in the middle of the fairway, but not wishing to quench her newfound enthusiasm, repositioned the flag so that the jam stain was at the edge of the rough.

'We could put it here, I suppose.'

A hairbrush forest perched on a pillow and Sadie listened, for once captivated by Jack's fervour. Instead of the rose-patterned teacup, she saw the small pond and the flowers that she must plant for him around its banks. She began to understand the challenge of playing out of the rough and, as she stroked the coarse horsehair blanket, she appreciated the sweep from the fifth hole. The coverlet fell away and she could see all the way down the bedcloth valley into the Blackmore Vale, beyond the foot of the bed and out of the window.

WHILE JACK CONTINUED to plot his model course, Sadie stitched him new flags. Jack tuned the wireless and they worked companionably, neither speaking, each absorbed in their task. Sadie sat on the windowsill where the light was good and meticulously double stitched the neat edges of the flags—she did not want them fraying or coming apart in the wind. She paused and watched the pounding rain battering the plants in the flowerbeds below. She looked beyond the garden to the golf course, gratified to understand the brilliance of Jack's scheme at last. It was much better to share it with him; if he was a madman then at least they were crazy together.

Yet, as she gazed at the field through the rain it looked as though the land was sliding. Her eyes were tired—she rubbed them and blinked. No, it was moving—the hillside was falling forward and, above the sound of the drum of the rain, there was a rumble—the noise of earth moving.

'Jack, Jack!'

They looked in horror at the ground above the fifth hole. It was slipping away and sliding down the hill. The avalanche of earth gathered pace and there was a colossal roar as it crashed onto the fairway below. It juddered to a stop, leaving a brown river of devastation—trees were snapped in two from the force of the landslide; more were carried forth on the giant clump of earth.

Clad in oilskins, they rushed down to the field to survey the damage. Panting to keep up, Sadie followed Jack onto the course, and as they marched across the third fairway, she admired the smooth grass that had sprung up verdant from the wet. The fifth hole was another story. It was always Jack's favourite, but now it lay smeared across the land below—an enormous pile of mud, rock and trees. Jack did not know what to do. Without a word he turned round and walked back to the house.

Sadie hurried after him. A trail of wet boots led from the back door into the study and she found Jack slumped in his chair, swigging whisky from the bottle.

'*Verflixt!* It's a catastrophe. I'll never finish on time. I'd need hundreds of pounds for repairs and there's no more money.'

He took another gulp and in his despair told his wife everything.

'I took a loan out against the business. I can't take out any more. I'll never be an Englishman. Never.'

He drained the bottle and gave a half-hiccup, half-sob. 'I may as well burn my list. Toss it into the fire and be done.'

He looked pitiful sitting in his wet things with water streaming down his cheeks. Sadie was not used to him like this; he was the one with the ideas, the one who took care of things. The optimist. 'What about the house?'

'What about it?'

'Is it mortgaged?'

Jack sat up. What was she suggesting?

'Yes. I took out a little one, to help with cash flow.'

'So you can take out another?'

Jack hesitated. 'I could. But I have nothing to pay it back with. And the bank will want the business loan repaid in a few months. It's a big risk, doll.'

Sadie tried to understand. 'If we don't take out another mortgage on this house then we cannot finish the golf course?'

'No.'

Sadie sat down on the stone floor, thinking hard before she began to speak. 'The course will be the greatest in England. There will be white doves and strawberry fields, streams filled with golden fish. It must be finished. You said so yourself.'

Jack stared at his wife in amazement. 'If the course does not make money and we cannot pay back the mortgage, we will lose the house. Do you understand that, darling?'

She met his blue eyes and nodded.

LATER THAT EVENING, Jack found himself in his study and composed his weekly epistle to Bobby Jones.

Dear Mr Jones,

Today, my wife surprised me. We've been married for a long time, Sadie and I, and we'd fallen into bad habits. I don't mean the leaving of socks on the bathroom floor and forgetting to close the chicken coop (though there is that, too). I thought I'd lost her, but now she has come back to me.

I'm in a spot of bother over the golf course (boring finances and what have you). We sat together and worked out all the sums.

Providing that the course is finished in time for the coronation and that we get fifty members (at the price of one guinea each), we should just get by. I'll have a golf course yet, Mr Jones!

Your servant and fellow golfing enthusiast, Jack Rose

THE NEXT MORNING the rain stopped, the men returned to work and Jack showed them the damage. Basset shook his head ruefully, 'A'ways knew there wis bad drainage in them fields. A'ways knew.'

Jack's optimism had returned—every time there was a disaster he met it, and now even Sadie had faith in his vision. He was not like those unfortunates in the books by Mr Thomas Hardy—he did not believe in fate; rather, one had to make one's own good luck.

The fifth hole had been swept away, so he ushered the men to the point just above the landslip. He balanced on a tree root and swept his arms out wide, motioning to the landscape below. His battered greatcoat—five sizes too big—hung around his ankles and his eyes shone with purpose. He looked like an Old Testament prophet to the Dorset men, who gazed at him curiously.

'Disaster has struck and still we stand firm! We shall not be dissuaded from our purpose, we men of England!'

Curtis mumbled appreciatively and Basset, Mike and Ed all spat on the ground, a sign of their approval. Jack rocked precariously on his tree root.

'We must continue apace! Full speed ahead! I need suggestions. I need inspired thought for how to mend and move forward.'

He gazed at the gathered men expectantly. They stared back.

Curtis was the first to speak. 'If you doesn't mind me sayin', I think we ran into difficulties, cos we went against the land 'imself. We needs to follow 'im more. Smooth out this mess for sure, but less diggin' and movin' of earth.'

He pointed to the fields below and suggested alterations to the run of the course, taking advantage of the natural hazards of the land, so that only the greens were to be smoothed and levelled. Jack listened, rapt. It was true—while he no longer wished to demolish the side of Bulbarrow as he had in the early days, he was still cutting into the land too much. He hated Wilson's Housing Corporation and their wretched concrete bungalows spoiling the meadows, but was he not as guilty?

Curtis's plan seemed like a good one, but even if they stuck to it and worked ten hours a day, seven days a week, the course would not be finished until the end of August, and that was too late. He watched the men, as small as mice from this distance, labouring mightily on the concrete houses. He needed them for his golf course. 'Basset, Curtis, Ed, Mike. We need to poach some Wilson men,' he said quietly.

Basset nudged a butterfly off his lapel. 'We needs more than that. I 'as got a plan.'

AT MIDNIGHT, Jack met Curtis, Basset, Ed and Mike at the bottom of the lane by the signpost known locally as Charing Cross. The night was smuggler's dark, useful for their purpose. Jack felt nervous about what they were going to do and hadn't been able to eat any dinner. His stomach growled.

'What the bloomin' heck were that?'

'Sorry.'

'Right. Is everyone ready?'

There was a chorus of 'ayes' and the party headed down the hill into the blackness. They stole through the village until they reached the fork leading to Wilson's Housing Corp. The building site was half a mile down the road, situated on the outskirts of the parish. The men walked quickly, Jack panting to keep up with their swift strides. They stopped outside the entrance to the construction site. The large wooden gates were padlocked and a sign reading KEEP OUT was stapled to a post. Jack gave a worried huff.

'Be 'ere in minute or two,' whispered Basset, exuding confidence.

Jack stamped his feet to keep warm and pulled his coat around him. He could see Curtis only by the twinkling of his eyes; one green eye gave him a conspiratorial wink. There was rustling in the bushes behind them and Jack jumped, his heart beating loudly in his ears.

Two figures appeared from the shadows and Jack could make out a slim man wearing a trilby hat and a stocky fellow sucking on a pipe.

Basset took charge once more, 'Mr Rose-in-Bloom, this 'ere is Freddie Wainwright and Matt Baxter. They is workin' for Wilson's but would like very much to join us in our endeavours on the Pursebury golf course.'

Jack reached into his pocket and retrieved a brown envelope.

'The bonus we discussed.'

'Thank ee.'

There was a jingle as Freddie produced a set of keys and proceeded to unfasten the padlock.

'Is there no security?' Jack wondered in a low voice.

'Oh, shouldn't think so,' answered Matt.

There was a click as Freddie eased off the padlock and swung the gates open. They squealed horribly and Jack shuddered. But no one came. One by one they slipped into the still yard. It glittered with machinery: there was a small crane, cement mixers, towering poles of scaffolding and a small army of diggers. Half concealed in the shadows like a glowering beast of mythological power was the mechanical digger, its bulk hidden in the darkness and its vast outstretched claw slumped against the wall.

'Is it sleeping?' Curtis hissed softly.

Freddie dangled the keys, 'Aye, till I use these.'

The others observed from a distance as the young man leaped up into the square box cab and turned on the engine. It stuttered, then gave a low roar.

'Best move, he's not terribly good at reversin',' advised Matt.

The men stood flat against the fence and watched the creature crawl backwards on its metal tracks. Jack felt a pang of conscience—this was too much like stealing for his blood (list item 33: The Englishman is scrupulously honest). Which was why, unbeknownst to the others, he had brought another envelope of more cash. He scanned the yard for somewhere to stash it, spied a makeshift cabin and determined this to be the site office. While the digger entranced the others, he shoved his envelope underneath the door. Now he wasn't stealing, only renting.

'Mr Rose-in-Bloom!' hollered a voice.

Jack stood up quickly, banging his head on the door handle.

'Don't you want to ride in 'im?' Freddie called across the yard, apparently abandoning all attempts at secrecy.

Jack saw that all the others had crammed into the machine: Freddie and Matt sat on the seat; Basset, Ed and Mike hung out the windows; and Curtis was perched on the roof, like a strangely shaped hat. Jack waved and hurried over. Basset reached down and pulled him up with a strong arm.

The machine could only creep along and Jack believed he could have gone faster if he were participating in a three-legged race. He was balanced precariously on the running board at the side of the cab, and only Basset's restraining arm stopped him from tumbling onto the tarmac. Sweat trickled along his spine and he fully expected to hear at any moment the bells of a police car and for a Black Maria to pull up and cart him away. The others would be all right. He would be the one to go to prison—he was the Jew and the boss and would be blamed for corrupting these good English men. He considered whether it would be undignified to be sick.

'And we're 'ere,' said Basset, giving him a friendly pat on the arm.

Ed climbed down and swung open the gate leading to the bottom field, but the space was just too narrow and the digger tore one of the gate posts clean from the ground, leaving an unsightly scar along the metalwork. No one apart from Jack seemed in the slightest bit concerned. The beast was quieter in the field; its metal claws made less noise on the earth than the road.

Freddie was the only one who knew how to drive the beast, so Basset explained to him what needed to be done. Jack stared in awe as it dug a huge hole in the rough and deposited a tree, roots and all, into the chasm. The men gathered around the monster in the murk, clutching their hats and shaking their heads in respect.

'See how much stuff he can carry.'

'Aye. Aye. Fifty bloody horsepower.'

'*Fifty*. My God. My God. Never thought I'd see the day.'

'An' they do bigger ones, too.'

'Bigger'n him? Be bigger'n God.'

'He really is some-att.'

'It's a nice mustard colour,' added Jack, feeling left out.

Under Basset's direction, the machine manoeuvred the hillside back into place. The land was removed from the fairway and piled piece by piece upon the spot where the fifth hole used to be. Jack and Curtis sat on upturned buckets by the ponds and watched the machine work in its own pool of artificial light. While the others were entranced by the sheer power of the contraption, Jack was disconcerted. He was used to machines in his factory—great electric looms that wove the carpets and vats of industrial dye. He had imagined the countryside to be a rural idyll, free from the clamour of mechanisation. Unthinkingly, he took the flask Curtis proffered and took a hefty swig, 'Change, I suppose, has to come everywhere.'

Curtis stared through half closed lids, his lined skin looking like chestnut bark in the gloom. 'Aye. He comes alrigh' whether we wants 'im or not. I remembers the days afore t' railways. Back in them days, every village had 'is songs an' each one were a bit differen' than 'is next door. Then, one day trains come, like bleedin' griffins, an' Dorsit isn't jist Dorsit no more, but a piece of big England. No one sings the ol' songs any more 'cept me.'

Jack had no reply for the old man. He glanced to the east and saw that there was the thought of dawn in the sky, and behind him a wren began to chirp. He scrambled to his feet, offering Curtis a soil-stained hand.

'Come on. It's time.'

Jack walked briskly up the rise to the others, with Curtis bleary-eyed, trying to keep pace. Feeling rather brave, Jack stood in the path of the machine and, waving both arms wildly, forced it to come to a stop.

'Eh, what you do that fur?' said Basset crossly.

Jack pointed at the sky. 'It's dawn. We must take it back.'

Basset studied the east sceptically. 'Got least an hour.'

'No.'

'Don't yer want some of them bunkers? 'Ee could dig you some in a minute. Bob's your uncle.'

'My uncle was Morris. And no bunkers. We must take it back right now.'

Jack was resolute; he stood very upright and looked Basset in the eye. The other man met his gaze and then shrugged.

'What ever yer wants.'

Basset whistled and signalled towards the road. In the cab, Freddie stuck up his thumb and the machine began its slow descent towards the lane.

Jack walked beside the digger as it crept along the road. The metal treads clattered horribly against the hard surface making him wince; he had studiously avoided trouble for more than fifty years and here he was actively inviting it—he could not be less invisible than he was at that moment, walking slowly next to a giant yellow mechanical digger.

It took him a moment to realise that the digger had stopped and its vast engine had fallen silent. Up in the cab, Freddie fumbled with the keys.

'Out o' juice,' he announced.

'I'll get the spare can,' said Matt and climbed up to rummage around behind Freddie's seat. 'Ent 'ere.'

'Aw, shit.'

'This is it. I'm going to prison,' said Jack, and turned white.

Nimbly, Freddie climbed down and joined the others. They were at the bottom of the hill by Charing Cross. The hulking digger looked out of place, marooned in the middle of the road and blocking the narrow lane in both directions, its yellow sides brushing the hedge.

'Let's jis leave it here. Leave key's in 'im an' bugger off,' suggested Matt.

'Suppose someone nicks 'im?'

'Won't budge, will 'ee. No juice.'

'Well, that's settled then,' said Basset and marched up the lane.

The others muttered assent and began to follow, until Jack was left alone. He stared at their departing backs as they sauntered up the hill, then, with a final glance at the stationary digger, he trailed after them, as the red fingers of dawn streaked the morning sky.

THE MACHINE had done a splendid job clearing the debris from the fairway, but the green still needed to be levelled and reseeded and the tee rebuilt. The eighth and ninth holes had not been started and the seventh was not quite finished. All in all, there was a mountain of work still to do but Jack vetoed absolutely the illicit borrowing of any more machinery—they must continue by hand, a course of action made easier by Freddie and Matt bringing with them another dozen men from Wilson's Housing Corp. Sadie ordered rosebushes from Dorchester and planted them in clumps around the ponds and along the edges of the hazards. She threw seeds for wild flowers among the grasses in the rough. Jack faithfully recorded their progress in his weekly letter to Bobby Jones.

Dear Mr Jones,

Today we finished the seventh hole and toasted it (and poured a healthy drop into the hole—no doubt giving some poor earthworm a punchy breakfast). There was much laughter and even the womenfolk came along. My wife baked some excellent pear tarts and we ate them with the local clotted cream. It's strange, I've eaten those tarts many times—they're from an old Bavarian recipe—but they've never been so delicious as with that little Dorset addition. The damage (from a landslide this time, not the woolly-pig) has been repaired and the course looks simply marvellous. I wish you could see it. I'm crippled with bank loans. Any more disasters and we're up Stourcastle creek.

I've placed an advertisement in The Times—which I've taken the liberty of enclosing.

Yours sincerely etc. Jack Rose

ADVERTISEMENT

Brand New Golf Course at Pursebury Ash in Dorsetshire. Competition Match to celebrate the Coronation of Her Majesty The Queen Elizabeth to be held on June 2nd. Inaugural members: Sir William Waegbert (baronet) and Mr Henry Hoare Esq. (gentleman). Open to new members.

THERE WAS STILL the problem of the molehills. Knowing Jack would not approve, Basset waited until he was safely out of the way writing his letter, and then sent ferrets down the holes to root out the moles. The near-sighted creatures emerged terrified into the daylight, where Curtis and Basset crushed their skulls with hammers. The trimmed green was soon piled high with their minute, velvety corpses, which Curtis quickly skinned, carefully preserving the pelts. Moleskin gloves were much prized by fashionable ladies, and a few elderly women in the village still knew how to make them. Basset dug a grave at the bottom of the field and filled it with the tiny bodies. Jack remained cheerfully oblivious to their method, but was thrilled when his molehill problem mysteriously vanished.

On Wednesday morning, Sadie ambled down to the village hall carrying a fat chocolate sponge for the Coronation Committee. The sun beat down on the corrugated iron roof, and the ladies of the committee had abandoned the sweltering building for blankets on the village green. Sadie hovered unseen at the edge of the field, in the shade of a spreading chestnut.

'Has anyone heard back from the electrical store in Dorchester?' asked Lavender. A robust lady in a pair of olive slacks raised a hand. Lavender tipped her head imperiously, 'Yes, Mrs Hinton?'

'Tis as we feared, Mrs Basset. Bulbarrow Hill blocks all signals for the television. There is nothin' to be done.'

There was a collective sigh, and mutterings of 'What a pity', until Lavender raised her hand for silence. 'We need ideas, suggestions an' solutions, ladies,' said Lavender.

'We can a'ways listen in on t' wireless.'

'Whole village crowdin' round a wireless? It'll be a shambles.'

'Aye. No sense o' occasion.'

From the shade of the chestnut tree, Sadie listened to the swell of noise. She thought back to the last great Royal celebration, the marriage of Princess Elizabeth to Prince Philip of Greece, five years before. Then, there had been no possibility of watching the event on the television set. Jack and Sadie had scrutinised every photograph in the newspapers, and Elizabeth's school held a pageant a few days later, with a girl in a white frock acting the princess and another, hair slicked back, playing the part of the prince. That gave Sadie an idea. She stepped out from the shadow of the tree and into the midst of the chattering women, her chocolate cake held aloft. She cleared her throat.

'Aye, pop the cake indoors, Mrs Rose-in-Bloom,' said Lavender, preoccupied with the crisis.

'I . . . em . . . I . . . have an idea,' said Sadie, standing her ground.

The women on the rugs stared at her in surprise. Sadie's cheeks pinked under the scrutiny. 'At eleven o'clock, when Her Majesty Queen Elizabeth the Second receives the crown from the Archbishop of Canterbury, we should be crowning our very own queen.' She paused, and smiled at the others. 'The Queen of Pursebury Ash.'

Lavender jumped up in excitement. 'I like that idea, Mrs Rose-in-Bloom!' She flung her arms out wide, eyes shining, 'We, of Her Majesty's Coronation Committee, Pursebury Ash Branch, refuse to be defeated or to permit this village to go without a proper coronation at the proper time.'

There were shouts of agreement from the assembled women.

'Excellent idea. Marvellous,' said Mrs Hinton, taking the chocolate cake from Sadie and trying to shake her hand at the same time.

'Now,' said Lavender, 'Over elevenses, we must discuss the matter of the Coronation Chicken.'

'Aye,' agreed Mrs Hinton. 'If they're havin' it at Buckingham Palace, we are most certainly havin' it at Pursebury Village Hall.'

They spread a picnic out on the rug with Sadie's cake in pride of place. The sticky icing attracted a swarm of flies, which Lavender swatted away with a roll of newspaper.

'No, not 'im,' said Mrs Hinton, snatching the paper. 'He's the one with the instructions. I saved him special.'

Mrs Hinton passed it to Sadie, 'Here you take a look, Mrs Rose-in-Bloom. You are a handsome cook and you knows all about foreign food.'

Sadie settled down on the rug, and studied the paper. It was a page carefully cut from *The Times*:

CORONATION CHICKEN (COLD) (FOR 6–8)

2 roasting chickens; water and a little wine to cover; carrot; a bouquet garni; salt; 3–4 peppercorns; cream of curry sauce (recipe follows).

Poach the chickens, with carrot, bouquet, salt and peppercorns, in water and a little wine, enough barely to cover, for about 40 minutes or until tender. Prepare the sauce given below. Mix the chicken and the sauce together, arrange on a dish.

'Ahh,' said Sadie, giving a little murmur of recognition, 'I heard Constance Spry herself on the wireless. She explained how to make this. I have poached chicken before. In Berlin. I can show you—if you like?'

Lavender blinked, forced a tight smile and then relaxed. This was the first time Mrs Rose-in-Bloom had mentioned her German past. But, Lavender supposed, it wasn't sordid like Mrs Hinton's younger sister whose 'past' had been a sailor from Kentucky. Mrs Rose-in-Bloom's past wasn't her fault, and perhaps it was better that she spoke of it from time to time.

EARLY ONE MORNING, after planting a flag in the restored fifth hole, Jack gathered his workforce around the flagpole and climbed on top of an upturned seed crate so that they could all see him. There was a full score of faces staring back up at him and he gazed at them, and then at his golf course. The land was so beautifully restored that in a few months no one would ever know it had slid down the hillside. The green fields shone in the morning sunshine, while white puffs of cloud drifted across the blue sky. A cuckoo called from where apple trees and cricket willows had been planted to screen the bungalows.

'Thank you all for your hard work. Bobby Jones himself could not have laboured more mightily. There is only one more hole to be completed and then we will be triumphant!'

He took off his hat and waved it at the crowd, who bayed and whistled with enthusiasm. He noticed a balding man dressed in a grey flannel suit standing apart from the others, watching. Jack did not recognise him and, curiosity piqued, climbed down from his box. The others took this as the signal to go back to work, but the stranger in the suit did not move and instead addressed him in a confidential tone.

'Lovely spot you've got here.'

'Thank you,' said Jack, smiling proudly. In his view this was the most beautiful spot in all of England and hence the whole of the world.

'Means I am very sorry to give you these.' The man opened his briefcase and handed Jack a tightly bound document.

'What is it?'

'Afraid it is a cease and desist notice.'

'A what?'

'Cease and desist. Means you must stop all work immediately or face a large fine and possible imprisonment.'

Jack sank down on the box, gripping the papers in his hand and scanned the first few lines. Then it hit him: all this was his own fault. He always knew he shouldn't have stolen that mechanical digger.

'It's Wilson's Housing Corporation out for revenge. I know it,' he declared miserably.

The man looked surprised. 'It's the council, sir. Nothing personal. You need to apply for planning permission for golf courses.'

This was news to Jack and fury began to bubble inside him.

'It's a golf course! There are no buildings. Not even a stupid car park.'

The man gave a nasal groan. 'I understand. It does seem most unfair. But nowadays even golf courses need to apply for planning permission.'

'And how long will that take?'

'I can't tell you that, sir.'

Jack got to his feet and pointed furiously at the men working on the land. 'See them? Am I supposed to send them all home? They thought they were to have another month's solid work. Have some pity, Mr . . . ?'

The grey man looked at him, and relented. 'Brown. Mr Brown. I can try to call an emergency meeting at the planning commission. Try to get this resolved quickly.'

'Please,' said Jack.

'But you must halt all work.'

THE LETTER popped through the letterbox two days later, as Jack was quietly pretending to eat his breakfast. Sadie watched as he tore it open with the silver knife, slowly read the contents and wordlessly handed it to her:

> Dear Mr Rose,
>
> I am sorry to inform you that planning permission for the golf course at Pursebury Ash has been denied. A number of planning codes are in violation.
>
> Details of this decision may be obtained from the local planning officer, Mr G. Brown.
>
> Yours regretfully, Etc.

'Well, this is it. We're finished. *Fertig*.'

Sadie shook her head. This was not the Jack she knew. She watched as he rested his head on the kitchen table and shut his eyes.

'We'll sausage through,' she said.

'I am so tired. Too tired to fight any more.'

Sadie poked him in the ribs. 'Get up.'

He shuffled round the table to avoid her but she poked him harder.

'Stop it.'

'Not until you sit up and decide what we are to do next.'

Jack raised his head and gazed evenly at Sadie. She was wearing her floral apron and curlers but her eyes were full of ferocious determination. 'How much of the loan money do we have left?'

'Not much. Less than two hundred pounds.'

Sadie frowned. 'I think there is only one thing you can do,' she said.

JACK WAITED by the car at the top of Bulbarrow Hill, listening to a pair of magpies squabble. The evening was so warm that he was sweating in his jacket, and his silk tie choked him. A brown cow leaned on a gate chewing the cud and stared at him nonchalantly. After what seemed an endless wait, he watched as a red Morris Minor chugged its way up the steep slope. In pursuit of his golf course Jack had taken many risks, even pushed the law a little, but the thought of what he was about to do made him frightened. He watched as the red car crept closer and closer and hoped Sadie was right.

The car drew up next to Jack's Jaguar and Mr Brown climbed out. 'I would have preferred to meet in my office.'

Trembling, Jack reached into his pocket and drew out a brown envelope. Inside was all the money they had left, every last penny.

'I want to give you this. I hope it might encourage you to . . . reconsider.'

Mr Brown recoiled from Jack in revulsion. Slowly, he shook his head and his lips curled in contempt.

'Bloody Jews. You think you can buy us all. You disgust me.'

He hissed the words at Jack, his eyes narrow with hate. Jack stared in surprise. If it was not money they wanted, then why were they tormenting him? It was the same everywhere—they stopped Jews from doing business but when you paid your bribe, they let you go back to work.

'If you don't want my money, why do you refuse me planning permission?' Jack asked, bewildered.

The other man got into his car, started the engine and began to drive off but then, clearly having a change of heart, wound down his window.

'You, sir, were in violation of at least seventeen planning codes under section A, subsection fifty-nine, paragraphs twenty-six to ninety-one.'

'But . . . I didn't know there were planning codes for golf courses.'

'A poor excuse. The gentleman building the other course made no excuses. Submitted a nice set of *professional* drawings.'

Jack heard only the first part of Mr Brown's outburst. 'What other course?' he asked, colour draining from his face.

'I can't tell you that! It's confidential. But it's for eighteen holes with a modern clubhouse.'

Jack rubbed his forehead and his throbbing temples, trying to digest this new information. There couldn't possibly be demand for two golf courses in this area, and the other one had official approval, while his was outlawed. With a miserable sigh, he turned and slouched back to the top of Bulbarrow. He must find out who was building this new course—even though he was not sure what he would do then. He leaned against the gate and, closing his eyes, absent-mindedly stroked the ears of the cow, which began to lick him with its sandpaper tongue. How could he find out where this other *verdammt* course was? He thought of Sir William Waegbert. Jack was quite sure he would smooth out this altercation—Sir William was an important man.

JACK SIGHED as he drove to Piddle Hall. There had been money in carpets and he wished that he had paid more attention to his business, then he could have paid off his debts and the mortgage on the house. Now the factory needed a massive order, the sort that only ever came from governments—otherwise the bank loans would never be repaid. As he gripped the steering wheel, Jack realised that he'd been happy. That Sadie had been happy. More than anything, he didn't want to go back to the city. He liked it here, and he wanted to live where there were deer and badgers, and woolly-pigs.

Jack drove over the bridge across the River Piddle. It was called the Piddle here but became the River Puddle further downstream. It was said that the name was changed from Piddle to Puddle everywhere that Queen Victoria visited during her tour of Dorsetshire—the courtiers fearing that the word 'piddle' would make the Queen blush. Jack found this example of English prudery endearing—imagine being embarrassed by such a little word.

The stone eagles outside Piddle Hall glared down at him from their tall plinths, beaks still frozen open in silent shrieks. He gave a tiny shudder and wound along the curving driveway and drove straight to the stables at the rear, where he had been told to park the previous summer. The horses whinnied softly as he slammed the car door. His heart was beating fast. A little whisky and some good advice would help. There had been some changes since he was here last. What he presumed to be another stable had gone up.

He hurried to the main steps of the hall. Lights were on in the downstairs windows but the vast door was shut. Jack yanked a huge, cast-iron handle that dangled down at the side of the entrance and a shrill bell pierced the night. Instantly, there erupted a chorus of barking, followed by voices, until finally he heard footsteps entering the hall. The door clunked and he saw with surprise that Sir William opened the door himself, a pack of spaniels wagging at his feet. Sir William looked equally amazed to find Jack on his front steps. He still had his napkin tucked into his shirt and he stood there for a moment, paralysed, before his perfect manners took over.

'Come in, come in,' he said, ushering Jack inside.

'I am sorry to call like this,' said Jack apologetically, 'but disaster has struck and I need your help.'

Sir William stared for a moment. 'Oh, dear. Gosh. We'll sit in the library and you must tell me everything.'

Jack followed him into the dimly lit panelled hall and along a winding passageway into a cavernous library.

'I'll just be a moment. I must tell Lady Waegbert to continue without me.'

Left alone, Jack surveyed the faded volumes decorating the shelves. They were all bound in the same worn crimson bindings and coated in a thin layer of dust. He wondered whether Sir William used this room very often—it had the smell of something packed away and forgotten.

A few minutes later Sir William returned with apologies and without his napkin. He gestured for Jack to sit, and went across to a book shelf, where he pulled out several books, which turned out to be hollow carvings filled with a whisky decanter and glasses. His hand shook slightly as he poured two generous measures and gave one to Jack. His face was pale and troubled, causing Jack to wonder if he had been unwell and, guiltily, if he should be here bothering him with his troubles.

Sir William toyed with his glass, downed its contents, and helped himself to another. Then the baronet crossed his arms in his lap and closed his eyes. 'Well, man, let's have it then.'

'You're sure? I don't want to be a bother.'

'You've come all this way. May as well let it out.'

Taking the invitation, Jack leaned forward and in a low voice recounted his unhappy tale. Sir William let him speak without interrupting; his elegant face was impassive and Jack could not read his expression.

'I want this golf course so much. So very much,' he concluded, tears beginning to form in the corner of his eyes. 'Without it, I am ruined. I lose my house. *Everything*.'

Sir William said nothing.

Jack waited in agony for him to speak and made one final plea for his assistance. 'Can you help me to discover who this rival is? Please.'

Sir William got up and began to pace the room before moving to the stone mullioned window, where he stood gazing out into the darkness.

'It's me, Jack. It's my course.'

Jack did not hear him properly—could not understand his friend's words. 'Beg pardon?'

Sir William remained by the window with his back turned, so that Jack could see only the reflection of his face in the glass.

'I am building a golf course. Eighteen holes. Parking for a hundred automobiles. You must have seen the new clubhouse on your way in.'

Jack tried to speak and found he couldn't. He swallowed but his mouth had gone dry. At last, he managed a whisper. 'We were friends.'

'Come. We were acquaintances,' said Sir William smoothly.

'I gave you membership to my golf course.'

'And you may have membership to mine. It will be the finest course and the most exclusive in the South-West.'

Jack reeled. He barely registered that Sir William was offering him membership to an exclusive English golf club: the last item on his list and the reason for moving to the countryside. Now he was being beseeched to join an elite club by a knight of the realm and he did not care. He spoke softly but his voice quivered with hate.

'I will never be a member of your club. I do not wish to be part of any society that includes you. You are *ein Landesverräter*.'

Sir William did not understand the word but he comprehended the tone, and it was true; he had used Jack and then betrayed him. After making enquiries, he had discovered that there really was demand for a golf course out here in the sticks, and if someone was going to make money, Sir William was going to make damn sure it was he. These country piles took a fortune to run, and the Waegbert fortune was running low. Jack interrupted his thoughts with another furious tirade.

'I can never be English to you, can I? Did you want to teach the shitty little Jew-Kraut a lesson?'

The venom of the small man took Sir William aback. He disliked conflict of any kind—when he got the council to stop the building on Jack's land, they had promised him that they would not reveal who had lodged the objection. It made him angry.

'How dare you address me like this? You're nothing but a vulgar counter-jumper. Go back to your tailor's shop.'

Jack blinked, opened his mouth and closed it again.

Aware of his guilt, Sir William became full of self-justification, 'You built a golf course on the side of a hill. It's preposterous. You can't have played a round in your life. It would never have worked. I admit that, yes, you gave me an idea, but I am going about it in the proper way. Your scheme was never anything more than a ludicrous pipe dream.'

Jack stared at Sir William in dismay. He ached with the betrayal.

'I may not have played, but I studied Robert Hunter and Bobby Jones.'

Sir William gave a laugh of derision. 'You read Bobby Jones. I *hired* him.'

'I don't believe you.'

Sir William stalked to a desk in the corner and pulled out a piece of paper, which he tossed to Jack.

Dear Sir William,

On behalf of Mr Jones, I would like to accept the commission to design the proposed course at Piddle Hall. Mr Jones's fee is $1,000 non-negotiable. Please forward all maps, land surveys and—

Jack read no more. He felt a cracking in his chest and wondered if his heart could actually break.

He stood up and walked out of the library, along the panelled corridor and out into the hall. He opened the front door and descended the stone steps into the cool, black night.

WHEN JACK REACHED HOME, the house was quiet. Sadie must have given up waiting for him and gone to bed. He felt ill at the thought of telling her what had transpired. He had sacrificed everything for his golf course and the sake of finishing his list. Now, after twenty years in England, he was as poor as he had been when he first arrived, only now he was old and without hope.

Jack wandered forlornly into his study to write one last letter, and for the final time he pulled out a piece of heavy white paper from the sturdy desk. He grabbed his whisky and drank straight from the bottle as he wrote.

Dear Mr Jones,

My heart is broken. After all this time, after all my letters, how could you agree to design Sir William Waegbert's course? You did not even write to tell me yourself. Sir William Waegbert has betrayed me. But your betrayal is worse. I thought golfers were honourable men. True gentlemen.

I am finished but alas my golf course will never be finished. I am empty. There is nothing left at all.

This is my last letter.

Jack Rose

With that, Jack sealed the envelope, put it out to be posted and wearily climbed the stairs to bed.

Sadie was fast asleep, sprawled on top of the covers, her hair fanned out across the pillow. Quietly, Jack got undressed, and then carefully lowered himself down onto the bed beside her. He slotted his body in beside hers, slid an arm round her waist and laid his head on her pillow.

'I am so sorry,' he whispered.

CHAPTER EIGHT

When they heard the awful news, the village suddenly remembered that Sir William was poor and had wasted his fortune on horses. The tales grew; Sir William turned into a vagabond who owed all the shopkeepers money and had letched over every daughter in the village. Lady Waegbert, it was said, was forced to pay her vast gaming debts in obscene favours, but none of this comforted Jack—it could not help him now. He had no pity left for Sir William—he needed it all for himself.

Jack lost his exuberance like a balloon the day after a birthday. He sagged and stooped so that Sadie felt she was watching him wither before her eyes. At first she baked him 'cakes to heal a broken heart' but either the recipe was faulty or he would not eat enough. The course was silent; no one returned to complete the last fairway and the flags drooped in the stillness of the May afternoon. Inconsolable, Jack refused to see any of his friends and when Basset arrived to offer words of condolence, he stole out to the course and would not be found.

Determined to reason with him, Sadie hunted him down to his favourite spot, hunched on a patch of grass by the fifth hole. In the late-May warmth, the fairway grass had sprouted thick and lush, and barely resembled any more the neat crop of a golf course. Sadie smoothed her skirt and sat down carefully beside him. 'Why don't we stay in the village?'

Jack looked at her with mild surprise but said nothing.

'I mean, the house must be sold, but there might be enough left over to buy a small cottage.' Sadie took his hand and rubbed the back of it. 'There is only two of us and I'm sure we could afford a box-room so that Elizabeth could visit.'

Jack gave an unhappy cry, 'I can't do it, Sadie. I can't.' He could not bear to remain and watch new people desecrate his golf course, his dream of England. 'And, really, darling, what can we afford to buy? We've not even two hundred pounds. I'm sorry, dolly. I gambled and I lost.'

He did not need to say it. They both knew that the price of defeat was to leave, never to return.

THE FOLLOWING EVENING, Sadie persuaded Jack to take a walk around the village, on the condition that it was late and the working folk were all in bed. The cherry blossom was nearly finished and it landed in her hair like brown confetti. Bluetits zoomed to and fro taking last meals to their hungry chicks. The grass had sprouted and was the glossy green of early summer and she could hear the evening rattle of crickets in the fields. Out of habit they walked down to the parish notice board at Charing Cross but they were both too melancholy to talk. A smart poster painted blue, white and red was carefully pinned to the board and the second she saw it Sadie tried to turn back. But it was too late: Jack had begun to read.

Coronation of Her Majesty, Queen Elizabeth the Second,
Tuesday, June 2nd, 1953. ~~Golf Match at~~
~~'The Queen Elizabeth Golf Club'. Tee off 6.30 a.m.~~
Celebrations Pursebury Ash Village Hall, 11 sharpish.
Latecomers not admitted.
Due to unforeseen circumstances the golf match is cancelled.

He stood bewildered, then rubbed his eyes, gave a loud cough and cleared his throat, 'Must be making hay nearby. Always bothers my eyes.'

Sadie looked at the forlorn figure and decided she could bear it no longer. 'I think we should simply pack up and go. The sooner we leave the better.'

'Yes. No goodbyes. We'll just disappear.'

JACK BROUGHT THE CAR to the front door and loaded the cases. Sadie came scurrying out, locked the front door with the giant iron key and hid it in a flowerpot. As the car bounced along the uneven driveway, Jack peered into the gloomy trees on either side and tried to resist taking a last look at the house. This part of his life was finished. He mustn't look back, he mustn't.

The car snaked along the narrow lanes as the moon caught the last of the cow parsley frothing in the hedgerows and the white wings of flitting moths. In his pocket, Jack had the brown envelope with all their remaining money: £129, 6s and 10d. He had already decided how to spend it—they would take a room at the Ritz. The old, confident Jack would have spent all his money in the belief that more would come, and so he decided to feign optimism in the hope that it would return to him, along with his good luck.

They drove in silence as Dorset smoothed into Wiltshire; then they were in Hampshire and the first of the Home Counties. The roads widened and they began to see other cars. Villages became towns, and then swelled into suburbs, until at last they were in London. The city was a vast construction sight: blocks of flats sprouted like weird concrete plants and great cranes hung over the West End. They tried to drive up the Mall but it was already cordoned off for the coronation. Thousands of flags lined every street and hung from all the windows. They waited at lights on Piccadilly and then, at last, they reached the Ritz. A bellboy held open the car door and Jack handed his keys to a porter wearing a smart pillbox hat, who swiftly unloaded the car and then whisked it away to be parked out of sight.

Sadie wanted to be thrilled by the glamour and decadence of the hotel and managed a smile. 'Well, this is a treat, *Broitgeber.*'

Jack offered her an arm and, each acting a game of jollity for the benefit of the other, they went into the smart lobby of the hotel. The tiled floor shone with polish, a new and sumptuous red carpet accentuated the curve of the room and a magnificent vase of exotic lilies rested on a circular table. The clerk at Reception, stiffly clad in tails, bowed his head as he saw Jack.

'Good to see you again, sir. It's been a while.'

'Too long. It's good to be back.'

The receptionist gestured to the bellboy, who ushered them into the lift and shut the cage, which with the stutter of machinery carried them to the fourth floor. He showed them into an elegant room, the ceilings high and the bed neatly turned down. The moment he left them alone, Sadie flopped onto the soft mattress and nestled into a pile of pillows, and watched as Jack went to the drinks cupboard.

'Toast our return?'

'I don't mind.'

'There's whisky, a twenty-five-year malt. Gin, vodka. I can call down for a cocktail if you prefer.'

What she really wanted was a glass of milk and perhaps a boiled egg. She thought of her hens and of collecting their warm eggs.

'I'll have a tonic water.'

He passed her a glass, which she didn't drink but held against her hot cheeks. She took in the creases around Jack's eyes, the shadow of grey stubble on his chin. He never used to be still—he was always moving, buzzing here and there with a scheme or a wild idea. Now, he sat with his whisky clasped on his lap, motionless as a heron watching goldfish in the pond.

This wasn't her Jack. Sadie wanted him spilling over at the edges with chaos and enthusiasm. She sensed that with his abandonment of his list, England could now never be home. They would live and die in exile.

She'd always done her best to ignore his list, but now she wondered. He'd almost succeeded in finishing it, and she had an inkling that if he had, they would have belonged to Pursebury Ash.

Sadie heaved herself up and went into the bathroom to get ready for bed. With a piece of cotton wool and a dab of cold cream she removed her lipstick. 'My name is Sadie Rose,' she said into the mirror.

The new name still tasted strange on her tongue, and though it was a little inelegant, she would prefer to be Sadie Rose-in-Bloom. During her life, she had had many names and had lived in many places but Rosenblum belonged to another Sadie—the one who lived in Berlin all those years ago. They would never go back now—*before* did not exist any more. She didn't belong anywhere: she wasn't English and she certainly wasn't German. *Jew*. It was such a small word and caused so much trouble. *Jewess*. That sounded more enticing, sexy even—but was not a word that fitted her, a plump woman born in the suburbs. She smoothed her blouse and tried to get the creases out of her skirt. It was tighter than it was a year ago—she needed to diet. Was it really only a year? In that time she had come to love the landscape and the seasons and the sky and the cows and the stories.

Sadie realised that she was crying. She chided herself, '*Du blöde Kuh*. This won't do. Pull yourself together, silly old woman.'

She combed her hair, wincing as the brush caught on a burr. She untangled it, placing it on the corner of the basin. It was a tiny piece of the countryside and, somehow, she couldn't quite bear to throw it away.

JACK COULD PUT IT OFF no longer—it was time to call at the carpet factory. He left Sadie after breakfast and drove to the East End. Even this corner of London was decorated with flags and coloured ribbons and the streets were teeming with stallholders selling *beigels*, buns, shoelaces, stinking fish, soap flakes and pickle jars. Jack picked his way through the crowd to the narrow street leading to his factory.

The men working on the looms did not look up when he came onto the factory floor; they were far too busy threading and cutting to see him, and the bang of the door was lost in the clamouring din. Jack had forgotten quite how loud the great looms were—the crash and clatter of the machines vibrated through him. One loom was broken and silent, its metal guts spewed across the floor.

He walked to his old office, where his name still hung on a brass plaque, now coated in a layer of dust. Wiping it off with his sleeve, he went inside. There was a scurry of movement and Fielding scrambled to his feet, sending a pot of tea flying in his haste.

'Mr Rosenblum, sir. I am sorry. Wasn't expecting you . . . did you call?'

Jack settled into the battered chair opposite the desk and motioned for the man to sit back down. The waste bin was overflowing, a dead plant rested on the windowsill and, judging by the snapshot of Fielding's family on the desk, it was clear that this was no longer Jack's office.

'I am sorry,' said Fielding. 'When you didn't come back, it was easier for me to work in here. It has a telephone.'

'It was the sensible thing to do.'

'Are you coming back?' asked Fielding, his voice betraying a note of desperation. 'Things have gone to the dogs without you.'

'I'm sure it's not so bad,' said Jack smoothly.

Fielding passed him a file. He opened it and read the contents in silence. When he had finished, he closed the folder and leaned back in his chair, wondering what to say. Fielding was right—it was bad, worse than bad.

'I know this is my fault. I took money out of the business to start another concern. But these figures are dreadful. We're not even in profit.'

'I wrote to you again and again and you never replied, Mr Rosenblum. I needed you to make decisions and you wouldn't. We need new machines like the other carpet factories. These looms are old and break down every other day.'

Jack said nothing. He was to blame and he needed to make it right.

JACK SAT IN THE HOTEL BAR thumbing through the *Financial Times*. He tried to interest himself in the headlines and failed, then noticed a copy of the *Daily Mail* on the table next to him and started to flip through that, instead. On page two, a news story caught his attention:

Blushes at Red Carpet Trip-Up

Officials organising the Coronation have been left red-faced after ordering insufficient carpet for the big day. More than a mile of carpet is needed but careless measurements by staff have left a shortage of hundreds of feet! So will the Queen break with tradition and be forced to walk up a Paisley swirl? A Palace spokesman declined to comment.

Jack felt a prickle of excitement as an idea began to emerge like a fox from its winter den. He seized the paper, and half an hour later arrived at the gates of Rosenblum's Carpet Factory. At a half run, he tore along the corridor to his old office and flung open the door. Fielding was still seated at the desk, speaking on the telephone, but he lowered the receiver in surprise on seeing Jack, who stood backlit in the doorway, white hair shining like some kind of elderly, bespectacled genie. Jack thrust the newspaper at him and paced anxiously while Fielding read the piece.

'Well?' He demanded, when the man had finished. 'Can the factory produce all that carpet in a week with one loom out of action?'

Fielding stared at him. 'It would be almost impossible.'

Jack banged the desk with a fist. 'But almost impossible is still possible.' He leaned towards the younger man. 'This order is big enough to save us. Imagine in a week's time, Her Majesty walking up a red Rosenblum carpet.'

Carried away by Jack's enthusiasm, Fielding leaped from his chair, 'Do you think we'd be able to have the Royal Warrant "*By Appointment to Her Majesty the Queen*" stamped on the side of the delivery pantechnicons?'

'I am sure we could.'

A flush of excitement suffused the pallor on the manager's face.

'When this is over, Mr Fielding, I'm going to retire. I'm making you partner. I should have done it years ago, and then we wouldn't be in this mess. The decisions are up to you. This is your office now.' Jack glanced at the 'Tulip Surprise' colour swatch on the wall. Perfect. 'And Mr Fielding—George—I'm sorry.'

Fielding stared at him for a moment in silence, and then nodded, 'Thank you.' He picked up the telephone receiver, 'Hullo, operator? Can you put me through to Buckingham Palace?'

WALKING INTO THE HOTEL, Jack knew he had done the right thing; his heart had gone out of the business and so it was right that he handed it on. He wasn't sure what he would do next, but he knew it wouldn't be carpets. The porter held open the door as Jack slipped inside. A second later, he dropped his hat in shock: there in the marbled lobby stood Jack Basset and Curtis.

For a moment Jack thought he was seeing things. Both men had dressed for the occasion: Curtis wore an ancient tweed suit and, for once, had used braces to hold up his trousers, rather than an old spotted tie; while Basset was in his Sunday suit but still seemed out of place in the mirrored lobby. He shifted awkwardly from foot to foot and gazed about him, spying Jack with relief. Skidding on the polished floor in his hurry, Basset enfolded the smaller man in a large embrace.

Jack eased himself free and shook hands with Curtis, bewildered.

'Let's go upstairs. Sadie will want to see you,' he said, guiding them towards the lift. Curtis started as the metal doors of the cage clanged shut. 'This is like them cattle cages at Stur market on a Monday. Feel like I is 'bout to be sold for 'alf a crown.'

When Sadie opened the door, her eyes went wide with surprise. It was nearly six and she was just beginning to wonder what had happened to her husband. She ushered them inside, wishing she had cakes to offer. Having visitors and not being able to feed them was a travesty.

Basset undid his top button, and sank into one of the deep armchairs with a grateful sigh. Underneath his weather-beaten suntan he looked exhausted. 'Traffic was terrible. N'er see sa many cars in all my life. An 'ee wasn't no bloody use,' he muttered, with a dirty look at Curtis.

'May I get you a drink?' Jack asked, ever the host.

Curtis produced from his pocket a large, familiar-looking flask. 'Brought 'ome brew.'

'Only thing 'ees good for. Stupid auld bugger's no good fer reading maps, that's fer sure,' complained Basset, snatching the flask. He unscrewed the cap and after taking a swig passed it to Jack, who took it gratefully and helped himself to a deep draught.

'So,' said Jack, trying to sound casual. 'What has brought you to town?'

'I 'as al'ays wanted to see Tower o' London. My great-great-great-uncle Billy got 'is 'ead chopped off there.'

Jack studied Curtis and saw a smile flicker at the corners of his mouth. Then, the old man's eyes narrowed. 'Yoos left without even a goodbye. I doesn't 'ave yer fancy ways, Mister Rose-in-Bloom, but where I is from, that's rude, that is. Enough to make you a ninnywally.'

'I'm sorry.'

'Right you are. 'Ave another.'

Curtis passed the bottle back to Jack, who took a gulp.

'We came to give yer this.'

Basset slid a hand into his breast pocket and proffered a telegram to Jack, who stared at it for a moment.

'Well, gowarn. Op'n it.'

'Yes, open it.'

Sadie, Curtis and Basset watched closely as Jack read the sender's name.

'It's from Bobby Jones.'

'Aye. Aye.'

Jack's hands began to tremble.

'Give it to me, Jack,' said Sadie.

Unable to speak, he passed her the telegram and she unfolded it.

Date: May 15, 1953
Post Office Telegraphs
No fees to be paid unless stamped hereon.
TO CHIEF EXECUTIVE DORSET COUNCIL FROM BOBBY JONES AUGUSTA GEORGIA USA

NO LONGER SUPPORT SIR WILLIAM WAEGBERTS GOLF COURSE STOP DID NOT REALISE MY FRIEND JACK ROSENBLUMS GOLF COURSE NEARBY STOP FULLY SUPPORT JACK ROSENBLUM STOP WILL PLAY IN CORONATION MATCH AT PURSEBURY ASH STOP

Jack took the paper from Sadie, read it and then read it again, all the while his head swimming. Basset decided that a little explanation was necessary.

'Clerk in council's office gave me this. Sold his dad some cows at good price last year like, an' 'ee thought it jist might interest me—yoos and me bein' friends like. Mr Jones sent this 'ere telegram to the council and another to Sir William. Auld Waegbert's shittin' a fury.'

Curtis could no longer keep quiet but jumped to his feet and began to prattle excitedly.

'Yer see, Jack, yer see? Din' I tell yer to keep an writin' to ol' Mister Jones? I said it were right thing to do an' look now! I bet it were the bit we told 'im 'bout the woolly-pig mischief what dun it, mind. That ud bring dew to a man's eye, right enuff.'

Jack swallowed hard, trying to take in this momentous news.

''Ee won't work no more for old Sir William cos 'ee don't want to spoil yer chances at success. Yoos alwa's said 'ee was a nice man, mind.'

'And he really wants to play in the Coronation match? You're quite sure?'

'Aye. Says so right 'ere in black 'n' white.'

Jack could hardly believe that his letters had achieved such a profound effect. He had confided everything to Bobby Jones—in part because he had come to accept that Bobby would never, ever read them. But he had, and they'd inspired in the greatest, most illustrious golfer of all time a feeling of friendship towards him, Jack Morris Rose. It was a miracle. He took the flask from Basset and drained it in a single swig. Was it possible? Could there be hope after all?

Curtis fixed Jack with a steady gaze. 'Come 'ome,' he pleaded.

Jack was struggling to absorb all of this new information and, when he started to speak, it was only to find he had forgotten his words.

'But what about the other course?' said Sadie.

Jack found his voice and wagged a finger. 'Yes, yes. Sir William will just hire another chap to design his perfect eighteen holes.'

Basset's nose twitched and he stared at his feet before looking up and meeting Jack's eye. 'Well, it's a funny thing, but Sir William Whatnot seems to 'ave a terrible woolly-pig problem.'

SIR WILLIAM WAEGBERT was sitting quietly in the breakfast parlour and sipping a cup of tea when he noticed a deep, muddy furrow slashed across his manicured fairway. He rushed outside, shirt-tails flapping, and stared aghast at the desecration of his perfect green turf. There, on a scraping of muck, was a fat, round trotterprint, bigger than that of any domestic pig. It was of such a size that it could belong only to a giant boar. Sir William had his gardeners rake over the damage and reseed the lawn but in the morning, as Sir William surveyed the garden from his bedroom window, he saw instantly that the woolly-pig had struck again.

Labourers had arrived at Piddle Hall from all over the county to prepare the estate for the plans drawn up by the new golf-course designer. They dug and they raked and they preened and they pruned, but every morning, all across the grounds, they were met with fresh marks left by the rampaging woolly-pig.

Several miles away, Jack arrived home to discover that his course was complete. Basset and Curtis led the Roses through the garden gate and out into the field where, fluttering in the summer breeze, were nine chequered flags. Jack stood on the newly rolled ninth green and surveyed the finished scene with awe. It was done: his very own golf course. Basset and Curtis watched with interest as he turned white then pink, and were briefly concerned he was going to cry, but then Jack simply seized Curtis and kissed him solemnly, while the old man made popping sounds of surprise.

'You've done it. I despaired, I gave up, but you didn't abandon me. This, this is friendship,' Jack concluded, gravely planting another kiss on the rough cheeks of the other man.

Sadie shook hands with each of them in turn, gratitude radiating from her eyes. The sun burned through the clouds and the air was filled with the scent of flowers. The buds on the rosebushes Sadie had planted around the pond were opening and formed clumps of crimson and cream against the green grass. Curtis produced his flask from his back pocket and held it up.

'A toast, to our very big success.'

Jack put out a hand. 'Yes. A toast to our success and to the Queen Elizabeth Golf Club. God save the Queen.'

Curtis grinned, took a swig and then passed the jar around the group. Each took a sip in turn, echoing the toast. Basset gave the flask to Sadie who, with scarcely a shudder, wetted her lips with the pungent liquid.

'God save the Queen,' she said, 'And all of you.' Unable to articulate her thanks further, she smiled and quietly retreated to her garden, leaving the men alone on the hillside.

'So how did you get the planning permission?' Jack asked in wonder.

Curtis and Basset exchanged looks and chuckled. Curtis sat down on a bank of daisies, sticking his leather boots out in front of him.

'This is an auld place. We doesn't care too much for these sniv'lin' rules. No busybody's tellin' me what to do with my land, or nothin'.'

The ancient man spoke slowly, while Basset harrumphed his agreement.

'But I can get arrested. Go to prison,' said Jack, still worried, as he settled down between them.

Basset chuckled, 'Aye, right. They takes you and they takes us all. They isn't goin' to do nothin'.'

From the top of the hill the church bell began to chime midday. As the deep note echoed around the valley, Basset got to his feet.

'Right you are, then. That's my dinner bell, that is. Best get 'ome or Lavender will give us a right earful.'

With a friendly wave, he disappeared across the meadow, while the other two lay down sleepily upon the mossy bank.

'Take a big breath, Jack, an' look at the gleam in the grass an' the sun in the sky.'

Jack filled his lungs with fresh air and looked at the light shimmering along the grass. He felt safe under this big blue sky. The village was at the edge of the world where the mundane rules did not apply. He remembered Curtis telling him months ago that this was part of the old world, an ancient place belonging to King Alfred, or was it Albert? Jack resolved to be like one of the men of old and ignore the piffling rules of planning departments. He disliked modernity and so he would be like the other men of the village and pretend it wasn't there. This was a corner of another place, with bluebells, willow herb, fat glossy cows and mythical pigs.

'No one tells us what to do but Jack,' murmured Curtis softly.

'Oh?' said Jack in surprise with a sideways glance at his friend, whose head was propped on an old molehill pillow.

'Not Jack Basset,' said Curtis. 'Jack-in-the-Green.'

'Jack-in-the-what?'

'Jack-in-the-Green. You know. The Green one. Robin of the Wood. 'Ee keeps everythin' in balance.'

He gestured to the concrete bungalows on the horizon. ''E'll flood out them houses, in time, turn 'em back to water meadow an' muck. Not these ten year perhaps, but 'ee will.' He pointed with a stubby thumb at Bulbarrow Ridge. 'Aye. That's 'is back.'

Jack turned to gaze once more at the jagged outline of Bulbarrow against the horizon and realised that if he shut one eye and squinted it did resemble a giant man sleeping. But, he wondered if this was the same as the tall tale of the woolly-pig. 'So, have you ever seen him, this Jack?'

Curtis chuckled. 'No one 'as seen Jack-in-the-Green. 'Ee's not a thing or a man. 'Ee is the trees, an' the gleam in the grass an' the damp mornin' dew an' that feelin' you gits in an evenin' when the wind's in the ash leaves.'

Jack felt a strange sensation in his belly, and when he closed his eyes he imagined that he could hear the worms churning the earth beneath the grass. There was something familiar about Curtis's words, as though he was telling a story that Jack already knew.

'A barn owl's white wings under a full moon,' he said.

'Aye. An' in the stink of badger shit on a nice summer's night—that's a good 'un.' Curtis sat up and looked straight at his friend. 'That's 'ow we knew yoos was all right. You'd seen Jack.'

'I had? But no one sees Jack.'

'Aye. Not as such. But yoos dug this land all by yerself for thirty days and thirty nights. We all watches you from top o' Bulbarrow. That were Jack.'

He stared at Curtis in wonder.

''Ee's in the earth an' in our flesh. When a man can work tireless like, beyond what is normal for a little man, that's Jack-in-the-Green,' Curtis explained, with a twitch in his smile. 'Did yer not wonder 'ow a chap like yoos managed it?'

Jack marvelled—he *had* worked with incredible energy, but he had not considered where this vigour had come from.

'So Jack must have wanted this golf course, then?'

'Aye,' Curtis pulled his hat over his eyes and added, 'Fer now.'

LATER THAT AFTERNOON, Jack sat at the kitchen table working out the playing order and the pairs for the Coronation tournament. Now everyone in the village wanted to play, so he was forced to decide the entrants by lottery—it was rather complicated and made his head ache. He needed a smoke to help him think and went outside to sit on the front porch. The garden had changed in the week they had been away. The jasmine around the front door had burst into flower and some of the white blooms had already withered.

Jack stubbed out the cigarette, stood up and pressed down the heavy iron latch on the door, only to find it was stuck and that he had locked himself out. Usually, Sadie would let him in but she was at the village hall with the Coronation Committee. He had an idea: he could stop writing the blasted tournament timetable and go and have a drink with Curtis instead—there were important things to discuss.

In all the time they'd been friends, he realised, he'd never been to Curtis's home and was not even sure exactly where the old man lived, although he had mentioned his orchard several times. Undeterred, he sauntered down the lane, admiring the colourful coronation posters, while women buzzed to and fro looking harassed. Curtis's orchard lay on the outskirts of the village, down a narrow dirt track. It was marshy and dank in the wet, while in the summer it swarmed with gnats and fearsome Blandford flies. Once, a long time ago, this had been a pleasant part of the village, with ten or more cottages and a stony lane leading to them. But then the river had changed its course and turned the road into a flowing stream. The cottages had flooded and, within a few years, the wattle walls were washed away and the families forced to relocate up the hill. He gave a low chuckle—Jack-in-the-Green must have wanted it back.

It had been a damp spring and the sodden water meadows were filled with wild flowers—pale pink spotted orchids, lemon balm and marsh marigolds. He tramped a path through the long grass towards a green shepherd's hut nestling in a far-off orchard that lay a good half-mile from even the dirt track. He was amazed that anyone lived in a place so isolated—the old man's nearest neighbours were a family of yellow wagtails nesting in an ancient sycamore tree that towered above the hedgerows.

Jack pushed open the wooden gate leading into the orchard and halted to gaze about him. There must have been a hundred trees but the grass around them was neatly trimmed, in contrast to the waving green of the surrounding meadows. The blossom on the branches had faded and early bees buzzed among the leaves. The shepherd's hut sat in the middle of the orchard, painted an olive colour that was starting to flake. It rested on four large iron wheels, red with rust, and a short ladder led to a small door in one end. A thin spiral of wood smoke rose from a narrow chimney on the side of the hut—Curtis must be at home. Jack paused on the top rung of the ladder to admire the view of Bulbarrow. He could make out the medieval church perched on the hilltop and the thatched roofs of the village and, while it might be lonely, no one could deny that Curtis had picked a magical spot for his home. Rousing himself, Jack rapped on the door. There was no answer.

He knocked again, louder this time. Nothing. He wondered if Curtis was sleeping and if he ought to come back later. He decided to try one last time and thumped on the door with his fist. The door creaked open. Gingerly, he pushed it open and crept into the cabin. It was warm and dark and, in the corner of the single room, he saw the red gleam of a wood-burning stove, throwing out a steady heat. There was almost no furniture—only a high-backed chair, a tattered fleece covering the wooden floor and a basket of logs. In a low cot, Curtis lay fast asleep with his mouth open. Jack knew he should turn around and leave the old man, but there was something about the stillness of the sleeping figure that unnerved him.

'Curtis,' he called softly.

He gave the small form a gentle nudge. It made no response. Jack sat on the edge of the cot and lowered his ear to Curtis's mouth. No breath tickled him. He touched his neck and felt for a pulse. The old man's skin was cool.

Curtis Butterworth, the last of the old Dorset men, was dead. His life had ended less than a mile from where it had begun, over a hundred years before.

Jack listened to the quiet of the afternoon. This strange old man was the greatest friend he had ever known, and yet he did not shed a tear. Curtis's stout boots were lined up next to the door and a bloodied brace of pheasant hung from a nail. He noticed something else. Pinned beneath the dead birds was an envelope with 'Meester Jack Rose-in-Blom' written upon it. He unfastened the letter, then, not knowing what he ought to do next, sat down by the cot, and opened the envelope. Inside was a note.

Deer Meester Ros In Blom

Yoos was the onlee one to trooly believe in dorsit woolly peg. Them others thinks it is only silly childers tail. Tis most unfortoonate. They is hignorant.

ONLY TROO DORSIT MEN CAN SEE IM, THAT WOOLY PEG (an Dorsit men is the bist of all English men).

Not them piles of cow mook. They is noggerheads, ninnywallies and effing turds. Ateeen deys after auwld midsommer Drink 5 pints cider as per instructshons (resipee on back of this paper) and look top bulbarrow. at noon. Yoos afectsionate frend,

Curtis

p.s Please take them pheasants. Tis a shame to waste em like.

Jack read the letter through three times. Curtis must have known he was dying. He had retreated into his hut like a wild animal that crawls into the hedgerow to die, and his last act had been to pass on his recipe to Jack.

THEY BURIED CURTIS with his last flask of special cider—everyone knew he could not face eternity without a good drink. Jack and Sadie had never been to a Christian burial before, and they stood by the grave with the rest of the village, ready to throw a handful of earth onto the coffin. Jack felt that there was a Curtis-shaped hole in the universe, an emptiness where once he had been. Curtis hadn't needed a list to be the best of all Englishmen.

After the service, Basset erected a temporary headstone fashioned out of wood, on which he had painted the words that would be transferred to the gravestone for posterity:

'Curtis. Born Last Century. Died May 28th, 1953, aged somewhere between eighty-nine and one hundred and thirteen-ish.'

In the now-deserted churchyard, Jack held the wooden board as Basset wedged it into the soft earth.

'He were one of a kind. Unique like.'

Jack nodded, dumb with grief.

Basset paused to stare into the horizon. 'I wish 'ee'd given 'is recipe to some 'un. It is awful sad that 'is cider dies with 'im.'

Jack reached into his pocket and felt the letter, but said nothing.

CHAPTER NINE

The kitchen at Chantry Orchard had been transformed into an alchemist's den, with cauldrons of simmering water and a mountain of feathers from the plucked chickens, now lying naked and headless, in piles ready for the pot.

'Oooh. I think 'ee's done,' said Mrs Hinton, prodding a fat bird poaching in a vat of water and Jack Basset's elderflower wine.

'Juices running clear?' said Sadie.

'Oh, yes, chief cook-lady,' replied Mrs Hinton with a toothy smile.

'Bring him out then,' commanded Sadie, handing her a fearsome carving fork and a large plate.

As one fowl was removed, Lavender plunged in the next.

'I'm right glad we is doin' 'im today. Imagine the kerfuffle if we was to make 'im on Coronation Day?' said Mrs Hinton.

Sadie raised an eyebrow—she quite agreed. Fortunately the recipe was clear: the chicken must be made in advance and chilled. This was most considerate of Constance Spry, as otherwise Sadie suspected all the ladies of England would miss the festivities in order to cook for the menfolk. On the great day, the entire country would eat the same luncheon, the nation transformed into a giant dining hall.

Mrs Hinton effortlessly jointed the chicken on a carving board. With a polished blade, she diced it into neat bites and scraped the meat into a vast china serving bowl. Lavender spooned in mounds of creamy mayonnaise, sprinkled on the curry powder and an entire jar of apricot jam.

'You got to check 'im, Mrs Rose-in-Bloom,' said Lavender.

Dipping her finger into the mixture, Sadie took a long lick.

'Good. But needs something more.'

Mrs Hinton fetched the torn page of newspaper and recited the ingredients. 'Tomato paste, curry powder, jam, cream, mayonnaise, onions . . . No, we've not forgotten anything.'

But Sadie knew when something was missing. She closed her eyes. 'Currants. It's wanting currants.' Emil's currants.

Lavender and Mrs Hinton watched curiously as she produced a box from her cavernous larder, and sprinkled in several handfuls. With a long-handled wooden spoon, she stirred the creamy-yellow mixture, and took another taste. Her teeth tingled. 'Yes. It's right now.'

Lavender plunged in a teaspoon and sampled a mouthful. There was something else in the mixture, a nameless something that wasn't there before. She met Sadie's gaze. 'Yes,' said Lavender, 'tis exactly right.'

LATER THAT AFTERNOON, Jack sat at the kitchen table and read Curtis's crumpled note for the hundredth time. Only Curtis believed the woolly-pig was real, but Jack remembered the grunting cry he had heard across the snow all those months ago. And that was why Curtis had left the recipe to him and him alone; the rest of the village were unbelievers.

'Well? Have you started making the cider?'

Jack looked up to find Sadie reading over his shoulder. 'I'm too busy. I'll get to it after the coronation.'

'You will do it right now, Jack Morris Rose-in-Bloom,' she declared, her hands lodged firmly on her hips.

Jack was surprised at her vehemence. 'Why? You don't think it's real?'

Sadie shook her head. 'It doesn't matter. This is how he wanted you to remember him. You must honour the wishes of the dead, and this is how he wants you to say Kaddish.'

'But what about the golf game?'

'What about it?'

'It's the same day. I'll have to drink all that cider, then play in a golf-match with Bobby Jones, watch the coronation and then climb up the hill—while I'm blind drunk.'

Sadie raised an eyebrow. 'I am sure you'll manage.'

Jack realised his wife was right—this was the way to remember his friend. He read through the recipe. There were some odd items that needed to be added to a regular batch of cider: enchanter's nightshade, mangel-wurzle, wolfsbane, water from Chantry Orchard spring collected at dawn.

With Sadie's help he managed to track all of them down, adding each as he found it to a vat of cider left in the stable from the autumn. It hissed and emitted noxious fumes that smelled a little like Curtis.

JACK SHOOK SADIE AWAKE at five in the morning.

'Wake up. Get up. You need to be ready.'

Thick with sleep, she opened her eyes to see Jack sitting on the edge of bed proffering a cup of tea.

'Did you sleep at all?'

'I sleep tomorrow. Today is the great day. Get up.'

Sadie gave a tiny groan and rolled out of bed.

While she dressed, Jack sat on the sill and gazed from the window towards the lane. Rows of red, white and blue bunting were tied to the trees; Union Jacks dangled from the eaves of all the houses and the whole village gave the appearance of having been scrubbed—cottages had been whitewashed, windows cleaned with vinegar, and sills given a lick of paint.

Elizabeth was waiting for her parents in the kitchen.

Sadie smothered her daughter in kisses. 'What a wonderful surprise—I thought you were watching the coronation in Cambridge.'

'Yes. But then, I thought I'd rather be here.'

Jack beamed. 'It is a little late to add you to the playing order.'

Elizabeth shrugged, 'I'd prefer to watch anyway.'

'Good, good.'

Jack rubbed his hands together in eager anticipation. Elizabeth's unexpected arrival was a sign—this was going to be a splendid day. He took his first sip of cider—five pints was a lot to get through, and a little nip might help his game. Soon, Basset arrived armed with the morning newspaper—he had declined the offer to play, preferring to caddy instead—and placed it on the table. The family crowded round to study the pictures of the Abbey set up for the coronation.

'Carpet looks good,' said Jack, 'but so it should. Highest-quality wool. Well, five hundred yards of it are anyway.'

Jack watched as the sun came up over the chicken shed. He was worried; it was nearly half-past six, the tournament was due to start, and there was no Bobby Jones. He took another draught from his flask.

Basset cleared his throat and pointed at the kitchen clock. 'Thinks we'd best go. Can't let the first match start late, now, can we?'

Effortlessly, Basset picked up both Jack and Sadie's clubs and walked down to the golf course. The little group heard the sound of the crowd before they could see them—the air vibrated with cheering voices and whooping shouts. The edges of the course were thronging with people, hundreds of them by the trees. Jack saw twinkling on the top of Bulbarrow and realised a moment later that it was the reflection of binoculars from hundreds more people, who had all flocked to watch from the hill.

'Good God,' he whispered. 'Everyone in Dorset's here.'

'Aye. An' there's a bus from Wiltshire,' added Basset.

Jack's stomach gurgled—now that the moment was here, he was more than a little anxious and, to crown it all, Bobby Jones was late. He felt Sadie slip her hand into his. Just then, there was an enormous rumble overhead and the sky seemed to shake. The trees shuddered and the cries of the crowd were drowned out as a small, very noisy biplane swooped down. It circled lower and lower, searching for a place to land and then, engine spluttering, touched down on the flat top of the hill. A moment later, a figure climbed out over the wing, pausing to pull out a bag of golf clubs, and then bounded down the hill. As the engine lapsed into silence, the crowd roared with excitement.

Jack, Sadie and the other golfers waited expectantly on the first tee, all watching as the figure drew closer until, finally, he reached them. He was immaculately clad in brown tweeds and polished golf shoes, his skin lightly tanned from the pleasant American sunshine.

'Bobby Jones,' announced the man, warmly clasping Jack's hand.

'Jack Rose-in-Bloom. We're so pleased you could make it.'

Bobby Jones continued to grip his hand firmly. 'Wouldn't have missed it for the world, Jack. I've kept every single one of your letters—sorry I'm not one for replying—and I savoured them all year long. Gee, at first, I couldn't believe you were for real.' Bobby opened his jacket just wide enough to display the letters carefully stashed in the inside pocket, and Jack puffed with pride like a robin with the fattest worm on the garden wall.

'Shall we?' Bobby Jones enquired politely, in his soft Augustan drawl.

As he gazed at the expectant faces in the crowd, Jack turned to Bobby Jones. 'Would you do me the honour of opening the match?'

'Why sure.'

Jack stood next to Sadie, keeping a respectful distance, as the great man walked to the first tee. A hush fell over the crowd. Bobby produced a wooden tee from his pocket, pushed it into the ground and then, with a motion of exactness, placed upon it a white ball. He stretched his arms above his head and swivelled his hips to loosen them. With unhurried calm, he selected his driver and, at last, assumed his famed stance. He was totally at ease, body balanced and poised; then he raised his club and, with the smoothest of movements, brought it down in a steady sweep. There was a satisfying click as the ball flew into the distance. Jack gazed in awe as it flew straight down the fairway and landed with a gentle thud at the edge of the green and rolled neatly to the base of the flagstick. The crowd clapped its raucous appreciation.

Now it was Jack's turn. He took another swig of cider to steady his nerves. His knees shook as Basset handed him his driver, and he walked up to the tee. He stood with legs shoulder-width apart and flexed his arms. This was the moment. He sensed everyone watching him as he placed the tee carefully in the earth and popped the small white ball on top. He settled over the ball, brought the club up high, and swung down with a powerful swoosh and then . . .

Nothing.

Jack glanced down to see the white ball still perched on the tee.

The crowed bellowed its approval. No one had ever seen a game of golf before and they were certain Jack's technique was masterful. 'Why doncha take another swing,' said Bobby Jones kindly.

Jack managed his second shot with slightly more dignity than the first: the ball rolled twenty yards down the hill before coming to rest in the rough, causing him to wonder if, perhaps, it might have been better to practise.

Now it was Sadie's turn. Jack had worked very hard to convince her to play; he had bought her a beautiful set of lady's clubs and at first only the knowledge that they would be wasted otherwise, had persuaded her. But now, to her surprise, she was rather looking forward to it. She had never held a club before; but, she reasoned, she couldn't be much worse than Jack. She had studied Bobby Jones very closely and, after slipping her tee into the ground, tried to mimic his stance. It felt surprisingly comfortable and she was quite relaxed as she filtered out the din of the crowd. She raised her club, and then brought it down in a seamless arc. There was a crack, and she watched in utter astonishment as the ball sailed through the air and landed in the middle of the fairway.

'Sweet Jesus,' said Bobby Jones in amazement. 'Your wife has a perfect swing. She's a natural.'

Jack turned scarlet with pride.

SADIE WON the women's match by twelve strokes and Bobby Jones the men's by a hundred and three. Jack was not the worst golfer in the competition and actually made it into the top three simply by not losing his ball. Twenty-seven balls were lost completely, but no one seemed to mind and the crowd hooted encouragement at every stroke. When the match ended there was a small celebration on the final fairway. The crowd cheered as Jack awarded the women's medal to his wife and the first-ever Queen Elizabeth Golf trophy to Bobby Jones. Bobby held it aloft and posed cheerfully for photographs before climbing back into his plane and taking off into the hazy sky.

After it had gone, Basset cleared his throat and raised himself to his full height for the final announcement.

'I wish to ask Mr Jack Rose-in-Bloom, with the full authority of the Coronation Committee, if he would do us the honour of crowning the Pursebury Queen at the coronation today in the village hall at eleven o'clock.'

Jack was dumbstruck—he took off his glasses and cleaned them again on his tie. He tried to speak but there was a strange feeling in his throat.

A SHORT WHILE LATER he sat down in the garden, enjoying the pleasant sunshine on his bald head. He was deeply touched at being asked to crown the village queen, but also a little concerned—considering the amount of cider he was supposed to imbibe. According to Curtis's instructions, he needed to scramble to the top of Bulbarrow before midday. The coronation was due to start at eleven, but Jack knew that village events rarely ran to time—he was also dubious about being able to make the steep climb after five pints of the brew. He concluded it was best not to think about it.

He took a gulp of cider now; it burned his throat and made him choke—this was the proper stuff all right. His eyes started to droop and he drifted off to sleep, and dreamed of Curtis. The old man was alive again and they sat on the grass above the fifth tee, sharing the flask.

'Ah. Now that's there is proper stuff,' Curtis said, giving a great yawn.

'I followed your instructions.'

'I know yer did. But tisn't many chaps what can make it. Takes a special summat.' Curtis chuckled. 'Yoos is a proper Dorsit man now. A real good Englishman. An' yoos knows what that means.'

'Dad.' Elizabeth roused him from his deep doze. 'Dad.'

Jack opened his eyes and was instantly filled with sadness—his friend was dead once more.

'It's half ten. You need to go down to the village hall.'

'All right. All right.'

Furtively, he took another gulp of the strange-smelling liquid. He had lost count now of how much he had drunk but supposed that this was a good sign. Gratefully, he leaned against his daughter and together they made their way down the lane.

Jack had a seat set up outside the village hall; it was the same wooden one as everyone else, but on his lay purple robes, a cardboard cut-out of a bishop's mitre and a shepherd's crook, all of which he sportingly donned. Behind the audience rows, twenty long tables covered with white cloths and strewn with red roses had been laid out on the village green, ready for the luncheon. Banners blew in the wind and children waved flags. The Pursebury Queen's throne rested in the centre of the green on a raised platform that was bedecked with a canopy of flowers and, Jack had to admit, it all looked rather wonderful. He took another drink. Elizabeth blew him a kiss and he beamed back; she was easily the prettiest girl in the crowd. Sadie came and sat beside him, and he cast an approving eye over her; she was wearing a crimson dress and looked very fetching. Then, as the Pursebury Players struck up the National Anthem and the village rose to its feet, Sadie gave Jack a peck on the cheek. 'Look, the parade is starting.'

She got up and went to the edge of the green for a better view, leaving Jack alone. He had been far too preoccupied with his golf tournament to listen to any other details. He knew only that it was all supposed to finish before twelve and that the woolly-pig would appear on the top of Bulbarrow at midday sharp. It was most strange; the more of the special cider he drank, the more certain he felt that the creature would come.

Jack glanced at the church clock. Eleven. Running late now. Never mind, he could walk fast. He got to his feet and swayed as Elizabeth caught his arm.

'Are you all right?'

Jack passed her his flask. 'Have a sip of that.'

Elizabeth choked. 'Daddy, what is it?'

'Secret.' He pressed a finger to his lips. 'I'll tell you when I'm dead.'

She looked a little worried as her father collapsed into his chair.

Basset ambled past and winked at him. 'A' right, Jack—ready?'

Jack tried to look official but Basset gave him a second glance—something wasn't right. He sat down in the empty seat next to him and sniffed.

'You got special cider.'

Jack handed him the flask and Basset took a loud slug of booze.

'I am confiscating this. You needs to be sober.'

Jack hiccupped happily. 'I'm fine. Just fine and dandelion.'

Jack tried to focus on the church clock—everything was getting a little fuzzy. Eleven thirty. He still might make it. The national anthem started again and the ladies-in-waiting took their places at the foot of the throne, while the children gathered on the grass.

Jack stared at the village clock. Eleven forty-five. If he left now—said he had a headache, a gangrenous leg or something—and ran to the top of Bulbarrow, then he might just make the woolly-pig. Two children began to sprinkle confetti petals on the grass up the central aisle, where the village Queen was to walk, and Jack got to his feet—it was almost his moment.

'Basset, you could crown the Queen.'

Basset's face fell. 'You is jist nervous, Jack. You'll be grand.'

There was a hush as the Queen descended from her horse-drawn carriage. She was a tall, buxom girl; and she understood the magnificence of the occasion and walked with a stately pride. All the faces on the green turned to watch her—they were filled with such hope and expectation, and Jack realised that he couldn't disappoint them. He would have to miss the woolly-pig. He hoped Curtis would understand, and muttered under his breath, 'I can't let them all down, my friend. It wouldn't be British.'

He grabbed Basset and lurched dangerously.

'Jack Basset. Walk with me.'

'I'd be honoured.'

Slowly, arm in arm, the two old men followed the Pursebury Queen up the aisle. All heads turned to watch them as they passed; the small, purple-robed bishop and the round, suited farmer. Sadie thought she would burst with pride.

Basset stopped at the end of the aisle. The Queen was already seated on her throne and Jack climbed the steps to kneel before her. She tapped him on the shoulder with her sceptre and he stood. Doing his best to remain steady, he turned to the crowd. He couldn't see any of their faces and colours had begun to pool together—there was a sea of white dresses, another of swaying grass and the sky was throbbing blue. Flying above them all was a squadron of jitterbugs. They cast their weird green light over the village and flitted in looping patterns among the trees. On the horizon Jack could see Bulbarrow Ridge. Was the woolly-pig there waiting for him?

A child knelt at his feet, holding a cushion on which lay a golden crown. Jack bent down and raised it up to the crowd. He took a step towards the Queen and she lowered her head to receive the diadem. It glinted in the sun, blinding him for a moment. He paused, crown held aloft, and turned once more to Bulbarrow. And there on the top he saw it: a giant boar with great carved tusks as white as bleached bone, its coat thick and matted like a sheep's fleece, its snout long and upturned like a pig's. It was a creature of majesty and magnificence, and it seemed to Jack that it saw him and met his gaze with its shining green eyes. As the clock struck midday, Jack placed the crown on the head of the Pursebury Queen. Then, the hour bell finished chiming and the woolly-pig was gone.

POSTSCRIPT

Elizabeth shaded her eyes with her hand, searching the garden for her father. She spied him sprawled on a deck chair under the shade of a cherry tree. He was fast asleep, the sound of his snores harmonising with the hum of the bees, his walking stick propped beside him. She watched as blossom rained down on his bald head like confetti.

The flowerbeds were overgrown with ragged robin, clouds of pale blue forget-me-nots and ground elder; bindweed choked the roses and ivy grappled with the clematis. The grass was long; it had not been cut for several weeks and had begun to go to seed under the creaking plum tree, but Elizabeth said nothing about the general state of neglect because Jack was insistent—Sadie had liked the weeds, so this was a garden where everything was allowed to grow.

As she watched, Jack woke, stretched luxuriantly and, seeing her, gave a great yawn. 'It's hard work being old. Very tiring.'

Elizabeth laughed. 'I know.'

'Poppycock. You're not even fifty.'

'I'm fifty-three.'

'Exactly. You've barely started. I only got going at fifty-three.'

He got to his feet, leaned on his stick and adjusted his hat. 'Shall we?'

They strolled through the garden and into the field where the meadow grass was speckled with wild flowers—scarlet herb robert, celandine and oxeye daisies. A stream meandered through the middle, trickling over pebbles and tiny pieces of broken crockery to fill the large pond at the bottom. Fat buttercup lilies trembled on the surface while lazy dragonflies flitted among the reeds.

Jack produced a flask from his jacket pocket, took a gulp, and then gave a loud hiccup.

'You shouldn't drink that stuff, Dad. Can't be good for you.'

'Nonsense. This is what's kept me alive so long. I'm completely pickled—like a herring.' His shoulders sagged. 'If only I could have got your mother to drink more of it.'

Elizabeth stroked the white hairs on his arm and watched as he knocked back another mouthful of cider. His eyes watered—she was not sure if it was the alcohol or the memory. With a shake of his head, he resumed the climb, and Elizabeth clambered up the slope behind him.

They came to a stop beside a neat grave, marked with a tattered flag. Jack dropped his stick and sat on the grassy mound. Elizabeth's breath was still coming in heaves and gasps.

'God, I'm unfit. Give me that,' she said snatching his leather flask. As she gulped down the fiery liquid, she felt her heart slow and her panting ease. She slumped beside her father and stared out across the fields. The land sloped smoothly to the bottom of the valley, where the River Stour dawdled among the trees. The only blight on the landscape was an ugly clump of concrete houses that were partly obscured by a copse of cricket willows. Several of the houses had fallen into the river when it flooded the year before. Jack fumbled in his pocket and handed her a package.

'A present.'

Elizabeth took it from him and peeled off the brown paper. Inside was a leather-bound volume, inscribed in a slanting, old-fashioned hand. It was Sadie's recipe book—all the women in her family had learned to cook from its pages. Closing her eyes, she sniffed the spine and remembered the first time she had used it, cooking meatballs for her mother. For a second, she imagined that it would smell like a glorious concoction of all the recipes inside: chicken soup with *kreplach*, vanilla crescents, beef *cholent* and honey, but it reeked only of dust and damp age.

Elizabeth wiped her hands on her jeans before leafing through the fragile pages. 'My German is just good enough . . . oh.'

A faded blue pamphlet was sandwiched between the pages of the Baumtorte recipe, like an extra layer in the cake. 'This is your list, Daddy.'

Jack peered at it over the top of his spectacles. 'So it is. Good bookmark.'

A woodpecker hammered at the bark of a gnarled oak and a pied wagtail trilled his flutelike tune. Jack smiled. This was his last summer. He couldn't explain how he knew, but he did. He sensed it, like the swallows knew dusk was coming, or the black-nosed badgers sought their winter hide-outs deep underground, sensing the coming snow.

'Tomorrow, bake a Baumtorte,' he said, turning to his daughter.

She smiled at him, 'All right.'

And bake one more layer. A layer for me. But he didn't say this aloud, not wanting to upset her. She'd find out soon enough. Besides, there was nothing to be sad about. This was the way of things. Jack was the last of them—they had all left for the churchyard at the top of the hill and weekenders from the city had taken over their homes. Even Basset had gone last spring, aged ninety-odd.

Sadie's grave was apart from the rest, nestled into the hillside and marked by a flagpole instead of a headstone. Jack knew that even after fifty years in England, his Sadie would not want to be buried in a churchyard. He sat for a moment in silence.

'This was the fifth hole. My favourite. Look at that sweep,' he said.

'It was a wonderful course, Dad.'

'No, it was the greatest course in all England,' he said, correcting her.

Elizabeth stared at the shining fields, trying to remember them as they had been—a series of fairways, smooth greens and waving chequered flags. Now, the land was a mixture of tangled grass, unkempt hedges and scrub. Yet, underneath lingered the remains of the golf course, slumbering like Sleeping Beauty. A long time ago, Bobby Jones had played here.

'What happened, Dad? Why did you let it go to ruin?'

Jack rubbed his nose. 'Well, we were open for quite a while. And then demand seemed to slip away and, of course, we got old. But we had a good time of it. Your mother was quite a golfer.'

He paused and gazed out at the fields below with a gleam in his eye.

'But the real reason is that Jack wanted it back.'

'Jack?'

'Jack-in-the-Green,' he said. 'He's a woolly-pig, a will-o'-the-wisp or the red sun sinking behind Bulbarrow Hill. Everyone should know Jack.'

He stood slowly, turned away and started his journey back down the slope, leaving Elizabeth alone on the hillside. She noticed a hulking oak at the edge of the rough with peculiar knobbles and calluses that looked weirdly like bone sticking through the bark. Then she saw that it was not bone, but dozens of golf balls embedded in the trunk, and that the bark, in time, had grown over the balls and absorbed them into the great rings of the tree. It was one of the strangest things she had ever seen.

The sunlight filtered through the leaves, casting green patterns on her skin. She inhaled the sudden scent of pine cones and peat, and remembered her mother telling her bedtime stories about a cabin in a dark wood and a boy named Emil.

A green acorn dropped onto the faded blue pamphlet in her hands. She looked down at the peeling cover—*Helpful Information and Friendly Guidance for Every Refugee* and, opening it, started to read her father's list. Each item was annotated with Jack's scrawl. Several extra pages had been inserted, all covered with his writing. There were more than a hundred points, detailing every aspect of daily life—'*An Englishman is scrupulously honest . . . An Englishman always says thank you . . . An Englishman apologises even when something is not his fault . . .*'

She turned to the final item, reading it aloud, '*Item 151—This last item supersedes all previous list items. If you see a Dorset woolly-pig you are a true Dorset man. And as any noggerhead or ninnywally knows, the Dorset man is the best of all Englishmen.*'

Elizabeth closed the leaflet, slipped it back inside the recipe book and hurried to catch up with the old man walking steadily down the hill.

natasha **solomons**

RD: Was there something personal or specific that fired you to write *Mr Rosenblum's List*?

NS: I grew up listening to my grandfather and his friends telling their stories. When I was very small, I'd quite literally sit at his feet as he settled in his battered armchair and talked with his old friends. There was always coffee in a Thermos flask, luncheon sausage and poppy seed cake and often a game of cards—but most of all I remember their voices. They all had that Mittel-European accent. You hear it less and less often these days, but that accent signalled a survivor, someone who had been born in one world and now lived in another. As much as wanting to write a story inspired by my grandparents' experiences, I wanted to capture their voices.

RD: Sadie, in your novel, cooks to remember her past. Are you a good cook?

NS: My grandmother, Margot, was a wonderful cook and Sadie's recipes are taken from her voluminous handwritten recipe books. I cannot bake. All the women in my family are wonderful bakers, from my mother to my sister, to all my great-aunts and cousins. We even have a family cookbook. It's only me who can't. My mother and sister have spent hours trying to teach me how to make *Baumtorte* and *Apfelkuchen*, but to no avail. All my cakes end up like pancakes or biscuits and have to be covered in liqueur, creamy custard and fruit and turned into trifle. My mother, sister and cousins are all a little embarrassed by my profound inadequacy in the kitchen.

RD: The landscape of Dorset becomes a major 'character' in your novel—it's where you live, and it surrounds the summerhouse where you write. What do you love most about it?

NS: Dorset is an ancient landscape. The Blackmore Vale, where the book is set, is a mixture of rolling hills and green woods carpeted with bluebells in the spring. History is etched on the countryside in a very physical way and I love the way that myth and legend blend with the landscape so that going for a walk here means walking through stories. I don't think there is any place more inspiring.

RD: What is your favourite Dorset legend?

The woolly pig of course! I once saw a vast wild boar in the woods one autumn. It was rooting around in the leaves for good things . . . but, sadly, it was not woolly.

RD: Where did your knowledge of Bobby Jones and Robert Hunter come from?

NS: I discovered Jones and Hunter in the British Library and loved their poetic descriptions of golf courses. I cannot play golf. My grandpa's enthusiasm for the game was matched only by his lack of competence, but my grandmother was very good and, like Sadie, she had a natural swing.

RD: To be a perfect Englishman in the 1930s, Jack was determined to get his suits from Savile Row, drive a Jaguar and be a member of a golf club. Do you think today's immigrants would view the Englishman in the same light?

NS: Ultimately the vision of England that Jack comes to embrace is friendship and a kinship with people and the landscape—something that transcends language or cultural barriers. I expect that immigrants today face many of the same prejudices as Jack, in addition to a cacophony of new ones. The leaflet Jack receives really was given to new Jewish refugees, and now it makes uncomfortable reading with its insistence on 'gratitude' and 'subservience' to the British. But the English are a peculiar bunch and explaining some of our more unusual habits might be useful to a new arrival.

RD: What's the best piece of advice you've ever been given?

NS: After a couple of attempts to write a city novel my husband told me to 'write about what you love. Write about Dorset.' And I did.

A carpet of bluebells

Bluebells prefer moist, shady and stable conditions, so Dorset woodlands are, of course, ideal. In more northern and westerly parts of Britain, bluebells can be found in all sorts of habitats, such as hedgerows, or even by the sea in Cornwall.

In recent years, bluebells have been seen in flower, and at their best, around the last week of April and the first week in May, depending upon their location and the local climate. A very cold winter can delay flowering by nearly two weeks.

Some estimates suggest that Britain has up to half the world's total bluebell population. Despite their name, bluebells can be white. If you catch sight of pink ones they are probably Spanish bluebells.

C.J. BOX

NOWHERE TO RUN

Joe Pickett is in his last week as temporary game warden in the isolated town of Baggs, Wyoming. He's about to make for home, but strange things have been going on in the surrounding mountains—camps looted, tents slashed, elk butchered—and his conscience won't allow him to leave without saddling up for one last recce.

The further Joe rides, the more he wishes he could turn around and call it a day. Because what awaits him is stranger than fiction—yet all too real and very deadly . . .

PART ONE
The Last Patrol

Tuesday, August 25

Three hours after he'd broken camp, repacked and pushed his horses higher into the mountain range, Wyoming game warden Joe Pickett paused on the lip of a wide, hollow basin and dug in his saddlebag for his notebook. The bow hunters had described where they'd tracked the wounded elk, and he matched the topography against their description. He glassed the basin with binoculars and noted the fingers of pine trees reaching down through the grassy swale and the craterlike depressions in the hollow they'd described. This, he determined, was the place.

He'd settled into a familiar routine of riding until his muscles got stiff and his knees hurt. Then he'd climb down and lead his geldings Buddy and Blue Roanie—a packhorse he'd named unimaginatively—until he could loosen up and work the kinks out. The second day of riding brought back all the old aches, and they seemed closer to the surface now that he was in his mid-forties.

Shifting his weight in the saddle towards the basin, he clicked his tongue and touched Buddy's sides with his spurs. The horse baulked.

'C'mon, Buddy,' Joe said, 'Let's go now, you knucklehead.'

Instead, Buddy turned his head back and seemed to implore Joe not to proceed.

'Don't be ridiculous. *Go*.'

Only when he dug his spurs in did Buddy shudder, sigh and start the descent. Joe turned to check that his packhorse was coming along as well. But on the way down into the basin, Joe instinctively reached back and touched the butt of his shotgun in the saddle scabbard to assure himself it was there.

It was to have been a five-day horseback patrol before the summer gave way to fall and the hunting season began in earnest, before a new game warden was assigned to take over the district; after a year away, Joe was finally going home.

He'd spent the previous weekend packing up and making plans to ride into the mountains on Monday, descend on Friday, and clean out his state-owned home in Baggs for the arrival of the new game warden the following week. Baggs was a tough, beautiful, raggedy mountain town so isolated it was known within the department as the 'warden's graveyard'—the district where game wardens were sent to quit or die. Governor Spencer Rulon had assigned Joe to districts all over the State of Wyoming as both game warden and scout. Then, as luck would have it, Phil Kiner in Saddlestring took a new district in Cody, and Joe quickly applied for—and received—his old district north in the Bighorns in Twelve Sleep County, where his family was.

Despite his excitement about moving back to his wife, Marybeth, and his daughters, Joe couldn't in good conscience vacate the area without investigating the complaint about the butchered elk. He'd leave the other reported crimes to the sheriff.

Joe Pickett was lean, of medium height and medium build. His grey Stetson Rancher was stained with sweat and red dirt. A few silver hairs caught the sunlight on his temples and unshaved chin. He wore faded Wranglers, scuffed lace-up boots with stubby spurs, a red uniform shirt and a badge over his breast pocket. A tooled leather belt that identified him as 'JOE' held handcuffs, his knife, bear spray and a service issue .40 Glock semiautomatic.

With every mile of his last patrol of the Sierra Madre of southern Wyoming, Joe felt as if he were going back in time to a place of immense and unnatural silence. And with each hoofbeat, the sense of foreboding got stronger until it enveloped him in a calm, dark dread.

The silence was disconcerting. It was late August, but the normal alpine soundtrack was switched to mute. There were no insects humming in the grass, no squirrels chattering in the trees to signal his approach, no marmots standing up in the rocks whistling.

'Stop spooking yourself,' he said aloud and with authority.

JOE WAS STILL unnerved by a brief conversation he'd had with a dubious local named Dave Farkus the day before, at the trailhead.

Joe had been pulling the girth tight on Buddy when Farkus emerged from the brush with a spinning rod in his hand. Short and wiry, with mutton-chop sideburns and a slack expression on his face, Farkus had opened with, 'So you're goin' up there?'

Joe said, 'Yup.'

The fisherman said, 'All I know for sure is I drink beer at the Dixon Club bar with four old-timers who were here long before you. They ran cattle up there and they hunted up there for years. But you know what? None of them old fellers will go up there any more. Ever since that runner vanished, they say something just feels wrong.'

Joe said, 'Feelings aren't a lot to go on.'

'That ain't all. What about all the break-ins at cabins in the area and parked cars getting their windows smashed in at the trailheads? There's been a lot of that lately.'

'I heard,' Joe had replied. 'Sheriff Baird is looking into that, I believe.'

Farkus snorted.

'Is there something you're not telling me?' Joe had asked.

'No. But we all heard the rumours. You know, camps being looted. Tents getting slashed. I heard there were a couple of bow hunters who tried to poach an elk before the season opened. They hit one, followed the blood trail for miles, but when they finally found the animal it had already been butchered and the meat all hauled away. Is that true?'

The bow hunters had come to Joe's office and turned themselves in. Joe had cited them for hunting out of season but had been intrigued by their story. They had seemed genuinely creeped out by what had happened. 'That's what they said.'

Farkus widened his eyes. 'So it's true after all. And that's what you're up to, isn't it? You're going up there to find whoever took their elk. Well, I hope you do. Man, nobody likes the idea of somebody stealing another man's meat. And this Wendigo crap—where did that come from? Bunch of Indian mumbo-jumbo. Evil spirits, flesh eaters, I ask you. This ain't Canada, thank God. Wendigos are up there, not here, if they even exist. Heh-heh.'

It was not much of a laugh, Joe thought. More like a way of saying he didn't believe a word of what he'd just said—unless Joe did.

JOE BROKE THROUGH the trees and emerged into a meadow walled by dark timber, stopping to look and listen. He squinted, looking for whatever was spooking his horses and him. What he saw were mountains that tumbled like frozen ocean waves south into Colorado, and wispy clouds that scudded over him.

The range ran south to north. He planned to summit the Sierra Madre by Wednesday, day three, and cross the 10,000-foot Continental Divide near Battle Pass. This was where the bow hunters said their elk had been cut up. Then he would head down towards No Name Creek on the west side of the divide and arrive at his pick-up and horse trailer by midday Friday. If all went well.

The terrain got rougher the further he rode, wild and unfamiliar. The mountain range was spectacular, with toothy rimrock ridges, dense old-growth forests, veins of aspen already turning gold, high alpine lakes and cirques like blue poker chips tossed on green felt, and hundreds of miles of lodgepole pine trees.

The cirques—semicircular hollows with steep walls filled with snowmelt and big enough to boat across—stair-stepped their way up the mountains. Those with outlets birthed tiny creeks; others were self-contained, bathtubs that would fill and never drain out.

Joe had been near the spine of the mountains only once, when he was a participant in the search-and-rescue effort for the runner Farkus had mentioned, Olympic hopeful Diane Shober, who'd vanished on a long-distance run on the canyon trail. Her body had never been found. Her face was haunting, though; it peered out from hundreds of handbills posted by her parents throughout Wyoming and Colorado. Joe kept her disappearance in mind as he rode, alert for scraps of clothing, bones or hair.

He dismounted once he was on the floor of the basin to ease the pain in his knees and let his horses rest. He led them through a stand of lodgepole pines that gradually melded into a pocket of rare, twisted knotty pine with softball-sized joints like swollen knees. The knotty pine stand covered less than a quarter of a mile of the forest, just as the elk hunters had described.

As he stood on the perimeter of the stand, he slowly turned and noted the horizon of the basin that rose like the rim of a bowl in every direction. He was struck by how many locations in the mountains looked alike, how without man-made landmarks like power lines or radio towers, wilderness could turn into a maelstrom of green and rocky sameness. He wished the bow hunters had given him precise GPS coordinates so he could be sure this was the place, but the hunters were purists and had not carried that kind of technology. Still, they'd accurately described the basin and the cirque, as well as the knotty pine stand.

He secured his animals and walked the floor of the basin looking for the remains of the elk. Although predators would have quickly stripped it of its remaining meat and scattered the bones, there should be evidence of hide and hair. The bow hunters said the bull had seven-point antlers on each beam, so the antlers should be nearby as well.

As he surveyed the ground, something in his peripheral vision struck him as discordant. He paused and carefully looked from side to side, visually backtracking. In nature, he thought, nothing is perfect. And something he'd seen—or thought he'd seen—was too vertical or horizontal or straight or unblemished to belong there.

After turning and retracing his steps, Joe saw it. It was an arrow stuck in the trunk of a tree. The shaft of the arrow was hand-crafted, with feather fletching on the end. The only place he'd ever seen a primitive arrow like that was in a museum. He photographed it with his digital camera, then pulled on a pair of latex gloves, grasped it by the shaft and pushed hard up and down while pulling on it. After a moment, the arrow popped free, and Joe studied it. The point was obsidian and attached to the shaft with animal sinew. The fletching was made of wild turkey feathers.

It made no sense. The bow hunters he'd interviewed were serious sportsmen, but even they didn't make their own arrows from natural materials. No one did. Who had lost this arrow?

He felt a chill roll through him. Slowly he rotated and looked behind him in the trees. He wouldn't have been surprised to see Cheyenne or Sioux warriors approaching.

He found the remains of the seven-point bull elk ten minutes later. Even though coyotes and ravens had been feeding on the carcass, it was obvious this was the elk the bow hunters had wounded and pursued. The hindquarters were gone and the backstraps had been sliced away. Exactly like the hunters had described.

So who had taken the meat?

Joe walked back to his horses with the arrow he'd found. He wrapped the point of it in a spare sock and the shaft in a T-shirt and put it in a pannier. He caught Buddy staring at him.

'Evidence,' he said. 'Something strange is going on up here. We might get some fingerprints off this arrow.'

Buddy snorted. Joe was sure it was a coincidence.

As he rode out of the basin, he couldn't shake the feeling that he was being watched. Once he reached the rim and was back on top, the air was thin and the sun was ruthless. Rivulets of sweat snaked down his spine beneath his uniform shirt. He couldn't stop thinking about the carcass he'd found. Or the arrow.

THAT NIGHT, he camped on the shoreline of an alpine lake and picketed the horses in ankle-high grass. He caught five trout, kept one, and ate it with fried potatoes over a small fire. After dinner he cleaned his dishes by the light of a headlamp and uncased his satellite phone from a pannier. He called home every night no matter what. Even if there was no news, it was the mundane that mattered; it kept him in touch with his family and Marybeth with him.

The signal was good, and the call went through. Straight to voicemail. He was slightly annoyed before he remembered Marybeth was taking the girls to the last summer concert in the town park. He'd hoped to hear her voice.

When the message prompt beeped, he said, 'Hello, ladies. I hope you had a good time tonight. I wish I could have gone with you. Right now, I'm high in the mountains, and it's a beautiful and lonely place. The moon's so bright I can see fish rising in the lake.'

He paused, and felt a little silly for the long message. He rarely talked that much to them in person. He said, 'Well, I'm just checking in. Your horses are doing fine, and so am I. I miss you all.'

He undressed and slipped into his sleeping-bag in the tent. He lay awake with his hands beneath his head and stared at the inside of the dark tent fabric. After an hour, he got up and pulled the bag out through the tent flap. There were still no clouds, and the stars and moon were bright and hard.

God, he thought, I love this.

And he felt guilty for loving it so much.

Wednesday, August 26

The rhapsody ended at noon the next day. There was a lone fisherman down in the small, kidney-shaped mountain lake, and something about him was wrong.

Joe reined to a stop on the summit and let Buddy and Blue Roanie catch their breath. The late summer sun was straight up in the sky, and insects hummed in the wild flowers. The sun had been relentless. There was little shade because he was on the top of the world, with nothing higher.

Joe raised his binoculars and focused in, trying to figure out what there was about the man that had struck him as odd. Several things popped up. The first was that the high-country cirques weren't noted for great angling. While hikers might catch a small trout or two for dinner along the trail, as he had, the area was not a destination fishing location.

Second, the fisherman wasn't dressed or equipped like a modern angler. The man—who at that distance looked very tall and rangy—was wading in filthy denim jeans, an oversized red plaid shirt with big checks, and a white slouch hat pulled low over his eyes. No waders, no fishing vest, no net. In these days of high-tech gear and clothing, it was extremely unusual to see such a throwback outfit.

Joe put away the glasses, clicked his tongue and started down towards the lake. Leather creaked, and horseshoes struck stones. Blue Roanie snorted. He was making plenty of noise, but the fisherman appeared not to have seen or heard him. In a place as big and empty and lonely as this, the fisherman's lack of acknowledgment was all wrong and made a statement in itself.

As he walked his animals down to the lake, Joe untied the leather thong that secured his shotgun in his saddle scabbard. He had often considered the fact that nearly every human being he encountered was armed, and it was rare when he could call for back-up. The only things on his side were his wits, his weapons, and the game and fish regulations of the State of Wyoming.

'Hello,' Joe called out as he approached the cirque lake from the other side of the fisherman. 'How's the fishing?'

His voice echoed round in the small basin until it was swallowed up.

'Excuse me, sir. I need to talk to you for a minute and check your fishing licence and habitat stamp.'

No response.

The fisherman cast, waited a moment for his lure to settle, then reeled in. The man was a spin-fishing artist, and his lure flicked out like a snake's tongue. *Cast. Pause. Reel.*

Joe thought, Either he's deaf and blind or has an inhuman power of concentration, or he's ignoring me, hoping I'll just get spooked and give up and go away.

As a courtesy and for his own protection, Joe never came at a hunter or fisherman head-on. He had learned to skirt them, to approach from an angle. Which he did now, walking his horses round the shore, keeping the fisherman firmly in his peripheral vision. Out of sight from the man, Joe let his right hand slip down along his thigh until it was inches from his shotgun.

Cast. Pause. Reel. Cast. Pause. Reel.

As Joe rode closer, he could see the fisherman was armed, as he'd suspected. Tucked into the man's belt was a long-barrelled Ruger Mark III .22 semiautomatic pistol.

The tip of the fisherman's pole jerked down and the man deftly reeled in a feisty twelve-inch rainbow trout. The sun danced off the colours of the trout's belly and back as the fisherman raised it from the water, worked the treble-hook lure out of its mouth, and studied it carefully. Then he bent over and released the fish. He cast again, hooked up just as quickly, and reeled in a trout of the same size and colour. After inspecting it, he bit it savagely behind its head to kill it. He spat the mouthful of meat into the water near his feet and slipped the fish into the bulging wet pack behind him. Joe looked at the pack—there were *a lot* of dead fish in it.

'Why did you release the first one and keep the second?' Joe asked. 'They looked like the same fish.'

The man grunted as if insulted. 'Not up close, they didn't. The one I kept had a nick on its tail fin. The one I threw back was perfect. The perfect ones go free.' He spoke in a hard, flat, nasal tone. The accent was upper Midwest, Joe thought. Maybe even Canadian.

Joe was puzzled. 'How many imperfect fish do you have there?' he asked. He was now behind and to the side of the fisherman. 'The legal limit is six. It looks like you may have more than that.'

The fisherman paused silently in the lake, his wide back to Joe. He seemed to be thinking, planning a move or a response. Joe felt a shiver roll through him despite the heat. It was as if something of significance was bound to happen.

Finally, the man said, 'I lost count. Maybe ten.'

'That's a violation. Tell me, are you a bow hunter?' Joe asked. 'I'm wondering about an arrow I found stuck in a tree.'

The fisherman shrugged. Not a yes, not a no. More like, *I'm not sure I want to answer*.

'Do you know anything about an elk that was butchered a few miles from here? The hunters who wounded it tracked it down, but someone had harvested the meat by the time they found it.'

The man coughed up phlegm and spat it over his shoulder. 'I don't know nothing about no elk.'

'The elk was imperfect,' Joe said. 'It was bleeding and probably limping.'

'For the life of me, I don't understand what you're talking about.'

'I need to see your licence,' Joe said.

'Ain't got it on me,' the man said, still not turning round. 'Might be in my bag.'

Joe turned in the saddle and saw a weathered canvas daypack hanging from a broken branch on the side of a pine tree.

'Mind if I look in it?'

The fisherman shrugged again.

'Is that a yes?'

'Yes. But while you look, I'm gonna keep fishing.'

'Suit yourself,' Joe said.

The fisherman mumbled something low and incomprehensible.

Joe said, 'Come again?'

The man said, 'I'm willing to let this go if you'll just turn your horses round and ride back the way you came. 'Cause if you start messing with me, well . . . it may not turn out too good.'

Joe said, 'Are you threatening me?'

'Nope. Just statin' a fact. You got a choice, is what I'm sayin'.'

Joe said, 'I'm choosing to check your licence. It's my job.'

The fisherman shook his head slowly, as if to say, *What happens now is on you.*

Joe dismounted but never took his eyes off the fisherman. He led his horse to the tree, tied him up and took the bag down. There were a few items in it—a knife in a sheath, some string, a battered journal, a pink elastic iPod holder designed to be worn on an arm but no iPod, an empty water bottle, and half a Bible—Old Testament only. It looked as if the New Testament had been torn away.

'I don't see a licence,' Joe said, stealing a look at the journal while the fisherman kept his back to him. There were hundreds of short entries made in a tiny, cramped hand. Joe read a few and noted the dates went back to March. Had this man been in the mountains for *six months*?

'Don't be reading my work,' the fisherman said.

On a smudged card inside the Bible was a note: For Caleb on his 14th birthday, from Aunt Elaine.

'Are you Caleb?' Joe asked.

Pause. 'Yeah.'

'Got a last name?'

'Yeah.'

Joe waited a beat, and the man said nothing.

'So, what is it?'

'Grimmengruber. Most people just say "Grim".'

'Who is Camish? I keep seeing that name in this journal.'

'I told you not to read it,' Caleb Grimmengruber said, displaying a flash of impatience.

'I was looking for your licence,' Joe said. 'I can't find it. So who's Camish?'

Caleb sighed, 'My brother.'

'Where is he? Is he up here with you?'

'None of your business.'

'You wrote that he was with you yesterday. It says, "Camish went down and got some supplies. He ran into some trouble along the way." What trouble?' Joe asked, recalling what Farkus had said at the trailhead.

Caleb Grim lowered his fishing rod and slowly turned round. He had close-set dark eyes, a tiny pinched mouth glistening with fish blood, a stubbled chin sequined with scales, and a long, thin nose sunburnt so badly that the skin was mottled grey and had peeled away down to yellow cartilage. Joe felt his toes curl in his boots.

'What trouble?' Joe repeated, trying to keep his voice strong.

'You can ask him yourself.'

'He's at your camp?'

'I ain't in charge of his movements, but I think so.'

'Where's your camp?'

Caleb chinned to the south, but all Joe could see was a wood-studded slope that angled up nearly a thousand feet.

'Up there in the trees?' Joe asked.

'Over the top,' the man said. 'Down the other side and up and down another mountain.'

Joe surveyed the terrain. He estimated the camp to be at least three miles the hard way. *Three miles.*

'Lead on,' Joe said.

'What you gonna do if I don't?'

Joe thought, There's not much I can do. He said, 'We won't even need to worry about that if you cooperate. You can show me your licence, I can have a word with Camish, and if everything's on the level, I'll be on my way and I'll leave you with a citation for too many fish in your possession.'

Caleb appeared to be thinking it over, although his hard, dark eyes never blinked. After a moment, he waded out of the lake. As he neared, Joe was taken aback by how tall he was, maybe six-foot-five. Joe could smell him approaching. Rancid—like rotten animal fat. Without a glance towards Joe, Caleb swept up the fish bag, took the daypack, threw it over his shoulders and started up the mountain. Joe mounted up, breathed in a gulp of clean air, and clucked at Buddy and Blue Roanie to get them moving.

A quarter of a mile up the mountain, Caleb stopped and turned round. His tiny dark eyes settled on Joe. He said, 'You coulda just rode away.'

NEARLY AT THE TOP, Joe prodded on his pack animals. They were labouring on the steep mountainside. Caleb Grim wasn't. The man long-strided up the slope at a pace that was as determined as it was unnatural.

Joe said, 'The Brothers Grimm?'

Caleb, obviously annoyed, said, 'We prefer the Grim brothers. One "m".'

'How long have you been up here? This is tough country.'

Nothing.

'Why just the Old Testament?'

Dismissive grunt.

'What kind of trouble did Camish run into yesterday?'

Silence.

'Some of the old-timers down in Baggs think someone's been up here harassing cattle and spooking them down the mountains. There have been some break-ins at cabins and cars parked at the trailheads. You wouldn't know anything about that, would you?'

Caleb grunted. Again not a yes, not a no.

'The elk that was butchered confounds me,' Joe said. 'Whoever did it worked fast and knew what they were doing. You wouldn't know who up here could've done that, then?'

'I already told you. I don't know about no elk.'

'Have you heard about a missing long-distance runner? A girl by the name of Diane Shober?'

Another inscrutable grunt.

They were soon in dense timber. Joe wondered if Caleb was leading him into a trap or trying to lose him, and he spurred Buddy on harder than he wanted to, noting the lather creaming out from beneath the saddle and blanket. 'Sorry, Buddy,' he whispered to his gelding, patting his wet neck, 'it can't be much further.'

JOE COULD SMELL the camp before he could see it. It smelled like rotten garbage and burnt flesh.

For a moment, he thought he was hallucinating. How could Caleb Grim have made it into the camp so much before him that he'd had the time to sit on a log and stretch out his long legs and read the Bible and wait for him to arrive? Then he realised the man on the log was identical to Caleb in every way, including his clothing, slouch hat and deformed nose, and he was reading the missing half of the book he'd seen in Caleb's daypack—the *New* Testament.

Caleb Grim emerged from a thicket of brush and sat down next to his brother.

'Why'd you bring *him*?' the brother—Joe assumed it was Camish—asked without looking up.

'I didn't,' Caleb said. 'He followed me.'

'I thought we had an agreement about this sort of thing.' Camish's voice was nasal as well, but higher-pitched. 'You know what happened the last time you did this.'

'That was different, Camish. You know that.'

'I didn't know it at the time.'

'You should have known. They're all like that—every damned one of them.'

'Especially when they got a badge to hide behind,' Camish said.

'What happened last time?' Joe asked. He was ignored. The brothers talked to each other as if Joe wasn't there.

The camp was a shambles. Clothing, wrappers, empty cans and food containers, bones and bits of hide littered the ground. Their tent was a tiny Boy Scout pup tent, and he could see two stained sleeping-bags extending out past the door flap. The bones meant the brothers were poachers, because there were no open game seasons in the summer. He could arrest them for wanton destruction of game animals and multiple other violations on the spot. And then what? he wondered. He couldn't just march them for three days out of the mountains to jail.

Said Caleb to Joe, 'You gonna stay up there on that horse?'

'Yup. I'll just take a look at your fishing licence and get going.'

The brothers exchanged looks and seemed to be sharing a joke.

'Well, then,' Caleb said, long-striding towards the pup tent, 'I'll go see if I can find it.'

Joe said to Camish, 'How long have you been up here?'

Camish looked up and showed a mouthful of stubby yellow teeth. 'Is that an official question?'

'An *official* question?'

'Like one I have to answer or you'll give me a dang ticket or something? I don't care to incriminate myself in any way. If it ain't an official question and all.'

'OK,' Joe said. 'It's an official question.'

'If I don't agree to see you as an authority, it ain't official. You know, game warden, this place ain't called Rampart Mountain for no reason. A rampart is a protective barrier. A last stand, kind of.' Camish shook his half of the Bible at Joe. 'I been reading this. I'm not all that impressed, to tell you the truth. I find it to be an imperfect book. At least the first part has lots of action in it. Lots of murder and killings and sleeping around and such. It keeps you entertained. This part, though, it's just too soft, you know? I'd not recommend it. Instead, I'd read the US Constitution. It's shorter, better, and up until recently it was pretty easy to find.'

Caleb crawled backwards out of the tent, stood up, said, 'Damned if I can't find it, officer. But we got a couple of caches back in the trees. I might have put my licence in one of 'em.'

Joe said, 'I'll follow you.'

That seemed to surprise Caleb, and again the brothers exchanged a wordless glance.

'Come on, then,' Caleb said. 'But you'll have to get down. The trees are too thick to ride through.'

Joe studied the trees behind Caleb. They *were* too closely packed to ride through. He considered telling Caleb he'd wait where he was. But he wondered if he let Caleb go if he'd ever see him again. And he didn't want to be stuck with Camish, who asked suddenly, 'You ever hear of the Wendigo?'

Joe looked over. He'd now heard the word twice—once from Farkus, now from Camish Grim. 'What about it?'

Again the stubby teeth, but this time in a sort of painful smile.

'Just wonderin',' he said.

Joe waited for more but nothing came. Then Camish said, 'So who owns these fish you're so worked up about?'

'What do you mean, who owns them?'

'Exactly what I asked. These fish are native cutthroats, mainly, and a few rainbows. So who owns them? Do you own them?'

'Technically . . . no. But I work for the Wyoming Game and Fish Department,' Joe said. 'We're in charge of managing our wildlife.'

'Maybe,' Camish said. 'But I like to get things clear in my mind. What you're saying is that American citizens have to go out and buy a piece of paper from the state in order to catch native fish. So you're sort of a tax collector for the government, then?'

Joe shook his head, lost in the logic.

'So if you don't own the fish, what gives you the right to collect a tax on folks like us?'

'I guess you can complain to the judge,' Joe said.

'Sounds like a racket to me. You've got me wondering who the criminal is here and who isn't.'

Joe climbed down quickly and tied Buddy to a tree. He said to Caleb, 'Let's go.'

Caleb grinned. Same teeth as Camish. 'Pissed you off, didn't he?'

Joe set his jaw and made a wide arc round Camish, who looked amused.

JOE FOLLOWED CALEB on a nearly imperceptible trail through the pine trees. The footing was rough because of the roots that broke the surface. Not that Caleb was slowed down, though. Joe found it remarkable how a man of his size could glide through the forest as if on a cushion of air.

'So,' Joe said to Caleb's back, 'where are you boys from?'

'You ever heard of the UP?'

Joe said, 'The Union Pacific?'

Caleb spat. His voice was laced with contempt. 'Yeah, game warden, the Union Pacific. OK, here we are.'

The trail had descended, and on the right side of it was a flat granite wall with large vertical cracks. Caleb removed a gnarled piece of pitchwood from one of the cracks and reached inside up to his armpit. He came out with a handful of crumpled papers.

Joe tried to see what they were. They looked like unopened mail. When Caleb caught Joe looking, he quickly stuffed the wad back into the rock.

'Nope,' he said. 'No licence here.'

'Is this a joke?' Joe asked. 'You didn't even look.'

'The hell I didn't.'

Joe shook his head. 'If you've got a valid licence, I can look it up when I get to a computer. In the meanwhile, though, I'm giving you another citation. The law is you've got to have your licence in your possession. Not in some rock hidden away.'

Caleb said, 'You giving me another ticket?' He laughed and shook his head.

'There'll be a court date,' Joe said, unnerved by Caleb's casual contempt. 'If you want to protest, you can show up with your licence and make your case. And I'm going to write up both of you for wanton destruction of game animals. I saw all the bones back there. You've been poaching game all summer.'

'OK,' Caleb said, as if placating Joe.

'So why don't we get back,' Joe said.

Caleb nodded, shouldered round Joe and strode back up the trail.

As Joe followed, he wondered if he'd been suckered, and why.

Camish was still on his seat on the log, and he watched with no expression on his face as Joe emerged from the woods.

'Guess what,' Caleb said to Camish, 'he's going to give us *tickets*.'

'Tickets?' Camish said, placing his hand over his heart as if pretending to ward off a stroke.

Joe felt his ears get hot, but said, 'Wanton destruction of game animals, hunting and fishing without licences, and exceeding the legal limit of fish.' He wrote out the citations while the Grim brothers watched him and smirked.

Caleb said to his brother, 'I told him we were from the UP. And you know what he said? He said, "*Union Pacific?*"'

Camish laughed out loud and slapped his thigh.

'Oh, and earlier, you know what he asked me?'

'What?'

'He asked if we'd ever run across any remains of that girl runner. You know, the one who took off running and never came back?'

'What did you tell him?'

'I said sure, we raped and killed her.'

Camish laughed again, and Caleb joined him, and Joe looked up from the last citation he was scribbling and wondered when he'd left planet earth for Planet Grim.

He handed the citations to the brothers. 'I'd suggest you boys get out of the mountains and straighten up and fly right,' he said. 'You're gonna have big fines to pay.'

'Straighten up and fly right,' Camish repeated in a mocking tone.

'What's the reason you're up here, anyway?' Joe asked. 'What's the story with you two?'

Camish turned to Joe. 'Let's just say this is the best place for us. I really don't want to go into detail.'

Joe reverted to training and said, 'If you want to contest the citations, I guess I'll see you boys in court.'

Caleb said, 'But we got folks to look after.'

Camish shot Caleb a vicious glance, which shut his brother up.

'What folks?' Joe asked.

'Never mind my brother,' Camish said. 'He knows not what he says sometimes.'

Caleb nodded and said, 'I just babble sometimes.'

'Is there someone else up here?' Joe asked.

'Ain't nobody,' Camish said.

'Ain't nobody,' Caleb repeated.

Joe mounted Buddy, clucked his tongue to get him moving, and started back up the hill. He was never so grateful to ride away. He tried not to look over his shoulder, but he found he had to if for no other reason than to make sure they weren't aiming a rifle at him.

They weren't. Instead, the Brothers Grimm were laughing and feeding the citations into the fire, which flared as they dropped the tickets in.

THAT NIGHT Joe discovered his satellite phone was missing. He emptied both panniers and checked his daypack and saddlebags looking for it. He thought, They took it. He re-created the encounter with the brothers and pinpointed when it was likely to have happened. When he'd followed Caleb to the cache.

'The arrow,' he said aloud and rooted through all of his gear again. It was gone as well.

His anger turned to thoughts of revenge. If the brothers used the phone, their exact location could be determined. Joe could bring a team back up into the mountains and nail those guys.

Being out of radio contact was not unusual in itself, and often he didn't mind it one bit. This time he did. Marybeth would worry about him. In fact, he was worried himself.

Later, as grey wisps of cloud passed over the moon, he lay outside his tent in his sleeping-bag, with the shotgun across his chest, and he thought how differently things could have turned out if he'd taken Caleb's advice and simply ridden away when he'd had the chance.

This was not how it was supposed to be on his last patrol. It was like walking into a convenience store for a quart of milk and realising there was an armed robbery in progress. He didn't feel prepared for what he'd stumbled into. There were countless times he'd entered hunting and fishing camps outnumbered, outgunned and without back-up, but he'd never felt as vulnerable and out of his depth.

He thought how strange it was that no one had ever reported seeing the Grim brothers. How was it possible these two had lived and roamed in these mountains and not been seen? Two six-and-a-half-foot identical twins in identical clothing? It was exactly the kind of tale repeated by men like Farkus at the Dixon Club bar. So how could these brothers have stayed out of sight?

Then Joe thought, Maybe they hadn't. But whoever had seen them felt compelled to keep their mouths shut. Or maybe they never lived to tell.

Joe dragged his bag a hundred yards from the camp into a copse of thick mountain juniper on a rise that overlooked the tent and his horses. If they came for him, he figured, he'd see them first on the approach. He sat with his back against a rock and both the shotgun and his .308 M-14 carbine within reach. Finally, deep into the night, he drifted into an exhausted sleep.

Thursday, August 27

The only sounds Joe could hear as he rode from the trees into a sun-splashed meadow were from a breeze that made far-off watery music in the tops of the lodgepole pines, and the huffing of his horses.

That was until he heard a hollow *thwap* somewhere in the dark trees to his right, the sizzle of a projectile arcing through the air, and the *thunk* of the arrow through the fleshy top of his thigh, which pinned him to the saddle and the horse. The pain was searing, and he fumbled and dropped the reins. Buddy screamed and crow-hopped, and Joe would have fallen if the arrow hadn't been pinning him to the saddle. He felt Buddy's back haunches dip and dig in, and suddenly the gelding was bolting across the meadow.

Joe held on to the saddle horn with both hands. The underbrim of his weathered Stetson caught wind and came off. Blue Roanie followed, hooves thundering, gear shaking loose as the canvas panniers caught air and crashed back against his ribs.

Joe threw himself forwards until his cheek was hard against Buddy's neck, and he reached out in order to try for a one-rein stop. In his peripheral vision he saw Blue Roanie suddenly sport an arrow in his throat and go down in a massive dusty tumble of spurting blood, flashing hooves and flying panniers.

Joe thought, This is it. They never had any intention of letting me get away. And: This is not where I want to die.

Joe managed to slow Buddy to a lope just before the horse entered the wall of trees on the edge of the meadow, and he welcomed the plunge into shadowed darkness because he was no longer in the open. Buddy seemed to read his mind, and he continued jogging his way through the thick lodgepole pine forest.

The shaft of the arrow jerked back on a skeletal branch that seemed to reach out and grasp it. Joe gasped from the electric jolt of pain. Buddy cried out, shimmied to the left and thumped hard into the trunk of a lodgepole, crushing Joe's left leg as well.

Finally, Buddy stopped and breathed hard from exertion and pain.

'It's OK, Buddy,' Joe whispered, reaching forward and stroking Buddy's mane. 'It's OK.'

But it wasn't.

'Let's turn round, OK, Buddy?' Joe asked. 'So we can see if anyone's following us.'

Joe pulled steadily on the rein until Buddy grunted and swung to the left. Joe could see no pursuers.

Then, in the distance, back in the open meadow, Joe heard a whoop. They were still out there. Joe tried to clear his head, to think. Buddy's laboured breathing calmed, but the forward angle of his ears indicated he was still on alert. Joe was thankful his horse would be able to see, hear or smell danger before he could.

Grasping the rough shaft of the arrow in order to steady it, Joe leaned painfully forward in the saddle. His Wranglers were black with blood that filled his boot and coursed through Buddy's coat and down his front leg to the hoof. He couldn't tell if it was all his blood or mixed with his horse's.

Taking a big gulp of air, Joe pulled cautiously on the arrow and was rewarded with another bolt of pain. Buddy crow-hopped again and made an ungodly sound. The arrowhead was buried in the leather of the saddle and Buddy's side, and the barbs held. Joe let go and eased back, grimacing. He couldn't gauge how far the arrow had penetrated Buddy's side.

Joe did a quick inventory of what gear was still with him. His saddlebags were filled with gloves, binoculars, granola bars, a packet of plastic tag Flex-Cuffs and a citation book. His .40 Glock semiauto and knife were on his belt. He cursed when he reached back for his shotgun and found an empty saddle scabbard. He'd lost his weapon of choice on the wild ride across the meadow. If only Blue Roanie had been able to follow, he thought. His first-aid kit was in the panniers. So was his .308.

He had to get out of the saddle to assess the wounds to his horse and to his leg. The arrow wouldn't come out as it was. He took another gulp of air, leaned forward again, grasped the shaft with both hands, broke the back end off, and tossed the piece with the fletching behind him. Then, grasping his own leg like he would heave a sandbag, he slid it up and off the broken shaft. The movement and the pain convulsed him when his leg came free, and he tumbled off the left side of the horse onto the forest floor, out cold.

When he awoke, he was surprised it wasn't raining, because he thought he'd heard the soft patter of rain in his subconscious. Joe had no idea how long he'd been out, but he guessed it had been just a few minutes. He was on his side with his left arm pinned under him. His right leg with the holes in it was now largely numb except for dull pulses of pain that came with each heartbeat. His left leg throbbed from being crushed against the tree.

Joe groaned and propped himself up on an elbow. Buddy stood directly over him. That's when Joe realised it wasn't rain he'd heard, but drops of blood from his horse striking the forest floor.

He rose by grasping a stirrup and pulling himself up the side of his horse. He paused with both arms across the saddle as he studied the dark tangle of trees they'd come through. He saw no one. Yet.

The saddle was loose due to Buddy's exertion, and it was easy to release the girth. He stood on his horse's right side where the arrow was and gripped the saddle horn on the front and the cantle on the back and set his feet. 'I'll make this as painless as I can, Buddy,' he said, then grunted and swung the saddle off, careful to pull it straight away from the arrow so the hole in the leather slid up the shaft and didn't do any more side-to-side damage. Buddy didn't scream again or rear up, and Joe was grateful.

He examined the wound and could see the back end of the flint point. It wasn't embedded deeply after all. Apparently, the leather—and Joe's leg—had blunted the penetration. So why all the blood? Then he saw it: another arrow was deep in Buddy's neck on the other side. So both brothers had been firing arrows at him from opposite sides of the meadow. The neck wound was severe.

The first-aid kit in Blue Roanie's panniers had the hydrogen peroxide to clean out wounds, and compresses to bind them and stop bleeding. He had to stop the flow. But how?

JOE SAT in the grass with his jeans pulled down to his knees. His left leg was bruised and turning purple. There were two holes three inches apart in the top of his right thigh. The holes were rimmed with red and oozing dark blood. He clumsily wrapped his bandana over the holes and made a knot.

Joe stood with the aid of a tree trunk and pulled his jeans back up. Buddy watched with his head down and his eyes going gauzy as his blood dripped.

'I'll take care of you first, Buddy,' Joe said in a whisper, 'then I'll take care of me.'

Before limping back towards the meadow and Blue Roanie's body, Joe emptied his canteen over the wound in Buddy's neck until the water ran clear. He drank the last of the water, then tied Buddy's reins to a tree trunk.

'Hang in there and don't move.'

Buddy's head was down and his ears weren't as rigid. It might mean the brothers had left the area. Or it might mean his horse was dying.

Joe lurched from tree to tree, holding himself upright by grabbing trunks and branches, anything that would help him take the weight and pressure off his leg. It took twenty minutes before he neared the meadow where he'd been bushwhacked.

Joe hated the fact that his only available weapon was his .40 Glock service piece. He was a poor pistol shot. Joe's proficiency was with a shotgun. He could wing-shoot with the best of them. His accuracy and reaction time were excellent as long as he shot instinctively. It was the slow, deliberate aiming he had trouble with.

As he staggered towards the meadow, Joe felt oddly disengaged. He seemed to be floating above the trees, looking down at the man in the red shirt moving towards what any rational observer would view as certain death. But he kept going, hoping the numb otherworldliness would continue to cushion him and act as a narcotic. As he moved, left hand on a tree trunk or branch and right hand on the polymer grip of his Glock, he realised how loud he was, how obvious. And how silent it was, which meant the brothers were still there.

ON HIS HANDS and knees, Joe crawled over fallen logs to the meadow. His wounded leg alternated between heat and cold, pain and deadness. The pine trees thinned. The meadow pulsed green and bright in the sunlight. Joe heard one of the brothers laugh like a hyena: *Cack-cack-cack-cack-cack.* The sound made the hairs on the back of his neck prick up.

What he saw through the tumbled pick-up sticks of untrammelled timber made his skin crawl. The brothers were on either side of Blue Roanie. They were laughing their blunt and brutal laugh.

Blue Roanie was dead. He'd bled out, and the black blood formed a large pool in the grass. Joe was grateful his end had come quickly.

The Grim brothers had stripped the body, taking the saddle and bridle and tossing them to the side. Camish produced his bowie knife and used it to pry Roanie's horseshoes off. As they came off, they were tossed into a pile near the saddle.

With brutal efficiency, they skinned the horse. Then, with the skill of a butcher, Camish severed the front quarter, barely touching a bone or joint with his blade.

Joe knew he was up against a force he'd never faced before. He didn't like his chances.

He briefly closed his eyes and thought of Marybeth, how she'd miss him. Worse, he thought of his daughters, who simply assumed he'd always prevail and come home and be Dad. He didn't want them to think of him as the man who failed. As the dad who failed and let himself die.

He thought, I've got more to live for than just me.

The Brothers Grimm had his shotgun, carbine, gear, first-aid kit; they had intimate knowledge of the mountains, and a violent sense of purpose. All he had was a sidearm he was no good at shooting, and his determination to help his horse, fix his leg and get home to his family.

Still watching himself from above, still not able really to believe what was happening before him, he could tell by the way the brothers shot wary glances at the trees for him that when they were done, he'd be next on their schedule.

AT THE SAME TIME, in Saddlestring, Wyoming, Marybeth Pickett saw through the living-room window the last thing she wanted to see: her mother's black Hummer as it roared into the driveway.

'Crap,' Marybeth said.

'Excuse me?'

Marybeth turned quickly from the window. 'I'm sorry,' she said into the telephone to Elizabeth Harris, the vice-principal of Saddlestring High. 'I just saw something outside that . . . alarmed me. But you were saying?'

What Mrs Harris was saying was that April Keeley, their fifteen-year-old foster daughter, was absent again from her maths class. It was the third time she hadn't shown up since summer catch-up courses had begun.

'I'm sorry,' Marybeth said. 'I had no idea. I mean, she left for school on time after breakfast . . .'

She looked up to see Sheridan, eighteen, standing in the hallway in a maroon smock, about to go to work for the afternoon. Sheridan had overheard her mother and mouthed, '*April, again?*'

Marybeth nodded and said to the vice-principal, 'I'll make sure it doesn't happen again. I'll drive her there myself. And my husband will be back next week. If I can't bring April in, I'll ask Joe to do it. He's used to shuttling kids.' And thought, Wherever he is. That Joe hadn't called the night before bothered her. There were so many things they needed to talk about, starting with the fact that their foster daughter's behaviour was spinning out of control.

Mrs Harris thanked Marybeth, and Marybeth said 'Bye' and disconnected the call. She placed the phone in the charger and asked Sheridan, 'What is she doing, that girl? Do you know what's going on?' Putting Sheridan in the position of ratting out her foster sister or deciding to maintain the shared silence of sisterhood.

Sheridan took a deep breath and was preparing to say something when Missy knocked sharply on the front door.

'Later,' Sheridan said.

'For now,' Marybeth said, dourly. 'Later, we talk.' She gestured to the front door. 'Would you please let your grandmother in?'

Sheridan welcomed the reprieve and shouted over her shoulder to her thirteen-year-old sister: 'Lucy, there's somebody here for you!' She ducked back down the hallway with a satisfied smirk.

'I WAS SURPRISED to see your car home on a Wednesday,' Missy said, sweeping into the house with a full-sized presence that belied her sixty-four years and petite figure. She wore a black silk trouser-suit embroidered with dragons, a purchase from China when she'd attended the 2008 Olympics with her fifth husband, Earl Alden, known as the 'Earl of Lexington', a multimillionaire media mogul. With each husband, Missy had traded up. Her last husband, Bud Longbrake, had lost his ranch in the divorce when he'd discovered the handover was in small print in the prenuptial agreement.

'I took the day off,' Marybeth said. 'Joe will be back next week, as you know. I've been putting boxes of the girls' things in his office, and I needed to clean it all up.'

'Oh,' Missy said, 'Joe. I'd *so* forgotten about him. I've gotten used to just you and the girls.'

'I'll bet,' Marybeth said.

'There you are!' Missy said, turning and seeing Lucy behind her.

'Hi, Grandma Missy,' Lucy said.

Missy enveloped Lucy in her arms and said, 'How's my favourite granddaughter?'

'I'm fine,' Lucy said, forcing a girlish smile she reserved for photographs and her grandmother.

The animosity between Sheridan and her grandmother had reached almost the same level of acrimony as that between Joe and Missy. So Missy no longer made an effort to pretend that she didn't prefer Lucy. Like Missy, Lucy went for fine clothing and fine things. Missy disapproved of Sheridan's interest in falconry and science and her lack of interest in all things Missy.

To Lucy, Missy said, 'And are you wearing that silk dress I brought you from Paris? The electric blue one?'

'School hasn't started yet,' Lucy said. 'But I will.'

Missy nodded with satisfaction.

Marybeth knew Lucy was fibbing. Lucy had told her she was embarrassed by the dress. That it might as well have had 'My Grandmother Is Rich' embroidered on the back of it. She'd also confessed she was getting more embarrassed in general by her grandmother, who sometimes acted as if they were contemporaries as well as allies. Marybeth still bristled at the memory of Lucy telling her that Missy had said one of the bonds between them included the fact that they 'shared common enemies'. Meaning Marybeth and Joe.

Marybeth thought, Not now . . . I don't have time for this.

MBP, MARYBETH'S business-management company, had been purchased by a local accounting firm. They'd retained her for a year while they incorporated her employees into the business. Managing the sale of her livelihood, the transition into a larger and entrenched company, the running of the household with three teenage girls, and Joe's year-long absence, had become almost unbearable.

Marybeth and Missy had sat down at opposite sides of the dining-room table, coffee in front of them. Suddenly, her mother reached over, grasped her hand and said, 'You haven't heard a word I've been saying, have you?'

'I thought you were talking to Lucy,' Marybeth said.

'No, Lucy managed to slip away,' Missy said, through a cold smile. 'She's never going to wear that blue dress, is she?'

'Mom, I don't *know*,' Marybeth said with a sigh.

Missy pulled her hand away and dramatically studied Marybeth over the rim of her coffee cup. 'You're killing yourself,' she said, putting the cup down. 'You have weary eyes, and I can see wrinkles where I've never seen them before. It just saddens me that—'

'You don't have to finish,' Marybeth said sharply. 'I know what you're going to say.' She set her cup down with enough force that both women looked to see if she'd cracked it. 'So what do you need, Mom? I mean, it's nice you dropped by and all, but I took the day off work so I could get some things done round here. I'm on edge waiting for Joe to call. And I know you well enough to guess that you didn't just drop by.'

Missy nodded and said, 'I'll get to the point. You know that friend of yours—Nate? The falconer who got in so much trouble a while back? I need to talk with him.'

'Why do you want to talk to Nate?' Marybeth said, surprised.

'Well, actually, the Earl thought of him,' Missy said. 'I was thinking I'd take care of the problem myself.'

'What problem?'

'Bud.'

'What about Bud?'

'He can't let go. He just stays in Saddlestring and drinks the Stockman's Bar dry every night. He tells anyone who will listen his pathetic story, and he says terrible things about the Earl and me.'

'Mom, you broke his heart and *stole* his ranch,' Marybeth said.

Missy made a tut-tut sound with her tongue. 'The transfer was perfectly legal, sweetie. Anyway, Bud's been calling and threatening me. I want to hire Nate Romanowski to scare him off.'

'Nate doesn't do things like that,' Marybeth said.

Missy smiled. 'Then there are obviously things about your friend that you don't know all that well. You see, The Earl had some research done.'

Marybeth looked at the clock above the stove. 'I've got to get some work done now. You've got to go home.'

'I'm not asking you to do anything to Bud,' Missy said. 'All I'm asking is for you to pass a message to Mr Romanowski that I'd like to speak to him.'

'I don't see Nate any more,' Marybeth said. 'He's in hiding. There are federal warrants out on him. Besides, Nate's in love these days. He's different. He'd never consider your proposition.'

Missy was undeterred. 'Your husband talks to him. And Sheridan still does, doesn't she?'

'I don't know,' Marybeth lied as she picked up both cups from the table and took them to the sink so she could keep her back to her mother.

'Honey,' Missy said, 'how do you think he makes a living? Haven't you ever wondered about that?'

Marybeth had. But like Joe, she never wanted to find out.

'Thank you for the coffee,' Missy said. 'Have Nate call me.'

Marybeth didn't turn round. She heard her mother call goodbye to Lucy and go outside. In a moment, the black Hummer roared to life.

THE BROTHERS WORKED in a quiet rhythm of flashing knives and strong, bloody hands.

All Joe's gear had been piled a few yards from the carcass. He could see everything he needed but couldn't get close enough to get it. A hundred yards was too far for an accurate shot with his handgun. If he missed, which he surely would, he would reveal his position and the brothers could make short work of him with the .308 or his shotgun. His Glock had fourteen rounds in the magazine. His spare magazines, like the first-aid kit, were in the panniers.

The wind reversed, and Camish suddenly stepped away and sniffed at the air like a wolf. They were trying to *smell* him. Then Camish suddenly pointed in Joe's direction in the aspen grove.

Oh, no, Joe mouthed. He wouldn't have thought it possible.

Caleb and Camish wordlessly retrieved their weapons and ran across the meadow in opposite directions. Caleb left with Joe's carbine, Camish right with his shotgun.

Instinctively, Joe scrambled back on his haunches. A hammer-blow of pain from his right thigh sat him back down, and he gulped air to recover. He glanced up to see Caleb dart into the left wall of trees. Camish was already gone. They obviously knew he'd been hit and they assumed—correctly—that he couldn't run. They were going to flank him, come at him in a pincer movement through the trees.

Gritting his teeth, Joe rose to his knees. He raised the Glock with both hands and swung it left, then right, looking over the sights towards the trees, hoping to catch one of them, get a clean shot.

His training trumped the urge to try to kill them without warning. He shouted, 'Both of you freeze where you are and toss your weapons out into the open. This is OVER. Don't take it any further.'

He paused, eyes shooting back and forth for movement of any kind, ears straining for sound. He continued, 'I hate to break it to you boys, but you think because you stole my satellite phone it means no one knows where I am. That's not the case. Twice a day I call in my coordinates. I called 'em in just before I rode up on Caleb. They know exactly where I was and which way I was headed. They'll be able to pinpoint this location within a mile or two, and they'll be worried. Help is on the way, boys. So let's end the game.'

No response, until Camish, a full minute later, said from where he was hidden to the right: 'You believe that, brother?'

Joe was shocked how close the voice was. Just beyond the thick red buck-brush; the voice so intimate it was as if Camish were whispering into his ear.

Caleb snorted from the dense juniper and pine on his left. 'No.'

'I don't believe him either. He's a liar.'

'Another damned liar,' Caleb said with contempt. 'After a while, a man starts to wonder if there's a single one of 'em who doesn't lie.'

And then the afternoon exploded. Joe threw himself to his belly as his shotgun boomed from the left. From the right, Camish fired the .308, squeezing off rounds as quickly as he could pull the trigger. Chunks of bark and dead branches fell round him. The air smelled sharply of gunfire.

The shots stopped. Joe did a mental inventory. He wasn't hit, which was a small miracle. But the proximity of the brothers, and the metal-on-metal sounds of them furiously reloading, convinced him he likely wouldn't survive another volley. An infusion of fear and adrenaline combined to propel him back to his knees, gun up.

A pine bough shuddered to his left, and Joe fired. *Pop-pop-pop.*

Through the ringing in his ears, he thought he heard someone cry out.

'Caleb,' Camish cried, 'you hit?'

Caleb's response was an inhuman moan ending in a roar, the sound of someone trying to shout through a mouthful of liquid.

Then Joe swung the Glock a hundred and eighty degrees to his right. The forest was silent, but he anticipated Camish to be at roughly the same angle and distance as his brother.

Pop-pop-pop-pop-pop.

No cries, no sounds. And it was silent again to the left.

Maybe he'd backed them off. Caleb was wounded, maybe fatally. Camish? Who knew?

A dry branch snapped to the left, and Joe wheeled and fired off four wild shots. Then he quickly lowered the Glock and cursed himself.

'Not many shots left, by my count,' Camish said from the shadows. 'Since your spare magazines were in those panniers, you may be out of luck.'

The slide on the Glock hadn't kicked fully back, which meant he had at least one round left. He tried to count back, to figure out how many rounds he still had. At least two rounds left, he hoped. He'd need that many . . .

LURCHING FROM TREE to tree, blood flowing again from the wounds in his right thigh, Joe crashed through the timber back towards where he'd left Buddy.

The Grim brothers couldn't be far behind.

He'd find his horse, apologise and spur him on. Push the horse down the mountain. Eventually, he'd hit water. He'd follow the stream to something, or somebody.

AN HOUR PAST SUNDOWN, Buddy collapsed onto his front knees. Joe slid off, and as soon as his boots hit the ground he was reminded sharply of the pain in his own legs, because they couldn't hold him up. He fell in a heap next to his horse.

Buddy sighed, and all four of his hooves windmilled for a moment before he relaxed and settled down on his side. Joe was heartbroken, but he did his best not to cry out. He stroked the neck of his gelding and cursed the Grim brothers. He knew that possibly, *possibly*, he could have saved his horse by not mounting up, that without Joe's weight Buddy could have walked slowly and maybe the blood would have stopped flowing out.

Buddy blinked at Joe.

'I'm sorry,' Joe said. 'I'm sorry for being selfish.'

Buddy deserved to go quickly. Joe unsheathed his knife.

He said a prayer. Asked both God and Marybeth to forgive him for what he was about to do.

USING A BROKEN BRANCH with a Y in the top of it as a crutch, Joe continued down the mountain in the dark. A spring burbled out from a pile of flat rocks. He kept the little creek to his right. He followed it until it joined a larger stream, which he guessed was No Name Creek.

The stillness of the night, the constant pain of his legs, the awkward rhythm of his descent, and the soft backbeat percussion of his own breath was an all-encompassing world of its own and nearly made him forget about the danger he was in.

His life became as simple as it had ever been because it was reduced to absolute essentials: *Place one foot before the other, keep weight off right leg, keep going, keep senses dialled to high.*

In the daylight, he might not have found it. If it weren't for the smoke which hung like a night-time shadow in the trees, he would have limped right past. But he stopped and turned slowly to the right. There was a cut in the hillside on the other side of the little stream. The cut went fifty yards back into the slope and doglegged to the right. The smoke came from where the dogleg ended.

Joe winced and nearly blacked out as he crossed the stream. He closed his eyes tightly and was entertained by fireworks on the inside of his eyelids. When he opened them, there was a cabin ahead. A faint square of light seeped through a small curtained window.

The curtain on the window quivered as he made a fist to knock on the rough pine door. Whoever was inside knew he was there. Then a wild thought: What if the Grims lived here?

He collapsed as the door opened and fell inside.

A woman said, 'Oh my God, no . . .' Then: 'Who *are* you? Why did you come here? Oh no, you'll be the *death* of me.'

Friday, August 28

When Joe awoke, he was on his back on the floor of the cabin in a nest of thick quilts. He reached up and rubbed the right side of his face, which was warm from the heat of an iron woodstove.

He could remember vivid nightmares reliving the attack, throwing off the quilts as he fought off demons, awaking with a fever and drinking water and broth, the touch of her fingers on his bare thigh as she bandaged it, her frequent prognostications of doom.

The cabin was small and old. Although it was only one room and was packed with possessions, it seemed clean and organised. Red curtains were drawn over small windows on each wall.

She was sitting at a table wearing thick trousers, a too-large man's shirt, and a fleece vest. It was hard to tell her age. Her long brown hair fell to her shoulders, and her forehead was hidden behind a thick fringe. Her clothes were so large and loose he couldn't discern her shape or weight. Her eyes were blue and cool and fixed on him, her mouth pursed with anticipation and concern.

'How long have I been out?' he asked.

'Eighteen hours,' she said. 'More or less.'

He let that sink in. 'So it's Friday night?'

She shrugged. 'I don't think in terms of days of the week any more.'

He nodded and tried not to stare at her. There was something pensive about her, as if she would melt away if he asked too many questions.

Joe folded the quilt back. His jeans were off, but she hadn't removed his boxers. He looked at the bandage on his right leg. It was tightly wrapped and neat. There were two small spots of dried blood where the holes in his thigh were. His other leg was purple and green with bruises.

'Thank you,' he said. 'You saved my life.'

She nodded quickly. 'I know.' She said it with a hint of regret, then shook her head. 'I really don't want you here one minute past when you can leave. Do you understand me?'

Joe nodded. 'Do you have a phone?'

'No, I don't have a phone.'

'Any way to communicate with the outside world?'

'This is my world,' she said, twirling a finger to indicate the inside of her cabin. 'What you see is my world. It's very small, and that's the way I like it. It's the way I want to keep it.'

He took in the contents of the cabin. There were burlap sacks in one corner: beans, coffee, flour, sugar. Canned goods were stacked near the sacks. A five-gallon plastic container on a shelf with a gravity-feed water-filter tube was dripping pure water into a bucket.

Dented but clean pots and pans hung from hooks above the stove. Several dozen worn hardback books stood like soldiers on a shelf above a single bed covered with homemade quilts. There was a heavy trunk under the bed and a battered armoire next to it.

'So you live alone?'

'Alone with my thoughts. I'm rarely lonely.'

'Have you lived here very long?' he asked, wondering why he'd never heard of a lone woman in a cabin in the mountains.

'Long enough,' she said. 'Really, I don't want to get into a discussion with you.'

Joe sat up painfully. His head swam, and it took a moment to make it stop spinning.

'I'm a Wyoming game warden. My name is Joe Pickett. I was attacked by two brothers up on top of the mountain. I wouldn't be surprised if they were still after me.'

She grimaced, but he could tell it wasn't news to her. Of course, he thought, she'd seen his badge and credentials. Which made him quickly start patting the folds of the quilts.

'I had a weapon,' he said.

'It's in a safe place.'

'I need it back,' he said. 'And my wallet and jeans . . .'

She put her hands palm-down on the table and fixed her eyes on something over Joe's head. She said, 'Your wedding ring—I saw it when you fell into my cabin. It got to me, I'm afraid. Otherwise I might have pushed you back outside and locked the door and waited for them to show up. I'm amazed they aren't here by now.'

He was taken aback by the casual way she said it.

He said, 'I think I hit one of them. Maybe I hit them both.'

Her eyes widened in fear, and she raised a balled fist to her mouth. She said, 'This isn't good.'

'So you know them—the Grim brothers.'

'Of course.'

There was something familiar about her face, Joe thought. He knew he didn't know her and hadn't met her before. But he'd seen her face. He wished his head were more clear.

'How do you know them?' he asked.

'They come by. They bring me firewood and meat. They look out for me. All they ask from me is my silence and my loyalty. You're making me betray them.'

Joe said nothing.

'They're not all bad,' she said. 'They provide me protection. They understand why I'm here, and they're quite sympathetic.'

'Tell me your name,' Joe said.

She hesitated. 'Terri,' she said finally. 'My name is Terri Wade.'

The name was unfamiliar to Joe. 'Look,' he said. 'This is national forest, and there shouldn't be any private dwellings. Aren't you worried forest rangers will find you and make you leave?'

She said, 'The brothers protect me. They wouldn't let that happen. This is *my* cabin. These are *my* things.' As her voice rose, she gestured by jabbing her right index finger into the palm of her left hand on the word *my.* 'No one has the right to make me leave.'

Said Joe, 'So why are you here?'

'You keep asking me questions. Look, I'm here to try to reassemble my life,' she said. 'I don't put my nose into anyone's business, and I expect the same from others. Including you,' she said, again jabbing her finger into her palm. '*Especially* you.'

'I understand,' Joe said.

Wade suddenly sat up straight and lifted her chin to the ceiling. 'Hear that?' she whispered.

Joe shook his head.

'There's someone on the roof,' she said softly.

He looked up. The ceiling was constructed of pine planks. As he stared, one of the planks bowed slightly inwards, then another did the same about a foot away. There was someone heavy up there.

Joe rocked forward, his leg screamed silently, and he reached out and touched her hand. He mouthed, 'Where's my gun?'

Her eyes glistened with tears, and she shook her head, but she inadvertently glanced towards the trunk under her bed.

He pulled himself painfully across the rough floor to the trunk. He slid it out and unbuckled the hasps. When he raised the lid, he found the Glock and his belt on top of folded piles of worn clothes. He worked the slide of his handgun and ejected a live cartridge. Another was in the magazine. So he still had two rounds. He let the magazine drop and loaded the loose cartridges again and jacked one of them into the chamber. Two shots, he thought. Just two shots.

They both jumped when there was a voice outside the door. 'Terri, do you have company in there?'

Joe recognised the voice as Camish. Which meant Caleb was on the roof. Which also meant that he wasn't dead and certainly wasn't wounded badly enough to take him out of circulation.

'Terri?' Camish repeated. 'I know you heard me.' His tone wasn't unkind.

'Not now,' Terri said loudly towards the door. 'Leave me alone.'

'Oh, Terri, it doesn't work like that. We know he's in there.'

'Please,' she said. 'Come back later. Come back tomorrow.'

'You mean after he's gone?' Camish asked, and Joe detected a slight chuckle. 'That's a crazy notion, Terri. He hurt my brother. And you know the situation. We can't let him go. You *know* that.'

'I don't want any violence,' Terri said. 'I told you before I don't want violence. You promised. You *promised* me.'

Camish said, 'Yes, we did. And there's no need for any violence at all. We just want that government man inside your place.'

Joe thought, Government man?

Then he looked at her and saw nothing other than torment. Her hands were knotted into white-knuckled fists and her shoulders were bunched and her mouth was pursed. She was in agony, and it was because of him. He felt sorry for her, grateful she'd displayed kindness and humanity towards him, and he wanted to save her.

He wanted to save himself as well.

Camish said, 'Then we have no choice, do we? Let the fumigation begin!'

Fumigation?

Suddenly, the cabin filled with an acrid, horrible steam that came from the woodstove. Terri sat back in her chair and buried her face in a napkin to try to avoid the foul-smelling steam.

Joe recognised the odour, shook his head, and whispered, 'Caleb is urinating down the chimney pipe.' He motioned for her to get down on the floor.

'I can't . . .' she said, glancing towards the closed door. She seemed frozen, conflicted.

He said, 'GET DOWN!'

Too loudly, he thought. Caleb no doubt heard him on the roof. Joe noted two particular ceiling planks bending downwards from Caleb's boots and visualised him up there, legs spread on either side of the chimney. Joe raised the weapon, calculated the height and stance of his target, aimed, squeezed the trigger . . . The .40 Glock barked out a bullet, but not where he'd aimed, because Terri had screamed 'No violence!' and launched up at him from the floor, hitting him clumsily with her shoulder. The impact threw him back, and the slug thudded into a log chest-high inside the cabin.

Joe fell back and then forward to his knees, both hands still round his gun. He was fully cognisant that he had only a single bullet left for the Grim brothers.

Camish shouted: 'Terri, get down!'

She dropped to her knees with her eyes locked in sympathy with Joe, then stretched out on the floor and covered her head with her hands.

Joe looked up.

The thick cabin door rocked with the force of a shotgun blast. Gun smoke filled the inside of the cabin and there were half-inch splinters of wood on every surface. Joe flung himself backwards, away from Terri Wade. He remembered the small curtained window over her bed. With Caleb on the roof and Camish in front of the cabin, it was his only escape.

Another blast punched a second hole through the front door. Wade screamed, begging them to stop, telling them they could come in and get the government man.

And Joe thought, once again, *Government man*? He didn't like to be thought of that way. He was a *wildlife* man.

The front door blew open. Caleb had come down off the roof and broken the door in with his shoulder. He stood in the threshold for a moment, eyes wide and mean, a blood-sodden bandage round the lower part of his face, and Joe realised he'd clipped the end of Caleb's chin off the day before.

Except he hadn't finished the job, which put him in a much worse situation now. Joe raised the Glock, centred the front and back sight on Caleb's chest, and fired.

Caleb winced and took a step back but didn't drop. He held the .308 at parade rest and seemed momentarily incapable of raising it and aiming at Joe. Joe thought, Why didn't he go down?

Camish blew through the front door, and when Terri Wade rose and threw herself at him, he greeted her with a stiff-arm that quickly got her out of the line of fire without flinging her to the floor.

Joe reared back, pitched his weapon through the glass of the back window and followed it.

Camish yelled, 'Hey, stop!' and raised his shotgun.

Joe glanced over his shoulder as he stepped on the bed, saw the O of the muzzle and steeled himself for the force of a shotgun blast in his back. But Terri Wade rammed Camish the way she'd thrown herself at him. The shotgun exploded, but the load smashed into the wall near Joe's left shoulder.

'Damn you, Terri,' Camish yelled as he shoved her aside again. He could have clubbed her with the butt of the shotgun, and Joe expected it, but he didn't.

Joe covered his face with his arms and dived through the broken window. The remaining glass gave way and he was outside, his arms and neck wrapped in the curtain, rolling in pine needles. He tossed the curtain aside and scrambled to his feet, his right boot tip thudding against something heavy on the ground—his empty gun. He recovered it and staggered downhill towards the creek he'd followed earlier. Behind him, he heard Camish rack the pump again and yell for Joe to stop.

Joe could hear glass breaking: Camish was probably using the barrel to knock down the remaining shards of glass so he could aim unimpeded. Joe stepped behind a tall pine tree just in time as the blast stripped the bark off the other side of the trunk.

Joe flung himself away, trying to keep the tree between the cabin and him, trying to get his legs to respond. Electric bolts of pain shot up into his groin from his wounds. Each tree and bush he passed provided more cover and protection, and he hoped he could vanish into the darkness before Camish could aim well and fire again. His shotgun was an extremely lethal short-range weapon, but it lost its punch with every step Joe made into the woods.

There was another shot, and pellets smacked trees and ripped through brush on both sides of him. He felt two sudden hot spots—one in his right shoulder and another under the scalp near his right ear. He tripped and pitched forwards, falling hard.

On the ground, he distinctly heard Camish say, 'Got him.' And a female voice say, 'Are you sure?'

Joe didn't pause to assess the new wounds, and he didn't stand up in case Camish could still see him. Instead, he crawled through the dirt on his hands and knees, plunging deeper into darkness.

After ten minutes of crawling, he used a fallen tree to steady himself and rise to his feet. As he ran, he swiped at the burn in his scalp and felt hot blood on his fingertips. His shoulder was numb except for a single burning ember buried deep in the muscle.

HE WAS SPLASHING through the creek before he realised it was there. The icy water shocked him but felt good at the same time. Joe paused and tried to catch his breath. He listened for the sound of footfalls but didn't hear them. Yet. Squatting on his haunches, he cupped his hands and filled them with icy water, which he drank and used to douse his neck wound.

Terri Wade had saved his life twice, yet he'd left her back there with them. He rose and turned in the creek, looking back in the direction of the cabin. What would they do to her?

He hoped they'd spare her. After all, it was him they were after, and Camish seemed to have chosen not to hurt her when he easily could have. But Camish was distracted at the time and Caleb was injured. What would happen now that Joe was gone and they had her to themselves?

Joe had an empty weapon, and again he was losing blood. His strength was fuelled by pure adrenaline and anger and nothing more. But he couldn't just leave her. Could he?

He waited fifteen minutes hidden in streamside buckbrush. They weren't coming. Which meant they'd stayed in the cabin with her.

Joe stood uneasily. It puzzled him that they hadn't pursued him or searched for his body to administer a kill-shot, if necessary. The brothers had pursued him for miles over rough terrain to find him at the cabin. Why would they simply assume he was dead?

As he limped back up the mountainside towards the cabin, he put his questions aside and made a plan.

Like before, he smelled wood smoke. He'd adjusted to the darkness and could see much better than when he'd run. If Camish or Caleb were searching for his body, Joe was confident he'd see them first.

It almost didn't register that the forest was getting lighter until he realised why: the cabin was burning.

'No,' he said aloud, and began to lope through the trees.

He stopped at the edge of the clearing. Tongues of flame licked out through the windows and illuminated the dark wall of trees that hid the cabin. The fire crackled angrily, and there were soft *POOM* sounds of the canned food exploding inside. Had they left her to burn to death?

Joe took a deep breath and prepared to move as quickly as possible towards the cabin when he suddenly froze. He'd seen something in his peripheral vision, three faces like faint orange moons, hanging low in the dark trees to his left. He stayed behind a tree trunk and turned away from the bright flames, trying to make his eyes adjust again.

Then he saw them: Caleb, Camish and Terri Wade, a hundred feet away. Watching the cabin burn. Tears streamed down Wade's face. She looked upset but unhurt. Most disturbingly, she appeared to be with them willingly, standing by their side. Caleb was stoic, likely in shock from his bullet wound. Camish looked demonic, his eyes reflecting the fire. They obviously hadn't seen him.

Wade turned away into the darkness, dousing her face.

Then a moment later, to Caleb's left, a fourth face appeared. The sight jarred him and he waited for another look, which didn't come. All had turned and were walking away and could no longer be seen.

He closed his eyes tightly, trying to visualise who he'd glimpsed, thinking: No. You've seen her face so many times in the past two years on fliers put up by her parents. Her face has been burned into your subconscious. You're seeing things. It couldn't have been her.

LATER, BEHIND HIM, he heard the cabin collapse in on itself with the rough crackling of timber.

The stream to his left, trees and boulders to his right, the sky filled with pulsing stars and a moon bright enough to see by, the injured game warden started walking slowly out of the Sierra Madre.

The stream would lead somewhere; a ranch house, a road.

He had no answers, only questions. He hoped his questions could keep him occupied and alive long enough to get off the mountain.

Saturday, August 29

Nate Romanowski tramped up the switchback canyon trail with a fifteen-pound mature bald eagle perched on a thick welder's glove. As he hiked, the eagle maintained its balance by clamping its talons on the glove and shifting its weight with subtle extensions of its seven-foot wingspan, often hitting Nate in the face.

'Stop that,' he said, flinching. The bird ignored him.

A satellite phone hung from a leather strap round Nate's neck, and his Freedom Arms .454 Casull, the second most powerful handgun in the world, was in a shoulder holster beneath his left armpit. It was a warm, late-summer day, and as he approached the rim of the canyon a slight breeze blew hot and dry. Two candy-floss cumulus clouds paraded across an endless light blue sky that opened up as he rose out of Hole in the Wall Canyon, where he lived in a cave once occupied by Old West outlaws. He'd chosen the location a year before, when the FBI office in Cheyenne had declared him a first-priority suspect in crimes he'd committed and in some he hadn't. Hole in the Wall was perfect for him to hide out in, due to its remote location on private land in north-central Wyoming, and due to the fact that no one could descend into it unseen. Only three people knew of his existence there: his lover, Alisha Whiteplume; his friend Joe Pickett; and Sheridan Pickett, his apprentice in falconry.

Nate was a master falconer: tall, lean, with broad shoulders, long legs and a foot-long blond ponytail that hung down his back. He had a hawk nose and icy blue eyes, and he went weeks without talking except to himself and his birds of prey. The eagle had been shot the year before and was seriously damaged. It had no desire to fly, to hunt, or to become independent and eagle-like. Nate was beginning to suspect the eagle was an incorrigible head case.

He emerged from the canyon and sat down in the grass, sweating from the exertion of the climb. He let the bald eagle step off his gloved hand and it stood next to him, inert and majestic. No bird, he thought, looked better on principle than a bald eagle. But if the eagle wouldn't fly or hunt or protect itself, what could he do?

There was a single message on his satellite phone from Marybeth Pickett. He dialled her phone number in Saddlestring.

'Nate?' she answered.

'You sound agitated. Is everything all right?'

'I'm worried about Joe. He went on a horseback patrol on Monday. He left a message saying everything was OK on Tuesday night, and I haven't heard from him since.'

'Maybe his phone went out. You know things like that happen.'

'Yes, I know. But I have a feeling something's terribly wrong. I can't shake it. I'm really worried about him. We've been married a long time, and sometimes you just know things. I can't explain it.'

Nate said, 'Where did you hear from him last?'

'Some lake in the Sierra Madre. I keep listening to that message over and over. He says everything's fine, but I get a bad vibe.'

Nate scrunched his face. This was unusual. Marybeth was a tough woman, not prone to panic. He had a soft spot for her. He said, 'Have you talked to anyone else?'

'Everyone I can think of. I called Game and Fish dispatch in Cheyenne, and they hadn't heard from him, either. And I also left a message for Governor Rulon.'

'You did?'

'I'm desperate,' she said. 'He expects Joe to be on call for him whenever *he* needs something. I told him he needs to be on call for *us* this time.'

'So Joe's by himself as far as you know?'

'Yes, damn it. Some hunters said they shot an elk and somebody butchered it before they could tag it. He was going up into the mountains to find whoever might have done it.'

'No back-up?' Nate said.

Marybeth groaned. 'He never has back-up. That's the way game wardens work, Nate. It drives me crazy.'

'What else have you done?'

'I called the sheriff down in Baggs. He didn't help my state of mind, because he said there were all sorts of weird things happening down there. He said ranchers had pulled their cattle from the mountains and there'd been break-ins at cabins and trailheads.'

'So the sheriff didn't give you any help?'

'It's not that he refused,' she said. 'He just wasn't sure what to do. Joe didn't exactly file a flight plan, which sounds like Joe.'

'When is he supposed to be down?'

'Today. This morning.'

Nate said, 'I don't want you to take this the wrong way, but shouldn't you give him the chance to call before you conclude something's wrong? Maybe his phone went bad up in the mountains and he just hasn't been able to reach you.'

Marybeth exhaled and said, 'Are you suggesting I'm hysterical? That I'd call you with no good reason?'

He thought about it. 'No.'

'I told you, I have a bad feeling. Something's happened.'

'OK,' he said. 'Call me again if you hear anything.'

'I will. And I know the situation you're in. I'd never compromise you unless I thought we needed help. You know that, don't you?'

'Yes.'

'I've got to go now.'

He punched DISCONNECT.

'MARYBETH-SHERIDAN-LUCY-APRIL, Marybeth-Sheridan-Lucy-April . . .' Joe muttered in a kind of hypnotic cadence as he walked. The mantra gave him comfort and strength and a reason to keep going.

It was approaching dusk. He'd walked through the night and for the entire day, scared to stop and rest for more than a few minutes. As he walked and chanted, he'd turn periodically, searching behind him for followers. He doubted he'd been followed, because the Grim brothers didn't know he'd survived the shotgun blast. Still, he couldn't be certain.

Joe tried not to pay attention to his injuries. He had no idea how much blood he'd lost, but he knew it was too much. He was light-headed and weak. His body was broken yet still functional, as if his muscles had a will of their own.

He trudged and chanted in a pain-dulled daze. 'Marybeth-Sheridan-Lucy-April, Marybeth-Sheridan-Lucy-April . . .'

Joe kept thinking about what had happened, what he'd seen, what he didn't know.

Why was Terri Wade in an isolated cabin? What was her relationship with the Grim brothers? And could that have possibly been who he thought it was with them? The girl? He shook his head. He'd imagined her, he was sure.

And what about the brothers themselves? Why were they up there? What caused them to hide in one of the roughest and most remote sections of the least populated state in the union?

It was almost imperceptible how the terrain changed, how cottonwoods took over from the pine trees, how bunches of cheater grass replaced the pine-needle floor. Joe knew he'd descended from the mountains into a valley. He veered away from the creek and the trees and, as the sun set, instead of the smell of pine, he smelled sweet cut hay and thought he caught a whiff of gasoline.

As he broke over a rise, the hay meadow was spread out before him. Cut hay lay in long, straight channels. After days of mountain randomness, he was impressed by the symmetry of the rows.

A half-mile away, a hay baler crawled across the field, its motor humming as it turned rows of cut hay into fifty-pound bales which it left behind like tractor droppings.

As Joe walked towards the baler, something in his brain released and his wounds exploded in sudden pain. It was as if now that his rescue was at hand, the mental dam holding everything back for three days suddenly burst from the strain.

His legs gave way and he fell to his knees and pitched forwards.

IN THE DARK, what seemed like hours later, he heard a boy say, 'Hey, Dad, look. It's that game warden everyone's looking for.'

PART TWO

Reloading Without Bullets

Tuesday, September 1

On the third day of his stay in the Billings Hospital, Joe awoke to find a tall, thin man in ill-fitting clothes—white dress shirt, open collar, loose tie, over-large blazer—hovering near the foot of his bed. The man had world-weary brown eyes, and his hair was light brown, peppered with silver. A pair of smudged reading glasses hung from a cord round his neck. His aura of legal bureaucracy was palpable. He said, 'Joe Pickett? I'm Bobby McCue, DCI.'

Wyoming Department of Criminal Investigation.

'I read the statement you gave the sheriff down in Carbon County,' McCue said. 'I was hoping I could ask you a few more questions. We're trying to fill in some of the gaps.'

'What gaps?' Joe raised his eyebrows, which elicited a sharp pain where they'd removed the shotgun pellet behind his ear.

He had given statements to Carbon County sheriff Ron Baird, Baggs police chief Brian Lally and his departmental supervisor. Each had asked basically the same questions but in different ways, and Joe had no control over what they wrote down when he answered. Even though what had happened in the mountains was clear in his mind, it was possible that his statements, when laid side by side, might not completely tally. It was the nature of the game, and one played—sometimes unfairly—by investigators and prosecutors. So he knew to be alert and careful each time he was questioned.

McCue slid Joe's tray table towards him and opened a manila folder on top of it. He fitted his glasses to his face, then slid them as far down his nose as they would go before they fell off.

'Just a couple of questions,' McCue said, peeling back single pages within the file. Joe recognised them as copies of the original sheriff's department statement given to Ron Baird.

'About Caleb Grim, the one you encountered at that lake. It says here he gave you permission to look through his possessions.'

Said Joe, 'Yes, he let me look through his bag.'

McCue read from the statement, '"The suspect's daypack contained several items, including a water container, a knife, a diary, half a Bible, and an iPod holder."' He looked up. 'Can you describe the iPod holder to me?'

Joe searched his memory. 'It was one of those things that strap to your upper arm. My wife Marybeth has one for the gym.'

'What colour was it? Can you recall?'

'Pink.'

'You're sure?'

Joe nodded. 'Why is that important?' he asked.

'It may not be at all. I'm just covering all the bases. You know how this works,' McCue said, then quickly flipped over the page to another. 'You say Caleb claimed he was from the UP.'

'Yes.'

'And you thought, being from the Rocky Mountain West, that UP meant "Union Pacific". Did you know it could have meant the Upper Peninsula of Michigan? That's what they call it there.'

'I know that now,' Joe said. 'One of the sheriff's deputies down in Baggs told me. I feel kind of stupid, not knowing it.'

McCue nodded, apparently agreeing with Joe's assessment of himself. He flipped another page and stabbed at a note.

'You say there were four people besides you at the cabin that burned down. Caleb and Camish Grim, Terri Wade, and one other. You suggest that when you saw the profile of the fourth person you thought of Diane Shober. Is that correct?'

Joe felt his face get hot. He realised how ridiculous it sounded when McCue said it. 'Her name came to mind, probably because I'd seen her photo on so many fliers in that part of the state. Plus, I knew that's where she went missing. So when I caught a glimpse of a youngish female in the dark down there, I think I naturally thought of her. I've never once said it *was* her.'

McCue bored in. 'Do you stand by your impression, though?'

Joe shook his head. 'I stand by the fact that I thought of her at the time. But the more I think about it, the more I think my mind might have jumped to conclusions.'

'Can you describe her?'

'I didn't get a clear look. I can recall I thought she was blonde, female, and younger than Caleb and Camish and Terri Wade.'

'Her build?'

'Thin,' Joe said. 'Like you.'

McCue nodded to himself, as if Joe had confirmed something. 'Fine,' he said, closing the folder. 'I've got what I need for now.'

'That's it?'

McCue unhooked his reading glasses from his ears and let them drop on the cord. 'That's it.'

'Where can I contact you?' Joe asked. 'Cheyenne? One of the other offices? Where are you out of? I've never seen you around.'

McCue simply nodded. 'Thanks for your time,' he said. 'I'm sure we'll be seeing each other again.'

'Leave me your card,' Joe said. 'I may think of something later.'

McCue said over his shoulder, 'I'll leave one for you at the nurses' station.' And he was gone.

Ten minutes later, Joe pressed his nurse call button and asked for Agent McCue's DCI business card.

'What?' she said. Then: 'There's no card here. I didn't see him stop by on his way out. I'll ask around and let you know.'

TALKING WITH THE GIRLS was awkward. Joe got the feeling they agreed with that sentiment because they seemed to look at everything in the room besides him. They didn't like seeing him injured in a hospital bed any more than he liked being seen by them in one.

'You look like you're doing better,' Sheridan said.

'I am.'

'Billings sucks,' April said.

'There's a nice mall,' Lucy said.

'Wow,' April said, 'a *mall*. These people in Montana have thought of everything.'

'April,' Sheridan moaned.

'I just want everyone to be happy,' Lucy said, grinning. 'Starting with me.'

'It always starts with you,' April said.

'It's got to start somewhere.' Lucy grinned again.

'Nice one,' Sheridan said.

'Get me out of here,' April said to no one in particular.

Marybeth took them to the Rimrock Mall.

TWELVE SLEEP COUNTY SHERIFF McLanahan said 'Knock knock' but didn't actually knock when he entered Joe's hospital room.

Joe knew McLanahan disliked him. He hadn't seen McLanahan in the year he'd been in Baggs, but their relationship resumed where it had left off when the sheriff said, 'I'm startin' to wonder if they've got you in the right kind of hospital here, Joe. I'm startin' to think maybe it might be best to put you in one of those facilities with the rubber walls, because there's a bunch of us fellers startin' to believe you've gone crazy as a damned tick.'

He ended the sentence with a tinny uplift and a rural flourish.

Joe winced and fished for the control that powered his hospital bed so he could raise the head of it. He didn't like the sheriff seeing him prone or in his stupid cotton gown. As the head of the bed rose, Joe said, 'I could have gone the rest of my life without seeing you again, Sheriff.'

McLanahan clucked his tongue as if to say, *Too bad for you*, then settled heavily in a straight-backed chair to Joe's right.

'Two hours ago, I got off the phone with the state DCI boys and Sheriff Baird down in Carbon County,' McLanahan said. 'They're coming down the mountain as we speak. What they told me made me climb in my rig and drive two hours so I could tell you in person.'

Joe nodded. After he had given his version of events to the sheriff, Baird had quickly requested a team of investigators from the state to ride with him into the mountains after the Grim brothers.

'Does this have to do with some kind of inconsistency in my statements?' Joe asked. 'An agent named McCue from DCI was asking me more questions earlier today.'

'No, it has nothing to do with him,' McLanahan said, 'whoever the hell he is. Naw, what I heard I found out from the search team themselves. I've been getting updates for the past three days. There's eleven men on horseback been all over those mountains. Guess what they've found?'

Joe felt his mouth go dry.

'Nothin',' McLanahan said. 'Not a single damn thing to corroborate your tall tale.'

Joe stared. 'That's impossible,' he said. 'They didn't find *anything*?'

McLanahan said, 'Nope.'

'My horses and my tack?'

'Nope.'

'I don't understand. I mean, I can see how it might be hard to find the brothers' little pup-tent camp. It was deep in the timber and there wasn't a good trail to it. But on top they should have found the remains of my horses and where that cabin was burned down.'

'Provided those things exist somewhere other than your imagination,' McLanahan said. He raised a large hand with his fingers out and used his other index finger to count out and bend the fingers down one by one. 'No brothers. No burned-down cabin. No crazy woman. No long-lost girl runner. No—'

'They must be in the wrong area,' Joe said. 'I'm not lying.'

'I'm sure you're convinced of that. Fabulists become convinced of their own stories.'

'Why would I make up a story?' Joe said. 'Look around you, McLanahan. We're in a hospital. These injuries are real. I need to talk to Sheriff Baird. I need to hear this from him myself.'

'Feel free. I'm sure he'd love to talk with you, too. This search they just been on wiped out his discretionary budget for the rest of the year, payin' all those men to find a whole lot of nothing.'

Joe wasn't sure what to say. The news had taken the wind out of him.

'Well,' McLanahan said, sitting up in his chair and slapping his thighs,

'I best be getting back to the office. I just wanted to make sure you heard the happy news straight from the horse's mouth.'

'Look,' Joe said, 'I'll talk with Baird and try to figure out where they went wrong up there. It doesn't make any sense, unless the Grim brothers were able to wipe out all the evidence.'

'Yeah,' McLanahan said, 'according to your statement they seem larger than life itself. You shoot 'em in the face and in the chest and they still keep coming, like . . . mountain *zombies*!'

'What are you saying?' Joe asked. 'That I put myself in here for some reason and made it all up?'

McLanahan raised his hand and formed a pistol with his fist and fired it at Joe. 'Bingo,' he said. 'I can see a scenario where maybe you dropped your shotgun. It went off, peppering your shoulder and neck. Your horses reared and dumped you and you injured your leg. Then the horses ran off and left you there with nothin' at all. You didn't want to tell the governor what happened, so you made up one hell of a good story.'

'Get out,' Joe said.

McLanahan's eyes flashed, and he said, 'The easiest way to eat crap is while it's warm. The colder it gets, the harder it is to swallow.'

'Let me give you some of your own advice,' Joe said. 'Never miss a chance to shut up. Now get out.'

'And give my best to the lovely Mrs Pickett.'

JOE GRIPPED THE RAILINGS of his bed and stared at the blank screen of the television.

How was it possible a team of eleven men couldn't confirm his story? Where had the Grim brothers gone? Was it possible that everything Joe recalled was some kind of a fever dream?

A phone burred on a stand next to his bed. Until it rang, he hadn't known there was one there.

A crisp female voice said, 'Hold for Governor Rulon.'

Joe closed his eyes. How much worse could this day get?

'Joe! How in the hell are you?' The governor's voice was deep and raspy.

'Hello, sir. I'm fine.'

'Good, good. I'm in Washington giving hell to these bastards, and I've got a few minutes between meetings. I don't have long, so we need to get to the point.'

'OK.'

'Tell me straight: are you nuts? Did you go goofy down there in Baggs?'

Joe swallowed. 'No.'

'I got part of the story from my chief of staff, who's in touch with DCI. I've been anxiously awaiting news of a bloody shootout where two brothers are killed and two women are rescued in the mountains. Instead, I hear they can't find anything or anybody.'

'They must have been searching in the wrong places.'

'Hmm.'

Joe asked, 'Do you know a DCI investigator named Bobby McCue? He was in here earlier today asking me a bunch more questions. Do you know why DCI is questioning my story?'

'The name is familiar somehow, but I can't say I place him. We have too many damned employees.' Rulon huffed. 'I can't know every one of 'em.'

Strike two, Joe thought.

Rulon said suddenly, '*The Brothers Grimm?*'

'They prefer "the Grim brothers".'

'Diane Shober?'

'I don't swear it was her. I made that clear to the DCI. C'mon, governor. How can you doubt me? Have I ever lied to you?'

'Well, no,' Rulon said. 'You haven't. Sometimes I wish you would. An honest man can be a big pain to a politician, you know.'

Joe smiled.

'Have you been contacted by the press yet?' Rulon asked.

'No.'

'Do not under any circumstances talk to them. Say "No comment" and direct any enquiries to my office.'

'OK,' Joe said.

'It's gonna be damage-control mode. If this story gets out—'

'It's not a story,' Joe said, gritting his teeth. 'It's the truth. It's what happened. I'm in a hospital bed because of those brothers.'

Rulon paused. 'OK, then. I've got two calls I need to return. They both have to do with you. The first is from Chuck Coon at the FBI. He says he wants to be briefed, but I think he may know something about those brothers that he doesn't want to reveal. I'll have my staff talk to Coon. We may find out something that way that could benefit us. And then I have a harder call to return. To Diane Shober's parents. Somehow, they found out about your story. They want to find their daughter and bring her home.'

Joe felt his stomach clench.

'Look,' Rulon said. 'I'm officially placing you on administrative leave until we can get a handle on all of this. So go home and don't answer the door or the phone. That's an order. Stay inside and don't come out until you hear from me. Got that?'

'Yes, sir.' Joe swallowed. 'But—'

'No buts. I'm not hanging you out to dry, because you've never lied to me, even when I wanted you to. Right now, though, we've got to go to ground until we can figure out the best course of action.'

Joe said, 'I never got to thank you for letting me go home.'

'Oh, this is thanks enough.' The governor snorted, and laughed bitterly at his own joke. 'It looks like you're going to be seeing plenty of it in the next few days.'

Rulon punched off. Joe lowered the phone to his lap and looked back up at the blank television screen.

ON THE EASTERN SIDE of the Sierra Madre, on the opposite side of the range where Joe Pickett had ascended days before, Dave Farkus crept his pick-up through the timber towards his fall-time elk camp.

He'd had a bad day so far, but being in the mountains on a nice summer day was always an improvement over just about anything. He'd spent most of the day in Encampment, where he'd had a miserable lunch with his soon-to-be-ex-wife, Ardith. He'd been disappointed to find her not despondent. Farkus wasn't sure he wanted her back, but if she did come back, he would leave this time. At least then the fellows would think it was his idea, not hers.

And even though he'd taken the day off, driven all the way over the top, and delivered a stack of mail as well as her Book-of-the-Month packages, she said she had no intention of ever coming back. The divorce paperwork was filed and wouldn't be recalled.

So he'd bought a twelve-pack of Keystone Light and drunk six of them on the way up. In the bed of his pick-up were canvas tents, cooking stoves, an eating table and grates for the fire pit. Farkus's objective today was to 'claim' the camp before other elk hunters could do the same thing.

Officially, he and his buddies had no real ownership of their camp. The forest was public land, and reservations weren't taken by the US Forest Service. But elk hunters didn't like setting up camp next to other hunters.

So the idea was to get up into the mountains before any other party and stake out their traditional site. This year, it was Farkus's turn to be the scout.

The last week had been interesting. He'd been somewhat of a celebrity because he'd been the last person to talk to the game warden before all hell broke loose in the mountains. He'd been interviewed by the sheriff, state boys from DCI, a lone investigator named Bobby McCue and the local newspaper.

Like everyone else, he'd waited anxiously to find out what Sheriff Baird and the search team found. When the search team returned and said they'd found nothing—*nothing*—to corroborate Joe Pickett's story, it was like the air went out of the balloon. Secretly, Farkus had hoped they would find some mutilated or cannibalised bodies. Despite the fact they hadn't, he still floated his speculation of the Wendigo. In fact, he'd told the fellows at the bar the fact the search team hadn't found anything supported his theory even more. Wendigos, he explained, weren't human. They could vanish and reappear. What Pickett had encountered were two Wendigos up there. They came out when they could do harm. But when they saw the size of the search team and the amount of weaponry, they'd vanished. The Wendigos would be back, eventually.

Which made Farkus grateful that his elk camp was on the *other* side of the mountain.

He cursed when, through the trees, he saw a late-model pick-up and an eight-horse trailer parked right in the middle of his elk camp. He hoped whoever had stumbled into the site had it just for day use and had no plans to set up camp. If so, Farkus could at least dump the tents and stoves there and come back in a day or two.

But the men who turned as he approached looked like neither fishermen nor hunters. There were four of them. Two wore black, two wore camouflage. The men in black had buzz cuts and chiselled, lean features. One was tall with red hair and the other was dark and built like a linebacker. Both had holsters strapped to tactical vests. The men in camo were not as threatening-looking but certainly seemed fit and serious.

'Jeez,' Farkus whispered, slowing his pick-up to a stop twenty yards from the site.

Rifle barrels poked out from piles of gear on the forest floor. Cases of electronic equipment were stacked, along with duffle bags. Farkus didn't like the look of what he'd stumbled upon. These men didn't jibe with a bucolic late-summer afternoon, and he didn't want to find out why they were there.

The tall, red-haired man approached Farkus with his hand on the grip of his pistol. The others fell in behind him, then fanned out, making it impossible for Farkus to keep track of them all at once.

'Can I help you with something?' the man asked.

'You fellas seem to be in my elk camp,' Farkus said, voice cracking. Then he added, 'Not that there's any problem with that.'

'Your elk camp?' the man said.

Said Farkus, 'Never mind. I'm sure you'll be gone by the season opener. So I'll just be going now.'

Before he could jam his truck into reverse and hightail it out of there, his rearview mirror filled with the chrome grille of a black SUV with smoked windows. Farkus saw the red-haired man turn to whoever was driving the SUV and arch his eyebrows. Like awaiting the word. In the rearview, Farkus could see the driver nod once.

Instantly, the red-haired man mouthed, 'Get him.'

The driver stayed behind the wheel while the men in position broke and streaked directly at him from all four directions.

Suddenly, the open driver's window was blocked by the body of the linebacker. He'd leapt on the running board and was reaching through the open window into the cab for the wheel. The man's other hand grasped the shifter and shoved it into park. The passenger door flew open, and the red-haired man launched himself into the cab. Farkus felt a sharp pain as a high-topped fatigue boot kicked his leg away from the accelerator and brake pedals. The man plucked the keys out of the ignition and palmed them.

A cold O from the muzzle of a pistol pressed into his temple from the linebacker on the left. He squirmed as the man in the cab shoved his handgun into his rib cage.

Farkus thought, No one is ever going to believe this in the Dixon Club bar. He got out of his pick-up at gunpoint. He was patted down—none too gently—by the black-clad linebacker, who found and pocketed his Leatherman tool and knife.

The man who'd been driving the SUV left it parked behind the pick-up, and Farkus realised with a start that he knew him. It was that state guy, McCue. What was he doing here?

The red-haired man said, 'Got a second, Mr McCue?' To Farkus, 'Don't move a muscle.'

'OK,' Farkus said. Then, pleadingly to McCue: 'Aren't you with the state cops? Shouldn't you be helping me here?'

McCue rolled his eyes, dismissing the notion. Farkus felt the floor he thought he was standing on drop away.

As the two men walked out of earshot, Farkus rotated his head slightly so he could see them out of the corner of his eye. He got the gist of what they were discussing: *him.* He'd obviously stumbled onto something he wasn't supposed to see. He knew his life rested on the decision McCue would make and wondered how he could influence that. While he searched for an angle—Farkus's life was an endless procession of angle location—he craned his neck round further and sneaked a look at the back of their vehicle and the horse trailer. Michigan plates.

'Damn,' he said. 'You boys came a long way. Where you from in Michigan?'

They didn't answer him.

But Farkus had his angle. He said, 'Boys, I don't know what you're doing here, but it's obvious you're about to head off into the mountains. I know these mountains. I grew up here and I've guided hunters in this area every fall for twenty-five years, and let me tell you something: it's easy to get lost up here.'

He felt like whooping when McCue turned to him, listening.

Farkus said, 'These mountains are a series of drainages. The canyons look amazingly similar to each other when you're in them. People get lost all the time because they think they're walking along Cottonwood Creek when it's actually Bandit Creek or No Name Creek. Even with a GPS it's easy to get rimrocked or turned round. You know what I'm saying here. Dave Farkus can help you find what it is you're looking for. Trust me on this.'

McCue said, 'He's got a point.'

The red-haired man said, 'Mr McCue, we have all the men and equipment we need. Taking along another guy will slow us down.'

McCue waved him off. 'That sheriff over in Baggs had more men and more equipment, and they didn't find them. Maybe having someone along who knows the mountains will help.'

The red-haired man was obviously in no position to argue with McCue. But he was unhappy. He pointed to Farkus. 'You can come along as long as you're actually useful. But you need to keep your mouth shut. And when you turn into dead weight—'

'I'm dead meat,' Farkus finished his sentence for him. 'I understand.' He had no idea what was going on or what these men were after. But that didn't matter now. What mattered was getting through the next ten minutes before McCue changed his mind.

JOE SAID TO MARYBETH, 'I chanted your name for two straight days. It helped me to keep going.'

It was nearly midnight. Sheridan, Lucy and April were back in the motel they were staying at while Joe was in hospital. Marybeth had come to say good night. She looked at Joe with sympathy and curiosity.

'You chanted my name?' she said.

'It was my mantra. You and the girls. I said your names over and over again to myself. Like this: "Marybeth-Sheridan-Lucy-April." '

'I'm touched,' she said, but he knew from her furrowed brow she was holding something back.

'What?' he asked.

She rose, took his right hand, and squeezed it with both of hers. 'This thing you went through with those brothers. It really seems to have affected you. Are you sure you're OK?'

'I'm fine.'

She breathed deeply. 'Not really,' she said.

He waved it off. 'Look, I'm hurting. I have holes all over me. I've been through quite an experience, and I'm trying to sort it all out.'

'Is it because they hurt you, those brothers?'

'I've been hurt before.'

'Then what?' Marybeth kneaded his hand and pursed her lips.

Finally, he said, 'I guess I feel like I left a piece of me up there on that mountain. I don't feel completely whole.'

'You'll heal up.'

'It's not that.'

'Then what?'

Joe shook his head. 'I feel like I missed something obvious. But for the life of me, I can't figure out what it was. But those brothers—they beat me at every turn. They were faster, smarter and meaner.'

Marybeth frowned at him. 'Don't say that.'

'It's true. Plus it doesn't help that McLanahan and the sheriff in Baggs think I made it all up.'

'McLanahan's an idiot.'

'There was a DCI agent here today,' Joe said. 'Or someone claiming to be a DCI agent. He asked some pretty strange questions, and I felt he was trying to trip me up for some reason. And no one seems to have ever heard of this guy before.'

'That's odd,' she said.

'To be honest, I heard some doubt in the governor's voice, too.'

'Joe,' she said, 'Rulon's a lot of things, but he's still a politician.'

He tried to shrug, but his right shoulder screamed at him. 'Ow,' he moaned.

'Are you in pain? Do you want me to call a nurse?'

He shook his head.

'Joe,' she said. 'You're tired. You need some sleep. We can talk about all of this tomorrow.'

He said, 'How are we affording the motel? How much are you paying per night?'

'Don't worry about that. You need to rest and not worry about things. You'll be back at home in no time, rested and healed.' She paused. Then: 'I hope you don't think you need to go back up there after them. The sheriff down in Baggs will catch them eventually. You don't have to make this a personal quest.'

He nodded, but he didn't mean it.

DAVE FARKUS had spent most of his adult life working hard to avoid hard work. Additionally, he'd made it a point to avoid anything to do with horses, like ranch work. Horses were unpredictable, and involved after-hours maintenance. So after three hours of riding up into the timber nose-to-tail with the four men and their horses, he decided to risk a question: 'If we find whatever it is you're looking for, will you let me go home?' Which made the red-haired rider in black, named M. Whitney Parnell, according to the nametag on his rifle scabbard, snort.

Farkus gathered from observation that Parnell was in charge. Smith—the other man in black—and the two camo-clad men, Campbell and Capellen, were subservient to Parnell.

Parnell rode out ahead, followed by Smith. It was necessary to ride single-file because the trail was narrow and trees hemmed in both sides. Farkus rode a fat sorrel horse in the middle. Behind him were Campbell, Capellen and two packhorses.

'You see,' Farkus explained, 'I'm just thinking my role here is to help you out, but if in the end you're not going to let me go, well, you know what I'm saying. Where's my motivation, you know?'

This time, Smith snorted derisively and touched the butt of his rifle. '*Here's your motivation.*'

Farkus craned round in his saddle to see if the riders behind him were more sympathetic. Campbell simply glared at him, his face a mask of contempt. Capellen, though, looked miserable. His face was bone-china white, and his eyes were rimmed with red. He clutched the saddle horn with both hands as if to remain mounted.

'Capellen looks bad,' Farkus said.

'He's fine,' Campbell said through gritted teeth. 'Turn round.'

'Besides,' Farkus said, turning back round, 'shouldn't you let me know what we're after? I can't help guide if I don't know what we're hunting for.'

Parnell said, 'We'll tell you what you need to know when you need to know it.'

They continued climbing. Farkus recognised a couple of the mountain parks, but he knew if they kept riding west he'd soon run out of country with which he was familiar. The fact was that Farkus had always hunted with the same philosophy he used at work. He was happy to let his buddies pore over maps and determine where they'd hunt. Farkus would just go along. He'd never actually guided hunters in these mountains, as he'd let on earlier.

His butt hurt, and his knees ached. He was hungry, and the beer buzz he had going earlier was being replaced by a dull headache.

Farkus looked furtively over his shoulder again, making it a point not to establish eye contact with Campbell. Capellen had drifted further back. He was leaning forward in his saddle with his head down and looked to be in great pain. Then he listed to the side and vomited up a thin, yellow-green stream into the high grass.

'Excuse me,' Farkus said, trying to get Parnell's attention.

'Shut up, Dave,' Smith said.

The men didn't talk much, except to make random observations that were answered by grunts from the others.

Campbell said, 'This is a live game trail, judging by the fresh deer scat.'

'That's elk,' Farkus corrected. 'The pellets are twice the size of deer.'

'Oh.'

Smith walked his horse out of the line and let everyone pass him. 'Gotta piss,' he said. 'Go ahead. I'll catch up.'

Farkus used the opportunity of the temporary opening ahead of him to catch up with Parnell and get the man's attention.

'Let me get this straight,' Farkus said. 'You guys aren't with the sheriff's team that came up here from the other side a few days ago, and you're not with the state cops.'

'Correct.'

'So who are you with? Does this have to do with what that game warden said happened to him? I was the last one to see him before he went up. I told him my theory. Do you want to hear it?'

Parnell said, 'You're talking too much.'

'Ever hear of a Wendigo?'

'Of course,' Parnell said. 'I'm from the UP.'

'The Union Pacific?'

From behind him, Campbell barked, 'Shut *up*, Dave.'

Farkus shut up. Pork-bellied cumulus clouds floated across the sky. When they crossed the sun, the temperature cooled instantaneously, and he shivered. The air was thin at this altitude, and temperature fluctuations were extreme.

Then he realised what was wrong with Capellen. 'He's got altitude sickness. I recognise it. It always happens above eight thousand feet. It hits guys from flatland states like Michigan.'

'What can be done for it?' Smith asked Farkus.

'Keep him drinking water, for one thing. But really the only thing that will cure him is to get off the mountain.'

Parnell said, 'We aren't leaving him, and we aren't going back.'

So Capellen rode in agony, complaining that he had the worst headache he'd ever had in his life and that he was so dizzy they might have to tie him to his saddle to keep him from falling off.

Farkus said, 'I'm not gonna ask whether you're after the woman that game warden described or the girl runner if that's really her, or the Grim brothers themselves. I'm not gonna ask that.'

Parnell nodded. *Good.*

'And I'm not gonna ask who you work for or why you aren't in contact with the locals in this area. I'm not going to ask you where you're from in Michigan or why you came this far.'

'Shut *up*, Dave,' Campbell growled from behind him.

He sounded very annoyed, Farkus thought.

'All I'm gonna ask again,' Farkus said quickly, pushing, 'is if you're gonna let me go after all of this is over.'

Parnell shrugged, said, 'Probably not.'

Farkus felt the blood drain out of his head and pool like dirty sludge in his gut.

FROM WHAT FARKUS could observe, the expedition was heavily armed and expensively geared up. He counted three AR-15s and a heavy sniper's rifle and scope. All of the riders packed at least one semiauto in a holster. And that was just what Farkus could see. He had no idea how much additional weaponry they had in the heavy panniers carried by the packhorses. He'd seen plenty of electronic equipment when he'd stumbled into the camp. He'd recognised radios, GPS devices, sat phones, range finders. Other pieces were unfamiliar to him, but they looked like tracking devices of some sort.

Tracking what? he wondered.

They rode through a stand of knotty pine. The trees were twisted and beautifully grotesque, with football-sized growths bulging out from the trunks and branches. Farkus said, 'Do you realise what this wood is worth? I know furniture makers who'd pay a fortune for this stuff.' Then, remembering that he'd claimed knowledge of the area, he said, 'Every time I come here, I try to figure out how to get a vehicle into the area to gather up some of this knotty pine. But as you can see, there aren't any roads.'

He got silence in response, except for the inevitable *Shut up, Dave.* He was grateful no one had challenged him.

They cleared the knotty pine stand and rode into a mountain park where the trees opened up to the now-leaden sky. Parnell looked up at the sky as if it were sending him a message.

Smith said to Parnell, 'Think we'll get a reading yet?'

'That's what I want to find out.'

Parnell had an electronic instrument of some kind about the size and thickness of a hardback book. Farkus could see a screen that glowed like a GPS display.

Parnell unfolded a stubby antenna from the unit and adjusted a dial. To Smith and the others, he said, 'I've got a faint signal. We're headed in the right direction.'

From behind Farkus, Campbell said, 'Any idea how far?'

Parnell adjusted the metal knob. 'Nearly ten miles. Over the top and down the other side of the mountain.'

'Where we thought they'd be,' Smith said, nodding.

Farkus moaned. 'Ten more *miles*? On horseback?'

'Shut up, Dave,' Smith said casually.

Even with the overcast day, Farkus could tell there was only an hour of daylight left, at most. He said, 'Don't tell me we're gonna keep riding in the dark? I'm tired and hungry, and I could use a rest.'

Suddenly, Campbell was right beside him. He had his sidearm out, a deadly looking semiauto with a gaping muzzle that he pressed against Farkus's cheekbone.

'Do you know what this is?' Campbell hissed. 'This is a Sig Sauer P239. I've been wondering what it would do to a man's head from an inch away. Do you want me to find out?'

'*Please, no,*' Farkus said, his voice cracking. 'Put the gun away. You see, I've always been a talker. I'm sorry. I'll shut up. I'll start now.' To himself, Farkus said, '*Shut up, Dave.*'

Wednesday, September 2

With Marybeth at work and the girls at school, Joe had the revelation that he'd never been alone in his own house before. It was remarkably quiet. He felt like both a voyeur and a trespasser as he limped through the rooms carrying a five-gallon bucket filled with tools and equipment. His only company was their dog, Tube, who since he'd returned had not let Joe out of his sight.

At dinner the previous night, Joe had asked Marybeth and his daughters for their wish lists of repairs and projects. He listed them on a legal pad and begged them to stop after he filled the first page. He was embarrassed there was so much to get done, which was testament to his long absences over the past two years. Joe figured he had at least a week's worth of projects ahead of him. By then, he hoped, Governor Rulon would lift his order of administrative leave.

After he turned off the water to the toilet so he could reset the float to make it stop trickling constantly, Joe parted the bathroom curtain and checked to see if his neighbour, Ed Nedney, was still out in his garden. He was. He was reseeding a patch of slightly bare earth so it would grow to be as perfect as the rest of his garden. Nedney was a former town administrator who'd retired solely, Joe believed, to keep his lawn and home immaculate, and because it gave him more time to disapprove of Joe's home-maintenance regimen.

When the toilet was fixed, Joe called Sheriff Baird in Carbon County. He wasn't in his office, but the dispatcher patched Joe through to Baird's county pick-up.

'So, it's the fabulist,' Baird said.

'I'm not sure what to say to that, Sheriff.'

'Don't say anything. When you talk it costs me too much damned money.'

'The Grim brothers must have covered their tracks,' Joe said. 'They knew you'd be looking for them, I guess.'

'Then they did a hell of a good job, because my team couldn't confirm a single thing you said. Do you know how much it costs to mount an eleven-person search-and-rescue team and outfit them for the mountains? Do you have any idea?'

Joe looked out of the window again. Ed Nedney was standing on the dividing line between his perfect lawn and Joe's matted and leaf-strewn grass. Nedney was shaking his head and puffing on his pipe.

'I'd guess quite a bit,' Joe said.

'Damn straight. Plus, I had personally to call the parents of Diane Shober and tell them their daughter wasn't found. That was not a pleasant experience.'

Joe felt his neck get hot. 'I never claimed I saw her. You must have put that out.'

'Yeah, stupid me,' Baird said. 'I believed what you told me. I'm spending way too much time trying to defend your story. The state even sent a man to interview me this morning.'

Joe felt a twinge in his belly. 'Was it McCue?' Joe asked. 'Bobby McCue?'

'Yeah, that's him. An odd duck, I thought. I don't like the state looking over my shoulder.'

Joe shook his head. 'He came to talk to me in the hospital. Same guy. I can't figure out what his game is or who he's really with.'

Baird snorted. 'That's all I need is some rogue investigator running round down here. Maybe I'll have to set the FBI on him.'

'The FBI?'

'Let me find that message,' Baird said. 'I grabbed it at the office before I left.' Joe could hear paper being unfolded. 'Special Agent Chuck Coon called. He wants me to call him back regarding what we found or didn't find in the mountains.'

'I know Coon,' Joe said, remembering that the governor had also mentioned federal interest. 'He's a good enough guy, but I don't know why they're interested.'

Said Baird, 'DCI, FBI, the *National Enquirer.* You sure as hell know how to stir up a hornet's nest. For nothing, I might add.'

'They're up there,' Joe said. 'The Grim brothers, Terri Wade and the mystery woman. You just didn't manage to find them. Come on, Sheriff. You're well aware of all the break-ins and vandalism over the last couple of years. You *know* they're up there.'

Baird was silent.

'Look,' Joe said, 'I'm sorry you couldn't find them. But those brothers will stay up there and something else will happen unless they're located. We both know that.'

'I don't know a damned thing, Joe, other than I'm pulling into the parking lot of the county building where I've got to tell the county commissioners that I've blown the entire annual discretionary budget of the Sheriff's Department and it's just September.'

'I'm sorry,' Joe said.

'You sure are.' With that, Baird punched off.

THE WOMAN who answered the phone in the state Department of Administration and Human Resources office in Cheyenne said, 'I've got three minutes to help you or you'll need to call back.'

Joe glanced at the digital clock on his desk. It was 11:57.

'You go to lunch in three minutes?' Joe asked.

'Two minutes now,' she said.

Joe closed his eyes briefly, took a breath, and asked her to confirm that either Bobby McCue or Robert McCue was employed by the State of Wyoming. Joe knew that the state was obligated to provide the names of employees because it was public record.

'Spell it,' she said. Joe tried M-C-C-U-E to no avail. He suggested M-C-C-E-W, then M-C-H-U-G-H. No hits on her computer system. 'You'll have to try back later,' she said, and hung up.

At 12:01, Joe called the Department of Criminal Investigation and asked for Bobby McCue's voicemail.

'We don't have an employee with that name,' the receptionist said.

'Thank you.' Joe slammed down the phone and moaned. Tube raised his head and cocked it inquisitively.

Joe threw back the curtains and shoved the window open. Nedney looked up, surprised.

'Hey, Ed,' Joe said. 'Get off my lawn.'

Nedney looked down at his feet. The tips of his shoes had crossed the property line.

'You're trampling my grass,' Joe said.

'Is that what it is?' Nedney said, a self-satisfied smile on his lips.

'Good one,' Joe conceded, and closed the window, already sorry he'd taken his frustration out on his neighbour.

As he limped through the kitchen with his bucket of tools, he felt he was being watched. Joe paused and slowly turned round.

Had Nedney entered his garden?

Joe raised his eyes to the window above the sink that overlooked his back lawn.

Nate Romanowski cocked his eyebrows at him from outside. Through the glass, he mouthed, 'Hey.'

Joe grinned. It had been a long time.

JOE AND NATE worked together on dinner. Joe had pronghorn antelope backstraps in the freezer from the previous fall, and Nate rubbed the meat with sage, garlic, salt and pepper and prepared it for the grill. As Joe roasted green beans in the oven and boiled potatoes on the stove, Nate said, 'This is uncomfortably domestic.'

Said Joe, 'This is the least I can do since I'm rattling round the house all day. At some point in the near future, though, I may need to learn how to do something besides grill red meat every night.' Joe chinned towards the kitchen window where Nate had stood earlier and said, 'Why'd you scare me like that?'

'I couldn't let anyone see me come in the front door,' Nate said. 'I'm still a wanted man, remember?'

While Joe plucked the potatoes out of the pot, he told Nate the story of what had happened in the Sierra Madre. Nate was intensely interested but listened in silence while nodding his head. Finally he said, 'I've got a couple of questions.'

'I'm sick of answering questions about it,' Joe said. 'Nobody seems to believe me, anyway.'

'I can see why,' Nate said. 'So I'll boil them all down to one. When are we going back up there to find those bastards?'

Before Joe could answer, the front door opened and Marybeth stepped in, trailed by the girls.

'Oh, my,' Marybeth said, her eyes wide.

They all stood taking in Nate from his ponytail to his scuffed boots. And then Sheridan ran across the room and hugged her master falconer.

AFTER THE DISHES were cleared and cleaned, Joe went out on the front porch. Although it was barely September, there was already a fall-like snap to the air. Nevertheless, he thought he'd suggest to Nate and Marybeth that they sit outside in the back. He knew Nate had more questions, and he wanted to answer them out of earshot of the girls. Marybeth should be there because she often provided insight he never considered.

Joe went back inside the house and nearly ran into Lucy. She said, 'I think I saw someone in the garden.'

'Was it Nate?'

'No, Nate's in the kitchen talking with Mom.'

As she said it, there was a heavy thump against the siding outside. Joe continued down the hall with Lucy padding behind him. Sheridan stuck her head out of her bedroom door and said, 'What was *that*?'

'I'm not sure, but I'm going to find out.'

He looked up to see Marybeth rising from the table and Nate striding across the living room to where he'd hidden his .454 on the top shelf of the coat closet.

Joe snatched a 12-gauge Mossberg pump from his gun rack. His six-battery steel Maglite slipped into his belt. He turned to Marybeth and said, 'Make sure the curtains are closed in the back bedrooms and the girls are in our room in the front of the house.'

He waited while Marybeth shooed Sheridan, April and Lucy into the master bedroom. When the girls were across the hallway, Marybeth leaned out and silently mouthed, 'OK.'

Nate said, 'Let's go out of the front door and come round to the back on both sides.'

Joe nodded and said, 'I'll take the left side.'

As they slipped out of the front door into the dark, Nate whispered, 'When we get in position, I'll make a noise to get their attention. You be ready on the back side and come up behind them.'

'OK.'

Joe kept low to avoid being illuminated by the house windows. He went left, reminded painfully of the injuries in his legs. He turned the corner, then paused at the back gate and tried to see into the garden through gaps in the wood slats. He couldn't see who had made the noise, but then Joe heard a rhythmic wheezing sound. Somebody breathing, but not easily.

From the other side of the house came an eerie, high-pitched call mimicking the sound of an angry hawk: *skree-skree-skree-skree.*

Joe quickly pushed through the gate and dashed into the garden. There was only one human form he could see, and the man was standing in the muted light beneath the kitchen window with his back to Joe, looking in the direction of the hawk sound. The man was big and blocky, wearing a cowboy hat, an oversized canvas ranch coat and jeans.

Joe said, 'Freeze where you stand or I'll cut you in half with this shotgun.'

Suddenly he recognised the hat, boots and pistol. He raised his Maglite alongside the barrel of his shotgun so he could see clearly down the sights and said, 'Bud, is that *you*?'

Bud Longbrake, Missy's ex-husband and Joe's ex-father-in-law, stood like a bronze statue of a washed-up cowboy. Slowly, Bud turned his head a little so he could talk to Joe over his shoulder. 'Hey, Joe. I didn't know you were home.'

His voice was bass and resigned, and his words were slurred.

'I live here, Bud,' Joe said. 'You know that. So what are you doing sneaking round in my garden?'

Joe put the beam of his flashlight on Bud's face. He was shocked by what he saw. Bud's eyes were rimmed with red, and his cheeks were puffy and pale. A three-day growth of beard sparkled like silver sequins in the beam of the flashlight.

'You look like hell, Bud,' Joe said, lowering the shotgun but keeping the flashlight on the old rancher.

Bud said, 'You know, I feel like hell, too.' He swayed while he said it. His arms circled stiffly in their sockets, and he took a step forward to regain his balance. 'Whoa,' he said.

'Sit down,' Joe said. 'Grab one of those lawn chairs.'

'I'll do that,' Bud said, pulling a chair over and collapsing into it.

Nate remained hidden, and Joe purposely didn't look in his direction. Although Bud seemed completely harmless now, it was good to have Nate there monitoring the situation.

'So what are you doing here?' Joe asked. 'I don't appreciate you sneaking round my house at night.'

'I'm sorry,' Bud said, shaking his head. 'I really am.' He looked up, trying to focus. 'Missy told me she'd hired that Nate Romanowski to put the hurt on me. She said he was coming here, to this house, and he was going to kick the living crap out of me in front of my friends and buddies.'

'She said that, did she?'

Bud nodded. 'She called me yesterday and told me she was giving me fair warning to get the hell out of town and stop bothering her. I couldn't sleep last night, and I had a beer for breakfast to help me decide what to do. I been on a tear ever since. Then I said to myself, the hell with it. I ain't scared of no Nate Romanowski. I came here to get the drop on him and maybe bring this thing to a head.'

Joe sighed. 'It's probably hard to sneak up on guys when you can hardly stand up.'

Bud nodded.

Joe said, 'Bud, Nate's not after you. That's all in Missy's imagination. That's not what Nate does.'

Bud said, 'What does he do?'

Which momentarily left Joe at a loss for words.

'I asked what he did,' Bud repeated.

'I take drunk old ranchers home,' Nate said, stepping out from the shadows. His .454 was low at his side but not in the holster.

At the sound of Nate's voice, Bud's arm rose stiffly and his boots kicked out in alarm.

'Calm down,' Nate said to Bud, putting a hand on his shoulder. 'If I was going to kill you, you'd already be dead.'

Joe shrugged to Bud, as if to say, *You know he's right.*

'Where's your pick-up, Bud?' Nate asked.

Bud gestured vaguely. 'Out there somewhere,' he said.

'Why don't we go find it? Then I'll take you home.'

'Can I at least see the girls?' Bud asked Joe. 'I miss them girls.'

'They're in bed,' Joe fibbed. 'It's a school night, Bud.'

'I do miss them girls.'

'They miss you, too,' Joe said. 'You were a good grandpa to them.'

'Come on,' Nate said. 'Can you find your keys?'

Bud clumsily started patting himself and located his keys. As Nate guided Bud out of the garden towards Bud's distant truck, Joe heard Bud say, 'If you really want to kill me, I probably wouldn't put up too much of a fight.'

'Shut up,' Nate responded.

LATER, AS JOE crawled into bed, Marybeth said, 'It's so sad what's happened to Bud. Do you think he'll come back?'

Joe pulled her closer. Her body felt warm and soft. He buried his face in her hair. 'I doubt it. He knows now Nate's not after him. And deep down, Bud's a good man. He'll wake up and be ashamed of himself for showing up here, I think.'

'Mmm.'

'Marybeth,' he whispered into her ear, 'I was wondering . . .'

'Joe,' she said, cutting him off. 'First, we need to talk.'

'About what?'

She took a deep, soft breath and paused. 'I can see the direction this is all headed. I could see it tonight when you and Nate got your guns and went outside. It was like your sails were full. I know it was me who called Nate for help, but at the time I wasn't sure when I'd see you again, if at all. You're thinking of going back up into those mountains, aren't you? You want to find those brothers.'

He closed his eyes. 'I keep thinking about everything that happened—how they whipped me. I keep thinking about Terri Wade and . . . that other woman. Something was going on up there and I couldn't see it at the time. I still can't. But whatever it is, it's still there. That the sheriff in Carbon County and all those DCI boys couldn't find the Grim brothers puzzles the heck out of me. That the FBI seems to be monitoring the situation makes no logical sense. And who is this Bobby McCue? There are a load of unanswered questions, starting with why the Grim brothers are up there in the first place. Plus, there are lives at stake. Even though Terri Wade and the mystery woman seemed to be there willingly, I just don't buy it. No woman would choose to be alone in the wilderness with those two brothers. Just walking away doesn't feel right.'

She turned to face him. 'Be thankful you were able to walk away, Joe. You may not be so lucky the next time.'

He said nothing for a long time. Then: 'I'll tell you something I have trouble putting into words. I'm *scared* to go back up there. I've been scared a lot in the past. But this one is different somehow. I don't think I can beat them.'

She reached out and touched his cheek. She spoke softly. 'Eventually, those brothers will get caught or turn themselves in. And who knows—maybe those women are up there of their own accord. But you've been reassigned, so they're someone else's problem now. We both know the governor wants you to stay out of it. And the sheriff down there probably never wants to see you again. If you went after them, it would be purely personal, and that's not good.'

'Still,' he said.

'Look,' she said, 'I've never asked this before. But I'm asking now: promise me you won't go after them.'

Joe sighed and rubbed his eyes hard.

'I know it's against your nature,' she said. 'I know you think your advantage is your inability to simply let things go. But something happened up there. They got into your head and under your skin and they stole a part of you. You can't get it back, Joe. You've just got to heal. And you've got to be home to heal.'

He said, 'You're serious, aren't you?'

'Yes.'

'OK,' he said. 'I promise.'

He was shocked how relieved he was when he said it, how a tremendous downward pressure on him seemed to release and dissipate. He felt lighter and slightly ashamed of himself.

The truth was, he needed her permission *not* to go after the Grim brothers. Because from what he'd experienced, they'd likely beat him again. And this time, he doubted they'd let the job go unfinished.

'Come here,' he said, pulling her to him.

DAVE FARKUS rode in the dark with his left arm up in front of his face in case the fat horse walked under a branch. He couldn't see a thing, and he was terrified. He was also severely chilled, because the temperature had dropped once the sun went down.

'I'm freezing,' Farkus said.

Ahead of him, Smith turned and said, 'Shut up, Dave.'

Earlier, Parnell had ordered them all to put on body armour and night-vision goggles—except for Farkus, of course. Where Smith's eyes should have been, there were dark holes. Occasionally, if the riders adjusted their goggles or briefly removed them, he could see their faces bathed in an eerie green.

Farkus said, 'I feel like I'm in a zombie movie.'

As they rode, Farkus could see Parnell consulting his equipment. Based on the readings, Parnell would subtly shift direction. The others would adjust as well. Farkus simply trusted his horse to want to stay with the others.

Parnell said, 'They're on the move. Away from us. And they're moving at a pretty good clip.'

Said Smith, 'I'm surprised they're moving at night. Do you think they know we're coming?'

'Those guys have always been unpredictable,' Campbell said from behind Farkus. 'They've adapted well.'

Parnell said, 'Not well enough to turn off the sat phone they took off that game warden.'

Ah, Farkus thought, that's what he's tracking.

'Is the signal still strong?' Smith asked.

'Strong enough. We've closed within three miles, and we seem to be holding at that distance as they move. Those guys can cover a lot of ground, as we know.'

So, Farkus thought, we're after the Brothers Grimm after all. But why?

'Hold it,' Farkus said. 'If it's just a matter of tracking these guys down through their sat phone, why couldn't the sheriff and his boys find 'em?'

Said Parnell, 'Because the brothers didn't turn it on until just a day or so ago.'

A strong and pungent smell wafted through the trees. Parnell and Smith pulled their horses up short.

'What *is* that?' Smith asked.

'Something dead,' Parnell said.

'This way,' Campbell said, peeling off from the line of horses to his right. 'Stay here, Mike,' he said to Capellen. 'No reason to get any sicker smelling this than you already are.'

Farkus spurred the fat horse into the trees with the others. The smell got stronger. He winced and pulled his T-shirt collar up out of his shirt and tried to breathe through the fabric. Back on the trail, he heard Capellen cry out with a short, sharp yelp.

'Probably getting sick again,' Campbell said. 'Poor guy.'

'Here they are,' Parnell said up ahead. 'The game warden's story checks out so far.'

'Here what is?' Farkus asked. 'I can't see anything, remember?'

'At least two dead horses,' Parnell said. 'Maybe more. I can see skulls and ribs and leg bones, but it looks like the carcasses are cut up. They must have had to cut up the bodies to move them here so the sheriff's team wouldn't find them. Since these guys were butchers, it probably wasn't a big deal to cut the horses apart.'

'*Butchers?*' Farkus said. No one replied.

'And they buried them,' Smith said. 'So they probably didn't stink at the time those other guys were up here. But something's been digging them up.'

Campbell said, 'Probably a bear. They've got bears here—black and grizzly. Mountain lions too. They've got lots of critters that like horsemeat.'

'Whatever it was eating on this horse, it hasn't gone far,' Smith said, shifting in his saddle. 'The damage looks fresh.' Farkus saw the dull red orbs of Smith's goggles sweep past him as the man looked around.

'Let's get back,' Parnell said. 'And see how Capellen is doing.'

'That's a good idea,' Farkus said.

'DAMN,' CAMPBELL SAID as they walked their horses through the trees back to the trail. 'Capellen fell out of the saddle. We should have tied him in it, like he asked.'

Smith said, 'There's something sticking out of him.'

The way he said it made Farkus hold his breath.

'It's an arrow,' Parnell whispered. 'Those brothers found *us.*'

Farkus couldn't see Parnell, Smith or Campbell, but he could tell from the creaking leather that all three men were turning in their saddles, trying to get a view of what might be out there in the trees.

Capellen was alive, but the arrow was buried deep in his chest. His breathing was harsh, wet and heavy. The shot had been perfectly placed in the two-inch gap between the ceramic shoulder pad and the armoured strap of the body armour. Farkus stayed on his horse while the others lifted the wounded man and shoved him back onto his saddle. He simply fell off the other side into the dirt, snapping off the shaft of the arrow in the fall.

Farkus said, 'Put him behind me. This old horse is stout enough to carry us both. I'm sure he can hold on.'

The men gathered Capellen up, and Farkus felt the weight and heat of the man behind him. Capellen leaned into Farkus with his arms round his ribs and dropped his face into his back.

'Get his gun,' Parnell said. Smith pulled Capellen's weapon out of his holster, and Farkus fought an urge to mouth curses.

There was a wet *cack-cack-cack* liquid sound when Capellen inhaled. Farkus recognised the sound from hunting. The arrow had pierced a lung. Capellen's chest cavity was filling up with blood. He would drown from the inside. It was a miserable and drawn-out way to die.

'Let's move back to the rock face where we've got an advantage,' Parnell said, turning his horse round and riding past Farkus and Capellen, back down the trail they'd come on.

Just below the summit, the trail had switchbacked through a massive rockslide where it looked like an entire wedge of the mountainside had given way and fallen, leaving a long treeless chute of rubble and scree. And a few room-sized boulders. It would be a perfect place for them to go: treeless so they could see for half a mile with their night-vision goggles, and well beyond arrow range from an archer in the trees.

Farkus had had his reasons to take Capellen. The first was his hope that they'd forget about the handgun, which they hadn't. But Capellen still wore his night-vision goggles, and Farkus reached over his shoulder and snatched them off. After fumbling with the straps, he managed to pull them on. The pitch-black night turned ghostly green, and he could see everything. The clarity was astonishing. He was shocked how dense the forest was as the trees moved by on both sides. Up ahead, he could see Parnell and Smith pushing their horses.

The third reason he'd volunteered to take Capellen was still forming in his mind. But by taking their buddy, they might decide he was all right after all. He was on their side. And he could work the new angle and get the hell away from them before the Grim brothers killed them all.

'THEY MUST HAVE split up,' Parnell said, a note of puzzlement in his voice. He adjusted the dial on his equipment. 'One of them has the sat phone and has finally stopped moving. The other one is down there somewhere.' He motioned towards the dark wall of trees. 'They split up so we'd march right towards the guy with the sat phone while the other one waited for us here.'

'What is it with those guys?' Smith asked no one in particular. 'We couldn't see a damned thing without our night-vision equipment, but whoever went after Capellen didn't seem to have that problem. And I doubt those guys have any real technology to use.'

'They're not human,' Farkus said.

THEY'D MADE IT to the rock slide without being attacked. The horses were picketed on a grassy shelf above them, and Capellen lay dying with his back to a slick rock. There had been no movement on the scree beneath them or in the trees below since they'd arrived an hour before.

Smith said to Farkus, 'If they aren't human, then what the hell are they?'

'They're Wendigos,' Farkus said, pleased finally to be able to introduce his theory. 'I know it sounds crazy, but things have been happening up here in these mountains for the last year that don't make sense. One night I asked an old Indian I know. He's a Blackfoot from Montana. That's the first time I heard about Wendigos. Then I did some research on the Internet. It's scary stuff, man. Wendigos look like walking skeletons with their flesh hanging off their bones. They stink like death—like those horses we found back there. And they feed on dead animals and living people. And they can *see in the dark*.'

AS THE EASTERN SKY lightened enough for Farkus to shed his night-vision goggles, Capellen died with a sigh and a shudder.

'Poor bastard,' Parnell said. 'There was nothing we could do to save him.'

Farkus didn't say, *Except maybe take him to a hospital.*

Parnell stood up and peeled his goggles off, said, 'We'll pick up his body on the way out. He's not going anywhere.' Then: 'Let's get this thing over with so we can go home.'

Thursday, September 3

It had been a long time since Joe had got up earlier than the rest of his family. He'd drunk half a pot of coffee and his nerves were jangling by the time Marybeth came down the hall in her robe. He poured her a mug of coffee.

'Thank you,' she said. 'Any sign of Nate?'

'Nope. My guess is he's staying with Alisha.'

She said, 'I'm glad we talked last night.'

'For starters,' he said.

She smiled and looked away. He watched as she peered through the front room towards the window, squinted and turned to him. 'Who's parked in front of our house?'

'What?' There was a massive red Ford Expedition with Colorado plates blocking Marybeth's van in the driveway.

Joe walked to the front window just in time to see the passenger door open and Bobby McCue swing out. Marybeth joined him at the window, and they both watched as another man and a woman got out of the Expedition. The man was tall and red-faced, and his movements were swift and purposeful. He wore an open safari jacket, jeans and heavy boots. The woman, in a navy blue jacket, wrapped her arms round herself as if trying to make herself smaller. She was short, thin, dark and furtive. She appeared uncomfortable, and she looked to the red-faced man for their next move. He gestured towards the house with a brusque nod and walked right by her. She followed him up the concrete walkway in front of Bobby McCue.

'Do you know them?' Marybeth asked.

'I know the guy at the back. He's the one who came to see me in the hospital and lied about being from DCI.'

'What do you suppose they want?'

'I don't know,' Joe said, 'but if they want to talk, I'll steer them into my office. Do you mind feeding the girls?'

Marybeth said, 'That's what I do every day, Joe. I think I can handle it.'

THE RED-FACED MAN said, 'Brent Shober,' and stuck out his hand.

Joe reached out and shook it. 'I was wondering when I might hear from you.'

'This is my wife, Jenna.'

She smiled tightly and looked away.

'And our investigator, Bobby McCue.'

'We've met,' Joe said. McCue winked, as if he and Joe were brothers-in-arms in law enforcement subterfuge. Joe shook his head, denying the bond.

Joe had to clear papers from his two office chairs and fetch a folding chair from a hall closet so all three could sit down in his cramped home office. They filled the room. He closed the door, sidled past them and round his desk, and sat in his office chair.

'What can I do for you?' he said.

Brent snorted and sat forward, putting his elbows on Joe's desk. 'We're here because Bobby got a hold of the statement you made to the sheriff in Carbon County, right?'

Joe said, 'Now before you jump to conclusions, I never said I positively identified your daughter. I'm sorry to say that, but—'

'Look, Pickett,' Brent said, cutting Joe off. 'We're here because we need you to help us locate Diane.'

'Didn't you just hear what I said?'

Brent shook his head as if it didn't matter. 'We've spent the last week in agony while that search team went up into the mountains. When they found nothing—nothing at all—it was like another twist of the knife in my back, right? And I'm getting sick and tired of having my hopes raised up and smashed back down. You're the only one, apparently, who knows where to find her. We need you to do just that. If necessary, I'll hire you. Just name your price.'

'It isn't about money,' Joe said.

'Everything's about money, right?' Brent said. 'I can see how you live here,' he said, gesturing vaguely round Joe's cluttered office. 'I also know your personal situation from Bobby here. You've been put on the shelf, and who knows if you'll even get your job back. You've got nothing to do. Right?'

Joe didn't like talking to people who ended statements with the word 'Right?' for the reason of pre-empting any possible disagreement. But before he could speak, Brent said, 'For two long, hard years, Jenna and I have done everything we could to find our daughter. Finding her is my obsession, Pickett. I know she's alive and well. I just know it, right?'

Joe had learned not even to try to talk to Brent Shober, so he didn't. Brent stood up. He clearly wanted to pace, but there was no room. He bent over Joe's desk so his face was close to Joe's.

'My little girl was on schedule to go to the Olympics, something her old man barely missed out on. I was a thousand-metre man. A month before the trials, I screwed up my knee. Diane, though, was getting stronger by the month. That's why we moved part of our company from Michigan to the mountains out here, so she could train at high elevation. Then she goes for a long run and never comes back. We haven't seen her or talked with her in *two years*. It's been eating us up, Jenna and me. I nearly lost my company—I build super high-end office parks—because I spent so much time listening to every crackpot who said they might have seen her.'

McCue sat in his chair like a good hired soldier. There was a slight smile on his face, as if he enjoyed seeing someone else on the other end of Brent Shober for a change. Jenna, on the other hand, made a point not to look at Joe or her husband, even when he referred to her. No doubt she shared his pain, Joe thought, but she didn't share his bombast.

'So,' Brent continued, 'for two years this has been our quest—to find our Diane. Her no-good fiancé used to work with us, but that little rat bastard picked up and moved to Baja, and we haven't heard from him in months. But I'm not giving up, Pickett. So we need you to go back up there. Take as many men as you need. You are the only soul alive who has seen her in the past two years, and you are the only one who has a chance of finding her again, right?'

'Wrong.'

Brent Shober sputtered, 'What did you say?'

'I said "wrong",' Joe repeated. He pointed at McCue. 'I told your guy and every investigator since I made the initial statement that I didn't get a good look at the fourth person up there. It was dark, I was hurt and her name popped into my mind, is all.'

Brent shook his head. 'You're backing out on me.'

Joe said, 'I was never *in*. Look, at least let me ask you a couple of questions before we end here.' He was fully aware of his promise to Marybeth, and he was honour-bound to keep it. But his curiosity was up. 'Did you or Diane ever know a couple of brothers named Grim? Or Grimmengruber? Is there any reason to believe if this person I saw was your daughter that she'd be with them?'

'That's the most ridiculous question anybody has ever asked me. We'd never know trash like that, right?'

Joe paused. He looked at McCue, then back to Brent Shober. 'How do you know what they're like?' Joe asked. 'I never said a word about them. I never used the term "trash".'

Brent's face got redder, and Joe could see the cords in his neck pull taut.

McCue said quickly, 'I told him what's in your statement and the report. Those are my words.'

Joe wasn't sure. He looked to Brent's face for clues but read only fury. Jenna wouldn't meet his eyes.

Brent closed his eyes and took several deep breaths, obviously to calm himself. Finally he said, 'To accuse me of anything is beyond ridiculous. I love my Diane more than life itself.'

'I didn't mean to imply you were guilty of anything.'

Brent waved him off and continued. 'Do you realise what a special girl she is? That she has the capability of representing her family and her country in the Olympics? Do you realise that in the life of a long-distance runner, you get maybe two shots at the Games? And if you miss your chance, you never get it back. You grow old knowing you had your shot and you didn't take it.'

Joe said, 'Are we talking about Diane here?'

McCue was faster than he looked and was able to throw himself in front of Brent Shober before the man could leap over the desk and throttle Joe.

McCue and Jenna managed to get Brent turned round, and McCue wrapped him up and guided him out of the door. Brent yelled over his shoulder, 'YOU'VE GOT TO HELP ME! *YOU'VE GOT TO HELP ME!*' even as McCue pushed him across Joe's lawn towards the Expedition. Jenna followed, her head down.

After they drove away, Joe moaned, collapsed on the couch, and put his head in his hands. He ached for Brent and Jenna Shober. What torment they'd gone through. Torment like that would likely turn him into someone like Brent, or worse. He didn't have to like the man to feel sorry for him.

AFTER CLEARING AWAY the breakfast dishes, Joe called FBI Special Agent Chuck Coon.

'Hello?' Coon said.

'It's me, Joe. You know why I'm calling,' Joe said. 'The Grim brothers.'

'I was afraid that was what you'd say.'

'Tell me about them.'

'There's nothing to be said. The Grim brothers don't exist.'

'Are you saying they don't exist because you can't find them in your database? Or that you think I made them up?'

Coon sighed. 'They're not in the database, Joe. Caleb, Camish Grim, or G-R-I-M-M, or Grimmengruber, or any combination thereof. They gave you a false name, Joe.'

'Why would they do that?'

Coon exhaled, as if he were going to answer Joe, but he caught himself. 'I've already said enough, I think.'

'But I'm investigating them too. So's the governor and DCI. I thought we shared information these days.'

Coon laughed, 'When did you come up with that one? Nice try, though.'

Said Joe, 'Chuck, why are you guys so interested in what happened up there? From what I know, it's a local or state matter.'

'The FBI doesn't comment on ongoing investigations.'

'Sheesh, I know. But why is there federal interest?'

'I'm sorry, Joe. That's the best I can do. My best to Marybeth and the girls.' With that, he punched off.

Joe closed his phone and stared out of the window. Despite what Coon withheld, he'd inadvertently confirmed a couple of things. There *was* an investigation going on, and it was obviously big enough that he'd felt the need to play it coy. But Joe was heartened that they believed him and his story after all.

Joe spent the afternoon walking aimlessly through the house with his tools, but his mind was back up in the Sierra Madre. He tried scenario after scenario and came up with nothing plausible. When he tried to link the Grim brothers, the FBI, Terri Wade, the mystery woman, the UP . . . he got nowhere.

He realised he'd forgotten about dinner, and he looked at his watch. There was an hour before Marybeth and the girls got home. He'd told Marybeth he'd cook burgers on the grill, but he'd forgotten to get the meat out of the freezer. On the way to the kitchen to see what he could rustle up, the doorbell rang.

It was Jenna Shober. She was alone and crying.

'HOW MANY MORE of these are there?' Smith asked, gesturing towards the round lake in the bottom of the alpine cirque.

'There's at least two more cirques,' Farkus said. 'They kind of stair-step their way down the mountain.'

The sky had cleared, and the morning was warming up. They'd been riding for five hours, rimming the series of spectacular cirques Farkus had surprised himself by knowing about. His lone trip up here was years before, but at last he had an idea where he was. He knew that if they kept travelling in a westerly direction, they'd eventually hit the creek and trailhead where he'd originally met Joe Pickett. Problem was, it was this area where the game warden had encountered the Grim brothers.

Parnell's tracking device chirped. He read the display and announced that they were practically on top of their target.

'How close?' Smith asked.

'Half a mile, maybe. Over the next ridge, I'd guess.'

'Are they still going the other way?'

'No,' Parnell said. 'He's coming at us right now.'

Smith drew his AR-15 rifle out of his saddle scabbard and laid it across the pommel of his saddle. Campbell checked the loads of his rifle, even though Farkus had seen him do it at least twice before.

Farkus felt a knot tighten in his stomach as they got close to the ridge. Parnell had veered from the established trail into a thick stand of gnarled pine trees. When they were in the cover, Parnell dismounted, and Smith, Campbell and Farkus did the same.

Parnell motioned for them to come close. He whispered, 'Let's get our weapons ready and tie up the horses here. When we're locked and loaded, we'll crawl through the trees to the edge of the ridge.' He turned to Farkus. 'You stay here and don't even think of trying to get away. If you try to run, I'll shoot you.'

Farkus swallowed and looked away.

'So,' Smith said to Parnell, 'you're thinking they're down in this cirque?'

'That's what I think,' Parnell whispered.

'Let's not miss,' Smith said. 'The last thing we need is a wounded Cline brother coming after us.'

Farkus said, 'Cline? I thought their name was Grim?'

'Shut up, Dave,' Parnell said, shooting Smith a punishing look.

When Parnell's tracker chirped again, he read it and appeared startled.

'What?' Smith asked.

'He's on top of us,' Parnell whispered. 'He's coming up the rim right at us. He's *running* up the side of the cirque.'

Parnell and Smith raised the barrels of their AR-15s, pointing them through the trees towards the lip of the rim. Campbell pulled his Sig Sauer and steadied it out in front of him with two hands.

Farkus heard the rapid thumping of footfalls and saw a flash of spindly movement from the other side of the rim and then a full set of antlers. A big five-point buck mule deer with a satellite phone wired to its antlers came lurching up over the side in a dead run.

Parnell and Smith turned it into hamburger.

'WE DIDN'T KNOW Diane was missing until she'd been gone for four days,' Jenna Shober said in a low, soft voice rubbed raw from two years of crying. 'Can you imagine that?'

'No,' Joe said.

They were in the living room. She'd folded into the far corner of the couch with her hands clamped tightly between her legs. She spent most of the time staring at her knees, recalling what happened from a script obviously seared into her being.

'She started her last run on a Tuesday. We didn't find out she was missing until Friday night, when her fiancé finally called.'

'Tell me about him,' Joe said.

She looked up. 'His name is Justin LeForge. He's a triathlete. Justin and Diane seemed like the perfect couple. They were beautiful—thin, fit, athletic, attractive. A little odd when it came to politics and world view, but young people can be like that. Brent thought Justin was the greatest, and he bragged constantly about his future son-in-law. But everything wasn't as it seemed.'

Joe said, 'What do you mean when you say they had odd political beliefs?'

She laughed a dry laugh. 'They were certainly counter to her father's, for one. Brent has always been very involved politically. We give a lot of money to candidates, and as a big developer he is used to being, um, close with them. There's a lot of federal money these days, you know. It has to go to somebody, is the way Brent puts it, so it might as well be him. Anyway, Justin was a big fan of that writer Ayn Rand. You know her?'

Joe said, 'I read *Atlas Shrugged* in college.'

'Justin said he was an Objectivist, like Ayn Rand. You know, staunch capitalist, anti-big government. Lots of kids go through that.'

Joe nodded, urging her on.

'Justin and Brent butted heads a few times, and Diane was right there in the thick of it. I always wondered how much of her new philosophy she truly held and how much was because of Justin. And how much of it was simple rebellion, mainly against her dad. They're both strong-willed people, Brent and Diane. The funny thing is Justin is just as bullheaded as Brent, but Diane never seems to see the similarity.'

Joe said, 'Back to the four days between her disappearance and you finding out about it.'

'Oh,' she said. 'I'm sorry. I went on a tangent.'

'It's OK,' he said, stealing a look at his wristwatch and deciding: *Pizza tonight. Delivered.*

'Well, as I said, we didn't hear from Justin until Friday night. He said he didn't have time to talk because he had to catch a flight for a race in Hawaii. It was like, "By the way, I'm not sure where Diane is. I haven't seen her since Tuesday. Gotta go, wish me luck."'

'Man,' Joe said, sitting back. 'How did he explain it?'

'He didn't, really. He said she'd left him a note on Tuesday morning saying she was going to drive north of Steamboat Springs and go for a run in the mountains. This in itself wasn't unusual. Later, he said he figured she decided to get a room in Steamboat and use it as her base for a few days. He said they'd been fighting and she probably needed a little time away, that it had happened before and it was no big deal.

'Brent contacted the authorities. We didn't have much to go on, and you can imagine how angry and scared we were. We didn't even know which mountains or in which *state.* On Monday, the sheriff in Walden, Colorado, got a report that her Subaru was reported at a trailhead in Wyoming. That's when things finally started to happen. Search-and-rescue teams, helicopters, news alerts, all of it.'

Joe nodded. 'I was on the search team.'

'Thank you,' she said sincerely. 'A lot of good men and women spent days trying to find her. But by that time, she'd been gone over a week. All I could think about was that she'd fallen and broken her leg and was waiting for help that never came. I was terrified she was suffering up there somewhere. I was horrified that she wouldn't be found at all or that her body would be found. I can't even tell you how awful that week was. Or how everything is coming back now.'

Joe said, 'About Justin . . .'

She waved her hand. 'I know what you're probably thinking, that maybe he had something to do with it. We did, too. Especially when he just stopped calling. When my husband hired Bobby to investigate, the first thing we asked him to do was to check out Justin's alibi. But Bobby said Justin's story held. A girl—another runner—testified he was with her from Tuesday through Thursday. He was cheating on my daughter, Mr Pickett.'

She looked at her hands. 'I no longer suspect Justin, even though I despise him. As tough as it was for me to accept, I realised he didn't care enough about Diane to hurt her.' She looked up. 'I hope you can forgive my husband for the way he acted earlier. If there is such a thing as being obsessed to the point of insanity, that pretty much describes Brent now. He worshipped his daughter, even though she distanced herself from him in the end.'

She took out a large envelope from her bag. 'We meant to show you these earlier,' she said. 'But things got heated and Brent forgot. He just assumed you'd jump up and go and find our daughter. When you didn't, he lost it and forgot about the envelope. When we got to the motel, I slipped it into my bag and lied about going shopping. Brent would never have approved of me coming here myself to talk with you.'

Joe nodded and looked at a postcard she handed to him.

'This was sent to our Michigan address a year ago,' she said.

The card was a 'Colourful Colorado' postcard with faded images of Pikes Peak and the Denver skyline. He flipped it over. It was postmarked from Walden, Colorado. The handwriting was cramped and severe. He guessed the sender was male.

Jenna:

I'm sending this to you on behalf of your daughter, Diane. I saw her and she is fine. She says not to worry about her. She asks that you not share this message with her dad.

It was signed, *A Friend.*

Joe handed the card back. 'Any idea who sent it?'

'No. But it gives me hope.'

He kept his voice soft. 'Her disappearance wasn't a secret. I mean, anyone could have sent this to you. It could be a cruel hoax, or it could be someone well-meaning trying to ease your pain.'

She looked down. 'I know that. But I want to think it's real.'

A moment went by as Joe tried to form his question as diplomatically as possible. 'So, did you show it to Brent?'

She shook her head quickly but didn't look up. He could see moisture in her eyes.

'You didn't want him to know,' Joe said.

She whispered, 'It's tough.'

Joe was confused. He knew he was on thin ice. Finally he said, 'Jenna, is it possible the relationship between your husband and your daughter was, you know, a little too close when she was growing up?'

Jenna refused to answer, which was an answer in itself, Joe thought. Minutes passed. Joe didn't press. And he tried not to stare at her while she sat silently, looking away.

At last, she said, 'Would you like to look at some photos?'

'Sure,' he said. Anything to move past his last question.

Most of the shots were of Diane running in competitions. She had a determined set to her face, and her blonde hair flew back like frozen flames.

'Here,' Jenna said, 'this is the one we wanted you to see.'

Joe took it. The photo was not from a track meet, but from training. In it, Diane looked happy and relaxed, and she had a nice, open smile. The front fender of her Subaru poked out from the bottom left corner of the photo, and behind her were lodgepole pine trees and a glimpse of a blue sky between openings in the branches.

'Justin sent us that picture,' Jenna said. 'He said he took it a week or so before she disappeared.'

Joe nodded. As he studied the photo, it hit him. He jabbed at the shot with his index finger. 'Oh, man,' he said.

On Diane's left arm was an iPod in a pink case.

'This looks *exactly* like the case Caleb had in his daypack,' Joe said softly.

'Bobby made the connection,' she said. 'He said he asked you about it when you were in the hospital.'

'Yes, he did.'

Joe shook his head. What was the possibility the case he'd seen in Caleb's daypack was similar but different? Given the remoteness of the tableau, the odds were good they were the same item.

He looked up. 'Mrs Shober, they look the same. But that doesn't mean she's up there with them. There's the possibility they found this case on a trail or even stole it from a car or something.' Or found it on her body and took it, he thought but didn't say.

He started to hand the photos back, but one of them nagged at him. He flipped through the stack again to a shot of Diane in a heated discussion with two other women runners in what was obviously a track meet at a stadium. Joe looked up for an explanation.

'Oh, that one,' Jenna said. 'It's from college. I have that one in there because I think it shows Diane's passion. Those other two girls are on her team, and one of them had lost a race because a competitor tripped her deliberately. Diane was *so* angry . . .'

But what Joe was struck by was the gesture Diane was making: stabbing her right index finger into the palm of her left hand to make a point. 'Your daughter,' he said, 'has she always been blonde?'

'Since high school, anyway. She dyes it religiously.'

Joe took his index finger and placed it along the brow of Diane's face in the photo, creating a fringe. 'So if she doesn't colour her hair, it turns back to the original dark brown,' he said.

'Yes.'

Joe looked up. 'Do you know the name Terri Wade?'

Jenna looked back quizzically. 'Of course I do. She was our housekeeper when Diane was growing up. Diane loved her, we all did. But she left us years ago. She and Brent had a disagreement.'

Joe's jaw and shoulders dropped. He flashed back to that moment when he saw the faces reflected in flame.

Jenna saw his reaction, said, '*What?*'

'Mrs Shober—I saw Diane. She's using the name of your old housekeeper,' he said. 'She's let her hair go brown and she's dressed frumpily. But at one point outside that burning cabin, she turned away and then turned back. The angle of her face or the fire made her hair look lighter and her face look younger. It made me think there were two women when there was only one.' He thought back again to that scene in the woods, that one quick glimpse of the 'fourth face'. Wade turning away into the darkness, then the flash of one he'd thought was a different woman. Except it hadn't been. It had been Diane all along. He shook his head in amazement. 'I told you earlier I was probably mistaken, but I don't think so now. She was alive when I saw her last. So you need to know that. But . . .'

Her eyes glistened with tears. 'So you won't help us?'

He couldn't look into her eyes any longer. He handed the photo back and said, 'I'm sorry.'

She started to say something, but her throat caught with a sob and she snatched the photo back and turned angrily away. As she shoved the photos back into the envelope, Joe stared at the ceiling.

'Joe?' It was Marybeth, from behind him. He hadn't heard her come into the house. And he didn't know how long she'd been there or how much she'd heard.

He turned.

'Go,' she said. 'Go find her.'

Joe said, 'But I promised you.'

'You promised me when we didn't know it was really Diane up there,' she said. 'And when I put myself in Mrs Shober's shoes, if Sheridan or April or Lucy were missing . . .'

Joe nodded. 'If you're sure . . .'

'Take Nate,' she said.

'Of course.'

THEY WERE RIDING BLIND, still bearing west towards the high rim of the last cirque, Parnell in the lead, when Farkus said, 'So all this time we were tracking a deer?'

Parnell started to answer as he approached the edge of the rim, but he suddenly reined his horse to a stop. 'There's someone down there.'

'Is it one of the Clines?' Smith asked.

Parnell shook his head slowly. 'It isn't one of them. You are *not* going to believe the scene down there.'

Intrigued, Farkus, Campbell and Smith nudged their horses forward. As his horse walked, Farkus stood in his stirrups and strained to see over the rim. On the other side of the cirque, the wall wasn't as steep. There was a trail through scree on the other side of a pure blue mountain lake. And then he saw her.

'It looks like a naked woman,' he said, a smile stretching across his face. 'Finally something good has happened.'

It took half an hour for the four horsemen to circumnavigate the last cirque to the trail down to the lake. Occasionally, as they rode near the rim, Farkus would rise up in his stirrups and catch a glimpse of the woman. It was too far to see her clearly, but what he could see was as interesting as it was baffling. She was swimming. He caught flashes of pale white skin, long dark hair fanning in the water, and a glimpse of bare shoulders, small breasts and long limbs. There was a pile of clothing in the rocks near the shore of the alpine lake.

'Don't let her see you,' Parnell said. 'We're staying just long enough to find out if she knows anything about the Clines.'

The trail down to the lake was wide enough at first that the horsemen could ride two abreast. Parnell and Smith led; Farkus rode with Campbell. The trail narrowed about twenty yards from the lake and looped between two large boulders. The steel shoes of the horses clicked on the crushed rock of the scree. Farkus could feel his heart beat faster. He held back on the reins so Parnell and Smith could squeeze through the opening in the boulders first. He wondered if the woman would scream when she saw four men coming towards her on horseback.

But the whistling sound he heard was not a scream, and he looked up just in time to see a thick green branch slice through the air on the other side of the boulders at chest height. On the end of the branch was a two-foot pointed stake, which thumped into Parnell with a hollow sound. While the stake didn't penetrate his body armour, the impact threw him off his horse, and he hit hard on the rocks in front of Farkus.

'*Ambush!*' Smith hollered a half-second before a shotgun blast blew him out of the saddle.

Farkus's horse reared, and he flew backwards out of his saddle. He landed hard in the loose shale.

Two heavy *booms* came from behind a man-sized slab of rock to the right of the boulders, and Farkus was crushed under Campbell's dead body as it fell on him, pinning him to the ground.

The last thing he saw before his eyes closed was the figure of a very tall man rise out of the rocks. There was something wrong with the man's face, like there was a dried red rose on the tip of his chin. The man was thin and gaunt. His face was pale and sunken, and flesh peeled away from his nose. He wore a red plaid shirt and a white slouch hat pulled low over his eyes. Farkus watched him limp over from where he'd hidden in the rocks to where Parnell was writhing on the ground, trying to get his breath. He shot him point-blank in the head.

Then Farkus heard, 'You all right, Caleb?'

He turned his head towards the voice and saw the same man. He thought he was seeing double.

And from the lake he heard a scream. Or was it a shriek of joy?

He thought, Wendigo. And there's more than one of 'em.

'OPEN YOUR EYES,' a voice growled. 'I know you ain't dead.'

Farkus felt pure terror course through him. For the past hour, he'd lain still on his back. Campbell's heavy, lifeless body crushed him, and as time went by it seemed to get heavier. Beneath him, several sharp stones poked into his lower back and thighs.

He'd kept his eyes closed and tried to keep his breathing relaxed.

He'd heard a few voices. One of them, female, asked, 'Who are they? Are they the ones from Michigan?'

And Caleb or Camish said, 'Yup, I recognise two of 'em. The other two I don't know. That one doesn't look like he should be with them.'

There were other conversations, but the roaring of blood through his ears blocked them out. He tried to stay calm, play dead.

Then the voice telling him to open his eyes. He was *caught.*

Something sharp tugged at the skin on his cheek, and he flinched. There was no way of pretending any more.

He opened his eyes as the brother with the dirty compress on his chin—it wasn't a red rose after all—withdrew the point of a knife. Both brothers hovered over him, looking down. They were mirror images of one another, except for the bandage on the face of one.

'This probably isn't going to be your best day ever,' one of them said in a flat Midwestern accent.

PART THREE

Outliers Among Us

Friday, September 4

Joe drove his pick-up, towing the horse trailer. They had stopped off to select and hire two geldings from Alisha's uncle's ranch, and now Nate sat in the passenger seat, running a BoreSnake cleaning cable through the barrel and five cylinders of his .454 Casull.

Nate said, 'Is the governor aware of what we're doing?'

'I thought it best not to tell him,' Joe said.

'What about your director? What does he know?'

'Nothing. As far as he's concerned, I'm on administrative leave.'

Nate said, 'Something I learned years ago is, it's always better to apologise than to ask permission.'

'Exactly. I'll call Sheriff Baird as we start up into the mountains. He needs to know we're in his county, but he really can't prevent us from going back up there.'

Nate loaded the cylinder with cartridges the size of cigar stubs, snapped it closed and holstered the revolver. 'I'm ready,' he said. 'What're you packing?'

'I picked up a new twelve-gauge,' Joe said. 'And my service weapon.'

Nate narrowed his eyes. 'Are you *ever* going to take the time to learn how to hit something with that? You drive me crazy.'

Joe shrugged. 'I've done some damage with it.'

'From an inch away and by spraying the landscape with slugs.' Nate snorted. 'A *monkey* could do that.'

Joe smiled, 'Every time I pull this gun, I think it's the last time I'll ever do it. Not because I think there will be world peace—I just never think trouble will come my way again.'

'But it always does,' Nate said, smiling a little.

Joe nodded. 'Yup, it seems to.'

Nate shook his head and looked away. They eventually settled into a comfortable and familiar silence.

Joe's phone burred, and he plucked it from his breast pocket and looked at the display. 'Uh-oh,' he said. 'It's a 777 number I don't recognise. But 777 is the state phone prefix. It's probably the governor.'

'Are you going to answer it?' Nate asked.

Joe dropped the phone back into his pocket, then bent forward and clicked off his radio under the dashboard as well.

'Radio silence,' Nate said. 'I like radio silence.'

'Unless, of course, Marybeth calls,' Joe said.

'Obviously,' Nate said.

'THIS ONE'S got a lot of moving parts, doesn't it?' Nate said thoughtfully, a little later.

Joe knew he was referring to the situation in general. 'Yup.'

'And a bunch of parts we don't even know yet. Are the Feds with us or against us?'

Joe shrugged. 'That's something I can't quite figure out yet. The FBI seems very interested in it, but from the outside. Usually, they move in and try to take over. This time, it's like they're trying to stay out of it but control things at the same time.'

'Have you talked to Coon?'

'Yup, I called him, but he didn't tell me much. He said he couldn't comment on ongoing investigations.'

'Ongoing investigations? That tells me something right there,' Nate said.

Joe nodded. 'Plus, Coon was adamant that the Grims didn't exist. At the time, I thought he was telling me I was nuts. In retrospect, I think he was telling me the names didn't fit with his investigation. In other words, he knows these brothers exist, but not under those names.'

'I wonder what he's hiding,' Nate said. 'And I wonder how far it goes up the chain.'

Joe's phone rang again. He said, 'Another 777 number.'

Nate said, 'It's always better to apologise than to ask permission.'

Joe breathed deeply and again dropped the phone back into his pocket without answering it.

AS JOE AND NATE approached Muddy Gap, Nate said, 'I don't see where the woman fits. Is she a hostage, a kidnap victim or a willing accomplice?'

Joe shrugged. 'I don't see how those guys could have taken her up into the mountains if she didn't want to go. She didn't seem to fear them nearly as much as she regretted letting them down by taking me in. Are you thinking she's the key to all of this?'

Nate sat back and sighed. 'No. I can't figure out how she fits. Or why, of all the places on earth, she'd end up there.'

Joe grunted.

After a few more miles, Nate said, 'This thing spooked you, didn't it?'

No response.

'You don't have to be ashamed,' Nate said. 'You got your butt kicked over and over. These guys ran circles round you up there and took everything you had, including your confidence. I can tell. You don't want to go up there for revenge as much as to see if you can get your courage back, isn't that it?'

'I'd rather not talk about it,' Joe said.

'Like I said, they kicked your butt up one side of the mountain and down the other,' Nate said.

'You're really irritating sometimes,' Joe mumbled.

'But what I can't figure out is why they didn't finish the job. They had you down from that shotgun blast, but they didn't follow up. Guys like that, who hunt for a living, would know to find you and put one or two into your head. Why didn't they do that?'

Joe shrugged. 'I've been wondering that since I woke up in the hospital.'

'Maybe they aren't as bad as you think?' Nate said.

'Not a chance,' Joe said, decisively. 'They're *worse*. They've got a woman up there, possibly against her will. And who knows what else we'll find?'

Nate rubbed his chin. 'Maybe we'll find that lady wants to stay.'

'No way,' Joe said.

'Another thing,' Nate said. 'They called you a government man. I find that interesting. Not a game warden, but a *government man*.'

'I've never been called that before. I never thought of myself that way,' Joe said. 'I'm surprised they used that choice of words.'

'That says something about their world view, doesn't it?'

Before Joe could answer, his phone rang again. He expected a 777 number but saw on the display it was from MBP Management. Joe opened the phone, said, 'Yes?'

Marybeth said, 'Has the governor found you yet?'

'No.'

'He called here a few minutes ago. When I told him you weren't here, he didn't sound very happy.'

'I can imagine,' Joe said.

'When he asked me where you were, I couldn't lie to him,' Marybeth said. 'I mean, he's your boss. And he is the governor.'

'I understand.'

'He asked which route you were taking.'

Joe frowned, 'He did?'

'That's not all,' she said. 'He told me this thing is blowing up all of a sudden and he needed to find you. Then he hung up. You know how he is.'

'Yup,' he said, 'I know how he is.'

He closed his phone and dropped it to the seat. They topped a rise before dropping down into Rawlins. As they crested the hill, Joe saw the blue and red flashing lights, the phalanx of state-trooper vehicles and the long row of eighteen-wheelers directly ahead, all waiting to pass through the roadblock.

'Oh, no,' Nate said, sitting up straight.

Joe looked over and saw his friend strip off his shoulder holster and cram it beneath the bench seat.

'I'm not going back to Cheyenne,' Nate said softly.

Joe considered braking and turning round, but he was on a one-way exit and the ditches on either side of the road were too steep for him to pull the horse trailer through.

'I've got to keep going,' Joe said, 'unless you have any ideas.'

'You could let me out here,' Nate said. 'Let me run for it.'

Joe looked ahead. He counted four highway patrol cars and a Carbon County sheriff SUV.

'They'll run you down in two minutes,' Joe said.

'Not if I take them out,' Nate said.

'If you take them out, we're both going to prison,' Joe said, easing on his brakes so he wouldn't rear-end an eighteen-wheeler. At that moment, both of his side mirrors filled up with the grinning chrome grille of another truck.

'We're hemmed in,' Joe said.

Ahead of them, uniformed troopers walked along the shoulder of the road from car to car.

Nate sat back, his eyes glassy.

Two state troopers approached Joe's pick-up, one on each side of the road. The trooper on the left was tall and stoop-shouldered. The trooper on the right was short, and his hard, round belly strained at the buttons on his uniform shirt. When he looked up and saw Joe he put his right hand on the grip of his weapon.

Joe couldn't hear him speak to the other trooper, but he read his lips: '*It's him.*'

The tall trooper put his hand on his gun as well. As they walked up, Joe lowered the driver's and passenger side windows.

'You Joe Pickett?' the tall trooper asked.

'Yes, sir.'

'Governor Rulon is looking for you. Our orders are to take you to him.'

'To Cheyenne?' Joe said. 'That's three hours away.'

'Naw, not to Cheyenne,' the trooper said. 'He's at the airport. He flew in about an hour ago, and he's waiting for you.'

The squat trooper on the other side of the truck said to Nate, 'We were supposed to be looking for one guy. Pickett. Who might you be? Do you have some ID on you?'

'No.' Nate's voice was soft but firm. Joe knew it was the way he spoke just before he tore someone's ear off.

Joe said with false but distracting cheer, 'Lead the way, men, and I'll follow. The governor's waiting, remember?'

He was grateful that both troopers decided to drop their line of enquiry and depart with both ears attached.

TWO HIGHWAY PATROL CARS led the way to the small airport, and another trooper car followed Joe's truck and horse trailer.

A small Cessna jet was parked on the runway near a cinderblock building that served as the private terminal. On the tail of the airplane was a Wyoming bucking horse silhouette.

'There's Rulon One,' Joe said. 'He's here, all right.'

RULON WAS a big man, with a round face and silver-flecked brown hair that always looked barely combed. He had a ruddy complexion that could quickly turn fire-engine red. He stood at the head of a table in the conference room of the terminal wearing an open-collared shirt, casual trousers and a dark blue windcheater. Special Agent Chuck Coon of the FBI sat slumped at the table to Rulon's right, and the governor's new chief of staff, a trim, retired military man named Carson, sat at Rulon's left. Both of them looked uncomfortable.

'You,' Rulon said, pointing at Joe, 'need to answer your phone.'

'I get that,' Joe said.

'And look who's with him,' Coon said. 'The infamous Nate Romanowski.'

'None of that here,' Rulon said to Coon.

'But he's a fugitive,' Coon said to Rulon. 'For crying out loud, I can't just look the other way.'

'Yes, you can, for now,' Rulon said. 'Anyway, that's not why we're here.'

Joe said, 'Why are we here?'

Rulon pointed his finger at Coon and said, 'Because the Feds are dumping murderous miscreants into my state and not telling me about it.'

'It's not like that,' Coon said heatedly.

Joe shook his head, confused.

'Got a minute?' Rulon said to him, then answered his own question: 'Why, of *course* you do. Have a seat, both of you.'

'JOE,' GOVERNOR RULON SAID, 'I'm not one to believe in government conspiracies, and the longer I'm in the government the more I'm convinced they cannot exist, because government, by nature, is damned sloppy and incompetent. There's just too many people involved with too many agendas for any secret to be kept very long. The only conspiracy that exists is the conspiracy of incompetence.' He paused, pleased with his phrasing. 'Conspiracy of incompetence—I like that. Write that down, Carson.'

Carson dutifully wrote it down on a yellow legal pad.

'So,' Rulon continued, 'conspiracies don't exist in government for long. But a couple of things are timeless, especially in Washington: greed and corruption. Especially with certain senators and congressmen who've been there so long they've forgotten what it's like back in the real world. It gets to the point where it's all about *them*.'

Joe looked out of the window at the runway. Beyond the governor's plane several tumbleweeds rolled across the tarmac.

'Am I boring you, Joe?' Rulon asked suddenly.

Joe looked up. 'With all due respect, Governor, I was hoping you would get to the point.'

Rulon froze, his face turning crimson. But instead of yelling, a slow grin formed. He held his hands out, palms up.

'Why can't I be surrounded by sycophants who tell me how great I am?' Rulon said. 'Instead, I get guys like you, Joe.'

Joe shrugged. 'Sorry, sir.'

'OK,' Rulon said, 'I'll cut to the chase. Have you ever heard of Senator Carl McKinty of Michigan? Thirty-year senator, he is. He's chairman of the Natural Resources Committee. That's where I've tangled with him. He's on the Homeland Security Committee as well.'

Joe said, 'I've heard his name.'

'Have you heard of a woman named Caryl Cline?'

Joe rubbed his jaw. 'The name is familiar, but I'm not sure why.'

'Five years ago,' Rulon said, 'she was all over television. She was a self-proclaimed activist for private-property rights. She got that way because Senator McKinty worked a sweetheart deal in the Upper Peninsula in Michigan for a huge tract of land she owned. He convinced the local government to condemn the land her family had owned for a hundred and fifty years in order to give it to a hotshot developer. The local government did it because the developer promised a higher tax base than that obtained from the little meat-processing company run by the family. And it was perfectly legal, because our brilliant Supreme Court said it was just fine for governments to do that.

'The only way to stop it was through civil disobedience, with the hope that the local or state government would be shamed and give up. And that's what she did,' Rulon said. 'She took her fight public. She did all she could to call out the senator and the local commissioners who condemned her land. She and her three sons got their guns and said they'd fight for their property.'

Joe said, 'OK, I remember her now. The media kind of made fun of her.'

'That's right,' Rulon said. 'Because she looked and talked like what she was—a rural Midwestern white woman. She had crooked teeth, glasses that were taped together in the middle, bad hair, and she wore these big print dresses. They called her "Ma Cline". They did their best to make her unsympathetic, but she became a symbol with a few political commentators and just plain folks.'

Joe remembered the *I'm with Ma Cline* bumper stickers that were popular at the time. He still saw some around.

Rulon said, 'Do you remember what happened to her?'

Before Joe could speak, Nate said, 'She was murdered.'

'Murder is not the right word,' Coon interjected. 'She was killed, yes. But it happened in a firefight at the Cline compound in the UP.'

Nate shook his head. 'It always amuses me how a family home suddenly becomes a "compound" when you folks decide to attack it.'

The news story came back to Joe. He remembered how it had been reported. The Cline family was armed to the teeth and refused to leave their land. The local sheriff, as well as federal law enforcement, moved in on them after arrest warrants had been issued for firearms violations, refusal to comply with the condemnation order, and dozens of other charges. Gunfire greeted them, and two members of the strike force were wounded before the tactical units unleashed holy hell on the 'compound'. In the end, Caryl Cline, her husband, Darrell, and one of three sons were killed.

'I'm confused,' Joe said. 'What does this have to do with us?'

Rulon said, 'Up until yesterday, I would have asked the same thing. But at this point, I'll ask Special Agent Chuck Coon to pick up the story.'

Joe thought Coon looked as if he were racked with turmoil, as if it would physically hurt him to talk.

Rulon lowered his voice and looked kindly towards Coon. 'Mr Coon is one of the good guys in this whole situation. He came to me yesterday afternoon because his conscience was bothering him. I know how far out on a limb he is now and how much courage it's taken when he could have easily said nothing at all.'

Coon thanked the governor with his eyes, then turned to Joe and Nate. He said, 'Some background is necessary. Senator McKinty is on the

Homeland Security Committee, as mentioned. He knew the government was looking for land for a new counter-terrorism effort, a training facility far removed from any population centres. As you know, Michigan has been in a one-state depression for years, so anything he can deliver keeps him popular and gets him re-elected. The Upper Peninsula is pretty hard hit, so he wanted to locate the facility there, but there wasn't a big enough piece of state land that would meet all the specs. So he worked with the locals to identify several huge private holdings. He worked with the developer to target the land. What no one knew was that he'd arranged for his son to be a major shareholder in the development as well. You see, McKinty's largest campaign contributor is himself. This was a way of creating a permanent major donor. There are no laws preventing a senator from contributing to his own campaign.'

Nate said, 'Bastards.'

Coon said, 'So he delivered an eight-hundred-and-fifty-million-dollar defence facility to his constituents. Few knew he was personally going to benefit, and those who knew didn't care because that's how things are done. The Clines were a major problem, though, because they became grass-roots heroes for refusing to relocate their business or leave their land. That put pressure on Senator McKinty, and he wanted them gone. He used his pull with federal agencies to put the pressure on them. The Clines were well known as independent, backwoods renegade types, and it didn't take long for legitimate charges to be brought against them.'

'Still,' Joe said, 'it was their land. How can the government just take it?'

Coon shrugged. 'We can. We do.'

Nate spat, 'Bastards!' again.

'Anyway,' Coon said, 'not every member of the Cline family died that day. Two of them survived.'

Coon read Joe's face.

'That's right,' Coon said. 'The two surviving sons were arrested. They were belligerent and claimed they were political prisoners and they wouldn't spend one minute in jail. It was shaping up to be a major federal trial, but Senator McKinty again got involved. He didn't want a trial that could blow open his personal connection to the facility. So he sent his staff to the Justice Department and a deal was cut. If the two surviving Cline sons would drop their claim to the land, they'd be given new identities and be placed in the Federal Witness Protection Programme. Otherwise, federal prosecutors would go after them and send them to prison for the rest of their lives.'

'Hold it,' Joe said, shaking his head. 'Prosecutors wouldn't cut those brothers a deal based on what you've said, would they? If they really fired on federal officers?'

Coon said, 'Don't forget, federal prosecutors are political appointees. They know where their bread is buttered.'

'This stinks,' Joe said.

Coon nodded. 'Welcome to the big time, Joe.'

'And I bet I can guess the names of the brothers,' Joe said. 'Camish and Caleb. Grimmengruber was the name they were given for the witness-protection programme. They told me they were from the UP. And the fact that they ran a meat-processing company explains how they were able to butcher the elk and my horses.'

Coon nodded. 'They were supposed to go to Nevada. But en route, they overpowered their federal escort and took off. We lost track of them completely, but our agency was told to keep an eye out for them. Until you gave your statement, we had no idea where they ended up.'

Rulon said, 'And I would have never put this all together except for Senator McKinty himself. As I said, I've been tangling with him for a couple of years, because he's the chairman of the Natural Resources Committee and he refused to release mineral severance payments to the State of Wyoming that are owed to us. He wouldn't answer my letters or take my calls until this week. Now, all of a sudden, his staff said he's rethinking his opposition to releasing the funds. But there's a condition. He wants the Clines to be left alone up there in the mountains. They made up this goofy story of wanting to look out for their former constituents, but I saw right through that. He doesn't want them to resurface and start talking.'

Joe said to Coon, 'So why'd you talk to the governor?'

Coon shook his head. 'There's only so much I can take. I just want to do my job out here and solve crimes and put bad guys in prison. I don't want any part of deals cut in DC.'

Nate said to the governor, 'Hold it. McKinty just wants the Clines, or the Grim brothers, *left alone*?'

Rulon said, 'Yes, that's what his staff is asking.'

Nate shook his head. 'That doesn't make sense. He doesn't want them left alone. He wants them silenced. That's the only way he can skate on this.'

Rulon glared at Nate and said, 'He's a US senator. He's not a killer, for God's sake. Man, I thought *I* was cynical.'

Nate said, 'When did he approach you about the deal?'

The governor said, 'Last week. Why?'

Nate said, 'Because I think he wanted you to not put any more effort into finding those brothers until he could take care of it himself. I wouldn't be surprised if he sent a team up there to solve the problem once and for all. And it wouldn't surprise me if he reneged on his offer once he got confirmation that the Clines were no more.'

Rulon turned to Carson while pointing his finger at Nate. 'This son of a bitch should be our scout in Washington. He's got a vicious, devious mind.'

'No, thanks,' Nate said. 'I used to work for them. So I know how they think and how they operate. The question is, did the team he sent out find the Clines?'

Joe stood up, fighting a wave of nausea. He said, 'And is Diane alive and well? Or did they get her, too?'

Nate stood as well. 'I wouldn't be surprised, based on what Joe experienced, to find out that it's McKinty's team that's taking a dirt nap and not the brothers. But there's only one way we're going to find that out.'

Joe sighed wearily. He said, 'They called me a government man. Now I know why they went after me.'

Coon said, 'We're all government men, Joe.'

'Not me,' Nate said proudly.

'So,' Joe said to the governor, 'where do we stand?'

Rulon didn't hesitate. 'Go up there and rescue that woman and bring those brothers out dead or alive. Do you need more people? I could have a dozen DCI agents here by nightfall.'

Joe shook his head, said, 'Those brothers own those mountains, and they know when a big contingent is after them. A big group makes lots of noise and raises dust and quiets the wildlife. That's why I stumbled on Caleb on my own while Sheriff Baird and his men couldn't find them at all. I think the leaner the better.'

'Meaning you and Mr Romanowski here,' Rulon said.

Joe nodded. 'Plus, I have a pretty good idea where they hang out.'

'Go get those bastards, then,' Rulon said, narrowing his eyes. 'Send 'em back to Michigan, either vertical or horizontal—I don't have strong feelings either way.'

Nate was out of the room before Joe could speak.

Rulon said, 'Is he still with you?'

Joe shrugged. 'I'm not sure.'

'Would you go alone?'

'Probably not.'

Rulon blew out a long breath and looked to Carson for solace.

'Two questions,' Joe said. 'One, what was the name of the developer in Michigan?'

Coon smiled wearily. 'Brent Shober,' he said.

Joe said, 'Thought so. Second question. How will the state cope with the loss of money from the Feds if Senator McKinty finds out you sent me up there?'

Rulon said, 'That's a good question, Joe. Very politically astute. You're learning, aren't you?'

'Not that I'm proud of it,' Joe said.

Rulon put his beefy hands on Joe's shoulders and leaned his face close. 'If you bring those brothers down the mountain, we have a news story on our hands. The story can be spun however we want it to be spun. Meaning McKinty might just find himself in the news again for the wrong reason. It'll be up to him how he plays it.'

'But if we don't find the Cline brothers and Diane Shober?' Joe asked.

Rulon said, 'I'm screwed. You're screwed. We're all screwed.'

THE STOPOVER IN RAWLINS with the governor had cost Joe two hours and a big chunk of his sense of purpose, he thought. As he and Nate travelled west via I-80, Joe called Marybeth and filled her in on the meeting. He was keenly aware of Nate's presence in the passenger seat, sullen and still. He was no doubt thinking whether or not he even wanted to be on this adventure any more.

'So do you think the Shobers were withholding information from you?' Marybeth asked.

Joe said, 'I'm not sure yet. If they don't know it was the Cline brothers up there, there wasn't anything for them to come clean about. It's possible Mr Shober knows something, but I'm not sure.'

'But still,' Marybeth said, 'the Michigan connection is just too . . . convenient. There has to be something there.'

'I agree, but what?'

'I'm not sure. But I could do a little research.'

Joe grinned. 'I was hoping you would say that.'

Marybeth had assisted in a number of Joe's cases over the years. Joe found her a clear-eyed and determined researcher. She got information no one else seemed to be able to find, and she got it quickly.

'I'll call you back as soon as I have something,' she said.

He could hear computer keys clicking in the background.

'Wow—this looks like a target-rich environment. I'll call later,' she said, hanging up.

'OK,' NATE SAID after an hour of silence, 'this new development about the Clines puts a whole new angle on the situation.'

Joe grunted, noncommittal.

Nate said, 'From the standpoint of the Cline brothers, they hunt, they fish, they go back to subsistence level. No doubt they even maintain some contacts with some of their kind round the country. And believe me, there's more of them than you'd think.'

Joe shook his head. 'You've been thinking about this for a while.'

Nate said, 'Yes, I have. Hanging out in Hole in the Wall gives me plenty of time to think.'

'Maybe you should get out more,' Joe said.

'I don't even think it was the licence so much,' Nate said, ignoring Joe. 'It was your threat about seeing them in court. You didn't realise what buttons you were pushing.'

'No,' Joe said, 'how could I know that?'

Said Nate, 'You couldn't. But you *are* stubborn.'

'Yup, when it comes to doing my job. Besides, they stole that guy's elk, too.'

Nate shrugged. 'From their point of view, those hunters were in their territory and they didn't bother to ask permission. It's all a matter of how you look at it.'

'We can't have the rule of law if people can choose which laws they want to obey based on their point of view,' Joe said.

'Agreed,' Nate said. 'Which is why the big laws ought to be reasonable and fair, and neither the people nor the government should breach their trust. But when the government decides to confiscate private property simply because they have the guns and judges on their side, the whole system starts to break down, and all bets are off. These boys may be losers, but *damn.* This is what happens when the government gets too big for its britches. Some folks get pushed out, and they get angry.'

'You sound sympathetic to them,' Joe said.

Nate said, 'Damned straight.'

'Great,' Joe said.

'I'm sympathetic to outliers among us,' Nate said. 'I'm kind of one myself.' Then he paused and looked over at Joe and said, '*Government man*.'

Joe said, 'Quit calling me that.'

THEY WERE ROLLING DOWN the hard-packed gravel road into the forest when Marybeth called back. Joe snatched his phone from the seat between them and opened it. Nate looked on, interested.

'It wasn't hard to find a connection between Caryl Cline and Diane Shober,' Marybeth said. 'They appeared on the same local cable-news show years ago. They were both in Detroit the same day. According to the schedule, Diane was on at the top of the hour to talk about her chances to make the Olympic team, and Ma Cline was on at the bottom of the hour to talk about what it felt like to lose her appeal to the court. They very likely met in the green room before the show. Maybe they struck up a relationship there that continued.'

'Goodness,' Joe said, his mind swirling.

She said, 'So we've got a Michigan connection now between the Cline family, Diane Shober and Brent Shober. This is getting interesting.'

'Yup,' he said. Then, 'This thing between Diane and Brent. It smells bad. I can see the basis of real animosity there.'

Marybeth said, 'Me too. The guy is more than a creep. He's obsessed with her.'

'And the Clines somehow connect with both of them,' Joe said.

'Maybe Diane and the Clines figure they've got a common enemy,' Marybeth said.

'Can you keep looking into it?' Joe asked.

'I'll do some advanced searches and get creative. I'll also start adding in the Cline brothers and see what we get.'

Joe briefed Nate on what Marybeth had found.

Nate nodded his head, said, 'The dispossessed.'

Joe said, 'Talk about pure speculation, Nate.'

'Trust me on this. These are my people,' Nate said, only smiling a little.

THE SIERRA MADRE defined the muscular horizon of the west and south, and it appeared to flex slightly into the blue as Joe and Nate approached it. Joe used his service radio to call Sheriff Baird's office. The county dispatcher put him through to Baird's vehicle. Joe expected a rebuke for being back in his county. Instead, the sheriff sounded relieved. 'Are you close?' he asked.

'Yup,' Joe said. 'I wanted to let you know we're planning to take horses into the mountains this afternoon to go after those brothers.'

'How far are you from the trailhead?' Baird asked.

Joe looked at the dashboard clock. 'Twenty minutes.'

Baird said, 'Can you divert and take the road straight up into the mountains? I'm up here now on the eastern side of the mountains about an hour and a half from you. I may need some help.'

Joe frowned. 'What's going on?'

'I'm not real sure,' Baird said, his voice low. 'I got a call earlier today about some vehicles sitting empty on the side of the mountain. A couple of pick-ups and a stock trailer with out-of-state plates. That struck me as unusual since it's a little early for hunting season, so I thought I'd check them out. Looks like I'm not the only one.'

'Meaning what?' Joe asked.

'I'm parked up on a pullout where I can see into the trees below me where the vehicles and horse trailer are located. But as I started looking over the campsite, I saw two men dressed exactly alike come down out of the trees and walk towards the camp.'

Joe felt the hair rise on his forearms and on the back of his neck. He reached down while he drove and turned up the volume on the radio so Nate could hear clearly. 'What's their description?' he asked.

'Taller than hell, skinnier than poles,' Baird said. 'Red flannel shirts with big checks on them. Dirty denims. Goofy-assed hats.'

'It's them,' Joe said. 'The brothers. I wonder why they're on the wrong side of the mountain?'

'Beats me. Maybe they plan to take the trucks and hightail it out of here. That would be OK with me,' the sheriff said with a chuckle. 'One thing, though,' he said. 'I see a pick-up truck down there I recognise. It belongs to Dave Farkus. You know him?'

Joe said, 'Yup. He's on my watch list for poaching.'

'Good place for him,' Baird said. 'Anyway, his county supervisor called our office yesterday and said he was AWOL. I said I'd keep a lookout for him. I have no idea why he'd be over here with some out-of-staters, but that sure looks like his wheels.'

'The brothers,' Joe said. 'Do you still see them?'

'Naw. Once they went down into the trees, I lost 'em.'

Joe said, 'Maybe you ought to pull back.'

'I don't think they saw me.'

'Don't be too sure of that,' Joe said. 'Those boys don't miss much. In fact, you may want to back on out of there.'

'I don't back off,' Baird said, his voice hard.

'Sheriff, can you see the licence plates on the pick-up and horse trailer at all?'

'Not real well,' Baird said. 'I can barely make one of them out through the trees. I can't see the numbers clearly, though.'

Joe asked, 'Is the plate blue?'

'Yes.'

'I'd bet you a dollar it's a Michigan plate.'

'That sounds right.'

'We'll be there as soon as we can,' Joe said. 'Keep in radio contact. And back out of there if you see those guys again. You don't want to take them on without help.'

HALF AN HOUR later, Joe's radio crackled to life.

'Joe, you there?' Baird asked. Joe noted the urgency of Baird's tone and his complete absence of radio protocol.

'Yes, sheriff, what is it?'

'*Jesus!*' Baird said, and the transmission went to static.

Joe's pick-up was in a steady climb into the mountains, struggling with the weight of the horse trailer behind it. His motor was strained, and the tachometer edged into the red. He floored it. While he did so, he tried to raise the dispatcher who'd originally connected them.

When she came on she was weeping. 'Did you hear the sheriff?' she asked. 'I think those bastards got him.'

'I heard,' Joe said. 'But let's not speculate on what we don't know. Are you dispatching emergency services? Anybody?'

The dispatcher sniffed. 'Everybody,' she said. 'But you're the closest to him. I hope you can help him. I hope they didn't—'

'Hey,' Joe said. 'You don't need to talk about him that way yet. He may be OK.'

'OK,' she said, to placate Joe.

A few minutes later, Nate said, 'Wonder what'll be left of him.'

THE LACK OF WIND was rare and remarkable, Joe thought, and the single thin plume of black smoke miles away deep in the timber rose straight up in a line until it dissipated at around 15,000 feet.

Joe and Nate had just summitted the mountain, and the eastern slope was laid out before them. The vista was stunning: a massive undulating carpet veined with tendrils of gold and red.

'Black smoke like that usually means rubber is burning,' Joe said.

'Do you know how to get there?' Nate asked.

Joe nodded. 'There are quite a few old logging roads ahead. We should be able to find Baird's tyre tracks and follow him in.'

There was only one open road that went to the southeast towards the smoke, and there were fresh tyre tracks imprinted over a coating of dust. Joe made the turn and drove down as swiftly as he could.

'We need to be ready,' Nate said.

Joe nodded. In his peripheral vision, he saw Nate dig his weapon and holster out from under the seat and strap it back on.

'You loaded?' Nate asked, pulling Joe's new shotgun from behind the seat.

'Shells in the glove box,' Joe said.

Nate found the shells and fitted them into the receiver.

'I have mixed feelings about this thing we are about to do,' he said.

'I know.'

'You do, too.'

Joe grunted. 'If it weren't for Diane, I might be tempted to turn round.'

'But we can't let feelings get in the way,' Nate said, putting the shotgun muzzle-down on the floor. 'We've set our course. It doesn't matter what we think about politics or the law. If we find those brothers and you've got a shot, take it. These boys aren't going to let us lead them back to jail. They've left all that behind. Don't start talking or reading them their rights. Just shoot.'

When Joe started to object, Nate said, 'It isn't about who is the fastest or the toughest hombre in the state. It's about who can look up without any mist in their eyes or doubts in their heart, aim and pull the trigger without thinking twice. It's about killing. It's always been that way.'

SHERIFF RON BAIRD'S county Ford Excursion was parked twenty feet off the track in a grove of aspen trees that overlooked the campground below. It wasn't burning, but it had been worked over.

Joe pulled up beside it and jumped out of his pick-up with his shotgun. He circled the Excursion. The hood was open and all visible wires had been sliced in half or pulled out. The front windshield was smashed inwards and the tyres were flat.

Baird was nowhere to be found.

Joe said, 'I wonder where they took him.'

'They marched him down the hill,' Nate said, binoculars at his eyes. 'I see him.'

Joe felt a spasm of fear shoot through him. 'Is he alive?'

'I think so. But he doesn't look real good.'

'How so?' Joe asked.

'Looks like he's got an arrow sticking out of his ass.'

THE STENCH from burning tyres and plastic was nearly overwhelming. The pick-up that had towed the horse trailer, the trailer itself and Dave Farkus's pick-up were on fire. Baird was fifty yards off to the side of the camp, and he appeared to be hugging the trunk of a tree.

'Do you see any sign of the brothers?' Joe asked as they drove down the hill towards the scene.

Nate lowered the binoculars. 'Nope.'

'Think they're gone or using the sheriff to draw us in?'

'My guess is those boys are running back into the mountains. They probably came down to disable the vehicles and didn't expect to get surprised by the sheriff.'

Joe drove to Baird and hit the brakes and leapt out. He could feel the heat from the burning pick-up on his back.

Baird was conscious, his eyes wide open. He was hugging the tree because they'd cinched Flex-Cuffs round his wrists on the other side of the trunk. And, as Nate had observed, there was an arrow shaft sticking out of his left buttock. Joe recognised that it had been made by the Grim brothers. The arrow wasn't deep at all, although Joe guessed it probably hurt.

'Sheriff,' Joe said, 'you've got an arrow sticking out of your butt.'

'Why, thank you, Joe. I was wondering what it was that's bothering me back there.'

'You want me to pull it out or cut you down first?'

'Cut me down, please.'

As Joe removed his Leatherman tool and opened the blade, he said, 'How far are the brothers ahead of us?'

Baird nodded towards the forested slope on the other side of the burning pick-ups. 'Maybe thirty minutes,' he said.

'They on foot?'

Baird nodded. 'They are, but they cover ground like demons. I saw them coming out of the trees at me on both sides, but they were so fast I didn't get a chance to fight them off.'

'I understand,' Joe said, cutting the plastic cuffs free. 'I've tangled with them and lost, just like you.'

Baird stepped away from the tree and rubbed hard on his wrists.

'So,' Joe said, 'do you believe me now?'

Baird reached up and pushed his stringy hair back. 'I was waiting to see how long it took you to ask me that question.'

As the two men looked at each other, Nate strode behind Baird towards the burning vehicles. As deft as a swallow plucking a gnat from the air, he reached out and pulled the arrow from Baird.

'Ouch, dammit!' Baird said, spinning round, clutching himself. 'Who said you could do that?'

Nate smirked, handed Baird the arrow, and continued on his way.

'They had no intention of killing you,' Joe said to Baird as he helped the sheriff limp to a fallen log. 'Or you'd be dead.'

'I know,' Baird agreed. He straddled the log and leaned over it so his chest rested against the bark. His wound was open to the sky.

'Same with me,' Joe said to the sheriff. 'For whatever reason, they did some real damage, but they didn't feel compelled to finish the job.'

'It would have been easy,' Baird said, then gestured over his shoulder towards his wound. 'This thing hurts. How bad is it?'

Joe said, 'This is when you find out who your friends are.' He grimaced and turned for his pick-up truck to get his first-aid kit.

JOE RIPPED another strip of tape to bind the compress to the wound. As he applied it, Nate came down out of the trees.

'Did those boys say anything?' Nate asked Baird. 'Like, "*Stay off our mountain, sheriff*", or "*Damn, where'd you come from?*"'

Baird shook his head. 'They never said a word the whole time. Until the end, I mean.'

Joe paused, said, 'What did they say at the end?'

Baird cleared his throat. 'After they cuffed me to that tree, I expected them to just cut my throat and leave me there. One of 'em got right behind me and kind of whispered into my ear. He said, "The only reason we're letting you live is so you can tell anybody who will listen to leave us the hell alone." '

'That's all?' Joe said.

'Pretty much. He repeated himself, though. "*Just leave us the hell alone.*" Then he stepped back and said, "This is to show you how serious we are," and shot me in the butt with that arrow. I could tell he took it easy on me, though. He barely shot that at me with much force. I mean, he could have done all kind of damage.

'You know, I was scared at first. But when he said, "*Just leave us the hell alone*", I felt sorry for them. Ain't that strange?'

Nate didn't respond. To Joe, he said, 'I saddled the horses. They've got an hour on us at best, and they aren't on horseback. This may be the closest we'll ever get to them.'

Joe nodded and felt another prickle of fear.

'We'd best get going,' Nate said.

'I heard you,' Joe said. He told Baird to pull up his trousers.

AS THEY RODE UP out of the camp where the vehicles still burned, they could hear the distant thumping of a helicopter. The chopper was coming to get Baird. Various state troopers and DCI agents were on their way as well, but hours behind them.

Baird's hand-held had been propped against the log he was resting on and the volume was up. As Joe saddled the packhorse and packed gear into the panniers, he heard the chatter pick up as word spread of the ambush of Baird. Sheriff departments from four Wyoming counties and two Colorado counties were mobilising. DCI and FBI were being contacted.

Joe said to Nate, 'By this time tomorrow, this camp will be a small city.'

Nate said, 'I'm not a city-type guy.'

They rode their horses up into the mountains. Joe led, followed by Nate and the packhorse.

The feeling of dread seemed to increase in direct proportion to the altitude,

Joe thought. The sharp smell of pine and sweating horses, the gritty taste of dust from the trail—it was as if he'd never been away. Joe reached out and touched the butt plate of his shotgun with the tips of his fingers, reassuring himself it was there.

Nate said, 'So we're agreed that the best way to do this is to drive hard on our own, right? We're going to try to catch up with those boys while they're within striking distance? And we aren't going to give a damn about all of the drummers on their way here?'

Joe said, 'Yup. I feel like we owe it to those brothers to find them before they're cornered by the cavalry that'll be coming.'

'Even though the result may be the same,' Nate said.

THEY FOLLOWED the tracks of the horses that had been there before them. Joe determined that the men from Michigan had six horses.

But who were they, these men? And how did Dave Farkus get hooked up with them? Joe's best guess was that Farkus stumbled on the men and was taken along—or disposed of along the way.

As he rode, Joe continually scanned the trail up ahead of him and the trees lining both sides. His shotgun was within quick reach. If the brothers didn't know they were being pursued, it was possible he and Nate could simply ride up on them. He wanted to be ready.

A doe and her fawn stayed ahead of them on the trail, and Joe kept seeing her at each turn. She'd graze with the fawn until the horses came into sight, then startle with a white flap of her tail and bound ahead again. Joe wished she'd move off the trail for good, because each time she saw him and jumped, his heart did too.

An hour later, as dusk muffled the eastside slopes, Joe again spooked the doe and fawn. But rather than running ahead along the trail where it narrowed and squeezed through the trunks of two massive spruce trees, the deer cut into the timber to the right. Joe was pleased the deer had finally moved out of the way, but then he saw them reappear on the trail further up the slope.

Instinctively, he leaned back in the saddle and pulled back on the reins. He said, 'Hold it, Nate,' quietly over his shoulder.

Nate rode up alongside. 'Are you wondering if the packhorse and panniers are going to fit through that narrow chute?'

'No,' Joe said. 'I'm wondering why those deer went round in the trees instead of staying on the game trail.'

THEY APPROACHED THE TRAP from behind after tying off their horses in the trees. It was a brutal work of art, Joe thought. And if it weren't for the deer, he would have ridden right into it.

The brothers had cut down and trimmed a lodgepole pine about as thick as Joe's fist near the base. The base was wedged into the gap between two branches on the large spruce, then bowed back almost to the point of breaking before being tied off with wire. The wire was fed through a smooth groove round the tree trunk and stretched ankle-high across the trail. A foot-long sharpened stake was lashed to the tip of the lodgepole. If the wire was tripped, it would release the tension that held back the cocked arm and stake.

'Chest high for a rider,' Joe said, absently rubbing a spot just below his clavicle.

Nate found a stump in the timber and carried it towards the trap from behind. 'Stand back,' he said, and threw the stump with a grunt. It landed on the wire, which sent the lodgepole and stake slicing through the air with surprising speed and velocity.

While the pole and stake rocked back and forth, Joe said, 'This is more than a warning to stay away.'

'That it is,' Nate said, inspecting the cuts on the lodgepole where branches had been trimmed away. With his fingertip, he touched an amber bead of sap that oozed from one of the cuts. 'Fresh,' he said. 'The boys are expecting us.'

At that moment, far up the mountainside, was the harsh crackle of snapping branches. Joe and Nate locked eyes for a moment, then dived for the ground. They lay helplessly while a dislodged boulder the size of a small car smashed down the slope, levelling small trees and splintering big ones along its path. The boulder rolled end over end, coming within ten yards of where they were on the trail. Remarkably, the horses didn't snap their tethers and run away.

When the boulder finally stopped rolling and settled noisily below them, Joe stood up. '*Man . . .*' he whispered.

'They're real close,' Nate said. 'And they *know* we're right behind them.'

WHEN THEY RODE to the edge of the tree line, Joe and Nate paused on their horses before continuing up. The sun had sunk behind the western mountains an hour before. The trail they were on switchbacked up through a long expanse of treeless scree but dissolved into darkness near the summit.

'I can't see what's up there,' Joe whispered. 'But we'll be in the open.

This would be a great place to get ambushed.'

Nate said, 'If we can't see them, they can't see us, right?'

'I wish there was some other way to get over the top,' Joe said, trying not to ascribe powers to the Grim brothers that they didn't realistically possess.

'There isn't,' Nate said, nudging his horse on.

Joe had rarely felt as vulnerable, as much of a target, as he did riding up through the talus. He urged his horse on to keep him walking fast, hoping the jerky gait would make him less easy to hit if someone was aiming. There was nothing quiet about his ascent: his horse's lungs bellowed as they climbed, the gelding nickered from time to time to call to Nate's horse, and the gelding's steel shoes struck some of the shale rocks with discordant notes. By the time he made it to the summit, his horse was worn out and Joe had a slick of sweat between his skin and his clothing.

But no one fired, and nothing more happened.

He pushed the gelding on, over the top, so they'd no longer be in silhouette against the sky. Nate was soon with him, his own horse breathing hard as well. They tucked away in a stand of aspen.

In the shadows of the trees, Joe dismounted to let his horse get his breath back. Nate did the same. They stood in silence, holding the reins of their horses, eyeing the dark timber out in front of them, wondering where the Grim brothers were.

IT WAS APPROACHING MIDNIGHT when Joe's gelding stopped short. He recognised the horse's signals of fear or agitation: the low rumbling *whoof,* the whites of his eyes, the ears stiffly cocked forwards.

Nate whispered, 'What's wrong?'

Joe shook his head. 'Don't know. Something's spooked him.'

He spun his horse round, and when he looked up, he could see Nate grimacing, his face illuminated by a splash of starlight.

'Jeez,' Nate said. 'Look.'

Joe leaned forward and peered ahead on the trail, willing his eyes to see better in the dark. Something hung across the trail. He slipped his Maglite out of its holster and adjusted the beam on a moon-shaped human face—eyes open but without the gleam of life, a dried purple tongue hanging out of its mouth like a fat cigar.

Joe twisted the lens of his flashlight to increase the scope of the light. Three male bodies, two in black tactical clothing and one in camouflage, hung from ropes tied to a beam that crossed the trail. The bodies were hung by their necks, but they hadn't died from hanging. One of the men in black had a hole in his chest, one's skull was crushed in on the side, and the third had an arrow shaft sticking out of his throat. Joe recognised the style of the arrow.

He squelched the light of his flashlight and reached for the saddle horn to steady himself. 'Oh, God,' he said, fighting nausea.

Nate said, 'I think we found the boys from Michigan.'

Saturday, September 5

One by one, the glassy surfaces of the alpine cirques Joe and Nate rode past mirrored the stars and slice of moon. They'd cut down the bodies and stacked them on the side of the trail, then covered them with dead logs to try to prevent predators from feeding on them. Joe bookmarked the location in his GPS so he could later direct search teams to the exact place to recover the bodies. Dave Farkus had not been among the dead.

It was two in the morning when they rode by the dark opening where the cabin had been. Joe didn't so much see it as feel it—a creeping shiver that rolled from his stomach to his throat and made him rein to a stop and turn to his right in the saddle.

'Here,' he said. He nosed the gelding over, and the horse splashed through a shallow stream. When he reached the clearing where the cabin had been, he rode round it, puzzled. There was no sign of the burned cabin, just a tangled pile of deadfall.

Nate asked, 'Are you sure this is the right place?'

'It's got to be,' Joe said. He probed the deadfall with the beam of his flashlight. Sweeping the pool of light across the dead branches, he noted a small square of orange.

'Ah,' he said with relief, and dismounted. Joe tugged at branches and threw them away from the pile. He kicked away the last tangle to reveal a square foundation of bricks, which was where the woodstove had been.

'The Grim brothers carted away whatever was still here and covered the footprint of the cabin in fallen timber,' he said to Nate. 'No wonder Sheriff Baird and his men never found this.'

'I was starting to wonder myself,' Nate said with a grin. 'I was thinking maybe you made it all up.'

'Ha ha,' Joe said sourly.

JOE AND NATE sat on opposite ends of a fallen tree trunk at four in the morning, facing the slash pile that covered up the remains of the cabin, each with his own thoughts. Joe could hear Nate slowly crunching granola from a Ziploc bag on the other end of the log and their horses munching mountain grass. There was no more reassuring sound, Joe thought, than horses eating grass. Their *grum-grum* chewing sound was restful. If only everything else was, he thought.

That's when he clearly heard a branch snap deep in the timber. The sound came from the north, from somewhere up the wooded slope.

At the sound Joe rolled to his right, and he sensed Nate roll to his left. Joe had no doubt Nate was on his knees with the .454 Casull drawn by now. For his own part, he had the shotgun ready. He slowly jacked a shell into the chamber to keep the action as quiet as possible. He held his shotgun at the ready and felt his senses straining to determine if whoever had made the sound was now closer, further, or standing still.

Joe turned to his left to ask Nate if he could hear any more sounds, but Nate was gone. Joe squinted into the darkness, trying to find his friend. When he couldn't, Joe settled back on his haunches behind the fallen log, his shotgun muzzle pointed uphill.

There was another muffled snap, this one closer than the first. He estimated the sound to be coming from fifty feet away.

He raised the shotgun and lay the switched-off Maglite along the forward stock. His heart pounded in his chest, and he thought if it beat any harder everybody would be able to hear it. As he stared into the darkness of the trees, he saw a single small red dot six feet off the ground. It blinked out. Then he saw it again. The roaring of blood in his ears nearly drowned out the voice of the man who said, 'Joe, is that you?' Then, 'For God's sake, Joe, don't shoot me!'

Joe said, 'Farkus?' And then he heard the hollow sound of the heavy steel barrel of Nate's .454 smack hard into the side of Farkus's head, toppling him over.

'Don't kill him, Nate,' Joe said, getting to his feet. 'I know this guy. He's the local who owned one of the burned-up trucks back in the campground. The one who didn't fit into all of this.'

'Night-vision goggles,' Nate said. 'And unless I'm wrong, he's wearing body armour, too.'

Farkus moaned. Joe fixed his Maglite on him. The bright light through the lenses of the goggles must have burned his retinas, as Farkus winced and pulled them off.

'You didn't shoot,' Joe said to Nate, ignoring Farkus.

'No reason to,' Nate said. 'I watched him come down through the trees focused totally on you. He was watching you every second. I was behind a trunk, and he never even turned my way.'

Farkus croaked, 'Why'd you smack me?'

Nate squatted down next to Farkus. 'Because we've nearly been killed twice tonight by people who more than likely had night-vision gear. You're lucky I didn't blow your head off. Where did you get those goggles?'

'I took them off a dead guy,' Farkus said, sitting up. 'The vest, too.'

Said Nate, 'Who was the dead guy?'

'His name was Capellen. He was with the other guys from Michigan up here to find the Cline brothers. Capellen was killed first, and I took his stuff.'

Joe said, 'Start from the beginning, Dave. How did you get from the other side of the mountain to here?'

'They kidnapped me,' Farkus said. 'The men from Michigan, I mean. I drove up on them at my elk camp, and they took me along with them because I know the mountains. They were tracking those brothers, but the brothers ambushed us, and I was the only one left alive. Them brothers, they ain't human, I tell you. They ain't.'

Joe said, 'What are they if they aren't human?'

'Wendigos. Monsters. They can move through the trees like phantoms, and they can just appear wherever they want.'

'So how did you get away from them?' Nate asked with a smirk. 'Did you hold up a cross and just walk away?'

'I waited until they were gone,' Farkus said, 'and I managed to get untied. They've completely left the mountains. They ain't around no more. They had me tied up in a cave—I mean, a cabin.'

Nate slapped Farkus hard across his face.

'Why'd you do that?' Farkus protested.

Nate said, 'You're speaking gibberish. I *hate* gibberish. Nobody confuses a cabin with a cave. You'd better start telling us the truth about what's going on up here, or you won't see morning come.'

Joe nodded. 'Your story doesn't add up, Dave.' He had kept his flashlight on Farkus's face and noted how the man averted his eyes and blinked rapidly as he spoke—two signs of a lying witness. 'Somebody set a trap that could have killed us and later rolled a boulder down the mountain that could have taken us out. The brothers were seen this afternoon at the trail-head where they were in the process of burning your truck. No one else would match *that* description. Plus,' Joe said, lowering the beam of the flashlight to Farkus's hands in his lap, 'I don't see any marks on your wrists from rope or wire. Which says to me you weren't tied up at all. Now, I'm going to ask you some questions, and if I think you're lying, I'm going to get up and walk away and leave you with Mr Romanowski.' He nodded towards Nate. 'And whatever happens, happens. Got that?'

Farkus said, 'Yes.'

'Good. Let's start with the men from Michigan. We found three of them back on the trail. Who were they?'

'I told you. They were here to find the brothers and kill them.'

'Why?'

'They wouldn't explain it all to me outright,' Farkus said. 'But from what I could get, it had to do with something that happened back in Michigan. They were taking orders from this guy named McCue. He was at my elk camp with them, but—'

'McCue?' Joe broke in. 'Did I hear you right? Bobby McCue? Skinny guy? Older, kind of weary-looking?'

'That's him,' Farkus said, and continued. 'The guys I was with knew the brothers, or knew enough about them, anyway. I got the feeling they might have clashed at one time or other.'

'It was personal, then?' Nate said.

'Not really. I think they knew of the brothers, like I said. But it wasn't personal. They were hired and outfitted by someone with plenty of money.'

'Did you hear any names besides McCue?'

Farkus scrunched up his eyes and mouth. He said, 'McGinty. I think that was it. And Sugar.'

Joe felt a jolt. He said, 'Senator McKinty and Brent Shober?'

'Could be right,' Farkus said.

Nate's upper lip curled into a snarl. 'It's worse than we thought.'

Joe said, 'And all of you rode into a trap of some kind?'

'At the last cirque,' Farkus said, nodding. 'We rode down the trail to the water, and the lead guy rode through some rocks. He tripped a wire, and a spike mounted on a green tree took him out.'

'We're familiar with the trap,' Joe said. 'Go on.'

'The brothers were on us like ugly on an ape,' Farkus said. 'The horses blew up and started rearing and everybody got bucked off. The brothers finished off the wounded except for me.'

'Why'd they spare you?'

Farkus shook his head. 'I don't know, Joe. I just don't know.'

'So they took you to their cabin. Or was it a cave?'

'It was a cabin.'

'Why did you say "cave" earlier?'

'You might have noticed there's a big guy with a big gun right next to me. I was nervous and probably misspoke.'

'Ah,' Joe said, as if he was happy with the explanation. 'And then the brothers just left?'

'Yes. They packed up and left me to die. They are completely out of this county by now. Maybe even out of the state.'

'Were the brothers alone?'

'What do you mean?' When he asked, Farkus looked away and blinked.

'Was there a woman with them?' Joe asked softly.

'A woman?' Farkus said. 'Up here?'

'Terri Wade or Diane Shober. I'm sure you'll have heard of at least one of them.'

Farkus shook his head.

Joe said to Nate, 'We're done here,' and stood up. 'Should we dig a hole for the body or let the wolves scatter his bones?'

Nate said, 'I say we put his head on a pike. That kind of thing spooks Wendigos, I believe.'

Farkus looked from Nate to Joe, his mouth hanging open.

'I've got no use for liars,' Nate said.

Joe turned to say something to Nate, but his friend was gone. He was about to call after him but didn't. Nate's stride as he walked away contained purpose. And when Joe listened, he realised how utterly silent it had become in the forest. No sounds of night insects or squirrels or wildlife.

He quickly closed the gap with Farkus and shoved the muzzle of his shotgun into the man's chest. He whispered, 'They're here, aren't they?'

Farkus gave an unwitting tell by shooting a nervous glance into the trees to his left.

Joe said, 'They sent you down here to distract us and pin us to one place while they moved in,' Joe said.

Farkus looked at the shotgun barrel just below his chin. 'Hold it,' he stammered. 'You're law enforcement. You can't do this.'

Joe eased the safety off with a solid click.

'Don't do this to me, please. You can't do this . . .'

'Keep your voice down,' Joe hissed, shoving the muzzle hard into Farkus's neck.

From the shadows of the forest, Camish said, 'I'm real surprised you came back, game warden.'

And fifty feet to the right of Camish, Nate said, 'Guess what? I've got your brother.'

THE STANDOFF that occurred at four thirty-five on the western slope of the Sierra Madre transpired so quickly and with such epic and final weight that Joe Pickett found himself surprisingly calm. So calm, he calculated his odds. They weren't good. He knew the likelihood of his death was high and he wished he had called his wife on the satellite phone and said goodbye to her and his girls.

In this moment of clarity, Joe said, 'We all know the situation we've got here. Things can get western in a hurry. If they do, I'm betting on my man Nate here to tip the scales. But I think a better idea may be sitting down and hashing this out.'

After a beat, Camish said, 'You're one of these folks thinks everything can be solved by talking?'

Said Joe, 'No, I don't believe that. No one has ever accused me of excess talking. But I think something really bad will happen any second if we don't. I'm willing to sit down and discuss the possibility of more than two of us walking away from here.'

Camish said, 'Caleb, you OK?'

The response was a muffled groan.

Joe realised his initial shocked calm had slipped away and he was sweating freely from fear. He struggled to keep his words even, hoping Camish would give in.

'Tell you what,' Joe said. 'Let's meet at that fallen log a few feet from me. Camish can keep aiming at me. Nate can keep his gun at Caleb's head. I'll keep my shotgun on Farkus here. But when we get to the log we'll sit down. How does that sound?'

Camish said, 'Deal.'

CAMISH LOOKED EVEN THINNER than Joe remembered him. It had been a rough few days. The man's eyes seemed to have sunk deeper into hollows above his cheekbones, and the silver hairs in his beard made him look gaunt and wizened. Like a Wendigo, Joe thought.

Joe and Nate sat on one log, the Grim brothers on another. They faced each other. Caleb sat in pained silence. If anything, he looked more skeletal than his brother. A dirt-filthy bandage was taped to his lower jaw. He had an AR-15 with a scope across his lap. The weapon must have come from the Michigan boys, Joe thought.

In between them, they'd started a small fire. Farkus sat on a stump, positioned carefully equidistant from both logs.

Nate sat silently to Joe's left. He kept his .454 lying across his thighs with his hand on the grip and his finger on the trigger. Joe knew Nate was capable of raising the weapon and firing at both brothers in less than a second. Whether Nate could take them out before Caleb could fire at Joe and Nate was the question.

Joe said to Caleb, 'I see your tactical vest now. I guess you were wearing it when I shot you with my Glock. Now I know why you didn't go down.'

Caleb glared back at him, his eyes dark and piercing but his expression inscrutable.

'He can't talk,' Camish said. 'That shot to his lower jaw splintered his chinbone, and drove slivers of it into his talk box.'

Joe said, 'I fired blindly when I hit him in the face. Not that I wasn't trying to do damage. I would have been happy to have killed him given the circumstances.'

Camish nodded. 'The circumstances are different depending on where you stand, I guess,' he said.

Joe nodded. 'Maybe so. But what I know is you boys came after me and killed my horses.'

Camish made his eyes big, and there was a slight smile on his face. 'My version, game warden, is me and my brother were minding our own damned business and not bothering a soul when you rode up and wanted to collect a tax on behalf of the government, the tax being a licence to fish so we could eat. And when we didn't produce the licence, you threatened our liberty. We resisted you.'

Nate tipped his head towards Joe, but never took his eyes off Caleb. He said, 'Joe's kind of like that. It's his worst fault. He's damned stubborn.'

'My horses,' Joe said, glaring at Camish. 'They belonged to my wife. She loved them like only a woman can love horses. You two killed them and butchered them.'

'Better than letting them go to waste, eh, Caleb?' Camish said, as if it made all the sense in the world, Joe thought. 'Anyway,' Camish said, 'We didn't target your horses. They were collateral damage. We came after you so hard because there was something in your eyes when we met you: We knew you'd follow this stupid fishing-licence deal to the gates of hell. Otherwise, we'd just have let you ride away. We practically begged you to just ride out of there. But you wouldn't let it go. You said you'd march us into court. All for a stupid twenty-four-dollar licence.'

Joe said, 'Actually, you boys are out of state. It's ninety-four dollars for Michigan residents.'

Camish leaned back on his log and tipped his head back and laughed. Caleb snorted. Nate groaned.

Joe felt his neck get hot. He said, 'It's my job. I do my job.'

Camish finished his run of laughter, then cut it off. He leaned forwards on the log and thrust his face at Joe. 'That may be. But the things you set in motion . . .'

Joe stood up. He let the muzzle of the shotgun swing lazily past Camish, past Caleb, past Nate. He said, 'Tomorrow by this time, these mountains are going to be overrun. There will be hundreds of law-enforcement personnel. You boys assaulted a sheriff. You assaulted *me.* The people who'll be coming after you don't even know about those men you killed yet. You boys are done. Even if you figure out a way to hole up and not get caught tomorrow, this is only the beginning. You can't really think you can stay here? That you can set traps and hang dead men from cross-poles and the world will just stay away. What are you thinking?'

'You people,' Camish said, his eyes sliding off Nate and settling on Joe, 'You government people just keep coming. It's like you won't stop coming until you've got us all and you own everything we've got. It ain't right. It ain't American. All we want to do is be left alone. That's all. Hell, we know we make people nervous, me and Caleb. We know we look funny and act funny to some people. We know they judge us. They made my mom out into some kind of stupid hillbilly when they went after her.'

Joe studied Camish's face in the flickering firelight. Unlike Caleb's almost manic glare, Camish's attitude had softened from its initial ferocity.

'That's all,' Camish repeated. 'We thought you would leave us alone back in Michigan if we just paid our taxes and kept our mouths shut. Didn't we, Caleb?'

Caleb nodded and grunted.

Said Camish, 'When they tried to take our property the first time, we fought 'em off pretty good. We thought it was over, that there was just no damned chance in the United States of America that the government could take a man's land and give it to somebody just because they'd pay *more* taxes. But they was like you. They just kept coming. Those three things that are supposed to be our rights—life, liberty and the pursuit of happiness? Hell, the government's supposed to protect those things. Instead, they took our place from us and we lost our dad, our mom and our brother in the process.' He spoke in a flat, unsentimental way. 'We just wanted to find somewhere we could be left alone. Is that so much to ask?'

Nate said, 'No, it isn't.'

Joe sighed. 'No one can just walk away. Everyone has obligations.'

Camish said, 'You mean like paying taxes?'

'Yeah, I guess,' Joe said, slowly. 'Folks can't expect services and programmes without paying for them somehow.'

Camish said, 'Why the hell should we pay for things we don't want and don't get? Why should the government take our money and our property and give it to other people? What the hell kind of place has this become?'

Joe said, 'It's not that bad or that simple. This whole mountain range, for example. It's managed by the US Forest Service, a government agency. Taxes pay for that.'

'We do our part,' Camish said. 'We keep the riffraff out.'

Caleb snorted a laugh.

Joe said, 'You boys vandalised some vehicles and scared the hell out of some campers. Not to mention that elk you took.'

Joe saw a flash of anger in Camish's eyes as he said, 'We did that to keep people away. To *spook* 'em. We didn't want to have to hurt somebody or take things too far, so we laid down a marker: *Leave us alone.* It's our way of managing the place. We didn't disturb or hurt anything that was perfect. Fish, deer, elk—whatever. If anything, we helped cull the herd. That's management, too. It just ain't done by bureaucrats sitting on their asses. Like the Forest Service, you know? Or you guys.'

Joe could feel Nate's eyes on the side of his face, but he didn't look over. Instead, Joe said, 'Diane Shober. Tell me about her.'

'Yeah,' Camish said. 'I was expecting you might have recognised her that night. She thought so, too. I won't get too far into it, but Diane felt like she needed a refuge, too. So we offered her one.'

Joe said, 'I find that hard to believe.'

Camish said, 'Believe whatever the hell you want. But sometimes it's pretty damned nice to find a place where no one expects you to live up to a certain standard.'

'Her fiancé?' Joe said.

'Yeah, him. But especially Daddy,' Camish said. 'That man expected one whole hell of a lot. He lived his life through her, but she can't stand him. He's one of those parasites. He got rich taking other people's property and money. We'd tangled before. She knew we didn't like or respect the man. She knew we'd help her out.'

Joe nodded his head. 'You had a common enemy,' he said.

''Course we did,' Camish said. 'He's the developer who got our family property. Friend of a damned crooked Senator McKinty from Michigan and his no-good son.'

Joe sighed. He had no reason to disbelieve Camish.

Camish turned to Farkus. 'He's the one sent them Michigan boys after us, right, Dave?'

Farkus nodded, his eyes moving from Joe to Camish as if watching a tennis match.

Joe said, 'You mean the senator? Are you saying a US senator sent a private hit squad after you?'

'Naw,' Camish said. 'Diane's old man did that. They were supposed to take us out and take her back. And the way things work, I'd bet the senator and his son knew all about it, but nobody would ever be able to prove that.'

Joe thought, And when Shober heard about me, he tried to put me on the hunt for Diane, too, just for insurance.

'She stayed with you to rub her father's nose in it?' Joe said.

Caleb shrugged as if to say, Why not?

And Camish said, 'Why not?'

'So was it you who sent the postcard to Shober's mother?'

Camish sighed. 'That was a dumb idea. But Diane insisted. Like she made us agree to call her Terri Wade.'

'Is she OK now?' Joe asked.

Said Camish, as a slow smile built on his face, 'If you figure out how to get out of here alive, you can ask her yourself. She won't mind, I don't think, as long as you don't try to take her back with you. See, we got some caves up in the rimrocks. Indians used to live there, then outlaws. They're sweet caves.'

Joe looked over at Nate. His friend mouthed, 'We have to talk.' But because Joe knew what Nate wanted to talk about, he turned away.

Camish said, 'We ain't going back until things change. We want our property back, and we want to see that senator go to prison. We want to see Brent Shober tarred and feathered. And most of all, we want to be left alone. Simple as that. And we ain't going to argue about it, game warden. If you can promise us those things, we'll put down our guns and come down with you. Can you promise them?'

Joe said, 'I promise I'll try.'

Camish snorted. 'That's the way it is with you people. Good intentions are supposed to be the same as good works.'

Joe had no reply.

Camish said, 'Then it is what it is.'

OUT OF EARSHOT of the brothers, Nate said, 'This isn't what I signed up for.'

Joe said, 'I know it isn't.'

Nate had stood and backed slowly away from where the brothers and Dave Farkus sat. As he did, Caleb never took his eyes off him. Likewise, Nate didn't turn his back on Caleb, and he held the .454, muzzle down, near his side. Joe had stood and joined his friend. The eastern sky was rose-coloured. It was less than an hour before sunrise.

'We have a couple of options,' Nate said. 'We could get on our horses and ride away. Let the locals and the state boys and the Feds finish this. We're sort of signing the death warrants on these guys, but they know that and we won't have blood on our hands. And who knows, maybe they'll just fade into the timber if we leave.'

Joe said, 'I can't ride away. As long as they're up here, they'll keep breaking laws. More people will get hurt and die, and some of them will be innocent. If we leave, they won't stop.'

Nate said, 'Nope, they won't. But that doesn't have to be our problem. This isn't right, Joe. Let me put this as clearly as I can: we're on the wrong side.'

Joe winced.

'Maybe we can make a deal with them,' Nate said. 'If they agree to dismantle the traps and promise to lay low, we'll ride away.'

'I am what I am, Nate. I took an oath. I can't just ride away. Maybe you should go, Nate. I know how you feel, and I understand. You don't need to be any part of this. There'd be no hard feelings on my part if you rode away.'

Nate said, 'They'll kill you.'

'Maybe.'

'I'm sorry.'

JOE STEPPED FORWARD towards the logs, narrowing the distance between them. Caleb, Camish and Farkus watched him.

Joe said, 'Put down your weapons, get Diane Shober, and come with me. If we get to the trailhead before they get assembled and get their blood up, I promise you I'll do all I can to get you secured away so you've got a chance.'

Caleb and Camish looked at him without a change in their expressions. Farkus narrowed his eyes, again glancing between Joe and the brothers, trying to read what was going to happen.

Joe said, 'I'll tell the locals, the state and the Feds how you cooperated. I'll ask Governor Rulon to get involved—we're pretty close. Look, you've got a story to tell. There are a lot of folks out there who will support you.'

He waited.

Camish said, 'I reckon the only way we're going off this mountain now is feet first. And I don't think that's likely to happen.'

Even without turning round, Joe knew Nate was gone. Then, deep in the trees to the east, he heard Nate's horse whinny.

'TELL YOU WHAT,' Camish said, standing almost casually. 'Unlike your government, we believe in freedom and opportunity. We'll give you ten minutes to pack up and ride away. And if you ride on out of here, we won't follow you. I just hope we don't ever see you up here again.' He turned. 'Dave, you can go with him. No offence, but you're kind of useless. And if the game warden is correct, there will be a battle coming. You might get caught in the crossfire.'

Farkus hopped to his feet, nodding. 'OK,' he said. 'Thank you, Camish.'

Camish smirked and looked back to Joe. 'You shouldn't still be here,' he said.

Farkus had started to walk towards Joe but now he hesitated.

'Look,' Camish said, 'My brother and I are going to walk away and give you some space. Maybe then you'll think about what you're doing and take old Dave here and be gone. But if for some damned reason you want to force the issue, we'll meet you in that clearing over there.' He gestured towards a small meadow to the west. The morning sun was building behind the trees, ready to launch and flood the meadow with light. 'We'll finish it there, I guess,' Camish said, shaking his head.

He seemed almost sad, Joe thought.

As they backed away, Camish said, 'I think on some level you know we're right, game warden. But you sure are stubborn.'

'It doesn't have to be this way,' Joe said. 'It's your government too. You can work to change it.'

'Too late for that,' Camish said. 'This is Rampart Mountain. This is where we turn you people back or we quit trying.'

And they were gone.

Farkus looked from Joe towards where the brothers had melded into the trees. He said, 'Let's get out of here, Joe.'

Joe said, 'Go ahead.'

THE TEMPERATURE DROPPED fifteen degrees as the cold morning air started to move through the timber in anticipation of the sun. Joe felt a long shiver roll through his body. He stood to the side of his gelding, keeping the horse between himself and the meadow. The brothers couldn't be seen. Neither could Farkus, who'd dumped the panniers from the packhorse, mounted the animal bareback, and headed east in a hurry. He hadn't looked back.

Joe found the satellite phone, powered it up and punched in the numbers. He woke Marybeth up, and sleep clogged her voice for a moment.

Joe said, 'We found them.'

'Are you OK? Are you hurt?'

'Not yet. I'm going to try to bring them in,' he said. 'They don't want to come.'

'Oh, no. Oh, my. Please be careful.'

'I will.'

'Did you find Diane?'

'No, but I know where she is. She's OK, they say.'

'Thank God. Her mother will be so happy.'

'Yup. I'm not so sure about her dad, though.'

'Joe, there's something in your voice. Are you all right?'

'Sure,' he said.

Joe looked across the meadow as two yellow spears of sun shot through a break in the trees. Instantly, the clearing lightened. In the shadows of the pine-tree wall on the far side of the clearing, he could see Camish and Caleb. They were about fifty yards apart, about to enter the meadow. Caleb held the AR-15 across his chest. Camish worked the pump on Joe's old shotgun.

'I've got to go,' Joe said.

'Call me when you can,' Marybeth said.

'I want you to know how much I love you,' he said. 'I want you to know I think I'm doing the right thing for you and the girls.'

She was silent for a moment. Then he heard a sob.

'I'll call,' he said, and punched off. It felt like a lie.

He couldn't feel his feet or his legs, and his heartbeat whumped in his ears as he walked into the clearing with his shotgun. Camish and Caleb emerged from the trees. Joe guessed they were seventy-five yards away. Out of range for his shotgun or .40 Glock. He wondered when Caleb would simply raise the rifle and start firing.

Joe thought, They look silly, the Grim brothers, dressed in the same clothes, identical except for the bandage on Caleb's jaw. From another place and another era, and their ideas of the way things ought to be are old and out of date. They know, he thought, if they come down from this mountain they'll be eaten alive. The poor bastards.

He thought, This is their mountain. It's where they feel safe. It's the only place they feel free.

Camish said something, but Joe didn't quite catch it.

'What's that?' Joe called out.

'I said it's still not too late to leave,' Camish said. 'I admire your courage, but I question your judgment.'

Joe thought, Me too.

The brothers were within fifty yards.

Joe thought, Camish first. Shoot Camish first. He was the leader, the spokesman. Taking out Camish might stun Caleb for a split second—time for Joe to jack in another shell and fire.

Shoot, then run to the side, he thought. Make himself a moving target. Duck and roll. Come up firing. Run right at Caleb, confuse him. Caleb wouldn't expect Joe to come right at him.

Forty yards.

Joe remembered what Nate had told him: *It's about who can look up without any mist in their eyes, aim, and pull the trigger without thinking twice. It's about killing. It's always been that way.*

Thirty yards.

Not optimum for his shotgun, but close enough.

Without warning, he dropped to one knee, raised his weapon, and shot at Camish. Camish was hit with a spray of pellets, but he didn't fall. Joe caught a glimpse of Camish's puzzled face, dotted with fresh new holes. He was hurt, but the wounds weren't lethal. He seemed as surprised at what Joe had done as Joe did.

From the trees to Joe's left there was a deep boom and Caleb's throat exploded. A second shot blew his hat off, and it dropped heavily to the grass because it was weighted by the top of Caleb's skull. Caleb fell, dead before he hit the ground. Camish opened his mouth to call something but a third .454 round punctured the body armour over his heart and dropped him like a bag of rocks.

Joe rose unsteadily, his ears ringing from the gunshots. He was stunned by what had just happened and amazed by the fact that he wasn't hurt, that the brothers hadn't fired back.

From the trees, Nate walked out into the clearing, and the morning sun lit him up. He ejected three smoking, spent cartridges from the cylinder and replaced them with fresh rounds. He said, 'That may have been the worst thing we've ever done, Joe.'

Joe dropped his shotgun, turned away, bent over with his hands on his knees and threw up in the dew-sparkled grass.

THE SHARP SMELL of gunpowder held in place a few feet above the meadow. Gradually, it dissipated. The odour of spilt blood, however, got stronger as it flowed from the bodies of Caleb and Camish.

Nate found a fallen log at the edge of the timber and sat down on it, his .454 held loosely in his fist, his head down as if studying the grass between his boots. Joe walked aimlessly towards the timber from where the brothers had emerged. He stopped near to where Caleb had come out, noting a dull, unnatural glint on the edge of a shadow pool in the trees. Stepping closer, he took a deep breath. The glint came from a substantial pile of loose rifle cartridges in the pine needles, and something dark and square. He was puzzled.

Joe dropped and counted thirty .223 cartridges on the ground. A lot, he thought. In fact, Joe thought with a growing sense of dark unease, it was the entire quantity of a combat AR-15 magazine.

Short of breath, Joe lurched from tree to tree clutching a rifle bullet and the journal he recognised from the first time he'd encountered Caleb at the lake. It didn't take long to find the place a few yards away where Camish had unloaded his shotgun shells. Four of them, bright with their red plastic sleeves, lay in a single pile.

He opened the journal and thumbed through it as his eyes swam. The first three-quarters of the book were devoted to daily journal entries. The last quarter appeared to be an anti-government screed. Joe thought, Their manifesto. Hundreds of words that could be summed up as: Don't Tread on Me.

The last of Caleb's entries was a spidery scrawl that read, '*Please take good care of Diane. It ain't her fault. She done nothing wrong. She just wanted to be free of you people.*'

Nate had entered the trees with his gun drawn. Joe watched him as his eyes moved from the .223 bullets to the shotgun shells, and his upper lip curled into a frightening grimace.

Joe said, 'No wonder they didn't shoot. They unloaded before they walked out there.'

'Oh, man,' Nate whispered. 'It was bad before. It just got worse.'

JOE CALLED MARYBETH. She picked it up on the first ring. He said, 'I'm not hurt. Nate's not hurt. We're done here.'

She said, 'Joe, what's wrong?'

He took in a long breath of cool mountain air that tasted like pine, and he looked out on the meadow as the sun lit up the grass so green it hurt his eyes. 'I don't even know where to start.'

AT MID-MORNING, Joe could smell food cooking from above in the rimrocks. The aroma wafted down through the sparse lodgepole copse. He clucked at his gelding and led the animal up towards the source of the aroma.

They'd lifted the bodies of Caleb and Camish facedown over the saddles of their riding horses and lashed them to the saddles as if they were packing out game animals. Joe and Nate wordlessly tied lifeless hands and feet together under the bellies of their mounts to keep the bodies from sliding off.

Before they guided the horses and the bodies out of the meadow up towards the rimrocks, Joe had called dispatch on his satellite phone. The dispatcher offered to route him through to Sheriff Baird or Special Agent Chuck Coon of the FBI, who were both in place and in charge at the command centre that had been established at the trailhead.

Joe said, 'No need. I don't want to talk to either of them right now. Just pass on the word that the Grim brothers—or the Clines, or whatever the hell their real names are—are dead. There is no more threat. Tell them they can stand down. We'll be bringing the bodies out by nightfall.'

The dispatcher said, 'My goodness. They're going to want to talk directly with you.'

Said Joe, 'I'm not in the mood,' and powered down the phone so they couldn't call him back.

WHEN THEY CLEARED the trees, Joe spotted Diane Shober. She was a hundred yards above them, peering down out of a vertical crack in the rimrock wall. When she saw them—and what they had strapped to their horses—her hand went to her mouth and he heard her cry out.

Joe thought that if he hadn't been told specifically by Farkus where the cave was located, he never would have found it.

'See her?' Joe said over his shoulder to Nate.

'Yes.'

She slowly shook her head from side to side. The sun gleamed off the tears streaming down her face.

Joe called, 'We're here to take you home.'

The woman drew back a few feet into the shadow of the opening. After a few moments, she said, 'I *am* home.'

He said, 'Diane, the reason we're here is because your mom asked me to come. She misses you.'

Joe wanted to persuade, to cajole, and not to threaten in any way. He couldn't bear the thought of forcing another result like what had happened with the brothers.

'We didn't want to hurt them,' he said. 'We did everything we could to talk them into coming down with us. Caleb and Camish forced the issue. In a way, they committed suicide.'

Shober nodded. It wasn't news to her. Obviously, Joe thought, the brothers had indicated to her how things were likely to end if the first wave—Joe and Nate—wasn't turned back by the traps.

Behind Joe, the packhorse nickered. Out of sight, a horse called back, then another. The brothers had kept the horses ridden by the Michigan men and had picketed them up in the trees.

'If it's OK with you,' Joe said, 'we'll come on up there and get those horses and saddle them up for you. You can ride down with us.'

Diane Shober stepped out of the cave opening. Her dark hair was tied into a ponytail. Her clothing was more form-fitting than it had been before, and she looked younger than she had as Terri Wade.

She said, 'What if I don't come with you?'

Said Joe, 'Let's not find out. This mountain will be crawling with law enforcement within the hour. We know where you are, and they'll find you. They might not be as sympathetic as us.'

'Sympathetic?' Diane said, laughing bitterly. 'Like you were sympathetic with Camish and Caleb there?'

Joe's voice held when he said, 'They gave us no choice. You'll have to believe me when I tell you that. They must have decided they'd rather die up here than take their chances in court.'

Diane nodded. 'Yes,' she said, 'that's what they told me they might have to do.'

'Then come with us,' Nate said. 'We'll do our best to protect you.'

Again, Diane laughed. It was a high, plaintive laugh. 'You think you can protect me, do you? From the government? From the press? From my father and the kind of people he works with?'

Nate said, 'I know people who could help you. You aren't the only one who's gone underground.'

Diane studied Nate for a long time, as if trying to make up her mind about something. Finally, she withdrew back into the cave. Joe waited without moving for five minutes, then turned to look at Nate. Nate looked back at him as if he were thinking the same thing.

'Damn,' Joe said, and quickly tied his horse to a stump. Nate did the same. They ran up the slope, breathing hard.

Joe threw himself through the opening. The sudden darkness made him blink. It took a moment for his eyes to begin to adjust. He and Nate stood in the entrance of a surprisingly large cavern. There were beds, a stove, hand-made tables and chairs, fabric and hides on the interior walls. The food odours made it surprisingly comfortable. It reminded Joe of where Nate hid out, and he wondered how many others there were in the country in hiding. How many people had gone 'underground', as Nate said?

Diane Shober looked up from where she was packing items into a large duffle bag. 'What did you think—I wasn't coming out?'

AS THEY RODE down the mountain, Joe said to Diane, 'I'm glad you're coming down. I'll be eternally grateful you saved my life, but this isn't any way to live.'

Her mouth was tight, and she stared straight ahead. When she talked, her lips hardly moved. 'It's crude and lonely, I agree. But it's my choice. There's no one here to tell me what to do or how to think. The trade-off is worth it.'

Nate nodded, said, 'Did you know the brothers were up here before you went on your run?'

She took a minute, then said, 'Yeah. We'd been in touch. I felt really awful for all the people who donated their time to come looking for me. I really did. But yes, I was in communication with the brothers. After all, we had a common enemy.'

'Your father?' Nate said.

'Yeah,' she said, then asked, 'Will my mom be down there?'

'I'm not sure.'

She hesitated, asked, 'My dad?'

'It's possible,' Joe said. 'But we're in a pretty remote location. It would be hard for them to get here so fast.'

'If he tries to talk to me, I might have to kill him,' she said, tears welling in her eyes.

APPROACHING THE TRAILHEAD, Joe got glimpses of what was below. As he'd predicted, it was a small city. Dozens of vehicles, tents, trailers. Satellite trucks from cable-news outlets.

Nate walked up abreast and handed the reins of his gelding to Joe. 'Time for me to go,' he said.

Joe nodded.

'I'm taking her with me,' Nate said, gesturing towards Diane. 'I know people who will put her up. They'll treat her well.'

Joe opened his mouth to object.

'I know what you're thinking,' Nate said. 'You're thinking there's no way I can take the victim with me before she's interviewed. That it wouldn't be procedure. And you're right, it wouldn't. But Joe, I shoved everything I believed in to the side to help you out up there. Now it's your turn to help me.'

Joe studied his saddle horn. He said, 'You promise me she'll be OK? I have these visions of the underground that aren't so good.'

Nate smiled. 'The underground isn't underground at all. It's not about people in caves, really. They're all around us, Joe. Real people, good people, are the underground. Believe me, Diane will be fine.'

'I understand.'

Nate reached out and touched Joe on the back of his hand. Then he gave him the reins to Caleb's horse, so Joe now had both brothers behind him. Nate said, 'You know where to find me.'

Joe nodded but didn't say anything.

The last glance he got of Diane as she followed Nate into the timber was when she turned in her saddle and waved. There was something sad in the gesture. Thanking him for letting them go. He waved back.

Joe tied the ropes for Caleb's and Camish's horses together into a loose knot and wrapped them round his saddle horn. He smiled to himself in a bitter way and clucked his tongue. All the animals responded and started stepping down the mountain trail. No doubt, Joe thought, they sensed some kind of conclusion when they reached the trailhead. If only he felt the same, he thought . . .

BEFORE THE RIDERS from the trailhead could reach him—dozens streamed up the trail—Joe reached back and got his satellite phone and called the governor's direct line.

Rulon's chief of staff, Carson, came to the phone.

'The governor's in an emergency meeting,' Carson said. 'He asked me to talk with you. We understand you killed those brothers and rescued Diane Shober. That's outstanding.'

Joe grunted.

'And we've got good news of our own,' Carson said. 'Senator McKinty of Michigan announced this morning he's not running for re-election. We don't have a reason. He's been our biggest impediment for years now. The governor's ecstatic.'

'Interesting,' Joe said.

'Look, you need to be available this evening. The governor's planning a press conference about the rescue, and he wants you there. He's going to make you a hero, Joe.'

'Nope,' Joe said.

Carson coughed, 'But you *are* a hero. We want the state to know. We want the *country* to know.'

As Carson talked, Joe glanced over to make sure there was no sign of Nate. They were gone. He didn't know if he'd ever see Diane again and wondered where Nate would take her. Finally he said, 'They aren't with me.'

After a long pause, Carson said, 'Who isn't with you?'

'Diane Shober. I let her go.'

Carson stammered, 'I'm not sure what to say. The governor is going to be very disappointed in you, Joe. Very disappointed.'

Joe shrugged and said, 'He's not the only one.'

He rode down the trail to meet the throng of law-enforcement personnel, media and hangers-on who waited for him. At the side of the crowd he saw Brent and Jenna Shober. They looked anxious.

He turned in the saddle to make sure the bodies of the brothers were still tightly bound to the packhorses.

He thought, They're under control, at last. McKinty, Brent Shober and Bobby McCue would be pleased.

The sun doused as massive black thunderheads rolled across the sky. Storm coming.

c. j. box

In Saratoga, in his native Wyoming, Charles James Box (known to his friends as 'Chuck') is very much in demand in local circles now that one of his books, *Blue Heaven*, is about to get the Hollywood treatment. Even before that, he was a local celebrity, with neighbours and friends wanting him to personally sign their copies of the latest Joe Pickett adventure.

So how did this third generation Wyomingite become a literary star? Box began his writing career in journalism, winning his first job on a local paper, the *Saratoga Sun*, after an extraordinary interview with the newspaper's publisher that he still remembers well. It took place, very sensibly, on a fishing boat. 'Four, five hours we floated and fished and drank beer. By the end of it, I would have paid him for the job!'

During his working career, C. J. Box also did time as a ranch hand, a surveyor and a fishing guide—all of which entailed working out of doors in the kind of scenery that he lovingly describes in his books. Nowadays, he's fortunate enough to be able to forget the day job, and he dedicates himself full-time to the novel-writing. He happily fills his free hours with fishing, mostly on his property by the Encampment River—one of the best stretches of fly-fishing water in Wyoming and an angler's dream come true. 'There are no dams. It's all natural. From the Colorado state line to Saratoga, a survey of three hundred miles of river found three to four thousand catchable fish.'

The success of his books has meant, Box says, that he can generally do 'a lot more stuff that I've always wanted to do'. He can fish just about anywhere in Wyoming, for example, because when local people meet their favourite author they often ask, 'Want to come to my ranch and fish?' 'I love that,' says C. J. And he can say in all honesty that he's hunted, fished, hiked, ridden or skied in most parts of the 'Mountain West', an area he works to protect and promote through a tourism site that he runs with his wife, Laurie.

Box has said, at interview, that the settings of his books, from the Bighorn Mountains to Yellowstone National Park, are as important to him as characters, each carefully distinguished by its own particular weather patterns, landscape features and local culture. And whichever state he chooses, he engages with the things that matter to the locals. 'I always start with an issue, a topic that's in the news. I think it's very important that every book be about something, besides who did it, so that the reader learns . . . perhaps finds out both sides of an issue that they may have heard about.'

Nowhere to Run is the tenth Joe Pickett adventure (the series kicked off in 2001 with the award-winning *Open Season*), and it touches on the regulation of hunting licences, raising the question of how much control central government should have over wilderness areas. After all, the wilderness belongs to everyone. In the book, Joe Pickett runs into twin brothers who feel so strongly that the warden has no place in their world that they turn violently against him. '*Nowhere to Run* is the first one of my books that's actually based on real events,' C. J. explains. 'The brothers are modelled on a real set of brothers who were found in the mountains in Wyoming a few years ago by a game warden. They threatened him . . . And the strange thing about it is that those brothers disappeared off the face of the earth and no one has ever found them since.'

Joe Pickett's family life is also an integral and continuing element in all the books in the series. Mild-mannered Joe has been called the antithesis of the modern thriller hero, but Box sees it differently. 'Part of the appeal is that he's portrayed as a real human being. He works hard, doesn't get well paid, makes mistakes and frets about his family. I think people empathise with Joe.'

So, now that Hollywood has come calling, does C. J. believe that the writing may take over his entire life? 'Neh,' comes the response. 'I'd rather be a fly-fisherman.'

Wyoming

Wyoming's towering mountains and vast plains—home to C. J. Box—provide grazing lands for sheep and cattle, rich mineral deposits and spectacular scenery. Today, a majority of the state's revenues comes from tourism. Millions of visitors flock to Wyoming's national parks and monuments, with key attractions being Yellowstone National Park, Grand Teton National Park and Devil's Tower National Monument.

SAFE HAVEN

Nicholas Sparks

Love hurts. There is nothing so painful as heartbreak. But in order to learn to love again you have to learn to trust again. Because of all that's happened—all that she's fled from—Katie is afraid to form new relationships. Eventually, though, she realises that she must make a choice between a life of transient safety and one of riskier rewards . . . and that in the darkest hour, love is the only true safe haven.

1

As Katie wound her way among the tables, a breeze from the Atlantic rippled through her hair. Carrying three plates in her left hand and another in her right, she wore jeans and a T-shirt that read *Ivan's: Try Our Fish Just for the Halibut*. She brought the plates to four men wearing polo shirts; the one closest to her caught her eye and smiled. Though he tried to act as though he was just a friendly guy, she knew he was watching her as she walked away. Melody had mentioned the men had come from Wilmington and were scouting locations for a movie.

After retrieving a pitcher of sweet tea, she refilled their glasses before returning to the waitress station. She stole a glance at the view. It was late April, the temperature hovering just around perfect, and blue skies stretched to the horizon. Beyond her, the Intracoastal Waterway was calm despite the breeze and seemed to mirror the colour of the sky. A dozen seagulls perched on the railing, waiting to dart beneath the tables if someone dropped a scrap of food.

Ivan Smith, the owner, hated them. He'd already patrolled the railing twice wielding a plunger, trying to scare them off. Melody had leaned towards Katie and confessed that she was more worried about where the plunger had been than she was about the seagulls.

Katie started another pot of sweet tea, wiping down the station. A moment later, she felt someone tap her on the shoulder. She turned to see Ivan's daughter, Eileen. A pretty, pony-tailed nineteen-year-old, she was working part time as the restaurant hostess.

'Katie—can you take another table?'

Katie scanned her tables. 'Sure.'

Katie had been working at the restaurant since early March. Ivan had hired her on a cold, sunny afternoon when the sky was the colour of robins' eggs. When he'd said she could start work the following Monday, it took everything she had not to cry in front of him. She'd waited until she was walking home before breaking down. At the time, she was broke and hadn't eaten in two days.

She refilled waters and sweet teas, and walked back to the kitchen. Ricky, one of the cooks, winked at her as he always did. He'd asked her out, but she'd told him she didn't want to date anyone at the restaurant.

'Can I drive you home later?' Ricky asked. He was blond and lanky, perhaps a year or two younger than her, and still lived with his parents. He offered to drive her at least twice a week.

'Thank you, no. I don't live that far. Walking's good for me.'

Ricky located one of her orders. She carried the order back to her section and dropped it off at a table.

Ivan's was a local institution, a restaurant that had been in business for thirty years. She'd come to recognise the regulars, and as she crossed the restaurant her eyes travelled to the people she hadn't seen before. Couples flirting, other couples ignoring each other. Families. No one seemed out of place and no one had come asking for her, but there were still times when her hands began to shake.

Her short hair was chestnut brown; she'd been dyeing it in the kitchen sink of the tiny cottage she rented. After paying the rent, there wasn't much money left. Ivan's was a good job, but the food was inexpensive, which meant the tips weren't great. On her diet of rice and beans, pasta and oatmeal, she'd lost weight in the past four months. She could feel her ribs, and until a few weeks ago, she'd had dark circles under her eyes that she thought would never go away.

'I think those guys are checking you out,' Melody said, nodding towards the table with the four men from the movie studio. 'Especially the brown-haired one. The cute one.'

'Oh,' Katie said. Anything she said to Melody was sure to get passed around, so Katie usually said very little to her.

'What? You don't think he's cute?'

'I didn't really notice.'

'How can you not notice if a guy is cute?' Melody stared at her in disbelief.

'I don't know,' Katie answered.

Like Ricky, Melody was a couple of years younger than Katie, maybe twenty-five. An auburn-haired minx, she'd grown up in Southport, which she described as being a paradise for children, families, and the elderly, but the most dismal place on earth for single people. She seemed to know everything about everybody.

'I heard Ricky asked you out,' she said, 'but you said no.'

'I don't like to date people at work,' Katie said. 'I had a bad experience once and I've kind of made it a rule not to do it again.'

Melody rolled her eyes before hurrying off to one of her tables. Katie cleared empty plates. She kept busy, trying to be efficient and invisible.

Katie worked both the lunch and dinner shift. As day faded into night, she loved watching the sky turn orange and yellow. Abby and Big Dave replaced Melody and Ricky in the evening. Abby was a high school senior who giggled a lot, and Big Dave had been cooking dinners at Ivan's for nearly twenty years.

The dinner rush lasted until nine. When it began to clear out, Katie cleaned and closed up the wait station. She helped the busboys carry plates to the dishwasher while her final tables finished up. At one of them was a young couple and she'd seen the rings on their fingers as they held hands. They were attractive and happy, and she felt a sense of déjà vu. She had been like them once, a long time ago, for just a moment. Or so she thought, because she learned the moment was only an illusion. Katie turned away from the blissful couple, wishing that she could erase her memories forever.

THE NEXT morning, Katie stepped onto the porch with a cup of coffee, the floorboards creaking beneath her bare feet, and leaned against the railing. She savoured the aroma as she took a sip.

She liked it here. Southport was different from Boston or Philadelphia or Atlantic City, with their traffic and smells and people rushing along the sidewalks. The cottage wasn't much, but it was hers and out of the way and that was enough. It was one of two identical structures located at the end of a gravel road, former hunting cabins nestled at the edge of a forest that stretched to the coast. The living-room and kitchen were small, but the cottage was furnished, including rockers on the front porch, and the rent was a bargain. The place was dusty from years of neglect, but the landlord offered to buy the supplies if Katie was willing to spruce it up. She'd spent much of her free time doing exactly that. She'd painted the kitchen a cheery yellow, and put glossy white paint on the cabinets. Her bedroom was now a light blue, the living room was beige, and last week, she'd put a new slipcover on the couch, which made it look practically new.

With most of the work now behind her, she liked to sit on the front porch and read books from the library. She didn't have a television, a cellphone, or a car. She was twenty-seven, a former long-haired blonde with no real friends. She'd moved here with almost nothing, and months later she still had little. She saved half of her tips and every night she folded the money into a coffee tin she kept hidden beneath the porch. She kept that money for emergencies. The knowledge that it was there made her breathe easier because the past might return at any time. It prowled the world searching for her, and she knew it was growing angrier every day.

'Good morning,' a voice called out, disrupting her thoughts. 'You must be Katie.'

Katie turned. On the sagging porch of the cottage next door, she saw a woman with unruly brown hair, waving at her. A pair of sunglasses nested in tangled curls on her head. She looked to be in her mid-thirties and wore jeans and a shirt. She was holding a small rug and she seemed to be debating whether or not to shake it before finally tossing it aside and starting towards Katie's.

'Irv Benson told me we'd be neighbours.'

The landlord, Katie thought. 'I didn't realise anyone was moving in.'

'I don't think he did, either. He about fell out of his chair when I said I'd take the place.' By then, she'd reached Katie's porch and she held out her hand. 'My friends call me Jo,' she said.

'Hi,' Katie said, taking it. 'When did you move in?'

'Yesterday afternoon. And then, joy of joys, I pretty much spent all night sneezing. You wouldn't believe the dust in there.'

Katie nodded toward the door. 'My place was the same way.'

'It doesn't look like it. Sorry, I couldn't help sneaking a glance through your windows. Your place is bright and cheery.'

'Mr. Benson let me paint.'

'As long as Mr. Benson doesn't have to do it, I'll bet he lets me paint, too.' She gave a wry grin. 'How long have you lived here?'

Katie crossed her arms. 'A couple of months.'

'I'm not sure I can make it that long. If I keep sneezing like I did last night, my head will probably fall off before then.' She reached for her sunglasses and began wiping the lenses with her shirt. 'Do you like Southport? It's a different world, don't you think?'

'What do you mean?'

'You don't sound like you're from around here. I'd guess somewhere up north?'

After a moment, Katie nodded.

'That's what I thought. Southport takes awhile to get used to. I mean, I've always loved it. I grew up here, went away, and ended up coming back. The oldest story in the book, right?'

Katie smiled and sipped her coffee. Then she remembered her manners. 'Would you like a cup of coffee? I just brewed a pot.'

'I'd *love* a cup of coffee,' Jo said.

'Come on.' Katie waved her in.

After crossing the kitchen, Katie pulled a cup from the cupboard, filled it, and handed it to Jo. 'Sorry, I don't have cream or sugar.'

'Not necessary,' Jo said, taking the cup. She blew on the coffee before taking a sip. 'OK, it's official,' she said. 'As of now, you're my best friend in the entire world. This is soooo good.'

'You're welcome,' she said.

'So Benson said you work at Ivan's?'

'I'm a waitress.'

'Is Big Dave still working there?' When Katie nodded, Jo went on. 'He's been there since before I was in high school.'

'How about Melody? Is she still talking about how cute the customers are?'

'Every shift.'

'And Ricky? Is he still hitting on new waitresses?'

When Katie nodded again, Jo laughed. 'That place never changes.'

'Did you work there?'

'No, but it's a small town. Besides, the longer you live here, the more you'll understand that there are no such things as secrets in this place. Everyone knows everyone's business, and some people, like let's say . . . Melody . . . have raised gossip to an art form. It used to drive me crazy.'

'But you came back.'

Jo shrugged. 'Yeah, well. What can I say? Maybe I like the crazy.' She took another sip of coffee. 'So what brought you to Southport? Do you have any family around here?'

'No,' Katie said. 'Just me.'

'So you just . . . moved here?'

'Yes.'

'Why on earth would you do that?'

Katie didn't answer. They were the same questions that Ivan and Melody and Ricky had asked. She was never quite sure what to say, other than to state the truth.

'I just wanted a place where I could start over.'

Jo took another sip of coffee, mulling over her answer, but, surprising Katie, she asked no follow-up questions. Instead, she simply nodded.

'Makes sense to me. Sometimes starting over is exactly what a person needs. And I think it's admirable. A lot of people don't have the courage it takes to do something like that.'

'You think so?'

'I know so,' she said. 'So, what's on your agenda today? While I'm whining and unpacking and cleaning until my hands are raw.'

'I have to work later. But other than that, not much. I need to run to the store and pick up some things.'

'Are you going to visit Fisher's or head into town?'

'I'm just going to Fisher's,' she said.

'Have you met the owner there? The guy with grey hair?'

Katie nodded. 'Once or twice.'

Jo finished her coffee and put the cup in the sink before sighing. 'All right,' she said, sounding unenthusiastic. 'Enough procrastinating. If I don't start, I'm never going to finish. Wish me luck.'

'Good luck.'

Jo gave a little wave. 'It was nice meeting you, Katie.'

FROM HER kitchen window, Katie saw Jo shaking the rug she'd set aside earlier. She seemed friendly enough, but Katie wasn't sure whether she was ready to have a neighbour. Then again, she had to admit she'd enjoyed chatting with Jo. For some reason, she felt that there was more to Jo than met the eye, something . . . trustworthy.

She washed out the coffee cups then put them back into the cupboard. The act was so familiar—putting two cups away after coffee in the morning—and for an instant, she felt engulfed by the life she'd left behind. Her hands began to tremble, and she took a few deep breaths until they stilled. Two months ago, she wouldn't have been able to do that. While she was glad that these bouts of anxiety no longer overwhelmed her, it also meant she was getting comfortable here, and that scared her. Being comfortable meant she might lower her guard, and she could never let that happen.

Even so, she was grateful to have ended up in Southport. It was a small historic town of a few thousand people, located at the mouth of the Cape Fear River. It was a place with sidewalks and shade trees and flowers and Spanish moss. She had watched kids riding their bikes and playing in the streets, and had marveled at the number of churches. This place felt *safe*.

Katie slipped on her only pair of shoes, a pair of beat-up Converse sneakers. The chest of drawers stood largely empty and there was almost no food in the kitchen, but as she stepped out into the sunshine and headed towards the store, she thought to herself, *This is home*. She knew she hadn't been happier in years.

HIS HAIR had turned grey when he was in his twenties, prompting some good-natured ribbing from his friends. His two older brothers had been spared. Neither his mom nor his dad could explain it. Alex Wheatley was an anomaly on both sides of the family.

Strangely, it hadn't bothered him. In the army, he sometimes suspected that it had aided in his advancement. He'd been with Criminal Investigation Division, or CID, stationed in Germany and Georgia, and had spent ten years investigating military crimes. He'd been promoted regularly, finally retiring as a major at thirty-two.

After punching his ticket and ending his career with the military, he moved to Southport, his wife's home town. He was newly married with his first child on the way, and though his immediate thought was that he would apply for a job in law enforcement, his father-in-law had offered to sell him the family business.

It was an old-fashioned country store, with white clapboard siding, blue shutters, and a bench out front. The living quarters were upstairs. His father-in-law had started the business before Carly was born, stocking whatever people happened to need. Five or six aisles offered groceries and toiletries, refrigerated cabinets overflowed with soda, water, beer and wine. There was also assorted fishing gear, fresh bait, and a grill manned by Roger Thompson, who'd once worked on Wall Street and had moved to Southport in search of a simpler life. The grill offered burgers, sandwiches, and hot dogs as well as a place to sit. There were DVDs for rent, rain jackets and umbrellas, and a small offering of bestselling and classic novels. Alex had three gasoline pumps, and another pump on the dock for any boats that needed to fill up. Rows of dill pickles, peanuts, and baskets of fresh vegetables sat near the counter.

Never in his life had Alex imagined doing something like this, but it had been a good decision, if only because it allowed him to keep an eye on the kids. Josh was in school, but Kristen wouldn't start until the fall, and she spent her days with him in the store. He'd set up a play area behind the register, where his bright and talkative daughter seemed most happy. Though only five, she knew how to work the register and make change. Alex always enjoyed the expressions on strangers' faces when she started to ring them up.

Alex had to admit that taking care of kids and the store took all the energy he had. Sometimes, he felt as though he could barely keep up—dropping Josh off at school, ordering from his suppliers, and serving the customers, all while keeping Kristen entertained. Add in making dinner and cleaning the house, and it was all he could do to keep his head above water.

After the kids went to bed, he spent the rest of his evenings alone. Though he knew most everyone in town, he had few real friends. The couples that he and Carly sometimes visited for barbecues or dinners had slowly drifted away. Part of that was his own fault—working at the store and raising his kids took most of his time—but sometimes he got the sense that he made them uncomfortable, as if reminding them that life was unpredictable and scary.

It was a wearying and sometimes isolating lifestyle, but he remained focused on Josh and Kristen. Early on, all of them had seen a counsellor; the kids had drawn pictures and talked about their feelings. It hadn't seemed to help as much as he'd hoped it would. Their nightmares continued for almost a year. Once in a while, when he coloured with Kristen or fished with Josh, they'd grow quiet and he knew they were missing their mom. Kristen sometimes said as much, in a babyish, trembling voice while tears ran down her cheeks. When that happened, he was sure he could hear his heart breaking, because he knew there was nothing he could do or say to make things any better.

The counsellor had assured him that kids were resilient as long as they knew they were loved. Time proved the counsellor right, but now Alex faced another form of loss. The kids were getting better, he knew, because their memories of their mom were fading. They'd been so young when they'd lost her—four and three—and it meant that the day would come when their mother would become more an idea than a person to them.

He thought of Carly often, and he missed the companionship and the friendship that had been the bedrock of their marriage. And when he was honest with himself, he knew he wanted those things again. He was lonely, even though it bothered him to admit it. For months after they lost her, he couldn't imagine ever being in another relationship. But he knew somehow that he was finally beginning to heal. That didn't mean, of course, that he was ready to rush headlong into the single life. If it happened, it happened.

Still . . . there was one possibility, he supposed. A woman interested him, though he knew almost nothing about her. She'd been coming to the store since early March. The first time he'd seen her, she was pale and thin. She kept her head down as she walked toward the grocery aisles, as if trying to remain unseen. Unfortunately for her, it wasn't working. She was too attractive to go unnoticed. She was in her late twenties, he guessed, with brown hair cut above her shoulder. She wore no makeup and her high cheekbones and wide-set eyes gave her an elegant if slightly fragile appearance.

At the register, he realised that up close she was even prettier than she'd been from a distance. Her eyes were a greenish-hazel colour and flecked with gold, and her brief smile vanished as quickly as it had come. On the counter, she placed staples: coffee, rice, oatmeal, pasta, peanut butter, and toiletries. He sensed that conversation would make her uncomfortable so he began to ring her up in silence. As he did, he heard her voice for the first time.

'Do you have any dry beans?' she asked.

'I'm sorry,' he'd answered. 'I don't keep those in stock. I'd be happy to stock them, I just need to know what kind you want.'

'I don't want to bother you.' Her voice barely registered above a whisper. She paid him in small bills, and after taking the bag, she left the store. Surprising him, she kept walking out of the lot, and he realised she hadn't driven, which only added to his curiosity.

The following week, there were dry beans in the store. He'd stocked three types: pinto, kidney, and lima, and the next time she came in, he made a point of mentioning that they could be found near the rice. Bringing all three to the register, she'd asked if he had an onion. He pointed to a small bag he kept in a bushel basket, but she'd shaken her head. 'I only need one,' she murmured. Her hands shook as she counted out her bills, and again, she left on foot.

Since then, the beans were always in stock, there was a single onion available. In the weeks that followed, she'd become something of a regular. Though still quiet, she seemed less fragile as time had gone on and the dark circles under her eyes were fading. She had even begun to talk to Kristen when the two of them were alone. It was the first time he'd seen the woman's defences drop. Her open expression spoke of an affection for children. After she left, Kristen had told him that she'd made a new friend and that her name was Miss Katie.

That didn't mean, however, that Katie was comfortable with him. Last week, after she'd chatted with Kristen, he'd seen her reading the covers of the novels he kept in stock. When he offhandedly asked if she had a favourite author, he'd seen the old nervousness. 'Never mind,' he added quickly. 'It's not important.' On her way out the door, however, she'd paused and mumbled, *I like Dickens*. With that, she opened the door and was gone, walking up the road.

He'd thought about her with greater frequency since then. He wanted to get to know her better. Not that he knew how to go about it. Aside from the year he courted Carly, he'd never been good at dating. In college, between swimming and his classes, he had little time to go out. In the military, he'd thrown himself into his career, working long hours. Sometimes, he barely recognised the man he used to be, and Carly, he knew, was responsible for those changes. He missed his wife, and there were still moments when he could swear he felt her presence nearby, watching over him.

2

Because of the glorious weather, the store was busier than usual for a Sunday. By the time Alex unlocked the door at seven, there were already three boats tied at the dock waiting for the pump to be turned on. Roger—who was working the grill, as always—hadn't had a break since he'd put on his apron, and the tables were crowded with people eating sausage sandwiches and cheeseburgers and asking for tips about the stock market.

Usually, Alex worked the register until noon, when he would hand over the reins to Joyce, who, like Roger, was the kind of employee who made running the store much less challenging than it could be. Joyce had 'come with the business', so to speak. His father-in-law had hired her ten years ago and now, in her seventies, she hadn't slowed down. Her husband had died, her kids had moved away, and she viewed the customers as her family.

Even better, she understood that Alex needed to spend time with his children away from the store, and she didn't get bent out of shape by working on Sundays. As soon as she showed up, she'd tell Alex he could go, sounding more like the boss than an employee. He'd come to view Joyce as one of the best things in his life.

Waiting for Joyce, Alex walked through the store, checking the shelves. He wondered idly what he was going to do with the kids in the afternoon and decided to take them for a bike ride.

With a quick peek towards the front door to make sure no one was coming in, he hurried through the storeroom and poked his head out. Josh was fishing off the dock, which was his favourite thing to do. Alex didn't like the fact that Josh was out there alone, but Josh always stayed within visual range of the video monitor behind the register. It was a rule, and Josh adhered to it. Kristen, as usual, was sitting at her table behind the register. She'd separated her doll's clothing into separate piles, and seemed content to change her from one outfit to the next.

Alex was straightening some of the condiments when he heard the bell on the front door jingle. He saw Katie enter the store.

'Hi, Miss Katie,' Kristen called out, popping up from behind the register. 'How do you think my doll looks?'

'She's beautiful,' Katie answered. 'What's her name?'

'Vanessa,' Kristen said. 'She came with the name. Can you help me get her boots on? I can't get them on all the way.'

Alex watched as Kristen handed Katie the doll and she began to work on the soft plastic boots. From his own experience, Alex knew it was harder than it looked, but somehow Katie made it seem easy. She handed the doll back and asked, 'How's that?'

'Perfect,' Kristen said. 'Should I put a coat on her?'

'It's not that cold out.'

'I know. But Vanessa gets cold sometimes. I think she needs one.' Kristen's head vanished behind the counter and then popped up again. 'Which one do you think? Blue or purple?'

Katie brought a finger to her mouth, her expression serious. 'I think purple might be good.'

Kristen nodded. 'That's what I think, too. Thanks.'

Katie smiled before turning away, and Alex focused his attention on the shelves. From the corner of his eye, he saw Katie scoop up a small shopping basket before moving to a different aisle.

Alex headed back to the register. When she saw him, he offered a friendly wave. 'Good morning,' he said.

'Hi. I just have to pick up a few things.'

'Let me know if you can't find what you need.'

She nodded before continuing down the aisle. As Alex stepped behind the register, he glanced at the video screen. Josh was fishing in the same spot, while a boat was slowly docking.

'What do you think, Daddy?' Kristen held up the doll.

'Wow! She looks beautiful.' Alex squatted down next to her. 'And I love the coat. Vanessa gets cold sometimes, right?'

'Yup,' Kristen said. 'But she told me she wants to go on the swings, so she's probably going to change.'

'Sounds like a good idea,' Alex said.

Lost in her own world, Kristen began to undress the doll again. Alex checked on Josh in the monitor just as a teenager entered the store, wearing board shorts. He handed over a wad of cash.

'For the pump at the dock,' he said before dashing out again.

Alex rang him up and set the pump as Katie walked to the register. Same items as always. When she peeked over the counter at Kristen, Alex noticed the changeable colour of her eyes.

'Did you find everything you needed?'

'Yes, thank you.'

He began loading her bag. 'My favourite Dickens novel is *Great Expectations*,' he said. He tried to sound friendly as he put the items in her bag. 'Which one is your favourite?'

She seemed startled that he remembered that she'd told him she liked Dickens. '*A Tale of Two Cities*,' she answered, her voice soft.

'I like that one, too. But it's sad.'

'Yes,' she said. 'That's why I like it.'

Since he knew she'd be walking, he double-bagged the groceries.

'I figured that since you've already met my daughter, I should probably introduce myself. I'm Alex,' he said. 'Alex Wheatley.'

'Her name is Miss Katie,' Kristen chirped from behind him. 'But I already told you that, remember?' Alex glanced over his shoulder at her. When he turned back, Katie was smiling as she handed the money to him.

'Just Katie,' she said.

'It's nice to meet you, Katie.' He tapped the keys and the register drawer opened with a ring. 'I take it you live around here?'

She never got around to answering. Instead, when he looked up, he saw that her eyes had gone wide in fright.

Swivelling around he saw what she'd caught on the monitor behind him: Josh in the water, arms flailing. Alex rushed out from behind the counter and raced through the store and into the storeroom. He flung open the back door and hurdled a row of bushes, taking a short cut to the dock. He hit the wooden planks at full speed. As he launched himself from the dock, Alex could see Josh thrashing in the water.

His heart slamming against his rib cage, Alex sailed through the air, hitting the water only a couple of feet from Josh. The water wasn't deep—six feet or so—and as he touched the soft, unsettled mud of the bottom, he sank up to his shins. He fought his way to the surface, feeling the strain in his arms as he reached for Josh.

'I've got you!' he shouted. 'I've got you!'

But Josh was unable to catch his breath, and Alex fought to control him as he pulled him into shallower water. Then, with an enormous heave, he carried Josh up onto the grassy bank. He tried to lay Josh down, but Josh resisted. He was still struggling and coughing, and though Alex could still feel the panic in his own system, he had enough presence of mind to know that it probably meant that Josh was going to be OK.

Josh gave a rattling cough, emitting a spray of water, and for the first time was able to catch his breath. He inhaled sharply and coughed again, then drew a few long breaths, still panic-stricken. Only then did he seem to realise what had happened. He reached for his dad and Alex folded him tightly in his arms. Josh began to cry, his shoulders shuddering, and Alex felt sick to his stomach at the thought of what might have been.

'I'm sorry, Daddy,' Josh choked out.

'I'm sorry, too,' Alex whispered, and still, he held on to his son.

When he was finally able to loosen his hold on Josh, Alex found himself gazing at a crowd behind the store. Roger was there, as were the customers who'd been eating. And of course, Kristen was there, too. Suddenly he felt like a terrible parent again, because he saw that his little girl was crying and afraid and needed him, too, even though she was nestled in Katie's arms.

IT WASN'T until Josh and Alex had changed into dry clothes that Alex pieced together what had happened. Roger had cooked both kids hamburgers and fries, and they were sitting in the grill area.

'My fishing line got snagged on the boat as it was pulling out, and I didn't want to lose my fishing rod. I thought the line would snap right away but it pulled me in.' Josh hesitated. 'I think I dropped my rod in the river.'

Kristen was sitting beside him, her eyes still red and puffy. She'd asked Katie to stay with her for a while, and Katie had remained at her side, holding her hand even now.

'It's OK. I'll head out there in a little while and if I can't find it, I'll get you a new one. But next time, just let go, OK?'

Josh sniffed and nodded. 'I'm really sorry,' he said.

'It was an accident,' Alex assured him.

'But now you won't let me go fishing.'

And risk losing him again? Alex thought. Not a chance. 'We'll talk about that later, OK?' he said instead.

Josh reached for a French fry and took a small bite.

Alex turned to Katie. He swallowed, feeling suddenly nervous. 'Can I talk to you for a minute?'

She stood up and he led her away from the kids. When he was sure they wouldn't hear, he cleared his throat. 'I want to thank you for what you did. Had you not been looking at the monitor, I might not have reached him in time.' He paused. 'And thank you for taking care of Kristen. I'm glad you didn't leave her alone.'

'I did what anyone would do,' Katie said. In the silence that followed, she suddenly seemed to realise how close they were standing and took a half step backward. 'I should really be going.'

'Wait,' Alex said. He walked towards the refrigerated cabinets at the rear of the store. 'Do you like wine?'

She shook her head. 'Sometimes, but—'

Before she could finish, he turned around and opened the case. He reached up and pulled out a bottle of Chardonnay.

'Please,' he said, 'I want you to have it. It's actually a very good wine.

When I was in the army, I had a friend who introduced me to wine. He's kind of an amateur expert, and he picks what I stock. You'll enjoy it.'

'You don't need to do that.'

'It's the least I can do.' He smiled. 'As a way to say thank you.'

For the first time she held his gaze. 'OK,' she finally said.

After gathering her groceries, she left the store. Josh and Kristen finished their lunches, while Alex went to the dock to retrieve the fishing pole. By the time he got back, Joyce was already slipping on her apron, and Alex took the kids for a bike ride. Afterward, he drove them to Wilmington, where they saw a movie and had pizza.

The sun was down and they were tired when they got home, so they showered and put on their pyjamas. He lay in bed between them for an hour, reading stories, before finally turning out the lights.

In the living room, he turned on the television, but he wasn't in the mood to watch. Instead, he thought about Josh again. He was doing the best he could, but he couldn't help feeling that it wasn't enough.

Later, he went to the kitchen and pulled out a beer from the refrigerator. He nursed it as he sat on the couch. The memories of the day played in his mind, but this time, his thoughts were of Kristen and the way she'd clung to Katie, her face buried in Katie's neck. The last time he'd seen that was when Carly had been alive.

APRIL GAVE WAY to May and the days continued to pass. The restaurant got steadily busier and the stash of money in Katie's coffee tin grew reassuringly thick. Katie no longer panicked at the thought that she lacked the means to leave this place if she had to.

Even after paying her rent and utilities, along with food, she had extra money for the first time in years. On Friday morning, she stopped at Anna Jean's, a thrift shop that specialised in secondhand clothes. She bought two pairs of shoes, a couple of pairs of trousers, shorts, three stylish T-shirts, and a few blouses.

Jo was hanging a wind chime when Katie got home. Since that first meeting, they hadn't talked much. Jo's job, whatever it was, seemed to keep her busy and Katie was working as many shifts as she could.

'Long time, no talk,' Jo said with a wave.

Katie reached the porch. 'Where've you been?'

Jo shrugged. 'You know how it goes. Late nights, early mornings, going here and there.' She motioned to the rockers. 'You mind? I need a break. I've been cleaning all morning.'

'Go ahead,' Katie said.

Jo sat and rolled her shoulders, working out the kinks. She nodded towards Katie's bags. 'Did you find anything you liked?'

'I think so,' Katie confessed.

'Well, don't just sit there, show me what you bought.'

Katie pulled out a pair of jeans and handed them over.

Jo held them up, turning them from front to back. 'Wow!' she said. 'You must have found these at Anna Jean's. I love that place.'

'How did you know I went to Anna Jean's?'

'Because it's not like any of the stores around here sell things this nice. This came from someone's closet. A rich woman's closet.' Jo peeked toward the bag. 'What else did you get?'

Katie handed over the items, listening as Jo raved about every piece. 'OK, it's official. I'm jealous. These are treasures,' Jo said.

Katie nodded toward Jo's house. 'How's it coming over there?' she asked. 'Have you started painting?'

'Not yet.' Jo made a face. 'It's a good thing you're my friend, so I can come over here where it's bright and cheery.'

'You're welcome anytime. Do you want me to come and help?'

'Absolutely not. I'm an expert in procrastination, but the last thing I want you to think is that I'm incompetent, too. Because I'm actually pretty good at what I do.'

'What *do* you do?' Katie asked.

'I'm a grief counsellor.'

'Oh,' Katie said. She paused. 'I'm not sure what that is.'

Jo shrugged. 'I visit people and try to help them. Usually, it's because someone close to them has died.' She paused. 'People react in different ways and it's up to me to figure out how to help them accept what happened. Sometimes, when I'm with someone, other issues come up. That's what I've been dealing with lately.'

'That sounds rewarding.'

'It is.' She turned towards Katie. 'But what about you?'

'You know I work at Ivan's.'

'But you haven't told me anything else about yourself. For instance, what really brought you to Southport?'

'I already told you,' Katie said. 'I wanted to start over.'

Jo seemed to stare right through her. 'OK,' she finally said, her tone light. 'You're right. It's not my business.'

'That's not what I said . . .'

'Yes, you did. You just said it in a nice way. And I respect your answer. But when you say you wanted to start over, the counsellor in me wonders why you felt the need to start over. And more important, what you left behind. If you ever want to talk, I'm here, OK? I'm good at listening. And sometimes talking helps.'

'What if I can't talk about it?' Katie said in a whisper.

'Then how about this? Ignore the fact that I'm a counsellor. We're just friends, and friends can talk about anything. Like where you were born or something that made you happy as a kid.'

'Why is that important?'

'It isn't. And that's the point. You don't have to say anything at all that you don't want to say.'

Katie squinted at Jo. 'You're very good at your job, aren't you?'

'I try,' Jo conceded.

Katie laced her fingers together in her lap. 'All right. I was born in Altoona,' she said.

Jo leaned back in her rocking chair. 'Is it nice there?'

'It's one of those old railroad towns,' she said. 'A town filled with good, hardworking people. It was pretty, too, especially in the fall.' She lowered her eyes, half lost in memories. 'That's where I went to school. I ended up graduating from high school there, but by then I was tired of it. I wanted something more, but college didn't work out and I ended up in Atlantic City. I worked there for a while, moved around a bit, and now, years later, here I am.'

'In another small town where everything stays the same.'

Katie shook her head. 'It's different here. It makes me feel . . .'

When she hesitated, Jo finished the thought for her. 'Safe?'

When Katie's startled gaze met hers, Jo seemed bemused. 'It's not hard to figure out. You're starting over and what better place to start over than a place like this? Where nothing ever happens?' She paused. 'That's not quite true. I heard there was a little excitement a couple of weeks back. When you dropped by the store?'

'You heard about that?'

'It's a small town. It's impossible not to hear. What happened?'

'It was scary. One minute, I was talking to Alex, and when I saw what was happening on the monitor, I guess he noticed my expression because in the next instant, he was racing past me. Then Kristen saw the monitor and started to panic. I scooped her up and followed her dad. By the time I got out there, Alex was already out of the water with Josh. I'm just glad he was OK.'

'Me, too.' Jo nodded. 'What do you think of Kristen? Isn't she sweetest thing?'

'She calls me Miss Katie.'

'I love that little girl,' Jo said. 'It doesn't surprise me that she reached for you when she was scared.'

'Why would you say that?'

'Because she's perceptive. She knows you've got a good heart.'

Katie made a sceptical face. 'Maybe she was just scared about her brother, and when her dad took off I was the only one there.'

'Don't sell yourself short. Like I said, she's perceptive.' Jo pressed on. 'How was Alex? Afterwards, I mean?'

'He was still shaken up, but other than that, he seemed all right.'

'Have you talked to him much since then?'

Katie gave a noncommittal shrug. 'Not much. He's nice when I come into the store, and he stocks what I need, but that's about it.'

'He's good about things like that,' Jo said with assurance.

'You sound like you know him pretty well.'

Jo rocked a little in her chair. 'I think I do.'

Katie waited for more, but Jo was silent.

'You want to talk about it?' Katie inquired innocently. 'Because talking sometimes helps, especially with a friend.'

Jo's eyes sparkled. 'You know, I always suspected you were a lot craftier than you let on. Throwing my own words back at me.'

Katie smiled but said nothing, just as Jo had done with her. And, surprising her, it worked.

'I'm not sure how much I should say,' Jo added. 'But I can tell you this: he's a good man. He's the kind of man you can count on.'

'Did you two ever see each other?'

Jo seemed to choose her words carefully. 'Yes, but maybe not in the way you're thinking. And just so we're clear: it was a long time ago and everyone has moved on.'

Katie wasn't sure what to make of her answer but didn't want to press it. 'What's his story? I take it he's divorced, right?'

'You should ask him.'

'Me? Why would I want to ask him?'

'Because you asked me,' Jo said, arching an eyebrow. 'Which means, of course, that you're interested in him.'

'I'm not interested in him.'

'Then why would you be wondering about him?'

Katie scowled. 'For a friend, you're kind of manipulative.'

Jo shrugged. 'I just tell people what they already know, but are afraid to admit to themselves.'

Katie thought about that. 'Just so we're clear, I'm officially taking back my offer to help you paint your house.'

Jo laughed. 'OK. Hey, what are you doing tomorrow night? Are you working?'

'No. I have the weekend off.'

'Then how about I bring over a bottle of wine?'

'Actually, that sounds like fun.'

'Good.' Jo stood up from the chair. 'It's a date.'

3

Saturday morning dawned with blue skies, but soon clouds began rolling in. The temperature began to plummet, and by the time Katie left the house, she had to wear a sweatshirt. The store was a little shy of two miles from her house, and she knew she'd have to hurry if she didn't want to get caught in a storm.

She reached the main road just as she heard thunder rumbling. The steady rhythm of her footfalls set her mind adrift and she found herself reflecting on her conversation with Jo and the things she had said about Alex. Jo, she decided, didn't know what she was talking about. Granted, Alex seemed like a nice guy, but she wasn't *interested* in him. She barely knew him. And the last thing she wanted was a relationship of any kind.

So why had it felt like Jo was trying to bring them together? She wasn't sure, but it didn't matter. She was glad Jo was coming over tonight. Just a couple of friends, sharing some wine . . . how long had it been since she'd done something that felt normal?

Since her childhood, she admitted. But she hadn't been completely truthful with Jo. She hadn't told her that she often went to the railroad tracks to escape the sound of her parents arguing, their slurred voices raging. She didn't tell Jo that her dad was mean when he was drunk, or that her parents had kicked her out of the house on the day she'd graduated from high school.

Maybe, she thought, she'd tell Jo about those things. Or maybe she wouldn't. So what if she hadn't had the best childhood? Yes, her parents were alcoholics and often unemployed, but they'd never hurt her. At eighteen, she didn't consider herself scarred. A bit nervous about having to make her way in the world, maybe, but not damaged beyond repair.

No, she reminded herself, her childhood hadn't defined her, or had anything to do with the real reason she'd come to Southport. Even though Jo was the closest thing to a friend that she had in Southport, Jo knew absolutely nothing about her. No one did.

'HI, MISS KATIE,' Kristen piped up from her little table. She was bent over a colouring book, working on a picture of rainbows.

'Hi, Kristen. How are you?'

'I'm good.' She looked up. 'Why do you always walk here?'

Katie squatted down to Kristen's level. 'I don't have a car.'

'Why not?'

Because I don't have a licence, Katie thought. 'I'll tell you what. I'll think about getting one, OK?'

'OK,' she said. 'What do you think of my picture?'

'It's pretty. You're doing a great job.'

'Thanks,' she said. 'I'll give it to you when I'm finished. You can hang it on your refrigerator.'

Katie smiled and stood up. 'OK,' she agreed.

Retrieving a basket, Katie saw Alex approaching. He waved, and she had the feeling that she was really seeing him for the first time. Though his hair was grey, there were only a few lines around the corners of his eyes. His shoulders tapered to a trim waist, and she had the impression that he was a man who neither ate nor drank to excess.

'Hey, Katie. How are you?'

'I'm fine. And yourself?'

'Can't complain.' He grinned. 'I'm glad you came in. I wanted to show you something.' He pointed towards the monitor and she saw Josh sitting on the dock holding his fishing pole. 'See the vest he's wearing?'

She leaned closer, squinting. 'A life-jacket?'

'He was miserable not being able to fish. I thought this was a solution. A better father would have figured it out beforehand.'

She looked at him. 'I get the sense you're a pretty good father.'

Their eyes held for a moment before she turned away. Alex, sensing her discomfort, began rummaging behind the counter.

'I have something for you,' he said, placing a bag on the counter. 'There's a small farm I work with that has a hothouse. They just dropped off some fresh vegetables yesterday. Tomatoes, cucumbers, some squash. You might want to try them out. My wife swore they were the best she'd ever tasted.'

'Your wife?'

He shook his head. 'I'm sorry. I still do that sometimes. I meant my late wife. She passed away a couple of years ago.'

'I'm sorry,' she murmured, her mind flashing back to her conversation with Jo.

What's his story?

You should ask him, Jo had countered. Jo had obviously known that his wife had died, but hadn't said anything. Odd.

Alex didn't notice that her mind had wandered. 'Thank you,' he said. 'She was a great person. You would have liked her.' A wistful expression crossed his face. 'But anyway,' he added, 'she swore by the place. Usually, the produce is gone within hours, but I set a little aside for you.' He smiled. 'Besides, you're a vegetarian, right? A vegetarian will appreciate these. I promise.'

'Why would you think I'm a vegetarian?'

'You're not?'

'No.'

'Oh,' he said. 'My mistake.'

'It's OK,' she said. 'I've been accused of worse.'

'I doubt that.'

Don't, she thought to herself. 'OK.' She nodded. 'I'll take the vegetables. And thank you.'

AS KATIE SHOPPED, Alex fiddled around the register, watching her from the corner of his eye. She'd changed in recent weeks. She had the beginnings of a summer tan and her skin had a glowing freshness to it. She was also growing less skittish around him, today being a prime example. No, they hadn't set the world on fire with their scintillating conversation, but it was a start, right? But the start of what?

From the very beginning, he'd sensed she was in trouble, and his instinctive response had been to want to help. And of course she was pretty. But it was seeing the way Katie had comforted Kristen after Josh had fallen in the water that had really moved him. It had reminded him that as much as he missed having a wife, his children missed having a mother. Their loneliness mirrored his own.

As for Katie, she was something of a mystery. He wondered who she really was and what had brought her to Southport.

She was standing near one of the refrigerated cabinets. As she debated what to buy, he noticed the fingers of her right hand twisting around her left ring finger, toying with a ring that wasn't there. The gesture triggered something familiar and long forgotten.

It was a tic he'd noticed during his years at CID and sometimes observed with women whose faces were bruised. They used to sit across from him, compulsively touching their rings. Usually, they denied their husband hit them. In the rare instances they admitted the truth, they usually insisted that it wasn't his fault, that they'd provoked him. They usually didn't want to press charges because his career would be ruined. The army came down hard on abusive husbands.

Some were different, though, and wanted to press charges. He would write up the report and read their own words back to them before asking them to sign it. It was then, sometimes, that their bravado would fail, and he'd catch a glimpse of the terrified woman beneath the angry surface. Alex came to understand that only those who pressed charges ever became truly free.

Still, there was another way to escape the horror of their lives, though he'd come across only one who actually did it. He'd interviewed the woman once and she'd taken the usual route of denial and self-blame. But a couple of months later, he'd learned that she'd fled. Not to her family and not to her friends, but somewhere else, a place where her husband couldn't find her. When he'd heard the news Alex remembered thinking, *Good for you*.

Now, as he watched Katie toying with a ring that wasn't there, he felt his old investigative instincts kick in. There'd been a husband, he thought. Either she was still married or she wasn't, but he had an undeniable hunch that Katie was still afraid of him.

The sky exploded while Katie was reaching for a box of crackers. Lightning flashed, and a few seconds later thunder cracked. From across the store, Alex saw her flinch, her face a mask of surprise and terror, and he found himself wondering whether it was the same way her husband had once seen her.

Katie picked up the crackers and carried her basket to the register. When Alex finished ringing up and bagging her items, she drew a fortifying breath and reached for her bags.

'Miss Katie!' Kristen cried, brandishing the picture she'd coloured. 'You almost forgot your picture.'

Katie reached for it. 'This is beautiful,' she murmured.

'I'll colour another one for you the next time you come in.'

'I'd like that very much,' she said.

Kristen beamed as Katie tucked the picture into the bag. Lightning and thunder erupted simultaneously. Rain hammered the ground. People lingered in the grill. Alex could hear them mumbling to themselves about waiting for the storm to stop.

Katie stared out the door, toying again with the nonexistent ring. In the silence, Kristen tugged at her dad's shirt.

'You should drive Miss Katie home,' she told him. 'She doesn't have a car. And it's raining hard.'

Alex looked at Katie. 'Would you like a ride home?'

Katie shook her head. 'No, that's OK. I don't want to impose.'

'You're not imposing.' He patted his pocket and pulled out his car keys before reaching for her bags. 'Roger?' he called out. 'Watch the store and the kids for a bit, would you?'

'No problem.' Roger waved.

Alex nodded towards the rear of the store. 'My car's out back.'

They made a frantic dash for the jeep. Once they had settled into their seats, Katie wiped the condensation from the window.

'I didn't think it would be like this when I left the house.'

'No one ever does, until the storm hits, anyway. We get a lot of *the sky is falling* on the weather reports, so when something big does hit, people never expect it. If it's not as bad as the reports predicted, we complain. If it's worse than expected, we complain. It just gives people something to complain about.'

'Like the people in the grill?'

He nodded and grinned. 'But they're basically good people. They're hardworking, honest, and as kind as the day is long. Any one of them would have been glad to watch the store for me if I'd asked, and they'd account for every penny. It's like that down here. It's great, even if it did take some time for me to get used to it.'

'You're not from here?'

'No. My wife was. I'm from Spokane. When I first moved here, I remember thinking I'd never stay in a place like this. But it grows on you. It keeps me focused on what's important.'

Katie's voice was soft. 'What's important?'

'Depends on the person. But right now, for me, it's about my kids. After what they've been through, they need predictability.' He paused, feeling self-conscious. 'By the way, where am I going?'

'Keep going straight. There's a gravel road that you'll have to turn on. It's a little bit past the curve.'

'You mean by the plantation?'

Katie nodded. 'That's the one.'

'I didn't even know that road went anywhere.' He wrinkled his forehead. 'That's quite a walk. What is it? A couple of miles?'

'It's not too bad,' she demurred.

'Maybe in nice weather. But today, you'd have to swim home. And Kristen's picture would have been ruined.'

He noted the smile at Kristen's name, but she said nothing.

'Someone said you work at Ivan's?' he prompted.

She nodded. 'I started in March.'

'How do you like it?'

'It's OK. It's just a job, but the owner has been good to me.'

'Ivan? He's a good man. Kristen and Josh love the hush puppies there. Next time we come in, we'll ask for you.'

She hesitated. 'OK.'

'She likes you,' Alex said. 'Kristen, I mean.'

'I like her. She's a bright spirit. How old is she?'

'She's five. When she starts school in the fall, I don't know what I'm going to do. I kind of like having her around.'

As he spoke, rain continued to sheet against the windows. Katie peered out, lost in her thoughts.

'How long were you married?' Katie finally asked.

'Five years. I met my wife when I was stationed at Fort Bragg.'

'You were in the army?'

'Ten years. It was a good experience and I'm glad I did it. At the same time, I'm glad I'm done.'

Katie pointed through the windshield. 'There's the turn ahead.'

Alex turned onto Katie's road, steering through the deep puddles. 'Which one is it?' he asked, squinting at the two cottages.

'The one on the right,' she said.

He pulled as close to the house as he could. 'I'll bring the groceries to the door for you,' he said.

'You don't have to do that.'

'You don't know the way I was raised,' he said, jumping out before she could object. He grabbed the bags and ran to her porch. By the time he set them down, Katie was hurrying towards him,

'Thank you,' she said, her eyes fixed on his. 'And thanks for driving me home.'

He tipped his head. 'Any time.'

WHAT TO DO with the kids: it was the endless question he faced on weekends, and as usual, he had absolutely no idea.

With the weather showing no signs of letting up, doing anything outside was out of the question. He pondered the options as he made grilled cheese sandwiches, but he soon found his thoughts drifting to Katie. While she was doing her best to maintain a low profile, he knew it was almost impossible in a town like this. She was too attractive to blend in, and it was inevitable that talk would start and questions would be asked about her past.

He didn't want that to happen. She was entitled to the kind of life she'd come here to find. A normal life. A life of simple pleasures, the kind that most people took for granted: the ability to go where she wanted and live in a home where she felt safe and secure. She also needed a way to get around.

'Hey, kids,' he said, putting their sandwiches on plates. 'I have an idea. Let's do something for Miss Katie.'

'OK!' Kristen agreed.

Josh, always easygoing, simply nodded.

WIND-DRIVEN RAIN blew across dark North Carolina skies. In the kitchen, Katie sliced cheddar cheese, nibbling as she moved about. On a yellow plastic plate were crackers and slices of tomatoes and cucumbers. In her previous home, she'd had a pretty wooden serving board and a silver cheese knife. She'd had a dining room table made of cherry, but here the table wobbled and the chairs didn't match. As horrible as her life had been, she'd loved assembling the pieces of her household, but as with everything she'd left behind, she now viewed them as enemies.

Through the window, she saw one of Jo's lights blink out. Opening the front door, Katie watched as Jo splashed through puddles on the way to her house, umbrella in one hand and wine in the other. Another couple of stomps and she was on the porch.

'Now I understand how Noah must have felt. Can you believe this storm? Here,' she said, handing over the wine. 'Just like I promised. And believe me, I'm going to need it.'

'Come on in.'

Jo tossed her yellow slicker on the rocker along with the umbrella and followed Katie inside as she led the way to the kitchen.

Katie set the wine on the counter. As Jo wandered to the table, Katie pulled out a Swiss Army knife and readied the opener.

'This is great. I'm starved. I haven't eaten all day,' said Jo.

'Help yourself. How did it go with the painting?'

'Well, I got the living room done. But after that, it wasn't such a good day. I'll tell you about it later. I need wine first. How about you? What did you do?'

'Nothing much. Ran to the store, cleaned up.'

Jo took a seat at the table. 'In other words, memoir material.'

Katie laughed as she began to twist the corkscrew. 'Oh, yeah. Real exciting.' The cork came out with a pop.

'Seriously, though, thanks for having me over.' Jo sighed. 'You have no idea how much I've been looking forward to this.'

'Really?'

'Don't do that.'

'Don't do what?' Katie asked.

'Act surprised that I wanted to come over and bond over a bottle of wine. That's what friends do.' She raised an eyebrow. 'And by the way, yes, I consider you a friend. Now how about some wine?'

The storm finally ended in the early evening, and Katie opened the kitchen window. The temperature had dropped and the air felt cool and clean. The wine had hints of oak and apricots and tasted wonderful. Katie finished her glass and Jo poured her another. Katie cut more cheese and added more crackers to the plate. They talked about movies and books, and Jo shrieked with pleasure when Katie said her favourite movie was *It's a Wonderful Life*, claiming that it was her favourite movie, too. Katie finished her second glass of wine, feeling as light as a feather on a summer breeze.

Jo asked few questions. Instead, they stuck to superficial topics. When silver highlighted the world beyond the window, they stepped out onto the porch. Katie could feel herself swaying and she took hold of the railing. The sky filled with stars. Katie pointed out the Big Dipper and Polaris, the only stars she could name.

Back in the kitchen, Katie poured the last of the wine and took a sip. It made her feel dizzy. She felt happy and safe and thought again how enjoyable the evening had been.

She had a friend, someone who laughed and made jokes, and she wasn't sure if she wanted to laugh or cry because it had been so long since she'd experienced something so easy and natural.

'Are you OK?' Jo peered at her. 'I think you might be tipsy.'

'I think you might be right,' Katie agreed.

'Well, OK then. Since you're obviously tipsy and ready for fun, do you want to head into town, find someplace exciting?'

Katie shook her head. 'No.'

'You don't want to meet people?'

'I'm better off alone.'

Jo ran her finger around the rim of the glass before saying anything. 'Trust me on this: no one is better off alone.'

'I am.'

Jo thought about Katie's answer before leaning closer. 'So you're telling me that—assuming you had food, shelter, and clothing—you'd rather be stranded on a desert island in the middle of nowhere, all alone, forever, for the rest of your life? Be honest.'

Katie blinked. 'Why would you think I wouldn't be honest?'

'Because everybody lies. It's part of living in society. People lie by omission all the time. People will tell you most of the story . . . and I've learned that the part they neglect to tell you is often the most important part. People hide the truth because they're afraid.'

With Jo's words, Katie felt a finger touch her heart. All at once, it seemed hard to breathe.

'Are you talking about me?' she finally croaked out.

'I don't know. Am I?'

Katie felt herself pale, but before she could respond, Jo smiled.

'Actually, I was thinking about my day today. It gets frustrating when people won't tell the truth. I mean, how am I supposed to help people if they hold things back? If I don't know what's going on?'

Katie could feel something tightening in her chest. 'Maybe they know there's nothing you can do to help,' she whispered.

'There's always something I can do.'

In the moonlight shining through the kitchen window, Jo's skin glowed a luminous white, and Katie had the sense that she never went out in the sun. The wine made the room move, the walls buckle. Katie could feel tears beginning to form in her eyes.

'Not always,' Katie whispered. When she began to speak, her voice didn't seem to be her own. 'I had a friend once. She was in a terrible marriage and she couldn't talk to anyone. He used to hit her, and in the beginning, she told him that if it ever happened again, she would leave him. He swore that it wouldn't and she believed him. But it only got worse, like when his dinner was cold. That night, her husband threw her into a mirror.'

Katie stared at the floor. Linoleum was peeling up in the corners.

'He always apologised, and sometimes he would cry because of the bruises he'd made on her. He would say that he hated what he'd done, but in the next breath tell her she'd deserved it. She worked hard to do things the way he wanted, but it was never enough.'

Katie could feel tears sliding down her cheek. Jo was motionless across the table, watching her without moving.

'And she loved him! In the beginning, he was so sweet to her. He made her feel safe. On the night they met, she'd been working, and after she finished her shift, two men were following her. One of them grabbed her. She didn't know what would have happened except that her future husband came around the corner and hit one of them on the back of the neck and he fell to the ground. Then he threw the other one into the wall, and it was over. Just like that. He walked her home and the next day he took her out for coffee. He treated her like a princess, up until she was on her honeymoon.'

Katie knew she shouldn't be telling Jo any of this, but she couldn't stop. 'My friend tried to get away twice. One time, she came back on her own because she had nowhere else to go. And the second time she ran away, she thought she was finally free. But he hunted her down and dragged her back to the house. At home, he beat her and put a gun to her head and told her that if she ever ran away again, he'd kill her. He'd kill any man she cared for. And she believed him, because by then, she knew he was crazy. But she was trapped. He never gave her any money, he never allowed her to leave the house. He used to drive by the house when he was supposed to be working, to make sure she was there. He monitored the phone records and he wouldn't let her get a driver's licence. She knew that if she stayed, the husband would eventually kill her.'

Katie swiped at her eyes. She could barely breathe but the words kept coming. 'She started to steal money from his wallet. Never more than a dollar or two. It took so long to get enough money for her to escape. Because that's what she had to do. Escape. She had to go someplace where he would never find her, because she knew he wouldn't stop searching for her. And she couldn't tell anyone, because her family was gone and she knew the police wouldn't do anything. And if he had so much as suspected anything, he would have killed her.'

Katie wasn't aware of when it had happened, but she realised that Jo had taken her hand. She could taste salt on her lips and imagined that her soul was leaking out. She wanted desperately to sleep.

'Your friend has a lot of courage,' Jo said quietly.

'No,' Katie said. 'My friend is scared all the time.'

'That's what courage is. If she weren't scared, she wouldn't need courage in the first place. I admire what she did.' Jo squeezed her hand. 'I think I'd like your friend. I'm glad you told me about her.'

Katie glanced away. 'I shouldn't have told you all that.'

Jo shrugged. 'I wouldn't worry too much. One thing you'll learn about me is that I'm good with secrets. Especially when it comes to people I don't know, right?'

Katie nodded. 'Right.'

Jo stayed with Katie for another hour, but steered the conversation towards easier ground. Katie talked about working at Ivan's and some of the customers she was getting to know. With the wine gone, Katie's dizziness began to fade, leaving in its wake a sense of exhaustion. Jo, too, began to yawn, and they finally rose from the table, and Katie walked Jo to the door.

As Jo stepped onto the porch, she paused. 'I think we had a visitor,' she said. 'There's a bicycle leaning against your tree.'

Katie followed her outside. Squinting, she realised Jo was right.

'Whose bicycle is that?' Katie asked.

'I don't know. But I think someone left it for you. See?' She pointed. 'Isn't that a bow on the handlebars?'

Katie spotted the bow. A woman's bike, it had wire baskets on each side of the rear wheel, as well as another wire basket on the front. 'Who would bring me a bicycle?'

'I don't know what's going on any more than you do.'

Katie and Jo stepped off the porch. The grass dampened her shoes as Katie moved through it. She touched the bicycle, then the bow. A card was tucked beneath it, and Katie reached for it.

'It's from Alex,' she said, sounding baffled.

'What does it say?'

Katie shook her head. *I thought you might enjoy this.*

'I guess that means he's as interested in you as you are in him.'

'I'm not interested in him!'

'Of course not.' Jo winked. 'Why would you be?'

4

Alex was sweeping the floor when Katie entered the store. He had guessed that she would show up to talk to him about the bicycle first thing in the morning. He tucked in his shirt and ran a quick hand through his hair. Kristen had been waiting for her all morning and she'd already popped up before the door had even closed.

'Hey, Miss Katie!' Kristen said. 'Did you get the bicycle?'

'I did. Thank you,' Katie answered. 'That's why I'm here.'

'We worked really hard on it.'

'You did a great job,' she said. 'Is your dad around?'

'Uh-huh. He's right over there.' She pointed. 'He's coming.'

Alex watched as Katie turned towards him.

'Hey, Katie,' he said.

She crossed her arms. 'Can I talk to you outside for a minute?'

He could hear the coolness in her voice and knew she was doing her best not to show her anger in front of Kristen.

'Of course,' he said, reaching for the door. Pushing it open, he followed her outside and headed towards the bicycle.

Stopping near the bike, she turned to face him. She patted the seat, her face serious. 'Can I ask what this is about?'

'Do you like it?'

'Why did you buy it for me?'

'I didn't buy it for you,' he said. 'It's been in the shed for the last couple of years.'

Her eyes flashed. 'That's not the point! I don't want anything from you. And I don't need a bike!'

'Then give it away. Because I don't want it, either.'

She shook her head and turned to leave.

Before she could take a step, he cleared his throat. 'Before you go, would you do me the favour of listening to my explanation?'

She glared at him over her shoulder. 'It doesn't matter.'

'It might not matter to you, but it matters to me.'

When she sighed, he motioned to the bench in front of the store. Katie took a seat, and Alex laced his fingers together in his lap.

'It used to belong to my wife,' Alex said. 'She rode it all the time. Once, she even rode it all the way to Wilmington, but by the time she got there, she was tired and I had to go pick her up.'

He paused. 'That was the last ride she took. That night, she had her first seizure and I had to rush her to the hospital. After that, she got sicker, and she never rode again. I put the bike in the garage, but every time I see it, I think back on that horrible night.' He straightened. 'I should have already gotten rid of it, but I wanted it to go to someone who would appreciate it as much as she did. That's what my wife would have wanted. You'd be doing me a favour.'

Katie's voice was subdued. 'I can't take your wife's bike.'

'So you're still giving it back?'

When she nodded, he leaned forward, propping his elbows on his knees. 'You and I are a lot more alike than you realise. In your shoes, I would have done exactly the same thing. You want to prove to yourself that you can make it on your own, right?'

She opened her mouth to answer but said nothing.

'After my wife died, I was the same way. People would drop by the store and tell me to call them if I ever needed anything. I never called anyone because it just wasn't me. For a long time, I was barely hanging on. All at once, I had to take care of two young kids as well as the store. Then one day, Joyce showed up.' He looked at her. 'Have you met Joyce yet? Works Sundays, older lady.'

'I'm not sure.'

'It's not important. But anyway, she showed up one afternoon, and she simply told me that she was going to take care of the kids while I spent the next week at the beach. She'd already arranged a place for me and she told me that I didn't have a choice in the matter because I was heading straight for a nervous breakdown.'

He pinched the bridge of his nose. 'I was upset about it at first. What kind of father was I to make people think that I couldn't handle being a father? But unlike anyone else, Joyce didn't ask me to call if I needed anything. She went ahead and did what she thought was right. The next thing I knew, I was on my way to the beach. And she was right. By the time I got back, I was more relaxed than I'd been in a long time . . .'

He trailed off, feeling the weight of her scrutiny.

'I don't know why you're telling me this.'

He turned towards her. 'Both of us know that if I'd asked if you wanted the bicycle, you would have said no. So, like Joyce, I just went ahead and did it because it was the right thing to do.' He nodded towards the bike. 'Take it,' he said. 'You have to admit that it would make getting to and from work a lot easier.'

It took a few seconds before he saw her shoulders relax and she turned to him with a wry smile. 'Did you practise that speech?'

'Of course.' He tried to look sheepish. 'But you'll take it?'

'A bike might be nice,' she finally admitted. 'Thank you.'

For a long moment, neither of them said anything. As he stared at her profile, he noted again how pretty she was, though he had the sense that she didn't think so. Which only made her more appealing.

'You're welcome,' he said.

'But no more freebies. You've done enough for me already.'

'Fair enough.' He nodded towards the bike. 'Did it ride OK? With the baskets, I mean?'

'It was fine. Why?'

'Because Kristen and Josh helped me put them on yesterday. One of those rainy-day projects. Kristen picked them out. Just so you know, she thought you needed sparkly handlebar grips too, but I drew the line at that.'

'I wouldn't have minded sparkly handlebar grips'

He laughed. 'I'll let her know.'

She hesitated. 'You're doing a good job, you know. With your kids, I mean.'

'Thank you.'

The door to the store opened, and as Alex leaned forward he saw Josh scanning the parking lot, Kristen close behind him.

'Over here, guys.'

Josh shuffled towards them. Kristen beamed, waving at Katie.

'Hey, Dad?' Josh asked. 'We wanted to ask if we're still going to the beach today. You promised to take us.'

'That was the plan.'

'OK,' he said. He rubbed his nose. 'Hi, Miss Katie.'

Katie waved at Josh and Kristen.

'Do you like the bike?' Kristen chirped.

'Yes. Thank you.'

'I had to help my dad fix it,' Josh said. 'He's not too good with tools.'

Katie glanced at Alex with a smirk. 'He didn't mention that.'

Kristen fixed her gaze on Katie. 'Are you going to come to the beach, too?'

Katie sat up straighter. 'I don't think so.'

'Why not?' Kristen asked.

'She's probably working,' Alex said.

'Actually, I'm not,' she said. 'I have things to do around the house.'

'Then you have to come. It's really fun. Please?' Kristen begged.

Alex stayed quiet, loath to add pressure. He assumed Katie would say no, but surprising him, she nodded slightly. 'OK,' she said.

AFTER GETTING back from the store, Katie parked the bike at the back of the cottage and went inside to change. She didn't have a bathing suit, but she wouldn't have worn one even if she did. She wasn't comfortable wearing something like that in front of Alex.

Though she resisted the idea, she had to admit he intrigued her. There was a loneliness within him, and she knew that in some way it matched her own. She knew he was interested in her. She'd been around long enough to recognise when men found her attractive. But that life was gone now, she reminded herself.

Opening the drawers, she pulled out a pair of shorts and the sandals she'd picked up at Anna Jean's. As soon as she finished dressing, she saw Alex's jeep coming up the gravel road and she drew a long breath as he pulled to a stop in front of her house. Now or never, she thought to herself as she stepped out onto the porch.

Alex looked at her, as if to say, *Are you ready for this?* She gave him her bravest smile.

'OK,' he said, 'let's go.'

THEY REACHED the coastal town of Long Beach in less than an hour. Alex pulled into a small parking lot nestled against the dunes. Katie got out of the car and stared at the ocean, breathing deeply.

The kids climbed out and made for the path between the dunes.

'I'm going to check the water, Dad!' Josh shouted.

'Me, too!' Kristen added, trailing behind.

Alex was busy unloading the back of the jeep. 'Hold up,' he called out. 'Just wait, OK?'

'Do you need some help?' Katie asked him.

He shook his head. 'I can handle this. But would you mind putting some sunscreen on the kids and keeping an eye on them for a few minutes? I know they're excited to be here.'

'That's fine.' She turned to Kristen and Josh. 'Are you ready?'

Alex spent the next few minutes ferrying the items from the car to the picnic table closest to the dune. For the most part they had this section of beach to themselves. Katie was standing at the water's edge as the kids splashed in the shallows. Alex noticed a rare expression of contentment on her face.

He slung a couple of towels over his shoulder as he approached. 'It's hard to believe there was a storm yesterday, isn't it?'

She turned. 'I forgot how much I missed the ocean.'

'Been awhile?'

'Too long,' she said.

Josh ran in and out of the waves, while Kristen came splashing towards them, holding a fistful of seashells.

'Miss Katie!' she cried. 'I found some really pretty ones!'

Katie bent lower. 'Can you show me?'

Kristen held them out, dumping them into Katie's hand before turning towards Alex. 'Hey, Daddy?' she asked. 'Can we get the barbecue started? I'm really hungry.'

'Sure, sweetie.' He took a few steps down the beach, watching his son diving in and out of the waves. As Josh popped back up, Alex cupped his mouth. 'Hey, Josh?' he shouted. 'I'm going to start the coals, so why don't you come in for a while.'

'Now?' Josh shouted back. Alex saw his son's shoulders droop.

'I can stay down here if you want,' Katie assured him. 'Kristen's showing me her seashells.'

He nodded and turned back to Josh. 'Miss Katie's going to watch you, OK? So don't go out too far!'

'I won't!' he said, grinning.

A LITTLE WHILE later, Katie led a shivering Kristen and excited Josh back towards the blanket Alex had spread out earlier. The grill had been set up and the briquettes were already glowing.

Alex watched them approach. 'How was the water, guys?'

'Awesome!' Josh answered. 'When's lunch?'

Alex checked the coals. 'Give me about twenty minutes.'

'Can me and Kristen go back to the water? We want to build sandcastles,' he said.

Alex noted Kristen's chattering teeth. 'All right. But let's throw shirts on you two. And stay where I can see you,' he said, pointing.

'I know, Dad.' Josh sighed. 'I'm not a little kid anymore.'

Alex helped both Josh and Kristen put their shirts on. When he was finished, Josh grabbed a bag full of toys and ran off, stopping a few feet from the water's edge. Kristen trailed behind him.

'Do you want me to head down there?' Katie asked.

He shook his head. 'No, they know to stay out of the water.'

Moving to the cooler, he squatted down and opened the lid. 'Are you getting hungry, too?' he asked.

'A little,' she said.

'Good. I'm starved.' As Alex began rummaging through the cooler, Katie noticed the sinewy muscles of his forearm. 'I was thinking hot dogs for Josh, a cheeseburger for Kristen, and for you and me, steaks.' He pulled out the meat and set it aside.

'Can I help with anything?'

'Would you mind putting the tablecloth on the table?'

'Sure,' Katie said. She unfolded the plastic tablecloth. 'Do you want me to put everything on the table?'

'We've got a few minutes. I'm ready for a beer,' he said. 'You?'

'I'll take a soda,' she said.

When he passed the can to her, his hand brushed against hers, though she wasn't sure he even noticed.

He motioned to the chairs. 'Would you like to sit?'

She hesitated before taking a seat next to him. When he'd set them up, he'd left enough distance between them so that they wouldn't accidentally touch. Alex twisted the cap from his beer and took a pull. 'There's nothing better than a cold beer at the beach.'

She smiled. 'I'll take your word for it.'

'You don't like beer?'

Her mind flashed to her father and the empty cans of Pabst Blue Ribbon that usually littered the floor next to the recliner where he sat. 'Not too much,' she admitted.

'Just wine, huh?'

It took her a moment to remember that he'd given her a bottle. 'I had some wine last night, as a matter of fact. With my neighbour.'

'Yeah? Good for you.'

She searched for a safe topic. 'You said you're from Spokane?'

He stretched his legs out in front of him. 'Born and raised. I lived in the same house until I went to college.' He cast a sidelong glance at her. 'University of Washington, by the way. Go, Huskies.'

She smiled. 'Do your parents still live there?'

'Yes.'

'That must make it hard for them to visit the grandkids.'

'They're not the kind of grandparents who would come by, even if they were closer. They've seen the kids only twice, once when Kristen was born and the second time at the funeral.' He shook his head. 'Don't ask me to explain it, but my parents have no interest in them. They'd rather travel or do whatever it is they do. I can't say they were all that different with me.'

'What about the other set of grandparents?'

He scratched at the label on his beer. 'That's trickier. They had two other daughters who moved to Florida, and after they sold me the store, they moved down there. They come up once or twice a year, but it's still hard for them. I think it reminds them of Carly.'

'In other words, you're pretty much on your own.'

'It's just the opposite,' he said, nodding towards the kids. 'I have them, remember?'

'It has to be hard, though. Running the store, raising your kids.'

'It's not so bad. As long as I'm up by six in the morning and don't go to bed until midnight, it's easy to keep up.'

She laughed easily. 'Do you think the coals are getting close?'

'Let me check,' he said, and walked over to the grill. The briquettes were white and heat rose in shimmering waves. 'Your timing is impeccable,' he said. He threw the steaks and the hamburger on the grill while Katie went to the cooler and started bringing items to the table: potato salad, coleslaw, a green bean salad, sliced fruit, bags of chips, slices of cheese, and assorted condiments. She shook her head, thinking that there was more food here than she'd kept in her house the entire time she'd lived in Southport.

As Alex hovered over the grill, they settled into easy conversation. The more Alex talked, the more Katie realised that he was the kind of man who tried to find the best in people. He talked about growing up in Spokane; he told her that once he discovered swimming, it became an obsession. He swam four or five hours a day and had Olympic dreams, but a torn rotator cuff in college put an end to those. As he talked, Katie noticed that he didn't seem to either embellish or downplay his past, nor did he appear preoccupied with what others thought of him.

She could see the traces of the élite athlete he once had been, noting the fluid way he moved. When he paused, she worried that he would ask about her past, but he seemed to sense that it would make her uncomfortable and would instead launch into another story.

When the food was ready, he called the kids and they came running. They were covered in sand, and Alex brushed them off. Watching him, she knew he was a good father in all the ways that mattered. He was different from anyone she'd met before, and any vestiges of the nervousness she'd once felt began to slip away.

The food was delicious, a welcome change from her austere diet. When they finished eating, Josh and Kristen wanted to go boogie boarding, and Alex followed them into the waves.

Katie carried her chair to the water's edge and spent the next hour watching as he helped the kids catch the waves. They were squealing with delight, having the time of their lives. As the afternoon wore on, she found herself smiling at the thought that for the first time in many years, she felt completely relaxed. And not only that, she knew she was having as much fun as the kids.

After they got out of the water, Kristen declared that she was cold and Alex led her to the public restrooms to help her change into dry clothes. Katie stayed with Josh while he scooped sand into piles.

'Hey, do you want to help me fly my kite?' Josh suddenly asked.

'I don't know that I've ever flown a kite before . . .'

'It's easy,' he insisted. 'I can show you how. C'mon.'

He took off running down the beach, and Katie jogged a few steps before settling back into a brisk walk. By the time she reached him, he was already beginning to unwind the string and he handed her the kite. 'Just hold this above your head, OK?'

She nodded as Josh started to back up slowly, continuing to loosen the string with practiced ease.

'Are you ready?' he shouted as he finally came to a stop. 'When I take off running and yell, just let go!'

'I'm ready!' she shouted back.

Josh started running, and when Katie felt the tension in the kite and heard him shout, she released it. The kite shot straight to the sky. Josh stopped and turned around, letting out even more line.

Reaching his side, Katie watched the rising kite. 'I'm pretty good at flying kites,' Josh said. 'How come you've never flown one?'

'I don't know. It just wasn't something I did as a kid.'

'You should have. It's fun.'

Josh stared upward, his face a mask of concentration.

'How do you like school? You're in kindergarten, right?'

'It's OK. I like recess best. We have races and stuff.'

Of course, she thought. 'Is your teacher nice?'

'She's really nice. She's kind of like my dad. She doesn't yell.'

'Your dad doesn't yell?'

'No,' he said with conviction. 'Do you have a lot of friends?' he asked.

'Not too many. Why?'

'Because my dad says that you're his friend. That's why he brought you to the beach.'

'When did he say that?'

'When we were in the waves.'

'What else did he say?'

'He asked us if it bothered us that you came.'

'Does it?'

'Why should it?' He shrugged. 'Everybody needs friends, and the beach is fun.'

No argument there. 'You're right,' she said.

'My mom used to come with us out here, but she died.'

'I know. And I'm sorry. You must miss her very much.'

He nodded. He looked both older and younger than his age. 'My dad gets sad sometimes. He doesn't think I know, but I can tell.'

'I'd be sad, too.'

He was quiet as he thought about her answer. 'Thanks for helping me with my kite,' he said.

'YOU TWO seemed to be having a good time,' Alex observed.

After Kristen had changed, Alex helped her get her kite in the air and then went to stand with Katie near the water's edge.

'He's sweet. So this is what you do on weekends after you leave the store. You spend time with the kids?'

'Always,' he said. 'I think it's important. And I enjoy it.'

Katie found herself remembering her own childhood, trying and failing to imagine either of her parents echoing Alex's sentiments.

'Why did you join the army after you got out of school?'

'I wanted to try something different, and joining gave me an excuse to leave Washington.'

'Did you ever see . . . ?'

When she trailed off, he finished her sentence. 'Combat? No, I was a criminal justice major in college and I ended up in CID.'

'What's that?'

When he told her, she turned towards him. 'Like the police?'

He nodded. 'I was a detective,' he said.

Katie turned away abruptly, her face closing down.

'Did I say something wrong?' he asked.

She shook her head. Alex stared at her, wondering what was going on. His suspicions about her past surfaced immediately.

'What's going on, Katie?'

'Nothing,' she insisted, but as soon as the word came out, he knew she wasn't telling the truth.

'We don't have to talk about it,' he said quietly. 'And besides, it's not who I am anymore. I'm a lot happier running a general store.'

She nodded, but he could tell she needed space. 'Listen, I forgot to add more briquettes to the grill. If the kids don't get their s'mores, I'll never hear the end of it. I'll be right back, OK?'

'Sure,' she answered, feigning nonchalance. When he jogged off, Katie exhaled. *He used to be a police officer*. It took almost a minute of steady breathing before she felt in control again.

She heard Alex approaching behind her.

'Told you it wouldn't take long,' he said easily. 'After we eat the s'mores, I was thinking about calling it a day. I'd love to stay out until the sun sets, but Josh has school tomorrow.'

'Whenever you want to go is fine with me,' she said.

Noting her rigid shoulders, he furrowed his brow. 'I'm not sure what I said that bothered you, but I'm sorry, OK?' he finally said.

She nodded without answering, and though Alex waited for more, there was nothing. 'Is this the way it's going to be with us?' he asked.

'What do you mean?'

'I feel like I'm suddenly walking on eggshells around you, but I don't know why.'

'I'd tell you but I can't,' she said. 'You didn't say or do anything wrong. But right now, I can't say any more than that, OK?'

'OK,' he said. 'As long as you're still having a good time.'

It took some effort, but she finally managed a smile. 'This is the best day I've spent in a long time. Best weekend in fact.'

'You're still mad about the bike, aren't you?' he said, narrowing his eyes in mock suspicion. Despite her tension, she laughed.

'Of course,' she said, pretending to pout.

Turning his gaze to the horizon, he seemed relieved.

'Can I ask you something?' Katie asked, turning serious again.

'Anything,' he said.

'What happened to your wife? You said she had a seizure, but you haven't told me why she was sick.'

He sighed, as if he'd known all along she was going to ask but still had to steel himself to answer. 'She had a brain tumour,' he began slowly. 'The doctors did the best they could, but when they walked out of surgery and told me that it had gone as well as it could, I knew exactly what they meant.'

'I can't imagine hearing something like that.'

'It was so . . . unexpected. I mean, the week before, we were a normal family, and the next thing I knew, she was dying. The left side of her body started to get weaker and she was taking longer and longer naps. The worst part for me was that she began to pull away from the kids. Like she didn't want them to remember her being sick; she wanted them to remember the way she used to be.' He shook his head. 'I'm sorry. I shouldn't have told you that. She was a great mom. I mean, look how well they're turning out.'

'I think their father has something to do with that, too.'

'I try. But half the time, it doesn't feel like I know what I'm doing. It's like I'm faking it.'

'I think all parents feel like that.'

He turned towards her. 'Did yours?'

She hesitated. 'I think my parents did the best they could.' Not a ringing endorsement, but the truth.

'Are you close to them?'

'They died in a car accident when I was nineteen.'

'I'm sorry to hear that. Do you have any brothers and sisters?'

'No,' she said. She turned towards the water. 'It's just me.'

A FEW MINUTES later, Alex helped the kids reel in their kites and they headed back to the picnic area. Alex pulled out what he needed for the s'mores. Following the kids' lead, Katie pushed three marshmallows onto her prong and the four of them stood over the grill. When the sugary puffs were golden brown, Alex helped the kids finish the treat: chocolate on the graham cracker, followed by the marshmallow and topped with another cracker. It was sticky and sweet and the best thing Katie had eaten in as long as she could remember.

Sitting between his kids, she noticed Alex struggling with his crumbling s'more, making a mess. The kids found it hilarious, and Katie couldn't help giggling as well, and she felt a sudden surge of hope. Despite the tragedy they'd all gone through, this was what a happy family looked like. For her, there was something revelatory about the notion that wonderful moments like these existed. Maybe it would be possible for her to experience similar days in the future.

5

'Then what happened?'

Jo was sitting across from her at the kitchen table. After Katie had returned, she'd come over, specks of paint in her hair. Katie had started a pot of coffee and two cups were on the table.

'Nothing, really. After finishing the s'mores, we drove home.'

'Did you kiss him good night?'

'Of course not. It wasn't a date. It was a family day.'

'It sounded like the two of you spent a lot of time talking.'

Katie leaned back. 'I think you wanted it to be a date. Ever since we've met, you've been trying to make sure I notice him.'

Jo set her coffee back on the table. 'And have you?'

Katie threw up her hands. 'See what I mean?'

Jo laughed before shaking her head. 'All right. How about this?' She hesitated, then went on. 'I've met a lot of people, and I've developed instincts I've learned to trust. Alex is a great guy, and I feel the same way about you. Other than that, I haven't done anything more than tease you about it. It's not like I dragged you to the store and introduced the two of you. Nor was I around when he asked you to go to the beach, an invitation you were more than willing to accept.'

'Kristen asked me to go . . .'

'I know. You told me that,' Jo said, arching an eyebrow. 'And I'm sure that's the only reason you went.'

Katie scowled. 'You have a way of twisting things around.'

Jo laughed again. 'Did you ever think that it's because I'm envious? Oh, not that you went with Alex, but that you got to go to the beach on a perfect day, while I was stuck inside painting.'

Katie poured another cup of coffee and held up the pot. 'More?'

'No, thank you. The caffeine would keep me up.' Jo stood and stretched. 'Are you working a lot this week?'

Katie nodded. 'Six nights and three days.'

Jo made a face. 'Yuck.'

'It's OK. I need the money and I'm used to it.'

'And, of course, you had a great weekend.'

Katie paused. 'Yeah,' she said. 'I did.'

THE NEXT FEW days passed uneventfully. It didn't take long before Katie admitted that the bicycle was a godsend. Not only was she able to come home between her shifts on the days she pulled doubles, but she could really explore the town. On Tuesday, she visited a couple of antique stores. On Wednesday, she visited the library, loading the bicycle baskets with novels that interested her.

In the evenings, though, as she lay in bed reading the books she'd checked out, she sometimes found her thoughts drifting to Alex. Katie realised that she was attracted to him. Beyond that, her feelings were complicated. The more time she spent with him, the more she had the sense that he knew more than he was letting on, and it frightened her. It was part of the reason she'd avoided going to the store this week. She needed time to think.

Unfortunately, she'd spent too much time dwelling on the way his eyes crinkled when he grinned or the graceful way he'd emerged from the surf. Early on, Jo had said something along the lines that Alex was a good man, and Katie's instincts told her he was a man she could trust.

She realised that she wanted him to know her. She wanted him to understand her, if only because she sensed he was the kind of man she could fall in love with, even if she didn't want to.

The following day, Katie pushed open the door to the store only half an hour after opening.

'You're here early,' Alex said, surprised.

'I was up early and thought I'd get my shopping out of the way.'

She smiled, reaching for a basket. As she did, she heard him clear his throat. 'Are you working next weekend?'

'I'm off Saturday. Why?'

He shifted his weight. 'Because I was wondering if I might be able to take you to dinner. Just the two of us this time. No kids.'

She knew they were at a crossroads, one that would change the tenor of things between them.

'Yes,' she said. 'I'd love dinner. But on one condition.'

'What's that?'

'You've already done so much for me that I'd rather do something for you. How about I make you dinner instead? At my house.'

He smiled, relieved. 'That sounds perfect.'

ON SATURDAY, Katie woke later than usual. She'd spent the past few days frantically shopping and decorating her house—a new lace curtain for the living room window, a few rugs. Friday night she'd worked until after midnight, giving the house a final cleaning. Despite the sun that slanted through her windows, she woke only when she heard the sounds of someone hammering. Checking the clock, she saw it was already after nine.

Stumbling out of bed, Katie walked towards the kitchen to switch on the coffeepot before stepping out onto the porch, squinting in the brightness of the morning sun. Jo was on her front porch, the hammer poised for another whack, when she spotted Katie.

Jo put the hammer down. 'I didn't wake you, did I?'

'Yeah, but I had to get up anyway. What are you doing?'

'I'm trying to keep the shutter from falling off.'

'How about coffee?'

'Sounds great. I'll be over in a few minutes.'

Katie went to her bedroom, slipped out of her pyjamas, and threw on a pair of shorts and a T-shirt. Through the window, she saw Jo walking towards the house. She opened the front door.

Katie poured two cups of coffee and handed one to Jo as soon as she entered the kitchen.

'Your house is really coming together! I love the rugs.'

Katie gave a modest shrug. 'Yeah, well . . . Southport is starting to feel like home. Where've you been? I haven't seen you around.'

Jo gave a dismissive wave. 'I was out of town for a few days on business, and then I was working. You know the drill.'

'I've been working a lot, too. I've had a ton of shifts lately.'

'You working tonight?'

'No. I'm having someone over for dinner.'

Jo's eyes lit up. 'Do you want me to guess who it could be?'

'You already know who it is.' Katie flushed.

'I knew it!' she said. 'Good for you. And you're going to cook?'

'Believe it or not, I'm actually a fairly good cook.'

'What are you going to make?'

When Katie told her, Jo raised her eyebrows.

'Sounds yummy,' Jo winked. 'It's too bad I can't stick around to spy on the two of you, but I'm heading out of town. As soon as I get back, I'm going to need the full play-by-play.'

'I think you need another hobby,' Katie said.

'Probably,' Jo agreed. 'But right now, I'm having plenty of fun living vicariously through you since my love life is pretty much nonexistent. A girl needs to be able to dream, you know?'

KATIE'S FIRST stop was the hair salon. There, a young woman trimmed and styled her hair. Across the street was the only women's boutique in Southport, and Katie stopped there next. She was pleasantly surprised not only by the selections, but by some of the prices.

She bought a couple of sale items, including a tan blouse with beading that scooped in the front, not dramatically but enough to accent her figure. She also found a gorgeous patterned skirt that complemented the blouse perfectly. After paying for her purchases, she wandered to the shoe store, where she picked up a pair of sandals. Again, they were on sale and she decided to splurge.

From there, she went first to the drugstore to buy a few things and then finally rode across town to the grocery store. When she was finished, she rode home and started the preparations for dinner.

She was making shrimp stuffed with crabmeat, cooked in scampi sauce. She had to recall the recipe from memory, but she'd made it a dozen times over the years and was confident she hadn't forgotten anything. As side dishes, she'd decided on stuffed peppers and corn bread, and as an appetiser, she wanted to make a bacon-wrapped Brie, topped with a raspberry sauce. It had been a long time since she'd prepared such an elaborate meal, but cooking was the one enthusiasm she'd been able to share with her mom.

She spent the rest of the afternoon hurrying. She mixed the bread and put it in the oven, then readied the ingredients for the stuffed peppers. Those went into the refrigerator along with the bacon-wrapped Brie. When the corn bread was done, she placed it on the counter to cool and started the raspberry sauce. By the time it was ready, the kitchen smelled heavenly.

She made a last tour of the house to make sure everything was in place. Finally, she slipped into the shower. After towelling off, she put on her new outfit, before reaching for the make-up she'd purchased from the drugstore. She didn't need much, just some lipstick, mascara, and a trace of eye shadow. She brushed her hair and stepped back from the mirror.

That's it, she thought to herself, that's all I've got. She turned one way, then the other, tugging at the blouse before finally smiling. She hadn't looked this good in a long time.

Though the sun had finally moved towards the western sky, the house was still warm and she opened the kitchen window. As she set the table, she heard the sound of an engine approaching.

She drew a deep breath and stepped out onto the porch. Dressed in jeans and a blue shirt, Alex was standing at the driver's door and leaning into the car, obviously reaching for something.

He pulled out two bottles of wine and turned around. Seeing her, he seemed to freeze, his expression one of disbelief. She stood surrounded by the last rays of the setting sun, perfectly radiant, and all he could do was stare. His wonder was obvious, and Katie let it wash over her, knowing she wanted the feeling to last forever.

'You made it,' she said.

The sound of her voice broke the spell, but Alex continued to stare. He found himself thinking, *I'm in serious trouble*.

He wasn't exactly sure when it had happened. It may have been the morning when he'd seen Kristen holding Katie after Josh had fallen in the river, or the rainy afternoon when he'd driven her home, or even during the day they had spent at the beach. All he knew for sure was that he was falling hard for this woman.

In time, he cleared his throat. 'Yeah,' he said. 'I guess I did.'

THE EARLY EVENING sky was a prism of colours as Katie led Alex through the small living room and towards the kitchen.

'I don't know about you, but I could use a glass of wine,' she said.

'Good idea,' he agreed. 'I brought both a sauvignon blanc and a zinfandel. Do you have a preference?'

'I'll let you pick,' she said.

In the kitchen, she leaned against the counter, while Alex opened the bottle of sauvignon blanc. Katie set the glasses on the counter next to him, conscious of how close they were standing.

'I should have said it when I got here, but you look beautiful.'

'Thank you,' she said.

He poured some wine, then handed her a glass.

Katie took a sip, feeling inordinately pleased about everything: how she looked and felt, the taste of the wine, the way Alex kept eyeing her while trying not to be obvious about it.

'Would you like to sit on the porch?' she suggested.

He nodded. Outside, they each sat in one of the rockers. In the slowly cooling air, the crickets began their chorus.

Katie savoured the wine, rocking back in the chair. 'When I'm not working, I like to sit out here and read. It's just so quiet, you know? Sometimes I feel like I'm the only one around for miles.'

'You are the only one around for miles. You live in the sticks.'

She playfully slapped his shoulder. 'Watch it. I happen to like my house.'

'You should. It's homey.'

'It's getting there,' she said. 'It's a work in progress. And best of all, it's mine, and no one's going to take it away.'

He looked over at her then. She was staring out over the gravel road, into the grassy field beyond.

'Are you OK?' he asked.

She took her time before answering. 'I was just thinking that I'm glad you're here. You don't even know me.'

'I think I know you well enough.'

Katie said nothing. Alex watched as she lowered her gaze.

'You think you know me,' she whispered, 'but you don't.'

Alex sensed that she was scared to say any more. 'How about I tell you what I think I know, and you tell me if I'm right or wrong?'

She nodded. When Alex went on, his voice was soft.

'I think you're intelligent and charming, and that you're a person with a kind heart. I know that when you want to, you can look more beautiful than anyone I've ever met. You're independent, you've got a good sense of humour, and you show surprising patience with children. You're right in thinking that I don't know the specifics of your past, but I don't know that they're all that important unless you want to tell me about them. Everyone has a past, but that's just it—it's in the past. You can learn from it but you can't change it. Besides, I never knew that person. The person I've come to know is the one I want to get to know even better.'

Katie gave a smile. 'You make it sound so simple,' she said.

'It can be.'

She twisted the stem of her wineglass, considering his words. 'What if the past isn't in the past? What if it's still happening?'

Alex held her gaze. 'You mean . . . what if he finds you?'

Katie flinched. 'What did you say?'

'You heard me,' he said. He kept his voice steady, almost conversational, something he'd learned in CID. 'I'm guessing that you were married once . . . and that maybe he's trying to find you.'

Katie jumped up from the chair, spilling the rest of her wine.

'Who told you?' she demanded. There was no way he could know those things. She hadn't told anyone except Jo. Her neighbour, she thought, had betrayed her. Her *friend* had betrayed her.

As fast as her mind was working, Alex's was working as well.

'No one told me,' he assured her. 'But your reaction makes it clear that I'm right. That's not the important question. I don't know that person, Katie. If you want to tell me about your past, I'm willing to listen. And if you don't want to tell me, that's OK, too. You must have a good reason for keeping it secret, and that means I'm not going to tell anyone, either. You can trust me on that.'

Katie stared at him as he spoke, absorbing every word.

'But . . . how?'

'I've learned to notice things that other people don't,' he went on. 'There was a time in my life when that was all I did. And you're not the first woman I've met in your position.'

'When you were in the army,' she concluded.

He nodded. Finally, he stood from the chair and took a cautious step towards her. 'Can I pour you another glass of wine?'

Still in turmoil, she couldn't answer, but when he reached for her glass, she let him take it. The porch door opened with a squeak and closed behind him, leaving her alone.

She paced to the railing, her thoughts chaotic. She fought the instinct to pack a bag and leave town as soon as she could. But what then? If Alex could figure out the truth simply by watching her, then it was possible for someone else to figure it out, too.

Behind her, she heard the door squeak again. Alex stepped onto the porch, joining her at the railing. He set the glass in front of her.

'Did you figure it out yet?'

'Figure what out?'

'Whether you're going to take off to parts unknown?'

She turned to him, her face registering shock.

He held open his hands. 'What else would you be thinking? But just so you know, I'm curious only because I'm kind of hungry. I'd hate for you to leave before we eat.'

It took her a moment to realise he was teasing, and she found herself smiling in relief. 'We'll have dinner,' she said.

'And tomorrow?'

Instead of answering, she said, 'I want to know how you knew.'

'It wasn't one thing,' he said. He mentioned a few of the things he'd noticed before finally shaking his head. 'Most people wouldn't have put it all together.'

She studied the depths of her glass. 'But you did.'

'I couldn't help it. It's kind of ingrained.'

'And you still wanted to go out with me?'

His expression was serious. 'I've wanted to go out with you from the first moment I saw you. I just had to wait until you were ready.'

They stood at the railing and Alex watched as the breeze gently lifted strands of her hair. She gazed into the distance, and Alex felt his throat catch as he wondered what she was thinking.

'You never answered my question,' he finally said.

She stayed quiet before a shy smile finally appeared.

'I think I'm going to stay in Southport for a while,' she said.

He breathed in her scent. 'You can trust me, you know.'

She leaned into him, feeling his strength as he slipped his arm around her. 'I guess I'm going to have to, aren't I?'

THEY RETURNED to the kitchen a few minutes later. Katie slid the appetiser and stuffed peppers into the oven. Still reeling from Alex's disturbingly accurate assessment of her past, she was glad for tasks to keep her busy. It was hard to fathom that he *still* wanted to spend an evening with her. Deep in her heart, she wasn't sure she deserved to be happy. That was the dirty secret associated with her past. Not that she'd been abused but that somehow she felt that she deserved it because she'd let it happen.

But here and now, it mattered less than it once had, because she suspected that Alex understood her shame. And accepted that, too.

From the refrigerator, Katie pulled out the raspberry sauce to reheat. It didn't take long, and after setting it aside, she pulled the bacon-wrapped Brie from the oven, topped it with the sauce, and brought the cheese to the table.

'This is just to start,' she said.

Alex leaned towards the platter. 'It smells amazing.' He took a bite of brie. 'Wow,' he said. 'It's delicious. I'm glad you're staying in Southport. I can easily imagine myself eating this regularly, even if I have to barter items at my store to get it.'

'The recipe isn't complicated.'

'You haven't seen me cook. I'm great with kid food, but after that, it starts going downhill fast.'

When the appetiser was finished, Katie went to the oven to peek at the peppers. She got the scampi sauce started, then began to sauté the shrimp. By the time the shrimp were done, the sauce was ready as well. She put a pepper on each plate and added the main course.

They ate and talked while, outside, the stars emerged. Alex praised the meal, claiming that he'd never tasted anything better. As the candle burned lower and the wine bottle emptied, Katie revealed bits and pieces about her life growing up in Altoona. She gave Alex the unvarnished version: the constant moves, her parents' alcoholism, the fact that she'd been on her own since she'd turned eighteen. Alex listened without judgment. When she finally trailed off, she found herself wondering whether she'd said too much. But it was then that he reached over and placed his hand on hers. They held hands across the table, neither of them willing to let go.

'I should probably start cleaning the kitchen,' Katie said finally, pushing her chair away from the table. Alex was aware that the moment had been lost and wanted nothing more than to get it back.

'I want you to know I've had a wonderful time,' he began.

'Alex . . . I . . .'

He shook his head. 'You don't have to say anything—'

She didn't let him finish. 'I want to, OK?' Her eyes glittered with emotion. 'I've had a wonderful time, too. But I know where this is leading. I don't want you to get hurt. I can't make promises. I can't tell you where I'll be tomorrow, let alone a year from now. As much as you know about me, there's a lot you don't know.'

Alex felt something collapse inside him. 'Are you saying that you don't want to see me again?'

'No.' She shook her head vehemently. 'I'm saying all this because I do want to see you and it scares me because I know that you deserve someone better. You deserve someone you can count on. Like I said, there are things you don't know about me.'

'Those things don't matter,' Alex insisted.

'How can you say that?'

'Because I know me,' he said, realising that he was in love with her. He loved the Katie he'd come to know and the Katie he'd never had the chance to meet. He rose from the table, moving to her.

'Alex . . . this can't . . .'

'Katie,' he whispered. He put a hand on her hip and pulled her closer. Katie exhaled, and when she looked up at him, it was suddenly easy for her to imagine that her fears were pointless. That he would love her no matter what she told him, and that he was the kind of man who loved her already and would love her forever.

And it was then she realised that she loved him, too.

With that, she let herself lean into him. She felt their bodies come together as he raised a hand to her hair. His touch was gentle and soft. He tilted his head, their faces drawing close.

When their lips finally came together, she could taste the wine on his tongue. She gave herself over to him then, allowing him to kiss her cheek and her neck, revelling in the sensation.

This is what it feels like to really love someone, she thought, and to be loved in return, and she could feel the tears beginning to form. She blinked, but they were impossible to stop. She loved him and wanted him, but more than that, she wanted him to love the real her, with all her flaws and secrets. She wanted him to know the truth.

They kissed for a long time in the kitchen, his hand moving over her back and in her hair. When he ran a finger over the skin of her arm, she felt a flood of liquid heat course through her body.

'I want to be with you but I can't,' she finally whispered, hoping that he wouldn't be angry. 'There's something you should know.'

'It's OK. Whatever it is, I'm sure I can handle it.'

She leaned into him again. 'I can't be with you tonight for the same reason I could never marry you. I have a husband.'

'I know,' he whispered.

'It doesn't matter to you?'

'It's not perfect, but trust me, I'm not perfect, either, so maybe it's best if we take all of this one day at a time. And when you're ready, if you're ever ready, I'll be waiting.' He brushed her cheek with his finger. 'I love you, Katie. You might not be ready to say those words now, but that doesn't change how I feel about you.'

'Alex . . .'

'You don't have to say it,' he said.

'I want to tell you something. I want to tell you about me.'

6

Three days before Katie left New England, a brisk early January wind made the snowflakes freeze, and she had to lower her head as she walked towards the salon. Her long blonde hair blew in the wind. Behind her, Kevin sat in the car watching her. She could imagine his mouth set into a hard, straight line.

The crowds that had filled the mall during Christmas were gone. When Katie pulled the door open, chilled air followed her into the salon. She slipped off her gloves and jacket, turning around as she did so. She waved good-bye to Kevin and smiled. He liked it when she smiled at him.

Her appointment was at two with a woman named Rachel. It was her first time here and she was uncomfortable. None of the stylists looked older than thirty and most had wild hair with red and blue tints. She was approached by a girl in her mid-twenties, tanned and pierced with a tattoo on her neck.

'I'm Rachel. Are you my two o'clock? Colour and trim?'

Katie nodded.

'Follow me.' Rachel led her to a station near the corner and put a smock over her. 'Are you new in the area?' she asked.

'I live in Dorchester,' Katie said.

'That's out of the way. Did someone give you a referral?'

Katie had passed by the salon two weeks earlier, when Kevin had taken her shopping, but she didn't say that. Instead, she simply shook her head.

'I guess I'm lucky I answered the phone then.' Rachel smiled. 'What sort of colour do you want?'

Katie hated to stare at herself in the mirror but she didn't have a choice. She had to get this right. She *had* to.

'I want it to look natural, so maybe some lowlights for winter?'

Rachel nodded into the mirror. 'Easy as pie,' she said. 'Just give me a couple of minutes to get things ready and I'll be back, OK?'

Katie nodded.

Rachel returned with the foil and the colour. Near the chair, she stirred the colour, making sure the consistency was right.

'Was that your husband who dropped you off?' Rachel asked as she coated and wrapped a strand of hair.

'Yes.'

'How long have you been married?'

'Four years.'

Rachel kept up her patter. 'So what do you do?'

Katie stared straight ahead, trying not to see herself. Wishing that she were someone else. She could be here for an hour and a half before Kevin came back and she prayed he wouldn't arrive early.

'I don't have a job,' Katie answered.

'I'd go crazy if I didn't work. Not that it's always easy. What did you do before you were married?'

'I was a cocktail waitress.'

'Is that where you met your husband?'

'Yes,' Katie said.

'So what's he doing now? While you're getting your hair done?'

He's probably at a bar, Katie thought. 'I don't know.'

'Why didn't you drive? Like I said, it's kind of out of the way.'

'I don't drive. My husband drives me when I need to go somewhere.'

'I'd hate to have to depend on someone else like that.'

'I never learned to drive.'

Rachel shrugged as she worked another piece of foil into Katie's hair. 'It's not hard. Practise, take the test, and you're good to go.'

She worked in silence for the next few minutes before finally leading

Katie to another seat. Rachel turned on a heat lamp.

'I'll be back to check in a few minutes, OK?'

Rachel wandered off towards another stylist. Katie glanced at the clock. Kevin would be back in less than an hour. Time was going too fast. She tried not to stare at the clock. Finally, Rachel removed the foil and led Katie to the sink. She massaged the shampoo into Katie's scalp and rinsed, then added conditioner and rinsed again.

'Now let's trim you up, OK?'

Back at the station, Rachel combed Katie's hair. There were forty minutes left. Rachel stared into the mirror at Katie's reflection.

'How much do you want taken off?' Rachel asked.

'Not too much,' Katie said. 'My husband likes it long.'

'Will do,' Rachel said.

Katie watched as she snipped it with the scissors. Finally Rachel reached for the hair dryer and a circular brush. She ran the brush through Katie's hair. Over the noise of the dryer in her ear. Katie asked for some light curls and Rachel brought out the curling iron. There were twenty minutes left.

Rachel curled and brushed until she was finally satisfied and studied Katie in the mirror. 'How's that?'

Katie examined the colour and style. 'Perfect. How much is it?'

Rachel told her and Katie dug into her purse. She pulled out the money she needed, including the tip. 'Could I have a receipt?'

'Sure,' Rachel said. 'Just come with me to the register.'

The girl wrote it up. Kevin would check it and ask for the change when she got in the car. She glanced at the clock. Twelve minutes.

Kevin had yet to return and her heart was beating fast as she slipped her jacket and gloves back on.

She left the salon while Rachel was still talking to her. Next door, at Radio Shack, she asked the assistant for a disposable cellphone and a card that allowed her twenty hours of service. She felt faint as she said the words, knowing that after this, there was no turning back.

He pulled one out from under the counter and began to ring it up while he explained how it worked. She had extra money in her purse tucked into a tampon case because Kevin would never look there. She pulled it out, laying the crumpled bills on the counter. The clock was continuing to tick and she began to feel dizzy.

It was taking forever. She wondered if Kevin would see her leaving the store. The assistant asked if she wanted a bag but she was out of the door without answering. She jammed the phone into her jacket pocket along with the prepaid card. The phone felt like lead, and the snow and ice made it hard to keep her balance.

She opened the door of the salon and went back inside. She slipped off her jacket and gloves and waited by the register. Thirty seconds later, she saw Kevin's car turn into the lot.

Rachel came towards her. 'Did you forget something?' she asked.

Katie exhaled. 'I was going to wait outside but it's too cold,' she explained. 'And then I realised I didn't get your card.'

Rachel's face lit up. 'Oh, that's right. Hold on a second.' She walked towards her station and pulled a card from the drawer. Katie knew that Kevin was watching her from inside the car.

Rachel returned with her business card and handed it over. 'I usually don't work on Sundays or Mondays,' she said.

Katie nodded. 'I'll give you a call.'

Behind her, she heard the door open and Kevin was standing in the doorway. She slipped her jacket back on, trying to control the trembling of her hands. Then, she turned and smiled.

THE SNOW WAS falling harder as Kevin Tierney pulled the car into the driveway. There were bags of groceries in the backseat and Kevin grabbed three of them before walking towards the door. He'd said nothing on the drive from the salon, had said little to her in the grocery store. Instead, he'd walked beside her as she scanned the shelves looking for bargains and trying not to think about the phone in her pocket. Money was tight and Kevin would be angry if she spent too much. When Kevin paid for the groceries, she handed him the change from the salon and the receipt. He counted the money, making sure everything was there.

At home, she rubbed her arms to stay warm. The house was old and frigid air wormed its way beneath the front door, but Kevin never let her adjust the thermostat.

Kevin placed the groceries on the kitchen table. Opening the freezer, he pulled out a bottle of vodka and ice cubes. He dropped the cubes into a glass and poured the vodka. Leaving her alone, he went to the living room and she heard the sounds of the television.

Katie slipped her jacket off and reached into the pocket. After peeking in the living room, she hurried to the sink. In the cupboard below, there was a box of scrubbing pads. She placed the cellphone at the bottom of the box and put the pads over the top of it.

She began to put the groceries away, knowing she had to act normal. Kevin liked a tidy house. She kept out some green beans and found a dozen red potatoes in the pantry. She left a cucumber on the counter, along with iceberg lettuce and a tomato for a salad. The main course was marinated steaks. She'd put the steaks in the marinade the day before.

She cut the potatoes in half, only enough for the two of them. She oiled a baking pan, turned the oven on, and seasoned the potatoes with salt, pepper, and garlic. They would go in before the steaks.

Kevin liked his salads finely diced. She cut the tomato in half and cut the cucumber. As she opened the door, she noticed Kevin in the kitchen behind her, leaning against the doorjamb that led to the dining room. He finished his vodka and continuing to watch her.

He didn't know she'd left the salon, she reminded herself. He didn't know she'd bought a cellphone.

'Steaks tonight?' he finally asked.

'Yes. It'll be a few minutes. I've got to put the potatoes in first.'

Kevin stared at her. 'Your hair looks good,' he said.

'Thank you. She did a good job.'

Katie began to cut the tomato, making a long slice.

'Not too big,' he said, nodding in her direction.

'I know,' she said. She smiled as he moved to the freezer. He pulled the bottle of vodka out again and watched as she diced the tomatoes. She tried not to cringe as he placed his hands on her hips. Knowing what she had to do, she turned towards him, putting her arms around his neck. She kissed him, and didn't see the slap coming until she felt the sting against her cheek. It burned, red and hot.

'You made me waste my entire afternoon!' he shouted at her. He gripped her arms tight, squeezing hard. She could smell the booze on his breath. 'My only day off and you pick that day to get your hair done in the middle of the city! And then go grocery shopping!'

She wiggled, trying to back away, and he finally let her go.

'I'm sorry,' she said, holding her cheek. She didn't say that she'd checked with him twice earlier in the week if it would be OK, or that he was the one who made her switch salons because he didn't want her making friends.

'I'm sorry,' he mimicked her. He shook his head. 'Is it so hard for you to think about anyone other than yourself?'

He tried to grab her, and she turned, trying to run. There was nowhere to go. He struck fast and hard, his fist a piston, firing at her lower back. She gasped, her vision going black. She collapsed to the floor, her kidney on fire, the pain shooting up her spine. When she tried to get up, the movement only made it worse.

'You're so damn selfish!' he said, towering over her.

She said nothing. She bit her lip to keep from screaming and wondered if she would pee blood tomorrow.

He continued to stand over her, then let out a disgusted sigh. He grabbed the bottle of vodka on the way out of the kitchen.

It took her almost a minute to get up. When she started cutting again, her hands were shaking. The week before, he'd hit her so hard in the stomach that she'd spent the rest of the night vomiting.

Tears were on her cheeks and she had to keep shifting her weight to keep the pain at bay as she finished dicing the tomato. She diced the cucumber as well. Small pieces. Lettuce, too, diced and chopped. The way he wanted it.

The oven was ready and she put the baking sheet in and set the timer. She rinsed and cut the green beans and put some olive oil in the frying pan. She would start the beans when the steaks went in the broiler. She was removing the baking sheet from the oven when Kevin came back in the kitchen. His eyes were glassy.

'Just a little longer,' she said, pretending that nothing had happened. She'd learned that if she acted angry or hurt, it only enraged him. 'I have to finish the steaks and then dinner will be ready.'

'I'm sorry,' he said. He swayed slightly.

She smiled. 'It's OK. It's been a hard few weeks.'

He took a step towards her. 'You're so beautiful. You know I love you. I don't like hitting you. You just don't *think* sometimes.'

She nodded, trying to think of something to do, then remembered she had to set the table. She moved to the cupboard near the sink.

He moved behind her as she was reaching for the plates and rotated her towards him, pulling her close. She inhaled before offering a contented sigh, because she knew he wanted her to make those sounds. 'You're supposed to say you love me, too,' he whispered.

'I love you,' she said.

His hand travelled to her breast. 'God, you're beautiful,' he said. He pressed himself harder against her. 'Let's hold off on putting the steaks in. Dinner can wait.'

'I thought you were hungry.' She made it sound like a tease.

'I'm hungry for something else right now,' he whispered. He kissed her once more before leading her to the bedroom.

He was almost frenzied as soon as they got there. She panted and moaned and called his name, knowing he wanted her to do those things, because she didn't want him to be angry. When it was over, she got dressed, went back to the kitchen and finished making dinner.

Kevin went back to the living room and drank more vodka before going to the table. He told her about work and then went to watch television again while she cleaned the kitchen. Afterward, he wanted her to sit beside him and watch television so she did, until it was finally time to turn in.

In the bedroom, he was snoring within minutes, oblivious to Katie's silent tears, oblivious to her hatred of him, her hatred of herself. Oblivious to the money she'd been stashing away for almost a year or the hair dye she'd snuck into the grocery basket a month ago and hidden in the closet, oblivious to the cellphone hidden in the cupboard beneath the kitchen sink. Oblivious to the fact that in just a few days, he would never see or hit her ever again.

KATIE SAT beside Alex on the porch, the sky above them a black expanse dotted with light. For months, she'd tried to block out the specific memories, focusing only on the fear that had been left behind. She didn't want to remember Kevin, didn't want to think about him. She wanted to erase him entirely, to pretend he never existed. But he would always be there.

Alex had stayed silent throughout her story. She'd told him without emotion, almost in a trance, as if the events had happened to someone else. He felt sick to his stomach by the time she'd trailed off. He'd heard versions of the same story before, but this time it was different. She wasn't simply a victim, she was his friend, the woman he'd come to love.

'You did the right thing by leaving,' he said. His tone was soft.

It took her a moment to respond. 'I know,' she said.

'It had nothing to do with you.'

She stared into the darkness. 'Yes it did. I chose him. I married him. I let it happen once and then again, and after that, it was too late. I still cooked for him and cleaned for him. I slept with him whenever he wanted. I made him think I *loved* it.'

'You did what you had to do to survive,' he said.

She grew silent again. The crickets were chirping and locusts hummed from the trees. 'I never thought something like this could happen, you know? My dad was a drunk, but he wasn't violent. I was just so . . . weak. I don't know why I let it happen.'

His voice was soft. 'Because at one time you loved him. You believed him when he promised it wouldn't happen again. You felt like he would change until you finally realised he wouldn't.'

With his words, she inhaled sharply and lowered her head, her shoulders heaving up and down. The sound of her anguish made his throat clench with anger. He wanted to hold her, but knew that right now, at this moment, he was doing all she wanted. She was fragile.

It took a few minutes before she was able to stop crying. 'I'm sorry I told you all that,' she said, her voice still choked up. 'The only reason I did was because you already knew.'

'I know. I'm glad you did.'

'I hate him,' she said. 'But I hate myself, too. I'm not the woman you think you know.'

She was on the verge of crying again and he finally stood. He tugged at her hand, willing her to stand. She did but wouldn't look at him. He kept his voice soft.

'Listen to me,' he said. He used a finger to raise her chin. She finally looked at him. He went on. 'There's nothing you can tell me that will change how I feel about you. Because that isn't you. You're the woman I've come to know. The woman I love.'

'But . . .'

'No buts,' he said, 'because there are none. You see yourself as someone who couldn't get away. I see the courageous woman who escaped. You see yourself as someone who should be ashamed because she let it happen. I see a kind, beautiful woman who should feel proud because she stopped it from happening ever again.'

He moved towards her, making sure it was OK before leaning in to kiss her. It was brief and soft. 'I'm just sorry you had to go through it at all.'

'I'm still going through it.'

'Because you think he's looking for you?'

'I know he's looking for me. And he'll never stop.' She paused, then said, 'There's something wrong with him. He's . . . insane.'

Alex thought about that. 'I know I shouldn't ask, but did you ever think of calling the police?'

Her shoulders dropped slightly. 'Yes,' she said. 'I called once.'

'And they didn't do anything?'

'They came to the house and talked to me. They convinced me not to press charges.'

Alex considered it. 'That doesn't make sense.'

'It made perfect sense to me.' She shrugged. 'Kevin warned me that it wouldn't do any good to call the police.'

'How would he know?'

She sighed, thinking she might as well tell him everything. 'Because he is the police,' she said. 'He's a detective with the Boston Police Department. He didn't call me Katie. He called me Erin.'

ON MEMORIAL DAY, hundreds of miles to the north, Kevin Tierney stood in the backyard of a house in Dorchester, wearing shorts and a Hawaiian-style shirt he'd bought when he and Erin had visited Oahu on their honeymoon.

'Erin's back in Manchester,' he said.

Bill Robinson, his captain, flipped burgers on the grill. 'Again?'

'I told you that her friend has cancer, right? She feels like she's got to be there for her friend.'

'That cancer's bad stuff,' Bill said. 'How's Erin holding up?'

'OK. I can tell she's tired, though. It's hard to keep going back and forth like she's been doing.'

'I can imagine,' Bill said. 'Emily had to do something like that when her sister got lupus.'

Kevin took a pull on his beer, and because it was expected of him, he smiled. Emily was Bill's wife and they'd been married almost thirty years. Bill hosted a barbecue at his house every Memorial Day and pretty much everyone who wasn't on duty showed up. Wives and husbands, girlfriends and boyfriends, and kids were clustered in groups, some in the kitchen, others on the patio.

'Next time she's back in town,' Bill added, 'why don't you bring her by for dinner? Em's been asking about her.'

Kevin wondered if the offer was genuine. Bill liked to pretend he was just one of the guys instead of the captain. But he was cunning. More a politician than a cop. 'I'll mention it to her.'

A group of kids ran across the patio. Two women exited the house carrying bowls of chips, probably gossiping. Kevin hated gossips.

'I need another beer,' Kevin said. 'You want one?'

Bill shook his head. 'I'm still working on mine. But thanks.'

Kevin stayed at the barbecue for a couple of hours. He talked with Coffey and Ramirez. They were detectives like him. Kevin didn't want to be the first one to leave, because he didn't want to offend the captain. He didn't like Coffey or Ramirez. Kevin knew they talked about him behind his back. Gossips. But Kevin was a good detective and he knew it. Bill knew it, and so did Coffey and Ramirez. He worked homicide and knew how to talk to witnesses and suspects. He knew when people were lying. He put murderers behind bars because the Bible says, *Thou shalt not kill* and he was doing God's work by putting the guilty in jail.

Later, back at home, Kevin walked through the living room. If Erin had been here, the mantel would have been dusted and there wouldn't have been an empty bottle of vodka on the couch. If Erin had been here, the dishes would have been washed and put away and dinner would have been waiting on the table and she would have smiled at him and asked him how his day had gone.

Though it was supposed to have been a relaxing day, he was tired. He hadn't wanted to go to the barbecue. It was hard to keep up the pretence that Erin hadn't left him. He'd invented a story and had stuck to it for months: that Erin called every night, that she'd been home the last few days but had gone back to New Hampshire, that the friend was undergoing chemotherapy and needed Erin's help. He knew he couldn't keep that up forever.

Kevin went to the bed and lay down. Next thing he knew, it was morning. He showered and had vodka and toast for breakfast. At the precinct, he was called out to investigate a murder. A woman in her twenties, most likely a prostitute, had been found stabbed to death, her body tossed in a Dumpster. He spent the morning talking to bystanders while the evidence was collected. When he finished, he went to the precinct to start the report while the information was fresh in his mind. He was a good detective.

The precinct was busy. Kevin walked towards his desk, one of four in the middle of the room. Through the open door, Bill waved but stayed in his office. Ramirez and Coffey were at their desks, sitting across from him.

'You OK?' Coffey asked. Coffey was in his forties, overweight and bald. 'You look like hell.'

'I didn't sleep well,' Kevin said.

'I don't sleep well without Janet, either. When's Erin coming back?'

Kevin kept his expression neutral. 'Next weekend. I've got a few days coming and we've decided to go to the Cape.'

'Yeah? My mom lives there. Where at the Cape?'

'Provincetown.'

'So does she. You'll love it there. Where are you staying?'

Kevin wondered why Coffey kept asking questions. 'I'm not sure,' he finally said. 'Erin's making the arrangements.'

Kevin would have to find the name of a bed-and-breakfast and a couple of restaurants, so if Coffey asked, he'd know what to say.

His days followed the same routine. He worked and talked to witnesses and finally went home. His work was stressful. He'd once believed that he would get used to the sight of murder victims, but their grey, lifeless faces were etched in his memory.

He didn't like going home. When he finished his shift, there was no beautiful wife to greet him at the door. Erin had been gone since January. Now, his house was dirty and he had to do his own laundry. There were no home-cooked meals. Instead, he grabbed food on the way home and ate on the couch.

After work he no longer bothered to store his gun in the gun box he kept in his closet; in the box, he had a second Glock for his personal use. Erin had been afraid of guns, even before he'd placed the Glock to her head and threatened to kill her if she ever ran away again. She'd screamed and cried as he'd sworn that he'd kill any man she slept with. Erin swore there wasn't a man. He'd never believed another man was involved. While they were married, he'd made sure of that. He never let her go to the store or to the hair salon or to the library by herself. She hadn't left because she wanted to commit adultery. She left because she was tired of getting kicked and punched. He knew he shouldn't have done those things and he always apologised but it hadn't mattered.

He went to the kitchen and pulled a bottle of vodka from the freezer. He knew he was drinking too much. He knew he should eat better and stop drinking, but all he wanted to do was take the bottle and sit on the couch and drink. He poured a glass of vodka, finished it, and poured another.

It was all so confusing. The house was a wreck. The casing around the bathroom door was splintered and cracked. He'd kicked the door in after she'd locked it, trying to get away from him. He'd punched her in the kitchen and she'd run to the bathroom. But now he couldn't remember what they'd been fighting about. He bought her flowers and apologised and promised it would never happen again. Afterward, he remembered thinking about how much he loved her and how lucky he was to have her as his wife.

7

Alex had stayed with Katie until after midnight, listening as she'd told the story of her prior life. When she was too exhausted to talk anymore, he kissed her good night. On his drive home, he thought that he had never met anyone braver or more resourceful.

They spent much of the next couple of weeks together. He anticipated his visits to her place with a sense of excitement he hadn't felt in years. Sometimes, Kristen and Josh went with him. Other times, Joyce would shoo him out the door with a wink.

They seldom spent time at his house and when they did, it was only for short periods. Part of him realised it had to do with Carly. Though he knew he loved Katie, he wasn't sure he was ready for that just yet. Katie didn't seem to mind, if only because it was easier to be alone at her place.

Even so, they'd yet to make love. Though he often found himself imagining how wonderful it would be, he knew Katie wasn't ready. For now, it was enough to kiss her, to feel her arms wrapped around him. He hadn't slept with anyone since his wife had died, and now he felt that he had unknowingly been waiting for Katie.

Since their dinner at her house, she hadn't broached her past again. He knew she was still working things out in her mind: whether or not she could trust him, what would happen if Kevin found her. Watching her, he would sometimes be overcome with an overwhelming rage at Kevin. He knew that if Kevin ever showed up, Alex would protect Katie, no matter what.

On most days, the spectre of Katie's past life didn't intrude, and they spent each day in a state of growing intimacy. The afternoons with the kids were particularly special. Katie was a natural with children. In this way she was like Carly, and he felt certain that Katie was the kind of woman Carly had once spoken about.

In the final weeks of Carly's life, he had maintained a vigil beside her bed, even though she slept most of the time. By then, speech was difficult. But one night, she'd reached for him.

'I want you to do something for me,' she said with effort.

'Anything.'

'I want you to be . . . happy.' At this, he saw the ghost of her old smile, the smile that had captivated him at their first meeting.

'I am happy.'

She gave a faint shake of her head. 'I'm talking about the future.' Her eyes gleamed. 'We both know what I'm talking about.'

'I don't.'

She ignored his response. 'Marrying you . . . having children with you . . . it's the best thing I've ever done.'

His throat closed up. 'Me, too,' he said. 'I feel the same way.'

'I know,' she said. 'And that's why this is so hard for me. I love you, Alex, and I love our kids. It would break my heart to think that you'll never be happy again. I want you to meet someone new.' She struggled to take a breath. 'I want her to be smart and kind . . . I want you to fall in love with her, because you shouldn't spend the rest of your life alone.'

Alex couldn't speak, could barely see her through his tears.

'The kids need a mom.' To his ears, it sounded almost like a plea. 'Someone who loves them as much as I do, someone who thinks of them as her own children.'

'Why are you talking about this?' he asked, his voice cracking.

'Because,' she said, 'I have to believe that it's possible.' Her bony fingers clutched at his arm. 'It's the only thing I have left.'

Now, as he saw Katie chasing after Josh and Kristen on the grassy shoulder of the duck pond, he felt a bittersweet pang at the thought that maybe Carly had got her last wish after all.

SHE LIKED HIM too much for her own good. Katie knew that she was walking a dangerous line. Telling him about her past had seemed like the right thing to do. But the morning after their first dinner, she was paralysed with anxiety. Alex used to be an investigator, which meant he could easily make a phone call or two. He'd talk to someone and they'd talk to someone and eventually, Kevin would learn of it. She hadn't told him that Kevin had an eerie ability to connect seemingly random information. When a suspect was on the run, Kevin almost always knew where to find him.

But gradually, over the next couple of weeks, she felt her fears ebb. The days passed with easy spontaneity. She couldn't help it: she trusted Alex. And when they kissed, her knees went shaky and it was all she could do to stop from dragging him into the bedroom.

On Saturday, two weeks after their first date, they stood on her front porch, his arms wrapped around her, his lips against hers. Josh and Kristen were at a swimming party hosted by a kid in Josh's class. Later, Alex and Katie planned to take them to the beach for an evening barbecue, but for the next few hours, they'd be alone.

When they finally separated, Katie sighed. 'Do you know what I like about you?'

'My body?'

'Yes. That, too.' She laughed. 'But I also that you make me feel special.'

'You are special,' he said. 'I'm glad you ended up in Southport.'

'Uh-huh.' For an instant she seemed to disappear inside herself.

'What?' He scrutinised her face, suddenly alert.

She shook her head. 'It was so close . . .' She sighed, hugging her arms around herself at the memory. 'I almost didn't make it.'

BRITTLE SNOW coated the yards of Dorchester, forming a glittering shell over the world outside her window. The January sky, grey the day before, had given way to an icy blue.

It was Sunday morning, the day after she'd had her hair done. Her kidney still throbbed. It had kept her up for hours as Kevin snored beside her. After closing the bedroom door behind her, she limped to the kitchen, reminding herself that in just a couple of days, it would be over. But she had to be careful not to arouse Kevin's suspicions, to play things exactly right.

Kevin had to go into work at noon, even though it was Sunday, and she knew he'd be up soon. She started the coffee and put the milk and sugar on the table, along with butter and grape jelly. After that, she put three eggs on the counter and placed six slices of bacon in the frying pan. They were sizzling when Kevin finally wandered into the kitchen. He took a seat and she brought him a cup of coffee.

'I was dead to the world last night,' he said. 'What time did we end up going to bed?'

'Maybe ten?' she answered. 'It wasn't late. You've been working hard and I know you've been tired.'

His eyes were bloodshot. 'I'm sorry about last night. I didn't mean it. I've just been under a lot of pressure lately. Since Terry's heart attack, I've been having to do the work of two people.'

Terry Canton had been Kevin's partner for the last three years, but he'd had a heart attack in December and had been off work since. Kevin had been working alone.

'It's OK,' she said. She could still smell the alcohol on his breath. 'Your breakfast will be ready in a few minutes.'

When the bacon was crispy, she put four pieces on Kevin's plate and two on hers. She put two pieces of bread in the toaster and cracked the eggs. He liked his over medium, with the yolk intact. The eggs cooked quickly. She slid two onto his plate and one onto hers. The toast came up and she placed both slices on his plate.

She sat across from him at the table because he liked them to have breakfast together. He buttered his toast and added grape jelly before using his fork to break the eggs.

She stared out the window, thinking of other things. She had learned to hate winter, with the endless cold, because she couldn't go outside. Kevin didn't like her to walk around the neighbourhood but he let her garden in the backyard because of the privacy fence. In the spring, she always planted flowers in pots and vegetables in a small plot near the back of the garage.

But winter made her life a prison. Most days were spent without setting foot outside the door because she never knew when Kevin would show up unexpectedly. She knew the names of one of her neighbours, the Feldmans, who lived across the street. In her first year of marriage, Kevin rarely hit her and sometimes she went for walks without him. The Feldmans, an older couple, liked to work in their garden, and she'd often stopped to talk to them. Kevin gradually tried to put an end to those friendly visits. Now she saw the Feldmans only when she knew Kevin was busy at work. She felt like a spy when she visited them. They showed her photos of their daughters growing up. One had died and the other had moved away and she had the sense that they were as lonely as she was.

After Kevin went to work, she vacuumed, dusted, and cleaned the kitchen. She tried not to think about the cellphone she had charged overnight and put under the sink. Even though she knew that she might never get a better chance, she was terrified because there was so much that could go wrong.

She made Kevin breakfast on Monday, just as she always did. He was grumpy and distracted and he read the paper without saying much. When he was about to leave, he put a coat on over his suit.

'Is there anything special you want for dinner?' she asked.

He thought about it. 'Lasagne and garlic bread. And a salad.'

When he left, she stood at the window watching as his car reached the corner. As soon as he turned, she walked to the phone, dizzy at the thought of what was to come next.

When she called the phone company, she was directed to customer service. Five minutes passed, then six. It would take Kevin twenty minutes to get to work, and no doubt he would call as soon as he arrived. She still had time. Finally, a rep got on the line.

'Is it possible to get call forwarding on my line?' she asked.

'It's an extra charge, but with that, you also get call waiting and voice mail. It's only—'

'That's fine. But is it possible to have it turned on today?'

'Yes,' the representative said. He took some more information and then told her it was done and that she would be able to use the service right away. She hung up and glanced at the clock. The whole transaction had taken eighteen minutes. Kevin called from the precinct three minutes later.

As soon as she got off the phone with Kevin, she called Super Shuttle, a van service that transported people to the airport and bus station. She made a reservation for the following day. Then, after retrieving the cellphone, she activated it. She called a local cinema that had a recording, to make sure it worked. Next, she activated the landline's call-forwarding service, sending incoming calls to the cinema. As a test, she dialled the home number from her cellphone. Her heart was pounding as the landline rang. On the second ring, the ring cut off and she heard the recording from the cinema. Something broke free inside her and her hands were shaking as she powered off the cellphone and replaced it in the box of scouring pads. She reset the landline. Kevin called again forty minutes later.

She spent the rest of the afternoon working steadily to keep from worrying. She scrubbed the bathroom until the floor was shiny. She started preparing the lasagne. She brushed four pieces of sourdough bread with butter, garlic, and oregano and diced everything she needed for the salad. At five, she put the pasta dish in the oven.

When Kevin got home, dinner was ready. He ate and talked about his day. After dinner, he drank vodka as they watched a basketball game. He fell asleep in front of the television and she wandered to the bedroom. She lay in bed, staring at the ceiling, until he finally woke and staggered in. He fell asleep immediately.

She made him breakfast on Tuesday morning. Kevin had been one of several detectives assigned to a big murder investigation and all were scheduled to testify Wednesday at the trial, which was in Marlborough, not Boston. He packed his clothes and toiletries and was finally ready to head to Marlborough. He loaded his things into the car, then went back to the front door and kissed her.

'I'll be home tomorrow night,' he said.

'I'll miss you,' she said, putting her arms around his neck.

'I should be home around eight.' He kissed her as she leaned into him. 'I'll call you,' he said, his hands caressing her.

'I know,' she answered.

IN THE BATHROOM, she took off her clothes. She'd placed a garbage bag in the sink, and naked, she stared at herself in the mirror. She fingered the bruises on her ribs and on her wrist. Dark circles beneath her eyes gave her face a hollowed-out look.

With the scissors, she began to chop savagely at her hair. Four inches of blonde hair fell onto the garbage bag. She seized another chunk, using her fingers to pull it tight, and snipped.

'I hate you!' she hissed. 'You degraded me all the time!' She lopped off more hair, her eyes flooding with rage-fuelled tears. 'Hit me because I had to go shopping!' More hair gone. 'Made me steal money from your wallet and kicked me because you were drunk!'

She snapped the scissors. 'I loved you!' She sobbed. 'You promised me you'd never hit me again and I believed you!' She cut and cried, and when her hair was all the same length, she pulled out the hair dye from behind the sink. Dark Brown. She tilted the bottle and began massaging the dye into her hair. She stood at the mirror and sobbed uncontrollably while it set. When it was done, she climbed into the shower and rinsed it out. She shampooed and conditioned and stood before the mirror. She added bronzer to her skin, darkening it. She dressed in jeans and a sweater and stared at herself. A dark, short-haired stranger looked back at her.

She cleaned the bathroom scrupulously. She had to hurry. She packed her things in a duffle bag. Three pairs of jeans, two sweatshirts, shirts. Panties and bras. Socks. Toothbrush and toothpaste. A brush. The little jewellery she owned. Cheese and crackers and nuts and raisins. A fork and a knife. She went to the back porch and dug out the money from beneath the flowerpot. The cellphone from the kitchen. And finally, the identification she needed to start a new life, identification she'd stolen from people who trusted her. She knew it was wrong, but she'd had no other choice.

She threw on a hat and her jacket, along with a scarf and gloves. She rounded the duffle bag and stuffed it beneath her sweatshirt, working it until it was round. Until she looked pregnant. She put on her long coat, one that was roomy enough to cover the bump.

She put on a pair of sunglasses, and on her way out the door, she turned on her cellphone and set the landline on call forwarding. She left the house through the gate at the side. She deposited the garbage bag in the neighbours' garbage can. She walked through their yard and past the side of the house, finally emerging onto the icy sidewalk. Snow had begun to fall again. By tomorrow, she knew, her footprints would be gone.

She had six blocks to go but she was going to make it. She kept her head down, trying to ignore the biting wind, feeling dazed and free and terrified. Tomorrow night, she knew, Kevin would walk through the house, calling for her, and he wouldn't find her because she wasn't there. And tomorrow night, he would begin his hunt.

SNOW SWIRLED as Katie stood at the intersection, just outside a diner. In the distance, she saw Super Shuttle's van round the corner and her heart pounded. Just then, she heard the cellphone ring.

She paled. She had to answer; there was no choice. But the van was coming and it was noisy on the street. If she answered now, he would know she was outside. He would know she'd left him.

Her phone rang a third time. The blue van stopped at a red light. She turned around, walking into the diner, the sounds muffled but still noticeable—plates clanking and people talking. Her legs went wobbly as she pressed the button and answered.

'What took you so long to answer?' he demanded.

'I was in the shower,' she said. 'What's going on?'

'I'm about ten minutes out,' he said. 'How are you?'

'I'm OK,' she said.

'You sound funny. Is something wrong with the phone?'

Up the street, the light turned green. The Super Shuttle's turn signal indicated that it was pulling over. She prayed it would wait.

'I'm not sure. But you sound fine,' she said. 'It's probably bad service where you are. How's the drive?'

'Not too bad. But it's still icy in places.'

'That doesn't sound good. Be careful,' she said. The van was pulling over to the kerb, the driver craning his neck, looking for her. 'I hate to do this, but can you call me in a few minutes? I still have conditioner in my hair and I want to rinse it out.'

'Yeah,' he grumbled. 'OK. I'll call you in a bit.'

'I love you,' she said.

'Love you, too.'

She let him hang up before she pressed the button on her phone. Then she walked out of the diner and hurried to the van.

At the bus terminal, she bought a ticket to Philadelphia. Twenty minutes later, she got on the bus. She stared out of the window as the bus pulled away from the station, feeling as if she were dreaming. On the highway, Boston began to recede into the distance.

She arrived in Philadelphia in the late afternoon. Passengers got off the bus and she hung back, waiting for them to leave. In the restroom, she removed the duffle bag and then went into the waiting room and took a seat on a bench. Her stomach was growling and she sliced off a little cheese and ate it with crackers. She knew she had to make it last though, so she put the rest of it away. Finally, after buying a map of the city, she stepped outside.

The terminal wasn't located in a bad part of town, which made her feel safe, but it also meant she could never afford a hotel room in the area. The map indicated that she was close to Chinatown, and for lack of a better plan she headed in that direction.

Three hours later, she'd found a place to sleep. It was dingy, and her room was barely large enough for the small bed that had been crammed inside. The communal bathroom was down the hall. Still, it was all she could afford. She had enough money to stay three nights.

She sat on the edge of the bed, her mind whirling. She couldn't do this, she thought. She wasn't strong enough. In three days, she'd have no place to stay. She lay down on the bed and drifted off to sleep almost immediately. Kevin called later, the bleating of the cellphone waking her up. It took everything she had to keep her voice steady. When he hung up, she fell asleep again within minutes.

In the morning, she had cheese and crackers for breakfast. She changed her clothes and brushed her teeth and hair. She repacked the duffle bag, and walked down the steps. The same clerk who'd given her the key was at the desk. She asked him to hold her room.

Outside, the sky was blue and the streets were dry. Despite her fears she found herself smiling. She'd done it. She'd escaped. Kevin would call a couple more times, then she'd throw away the cellphone and never speak with him again. Today, she told herself, she was going to start living the rest of her life.

SHE HAD RUN away twice. The first time was a little less than a year after she was married, after he'd beaten her while she was cowering in the corner of the bedroom. The bills had come in and he was angry because she'd turned up the thermostat to make the house warmer. When he'd finally stopped, he'd grabbed his keys and headed out to buy more liquor. Without thinking, she'd grabbed her jacket and left the house, limping down the road. Hours later, with nowhere to go, she'd called him and he went to pick her up.

The next time she'd got as far as Atlantic City before he found her. She'd taken money from his wallet and purchased a bus ticket, but he'd found her within an hour of her arrival. He'd driven his car at breakneck speed, knowing she would run to the only place where she might find friends. He'd handcuffed her in the backseat of the car on the drive back. He stopped once, pulling the car over, and beat her; later that night, the gun came out.

After that, he'd made it harder to leave. He kept the money locked away and started tracking her whereabouts obsessively. She knew that he would go to extraordinary lengths to find her. She had a head start, that was all.

She found a job as a cocktail waitress on her third day in town. She made up a name and social security number. She worked for two weeks, accumulated some tip money and quit without bothering to pick up her paycheck. Without identification, she wouldn't be able to cash it. She worked another three weeks at a small diner and moved out of Chinatown to a motel that rented by the week. She'd saved a few hundred dollars, but not enough to start over. Again, she left before picking up her paycheck. She found yet another job a few days later. She told the manager her name was Erica.

It was there, only four days after she started, that she'd rounded the corner on her way to work and saw a car that seemed out of place. She stopped. As she stared at the car, she noticed movement in the driver's seat. The engine wasn't running and it struck her as odd that someone would be sitting in a car on a cold morning.

Kevin. She knew it was him, and she backed around the corner, the way she'd come, praying that he hadn't seen her. As soon as the car was out of sight, she ran back to the motel, her heart hammering. Kevin didn't follow, but no matter. He knew she was here.

In her room, she threw her things into the duffle bag. She had the clerk call her a cab. It arrived ten minutes later.

At the bus station, she selected a bus to New York. It was scheduled to leave in half an hour. She hid in the women's restroom until it was time to board. When she got on the bus she lowered herself into a seat. It didn't take long to get to New York. Again, she scanned the schedules and bought a ticket to Omaha.

In the evening, she got off the bus somewhere in Ohio. She slept in the station, and the next morning she found her way to a truck stop. There she met a man who was delivering materials to Wilmington, North Carolina.

A few days later, after selling her jewellery, she wandered into Southport and found the cottage. After she paid the first month's rent, there was no money left to buy food.

8

Kevin Tierney didn't go to Provincetown at the weekend he'd told Coffey and Ramirez that he would. Instead, he stayed home brooding over how close he'd come to finding her in Philadelphia.

He wouldn't have succeeded in tracking her that far, except that she'd made a mistake in going to the bus station. He knew it was the only choice she could have made. Bus tickets were cheap and identification wasn't necessary, and though he wasn't sure how much she'd stolen from him, it couldn't have been much.

In the darkness, he chewed his lips, remembering his initial hope that she might come back. It was snowing and she couldn't get far.

On the night he realised she was missing last January, he drank two glasses of vodka while he waited for her to come back, but the phone didn't ring. He knew she hadn't been gone long. He'd spoken to her less than an hour before and she'd told him she was making dinner. But there was no dinner on the stove. No sign of her in the house.

Two more vodkas later and another half hour passed. By then, he was in a rage and he punched a hole in the bedroom door. He hopped in his car and drove up and down the streets looking for her. It was three a.m. before he finally went back home, and the house was empty. After another vodka he cried himself to sleep.

In the morning, he was enraged again. He called in sick, then went to the couch and tried to figure out how she'd got away. He was pouring himself a drink when he heard the phone ring. He lunged for it, hoping it was Erin. Strangely, however, the phone rang only once, and when he picked up he heard a dial tone.

How had she got away? He tried to piece together the sequence of events. Something seemed off, though he couldn't identify what it was. He focused on the telephone. It was then that the pieces suddenly came together and he pulled out his cellphone. He dialled his home number and listened as it rang once. The cellphone kept ringing. When he picked up the landline, he heard a dial tone and realised that she'd forwarded the calls to a cellphone. She'd been gone, he now knew, since Tuesday morning.

AT THE BUS station, she made a mistake, even if she couldn't really help it. She should have purchased her tickets from a woman, since Erin was pretty and men always remembered pretty women. It didn't matter whether their hair was long and blonde or short and dark. Nor did it matter if she'd pretended she was pregnant.

He went to the bus station. He showed his badge and carried a larger photograph of her. One of the ticket sellers said that it might have been her, except that her hair was short and brown and that she was pregnant. He didn't, however, remember her destination.

At home, Kevin found a photograph of her on the computer and used

Photoshop to change her hair from blonde to brown and then shortened it. He called in sick again on Friday. *That's her*, the ticket seller confirmed, and Kevin felt a surge of energy. He took a couple of vacation days the following week and continued to hang around the bus station, showing the new photograph to drivers.

On Saturday, eleven days after she'd left, he found the driver. He had taken her to Philadelphia. He remembered her because she was pretty and pregnant and she didn't have any luggage.

Kevin drove to Philadelphia. He parked at the bus station and tried to think like her. He was a good detective and he knew that if he could think like her, he'd be able to find her.

The bus had arrived a few minutes before four o'clock, and he stood in the bus station, looking from one direction to the next. She would need a place to stay. Not in this area. Too expensive. Where would she go? She'd have to walk. Which meant she'd need a map.

He went to the convenience store at the station and bought himself a map. He located the station. It bordered on Chinatown and he guessed she had headed in that direction.

He got back in his car and drove the streets of Chinatown. He drank his vodka and showed her picture around. He found the first place she'd stayed, but the owner didn't know where she'd gone.

Kevin had to go back to work on Monday, furious that she'd eluded him. But the following weekend, he was back in Philadelphia. And the weekend after that. He was patient and diligent. Another weekend passed. He widened his search.

Finally, a week after Valentine's Day, he met a waitress named Tracy who told him that Erin was working at a diner, except she was calling herself Erica. She was scheduled to work the following day.

He rented a car and waited up the block from the diner the following morning, before the sun was up. Employees entered through a door in the alley. He sipped from his Styrofoam cup in the front seat, watching for her. Eventually, he saw Tracy head down the alley. But Erin never showed, and she didn't show up the following day, either. She never came back to pick up her paycheck.

He found where she lived a few hours later. It was walking distance from the diner, a piece-of-crap hotel. The man knew nothing except that Erin had left the day before in a hurry. Kevin raced to the bus station but there were only women in the ticket booths and no one remembered her. Buses in the last two hours were going everywhere.

She'd disappeared again, and in the car Kevin screamed and beat his fists against the wheel until they were bruised.

In the months that Erin had been gone, he felt the ache inside grow more poisonous. He'd returned to Philadelphia and questioned the drivers over the next few weeks. He eventually learned that she'd gone on to New York, but from there, the trail went cold. He flew into rages and broke things; he cried himself to sleep. He was filled with despair and sometimes felt he was losing his mind.

THE THIRD week of June was a series of glorious summer days. Katie continued to work long shifts at the restaurant. She put half the money she earned in tips in the coffee tin, and it was almost filled. She had more than enough money to get away if she had to.

Lingering over her breakfast, she stared out the window. Alex, she knew, would be by later today. His visits had settled into something of a routine, and when they were together, she was constantly reminded of all the reasons she'd fallen for him. He treated her with a gentleness that astonished and touched her. But she wondered if she was being unfair to him. What would happen if Kevin showed up? How would Alex and the kids react if she disappeared? Was she willing to leave all of them behind?

Leaving her breakfast dishes in the sink, she walked through the small cottage, thinking how much had changed in the last few months. She felt loved for the first time in years. She'd never been a parent, but she found herself thinking and worrying about Kristen and Josh when she least expected it. She was struck with the sudden certainty that leaving this new existence behind was inconceivable.

What had Jo once said to her? *I just tell people what they already know but are afraid to admit to themselves.*

Reflecting on her words, she knew exactly what she had to do.

'SURE,' ALEX SAID to her, after she related her request. She could tell he was surprised, but he also seemed encouraged. 'When do you want to start?'

'How about today?' she suggested. 'If you have any time.'

He looked around the store. There was only one person eating in the grill area, and Roger was chatting with him.

'Hey, Roger? Could watch the register for an hour?'

'No problem, boss,' Roger said.

They left the store, walking towards his jeep. Climbing in, she could feel his gaze on her.

'Why the sudden rush to learn how to drive?' he asked. 'Is the bike not good enough?' he teased.

'The bike is all I need, but I want to get a driver's licence.'

He reached for the car keys before pausing. He turned back to her. 'Learning how to drive is only part of it. To get a licence, the state requires identification. Birth certificate, social security card.'

'I know,' she said.

He chose his words carefully. 'Information like that can be tracked. If you get a licence, people might be able to find you.'

'I'm already using a safe social security number,' she said. 'If Kevin knew about it, he would have tracked me down already. And if I'm going to stay in Southport, it's something I need to do.'

He shook his head. 'Katie . . .'

She leaned over and kissed him on the cheek. 'It's OK,' she said. 'My name's not Katie, remember?'

He traced the curve of her cheek with his finger. 'To me, you'll always be Katie. You don't look like an Erin.'

'No?'

'I knew one in sixth grade. You don't look anything like her."

She smiled. 'I have a secret,' she said. 'My hair isn't naturally brown. I'm really blonde.'

He sat back, processing this new information. 'What's this all about? Wanting to learn how to drive, volunteering information?'

'You told me I could trust you.' She shrugged. 'I believe you. I feel I can tell you anything.'

'Then I'll cut to the chase. Are you sure your documents will hold up? They have to be originals.'

'I know,' she said.

He knew better than to ask anything more. He reached for the keys but didn't start the engine.

'What is it?' she asked.

'Since you want to learn how to drive, we may as well start now.' He opened the door. 'Let's get you behind the wheel.'

They switched places. As soon as Katie was behind the wheel, Alex pointed out the basics: accelerator and brake pedals.

'You ready?' he asked.

'I think so,' she said, concentrating.

She did exactly as she was told, and they spent the next hour driving along rural roads. She had trouble with oversteering, but other than that, she did better than probably either of them expected. As they were getting close to finishing, Alex had her park on one of the downtown streets.

'Where are we going?'

He pointed to a small coffee shop. 'I figured you might want to celebrate. You did well.'

'Can I drive tomorrow?' she asked.

'Of course,' he said.

She reached out and gave him a hug. 'Thanks for this.'

He hugged her back. 'I'm glad to help. It's something you should probably know how to do. Why didn't you . . . ?'

'Learn to drive when I was younger?' She shrugged. 'Growing up, we had only one car and my dad was usually using it. After I moved out, I couldn't afford a car, so I didn't bother. Then, when I was married, Kevin didn't want me to have one. And here I am. A twenty-seven-year-old bike rider.'

'You're twenty-seven? You don't look a day over thirty.'

She punched him lightly in the arm. 'For that, I'm going to make you buy me a croissant, too.'

'Fair enough. And since you're in the mood for full disclosure, I'd like to hear the story of how you finally got away.'

She hesitated only briefly. 'OK,' she said.

At a small table outside, Katie related the account of her escape—the forwarded phone calls, the trip to Philadelphia, the eventual trip to Southport. When she finished, he shook his head.

'What?'

'I was just trying to imagine how you must have felt after hanging up on that final call from Kevin. When he still thought you were at home. I'll bet you were relieved.'

'I was. But I was also terrified. And at that point, I didn't have a job and didn't know what I was going to do.'

'But you made it.'

'Yes,' she said. 'I did.' Her gaze was focused on some distant point. 'It's not the kind of life I ever imagined for myself.' Her gaze was focused on some distant point.

Alex's tone was gentle. 'I'm not sure anyone's life turns out exactly the way they imagine. All we can do is to try to make the best of it. Even when it seems impossible.'

She knew he was talking as much about himself as he was about her, and for a long moment neither of them said anything.

'I love you,' he finally whispered.

She touched his face. 'I know. And I love you, too.'

BY LATE JUNE, the flower gardens in Dorchester were beginning to wilt. Kevin told Coffey and Ramirez that he and Erin were going to spend the weekend at home, doing a little gardening. Coffey had asked about Provincetown and Kevin had lied and told him about the bed-and-breakfast where they'd stayed and the restaurants they'd gone to. Coffey had said that he'd been to all of those places.

Erin was gone, but Kevin still looked for her everywhere. In Philadelphia, she'd used a phoney name and social security number, but that couldn't last forever. To this point, she hadn't used her own social security number. An officer from another precinct who had connections checked for him. That officer was the only one who knew that Erin was gone, but he'd keep his mouth shut because Kevin knew he was having an affair with his underage babysitter.

Kevin knew Erin wasn't running any longer. She liked nice things and wanted them around her. Which meant she had to be using someone else's identity. He knew the most common way was to find someone of a similar age who'd recently died, then take on the identity of the deceased. But even if she had found a name, how had she retrieved the identification? And where was she? These were the questions that tormented him.

July rolled in hot and moist. Kevin had a headache every morning. Trial and error proved that vodka worked better than Tylenol, but the pain was always there. Coffey and Ramirez asked about his wife again and he said that she was fine but said nothing else. He got a new partner named Todd Vannerty, who was happy to let Kevin do most of the questioning when they talked to witnesses and victims, and that was fine with Kevin.

At the end of their first week together, they were called out to an apartment where they found a ten-year-old boy who'd died of a bullet wound.

The shooter was a recent emigrant from Greece who had been celebrating a Greek soccer victory when he'd fired his gun at the floor. The bullet passed through the ceiling of the apartment below him and killed the boy just as he was taking a bite of pizza. The bullet entered the top of his head and the boy fell face-first into his pizza. When they saw the boy, there was cheese and tomato sauce on his forehead. His mother had cried and had tried to tackle the Greek as he was led down the stairs in handcuffs. She ended up tumbling down to the landing and they'd had to call an ambulance.

Kevin and Todd went to a bar after their shift ended and Todd tried to pretend he could forget what he'd seen, but he drank three beers in less than fifteen minutes. Kevin drank vodka, though because Todd was with him, he told the bartender to add a splash of cranberry.

When Kevin finally got home, he needed a drink but the thought of vodka made him sick. The house was messy and dirty. He paced the living room. Suddenly, he strode to the kitchen and found a garbage bag beneath the sink. He filled it with empty takeaway containers and magazines and empty bottles of vodka. It was well past midnight and he didn't have to work in the morning, so he stayed awake cleaning the house.

He put the dirty clothes in the washing machine and dried them and folded them. The sun came up and he scrubbed the toilet and mopped the linoleum. Dawn turned to morning and then to late morning. He mowed the lawn and went shopping and bought turkey and ham and fresh rye bread. He bought flowers and set them on the table. He added candles. When he was finished he poured himself a tall, icy glass of vodka and sat at the kitchen table and waited for Erin. They would trust each other and be happy and he would love her forever.

KATIE GOT HER driver's licence in the second week of July. She'd passed the test with a nearly perfect score. The licence arrived in the mail and when Katie opened the envelope, she felt dizzy. There was a photograph of her next to a name she'd never imagined having.

Though the store was as busy as ever, Alex took a vacation. It was his first in a while, and he spent most afternoons with Katie and the kids, relishing the lazy days of summer. He fished with Josh and built doll's houses with Kristen; he took Katie to a jazz festival. When Katie wasn't working evenings, Alex liked to fire up the grill. The kids would eat and then swim in the creek until it was dark. After they'd gone to bed, Alex would sit with

Katie on the dock out back, their legs dangling over the water. They sipped wine and talked about nothing, but Alex savoured those quiet moments.

Kristen particularly loved spending time with Katie. When the four of them were walking together, Kristen often reached for Katie's hand. When Kristen asked if Katie could take her shopping, Alex couldn't say no. After giving Katie some money, Alex handed her the keys to the jeep and waved from the parking lot as they left.

As happy as Katie's presence had made Kristen, Josh's feelings weren't as obvious. The day before, Alex had picked him up from a friend's party, and he hadn't said anything the rest of the evening. Alex knew that something was bothering him and suggested that they get out their fishing poles, just as dusk was settling in.

They cast their lines for an hour while the sky turned violet. Josh remained strangely quiet. Just when Alex was about to ask Josh about it, however, his son half-swivelled in his direction.

'Hey, Dad? Do you ever think about Mom?'

'All the time,' he said.

Josh nodded. 'I think about her, too. Do you miss her?'

'Of course I do. I loved her very much,' Alex said.

'What do you do when you go out with Miss Katie?' Josh asked.

Alex shifted slightly. 'It's kind of like what we did at the beach. We eat and talk and maybe go for a walk.'

Josh considered that. 'What do you talk about?'

'Just regular stuff.' Alex tilted his head. 'And we talk about you and your sister. How much fun it is to spend time with you two, and how well you did in school, or how good you are at keeping your room clean. Just so you know, she thinks you're a great kid.'

Josh sat up straighter and began reeling in his line. 'Good,' he said. 'Because I think she's pretty great, too.'

KRISTEN AND KATIE had returned to the house, full of excitement as they showed him the clothes they'd purchased. Alex sat on the couch as Kristen modelled an outfit for him, only to vanish back into her bedroom before returning wearing something different. Even Josh set his Nintendo game aside, and when Kristen had left the room, he approached Katie.

'Could you take me shopping, too?' he asked, his voice barely above a whisper. 'Because I need some new shirts and stuff.'

Afterward, Alex ordered Chinese food and they sat around the table, eating and laughing. At one point, Katie pulled a leather wristband from her purse and turned towards Josh. 'I thought this was pretty cool looking,' she said, handing it to Josh. His surprise gave way to pleasure as he put it on, and Alex noticed how Josh's eyes continually flickered towards Katie for the rest of the evening.

Ironically, it was at times like tonight that he missed Carly most. He found it easy to imagine her being at the table.

Perhaps that was the reason he couldn't sleep, long after Katie went home and Kristen and Josh were asleep in their beds. Tossing back the covers, he went to the closet and opened the safe he'd installed a few years earlier. In it were important financial and insurance documents, stacked beside treasures from his marriage: photos from their honeymoon, ultrasound images of Josh and Kristen. Since Carly's death, Alex had added nothing to the safe, except for the letters that she had written. One had been addressed to him. The second had no name on it, however, and it remained unopened. He couldn't open it—a promise was a promise.

He pulled out the letter he'd read a hundred times, leaving the other in the safe. He'd known nothing about them until she'd handed the envelopes to him less than a week before she died. By that point, she was bedridden. On the day she gave him the envelopes, he saw that they had been tucked into the blankets, appearing as if by magic. Later he learned that she'd written them two months earlier and her mom had been holding them.

Now, Alex opened the envelope and pulled out the much-handled letter. It was written on yellow legal paper. He remembered his surprise and the way her eyes pleaded with him for understanding.

'You want me to read this one first?' he remembered asking. He pointed to the one inscribed with his name and she nodded.

My dearest Alex,

How can I describe how much I love you? Is it possible to describe a love like that? I don't know, but I have to try.

When I think back on the night we first met, I think I realised even then that we were meant to be together. I remember that night clearly, just as I can every detail of the cloudy afternoon at the beach when you dropped to one knee and asked me to become your wife. You are, and always have been, everything I've always wanted in a husband.

You're kind and strong and caring and smart; you lift my spirits and you're a better father than you know.

It scares me to know that all of this will be ending soon. I'm not simply scared for me, though—I'm scared for you and our children, too. It breaks my heart to know that I'm going to cause you all such grief. But I truly believe that while love can hurt, love can also heal . . . and that's why I'm enclosing another letter. Please don't read it. It's not meant for you. You see, it is meant for the woman who eventually heals you, the one who makes you whole again.

Right now, I know you can't imagine something like that. It might take months, it might take years, but someday, you'll give that letter to another woman. Trust your instincts. You'll know when and where, just as you'll know which woman deserves it. And when you do, trust me when I say that somewhere, somehow, I'll be smiling down on both of you.

Love,

Carly

After reading the letter, Alex returned it to the safe. Beyond the window, the sky was filled with moonlit clouds. He stared upward, thinking of Carly and Katie. Carly had told him to trust his instincts; Carly had told him that he would know what to do with the letter.

And Carly, he suddenly realised, had been exactly right, about half of it, anyway. He knew he wanted to give the letter to Katie. He just wasn't sure whether she was ready to receive it.

9

'Hey, Kevin.' Bill gestured to him. 'Can you come into my office?'

Kevin had almost reached his desk, and Coffey and Ramirez followed him with their eyes. His new partner, Todd, was already at his desk and offered a weak smile, but it faded quickly.

His head was throbbing and he didn't want to talk to Bill first thing in the morning but Kevin wasn't worried. He was good with witnesses and victims and he made lots of arrests and the criminals were convicted.

Bill motioned for him to sit in the chair. Kevin took a seat. Bill closed the door before propping himself on the edge of his desk.

'How are you doing, Kevin?'

'I'm fine,' Kevin answered. He wanted to close his eyes to lessen the pain but he could tell Bill was studying him. 'What's up?'

Bill crossed his arms. 'I called you in here to let you know that we received a complaint about you. Internal Affairs is involved, and as of now, you're being suspended pending an investigation.'

The words sounded jumbled, making no sense. Kevin wished he hadn't woken with a headache and didn't need so much vodka.

'What are you talking about?'

Bill lifted a few pages from his desk. 'The Gates murder,' he said. 'The little boy who was shot through the floor?'

'I remember,' Kevin said. 'The boy had pizza sauce on his forehead. It was horrible.'

Bill furrowed his brow. 'An ambulance was called,' he said.

Kevin breathed in and out. Concentrating.

'It came for the mom,' Kevin said. 'She went after the Greek who'd fired the bullet. They struggled and she fell down the stairs. We called it in immediately . . . she was taken to the hospital.'

Bill stared at him. 'You talked to her beforehand, right?'

'I tried to . . . but she was pretty hysterical. It's all in the report.'

Bill reached for the papers again. 'I saw what you wrote. But the woman claims that you told her to push the perp down the stairs.'

'What?'

Bill read from the pages. 'She claims you were talking about God and told her, quote, "The man was a sinner and deserved to be punished because the Bible says, *Thou shalt not kill.*" She says that you also told her that the guy was probably going to get probation, even though he killed her kid, so she should take matters into her own hands. Does any of this ring a bell?'

'That's ridiculous,' Kevin said. 'You know she's lying, right?'

He expected Bill to agree with him. But he didn't. Instead, Bill leaned forward. 'What exactly did you tell her? Word for word.'

'I didn't *tell* her anything. She told me what happened and I saw the hole in the ceiling and went upstairs and I arrested the neighbour after he admitted to firing the gun. I cuffed him and started bringing him down the stairs; the next thing I know, she went after him.'

Bill held up the paper he had been reading from. 'You never said the words, *Vengeance is mine, I will repay, says the Lord.*'

Kevin felt the anger rising but forced it back down. 'Nothing. It's a lie. You know how people are. She probably wants to sue the city so she can get a big payday.'

Bill's jaw muscle was flexing.

'Had you been drinking before you talked to the woman?'

'No. I wouldn't do that. I'm a good detective.' Kevin held out his hands. 'C'mon, Bill. We've worked together for years.'

'That's why I'm talking to you instead of firing you. Because in the past few months, you haven't been yourself. And I've been hearing rumours that you're drunk when you come into work.'

'It's not true.'

'So if I gave you a Breathalyser, you'd blow a zero, right?'

Kevin could feel his heart hammering in his chest. 'Last night, I was up late with a buddy and we were drinking. There might still be some alcohol in my system, but I'm not drunk.'

Bill stared at him. 'Tell me what's going on with Erin,' he said.

'I've already told you. She's helping a friend in Manchester. We went to the Cape just a few weeks ago.'

'You told Coffey that you went to a restaurant in Provincetown with Erin, but the restaurant closed six months ago and there was no record of you checking into the bed-and-breakfast you mentioned. And no one has seen or heard from Erin in months.'

Kevin felt his head pounding. 'You checked up on me?'

'You've been drinking on the job and you've been lying to me.'

'I haven't—'

'Stop lying!' the captain suddenly shouted. 'I can smell your breath from here!' His eyes flared. 'As of now, you're suspended from duty. Leave your gun and badge on my desk and go home.'

'How long?' Kevin managed to croak out.

'Right now, suspension is the least of your worries.'

'Just so you know, I didn't say anything to that woman.'

'They heard you!' Bill shouted. 'Your partner, the medical examiner, the crime scene investigators.' He paused, trying to regain his calm. 'Everyone heard you,' he said, and Kevin felt as though he'd lost control of everything and he knew it was all Erin's fault.

August rolled in, and although Alex and Katie were enjoying the hot, slow summer days, the kids were beginning to get bored. Wanting to do something unusual, Alex took Katie and the kids to see the rodeo monkeys in Wilmington. Much to Katie's disbelief, it turned out to be exactly what it sounded like: monkeys, dressed in cowboy outfits, rode dogs and herded sheep for almost an hour before a show of fireworks that rivaled the Fourth of July. On their way out, Katie turned towards Alex with a smile.

'And next week?'

'That's easy. The carnival will be in town,' Alex said. 'That reminds me. Are you working next Saturday?'

'I'm not sure. Why?'

'I was hoping you'd come to the carnival with us. And I would like to ask a favour. I was hoping you'd watch the kids later that evening. Joyce's daughter is flying into Raleigh, and Joyce asked if I could drive her to the airport to pick her up.'

'I'd be glad to watch them. That sounds like fun.'

Alex walked in silence for a few steps before he asked, 'Do you ever want to have kids?'

Katie hesitated. 'I'm not sure,' she said. 'I haven't really thought about it.'

'Ever?'

She shook her head. 'In Atlantic City I was too young, with Kevin I couldn't bear the idea, and I've had my mind on other things the last few months.'

'But if you did think about it?' he persisted.

'I still don't know. I guess it would depend on a lot of things.'

'Like what?'

'Like whether I was married. And, as you know, I can't get married.'

'Erin can't get married,' he said. 'But Katie probably could. She has a driver's licence, remember.'

Katie took a few steps in silence. 'She might be able to, but she wouldn't do it unless she met the right guy.'

He laughed and slipped his arm around her.

The kids fell asleep before they reached the highway. Neither Alex nor Katie wanted to risk waking the kids, so they held hands in silence as they made the drive back to Southport. As Alex pulled to a stop in front of her house, Katie spotted Jo sitting on the steps of her porch, as if waiting for her. In the darkness, she wasn't sure whether Alex recognised her, but at that moment Kristen stirred and he turned around in his seat to make sure she hadn't woken up. Katie leaned over and kissed him.

'I should probably talk to her,' Katie whispered.

'Who? Kristen?'

'My neighbour.' Katie smiled, gesturing over her shoulder.

'Oh.' He nodded. 'OK.' He glanced towards Jo's porch and back again. 'I had a great time tonight.'

'I did, too.'

He kissed her and pulled out of the driveway. Katie started towards Jo's house. Jo smiled and waved.

'I saw you driving the other day,' Jo said.

'Hard to believe, isn't it? I still don't feel comfortable behind the wheel.'

'You will,' she said. 'I'm happy for you and Alex. And the kids. You're good for them, you know.'

'How can you be so sure?'

'Because I can see the way he looks at you. The two of you look like you're in love.' She squirmed under Katie's blushing gaze. 'OK, I'll admit it. Even if you haven't seen me, let's just say that I've seen the way the two of you kiss when you say goodbye.'

'You spy on us?' Katie pretended to be outraged.

'Of course.' Jo snorted. 'How else am I supposed to occupy myself?' She paused. 'You do love him, don't you?'

Katie nodded. 'And I love the kids, too.'

'I'm so glad.' Jo clasped her hands together, prayer-style.

Katie paused. 'Did you know his wife?'

'Yes,' Jo said.

Katie stared down the road. 'What was she like?'

'She was a lot like you. And I mean that in a good way. She loved Alex and she loved the kids. They were the most important things in her life. That's really all you have to know about her.'

'Do you think she would have liked me?'

'Yes,' Jo said. 'I'm sure she would have loved you.'

AUGUST, AND Boston was sweltering. Kevin vaguely remembered seeing the ambulance outside the Feldmans' home, but he hadn't thought much about it. Only now did he realise that Gladys Feldman had died and cars were parked along the street. Kevin had been suspended for two weeks and he didn't like cars parked in front of his house, but people were in town for the funeral later that afternoon.

He sat on the porch, drinking straight from the bottle, watching people walk in and out of the Feldmans' house. He knew the funeral was later in the afternoon and people were at the Feldmans house because they would be going to the funeral as a group. He drank until the Feldmans' house was a blur. Across the street, he saw a woman walk out of their house to smoke a cigarette. She was wearing a black dress.

The woman finished her cigarette. She scanned the street and noticed him sitting on the porch. She hesitated before crossing the street towards him. He didn't know her; had never seen her before.

He put the bottle down and climbed down the porch steps. She stopped on the sidewalk out front.

'Are you Kevin Tierney?' the woman asked.

'Yes,' he said.

'I'm Karen Feldman,' she said. 'My parents live across the street.' She paused but Kevin said nothing and she went on. 'I was just wondering if Erin was planning to attend the funeral.'

He stared at her. 'Erin?' he finally said.

'Yes. My mom and dad used to love it when she came by to visit. She used to make them pies and sometimes she helped them clean up, especially once my mom started getting sick. Lung cancer. It was awful.' She shook her head. 'Is Erin around? I've been hoping to meet her. The funeral starts at two.'

'No, she's not. She's helping a sick friend in Manchester. She's upset that she can't be here.'

'Oh . . . well. OK. That's too bad. I've always wanted to meet her. My mom told me that she reminded her of Katie.'

'Katie?'

'My younger sister. She passed away six years ago.'

'I'm sorry to hear that.'

'Me, too. We all miss her—my mom did especially. That's why she got along so well with Erin. They even looked alike. Same age and everything.' If Karen noticed Kevin's blank expression, she gave no sign. 'My mom used to show Erin the scrapbook she'd put together about Katie . . . She was always so patient with my mom. She's a sweet woman. You're a lucky man.'

Kevin forced himself to smile. 'Yes, I know.'

He'd been a good detective but in truth sometimes the answers came down to luck. In this case the lead came from a woman in black named Karen Feldman, who crossed the street on a morning he'd been drinking and told him about her dead sister.

Even though his head still ached, he poured the vodka down the drain, and thought about Erin and the Feldmans. Erin knew them and visited them, even though she'd never mentioned going to their house. He'd called her and dropped by unexpectedly and she'd always been home, but somehow, he'd never found out. She'd never told him and when he'd complained that they were bad neighbours, she'd never said a word. Erin had a secret.

His mind was clearer than it had been in a long time. He got in the shower and washed and put on a black suit. The street was filled with cars. Karen came outside and smoked another cigarette. While he waited, he tucked paper and a pen in his pocket.

In the afternoon, people started filing towards their cars. It was past one o'clock and they were going to the service. It took fifteen minutes for everyone to leave. Finally, there were no more cars on the street. He waited ten more minutes before walking out his front door. He headed for the Feldmans' house. The neighbours would simply remember a mourner wearing a black suit. He went to the front door and it was locked. He headed to the back. There, he found another door. It was unlocked and he stepped into the house.

It was quiet. He walked through the house and went into the study. In the corner, he spotted a small filing cabinet and opened it.

He found a file labeled KATIE. There was a newspaper article—she'd drowned after falling through the ice of a local pond—and there were pictures of her that had been taken at school. She looked remarkably like Erin. In the back of the file, he found an envelope. He opened it and found an old report card. On the front of the envelope was a social security number, and he took his pad and his pen and wrote it down. He didn't find the social security card. The birth certificate was a copy.

He had what he needed and he left the house. As soon as he reached home he called the officer from the other precinct, the one who was sleeping with the babysitter. The following day, he received a call in return. Katie Feldman had recently been issued a driver's licence, with an address listed in Southport, North Carolina.

Kevin hung up without another word, knowing he'd found her.

REMNANTS OF a tropical storm blew through Southport, rain falling most of the afternoon and into the evening. Katie worked the lunch shift, but the weather kept the restaurant only half full and Ivan let her leave early. She had borrowed the jeep and she dropped it off at the store. When Alex drove her home, she'd invited him to come by later with the kids for dinner.

She'd been on edge the rest of the afternoon. She wanted to believe it was the weather, but she knew it had more to do with the uneasy feeling that everything in her life these days seemed too perfect. She learned long ago that nothing wonderful lasted forever.

Earlier that day, at the library, she'd perused the *Boston Globe* online at one of the computers and had come across Gladys Feldman's obituary. She'd known about Gladys's terminal diagnosis of cancer before she left. The sparse description of Gladys's life and survivors struck Katie with unexpected force.

She hadn't wanted to take the identification from the Feldmans' files, hadn't even considered the possibility until Gladys had pulled out the file to show her Katie's graduation photo. She'd seen the birth certificate and the social security card and recognised the opportunity they presented. The next time she'd gone to the house, she'd excused herself to go to the bathroom and had gone to the filing cabinet instead.

A week later, after making a copy of the birth certificate at the library and wrinkling it to make it appear dated, she put the document in the file. She would have done the same with the social security card, but she couldn't make a good enough copy. She hoped they would believe it had been lost or misplaced.

She reminded herself that Kevin would never know what she'd done. He didn't like the Feldmans and the feeling was mutual. She suspected that they knew he beat her. She wanted to think that the Feldmans would have been OK with what she'd done, because they knew she needed the identification and wanted her to escape.

'YOU'VE BEEN quiet tonight,' Alex said. 'Is everything OK?'

She'd made tuna casserole for dinner and Alex was helping her with the dishes. The kids were playing in the living room.

'A friend of mine passed away,' she said. She handed him a plate to dry. 'I knew it was coming, but it's still sad.'

'It's always sad,' he agreed. 'I'm sorry.'

'How long do you think the storm is going to last?' she asked, changing the subject.

'Not long. Why?'

'I was just wondering whether the carnival tomorrow is going to be cancelled. Or whether Joyce's flight is going to be cancelled.'

Alex glanced out the window. 'It should be fine.'

'How long is it going to take you to pick up Joyce's daughter?'

'Probably four or five hours. Raleigh's not exactly convenient.'

'You're doing a good thing, you know. Helping Joyce like that.'

He gave a nonchalant shrug. 'Can I ask you something?' he said. 'I don't want you to take it the wrong way, but I've been curious.'

'Go ahead.'

He cleared his throat, buying time. 'I was wondering if you'd given any thought to what I said last weekend, after seeing the rodeo monkeys?

'You said a lot of things,' she said cautiously.

'Don't you remember? You told me that Erin couldn't get married, but I said that Katie probably could?'

Katie felt herself stiffen, less at the memory than the serious tone he was using. She knew exactly where this was leading. 'I remember,' she said with forced lightness. 'I think I said I would have to meet the right guy.'

At her words, his lips tightened, as if he were debating whether to continue. 'I just wanted to know if you thought about it. Us eventually getting married, I mean.'

'You'd have to ask first.'

'But if I did?'

'I suppose I'd tell you that I love you.'

'Would you say yes?'

She paused. 'I don't want to get married again.'

'You don't want to, or you don't think you can?'

'What's the difference?' Her expression remained closed. 'You know I'm still married. Bigamy is illegal.'

'You're not Erin anymore. You're Katie. Your driver's licence proves it.'

'But I'm not Katie, either!' she snapped. 'I stole that name from people I cared about! People who trusted me.' She stared at him, recalling with fresh intensity Gladys's kindness and pity, her escape, and the nightmarish years with Kevin.

'Why can't you just be happy with the way things are? Why do you have to push me to be the person you want me to be rather than the person that I am?'

He flinched. 'I love the person that you are.'

'But you're making it conditional!' She knew she was raising her voice but she couldn't seem to stop it. 'You have this idea of what you want in life and you're trying to make me fit into it!'

'I don't,' Alex protested. 'I simply asked you a question.'

'But you wanted a specific answer! You wanted the *right* answer, and if you didn't get it, you were going to try to convince me otherwise. That I should do what you want!'

Alex narrowed his eyes at her. 'Don't do this,' he said.

'Do what? Tell the truth? Tell you how I feel? Why? What are you going to do? Hit me? Go ahead.'

He physically recoiled as if she'd slapped him. She knew her words had hit their mark, but instead of getting angry, Alex took a step back.

'I don't know what's going on, but I'm sorry that I brought it up. I didn't mean to put you on the spot or try to convince you of anything. I was just trying to have a conversation.'

He paused, waiting for her to say something, but she stayed silent. Shaking his head, he started to leave the kitchen before coming to a stop. 'Thank you for dinner,' he whispered.

In the living room, she heard him tell the kids it was getting late, heard the front door open. He closed the door softly behind him and the house was suddenly quiet, leaving her alone with her thoughts.

KEVIN WAS having trouble staying between the lines on the highway. His head had begun to pound, so he'd stopped and bought a bottle of vodka. It numbed the pain, and as he sipped it through a straw, all he could think about was Erin.

He'd found her. He knew where Erin lived. Her address was scribbled on a piece of paper on the seat beside him, held in place by his Glock. On the back seat was a duffle bag filled with clothes and handcuffs and duct tape. He wanted to smash Erin's face with his fists as soon as he found her. He wanted to kiss her and hold her and beg her to come home.

He'd been on the road for hours. The engine droned, the noise steady in his ears. She had a driver's licence now and she was a waitress at a restaurant called Ivan's. It hadn't been hard to track her down because the town was small. *I'm coming*, he thought to himself. *You won't get away again.*

He would drive all night and find Erin tomorrow.

I'm coming, Erin, he thought. I'll be there soon.

KATIE AWOKE EXHAUSTED. She had tossed and turned for hours during the night, replaying the horrible things she'd said to Alex. She didn't know what had come over her. She'd known he hadn't been pressuring her to do anything she wasn't ready for. She knew he wasn't remotely like Kevin, but what had she said to him?

What are you going to do? Hit me? Go ahead.

Why would she have said something like that?

She eventually dozed off sometime after two a.m., when the wind and rain were beginning to taper off. By dawn, the sky was clear. It was going to be a scorcher. She made a note to herself to remind Alex not to keep the kids out in the sun too long before she realised that he might not want her with them. He was almost certainly mad at her. He hadn't even let the kids say good-bye last night.

She took a seat on the steps and turned towards Jo's, wondering if she was up. It was probably too early to knock on her door.

Her intuition told her that something was wrong but she couldn't pinpoint what it was, other than that her thoughts kept returning to the Feldmans. To Gladys. What would happen if someone realised Katie's information was missing?

'It's going to be OK,' she suddenly heard. Whirling around, she saw Jo standing in her running shoes, cheeks flushed.

'Where did you come from?'

'I went for a jog,' Jo said. 'I was trying to beat the heat, but it didn't work. I thought I was going to die of heatstroke. Even so, I think I'm doing better than you. You seem downright glum.' She motioned to the steps and Katie scooted over. Jo took a seat.

'Alex and I had a fight last night.'

'And?'

'I said something terrible to him.'

'Did you apologise?'

'No,' Katie answered. 'He left before I could. And now . . .'

'What? You think it's too late?' She squeezed Katie's knee. 'It's never too late to do the right thing. Go over there and talk to him.'

Katie hesitated. 'What if he won't forgive me?'

Jo tried to fan herself. 'He'll forgive you. He might be angry and you might have hurt his feelings, but he's a good man.'

Katie nodded. 'You're right. Thanks.'

Jo patted Katie's leg and stood. 'What are friends for, right? Now head on over there before you change your mind.'

Katie sat on the steps a few minutes longer before retreating into the house. She showered and changed into shorts and sandals before walking around the house and getting on her bicycle.

On the road, traffic was light. Katie pedalled on and the store came into view. She pulled to a stop in front and walked towards the door. Behind the register, Joyce smiled.

'Good morning, Katie,' she said.

Katie quickly scanned the store. 'Is Alex around?'

'He's upstairs with the kids. You know the way, right?'

Katie left the store and went towards the rear of the building. She hesitated at Alex's door before finally knocking. When the door swung open, Alex stood before her.

She offered a tentative smile. 'Hi,' she said.

He nodded, his expression unreadable. Katie cleared her throat.

'I'm sorry about what I said. I was wrong.'

'OK,' he said. 'I appreciate the apology.'

For a moment, neither of them said anything, and Katie suddenly wished she hadn't come. 'I can go. I just need to know whether you still need me to watch the kids tonight.'

Again, he said nothing, and in the silence Katie shook her head. When she turned to leave, she heard him take a step towards her.

'Katie . . . wait,' he said. He peeked over his shoulder at the kids before closing the door behind him.

'What you said last night . . .' he began. He trailed off, uncertain.

'I didn't mean it,' she said, her voice soft. 'I don't know what got into me. I was upset about something else and I took it out on you.'

'I admit it—it bothered me. Not so much that you said it, but that you imagined me capable of . . . that.'

'I don't think that,' Katie said. 'I would never think that about you.'

He seemed to take that in, but she knew he had more to say.

'I want you to know that I value what we have right now, and more than anything, I want you to be comfortable. I'm sorry for making you feel like I was putting you on the spot. That wasn't what I was trying to do.'

'Yes, you were.' She gave him a knowing smile. 'A little, anyway. But it's okay. I mean, who knows what the future might bring, right? Like tonight, for instance.'

'Why? What happens tonight?'

She leaned against the doorjamb. 'Well, once the kids are asleep and depending when you get back, it might be too late for me to ride back to my house. You might just find me in your bed . . .'

When he realised she wasn't kidding, he brought a hand to his chin in mock contemplation. 'That is a dilemma.'

'Then again, traffic might be light and you'll get home early enough to bring me home.'

'I'm a pretty safe driver. As a rule, I don't like to speed.'

She leaned into him. 'That's very conscientious of you.'

'I try,' he whispered, before their lips met. When he pulled back, he said, 'Have you had breakfast yet?'

'No.'

'Would you like to have cereal with me and the kids? Before we head off to the carnival?'

'Cereal sounds delicious.'

HE WAS IN Wilmington by ten. He drove through the city and turned onto a small, rural highway. He put the gun in his lap and then back on the seat again and kept on going. And finally, he was there, in Southport.

He drove slowly through town, detouring around a street fair, occasionally consulting the directions he'd printed out on the computer before he left. He pulled a shirt from the duffle bag and placed it over the gun to conceal it. Minutes later, he found the road where she lived.

On the left, up ahead, was a general store and he pulled in to buy some gas and a can of Red Bull. At the register, he paid the old woman. She smiled and thanked him for coming, and commented in that nosy way that old women have that she hadn't seen him around before. He told her he was in town for the fair.

As he turned back onto the road, his pulse raced at the knowledge that it wasn't far now. He rounded a bend and slowed the car. In the distance, a gravel road came into view. The directions indicated that he was supposed to turn but he didn't stop the car. If Erin was home, she would recognise his car immediately, and he didn't want that.

He turned the car around, searching for an out-of-the-way place to park. There wasn't much. The store parking lot, maybe, but wouldn't someone notice if he parked it there? The caffeine in the Red Bull was making him jittery and he switched to vodka to settle his nerves. For the life of him, he couldn't find a place to stash the car. He turned around again, getting angry. The store was the only option and he pulled back into the lot. It was at least a mile to the house from here but he didn't know what else to do.

When he opened the car door, the heat enveloped him. He emptied the duffle bag, tossing his clothes on the back seat. Into the bag went the gun, the ropes, the handcuffs, and the duct tape—and a spare bottle of vodka. Tossing the bag over his shoulder, he glanced around. No one was watching.

He left the lot, and as he walked down the road he could feel the pain starting in his head. The heat was ridiculous. He reached the gravel road and turned. The road seemed to lead nowhere until he finally spotted a pair of cottages a half mile down. He moved to the side of the road, hugging the trees.

From a distance neither cottage appeared occupied. Hell, neither one looked habitable. He didn't know which cottage was hers. He moved towards the better one.

It had taken thirty minutes to get here from the store. Once he surprised Erin, he knew she'd try to get away. He would tie her up and tape her mouth shut and then fetch the car. Once he returned with the car, he would put her in the trunk until they were far away.

He peeked around the back of the house and saw nothing. He crept forwards, watching. Ahead, there was a small window and he took a chance and looked in. No lights on, but it was clean and tidy, with a tea towel draped over the kitchen sink. Just like Erin used to do. He silently approached the door and turned the knob. Unlocked.

He opened the door and stepped inside, pausing to listen and hearing nothing. He entered the living-room—then the bedroom and bathroom. He cursed aloud, knowing she wasn't home.

In the kitchen, he rifled through the drawers until he found a utility bill. It was addressed to Katie Feldman. He stared at the name, feeling a sense of completion.

The only problem was that she wasn't here. He couldn't leave his car at the store indefinitely, but he was just so tired. He'd driven all night and his head was pounding. Instinctively, he wandered back to her bedroom. He crawled into the bed, breathing her in. He felt the tears flood his eyes as he realised how much he missed her.

He told himself that he would sleep for just a little while. Just enough so that his mind would be sharp and he wouldn't make mistakes and he and Erin could be husband and wife once more.

10

Alex, Katie, and the kids rode their bikes to the carnival because parking downtown was almost impossible. Booths displaying arts and crafts lined either side of the street, and the air was thick with the scent of hot dogs and burgers, popcorn and candyfloss. Alex stood in line to buy tickets while Katie followed behind with the kids, heading towards the bumper cars. Long lines were everywhere.

The kids wanted to ride everything, so Alex purchased a small fortune in tickets. The tickets went fast, because most of the rides required three or four. The cost was ridiculous, and Alex tried to make the tickets last by insisting they do other things as well.

They watched a man juggle bowling pins and cheered for a dog that could walk across a tightrope. They had pizza for lunch at one of the local restaurants. Afterward, they watched people racing jet skis in the Cape Fear River before heading back to the rides.

On the Ferris wheel, Alex and Josh sat in one seat and Kristen and Katie in another, hot wind in their faces. Katie draped her arm over Kristen's shoulders, knowing that Kristen was nervous about the height. Katie wasn't exactly thrilled with the height, either.

Katie occupied herself by staring at the throngs of people below. The carnival had become even more crowded as the afternoon wore on. She recognised a couple of people as regulars at Ivan's. Her eyes began to travel from group to group, and for some reason she remembered that she used to do the same thing when she first started working at Ivan's. Back when she was watching for Kevin.

KEVIN WOKE two hours later, his stomach knotted with cramps. His head felt like it was splitting in two. He staggered into the kitchen, slaking his thirst directly from the tap. He was dizzy and weak and felt more tired than when he lay down in the first place.

But he couldn't linger. He remade the bed, left the house and headed up the gravel road towards the store.

The roof of the car was scalding to the touch and when he opened the door, it felt like a furnace. No one was in the parking lot. Too hot to be outside. Sweltering, without a cloud or hint of breeze.

In the car, he drank more vodka, not caring that it was the temperature of a cup of coffee. As long as it made the pain go away. As he drank, the throbbing in his temples began to recede, but he started to see two of everything. He needed to keep his mind sharp, but the pain and the heat were making him sick.

He started the car and turned onto the main road, heading back to downtown Southport. Many streets were closed off and he made countless detours before he found a spot to park.

He changed his shirt and tucked the gun into the waistband of his jeans and started towards the waterfront. He knew that's where he'd find Ivan's, because he'd searched for the location on the computer.

Crowds of people were everywhere. Weaving among the people, he spotted the waterfront in the distance, and then Ivan's. His mouth was dry by the time he reached the door of the restaurant.

Ivan's was packed. He should have brought a hat and sunglasses, but he hadn't been thinking. He knew she would recognise him instantly, but he worked his way to the door and stepped inside.

'Is Erin working today?' he called out to the hostess.

She blinked at him in confusion. 'Who?'

'Katie,' he said. 'I meant Katie. Katie Feldman.'

'No,' the hostess shouted back. 'She's off.' She nodded towards the windows. 'She's probably out there along with everyone else.'

Kevin turned and left, bumping into people as he went. Outside, he paused at a sidewalk stall. He bought a baseball hat and a pair of sunglasses. And then he began to walk. He went past the booths that lined either side of the street, just wandering and trying to think like Erin. It was hard to keep reminding himself that she might have short brown hair. He could feel the gun in his waistband, pressing against his skin.

He moved around groups of people. People were stuffing their faces with food: pretzels and ice cream, nachos, cinnamon rolls. People talked and whispered all around him and he thought some of them were staring at him. He ignored them, focused on his search.

He worked his way through the crowd, studying people's faces. He wandered among the rides and noticed the Ferris wheel up ahead. He moved closer, checking the seats. Erin wasn't there.

He moved on, walking in the heat among the people, looking for Erin. With every step, he thought about the Glock.

THE SWINGS, spinning clockwise, were a big hit with the kids. They'd ridden them twice in the morning, and after the Ferris wheel Kristen and Josh begged to ride them once more. Alex agreed, explaining that after this last ride they would have to go home. He wanted to have time to shower before he had to drive to Raleigh.

Despite his best efforts, he couldn't stop thinking about Katie's earlier suggestive remark. She seemed to sense the direction of his thoughts, because he'd caught her staring at him a number of times, a provocative smile playing at the corner of her lips.

Now she stood beside him, smiling up at the kids. He slipped his arm around her, and felt her lean into him. She tilted her head, resting it against his shoulder, and Alex was struck by the notion that there was nothing better in the world.

The swings had begun to slow, but Kristen and Josh were still grinning with excitement. Alex was right about needing to call it a day; the heat had drained Katie and it would be nice to be able to cool off for a while.

The ride came to a stop and Josh unhooked the chain and jumped down. It took Kristen a little longer, but a moment later, the two children were scrambling back towards Katie and their dad.

KEVIN SAW the swings come to a stop and a bunch of kids jump down from their seats, but that wasn't where he focused his attention. He concentrated on the adults at the perimeter of the ride.

He kept walking, his eyes moving from one woman to the next. Blonde or brunette, it didn't matter. He watched for Erin's lean figure. He walked quickly. A family stood in front of him, holding tickets, debating where to go next, arguing in confusion. Idiots.

No skinny women, except for one. A short-haired brunette, standing next to a man with grey hair, his arm around her waist. She was unmistakable. Same long legs, same face, same sinewy arms.

Erin.

ALEX AND KATIE held hands as they walked towards Ivan's with the kids. They'd stored their bicycles near the back door, Katie's regular spot. On the way out, Alex bought some water for Josh and Kristen before they started for home.

'Good day, guys?' Alex asked, bending over to unlock the bikes.

'Great day, Daddy,' Kristen answered, her face red with the heat.

An overhang at the back of the restaurant provided some shade, but it was still warm. Katie was glad she'd taken the day off, even if she had to work a double shift tomorrow. It was worth it. It had been a good day, and she'd get to relax and watch a movie with the kids while Alex was away tonight. And later, when he got back . . .

'What?' Alex said. 'You were staring at me like you were going to eat me up.'

'Just drifting off there for a second,' she said with a wink. 'I think the heat kind of got to me.'

'Uh-huh.' He nodded. 'If I didn't know better . . .'

'I'd like to remind you that there are some young ears tuning in right now.' She kissed him before patting him lightly on the chest.

Neither of them noticed the man in the baseball hat and sunglasses watching them from the deck of the neighbouring restaurant.

Kevin felt dizzy as he watched Erin and the grey-haired man kiss. He saw her lean down and smile at the little girl. Watched as she tousled the hair of the little boy. Erin—his wife—was cheating on him with her new family.

They got on their bikes and started pedalling, heading around the side of the building, away from Kevin. Erin rode beside the grey-haired man. She was wearing shorts and sandals, looking sexy.

Kevin followed them. He rounded the corner. They were riding and he was on foot, but they were moving slowly to allow the little girl to keep up. He was closing the distance. He reached for the Glock in his waistband and pulled it out, then slid it beneath his shirt. His finger moved to the trigger and he slipped the safety off because the Bible says, *Let marriage be held in honour among all, and let the bed be undefiled*. But hitting moving targets from a distance was almost impossible with a Glock, and there were people everywhere. They would see the gun and scream, so he removed his finger from the trigger.

All at once, the kids turned the corner and they were followed by Erin and the grey-haired man.

Kevin stopped, panting and feeling ill. As she'd rounded the corner, her profile had flashed in the light and he thought again that she was beautiful. He started to jog, trying to reach the spot where they'd turned. He reached the corner and peered up the street.

No one in sight, but two blocks up, there were barricades blocking the road for the street fair. He figured they had turned right, the only way to leave the downtown area.

He had a choice. Chase them on foot and risk being spotted or run back to the car and try to follow them that way. His car was blocks away, but he turned and started to run. It took forever to get to his car. When he reached it, the sun was baking it like a loaf of bread. Heat spilled out in clouds, and the steering wheel was scalding to the touch. He started the car and opened the windows, making a U-turn back towards the carnival.

Detours again. Barricades. He wanted to blow through them, to blast them into pieces, but there were cops and they would arrest him. Stupid cops, fat and lazy cops. Idiots. None of them were good detectives but they had guns and badges. Kevin drove the side streets, trying to zero in on where Erin was heading.

He caught sight of them, tiny figures in the distance. They were just beyond another barricade, heading towards the road that led to her house. A cop was standing at the corner.

He turned, speeding up, heading through the neighbourhood. Turned left and sped up again. More barricades up ahead. He was stuck in a maze. He raced to the next intersection. It had to be close now and he turned left again, saw a line of traffic ahead, moving in the direction he wanted. He muscled his car between a couple of trucks. Up ahead, Erin and the grey-haired man were gone.

A DOZEN CARS were parked in front of the store as Katie trailed the kids up the stairs to the house. A burst of cool air as they opened the door was refreshing. Alex led Katie to the kitchen and she watched as he drenched his face at the kitchen sink. In the living room, the kids were already sprawled on the couch, the television on.

Alex retrieved two glasses from the cupboard and poured water from a pitcher he kept in the refrigerator.

'You're a trouper,' he said, handing her a glass. 'It's like a sauna out there.'

She glanced at the clock on the wall before taking a drink. 'What time do you have to leave?'

'In an hour or so. But I should be back before eleven.'

Five hours, she thought. 'Do you want me to make the kids anything special for dinner?'

'They like pasta. I've got a bottle of marinara sauce in the refrigerator.'

'What time do they go to bed?'

'Whenever. It's always before ten, but sometimes it's as early as eight. You'll have to use your best judgment.'

She held the cool glass of water against her cheek and glanced around the kitchen. She hadn't spent much time in their home, and now that she was here she noticed remnants of a woman's touch. Little things—red stitching on the curtains, china prominently displayed in a cabinet. The house was filled with evidence of his life with another woman, but to her surprise, it didn't bother her.

'I'm going to go hop into the shower,' Alex said. 'Will you be OK for a few minutes?'

'Of course,' she said. 'I can snoop around your kitchen and think about dinner.'

'The pasta's in the cupboard over there,' he said, pointing. 'But listen, when I get out, if you want me to drive you over to your place so you can shower and change, I'd be glad to do it. Or you can shower here. Whatever you want.'

She struck a sultry pose. 'Is that an invitation?'

His eyes widened and then flashed to the kids.

'I was kidding.' She laughed. 'I'll shower after you're gone.'

'Do you want to pick up a change of clothes first? If not, you can borrow sweats and a T-shirt. The sweats will be too big for you, but you can adjust the draw-string.'

Somehow the idea of wearing his clothes sounded extremely sexy to her. 'That's fine,' she assured him. 'I'm not picky.'

Alex kissed her, then headed towards the bedroom.

Once he was gone, Katie turned towards the kitchen window. She watched the road outside, feeling a nameless anxiety come over her. She'd felt the same way earlier in the morning and assumed it was an aftershock of the argument she'd had with Alex, but now she found herself thinking of the Feldmans again. And about Kevin.

She'd thought of him when she was on the Ferris wheel, as she'd scanned the crowd. But that was just her paranoia surfacing. There was no way he could know where she was. But why, then, had she felt all day like someone was following her?

She wasn't psychic and didn't believe in such things. But she did believe in the power of the subconscious mind to put together pieces that the conscious mind might miss. Standing in Alex's kitchen, however, the pieces were still scrambled, and after watching a dozen cars pass by on the road, she finally turned away. It was probably just her old fears raising their ugly head again.

Katie shook her head to clear it and went to the living room, where she took a seat on the couch next to Josh. They were watching a Disney Channel television show she didn't recognise. Once he finished with his shower, Alex made a sandwich and sat beside her on the couch as he ate.

When it was time for him to leave, he kissed the kids in the living room. She followed him to the door and when he kissed her goodbye, he let his hand wander lower, past her waist, his lips soft against hers. Obviously wanting her, making sure she knew it.

'See you in a bit,' he said, pulling back.

'Drive safely,' she whispered. 'The kids will be fine.'

When she heard his footsteps descending the steps outside, she leaned against the door. Good Lord, she thought. Vows or not, she decided that even if *he* wasn't in the mood, she definitely was.

She peeked up at the clock again, certain that this would be the longest five hours of her life.

'DAMN!' KEVIN kept saying. 'Damn!' He'd been driving for hours. He'd stopped to buy four bottles of vodka at the ABC store. One of them was half gone, and as he drove he saw two of everything unless he squinted, keeping one eye closed.

He was searching for bicycles. Four of them, including one with baskets. He might as well have been looking for a specific piece of plankton in the ocean. Up one road and down the next, as the afternoon wound down. He knew where she lived, knew he would eventually find her at home. But in the meantime the grey-haired man was out there with Erin.

Dusk turned the streets into shadowy mazes, making it difficult to see the spindly outlines of bicycles. His head throbbed in time with his heartbeats, a knife going in and out. Stab. Stab. Stab. He felt like he had been weeks without sleep, weeks without food. He couldn't understand why it was dark and he wondered when that happened. He remembered seeing Erin, remembered trying to follow her and driving, but he wasn't even sure where he was.

A store loomed on the right, looking like a house with a porch out front. GAS FOOD, the sign said. He remembered that from earlier, but how long ago he couldn't say. He slowed the car. He needed food, needed to sleep. His stomach lurched. He grabbed the bottle and tilted it, feeling the burn in his throat, soothing him. But as soon as he lowered the bottle, his stomach heaved again.

He pulled into the lot, fighting to keep the liquor down, his mouth watering. He skidded to a stop alongside the store and jumped out. Ran to the front of his car and heaved into the darkness. His body shivered, his legs wobbled. His stomach coming up. Somehow, he was still holding the bottle, hadn't put it down. He drank, using it to rinse his mouth, swallowing it. Finishing another bottle.

And there, like an image from a dream, in the darkened shadows behind the house, he saw four bicycles parked side by side.

KATIE GAVE the kids a bath before getting them into their pyjamas. Afterward, she showered, enjoying the luxurious feeling of shampoo and soap rinsing the salt from her body after a day in the sun.

She made the kids their pasta, and after dinner they watched *Finding Nemo*. She sat between Josh and Kristen on the couch, a bowl of popcorn in her lap. She wore a comfy pair of sweats that Alex had laid out and a Carolina Panthers jersey, tucking her legs up under her as they watched the movie, utterly at ease.

When the movie ended and Katie turned it off, Josh yawned and rose to his feet and, with Katie by his side, staggered to the bedroom. He crawled into bed and she kissed him good night.

Kristen was next. She asked Katie to lie beside her for a few minutes, and Katie did, staring at the ceiling. Kristen fell asleep within minutes, and Katie tiptoed out of the room.

She turned out the lights and collapsed on the couch. She picked up the remote and surfed TV channels, trying to find something interesting but not too demanding. It was coming up to ten o'clock, she noted. An hour to go. She lay back on the couch and started watching a show about volcanoes.

Katie watched for a few minutes, barely aware that every time she blinked, her eyes stayed closed a fraction longer. Images began to float through her mind, disjointed at first, thoughts of the carnival rides, the view from the Ferris wheel. People standing in clusters. And somewhere in the distance, a man in a baseball hat and sunglasses, weaving among the crowd. Something she'd recognised: the walk, the jut of his jaw, the way he swung his arms. She was drifting now, relaxing and remembering, the images beginning to blur, the sound of the television fading. The room growing darker. She drifted further, her mind flashing back to the view from the Ferris wheel. And to the man she'd seen, a man who'd been moving like a hunter through the brush, in search of game.

KEVIN STARED UP at the windows, nursing his half-empty bottle of vodka, his third of the night. No one gave him a second glance. He was standing on the dock at the rear of the house; he'd changed into a black long-sleeved shirt and dark jeans. Only his face was visible, but he stood in the shade of a cypress tree, hidden behind the trunk. Watching the windows. Watching the lights, watching for Erin.

Nothing happened for a long while. People came through the store every few minutes, often using their credit cards to buy gas at the pump. Busy, busy, even out here, in the middle of nowhere. He moved around to the side of the store, gazing up at the windows. He recognised the flickering blue glow of a television.

Everything hurt and he was tired and his stomach kept churning. He could have walked up the stairs and kicked the door in, could have killed them half a dozen times already, and he wanted to get it over with, but there were people in the store. He spotted her profile at the window, saw her smiling, and knew she was thinking about the grey-haired man. Thinking about sex and the Bible says, *Those who gave themselves over to fornication and strange flesh are set forth for an example and suffering the vengeance of eternal fire.*

In the Bible there was always fire because it purified and condemned, and he understood that. Fire was powerful. A car pulled up to the gasoline pumps and a man stepped out. He slid his credit card in and began to pump gas. The sign near the pump informed people it was illegal to smoke, because gasoline was flammable. Fire.

By ten o'clock the lot was nearly empty. It was just before closing time, and Kevin walked around to the front of the store. He pushed the door open and heard a bell jingle. At the register was a man in an apron, the name ROGER stencilled on the right.

Kevin walked past the register, trying not to slur his words. 'I ran out of gas up the road.'

'Gas cans are along the far wall,' Roger answered without looking up. When he finally did, he blinked. 'You OK?'

'Just tired,' Kevin said from the aisle, trying not to draw attention to himself. At the far wall, Kevin saw three five-gallon plastic cans and reached for two of them. He took them to the register and put money on the counter.

'I'll pay after I fill 'em,' he said.

Outside, he pumped the gas into the can. He filled the second and went back inside. Roger was staring at him.

'You sure you're OK to drive?'

'I've been sick,' Kevin muttered. 'Puking all day.'

He wasn't sure whether Roger believed him, but after a moment, Roger took the money. Kevin had left the cans near the gas pumps and went outside to pick them up. It was like lifting cans of lead. He started up the road, leaving behind the lights of the store. In the darkness, he set the cans down in the tall grass just off the road. After that, he circled back behind the store.

From his hidden vantage point, Kevin watched the lights in the store go out. He watched Roger lock the door and walk to a pick-up truck, rev the engine, then turn onto the road heading downtown.

Kevin waited five minutes. The road in front of the store was quiet now. He jogged over to the bushes, where he'd hidden the cans. Checked the road again, and then carried one of them to the back of the store. He did the same with the second can, setting them next to a couple of metal garbage cans.

Upstairs, the TV continued to bathe one of the windows in blue light. Now, he thought. It was time. When he reached for the gas cans, he saw four of them. He closed one eye and it was back to two. As he took a step, he stumbled and fell, landing hard, his head hitting the gravel. Sparks and stars, shooting pains. It was hard to breathe. Tried to stand up and fell again. He rolled over onto his back, staring up at the stars.

He wasn't drunk because he never got drunk, but something was wrong. Twinkling lights were whirling round and round. He squeezed his eyes shut, but the spinning got worse. He rolled to his side and vomited onto the gravel. Someone must have slipped him drugs because he'd barely had anything to drink all day and he'd never been sick like this.

He reached out blindly for the garbage can. He grabbed the lid and tried to use it for balance, but he pulled too hard. The lid clattered off and a bag of garbage spilled out, making an unholy racket.

Upstairs, Katie flinched at the sound of something crashing. She was lost in her dream, and it took a moment for her eyes to open. Groggy, she wasn't sure whether she'd dreamed the sound or not.

She leaned back, giving way to sleep again, and the dream picked up from where it left off. She was at the carnival, on the Ferris wheel, but it was no longer Kristen sitting beside her. It was Jo.

11

Kevin was finally able to struggle to his feet. He couldn't figure out what was happening to him, why he couldn't keep his balance. He concentrated on catching his breath. He spotted the cans of gas and stepped towards them. He lifted one, then staggered towards the stairs at the back of the house. He lugged the can of gas up the stairs. He finally reached the landing at the top, panting.

He removed the cap, picked up the can and doused the landing. He splashed left and right, trying to coat either side of the building. He started back down the stairs, splashing left and right.

There wasn't much gas left in the can when he reached the bottom. He tossed the empty can aside and reached for the other. He couldn't douse the upper reaches of the walls, but he did what he could. He splashed one side and then circled around the back to the other side. Above him, the window still flickered with light from the television but all was quiet.

He drained the can on the other side of the building and had nothing left for the front. He scanned the road; no cars were coming. He stood in front of the store, thinking about the windows. Maybe they were alarmed and maybe not. He didn't care. He needed lighter fluid, turpentine, anything that would burn.

He shattered the window with his elbow but heard no alarm. Pulling out pieces of glass, he barely felt his fingers getting cut and beginning to bleed. He thought the opening was big enough for him to climb inside, but his arm caught on a jagged shard, deep. He pulled, tearing flesh. But he couldn't stop now. Blood flowed from his arm.

The coolers along the back wall were still illuminated and he walked the aisles. He located the lighter fluid—only two cans, not enough. He spotted the grill in the rear of the store. Propane.

He turned a burner on, then another. Roger's apron hung on a rack and he tossed it onto the flame. He opened the can of lighter fluid and sprayed it on the walls of the grill. He hopped on the counter and squirted lighter fluid on the ceiling and got down again. The flames from the apron began leaping towards the walls and the ceiling. He went to the register and searched for a lighter and found a bunch of them. He climbed out the window he'd broken earlier, stepping on broken glass. Standing by the side of the house, he flicked the lighter and held it against the gas-soaked wall, watching as the wood caught fire. At the back of the house, he touched the flame to the stairs and flames rose quickly. Next came the far side.

Fire blossomed everywhere, the exterior rippling with flame, and Erin was a sinner and her lover was a sinner and the Bible says, *They will suffer the punishment of eternal destruction.*

He stood back, watching the fire start to consume the building, wiping his face, leaving trails of blood. In the glowing orange light, he looked like a monster.

IN HER DREAM, Jo wasn't smiling as she sat beside Katie on the Ferris wheel. She seemed to be searching the crowd below.

There, she said, pointing. *Over there. Do you see him?*

Katie looked but there were so many people, so much movement. Where? she asked. I don't see anything.

He's here, Jo said.

Who?

You know.

In her dream, the carnival scene dissolved. Katie was surrounded by darkness, broken only by an odd flickering at the periphery of her vision, and the sound of someone talking.

Katie heard Jo's voice again, almost a whisper.

Can you smell it?

Katie sniffed, still lost in the haze. Her eyes fluttered open, stinging for some reason. The television was still on and she realised she must have fallen asleep. Katie pushed herself to a sitting position and started coughing. It took only an instant to realise that the room was filled with smoke. She bolted off the couch.

Smoke meant fire, and now she could see the flames outside the window, dancing and twisting orange. The door was on fire, smoke billowing from the kitchen in thick clouds.

Oh, my God. The kids.

She ran towards the hallway, panicked at the sight of heavy smoke billowing from both rooms. Josh's room was closest and she rushed into the black fog. She grabbed Josh's arm, dragging him up.

'Josh! Get up! The house is on fire! We've got to get out!'

He immediately began to cough, doubled over as she dragged him out. The hallway was an impenetrable wall of smoke, but she rushed forward nonetheless, pulling Josh behind her. Groping, she found the doorjamb to Kristen's room across the hall.

It wasn't as bad as Josh's room, but she could feel the enormous heat building behind them. Josh continued to cough and wail, struggling to keep up, and she knew better than to let go. She raced to Kristen's bedside and pulled her out of bed with her other hand.

The roaring of the fire was so loud, she could barely hear the sound of her own voice. The entrance hallway crawled with fire, moving towards them. She turned and pushed the kids back down the hall to the master bedroom, where the smoke was less thick.

She rushed into the room, flicking on the light. Still working. Straight ahead was a rocking chair and windows, thankfully untouched as yet by fire. She slammed the door behind her.

Racked by coughing, she stumbled forward, dragging Josh and Kristen. They clung to her, wailing between bouts of coughing.

'I need to open the window!' she screamed. She tried to heave the heavy pane up. It wouldn't budge. Katie realised that the frame had been painted shut, probably years ago. She looked around, frantic, finally seizing the rocking chair. It was heavy, but somehow she heaved it at the window with all her might. It went flying out, crashing onto the overhang below. Moving fast, Katie raced to the bed and tore off the quilt. She bundled it around Josh and Kristen and began pushing them towards the window.

There was a loud splintering sound behind her as part of the wall burst into flame. Katie turned in panic, pausing long enough to notice the portrait that hung on the wall. She stared at it, knowing it was of Alex's wife, because there was no one else it could be. She blinked, thinking the eerily familiar face was an illusion. Then she heard a roar above her as the ceiling started to give way.

Whirling around, she pushed through the window, holding the kids in the circle of her arms and praying that the quilt would protect them from glass shards. They seemed to hang in the air for an eternity, Katie twisting as they fell so that the kids would land on top of her. She hit the overhang on her back with a whump. It wasn't far, maybe five feet, but pain rolled over her in waves.

Josh and Kristen were hiccupping in fear, wailing and coughing. But they were alive. She shook her head to clear her vision. Flames were everywhere now, and she knew they had only seconds to live unless she summoned the strength to move.

The ground was perhaps a ten-foot drop from the overhang, but Katie had to risk it. Josh sobbed but didn't protest as Katie quickly explained what was going to happen next. She seized his arms, trying to keep her voice steady.

'I'm going to lower you as far as I can, then you have to jump.'

He nodded, and she quickly scooted towards the edge, dragging Josh with her. He moved to the edge and she grabbed his hand. He climbed over, legs first, holding on, Katie sliding on her belly towards the edge. Lowering him . . . God, the agony in her arms . . . four feet, no more, she told herself. He wouldn't fall far and he would land on his feet.

She let go as the roof shuddered. Kristen crawled towards her, trembling.

'OK, baby, your turn,' Katie urged. 'Give me your hand.'

She did the same thing with Kristen, holding her breath as she let go. A moment later, both of them were on their feet, staring up at her. They were waiting for her.

'Run!' she screamed. 'Move back!' She grabbed the edge of the overhang and swung one leg off, then the other. She dangled for only an instant before her grip weakened.

She hit the ground and felt her knees buckle. Her legs screamed with pain, but she had to get the kids to safety. She scrambled towards them, seizing their hands and beginning to drag them away.

There was a sharp clap, loud enough to make her ears ring. She peeked over her shoulder, just in time to see the building collapse inwards. Then there was the deafening sound of an explosion, and Katie and the kids were knocked over in the scorching blast of air.

By the time the three of them caught their breath and turned to look, the store was nothing but a gigantic cone of fire.

But they'd made it. She pulled both Josh and Kristen towards her. They were whimpering as she put her arms around. 'You're OK,' she murmured. 'You're safe now.'

It was only when a shadow appeared before her that she realised she was wrong. It was him, looming over them, a gun at his side.

Kevin.

ON HIS way back from Joyce's house, Alex noticed the sky glowing orange just above the blackened tree line on the outskirts of town. He hadn't seen that as they drove into town and navigated the streets to Joyce's home. Now, however, he frowned as he turned in that direction. Something in his gut told him that danger lay ahead.

Though the fire was still too far away to pinpoint the location with accuracy, his stomach began to seize up. There weren't too many structures in that direction, mostly a few farmhouses. And, of course, the store. He leaned over the steering wheel. *Faster.*

KATIE HAD trouble processing what she was seeing.

'Where is he?' Kevin rasped out. The words came out slurred. In his hand the Glock shone, like it had been dipped in a barrel of oil.

He's here, Jo had said in Katie's dream.

Who?

You know.

Kevin raised the gun. 'I just want to talk to him, Erin.'

Katie got to her feet. Kristen and Josh clung to her. Kevin's eyes were feral, his movements jerky. He took a step towards them, almost losing his balance. The gun swung back and forth. Unsteady.

He was ready to kill them all, Katie realised. He'd already tried to kill them with the fire. But drunk, very drunk. Worse than she'd ever seen him. He was out of control, beyond reason.

She had to get the kids away, had to give them a chance to run.

'Hi, Kevin,' she purred. She forced herself to smile. 'Why are you holding that gun? Did you come to get me? Are you all right, baby? I love you, Kevin, and I always knew you'd come.'

Kevin blinked. The voice, soft and sultry, sweet. He liked it when she sounded like that, and he thought it was a dream. But he wasn't dreaming. Erin was standing in front of him, telling him that she loved him.

Closer, Katie thought. She took a step forward, pushing the kids behind her. 'Can you bring me home?' Her voice pleaded with him, begged like Erin used to, but her hair was short and brown and she was moving closer and he wondered why she wasn't scared and he wanted to pull the trigger but he loved her. If only he could stop the hammering inside his head—

Suddenly, Katie lunged, pushing the gun away. It fired, the sound like a vicious slap, but she kept moving forward, clinging to his wrist, not letting go. Kristen started to scream.

'RUN!' Katie shouted over her shoulder. 'Josh, take Kristen and run! He's got a gun! Get as far away as you can and hide!'

Josh grabbed Kristen's hand and took off running. They headed towards the road, racing for Katie's house. Fleeing for their lives.

'Bitch!' Kevin screamed, trying to free his arm. Katie lowered her mouth and bit down as hard as she could and Kevin screamed, letting go of the gun. It clattered to the ground and he punched her, knocking her to the ground. He kicked her in the back and she arched with pain. But she kept moving, crawling, gaining speed. Finally, she surged to her feet.

She ran as fast as she could, but she felt his body slam into her from behind and she lay breathless on the ground again. He seized an arm and twisted it, but she was slippery enough to turn onto her back She clawed at his eyes, catching one in the corner.

Fighting for her life, fighting now, for all the times she hadn't. Fighting to give the Josh and Kristen time to run. Screaming at him, hating him, refusing to let him beat her again.

He snatched at her fingers, tottering off balance, and she used the opportunity to wiggle away. Pulling her knee up towards her chin, she kicked him, connecting with his chin. He toppled sideways. She scrambled to her feet and started to run, but Kevin was up just as quickly. A few feet away, she saw the gun and lunged for it.

ALEX WAS DRIVING recklessly now, praying for the safety of Kristen and Josh and Katie, whispering their names in panic.

He passed the gravel road and rounded the bend, his stomach dropping as his premonition proved right. Before him the entire tableau spread out beyond his windshield, like a portrait of hell.

He noticed movement on the side of the road. Two small figures, dressed in pyjamas. Josh and Kristen. He slammed on the brakes. He was out of the car and rushing towards them almost before the jeep came to a halt. They cried out for him as they ran, and he bent down to scoop them into his arms.

'You're OK,' he murmured over and over. 'You're OK.'

Kristen and Josh were both sobbing and at first he didn't understand what they were saying because they weren't talking about the fire. They were crying about a man with a gun, that Miss Katie was fighting him, and then he suddenly knew what had happened.

He pushed them into the jeep and wheeled it around, racing towards Katie's house as his fingers punched the speed dial on his cellphone. He reached a startled Joyce and told her to have her daughter drive her to Katie's house now, that it was an emergency, that she should call the police immediately. Then he hung up.

He came to a skidding halt in front of Katie's house. He dropped the kids off and told them to run inside, that he would be back for them as quick as he could. He turned around and gunned the engine for the store, praying that he wasn't too late.

KEVIN SAW the gun in the same instant she did and dived for it, reaching it first. He snatched it up, grabbed her by the hair and put the gun to her head as he began dragging her across the lot. Behind the store, beneath a tree, she saw his car.

'Leave me? You can't leave me!' Kevin was raging at her, his voice slurred and raw. 'You're my wife!'

In the distance, she could faintly make out sirens.

When they reached the car, Kevin opened the trunk and tried to force her in. Somehow she turned and managed to drive her knee into his groin.

She heard him gasp and felt his grip loosen. She pushed blindly, tearing out of his grasp, and ran for her life.

He started staggering after her, raising the gun, aiming, but there were two Erins and both were running. He pulled the trigger.

Katie gasped as she heard the shot, waiting for the flash of pain, but it didn't come. She kept running and suddenly it occurred to her that he'd missed. She veered left and then right, still in the lot, desperate for some kind of shelter. But there was nothing.

She saw the headlights of a car on the road, moving as fast as a race car. The car began to slow, and all at once, she recognised the jeep as it careered into the lot, Alex behind the wheel.

Roaring past her, towards Kevin.

The sirens were getting closer now. She felt a surge of hope.

KEVIN SAW the jeep coming and raised the gun. He began firing, but the jeep kept coming towards him. He leapt out of the way as the jeep roared past, but it clipped his hand, breaking all the bones and knocking the gun somewhere into the darkness.

Kevin screamed in agony, instinctively cradling his hand as the jeep careered forwards, past the burning wreckage of the store, crashing headlong into the storage shed.

There were sirens in the distance. He wanted to chase Erin but he would get arrested if he stayed. The fear took over and Kevin began to limp and jog to his car, knowing that he had to get out of there, and wondering how everything had gone so wrong.

KATIE WATCHED Kevin tear out of the lot, gravel spinning, onto the main road. Turning around, she saw that Alex's jeep was half buried in the storage shed, its engine still spewing exhaust, and she raced towards it.

She was closing in on the car when her foot hit something hard, making her stumble. Spotting the gun she'd tripped on, she picked it up and started towards the car again.

Ahead, the door of the car pushed open slightly, but it was blocked by debris. She felt a surge of relief that Alex was alive.

'Alex!' she cried. She reached the back of the jeep and started to pound on it. 'You have to get out! The kids are out there—need to find them!'

The door was still jammed but he was able to roll down the window.

When he leaned out, she saw he was bleeding from his forehead. 'They're OK . . . I took them to your house . . .'

Ice flooded her veins. 'Oh, my God,' she croaked out, thinking, *No, no, no* . . . 'Hurry up!' She pounded the rear of the car. 'Get out! Kevin just left!' She could hear the raw fear in her voice. 'That's the direction he went!'

THE PAIN in his hand was beyond anything he'd ever experienced, and he felt dizzy from blood loss. Nothing was making any sense. He heard the sirens coming but he would wait for Erin at her house.

He parked behind the other, deserted cottage. He wanted so much to sleep. The world around him was growing faint and distant. He heard the trees swaying back and forth. He began to shiver, but he was sweating, too. So much blood, and it drained out of his hands and arm. He needed to rest, and his eyes began to close.

ALEX SLAMMED the jeep into reverse and revved the engine. The jeep began to move, debris scraping its body. It came free with a final lurch. Katie jumped into the passenger seat. Alex turned the jeep around and accelerated. He'd never been more frightened in his life.

Around the bend, the gravel road. Alex turned sharply. Up ahead, he spotted the cottages, lights glowing in the windows of Katie's. No sign of Kevin's car, and he exhaled.

KEVIN HEARD the sound of an engine coming down the gravel road and he jerked awake. The police, he thought. He got out of the car and looked up the road. The jeep pulled into view, the one from the store parking lot, the one that had almost killed him. It came to a stop and Erin and grey-haired man leapt out.

His good hand was shaking hard as he opened the trunk and removed the crowbar. He saw Erin and her lover racing to the porch. He staggered towards the house, unwilling to stop, because Erin was his wife and he loved her and the man had to die.

ALEX AND KATIE ran for the door, Katie still holding the gun. They reached the door just as Josh opened it, and as soon as he saw his son, Alex swept him up in his arms. Kristen came out from behind the couch and rushed towards them. Alex opened his arms to her as well, catching her as she jumped.

Katie stood just inside the doorway, watching with tears of relief in her eyes. Kristen reached out for her, too, and Katie moved closer, accepting Kristen's hug with a blind rush of happiness.

Lost in the tidal wave of emotion, none of them noticed Kevin appear in the doorway, crowbar raised high. He swung hard, sending Alex crashing to the floor and the kids stumbling and falling in horror and shock.

Katie rushed towards Kevin, driving him back out of the door. There were only two porch steps, but it was enough, and Kevin toppled backwards into the dirt. Katie spun around. 'Lock the door!' she screamed, and this time it was Kristen who moved first.

The crowbar had fallen to the side and Kevin struggled to roll over and stand. Katie raised the gun, pointing it as Kevin finally made it to his feet. He swayed, his face a skeletal white. He seemed unable to focus and Katie could feel the tears in her eyes.

'I used to love you,' she said. 'I married you because I loved you.'

He thought it was Erin, but her hair was short and dark, and Erin was a blonde. Why was she telling him this?

'Why did you start to hit me?' she cried. 'I never knew why you couldn't stop even when you promised.' Her hand was shaking and the gun felt so, so heavy. 'You hit me on our honeymoon because I left my sunglasses by the pool . . .'

The voice was Erin's and he wondered if he was dreaming.

'I love you,' he mumbled. 'I don't know why you left me.'

She could feel the sobs building in her chest. Her words flooded out in a torrent, years' worth of sorrow. 'You wouldn't let me drive or have any friends and you kept the money and made me beg you for it. I want to know why you thought you could do that to me. I was your wife and I loved you!'

Kevin could barely stay upright. He wanted to talk to Erin, wanted to find her, but this wasn't real. He was sleeping,

She hated him with a rage that had been building up for years.

'I cooked for you and cleaned for you and none of it mattered! All you did was drink and hit me! You shouldn't have come here! Why couldn't you just let me go? You never loved me!'

Kevin lurched towards her, reaching for the gun, trying to knock it away. He was weak now, though, and she managed to hold on. He tried to grab her, but he screamed in agony when his damaged hand connected with her arm. Acting on instinct, he threw his shoulder into her, driving her into the side of the house. He reached for the gun with his good hand, using his weight against her. He felt the barrel graze his fingertips and scrambled for the trigger. He tried to push the gun towards her, but it was moving in the wrong direction, pointing down now.

'I loved you!' she sobbed, fighting him with every ounce of rage and strength left in her, and he felt momentary clarity returning.

'Then you never should have left me,' he whispered, his breath heavy with alcohol. He pulled the trigger and the gun sounded with a loud crack and then he knew it was almost over. She was going to die because he'd told her that he'd find her and kill her if she ever ran away again. He would kill any man who loved her.

But strangely, Erin didn't fall. Instead, she stared at him with fierce green eyes, holding his gaze without blinking.

He felt something then, burning in his stomach, fire. He collapsed on the porch, reaching for his stomach.

'Come back with me,' he whispered. 'Please.'

Blood pulsed through the wound, passing between his fingers. Above him, Erin was going in and out of focus. Blonde hair and then brown again. She was always so beautiful, he thought, and then he was tired again. His breaths became ragged and then he started to feel cold, and he began to shake. He exhaled once more, the sound like air being released from a tyre. His chest stopped moving. His eyes were wide open, uncomprehending.

Katie stood over him, shaking as she stared down at him. Kevin was gone, and she realised then that it was finally, truly, over.

THE HOSPITAL kept Katie under observation for most of the night before releasing her. Afterward, she remained in the waiting-room, unwilling to leave until she knew Alex would be OK.

Kevin's blow had nearly cracked Alex's skull, and he was still unconscious. Every time she heard a doctor's voice, she looked up, hoping she would be allowed to see Alex.

Bruises mottled her face and arms, and her knee was swollen to almost twice its usual size, but after the requisite X-rays and exams, the doctor on call had merely given her ice packs and Tylenol. He was the same doctor who was treating Alex. 'Head wounds can be serious,' he'd told her. 'We'll know more in a few hours.'

She couldn't stop worrying. Joyce had taken the kids home from the hospital and Katie hoped they hadn't had nightmares. Hoped Alex was going to recover fully. Prayed for that.

She was afraid to close her eyes because every time she did, Kevin reappeared. Somehow, he'd found her. He'd come to Southport to take her home or kill her, and he'd almost succeeded.

She worried about Kristen and Josh. They'd be here soon; Joyce would bring them in to see their father. She wondered if they would hate her because of everything that happened. She covered her face with her hands.

'Katie?'

She looked up and saw the doctor who was now treating Alex.

'He woke up about ten minutes ago.,' he said. 'You can't stay long, but he wants to see you.'

'Is he OK?'

'He's about as good as can be expected. He took a nasty blow.'

She followed the doctor as they made their way to Alex's room.

The ICU was filled with machines and blinking lights. Alex was in a bed in the corner, a bandage wrapped around his head. He turned towards her. She moved to his bedside and reached for his hand.

'How are the kids?' he whispered. The words came out slowly.

'They're fine. They're with Joyce. She took them home.'

A faint, almost imperceptible smile crossed his lips.

'Love you,' he said.

It was all she could do not to break down.

'I love you, too, Alex.'

His eyelids drooped, his gaze unfocused. 'What happened?'

She gave him an abbreviated account of the past twelve hours, but mid-story she saw his eyes close. When he woke again later that morning, he'd forgotten parts of what she had recounted, so she told him again, trying to sound calm.

Joyce brought Josh and Kristen, and though children weren't normally allowed in ICU, the doctor let them visit their dad for a couple of minutes. Kristen had drawn a picture of a man lying in a hospital bed, complete with a crayon-scrawled, 'Get Well Daddy'. Josh gave him a fishing magazine.

As the day wore on, Alex became more coherent. By the afternoon, although he complained of a monstrous headache, his memory had returned. When he told the nurse he was hungry, Katie gave a smile of relief, finally sure that he was going to be OK.

12

Alex was released the next day, and the sheriff visited them at Joyce's to get their formal statements. He told them that the alcohol content in Kevin's blood was so high that he'd effectively poisoned himself. Combined with the blood loss he'd suffered, it was a wonder he had been conscious, much less coherent to any degree. Katie said nothing, but all she could think was that they didn't know Kevin or understand the demons that drove him.

After the sheriff left, Katie went outside and stood in the sunlight, trying to make sense of her feelings. Though she'd told the sheriff about the events of that night, she hadn't told him everything. Nor had she told Alex everything. She didn't tell them that in the moments after Kevin had died and she'd rushed to Alex's side, she'd wept for them both. It seemed impossible that even as she relived the terror of those last hours with Kevin, she also remembered their rare happy moments together.

She didn't know how to reconcile these conflicting pieces of her past and the horror of what she'd just lived through. But there was something more, too, something else she didn't understand: she'd stayed at Joyce's because she was afraid to go back home.

LATER THAT DAY, Alex and Katie stood in the parking lot, staring at the charred remains of the store. A couple of firemen were rooting through the remains. Alex had asked them to look for the safe he'd kept in his closet. He'd removed the bandage and Katie could see the spot where they'd shaved his head to apply stitches, the area black and blue and swollen.

'I'm sorry,' Katie murmured. 'For everything.'

Alex shook his head. 'It's not your fault. You didn't do it.'

'But Kevin came for me …'

'I know,' he said. He was quiet for a moment. 'Kristen and Josh told me how you helped them get out of the house. Josh said that after you grabbed Kevin, you told them to run. He said you distracted him. I just wanted to say thank you.'

Katie closed her eyes and said, 'You can't thank me for that. If anything had happened to them, I don't know that I could have lived with myself.'

He nodded but couldn't seem to look at her.

Katie kicked at a small pile of ash that had blown into the parking lot.

'What are you going to do? About the store?'

'Rebuild, I guess.'

'Where will you live?'

'I don't know yet. We'll stay at Joyce's for a bit, but I'll try to find someplace quiet, someplace with a view. Since I can't work, I might as well try to enjoy the free time.'

She felt sick to her stomach. 'I can't even imagine how you feel right now.'

'Numb. Sad for the kids. Shocked.'

'And angry?'

'No,' he said. 'I'm not angry.'

'But you lost everything.'

'Not the important things. My kids are safe. You're safe. This'—he said motioning—'is just stuff.' When he finished, he squinted at something in the rubble. 'Hold on for a second,' he said.

He walked towards a pile of debris and pulled out a fishing pole. It looked undamaged. For the first time since they'd arrived, he smiled. 'Josh will be happy about this,' he said. 'I just wish I could find one of Kristen's dolls.'

Katie felt tears in her eyes. 'I'll buy her a new one.'

'You don't have to. I'm insured.'

'But I want to. None of this would have happened if it hadn't been for me.'

He looked at her. 'I knew what I was getting into when I asked you out.'

'But you couldn't have expected this.'

'No,' he admitted. 'Not this. But it's going to be OK. We survived and that's all that matters.' He reached for her hand. 'I haven't had a chance to say that I'm sorry.'

'Why would you be sorry?'

'For your loss.'

She knew he was talking about Kevin. He seemed to understand that she'd both loved and hated her husband. 'I never wanted him to die,' she began. 'I just wanted to be left alone.'

'I know.'

She turned tentatively towards him. 'Are we going to be OK? I mean, after all this?'

'That depends on you. My feelings haven't changed. I still love you, but you need to figure out if your feelings have changed.'

'They haven't.'

'Then we'll find a way to work through all this together because I know I want to spend the rest of my life with you.'

Before she could respond, one of the firemen called out to them. He was holding a small safe.

'Do you think it was damaged?' Katie said.

'It shouldn't be,' Alex answered. 'It's fireproof.'

'What's in it?'

'Mainly records, but I'm going to need them. Some photo disks and negatives. Things I wanted to protect.'

'I'm glad they found it.'

'So am I,' he said. 'Because there's something in there for you.'

AFTER DROPPING Alex off at Joyce's, Katie finally drove back home, knowing she couldn't put off the inevitable forever.

Dust rose from the gravel and she bounced through the potholes before pulling to a stop out front. She sat in the jeep—dented and scraped, but still running fine—and stared at the door.

She was afraid that opening the door would remind her of the way Alex had looked after Kevin struck him. She could practically hear the sounds of Kristen and Josh crying hysterically as they clung to their father. She wasn't prepared to relive all of that.

Instead, she started towards Jo's. In her hand was the letter that Alex had given her. When she'd asked him why he'd written to her, he'd shaken his head. 'It's not from me,' he'd said. She'd stared at him, confused. 'You'll understand once you read it,' he'd told her.

As she approached Jo's, she felt the trace of a memory stir to life. Something that happened on the night of the fire. Something she'd seen but she couldn't quite place. She slowed as she drew nearer to Jo's house, a frown of confusion creasing her face.

There were cobwebs on the window. The porch railing was broken and weeds sprouted between the planks. She was unable to process the scene before her: a rusted doorknob, grime on the windows. No curtains, no entry mat, no wind chime . . .

She felt as if she were in a dream. The closer she got, the more the house seemed to decay before her. She climbed onto the porch. Leaning in, she peered through the windows into the cottage.

Dust and dirt, broken furniture, piles of garbage. Nothing painted, nothing cleaned. All at once, Katie stepped back on the porch, almost stumbling off the broken step. *No.* It wasn't possible. What had happened to Jo, and what about all the improvements she'd made on the small cottage? Katie had seen Jo hang the wind chime. Jo had been over to her house, complaining about having to paint and clean. They'd had coffee and wine and cheese.

Katie massaged her temples, searching for answers. She remembered that Jo had been sitting on the steps when Alex dropped her off. Even Alex had seen her . . . *Or had he?*

Katie backed away from the decaying home. Jo was real. There was no way she'd been a figment of her imagination.

But Jo liked everything you did: she drank her coffee the same way, she liked the clothes you bought, her thoughts about the employees at Ivan's mirrored your own.

A dozen random details suddenly began crowding her mind . . .

She lived here! *But why is it such a dump?*

We drank wine at my house! *You drank the bottle yourself, which was why you were so dizzy.*

She told me about Alex! She wanted us to be together! *She never mentioned his name until you already knew it, and you were interested in him all along.*

One by one, the answers came as quickly as she could think of them: the reason she'd never learned Jo's last name or saw her drive a car . . . the reason Jo never invited her over . . . how Jo had been able to magically appear at Katie's side in jogging clothes . . .

Katie felt something give way inside her as everything clicked into place. Jo, she suddenly realised, had never been there at all.

Still feeling as if she were in a dream, Katie stumbled back to her house. She took a seat in the rocker and stared at Jo's house.

She knew that the creation of imaginary friends was common among children, but she wasn't a child. And yes, she'd been under a great deal of stress when she arrived in Southport. Alone and friendless, on the run and terrified—who wouldn't be anxious? But was that enough to have prompted the creation of an alter ego?

She couldn't believe it because it had felt so . . . *real*. She could still see

Jo's expressions, still hear the sound of her laughter. She shook her head, frustrated and confused and yet . . .

There was something else nagging at her, something she couldn't put her finger on. She was forgetting about something important.

She looked up. Dusk was beginning to spread across the sky.

Looking away from Jo's house, Katie reached for the letter and examined it. The outer envelope was blank. Turning the envelope over, Katie lifted the seal. She ran her finger over the yellow legal paper before unfolding the pages. Finally, she began to read.

To the woman my husband loves,

If it seems odd for you to read these words, please believe me when I tell you that it feels just as odd to write them. There's so much I want to say. I'm not sure where to begin.

I can start by saying this: I've come to believe that in everyone's life, there's one undeniable moment of change, a set of circumstances that suddenly alters everything. For me, that moment was meeting Alex. Though I don't know when or where you're reading this, I know it means he loves you. It also means he wants to share his life with you, and if nothing else, we will always have that in common.

My name, as you probably know, is Carly, but for most of my life, my friends called me Jo . . .

Katie stopped reading and looked at the letter in her hands. *For most of my life, my friends called me Jo . . .*

She gripped the pages, feeling the memory she'd been struggling to retrieve come into focus at last. Suddenly, she was back in the master bedroom on the night of the fire. She felt the strain in her arms as she heaved the rocking chair through the window, felt the panic as she wrapped Josh and Kristen in the comforter. With sudden clarity, she remembered whirling around and seeing the portrait hanging on the wall, the portrait of Alex's wife. At the time, she'd been confused, her nerves short-circuiting. But she'd seen the face.

That looks a lot like Jo, she remembered thinking, even if her mind hadn't been able to process it. But now, she knew with certainty that she was wrong. Wrong about everything. It looked like Jo, she realised, because it was Jo. She felt another memory float free, from the first morning that Jo had come over. My friends call me Jo, she had said by way of introduction.

Oh, my God. Katie paled.

She hadn't imagined Jo. She hadn't made her up.

Jo had been here, and she felt her throat begin to tighten. Not because she didn't believe it, but because she suddenly understood that her friend Jo—her only real friend, her wise adviser, her supporter and confidante—would never come back.

They would never have coffee, they would never share another bottle of wine, they would never sit out on the front porch. She'd never hear the sound of Jo's laughter or hear Jo complain about having to do manual labour, and Katie began to cry, mourning the wonderful friend she'd never had the chance to meet in life.

She wasn't sure how much time passed before she was able to begin reading again. It was getting dark, and with a sigh, she stood and unlocked the front door. Inside, she took a seat at the kitchen table. OK, she thought, I'm ready to hear what you have to say.

. . . but for most of my life, my friends called me Jo. Just so you know, I already consider you a friend.

Dying is a strange business. Though it's a cliché, it's true that so many of the things I once believed to be important no longer are. I don't care about the stock market, or worry whether it's going to rain while I'm on vacation. Instead, I think about Alex and how handsome he looked on the day we were married. I remember when I first held Josh and Kristen in my arms. I'd never experienced a purer form of joy.

It wasn't until I had children that I really understood what love meant. Don't get me wrong. I love Alex deeply, but it's different from the love I feel for Josh and Kristen. Despite my illness, I feel blessed, because I've been able to experience both. I've lived a full, happy life and experienced the kind of love that many people will never know.

Alex is my dream and my companion, my lover and my friend. He's a devoted father, but more than that, he's my ideal husband. There's an unshakeable humanity about him, and it breaks my heart to imagine him alone. That's why I've asked him to give you this letter; I thought of it as a way of making him keep his promise that he would find someone special again—someone who loves him, and someone he could love. He needs that.

I was blessed to be married to him for five years and I've mothered my children for less time than that. Now, my life is almost over and you are going to take my place. You'll become the wife who grows old with Alex, and you'll become the only mother my children will ever know. Sometimes, I dream that I'll find a way to come back, that I can find a way to ensure they're going to be all right. I like to believe that I'll watch over them from heaven, or that I can visit them in their dreams. I want to pretend that my journey isn't over and I pray that the boundless love I feel for them will somehow make it possible.

This is where you come in. I want you to do something for me. If you love Alex now, then love him forever. Make him laugh again. Take walks and ride your bikes, curl up on the couch and watch movies. Kiss him and make love to him, and consider yourself lucky for having met him, for he's the kind of man who'll prove you right.

I also want you to love my children in the same way I do. Help them with their homework and kiss their scraped knees when they fall. Tuck them in at night and help them say their prayers. Adore them, laugh with them, help them grow into kind, independent adults.

Please. I beg you, do these things for me. After all, they are your family now, not mine.

I'm not jealous or angry that I've been replaced by you; as I mentioned already, I consider you a friend. You've made my husband and children happy, and I wish I were around to be able to thank you in person. Instead, all I can do is assure you that you have my everlasting gratitude.

If Alex has chosen you, then I have chosen you as well.

Your friend in spirit,

Carly Jo

When Katie finished reading the letter, she wiped her tears and ran her finger over the pages before slipping them back into the envelope. She sat quietly, thinking about the words that Jo had written, already knowing she would do exactly as Jo had asked.

Not because of the letter, she thought, but because she knew that in some inexplicable way, Jo was the one who'd gently urged her to give Alex a chance in the first place.

She smiled. 'Thank you for trusting me,' she whispered, and she knew that Jo had been right all along. She'd fallen in love with Alex and she'd fallen in love with the children and she already knew that she couldn't imagine a future without them. It was time to go home, she thought, it was time to see her family.

Outside, the moon was a brilliant white disc that guided her as she made her way towards the jeep. But before climbing in, she glanced over her shoulder in the direction of Jo's.

The lights were on and the windows of the cottage were glowing yellow. In the painted kitchen, she saw Jo standing near the window. Though she was too far away to make out much more than that, Katie had the sense she was smiling. Jo raised a hand in a friendly farewell, and Katie was reminded again that love can sometimes achieve the impossible.

When Katie blinked, however, the cottage was dark again. No lights were on and Jo had vanished, but she thought she could hear the words in the letter being carried on the gentle breeze.

If Alex has chosen you, then I want you to believe that I have chosen you as well.

Katie smiled and turned away, knowing it wasn't an illusion or a figment of her imagination. She knew what she saw.

She knew what she believed.

nicholas **sparks**

When his first novel, *The Notebook*, was published in 1996, Nicholas Sparks could not believe his luck. At the time he was working as a pharmaceutical salesman earning $40,000 a year and was astounded when Warner Books bought the rights to his novel for $1,000,000. 'If you think I was excited about that, you're severely underestimating my response. I jumped up and down so long I got a cramp in my calf. I was hoarse for two days from screaming. I could barely sleep. It didn't seem real, but it was. And it was absolutely wonderful.'

Incurable romantic that he is, the first thing Sparks did was to buy a new wedding ring for his wife. 'I remember getting down on my knees and telling her that our life just might be changing for ever and that I didn't know what the future would bring.'

In fact, it was the start of an extraordinary literary career. Fifteen books later, his work has been translated into over forty languages, six of his novels have been turned into major motion pictures, and he is one of only two contemporary authors who have had a novel staying on both the *New York Times* hardcover and paperback best-seller lists for more than twelve months—the other author being J. K. Rowling.

So where does he get the ideas for his deeply romantic novels? 'Different novels emphasise a different sadness. It's part of the emotion of life. A reader should feel they've experienced a mini-life between the covers, and to do that you have to include happiness, elation, love and betrayal—and sadness. It's part of life. If you don't have that, it doesn't feel real.' Many of the stories in his novels come from actual family events, albeit heavily fictionalised. *Message in a Bottle* was inspired by his father's experiences after the tragic death of Sparks's mother; *A Walk to Remember* by his sister's losing battle with cancer.

Generally, Nicholas Sparks writes five or six days a week, averaging about five hours a day. His daily goal is to write 2,000 words and it usually takes him about four or five months to finish a novel. Before he starts writing, he knows how the story will begin and end and has about five or six key events in mind that will act as turning points. 'I usually start with the age of a character, and ask myself lots of 'what-if' questions. What might the dilemmas of a fifty-year-old character be? They may have children leaving home for college, or aged parents to take care of, and I take it from there.'

But even now, every time Nicholas Sparks finishes a novel he wonders where the ideas for the next one will come from. 'Luckily for me, my publisher is very forgiving about the fact that I tend to be late in delivering my manuscripts. This lateness is not due to lack of effort or even procrastination; rather, it usually reflects the unpredictability of my creative process. In the case of *Safe Haven*, for instance, I started a novel in October 2009. The working title was *Saying Goodbye*, and though I felt that its basic premise was strong, I reached a point in January 2010 where I simply couldn't write any further. The story was lacking . . . something, but I couldn't figure out what. I spent torturous weeks trying to overcome this hurdle, but nothing seemed to work. So, knowing that I still had to write a novel for the fall, I put *Saying Goodbye* aside and spent a few weeks pondering a new story. That story eventually became the novel *Safe Haven*. I started writing it on February 17th, 2010, and though I hoped the book would take a simple and straightforward course, it ended up being one of the most challenging novels I've written. It has many of the same elements my readers expect—a moving love story and compelling characters—but this novel also features an element of danger.'

'A reader should feel they've experienced a mini-life between the covers, and to do that you have to include happiness, elation, love and betrayal—and sadness. It's part of life. If you don't have that, it doesn't feel real.'

Since completing *Safe Haven*, the author has written two screenplays, which are not based on his own novels. 'One is an action-adventure project, and the other is supernatural horror flick. I know that might strike some people as strange, but for me it's been a way of working on something different, which keeps the writing process interesting. The next question, of course, is *will they get made into movies*? Who knows? But that's OK—I wrote them because I wanted to, and it was a pleasure.'

As a father of five growing children, it's amazing that Nicholas Sparks finds enough solitude to pursue his writing career, but the author admits that he misses the noise and excitement when 'the kids' are at school or college. 'I like having my kids around. I like watching them grow up, and am always amazed at how fast it seems to happen. Time . . . we're always chasing it, and it's for ever slipping out of our grasp.'

Spine: illustration: Richard Merrit @ The Organisation. Front cover (from left) and page 4 (from top): William S. Helsel/Getty Images; Nathan Burton Design; Yellowj/Shutterstock.com; Colin Thomas. Page 5 (top) Matthew Peyton/Getty Images. 6–8: image of presidential seal: Dreamstime Stock Photos; illustration: Rhett Pedersoo@Advocate-Art; 156 © Doug Peters/Press Association images; 157: Peter Gridley/Getty Images. 158–60 illustration: Richard Merritt @ The Organisation; 314 © Tony Buckingham; 315 © Pixelbliss/ Shutterstock.com. 316–8 photo of cowboy on hill: © Keith Szafranksi/istockphoto; illustration: James Kessell; 444 © Dove Studios; 445 © Buddy Mays/Corbis. 446-8 illustration: Sonia Possentini @ Advocate-Art; 574 © Gasper Tringale Photograph.

Printed and bound by GGP Media GmbH, Pössneck, Germany

020-269 UP0000-1